SUMMER *by the* SEA

SUSAN WIGGS

Summer by the Sea

MIRA®

ISBN-13: 978-0-7783-2965-7

Recycling programs
for this product may
not exist in your area.

SUMMER BY THE SEA

For questions and comments about the quality of this book please contact us at
Customer_eCare@Harlequin.ca.

www.MIRABooks.com

Printed in U.S.A.

In memory of Trixie,
beloved companion, faithful friend.

ACKNOWLEDGMENTS

As always, I'd like to acknowledge my ever-patient critique group: Rose Marie, Anjali, Kate, Lois, P.J., Susan, Krysteen and Sheila, for their talent, wisdom and courage to sample a number of culinary experiments. I'm deeply grateful to my agent, friend and champion Meg Ruley, and to Martha Keenan and Dianne Moggy of MIRA Books. *Molto grazie* to Mike Sharpe of Four Swallows Restaurant on Bainbridge Island, Washington, for patiently answering my many questions. And finally, a very special thank-you to my Uncle Tommy, who has no idea why I'm thanking him: you've never heard the sound of my voice, but you've always had my love, admiration and respect.

PART ONE

Antipasto

Antipasto: The Italian word for a snack served before a meal. These are dishes to pique the appetite, not quench it. Antipasto literally means "before the meal." Mamma used to say it was the anti-noise course because my brothers, Robert and Sal, would be so busy stuffing their faces that they'd forget to complain about being hungry.

Caponata

This has an excellent flavor and makes a very nice presentation on a perfect leaf of lettuce, not that Robert and Sal ever gave a hoot about presentation. And it's even quite low in calories, not that guys care about that, either. Serve this as a traditional antipasto with a good crusty Italian bread and a glass of chilled Pinot Grigio.

Peel and dice an eggplant, toss with salt, put in a colander and drain for at least a half hour. Then heat up a heavy skillet and add 1/4 cup olive oil, a small onion, chopped, and a stick of celery, also chopped. Add the eggplant and sauté. Finally, add three chopped tomatoes, three minced anchovies, a pinch of sugar, 1/4 cup wine vinegar and a spoonful of capers (the best ones come from Pantelleria Island). If your family likes olives, add some of those, too, along with a pinch of red pepper flakes. Simmer for ten minutes. Cool, then store overnight in a glass container. For a smoother spreading consistency, you can whirl the mixture in the food processor, but don't overdo it. Things that are too smooth lose their character.

One

Rosa Capoletti knew that tonight was the night. Jason Aspoll was going to pop the question. The setting was perfect—a starlit summer evening, an elegant seaside restaurant, the sounds of crystal and silver gently clinking over quiet murmurs of conversation. At Jason's request, the Friday night trio was playing "Lovetown," and a few dreamy couples swayed to the nostalgic melody.

Candlelight flickered over their half-empty champagne flutes, illuminating Jason's endearingly nervous face. He was sweating a little, and his eyes darted with barely suppressed trepidation. Rosa could tell he wanted to get this right.

She knew he was wondering, *Should I reach across the table? Go down on one knee, or is that too hokey?*

Go for it, Jason, she wanted to urge him. Nothing's too hokey when it's true love.

She also knew the ring lay nestled in a black velvet box, concealed in the inner pocket of his dinner jacket, right next to his racing heart.

Come on, Jason, she thought. Don't be afraid.

And then, just as she was starting to worry that he'd chickened out, he did it. He went down on one knee.

A few nearby diners shifted in their chairs to look on fondly. Rosa held her breath while his hand stole inside his jacket.

The music swelled. He took the box from his pocket and she saw his mouth form the words: *Will you marry me?*

He held out the ring box, opening the hinged lid to reveal the precious offering. His hand shook a little. He still didn't know for sure if she would have him.

Silly man, thought Rosa. Didn't he know the answer would be—

"Table seven sent back the risotto," said Leo, the head-waiter, holding a thick china bowl in front of Rosa.

"Leo, for crying out loud," she said, craning her neck to see past him. "Can't you tell I'm busy here?" She pushed him aside in time to watch her best friend, Linda Lipschitz, stand up from the table and fling her arms around Jason.

"Yes," Linda said, although from across the dining room Rosa had to read her lips. "Yes, *absolutely.*"

Atta girl, thought Rosa, her eyes misting.

Leo followed her gaze to the embracing couple. "Sweet," he said. "Now what about my risotto?"

"Take it back to the kitchen," Rosa said. "I knew the mango chutney was a bad idea, anyway, and you can tell Butch I said so." She let Leo deal with it as she walked across the dining room. Linda was wreathed in smiles and tears. Jason looked positively blissful and, perhaps, weak with relief.

"Rosa, you won't believe what just happened," Linda said.

Rosa dabbed at her eyes. "I think I can guess."

Linda held out her hand, showing off a glittering marquise-cut diamond in a gold cathedral setting.

"Oh, honey." Rosa hugged Linda and gave Jason a kiss on the cheek. "Congratulations, you two," she said. "I'm so happy for you."

She'd helped Jason pick out the ring, told him Linda's size, selected the music and menu, ordered Linda's favorite flowers for the table. They'd set the scene in every possible way. Rosa was good at things like this— creating events around the most special moments in people's lives.

Other people's lives.

Linda was babbling, already making plans. "We'll drive over to see Jason's folks on Sunday, and then get everyone together to set a date—"

"Slow down, my friend," Rosa said with a laugh. "How about you dance with your fiancé?"

Linda turned to Jason, her eyes shining. "My fiancé. God, I love the sound of that."

Rosa gave the couple a gentle shove toward the dance floor. As he pulled Linda into his arms, Jason looked over her shoulder and mouthed a thank-you to Rosa. She waved, dabbed at her eyes again and headed for the kitchen. Back to work.

She was smiling as she crossed the nonskid mat and entered the kitchen through the swinging doors. Quiet elegance gave way to controlled chaos. Glaring lights and flaming grills illuminated the crush of prep workers, line cooks and the sous-chef hurrying back and forth between stainless steel counters. Waiters tapped their feet, checking orders before stepping through the sound-proofed doors that protected the serenity of the dining room from male shouts and clattering dishes.

The revved-up energy of the kitchen was fueled by testosterone, but Rosa knew how to hold her own here. She walked through a gauntlet of aproned men with huge knives or vats of boiling water, pivoting around each other in their nightly ballet. A stream from a hose roared against the dishwashing sink, and hot drafts from the Imperial grill licked like dragon's breath at precisely 1010°F.

"Wait," she said as a prep worker passed by with a plated steak that had been liberally sprinkled with tripepper confetti.

"What?" The worker, a recent hire from Newport, paused at the counter.

"We don't garnish the steaks here."

"Come again?"

"This is premium meat, our signature cut. Serve it without the garnish."

"I'll remember that," he said, and set the plate on the counter for a server to pick up.

She planted herself in front of him. "Go back and replate the steak, please. No garnish."

"But—"

Rosa glared at him with fire in her eyes. Don't back down, she cautioned herself. Don't blink.

"You got it," he said, scowling as he returned to the prep area.

"Well?" asked Lorenzo "Butch" Buchello, whose fresh Italian cuisine was drawing in patrons from as far away as New York and Boston.

"Yep." Rosa grinned and selected a serrated knife from the array affixed to a steel grid on the wall. "Went down on one knee and everything."

Neither of them stopped working as they chatted. He was coordinating dessert while she arranged fluffy white peasant bread in a basket.

"Good for them," said Butch.

"They're really in love," Rosa said. "I got all choked up, watching them."

"Ever the incurable romantic," Butch said, piping chocolate ganache around the profiteroles.

"Ha, there's a cure for it," Shelly Warren cut in, whisking behind them to pick up her order.

"It's called marriage," Rosa said.

Shelly gave her a high-five. She had been married for ten years and claimed that her night job waiting tables was an escape from endless hours of watching the Golf Channel until her eyes glazed over.

"Hey, don't knock it till you've tried it, Rosa," said Butch. "In fact, what about that guy you were dating— Dean what's his name?"

"Oh, actually, he did want to get married," she explained.

Butch's eyes lit up. "Hey! Well, there you go—"

"Just not to me."

His face fell. "I'm sorry. I didn't know."

"It's all right. He joins a long and venerable line of suitors who didn't suit."

"I'm starting to see a pattern here," Butch said. He took a wire whisk to a bowl of custard and Marsala, creating an order of his famous zabaglione. "You run them off and then say they didn't suit."

She finished up with the bread baskets. "Not tonight, Butch. This is Linda's moment. Send them a tiramisu and your congratulations, okay?"

She headed back to the dining room and went over to the podium, which faced the main entrance. It was a perfect Friday night at Celesta's-by-the-Sea. All the tables in the multilevel dining room were oriented toward the view of the endless sea, and were set with fresh flowers, crisp linens, good china and flatware.

This was the sort of scene she used to dream about back when the place was a run-down pizza joint. Couples danced to the smooth beat of a soft blues number, the drummer's muted cymbals shimmering with a sensual resonance. Out on the deck, people stood listening to the waves and looking at the stars. For the past three years running, Celesta's had been voted "Best Place to Propose" by *Coast* magazine, and tonight was a perfect example of the reason for its charm—sea breezes, sand and surf, a natural backdrop for the award-winning dining room.

"Did you cry?" asked Vince, the host, stepping up beside her. They'd known each other since childhood— she, Vince and Linda. They'd gone through school together, inseparable. Now he was the best-looking maître d' in South County. He was tall and slender, flaw-lessly groomed in an Armani suit and Gucci shoes. Rimless glasses highlighted his darkly-lashed eyes.

"Of course I cried," Rosa said. "Didn't you?"

"Maybe," he admitted with a fond smile in Linda's di-rection. "A little. I love seeing her so happy."

"Yeah. Me, too."

"So that's two of us down, one to go," he said.

She rolled her eyes. "Not you, too."

"Butch has already been at you?"

"What do you two do, lie awake at night discussing my love life?"

"No, sweetie. Your lack of one."

"Give me a break, okay?" She spoke through a smile as a party of four left the restaurant. She and Vince had per-fected the art of bickering while appearing utterly con-genial.

"Please come again," Vince said, his expression so warm that the two women did a double-take. Glancing down at the computer screen discreetly set beneath the surface of the podium, he checked the status of their tab. "Three bottles of Antinori."

Rosa gave a blissful sigh. "Sometimes I love this job."

"You always love this job. Too much, if you ask me."

"You're not my analyst, Vince."

"Ringrazi il cielo," he muttered. "You couldn't pay me enough."

"Hey."

"Kidding," he assured her. "Good night, folks," he said to a departing threesome. "Thanks so much for coming."

Rosa surveyed her domain with a powerful but weary pride. Celesta's-by-the-Sea was the place people came to fall in love. It was also Rosa's own emotional landscape; it structured her days and weeks and years. She had poured all her energy into the restaurant, creating a place where people marked the most important events of their lives—engagements, graduations, bar mitzvahs, anniversaries, promotions. They came to escape the rush and rigors of everyday life, never knowing that each subtle detail of the place, from the custom alabaster lampshades to the imported chenille chair covers, had been contrived to create an air of luxury and comfort, just for them.

Rosa knew such attention to detail, along with Butch's incomparable cuisine, had elevated her restaurant to one of the best in the county, perhaps in the entire state. The focal point of the place was a hammered steel bar, its edges fluted like waves. The bar, which she'd commissioned from a local artisan, was backed by a sheet of blue glass lit from below. At its center was a nautilus seashell, the light flickering over and through the whorls and chambers. People seemed drawn to its mysterious iridescence, and often asked where it came from, and if it was real. Rosa knew the answer, but she never told.

She checked the time on the screen without being obvious. None of the servers wore watches and there was no clock in sight. People relaxing here shouldn't notice the passing of time. But the small computer screen indicated 10:00 p.m. She didn't expect too much more business, except perhaps in the bar.

She could tell, with a sweep of her gaze, that tonight's till would be sky-high. "I'm so glad summer's here," she said to Vince.

"You know, for normal people, summer means vacation time. For us, it means our lives belong to Celesta's."

"This is normal." Hard work had never bothered Rosa. Outside the restaurant there was not much to her life, and she had convinced herself that she liked it that way. She had Pop, of course, who at sixty-five was as independent as ever, accusing her of fussing over him. Her brother Robert was in the navy, currently stationed with his family overseas. Her other brother, Sal, was also in the navy, a Catholic priest serving as chaplain. Her father and brothers, nieces and nephews, were her family.

But Celesta's was her life.

She stole a glance at Jason and Linda, and fancied she could actually see stars in their eyes. Sometimes, when Rosa looked at the happy couples holding hands across the tables in her restaurant, she felt a bittersweet ache. And then she always pretended, even to herself, that it didn't matter.

"I give you two months off every year," she pointed out to Vince.

"Yeah, January and February."

"Best time of year in Miami," she reminded him. "Or are you and Butch ready to give up your condo there?"

"All right, all right. I get your point. I wouldn't have it any other—"

The sound of car doors slamming interrupted them. Rosa sent another discreet look at the slanted computer screen under the podium. Ten-fifteen.

She stepped back while Vince put on his trademark smile. "So much for making an early night of it." The comment slipped between his teeth, while his expression indicated he'd been waiting all his life for the next group of patrons.

Rosa recognized them instantly. Not by name, of course. The summer crowds at the shore were too huge for that. No, she recognized them because they were a "type." Summer people. The women exuded patrician poise and beauty. The tallest one wore her perfectly straight golden-blond hair caught, seemingly without artifice, in a thin band. Her couture clothes—a slim black skirt, silk blouse and narrow kid leather flats—had a subtle elegance. Her two friends were stylish clones of her, with uniformly sleek hair, pale makeup, sleeves artfully rolled back just so. They pulled off the look as only those to the manor born could.

Rosa and Vince had grown up sharing their summers with people like this. To the seasonal visitors, the locals existed for the sole purpose of serving those who belonged to the venerable old houses along the pristine, unspoiled shore just as their forebears had done a century before. They were the ones whose charity galas were covered by *Town & Country* magazine, whose weddings were announced in the *New York Times*. They were the ones who never thought about what life was like for the maid who changed their sheets, the fisherman who brought in the day's catch, the cleaners who ironed their Sea Isle cotton shirts.

Vince nudged her behind the podium. "Yachty. They practically scream Bailey's Beach."

Rosa had to admit, the women would not look out of place at the exclusive private beach at the end of Newport's cliff walk. "Be nice," she cautioned him.

"I was born nice."

The door opened and three men joined the women. Rosa offered the usual smile of greeting. Then her heart skipped a beat as her gaze fell upon a tall, sandy-haired man. No, it couldn't be, she told herself. She hoped—prayed—it was a trick of the light. But it wasn't, and her expression froze as recognition chilled her to the bone.

Big deal, she thought, trying not to hyperventilate. She was bound to run into him sooner or later.

"Uh-oh," Vince muttered, assuming a stance that was now more protective than welcoming. "Here come the Montagues."

Rosa struggled against panic, but she was losing the battle. You're a grown woman, she reminded herself. You're totally in control.

That was a lie. In the blink of an eye, she was eighteen again, aching and desperate over the boy who'd broken her heart.

"I'll tell them we're closed," Vince said.

"You'll do nothing of the sort," Rosa hissed at him.

"I'll beat the crap out of him."

"You'll offer them a table, and make it a good one." Straightening her shoulders, Rosa looked across the room and locked eyes with a man she hadn't seen in ten years, a man she hoped she would never see again.

Two

~~~

"You asked for it." As though flipping a switch, Vince turned on the charm, stepping forward to greet the latest arrivals. "Welcome to Celesta's," he said. "Do you have a reservation?"

"No, we just want to drink," said one of the men, and the women snickered at his devastating wit.

"Of course," said Vince, stepping back to gesture them toward the bar. "Please seat yourself."

The men and their dates headed to the bar. Rosa thought about the nautilus shell, displayed like a museum artifact. Would he recognize it? Did she care?

Just when she thought she'd survived the moment, she realized one man held back from the group. He was just standing there, watching her intently, with a look that made her shiver.

Her task, of course, was simple. She had to pretend he had no effect on her. This was easier said than done, though, because she had trouble keeping her feelings in. Long ago, she'd resigned herself to the fact that she was a walking cliché—a curly-haired, big-breasted, emotional Italian American.

However, cool disregard was the only message she wanted to send at the moment. She knew with painful certainty that the opposite of love was not hate, but indifference.

"Hello, Alex," she said.

"Rosa." He lifted the corner of his mouth in a half smile.

He'd been drinking. She wasn't sure how she knew. But her practiced eye took in the tousled sandy hair, the boyish face now etched with character, the sea-blue eyes settling a gaze on her that, even now, made her shiver. He looked fashionably rumpled in an Oxford shirt, chinos and Top-Siders.

She couldn't bear to see him again. And oh, she hated that about herself. She wasn't supposed to be this way. She was supposed to be the indomitable Rosa Capoletti, named last year's Restaurateur of the Year by Condé Nast. Self-made Rosa Capoletti, the woman who had it all—a successful business, wonderful friends, a loving family. She was strong and independent, liked and admired. Influential, even. She headed the merchants' committee for the Winslow Chamber of Commerce.

But Rosa had a secret, a terrible secret she prayed no one would discover. She had never gotten over Alexander Montgomery.

"'Of all the gin joints in all the towns in all the world, he walks into mine,'" she said. She pulled it off, too, with jaunty good humor.

"You know each other?" The woman with the Marcia Brady hair had come back to claim him.

He didn't take his eyes off Rosa. She refused to allow herself to look away.

"We did," he said. "A long time ago."

Rosa couldn't stand the tension, although she struggled

to appear perfectly relaxed as she offered an impersonal smile. "Enjoy your evening," she said, every bit the hostess.

He looked at her a moment longer. Then he said, "Thanks. I will," and he stepped into the bar.

She held her smile in place as he and the others settled into an upholstered banquette. The women looked around the bar with surprised appreciation. The norm in these parts consisted of beach shacks, fried food, dated seaside kitsch. Celesta's one-of-a-kind bar, the understated handsomeness of the furnishings and the unparalleled view created an ambience of rare luxury.

Alex took a seat at the end of the table. The tall woman flirted hard with him, leaning toward him and tossing her hair.

Over the years, Rosa had kept up with his life without really meaning to. It was hard to ignore him when she spotted his face smiling out from the pages of a newspaper or magazine. "The thinking woman's hunk," one society columnist dubbed him. "Drives Formula One race cars and speaks fluent Japanese...." He kept company with billionaires and politicians. He did good works—funding a children's hospital, underwriting loan programs for low-income people. Getting engaged.

Pharmaceutical heiress Portia van Deusen was the perfect match for him, according to the people-watchers. With a slight feeling of voyeuristic shame, Rosa had read the breathless raves of society columnists. Portia was always described as "stunning" and Alex as "impeccable." Both of them had the social equivalent of champion bloodlines. Their wedding, of course, was going to be the event of the season.

Except that it never happened. The papers ceased to mention them as a couple. The engagement was "off." Ordinary people were left to speculate about what had happened. There was a whisper that she had left him. And she appeared so quickly on the arm of a different man—older, perhaps even wealthier—that rumor had it she'd found greener pastures.

"Vince said he offered to beat the crap out of him," said Shelly, holding aloft a tray of desserts and espresso.

So much for privacy. In a place like Celesta's, rumors zinged around like rubber bullets.

"As if he could stand to have one hair out of place." In spite of herself, Rosa smiled, picturing Vince in a fight. The sentiment was touching, though. Like everyone who had seen the wreckage Alex had left in his wake, Vince was protective of Rosa.

"Are you all right?" Shelly asked.

"I'm fine. You can tell that to anyone who's wondering."

"That would be everybody," Shelly said.

"For Pete's sake, we broke up eons ago," Rosa said. "I'm a big girl now. I can handle seeing a former boyfriend."

"Good," Shelly said, "because he just ordered a bottle of Cristal."

From the corner of her eye, Rosa saw the sommelier pop the cork of the bottle, listed at $300 on the menu. One of the women at Alex's table—the flirt—giggled and leaned against him as he took a taste and nodded to Felix to pour. The six of them lifted their glasses, clinking them together.

Rosa turned away to say good-night to a departing couple. "I hope you enjoyed your evening," she said.

"We did," the woman assured her. "I read about this place in the *New York Times* 'Escape' section, and have always wanted to come here. It's even nicer than I expected."

"Thank you," Rosa said, silently blessing the *Times*.

Travel writers and food critics were a picky lot, as a whole. But her kitchen had proven itself, again and again.

"Are you Celesta, then?" the woman asked as she drew on a light cotton wrap.

"No," Rosa said, her heart stumbling almost imperceptibly as she gestured at the lighted portrait that hung behind the podium next to the numerous awards. Celesta, in all her soft, hand-tinted beauty, gazed benevolently from the gilt frame. "She was my mother."

The woman smiled gently. "It's a wonderful place. I'm sure we'll be back."

"We'd love to have you."

When Rosa turned from the door, she used every bit of her willpower to keep from spying on Alex Montgomery. She knew he was watching her. She just knew it. She could feel his gaze like a phantom touch, finding her most vulnerable places.

They had said goodbye many years ago, and it was the sort of goodbye that was supposed to be permanent. She wondered what he was thinking, barging in on her like this.

"May I have this dance?" Jason Aspoll held out his hand to Rosa.

She smiled at him. It was a well-known fact that on most nights, near closing time, Rosa enjoyed getting out on the dance floor. It was good marketing. Show the public you like your place just as much as they do. Besides, Rosa did love dancing.

And she didn't like going home. There was nothing wrong with her place, except that it simply wasn't... lived in enough.

"I'd love to," she said to Jason, and slipped easily into his arms. The ensemble played "La Danza," and they swayed, grinning at each other like idiots.

"So you finally did it, you big goof," she said.

"I couldn't have done it without you."

"I know," she said breezily, then patted his arm. "Seriously, Jason, I'm honored that you asked for my help. It was fun."

"Well, I'm in awe. You managed everything perfectly, down to the last detail. Her favorite food was tonight's special, the ensemble kept playing songs she loves… You even had special flowers on all the tables. I didn't know Lily of the Valley was her favorite."

"In the future, knowing her favorites is your job." Rosa was always mystified that people simply didn't notice things about other people. She had once dated an airline pilot for five months, and he never learned how she took her coffee. Come to think of it, no man had ever bothered to learn that about her, except—

"How does Linda take her coffee?" she asked Jason suddenly.

"Hot?"

"Very funny. How does she like her coffee?"

"Linda drinks tea. She takes it with honey and lemon."

Rosa collapsed against him in exaggerated relief. "Thank God. You passed the test." She didn't mean to dart one tiny glance at Alex. It just happened. He was looking straight at her. Fine, then, she thought. Let him look.

"I didn't know there was a test," Jason whispered to her.

"There's always a test," she said. "Remember that."

The music wound down and then stopped. During the polite patter of applause, Linda joined them.

"I've come to claim my man," she said, slipping her hand into his.

"He's all yours." Rosa gave her a quick hug. "And that's for you. Congratulations, my friends. I wish you all the happiness in the world."

Linda jerked her head in the direction of Alex's table. "What the hell is he doing here?"

"Drinking a $300 bottle of champagne." Rosa held up a hand. "And that's all I have to say on the subject. Tonight is your night. You and Jason."

"You're meeting me for coffee tomorrow, though," Linda insisted. "And then you'll spill."

"Fine. I'll see you at Pegasus tomorrow. Now, take your man and go home."

"All right. Rosa, I know how much you did to make this night special," said Linda. "I'll never be able to thank you enough."

Rosa beamed. The look on Linda's face was reward enough, but she said, "You can name your first child after me."

"Only if it's a girl."

She and Linda hugged one more time, and the happy couple left. The music started up again, Rosa went back to work and pretended not to see Alex ask the tall woman at his table to dance.

This was absurd, she thought. She was an adult now, not a wide-eyed kid fresh out of high school. She had every right to go over to him this minute and demand to know what he was doing here. Or for that matter, what he'd been doing since he'd said, "Have a nice life" and strolled off into the sunset.

Did he have a nice life? she wondered.

He certainly looked as though he did. He seemed relaxed with his friends—or maybe that was the champagne kicking in. He had an air of casual elegance that was not in the least affected. Even when she first met him, as a little boy, he'd had a certain aura about him. That in-born poise was a family trait, one she'd observed not just in Alex, but in his parents and sister, as well.

The quality was nothing so uncomplicated as mere snobbery. Rosa had encountered her share of that. No, the Montgomerys simply had an innate sense of their place in the world, and that place was at the top of the heap.

Except when it came to loving someone. He pretty much sucked at that.

Maybe he'd changed. His date certainly appeared hopeful as she undulated her "Sex and the City" body against his on the dance floor.

"You want I should break his kneecaps?" inquired a deep voice behind her.

Rosa smiled. "Not tonight, Teddy."

Teddy was in charge of security at the restaurant. In another sort of establishment, he'd be called a bouncer. The job required a thorough knowledge of digital alarms and surveillance, but he lived for the day he could wield those ham-sized fists on her behalf. "I got lots of footage of him on the security cameras," he informed her. "You can watch that if you want."

"No, I don't want," Rosa snapped, yet she could picture herself obsessively playing the tape, over and over again. "So does everybody in the place know the guy who once dumped me is here tonight?"

"Oh, yeah," he said unapologetically. "We had a meeting about it. We don't care how long ago it happened. He was harsh, Rosa. Damned harsh. What a dickwad."

"We were just kids—"

"Headed to college. That's pretty grown-up."

She'd never made it to college. Her staff probably had a meeting about that, too.

"He's a paying customer," she said. "That's all he is, so I wish everyone would quit trying to make such a big deal out of it. I don't like people discussing my personal affairs."

Teddy gently touched her shoulder. "It's okay, Rosa. We're talking about this because we care about you. Nobody wants to see you hurt."

"Then you've got nothing to worry about," she assured him. "I'm fine. I'm perfectly fine."

It became her mantra for the remainder of the evening, which was nearly over at last. The bartender's final call circulated, and the ensemble bade everyone good-night by playing their signature farewell number, a sweet and wistful arrangement of "As Time Goes By."

The last few customers circled the dance floor and then dispersed, heading off into the night, couples lost in each other and oblivious to the world. Rosa couldn't keep count of the times she had stood in the shadows and watched people fall in love right here on the premises. Celesta's was just that kind of place.

How'm I doing, Mamma?

Celesta, twenty years gone, would undoubtedly approve. The restaurant smelled like the kitchen of Rosa's childhood; the menu featured many of the dishes Celesta had once prepared with warmth, intense flavors and a certain uncomplicated contentment Rosa constantly tried to recapture. She wanted the restaurant to serve Italian comfort food, the kind that fed hidden hungers and left people full of fond remembrances.

She pretended to be busy as Alex and his friends left. Finally she let out the breath she hadn't known she was holding. When the last patron departed, so did the magic. The lights came up, revealing crumbs and smudges on the floors and tables, soot on the candle chimneys, dropped napkins and flatware. In the absence of music and with the kitchen doors propped open, the clank and crash of dishes rang through the building.

"Ka-*ching*," Vince said as he printed out a spreadsheet

summarizing the night's receipts. "Biggest till of the year so far." He hesitated, then added, "Your dumbshit ex-boyfriend left a whopper tip."

"He's not my ex-anything," she insisted. "He's ancient history."

"Yeah, but I bet he's still a dumbshit."

"I wouldn't know. He's a complete stranger to me. I wish everyone would get that through their heads."

"We won't," he assured her. "Can't you see we're dying here, Rosa? We're starved for gossip."

"Find someone else to gossip about."

"We were all watching him with the new security cameras," Vince said.

"I can't believe you guys."

"Teddy can zoom in on anything."

"Good for him." Her head pounded, and she rubbed her temples.

"I got this, honey," Vince said. "I'll close tonight."

She offered a thin smile. "Thanks." She started to remind him about the seal on the walk-in fridge, the raccoons in the Dumpster, but stopped herself. She'd been working on her control-freak impulses.

As she left through the back entrance, she wished she'd thought to grab a sweater before rushing out today. The afternoon had been hot; now the chill air raised goose bumps on her bare arms.

Debris from last week's windstorm had been cleared away, but broken trees and fallen branches still lay along the periphery of the parking lot. The power had been knocked out for hours, but the cameras had come through unscathed.

Her heels rang on the pavement as she headed for her car, a red Alfa Romeo Spider equipped with an extravagant stereo system. As she used the remote on her key chain to unlock the driver's side door, a shadow overtook her.

She stopped walking and looked up to see Alex, somehow not surprised to find him standing in the dull glow of the parking lot lights. "What, you're stalking me now?"

"Do you feel stalked?"

"Yeah, I generally do when a man approaches me in a deserted parking lot at midnight. Creeps me out."

"I can see how that could happen."

"You should hear what they're saying about you inside."

"What's that?"

"Oh, all sorts of things. Dumbshit, dickwad. Stuff like that. Two different guys offered to break your kneecaps. They liked your tip, though."

He offered that crooked smile again, the one that used to practically stop her heart. "It's good to know you surrounded yourself with quality people."

She gestured at the security camera mounted on a light pole.

"What are you doing?" Alex asked.

"Trying to let my quality people know I don't need rescuing." It was late. She couldn't keep batting this pointless conversation back and forth. She just wanted to go home. Besides, it was taking every bit of energy she possessed to pretend he had no effect on her. "What are you doing here, Alex?" she asked.

He showed her his hand, which held a palm-sized cell phone. "I was calling a taxi. Is the local service as bad now as it used to be?"

"A taxi? You'd be better off hitchhiking."

"That's supposed to be dangerous. And I know you wouldn't want to put a customer in danger."

"Where are your friends, anyway?"

"Went back to Newport."

"And you're headed…?"

"To the house on Ocean Road."

No one in his family had visited the place in twelve years. It was like a haunted mansion, perched there at the edge of the ocean, an abandoned, empty shell. Wondering what had brought him back after all this time, she shivered. Before she realized what he was doing, he slipped his jacket around her shoulders. She pulled away. "I don't—"

"Just take it."

She tried not to be aware of his body heat, clinging to the lining of the jacket. "Your friends couldn't give you a ride?"

"I didn't want one. I was waiting for you…Rosa."

"What, so I can give you a lift?" Her voice rose with incredulity.

"Thanks," he said. "Don't mind if I do." He headed for the Alfa Spider.

Rosa stood in the amber glow of the floodlights, trying to figure out what to do. She was tempted to peel out without another word to him, but that seemed a bit juvenile and petty. She could always get someone from the restaurant to give him a ride, but they weren't feeling too friendly toward him. Besides, in spite of herself, she was curious.

She didn't say another word as she released the lock on the passenger side door. She waved goodbye to the security camera; then they got in and took off.

"Thanks, Rosa," he said.

Like he'd given her a choice. She exceeded the speed limit, but she didn't care. There wasn't a soul in sight, not even a possum or a deer. This area was lightly patrolled by the sheriff's department, and given her association with Sean Costello, sheriff of South County, she didn't have much concern that she'd get a ticket.

At the roadside, beach rose hedges fanned out toward the dunes and black water. On the other side lay marshes and protected land, an area mercifully untouched for generations.

"So I guess you're wondering why I'm back," Alex said.

She was dying to know. "Not at all," she said.

"I knew Celesta's was your place," he explained. "I wanted to see you."

His directness took her aback. But then, he used to be the most honest person she knew. Right up until he left, never looking back.

"What for?" she asked.

"I still think about you, Rosa."

"Ancient history," she assured him, reminding herself he'd been drinking.

"It doesn't feel that way. Feels like only yesterday."

"Not to me," she lied.

"You were dating that deputy. Costa," Alex said, referring to the day he'd briefly returned, about ten years ago, and she'd sent him away. He would remember that, along with the fact that she didn't need or want him.

"Costello," she corrected him. "Sean Costello. He's the sheriff now."

"And you're still single."

"That's none of your business."

"I'm making it my business."

Rosa drove even faster. "It was awkward, you showing up like that."

"I figured it would be. At least we're talking. That's a start."

"I don't want to start anything with you, Alex."

"Have I asked you to?"

She pulled into the crushed gravel and oyster shell drive of the Montgomery house. Over the years, the grounds had been kept neat, the place painted every five years. It was a handsome Victorian masterpiece in the Carpenter Gothic style, complete with engraved brass plaque from the South County Historical Preservation Society.

"No," she admitted, throwing the gear in Neutral. "You haven't asked me for anything but a ride. So here's your ride. Good night, Alex." She thought about tossing off a remark—*Say hi to your mother from me*—but couldn't bring herself to do that.

He turned to her on the seat. "Rosa, I have a lot to say to you."

"I don't want to hear it."

"Then you won't. Not right now. See, I'm drunk. And when I say what I want to say to you, I need to be stone-cold sober."

Three

＊＊＊

The next morning Rosa went to Pegasus, a coffeehouse furnished with overstuffed sofas and chairs, low tables and a luxurious selection of biscotti. The café offered the *New York Times* and *Boston Globe,* along with the *Providence Journal Bulletin* and local papers. Rosa was friendly with the proprietor, Millie, a genuine barista imported from Seattle, complete with baggy dress, Birkenstocks and a God-given talent for making perfect espresso.

While she fixed a double tall skinny vanilla latte, Millie eyed the stack of notebooks and textbooks Rosa had set on the table.

"So what are we studying now?" She tilted her head to the side to read the spines of the books. "*Neurolinguistic Programming and its Practical Application to Creative Growth.* A little light reading?"

"It's actually an amazing topic," Rosa said over the *whoosh* of the milk steamer. "Did you know there's a way to recover creative joy simply by finding pleasurable past associations?"

Millie set the latte on the counter. "Too advanced for me, Einstein. What school?"

"Berkeley. The professor even offered to read my final paper if I e-mail it to him."

Millie eyed her admiringly. "I swear, you have the best education money can't buy."

"Keeps me out of trouble, anyway." Rosa had never left home, but over the years she'd managed to sample the finest places of higher learning in the world—genetics at MIT, rococo architecture at the University of Milan, medieval law at Oxford and chaos theory at Harvard. She used to contact professors by phone in order to finagle a syllabus and reading list. Now the Internet made it even easier. With a few clicks of the mouse, she could find course outlines, study sheets, practice tests. The only cost to her was the price of books.

"You're nuts," Millie said with a grin. "We all think so."

"But I'm a very educated nut."

"True. Do you ever wish you could sit down and take an actual class?"

Long ago, that had been all Rosa had dreamed of. Then she'd found herself in the midst of an unspeakable tragedy, and the entire course of her life had shifted. "Sure I do," she said with deliberate lightness. "I still might, one of these days, when I find the time."

"You could start by hiring a general manager for your restaurant."

"I can barely afford my own salary." Rosa had a seat and opened one of the books to an article on Noam Chomsky's Transformational Grammar.

Linda showed up wearing a T-shirt that read What if the Hokey Pokey *is* what it's all about? and went to the counter to order her usual—a pot of Lady Grey with honey and a lemon wedge on the side. "Sorry I'm late," she said over her shoulder. "I tried to get off the phone with my mom, but she couldn't stop crying."

"That's sweet."

"I guess, but it might be a little insulting, too. She was just so…relieved. She's been worried that I'd never get married. A major tragedy in the Lipschitz family. So the fact that Jason's Catholic didn't even faze her." She held out her hand, letting the sunlight glitter through the facets of the diamond in her new engagement ring. "It looks even better in broad daylight, doesn't it?"

"It's gorgeous."

Linda beamed at her. "I can't wait to change my name to Aspoll."

"You're taking his name?"

"Hey, for me it's an upgrade. We can't all be born with names like Puccini opera characters, Miss Rosina Angelica Capoletti." Linda drizzled honey into her tea. "Oh, and I have news. The wedding has to be in August. Jason's company transferred him to Boise, and we're moving right after Labor Day."

Rosa smiled at her friend, though when Jason had told her that, she'd wanted to hit him. "So we have less than twelve weeks to plan and execute this wedding," she said. "Maybe that's why your mom was crying."

"She's loving it. She'll be flying up from Florida next week. There's nothing quite like my mom in event-planning mode. It's going to be fine, you'll see."

She seemed remarkably calm, Rosa thought. The reality of getting married and leaving Winslow forever probably hadn't hit her yet.

Linda lifted her cup. "How you doing, Ms. Rosa? Still recovering from the shock of seeing Mr. Love-'em-and-leave-'em?"

Rosa concentrated on sprinkling sugar in her latte. "There's nothing to recover from. So he showed up at the restaurant, so what? His family still owns that property out on Ocean Road. I was bound to run into him sooner or later. I'm just surprised it took so long. But it's no big—"

"You just put four packets of sugar in that coffee," Linda pointed out.

"I did not…" Rosa stared in surprise at the little ripped packets littering the table. She pushed the mug away. "Shoot."

"Ah, Rosa." Linda patted her hand. "I'm sorry."

"It was just weird, okay? Weird to see that someone who was once my whole world is a stranger now. And I guess it's weird because I had to imagine him having a life. I didn't do that when we were little, you know? He'd go away at the end of summer, and I never thought about him in the city. Then when he came back the next year, we picked up where we left off. I thought he only existed for the three months he was with me. And now he's existed for twelve years without me, which is completely no big deal."

"Oh, come on, Rosa. It's a big deal. Maybe it shouldn't be, but it is."

"We were kids, just out of school."

"You loved him."

Rosa tried her coffee and winced. Too sweet. "Everybody's in love when they're eighteen. And everybody gets dumped."

"And moves on," Linda said. "Except you."

"Linda—"

"It's true. You've never had anyone really special since Alex," Linda stated.

"I go out with guys all the time."

"You know what I mean."

Rosa pushed the coffee mug away. "I went out with Greg Fortner for six months."

"He was in the navy. He was gone for five of those six months."

"Maybe that's why we got along so well." Rosa looked at her friend. Clearly, Linda wasn't buying it. "All right, what about Derek Gunn? Eight months, at least."

"I'd hardly call that a lifelong commitment. I wish you'd stuck with him. He was great, Rosa."

"He had a fatal flaw," Rosa muttered.

"Yeah? What's that?"

"You'll say I'm petty."

"Try me. I'm not letting you out of my sight until you 'fess up."

"He was boring." The admission burst from Rosa on a sigh.

"He drives a Lexus."

"I rest my case."

Linda got an extra mug and shared her tea with Rosa. "He's got a house on the water in Newport."

"Boring house. Boring water. Even worse, he has a boring family. Hanging out with them was like watching paint dry. And I'll probably burn in hell for saying that."

"It's best to know what your issues are before going ahead with a relationship."

"You been watching too much Dr. Phil. I have no issues."

Linda coughed. "Stop that. You'll make me snort tea out my nose."

"Okay, so what are my issues?"

Linda waved a hand. "Uh-uh, I'm not touching that one. I need you to be my maid of honor, and it won't happen if we're not speaking. That's what this meeting's about, by the way. Me. My wedding. Not that it's anywhere near as interesting as you and Alex Montgomery."

"There is no me and Alex Montgomery," Rosa insisted. "And—not to change the subject—did I just hear you ask me to be your maid of honor?"

Linda took a deep breath and beamed at her. "I did. You're my oldest and dearest friend, Rosa. I want you to stand up with me at my wedding. So, will you?"

"Are you kidding?" Rosa gave her friend's hand a squeeze. "I'd be honored."

She loved weddings and had been a bridesmaid six times. She knew it was six because, deep in the farthest reaches of her closet, she had six of the ugliest dresses ever designed, in colors no one had ever seen before. But Rosa had worn each one with a keen sense of duty and pride. She danced and toasted at the weddings; she caught a bouquet or two in her time. After each wedding, she returned home, carrying her dyed-to-match shoes in one hand and her wilting bouquet in the other.

"…as soon as we set a date," Linda was saying.

Rosa realized her thoughts had drifted. "Sorry. What?"

"Hello? I said, keep August 21 and 28 open for me, okay?"

"Yes, of course."

Linda finished her tea. "I'd better let you go. You need to deal with Alex Montgomery."

"I don't need to deal with Alex Montgomery. There's simply no dealing to be done."

"I don't think you have a choice," Linda said.

"That's ridiculous. Of course I have a choice. Just because he came back to town doesn't mean it's my job to deal with him."

"It's your shot, Rosa. Your golden opportunity. Don't let it pass you by."

Rosa spread her hands, genuinely baffled. "What

shot? What opportunity? I have no idea what you're talking about."

"To get unstuck."

"I beg your pardon."

"You've been stuck in the same place since Alex left you."

"Bullshit. I'm not stuck. I have a fabulous life here. I never wanted to be anywhere else."

"I don't mean that kind of stuck. I mean emotionally stuck. You never got over the hurt and distrust of what happened with Alex, and you can't move on. Now that he's back, you've got a chance to clear the air with him and get him out of your heart and out of your head once and for all."

"He's not in my heart," Rosa insisted. "He's not in my head."

"Right." Linda patted her arm. "Deal with him, Rosa. You'll thank me one day. He can't be having an easy time, you know, since his mother—"

"What about his mother?" Rosa hadn't heard talk of Emily Montgomery in ages, but that was not unusual. She never came to the shore anymore.

"God, you didn't hear?"

"Hear what?"

"I just assumed you knew." Linda jumped up and rifled through the stack of daily papers. She returned with a *Journal Bulletin,* folded back to show Rosa.

She stared at the photo of the haughtily beautiful Emily Montgomery, portrait-posed and gazing serenely at the camera.

"Oh, God." Her hands rattled the paper as she pushed it away from her on the table. Then, in the same movement, she gathered the paper close and started to read. "Society matron Emily Wright Montgomery, wife of financier Alexander Montgomery III, died on Wednesday at her home in Providence…"

Rosa laid down the paper and looked across the table at her friend. "She was only fifty-five."

"That's what it says. Doesn't seem so old now that we're nearly thirty."

"I wonder what happened." Rosa thought about the way Alex had been last night—slightly drunk, coming on to her. Now his recklessness took on a different meaning. He'd just lost his mother. Last night, she had dropped him off at an empty house.

Linda leveled her gaze at Rosa. "You should ask him."

Four

Rosa drove along Prospect Street to the house where she'd grown up. Little had changed here, only the names of the residents and the gumball colors of their clapboard houses. Buckling concrete driveways led to crammed garages with sagging rooflines. Maple and elm trees arched over the roadway, their stately grace a foil for the homely houses.

It was nice here, she reflected. Safe and comfortable. People still tended their peonies and hydrangeas, their roses and snapdragons. Women pegged out laundry on clotheslines stretched across sunny backyards. Kids rode bikes from house to house and climbed the overgrown apple tree in the Lipschitzes' yard. She still thought of it as the Lipschitzes' yard even though Linda's parents had retired to Vero Beach, Florida, years ago.

She pulled up to the curb in front of number 115, a boxy house with a garden so neat that people sometimes slowed down to admire it. A pruned hedge guarded the profusion of roses that bloomed from spring to winter. Each of the roses had a name. Not the proper name of its variety, but Salvatore, Roberto, Rosina—each one planted in honor of their first communion. There were also roses that honored relatives in Italy whom Rosa had never met, and a few for people she didn't know—La Donna, a scarlet beauty, and a coral floribunda whose name she couldn't remember.

The sturdy bush by the front step, covered in creamy-white blooms, was the Celesta, of course. A few feet away was the one Rosa, a six-year-old with a passion for Pepto-Bismol pink, had chosen for herself. Mamma had been so proud of her that day, beaming down like an angel from heaven. It was one of those memories Rosa cherished, because it was so clear in her heart and mind. She wished all the past could be remembered this way, with clarity and affection, no tinge of regret. But that was naive, and by now, she had figured that out.

She used her ancient key to let herself in. Pop had given it to her when she was nine years old, and she had never once lost it. In the front hall, she blinked the lights a few times. Out of habit she called his name, though it had been some years since he'd been able to hear her.

An acrid odor wafted from the kitchen, along with a buzzing sound.

"Shit," she muttered under her breath, clutching the strap of her purse to her shoulder as she ran to the back of the house. On the counter, a blender stood unattended, its seized motor humming its last, rubber-scented smoke streaming from the base. She grabbed the cord—it felt hot to the touch—and jerked it from the wall. Inside the blender, the lukewarm juice sloshed. The kitchen smoke alarm blinked—what good was that if Pop wasn't looking?

"Jesus, Mary and Joseph, you're going to kill yourself one of these days," Rosa said, waving the smoke away from her face. She peered through the window and saw him out in the backyard, puttering around, oblivious.

On the kitchen table, a newspaper lay open to the Emily Montgomery obituary. Rosa pictured her father starting his breakfast, paging through the paper, stopping in shock as he read the news. He'd probably wandered outside to think about it.

She opened the windows and turned on the exhaust fan over the range, then emptied the blender carafe into the sink. As she cleaned up the mess, Rosa felt a wave of nostalgia. In the scrubbed and gleaming kitchen, her mother's rolled-out pasta dough used to cover the entire top of the chrome and Formica table. Rosa could still picture the long sleek muscles in her mother's arms as she wielded the red-handled rolling pin, drawing it in smooth, rhythmic strokes over the butter-yellow dough.

The reek of the burnt-out motor was a corruption here, in Mamma's world. The smell of her baking ciambellone used to be so powerful it drew the neighbors in, and Rosa could remember the women in their aprons and scuffs, sitting on the back stoop, sharing coffee and Mamma's citrusy ciambellone, fresh from the oven.

To this day, the sweet, dense bread was one of the signature brunch items at Celesta's-by-the-Sea. Butch prepared the dough directly on the countertop with his bare hands, no bowls or spoons, just like Mamma had. Rosa appreciated Butch's skill at cooking and his exquisite palate, but some subtle essence was missing; she could only put it down as magic. No one could capture that, though Rosa knew in some part of her heart that she would never stop trying.

She went out back to talk to her father. The yard had a long rectangular garden that had been laid out and planted by her mother before Rosa was born. Nowadays, her father tended the heirloom tomatoes, peppers, beans and herbs, happy to spend his silent hours in a place his young wife had loved.

He was seated on a wooden folding chair beneath a plum tree, smoking a pipe. A few branches lay around, casualties of the recent windstorm. He looked up when her shadow fell over him.

"Hi, Pop," she said.

"Rosa." He set aside the pipe, stood and held out his arms.

She smiled and hugged him, then gave him a kiss on the cheek, inhaling his familiar scent of shaving soap and pipe tobacco. When she stepped back, she made sure he was looking directly at her, and told him about the blender.

"I guess I forgot and left it on," he said.

"The house could have burned down, Pop."

"I'll be careful from now on, okay?"

It was what he always said when Rosa worried about him. It didn't help, but neither did arguing with him. She studied his face, noticing troubled shadows in his eyes, and knew it had nothing to do with the blender. "You heard about Mrs. Montgomery."

"Yes. Of course. It was in all the papers."

Pop had always been addicted to reading the newspapers, usually two a day. In fact, Rosa had learned to read while sitting in his lap, deciphering the funny pages.

He took her hand in his. He had wonderful hands, blunt and strong, callused from the work he did. His touch was always gentle, as though he feared she might break. "Let's sit. Want some coffee?"

"No, thanks." She joined him in the shade of the plum tree. He seemed…different today. Distracted and maybe diminished, somehow. "Are you all right, Pop?"

"I'm fine, fine." He waved off her concern like batting at a fly.

This wouldn't be the first time he'd lost a client. In the forty years since he had emigrated from Italy, he'd worked for scores of families in the area. But today he seemed to be particularly melancholy.

"She was still so young," Rosa commented.

"Yes." A faraway look came into his eyes. "She was a bride when I first saw her, just a girl, younger than you."

Rosa tried to picture Alex's mother as a young bride, but the image eluded her. She realized Mrs. Montgomery must have been just thirty the first time Rosa had seen her. It seemed inconceivable. Emily Montgomery had always been ageless in her crisp tennis whites, her silky hair looped into a ponytail. She wore almost no jewelry, which Rosa later learned was characteristic of women from the oldest and wealthiest families. Ostentation was for the nouveau riche.

Mrs. Montgomery had lived in terror for her fragile son and had regarded Rosa as a danger to his health.

"I wonder how she died," Rosa said to her father. "Did any of the obituaries say?"

"No. There was nothing."

She watched a ladybug lumber over a blade of grass. "Are you going to the service, or—"

"No, of course not. It is not expected. She doesn't need the gardener. And if I sent flowers, well, they would just get lost."

Rosa got up, pacing in agitation. She walked over to the tomato bushes, the centerpiece of the spectacular garden plot. In her mind's eye, she could see her mother in a house dress that somehow looked pretty on her, a green-sprigged apron, bleached Keds with no socks, a straw hat to keep the sun from her eyes. Mamma never hurried in the garden, and she used all her senses while tending it. She would hold a tomato in the palm of her hand, determining its ripeness by its softness and heft. Or she would inhale the fragrance of pepperoncini or bell peppers, test a pinch of flat leaf parsley or mint between her teeth. Everything had to be at its peak before Mamma brought it to the kitchen.

Rosa bent and plucked a stalk of dockweed from the soil. She straightened, turned to find her father watching her, and she smiled. His hearing loss broke her heart, but it had also brought them closer. Of necessity, he had become incredibly attentive, watching her, reading every nuance of movement and expression with uncanny accuracy. His skill at reading lips was remarkable.

And he knew her so well, she thought, her smile wobbling. "Alex came by the restaurant last night."

Pop's eyebrows lowered, but he didn't comment. He didn't have to. Years ago, he had thought Alex a poor match for her, and his opinion probably hadn't changed.

"He didn't say a word about his mother," she continued. That was when she felt a twist of pain. He'd been drinking last night because he was hurting. Surely his friends must've realized that. Why had they simply left him? Why didn't he have better friends? Why did it matter to her?

"Well." Pop slapped his thighs and stood up. "I must go to work. The Camdens are having a croquet party and they need their hedges trimmed."

Rosa removed his flat black cap and kissed his balding head. "You come up to the restaurant tonight. Butch is fixing bluefish for the special."

"I'm gonna get fat, I keep eating at your place all the time."

She gave his arm a playful punch. "See you, Pop."

"Yeah, okay."

She stepped through the gate and turned to wave. The

expression on his face startled her. "Pop, you sure you're doing all right?"

Instead of replying to her question, he said, "You shouldn't mess with that guy, just because he came back."

"Who says I'm messing with him?"

"Tell me I'm wrong, Rosa."

"Don't worry about me, Pop. I'm a big girl now."

"I always worry about you. Why else am I still here on this earth?"

She touched her hand to her heart and then raised it to sign *I love you*.

He'd learned American Sign Language after losing his hearing in the accident, but rarely used it. Signing in public still made him feel self-conscious. But they weren't in public now, so he signed back. *I love you more.*

As she pulled away from the curb, she let her father's warning play over and over in her head. *You shouldn't mess with that guy, just because he came back.*

"Right, Pop," she said, then turned onto Ocean Road, heading toward the Montgomery place.

Ciambellone

Ciambellone is a cross between a cake and a bread, with a nice texture well suited to be served at breakfast or with coffee. The smell of a baking ciambellone is said to turn a scowl into a smile.

  4 cups flour
  3 eggs
  1 teaspoon vanilla
  1 cup sugar
  1 cup milk
  1 teaspoon cinnamon
  1/2 cup oil
  1 teaspoon baking powder
  zest from 1 lemon, finely chopped
  garnish: milk, coarsely granulated sugar

Make a mound with the flour on a board, creating a well in the center. Using your fingers, begin alternating the liquid and other dry ingredients into the well, mixing until all the ingredients are combined, adding additional flour as needed and kneading to make a smooth dough. Divide into 2 parts and shape into fat rings. Brush the tops with milk and sprinkle with sugar. Place the coils on a buttered baking sheet and bake at 350° F for about 40 minutes or until golden brown.

PART TWO

Insalata

When she made a salad, Mamma used only the
most tender hearts and cores of the lettuce.
She tossed everything in a bowl so big and wide,
a small child could sit in it. That's the secret
of a great salad. Give yourself plenty of space
to toss. You always need more room than you
think you need.

Romaine and Gorgonzola Salad

Wash two heads of romaine lettuce in cold water, discarding the tough outer leaves. Shake dry and tear into bite-sized pieces. Add basil sprigs and cherry tomatoes, cut in half. Right before serving, toss the lettuce with Gorgonzola vinaigrette.

Gorgonzola Vinaigrette
1/4 cup white wine vinegar + 1/4 cup apple juice
1 Tablespoon minced shallots
2 Tablespoons mustard
2 teaspoons chopped basil
2 Tablespoons toasted pine nuts (pinones)
1/4 cup walnut oil + 3 Tablespoons olive oil
2 Tablespoons crumbled Gorgonzola—preferably
*   the aged variety from Monferrato*
freshly ground black pepper

Put everything in a jar and shake well. Makes about 1 cup. Store in the fridge for up to 5 days.

Five

Summer 1983

When Rosa Capoletti was nine years old, she learned two important lessons. One: after your mother dies, you should still remember to talk to her every day. And two: never put up a rope swing in a tree containing a beehive.

Of course, she wasn't aware of the hive when she coiled a stout rope around her shoulder and shinned up the trunk of a venerable elm tree by the pond in the Montgomerys' garden. The pond was stocked with rare fish from Japan and water lilies from Costa Rica, and had a burbling fountain. Pop had told Rosa she should never bother the fish. The pond was Mrs. Montgomery's pride and joy, and under no circumstances must it be disturbed.

Pop had told her to stay out of trouble. He was going to the plant nursery with Mrs. Montgomery and Rosa was not to leave the yard. That was fine with her, because it was a perfect summer day, third grade was behind her and she had nothing but lazy days ahead. When Mamma was alive, Rosa used to help her in the kitchen garden at home. Mamma's tomatoes and basil were so good they won prizes, and she always made Rosa wear a straw hat with a brim, tied on with a polka dot scarf. She said too much sun was bad for the skin.

Since Mamma died and the boys went into the navy, there was no one to look after Rosa once school let out for summer, so she went to work with Pop each day. The nuns from school urged Rosa's father to send her to a Catholic summer camp. Rosa had begged to stay home, promising Pop she'd stay out of the way.

Going to work with her father turned out to be the only thing that kept Rosa from shriveling up with sadness over Mamma. He used to be a familiar sight around the area, going from place to place on his sturdy yellow bicycle. Now they drove together in the old Dodge Power Wagon, with all his gardening tools in the back. During the summer, he worked from dawn to dusk at six places—one for each day of the week—mowing, pruning, digging and clipping the yards and gardens of the vast seaside estates that fringed the shoreline.

This was Rosa's first visit to the Montgomery place, a giant barge of a house with a railed porch on three sides and tall, narrow windows with glass so old it was wavy. She found all sorts of things to explore in the huge, lush yard that extended out to touch an isolated stretch of beach. Still, she was bored. She wanted to go to the beach, to take the little dinghy out, to go on adventures with her friends. But she was stuck here.

Spending the afternoon alone would be a lot more fun now that she had a rope swing, she thought, sticking one bare foot in the bottom loop and pushing off. She laughed aloud and started singing "Stray Cat Strut," which played on the radio at least once a day. She didn't really know what a "feline Casanova" was, but it was a good tune, and her big brother Sal had taught her all the words before he left.

He and her other brother, Rob, took the train early this morning. They were going to something called Basic Training, and who knew when she'd see them again?

She soared high enough to see the empty beach beyond the lavish gardens and then low enough to skim the soft, perfectly groomed carpet of grass. The sky was bluer than heaven, like Mamma used to say. In the garden below, the button-eyed daisies and fancy purple lobelias were reflected in the surface of the pond. Seagulls flew like flashing white kites over the breakers on the beach, and Rosa felt all the fluttery excitement of freedom.

Summer was here. Finally, endless days out from under the glare of Sister Baptista, whose stare was so sharp she could make you squirm like a bug on a pin.

The little seaside town of Winslow changed in the summer. The pace picked up, and people drove along the coast road in convertibles with the tops down. Pop would comment that the price of gas and groceries went sky-high and that it was impossible to get a table at Mario's Flying Pizza on a Friday night, even though Rosa and Pop always got a table, because Mario was Mamma's cousin.

Rosa came in for a landing, aiming her bare foot for the crotch of the tree. Her foot struck something dry and papery that collapsed when she touched it. A humming noise mingled with the rustle of the breeze through the leaves. Then Rosa's foot burst into flame.

A second later, she saw a black cloud rise from the tree, and the faint humming sound changed to a roar. A truly angry roar.

She didn't remember getting down from the tree, but later she would discover livid rope burns on the insides of her knees, along with a colorful variety of scratches and bruises. She hit the ground running, howling at the tops of her lungs, then stabbing the air with a separate shriek each time she felt another sting.

She headed straight for the pond with its burbling fountain.

Rosa took a flying leap for the clear, calm water. She couldn't help herself. She was on fire. It was an emergency.

The cool water brought relief as she submerged herself. The places she'd been stung were instantly soothed by the silky mud on the bottom. She broke the surface and saw a few bees still hovering around, so she sat in the shallow water, waving her arms and legs, stirring up brown clouds. She didn't know how long she sat there, letting the mud cool the stings. She could detect six of them, maybe more, mostly on her legs.

"What in heaven's holy name is going on?" demanded a sharp voice. A woman rushed out of the house and down the back stairs.

Rosa almost didn't recognize Mrs. Carmichael in her starched housekeeper's uniform. The Carmichaels lived down the street from the Capolettis, and usually Rosa only saw her in her housedress and slippers, standing on the porch and calling her boys in to dinner. Everything was different in this neighborhood of big houses overlooking the sea. Everything was cleaner and neater, even the people.

Except Rosa herself. As she slogged to the edge of the pond, feeling the smooth mud squish between her toes, she knew with every cell in her body that she didn't belong here. Muddy and barefoot, soaked to the skin, bee-stung and bruised, she belonged anywhere but here.

She waited, dripping on the lawn as Mrs. Carmichael bustled toward her. "I can explain—"

"What are we going to do with you, Rosa Capoletti?" Mrs. Carmichael demanded. She was on the verge of being mad, but she was holding her temper back. Rosa could tell. People tried to be extra patient with her, on account of her mother had died on Valentine's Day. Even Sister Baptista tried to be a little nicer.

"I can get cleaned off in the garden hose," Rosa suggested.

"Good idea. I hope you didn't do in any of the koi."

"The what?"

"The fish."

"I didn't mean to."

Mrs. Carmichael shook her head. "Let's go."

As she followed Mrs. Carmichael across the lawn, Rosa glanced at the house and saw a ghost in the window. A small, pale person with a round Charlie Brown head stood staring out at her, veiled by lace curtains. She looked again and saw that the ghost was gone, shy as a hummingbird zipping out of sight.

"Holy moly," she muttered.

"What's that?" Mrs. Carmichael cranked opened the spigot.

"Oh, nothing." It was kind of interesting, seeing a ghost. Sometimes she saw Mamma, but she didn't tell anyone. People would think she was lying, but she wasn't.

"Stand right there." Mrs. Carmichael indicated a sunny spot. The grass was as soft as brand-new shag carpet. "Hold out your arms."

Rosa's shadow fell over the grass, a skinny cruciform with stringy hair. An arc of fresh water from the hose drenched her. "Yikes, that's cold," she said.

"Hold still and I'll be quick."

She couldn't hold still. The water was too cold, which

felt good on the beestings but chilled the rest of her. She jumped up and down as though stomping grapes, like Pop said they used to do in the Old Country.

The ghost came to the window again.

"Who is that?" Rosa asked through chattering teeth.

"He's Mrs. Montgomery's boy."

"Is he all alone in there?"

"He is. Put your head back," Mrs. Carmichael instructed. "His sister went away to summer camp."

"I bet he's lonely. Maybe I could play with him."

Mrs. Carmichael gave a dry laugh. "I don't think so, dear."

"Is he shy?" Rosa persisted.

"No. He's a Montgomery. Now, turn around and I'll finish up."

Rosa squirmed under the impact of the cold stream of water. When the torture stopped, Mrs. Carmichael told her to wait on the back porch. She disappeared into the house, carefully closing the door behind her. She returned with a stack of towels and a white terry-cloth bathrobe. "Put this on, and I'll throw your clothes in the dryer."

As Rosa peeled off her wet clothes, Mrs. Carmichael stared at her legs. "Mother of God, what happened to you?"

Rosa surveyed the welts on her feet and legs. "Beestings," she said. "I kicked a hive. It was an accident, I swear—"

"Why didn't you tell me?"

Rosa thought it would be rude to point out that she had already tried to explain.

"Heavenly days," said Mrs. Carmichael, wrapping a towel around her. "You must be made of steel, child. Doesn't it hurt like hellfire?"

"Yes, ma'am."

"It's all right to cry, you know."

"Yes, ma'am, but it won't make me feel any better. The mud helped, though. And the cold water."

"Let me find the tweezers and get those stingers out. We might need to call a doctor."

"No. I mean, no, thank you." Rosa hoped she sounded firm, not impolite. While Mamma was sick, the whole family had had their fill of doctors. "I don't need a doctor."

"You sit tight, then. I'll get the tweezers."

A few minutes later, she returned with a blue-and-white first-aid kit and used the tweezers to pluck out at least seven stingers. "Hmm," Mrs. Carmichael mused, "maybe it wasn't such a bad idea, jumping in the pond. I think it'll keep the swelling down." She gently pressed the palm of her hand to Rosa's forehead, and then to her cheek.

Rosa closed her eyes. She had forgotten how good it felt when someone checked you for fever. It had to be done by a woman. A mother had a way of touching you just so. It was one of the zillion things she missed about Mamma.

"No fever," Mrs. Carmichael declared. "You're lucky. You're not allergic to beestings."

"I'm not allergic to anything."

Mrs. Carmichael treated the stings with baking soda and gave Rosa a grape Popsicle. "You're very brave," she said.

"Thank you." Rosa didn't feel brave. The beestings hurt plenty, like little licks of fire all over, but after what happened with Mamma, Rosa had a different idea about what was worth crying about.

Mrs. Carmichael got a comb and tugged it through Rosa's long, thick, curly hair. Rosa endured it in silence, biting her lip to keep from crying out. "This is a mass of tangles," Mrs. Carmichael said. "Honestly, doesn't your father—"

"I do it myself," Rosa said, forcing bright pride into her tone. "Pop doesn't know how to do hair."

"I see."

Rosa pressed her lips together hard and stared at the painted planks on the porch floor. "Mamma taught me how to make a braid. When she was sick, she used to let me get in bed with her, and she'd do my hair." Rosa didn't tell Mrs. Carmichael that by the end, Mamma was too weak to do anything; she couldn't even hold a brush. She didn't tell her that the sickness that had taken Mamma took some of Rosa, too, the part that was easy laughter and feeling safe in the dark at night, the security of living in a house that smelled of baking bread and simmering sauce.

"Dear? Are you all right?"

Rosa tucked the memories away. "Mamma said every girl should know how to make a braid. But it's hard to do on your own head."

Mrs. Carmichael surprised her by holding her close, stroking her damp head. "I guess it is hard, kiddo."

"I'll keep practicing."

"You do that." Like all grown-up women, Mrs. Carmichael was a champ at braiding hair. She made a fat, perfect braid down Rosa's back. "I'll put these things in the dryer. Wait here, and try to stay out of mischief."

Six

———ⴰⵖⴰ———

The housekeeper disappeared again and Rosa tried to be patient. Waiting was the pits. It was totally boring, and you never knew when it would end. She fiddled with the long tie that cinched in the waist of the thick terry robe. It was way too big for her, the sleeves and hem practically dragging.

Somewhere far away, the phone rang three times. Mrs. Carmichael's voice drifted through the house. Rosa couldn't hear the conversation, but Mrs. Carmichael laughed and talked on and on. She probably forgot all about Rosa.

The door to the kitchen was slightly ajar. Rosa pushed it with her foot and, almost all by itself, it swung open. She gasped softly at what she saw. Everything was white and steel, polished until it shone. There were miles of countertops, and Rosa figured the Montgomerys owned every tool and utensil that had ever been invented—strainers and oddly shaped spoons, gleaming pots hanging from a rack, a huge collection of knives, baking pans in several shapes, timers and stacks of snow-white tea towels.

Boy, thought Rosa, Mamma would love this. She was the world's best cook. Every night, she used to sing "Funiculi" while she fixed supper—puttanesca sauce, homemade bread, pasta she made every Wednesday. Rosa had loved nothing better than working side by side with her in the bright scrubbed kitchen in the house on Prospect Street, turning out fresh pasta, baking a calzone on a winter afternoon, adding a pinch of basil or fennel to the sauce. Most of all, Rosa could picture, like an indelible snapshot in her mind, Mamma standing at the sink and looking out the window, a soft, slightly mysterious smile on her face. Her "Mona Lisa smile," Pop used to call it. Rosa didn't know about that. She had seen a postcard of the Mona Lisa and thought Mamma was way prettier.

Rosa walked through the strange high-ceilinged kitchen, running her finger along the edge of the counter. She stood on tiptoe to peer out the window over the sink. It framed a view of the sea. Her mother would've gone nuts for this kitchen.

But it didn't smell like anything, just faintly of cleanser. Mamma's kitchen always smelled like roasting chicken or baking pizza or freshly squeezed lemons.

Rosa finished her Popsicle and put the stick in a shiny, bullet-shaped trash can. She tried to keep still, she really did, but curiosity poked at her. She knew it was wrong, but she was going to snoop. She had always wondered about these great big houses. She'd seen them from the outside, painted giants with white scrollwork trim, shiny cars in the circular drives and yards where people in summer hats and starched white shirts held garden parties.

She walked down a hallway, her bare feet soundless on the polished wood floor, the hem of the robe dragging. Her hand stole inside the bathrobe to clutch at the shiny new key Pop had given her. She was old enough to have a house key now, and he told her never to lose it.

She could hear snatches of Mrs. Carmichael's phone conversation, and when she realized it was about her, she froze right under a big painting of a sailboat in a rustic frame.

"...know what to do with that poor little girl all summer. Pete wasn't gone five minutes and she got in trouble."

Pete was Pop. It seemed like every woman who knew him was waiting for him to mess up now that he didn't have a wife anymore.

"Oh...no idea," Mrs. Carmichael was saying. "The kindest thing he can do for that child is remarry. She needs a mother."

No, thank you. Rosa buried her face in the overly long sleeves of the bathrobe to stifle a snort. She absolutely did not need a mother. She had the best mother in the world, and just because she wasn't around anymore didn't mean she was gone. She belonged to Rosa in a special way. That's what Father Dominic said, and everyone knew priests didn't lie.

I still talk to you, don't I, Mamma? She thought the words as hard as she could.

"At least Pete's got his work," Mrs. Carmichael went on. "He's happy when he works. He's like a different person." She gave a gentle laugh. "Hmm. I know. And with those looks of his..."

Rosa got bored with eavesdropping. Everyone was always saying how Pop was still young and good-looking, and that he ought to find another wife. Why did people think you could replace someone, like she was a lost schoolbook and all you had to do was bring a check to the office and they'd give you another?

She continued her silent exploration of the house, feeling as though she had stepped into an enchanted castle. The front room was all white and lemony-yellow, with white furniture and a seashell collection in a jar. Photographs in silver frames pictured people in white clothes without wrinkles, just like in a magazine ad. There was a huge bouquet of cut flowers, probably from the garden Pop took care of. The glass-topped coffee table displayed an important-looking scrimshaw collection. The mantel had a crystal candelabrum with long white tapers that had never been lit.

This wasn't like going over to Linda's house to play. Everything was so big and so incredibly quiet. The flowers made it smell like the funeral home where they took Rosa's mother.

She backed out of the room and tiptoed down the hall. Tall double doors with glass panes framed a room that had more books than the Redwood Library in Newport.

Rosa loved books. When Mamma got too sick to do anything else, and couldn't even braid hair anymore, Rosa used to get in bed with her and read and read and read—*The Indian in the Cupboard, Tales of a Fourth Grade Nothing, Charlotte's Web* and poems from *A Light in the Attic.* And of course, *Goodnight Moon,* which Mamma used to read to Rosa every night when she was tiny.

She stepped into the room and inhaled the musty sunshine smell of books. She walked over to the lace-paneled windows and discovered a view of the garden and pond. Rosa caught her breath. The ghostly boy had stood right there, at the window, watching her run from attacking bees.

She wanted to browse through the books on the shelves, but she became aware of a hissing-gurgling-sucking sound. A creepy chill slipped over her skin. This was a haunted library.

She spun away from the window and saw the ghost on the couch.

Rosa had to push both fists against her mouth to keep from screaming. He was doing a terrible thing, sucking steam from a snaky plastic tube into his mouth. The tube was attached to a box, which emitted the hissing sounds.

Finally she found her voice. "What are you doing?"

He pulled the tube away from his mouth. "This helps me breathe," he said. "It's a portable bronchodilator."

She edged a little closer, but still felt wary. He was very skinny, lying on a leather sofa with a sailboat quilt covering him up. He wore wire-rimmed glasses and had a nice face, nicer than you'd expect for a ghost boy. Pale yellow hair, pale blue eyes, pale white skin.

"You need help breathing?" she asked.

"Sometimes." He set aside the tube, hooking it into a holder on the side of the machine. A wisp of steam coughed from the mouthpiece. "I have asthma."

"Can you get rid of it?" Rosa tensed up, wishing she hadn't asked. Sometimes a person got sick and there was no way to get better.

"No one can tell," he said. "It can be controlled, and maybe it'll improve when I get bigger and my lungs grow. What's your name?"

"Rosina Angelica Capoletti, and everyone calls me Rosa. What's yours?"

"Alexander Montgomery."

"Does everyone call you Alex?"

He offered a mild, sweet smile. "No one calls me that."

"Then I think I will."

They verified that they were just a year apart in age, but in the same grade. Alex had started kindergarten a year late on account of having trouble with his asthma. He admitted that he disliked school, and she got the impression that he got bullied a lot. She declared that she, too, despised school.

"I know I have to go," she lamented. "It's the only way to get ahead."

"Ahead of what?" he asked.

She laughed. "I don't know. My brothers were in ROTC and joined the U.S. Navy for their education."

"You go to college to get an education," he said with a frown.

"If you go in the navy first, then the navy pays for it," she explained patiently. "I thought everybody knew that." She indicated the book that lay open across his lap. "What are you reading?"

He picked it up and showed her the spine. "*Bulfinch's Mythology*. It's a collection of Greek myths. This one is about Icarus. There's a picture."

Rosa sat beside him on the sofa and scooted over to see. Alex thoughtfully put half the book on her lap. "He's flying," she said.

"Yes."

"He doesn't look like he's having much fun."

"Well, he's in pain."

"Why would he fly if it hurts him?"

"Because he's flying," Alex said as if that explained everything.

Rosa stuck out her bare foot. The beestings formed red dots on her ankle and shin. "I tried flying, and trust me, it's not worth the pain."

"I saw you," he said. "I was watching from the window."

"I know. I saw you watching me."

"I was going to come and help, but I didn't know what to do."

"That's all right. Mrs. Carmichael came straightaway when she heard me yelling."

He nodded gravely, studying her with such total absorption that she felt like the only person on the planet. "Do the beestings hurt?"

"Not anymore. Mrs. Carmichael put baking soda on them. She said I'm lucky I'm not allergic."

"You are lucky," he said with a funny, dreamy look on his face. "You get to be outside and do whatever you want."

She thought about telling him just how unlucky she was. She was a girl without a mother. But she didn't want to say anything. Not just yet. It might be too scary for him, this sick boy, to hear about a sick person who had died.

"You mean you're not allowed outside?"

He pushed his glasses up the bridge of his nose. "Not without supervision. I might have an asthma attack."

"Going outside causes an attack?"

"Sometimes."

She'd heard of a heart attack. An attack of nerves. But not an asthma attack. "What's it feel like?"

"It's like…drowning. But in air instead of water."

Rosa had some knowledge of the sensation. More than once, while swimming, she'd gone out too far and under too deep, and she'd experienced the momentary panic of needing air. The feeling was horrifying. "Then you'd better not go outside."

He stared down at Icarus, whose mouth was twisted in agony as he flew too close to the sun. Then he looked up at Rosa, and there was a new light in his blue eyes. "Let's go anyway."

"Really?"

"My lungs were twitchy this morning, but I'm better now. I'll be okay."

She looked at him very closely. There were no lies in that face of his. She could just tell. "I have to get my clothes. Mrs. Carmichael put them in the dryer."

"I think that might be in the utility room."

As she followed him through the house, she marveled that he didn't know for sure where the dryer was. At her house, everyone knew, because laundry was everyone's business. He opened a painted door in the kitchen to reveal a dim, cavernous room dusty with dryer lint. "It's in there."

"You wait here."

"Are you sure?"

"I have to change. I sure don't need any help doing that." The room smelled of must and dryer lint, and a hissing sound came from the water heater. Her clothes were still damp, but she put them on anyway—undies, cutoffs and a T-shirt from Mario's Flying Pizza. The sun would finish the job of drying them. She left the bathrobe on top of the dryer and hurried back to the kitchen.

There, she found Alex and Mrs. Carmichael locked in a staredown. "I'm going," he said to the housekeeper.

She sniffed. "You're not to leave the house."

"That was this morning. I'm better now. I have my inhaler and my epi-pin, see?" He took a plastic thing in a yellow tube from the pocket of his shorts.

"I'll watch him," Rosa blurted out. "I will, Mrs. Carmichael. If he starts looking sick, I'll make him come right back inside."

The housekeeper kept her hands planted on her hips, though her eyes softened and there was a barely perceptible easing of her shoulders. Mothers were like that.

They gave in with their eyes and their posture before saying okay out loud. "You will, will you?" she asked.

"Yes, ma'am. I got my things from the dryer. Thank you, Mrs. Carmichael."

"You're very welcome." She looked from Alex to Rosa. "Try to keep your noses clean, all right?"

"Yes, Mrs. Carmichael," they said together, trying not to look too gleeful.

Out in the sunlight, Rosa noticed that Alex's eyes were ocean-blue, and they crinkled when he grinned at her. She vowed to be on her best behavior, just like Mrs. C had admonished them. If she got in trouble, Pop wouldn't let her come to work with him anymore. He'd make her stay with that dreadful Mrs. Schmidt, the widow with the mustache, whom Rosa likened to a circling buzzard. Even before Mamma died, Mrs. Schmidt had started coming around the house, bringing covered dishes and making eyes at Pop, which of course he never even noticed.

"Here. Have a cookie." As they headed for the door, Mrs. Carmichael held out a white jar in the shape of a sandcastle.

"Thank you." They each took one and stepped out into the sunshine. Rosa nibbled on the cookie as she grinned at Alex.

It was a store-bought sugar cookie. Not as good as Mamma's, of course. Mamma made hers with a secret ingredient—ricotta cheese—and thick, sweet icing. Now *that* was a cookie.

Ricotta Cheese Sugar Cookies

1 cup softened butter
2 cups sugar
1 carton full-fat ricotta cheese
2 eggs
3 teaspoons vanilla (the kind from Mexico is best)
1/2 teaspoon salt
1 teaspoon baking soda
1 teaspoon grated lemon zest
4 cups flour

For the glaze:
1 cup powdered sugar
2-4 Tablespoons milk
2 drops almond extract (optional)
sprinkles

Preheat oven to 350° F. Mix cookie ingredients to form a sticky dough. Drop by teaspoonfuls on an ungreased cookie sheet. Bake 10 minutes or until the bottoms turn golden brown (the tops will stay white). Transfer to wire racks to cool. To make the glaze, stir milk a few drops at a time, along with the almond extract if desired, into the powdered sugar in a saucepan. Stir over low heat to create a glaze. Drizzle over cooled cookies and top with colored sprinkles. Makes 3-4 dozen cookies.

Seven

"Too bad about the rope swing," Alex said, eyeing the rope that still hung from the tree branch.

"I took it from that shed behind the—what is that building, anyway? It's too big to be a garage," Rosa said, stopping to put on her flip-flops. The tall building was painted and trimmed to match the house. It had old-fashioned sliding wooden doors like a barn, an upper story at one end with a row of dormer windows facing the sea and a cupola with a wind vane on top.

"My mother parks her car there. She calls it the carriage house even though there's no carriage in it."

Sunlight glinted off the windows at the top of the house. "I knew it was way too fancy to be called a garage. Does somebody live there?"

"No, but somebody used to. In the olden days, a caretaker lived upstairs."

"What did he take care of?"

"The horses. And carriages, I guess, but that was a long time ago. My grandfather used it as an observatory. He showed me how to spot the Copernicus Crater with a telescope."

He sure did seem smart. Rosa nodded appreciatively, as though she knew what the Copernicus Crater was.

"My grandfather was teaching me about the stars, but he died when I was in first grade."

Rosa didn't quite know what to say about that, so she followed him across the property to the carriage house. The front doors were stuck, but they struggled together to push them along the rusted runners. Inside was a maze of spiderwebs, old tools and some sort of car under a fitted cover. "My mother's car," Alex said. "She calls it her beach car. It's a Ford Galaxy. She hardly ever drives it, though."

"My mother didn't like driving, either."

He shot her a quick look, and Rosa realized that now was her chance to tell him, because she'd said "didn't" instead of "doesn't." But she decided not to say anything. Not yet. She might later, though. She'd already decided he was that kind of friend.

Before he could question her, she ran up the stairs. Sure enough, there was a whole house up there, flooded with dusty sunshine. Alex sneezed, and she turned to him. "Is this going to cause an as—" She couldn't remember the word. "An attack?"

"Asthma attack. I don't think so." He stuck his hand into his pocket and she could see him feeling for the inhaler. Still, he seemed fine. So far, so good.

The furniture was stacked in a broken heap, like old bones on Halloween. The most interesting item was a spinning wheel. Rosa stepped on the pedal, and when the large wheel spun, she jumped back with a yell of fright.

Alex laughed at her, but not in a mean way.

"What are you going to do with all this stuff?" Rosa asked.

"I don't know. My mother says she keeps meaning to

clean it out, but she never gets around to it. I get to keep the telescope, though." It was on a table in front of the biggest window. He opened the long black case to reveal the instrument broken down in parts.

"Can you see the man in the moon with that?" Rosa asked.

"There's no such thing as the man in the moon."

"I know. It's just an expression."

He shut the case, and a cloud of dust rose. When he breathed, he made a scary wheezing sound, and his face turned red.

"Hey, what's wrong?" Rosa asked.

He waved his hand and headed for the stairs, gasping all the way like a cartoon character pretending to die. Rosa followed him in terror. When they got outside, she headed for the house to tell Mrs. Carmichael, but Alex grabbed her arm and pulled her back.

His touch felt desperate but not angry. "I'm okay," he said, though his voice was only a whisper.

"Are you sure?"

He nodded. "Cross my heart and hope to—I'm sure." His eyes looked brighter, somehow, than they had before. Magnified by the lenses of his glasses, they appeared huge.

"Was that an asthma attack?"

He grinned. "No way. That was just a little wheezing."

"I'd hate to see an attack, then."

"I'm all right. Let's go to the beach."

She hesitated, but only for a second. You just didn't say no to a kid who spent half his life cooped up like Alex did. "Okay," she said.

The Montgomery house overlooked a part of the shore almost no one visited, an area known as North Beach. It was a long, isolated curve of the coastline, a good hike from the nearest public beach. It was also a bird sanctuary, safe from development and a good distance from town. A path, overgrown by runners from wild roses and greenbrier, led through the sanctuary to the shore. The summer crowds had never discovered the marsh-rimmed beach, or if they had, it was too rocky to be popular.

"Too cold for swimming yet," Rosa said, running down to the water's edge. "But soon. Ever seen a tide pool?"

"In a book," he said, following more slowly, breathing hard.

"I can take you to see some real ones."

"All right."

His breathing worried her. "Can you make it?"

"Sure, I'm okay."

It was impossible to walk in a straight line on the beach; Rosa had never been able to do it. They darted back and forth, examining shells, overturning rocks to watch the tiny crabs run for cover, picking out a perfectly round, flat stone to skip.

Alex turned out to be a big talker. In fact, he was a funny, clever boy who took delight in everything she said and did, everything she showed him. And he knew things, too. He knew a dolphin swims at thirty-five miles per hour, and a baby gray whale drinks the equivalent of two thousand bottles of milk each day. So all that reading was good for something, after all.

He had a sister who was away at horseback riding camp. "Her name's Madison. She's fifteen. I'm not allowed to go to camp on account of my asthma."

"It's just as nice here," Rosa declared, though she had no idea whether or not that was true.

"My family's firm has offices in the city, and my

father comes to the beach house only on weekends and holidays," he said.

She didn't really get what a firm was, but it seemed to keep his father plenty busy. "Which city?"

"New York City. And Providence, too. Where do you live?"

"In Winslow."

"You're lucky. I wish I could live here all year around."

"I don't know. It gets pretty cold in the winter. Summers are the best. Do you like swimming or hiking, going out in boats?"

"I don't do things like that," he said. "I'm not allowed."

"That's too bad." What an odd boy, she thought. "Pop says when I'm twelve, I can go parasailing."

"See what I mean? Lucky."

"I guess. Maybe we could go down to the docks at Galilee and catch a ride on a fishing boat that's heading out for the day. Mrs. Carmichael's husband is a lobsterman. Did you know that?"

"No."

She had a feeling he didn't do much talking to the housekeeper. "My brothers' names are Roberto and Salvatore. We call him Sal but never Sally." She pointed out a firepit with the charred remains of a few logs. "My brothers used to build bonfires that would shoot sparks a mile high." Just saying it made her miss Rob and Sal, who were so much older than her. Her parents used to call her their last blessing. After the boys, they weren't really expecting to have a daughter, too, nine years later. Her parents had been older than the parents of her friends, but Rosa never cared about that. She was surrounded by love, she was the last blessing and she used to think she was the luckiest girl in the world.

"Maybe we could build a bonfire," Alex said.

It was nice, the way he seemed to feel her turning sad, and spoke right up. "Maybe," she said, and took him past the public beaches and parking lots to the rocky tip of Point Judith. "You have to be careful here," she warned him. "The rocks are slippery. Sharp, too."

He took a step and wobbled a little on his skinny white legs, then regained his balance. He looked very small, standing on the sharp-edged black rock with the waves exploding high into the sky.

Rosa put out her hand. "Hang on and watch where you step."

He grabbed on, and his strong grip surprised her. He studied each move with deliberation, but they made steady progress. When a fount of white foam erupted between the rocks he was straddling, Alex jumped, but not in time to avoid getting his shorts soaked.

"Are you all right?" asked Rosa.

"Yes." With his free hand, he straightened his glasses. "It's steep."

"Don't worry." She stepped down to the next rock. "I'll catch you if you fall."

"What if *you* fall?" he asked.

"I won't," she declared. "I never fall." Step by unsteady step, she led him down to the placid clear pools that stayed filled at low tide. They studied hand-sized starfish and sea cucumbers, neon-colored algae and clusters of black mussels clinging to the rock. Alex knew what everything was from his reading, but he didn't know how to make sunburst anemones squirt. Rosa showed him that. Splat, right on his eyeglasses.

Alex laughed aloud as he wiped his face, and the sound made her smile bigger than she'd smiled in weeks. Months, maybe. Crouched by the pool, she felt a slight change, like the wind shifting. They weren't just two kids anymore. They were friends.

She sat back on her heels and tilted her face up to the clear blue sky. A trio of seagulls swooped over them, and Rosa looked away. Mamma used to have a lot of superstitions. *Three seagulls flying together, directly overhead, are a warning of death soon to come.*

Until Mamma, Rosa had never known a person who died. She used to think she knew what death was: a bird fallen from the nest. A possum at the side of the road, buzzing with flies. She had grandparents who had died, but since she'd never met them, that didn't count. They were from a place in Italy called Calabria, which her parents called the Old Country.

One time, she asked Pop why he never went to Italy to see his parents while they were alive. You can't go back, he'd said dismissively. It's too much bother.

Rosa didn't really care. She didn't want to go to Italy. She liked it right here.

"What school do you go to?" asked Alex.

"St. Mary's." She wrinkled her nose. "I think classes are boring, and the cafeteria food makes me gag." When they had to say the blessing right after Second Bell, she used to give extra thanks for her mother's sack lunches—chicken salad with capers or provolone with olive loaf, sometimes a slice of cake and a bunch of grapes. There was always a funny little message on the napkin: "Smile!" Or "Only 12 more days to summer!"

"I like sports," she told Alex, not wanting him to think she was a total loser. "I can run really fast and I like to win. My big brothers taught me everything they know, which is a lot. I play soccer in the fall, swimming in the winter, softball in the spring. Do you play sports?"

"Not allowed," he said, trailing his hand in the crystal

clear water. "Makes me wheeze." Then he was quiet for several minutes. Rosa watched the way the breeze tossed his shiny white-blond hair. He looked like a picture in a book of fairy tales, maybe Hansel, lost in the woods.

He turned those ocean-blue eyes on her. "Your mom died, didn't she?"

Rosa felt a quick hitch in her chest. She couldn't speak, but she nodded her head.

"Mrs. Carmichael told me this morning."

Rosa drew her knees up to her chest, and as she watched the waves exploding on the rocks, she felt something break apart inside her. "I miss her so much."

"I was scared to say anything, but…it's okay if you want to talk about it."

She started to shake her head, to find a way to change the subject, but this time the subject refused to be changed. Alex had brought it up and now it was like the incoming tide; it wouldn't go away. And to her surprise, she kind of felt like talking. "Well," she said. "Well, it's a long story."

"The days are long in the summer," he reminded her. "The sun sets at 8:14 tonight."

She rested her chin on her knees and gazed out at the blue distance. Usually she tried not to bring up the subject of her mother's death. It made her brothers all awkward, and Pop sometimes cried, which was scary to Rosa. Now she could feel Alex staring right at her, and it didn't scare her at all.

"When Mamma first got sick," she said, "I didn't worry because she didn't really act sick. She went for her treatments, and came back and took naps. But after a while, it got hard for her to act like she was okay." Rosa thought about the day her mother came home from the hospital for the last time. When she took off her bright blue kerchief, she looked as gray and bald as a newborn baby bird. That was when Rosa finally felt afraid. "The nuns came—"

"Like Catholic nuns?" Alex asked.

"I don't think there's any other kind."

"Are you Catholic, then?" he asked.

"Yep. Are you?"

"No. I don't think I'm anything. I want to hear about the nuns."

"They used to sit and pray in the bedroom with my mother. My father got really quiet, and his temper was short." Rosa wasn't going to say any more about that. Not today, anyway. "My brothers had no idea what to do. Rob went to Mamma's garden, which she didn't plant last year because she was too sick, and he mowed down a whole field of brambles using only a machete." Rosa pictured her brother, sweat mingling with the tears on his face even though it was the middle of winter. "Sal lit so many candles at St. Mary's that Father Dominic had to tell him to put some of them out to avoid starting a fire."

None of it helped, of course. Nothing helped.

"Mamma said it was a lucky thing, to be able to say goodbye, but it didn't feel…lucky." Rosa pressed the heel of her hand into the rock hard enough to hurt. Her mother had been too weak to prop up a book, so Rosa got on the bed and lay down beside her and read *Grandfather Twilight,* and it felt strange to be the one reading it.

"She died on Valentine's Day," Rosa told Alex. "A week after my ninth birthday. All kinds of people came, and the neighbors brought food, but mostly it just spoiled in the refrigerator and then we threw it out because nobody was hungry. Some of the women got right to work on my father. They wanted him to marry again immediately." She shuddered.

"Mrs. Carmichael thinks he looks like Syvester Stallone. I heard her talking to somebody about it on the phone."

Rosa made a face. "He just looks like Pop."

The chill water sluiced in, breaking over Rosa's feet and Alex's checkered Vans sneakers.

"Tide's coming in. We'd better go back," he said.

"All right." She stood up and offered her hand.

"I can make it," he said.

As they headed back along the public beach, she glanced at the sky. It wasn't that late yet. "Do you think we should hurry?"

"No, but my mother doesn't like me to be late for dinner. At least when we're at the shore, we don't have to dress for dinner like we do in the city."

"You mean you eat naked?" Rosa fell down laughing, landing in the sun-warmed sand.

"Ha-ha, very funny," he said, trying to act serious. But he fell down next to her, clearly not in a hurry anymore. They watched Windsurfers skimming along, and families having picnics and feeding the seagulls. Alex found a piece of driftwood and dug a deep moat while Rosa formed the mound into a castle. It wasn't a very good one, so they weren't sorry when a wave sneaked up and swamped it. Rosa jumped up in time to avoid getting wet, but Alex got soaked to the skin.

"Yikes, that's cold," he said, but he was grinning. When he stood up, he had something in his hand. He bent and washed it in the surf. "A nautilus shell. I've never found one before."

It was a nice big one, a rare find, not too damaged by the battering waves. Alex couldn't know it, but it was Mamma's favorite kind of shell. The nautilus is a symbol of harmony and peace, she used to say.

"You can have it if you want," he said, holding the shell out to her.

"No. You found it." Rosa kept her hands at her sides even though she wanted it desperately.

"I'm not good at keeping things." He wound up as if to throw it back into the surf.

"Don't! If you're not going to keep it, I will," Rosa said, grabbing it from him.

"I wasn't really going to throw it away," he said. "I just wanted you to have it."

When they got back to Alex's yard and Rosa saw what awaited them, she closed her hand around the seashell. "I hope this thing brings me good luck. I'm going to be needing it," she said.

Mrs. Montgomery and Pop stood waiting for them, both their faces taut with worry and anger. Before either of them spoke, Rosa could already hear them. *Where have you been? Do you know how worried we've been?*

"Where on earth have you been?" demanded Mrs. Montgomery. Rosa was speechless at the sight of her. She had flame-red hair and wore a straight white summer dress and white sandals. Her long, thin fingers held a long, thin cigarette. Mrs. Montgomery herself looked like a cigarette. A giant human cigarette.

"What are you thinking, eh? I told you to stay out of trouble," said Pop.

"And you're soaking wet," Mrs. Montgomery declared as though being wet was the crime of the century. From her shiny white handbag, she took out a bunch of what appeared to be first-aid gear. "Honestly, Alexander, I can't imagine what you were thinking. Come over here and let me take your temperature."

He dragged his feet, but submitted to her with the resignation of long habit. Mrs. Montgomery didn't check for fever like a regular mother, by feeling with her hands. She stuck a cone-shaped thing in his ear and then took it out and read the number.

"All right for you," Pop said, marching Rosa toward the truck. "We're gonna get you home, talk some sense into you."

As their parents separated them, Rosa and Alex caught each other's eye. Neither of them could keep from grinning. They both knew this wasn't the end of their adventure.

Eight

Summer 1984

During the second summer Rosa and Alex spent together, she saw him suffer a full-blown asthma attack, and it made her weep with terror. She had never seen anything like it before. She had stopped thinking of him as being sick at all, because the medications and breathing apparatus kept his condition under control.

But not always. On a bright August day, they convinced his mother to allow them to fly kites on the beach, something that—incredibly—Alex had never done before. Rosa showed up with a kite her brother Sal had sent from Hong Kong, where the destroyer he was serving on had made port. She and Alex spent an entire morning putting the kite together, then headed for the beach.

At the long shoreline, isolated from the public beaches by a dense salt marsh, the wind was perfect for kite-flying. It blew strong and steady, a warm current up from the south. Rosa held the kite for Alex to launch. He got so excited and ran so fast along the beach that at first she had no clue there was anything wrong.

"Go, Alex, go!" she called, waiting to feel the wind fill the kite so she could launch it. "Faster!"

But he didn't go faster. He stumbled as though tripping over a log, yet there was nothing but sand beneath his feet.

"Hurry up," she urged.

He collapsed like a bird shot from the sky. His glasses flew off and landed in the sand.

"Alex!" she said, dropping the kite. She plunged to her knees beside him and touched his shoulder.

His face was turning blue and gray, like a ghost's. The rattle and wheeze of his struggling lungs terrified her, and she burst into tears. "Oh, Alex, I don't know what to do," she said, feeling helpless and horrible all at once. She looked around wildly, but there was nothing in sight except a pair of blue herons wading in the shallows. "Tell me what to do."

He shook his head and groped in the pocket of his khaki shorts. He took out his inhaler and inhaled three quick puffs. His eyes looked bright and desperate, but his coloring didn't improve and his wheezing grew worse. He couldn't seem to get his lungs working right.

Then he took something from another pocket. A black-and-yellow tube. He ripped open the plastic packaging and then, with his teeth, removed the gray cap from the end. Finally, in one smooth movement, he stabbed the black tip of the tube at his thigh and held it there for several seconds. He wheezed hard four times—in a panic, Rosa counted them—but then his breathing seemed to start working better.

He slowly removed the tube and inspected the black tip. Rosa was horrified to see a rather large needle sticking out of it. The whole business had taken only a few seconds. In the strange aftermath, Alex lay weak upon the sand, and Rosa was still crying.

"It's okay," he said, his voice soft and raspy. "I'm all right. Cross my heart and hope—"

"Are you going to be able to make it back home?"

"I need a minute."

Rosa started to scramble to her feet, but stopped when his cold hand touched hers. "No, wait," he said. "The kite—"

"You're not flying the kite."

"I know. But…how about you fly it for me? I need to rest." His voice was thin and pleading. "Come on, Rosa. She's going to take me straight to the hospital. That's the rule."

"Then I should go right now and get help."

"A few minutes won't make any difference one way or another. I'll be able to walk back if I can rest a little. The shot lasts twenty minutes, and I'm over the wheezing anyway. Fly the kite. *Please.*"

"I can do that. But only for a minute." She looked down at their hands—hers dark, his pale—and felt a wave of emotion moving through her. Then she gave him his glasses. Spying a mermaid's purse in the sand, she gave him that, too. "For luck," she explained, closing his hand around the small shell.

It felt particularly important to get it right. Like if she didn't, if she messed up, she would be letting him down along with the kite. It was a beautiful, one-of-a-kind kite, yellow with red streamers, and Pop had given her a brand-new spool of string to use. She refused to let Alex launch the kite, because he needed to rest. Instead, she planted it in the sand to catch the wind, and ran with the string shortened until the kite spiked up. Then she put on a full burst of speed and paid out the string.

She could hear Alex saying, "Go, Rosa," and that only made her run faster. Don't let him down, she thought. Don't let him down.

She managed to hoist the kite upward until it took off as though it had a will of its own, and would stay up no matter what she did on the ground. Breathless from running, she brought the string spool to Alex.

"It's up," she said.

"It's up," he echoed, taking hold and watching with shining eyes.

The moment they got back, there was a big fuss, just as Alex had warned her. They tried to act as though nothing had happened, but Alex's mother had an uncanny eye, and the minute she saw him, she said, "You were running on the beach, weren't you?"

"No, we just—"

"You were running, and you started wheezing."

He stared at the floor as he held out the autoinjection tube for her to inspect. Her face turned hard as alabaster marble. "I need to get my purse," she said. She brushed past Rosa as though she didn't see her at all.

Rosa and Pop stood on the porch and watched them go. Mrs. Montgomery hardly ever drove the car that was parked in the old carriage house, and when she gunned the engine, it coughed and wheezed worse than Alex. She didn't seem to be a very good driver, either, Rosa observed. The blue Ford Galaxy lurched and shuddered backward out of the driveway, and the engine banged and backfired all the way down Ocean Road.

"It's so sad that he's sick," Rosa said to her father. "When he couldn't breathe, I got really scared, like—" She stopped, not wanting to upset her father by mentioning Mamma. "Do you think Mrs. Montgomery is really mad at me?"

"She is afraid for her boy." Pop grabbed his pruning shears, ready to get back to work. "I think next week, you will stay with one of the neighbors."

"Pop, no." Rosa panicked. The neighbor ladies—those who stayed home instead of going to work—were old and smelled funny and some even had chin whiskers. Worse, the widowed ones all wanted to marry her father. "Please, Pop, I'll be good, I swear I will. Just give me a chance, okay, Pop. *Okay?*"

Returning from the doctor's a couple of hours later, Alex seemed to be having a similar argument with his mother. "It's no big deal, you know it's not," he said, banging the car door shut.

Rosa came running from the yard, where she had been watching the koi fish feed on hapless bugs. "Are you all right, Alex?" she asked. "Hello, Mrs. Montgomery."

Mrs. Montgomery was inspecting Alex fiercely; she didn't even seem to hear Rosa. "You're not to do anything but rest," she scolded. "You heard the doctor."

"Fine," Alex said. "I'll teach Rosa to play chess."

"I don't think Rosa—"

"I already know how to play chess," Rosa declared. "We could have a tournament."

"Then that's what we'll do," Alex said. "We'll have a chess tournament."

Rosa was aware of Mrs. Montgomery's stern disapproval, but she chose to ignore it.

So did Alex. He had the key to his mother. She would rather put up with Rosa than say no to Alex. He showed her that he had kept the mermaid's purse she'd given him. "I think it did bring me luck," he said.

He was good at chess, way better than she was. She was impulsive, he was deliberate. She moved by intuition while he applied his knowledge and intelligence. She didn't bother looking ahead at things; he studied the board as though it held the meaning of life.

Despite her poor skills, she managed to win a few victories. She improved quickly, and before long, she was asking about all the other interesting games stashed in a tall cabinet in the library.

"Canasta and backgammon," he said, then took down a long, narrow pegboard. "Cribbage."

She chuckled. "Sounds like something to eat."

"It's a good game. I'll show you."

Nine

Summer 1986

By their fourth summer together, Rosa and Alex had fallen into a routine. From mid-June until Labor Day, they were best friends. Mrs. Montgomery objected, but as usual, Alex knew how to handle her. He had all these long arguments about how being with someone his own age helped him manage his illness, because being alone was stressful and made his lungs twitchy.

Rosa couldn't believe his mother bought that. Maybe a mother's love made her putty in his hands. She was a severe woman but she adored Alex. She used to try to get him to invite other boys over, "other" meaning boys like him, summer people. Alex pitched such a fit that eventually his mother stopped trying. Rosa was just as glad about that. With the exception of Alex, summer people were snooty, and they seemed to have nothing better to do than work on their tans or shop. Pop said they were his bread and butter so she'd better be polite to them.

Each year at summer's end, Alex went away, and Rosa

felt bereft after he was gone. They always said they'd write to stay in touch, but somehow, neither of them got around to it. Rosa got busy with school and sports, and the year would speed past. When the next summer rolled around, they fell effortlessly back into their friendship. Getting together with Alex was like putting on a comfortable old sweater you'd forgotten you had.

That fourth summer, they were both going into the seventh grade, and they didn't ease back into the friendship as effortlessly as before. For some strange reason, she felt a little bashful around him that year. He was just plain old Alex, skinny and fair-skinned and funny. And she was just Rosa, loud and bossy. Yet there was a subtle difference between them that hadn't been there before. It was that stupid boy-girl thing, Rosa knew, because even the nuns were required to show kids those dumb videos, *Girl into Woman* and *Boy into Man*.

According to the videos, Rosa was still at least ninety percent girl, and Alex was definitely a boy. He had the same scrawny chest and piping boyish voice. She was pretty scrawny herself, and even though she sometimes yearned for boobs like Linda Lipschitz's, she also dreaded the transformation. Maybe if her mother was still alive, she'd feel differently, but on her own, she was more than happy for nature to take its time.

Mrs. Montgomery hadn't changed one bit, either. The whole first week of summer, Alex was confined to the house because his mother said he had a head cold. Fine, thought Rosa, trying not to feel frustrated about missing out on perfect weather. They'd find indoor things to do.

One day in June she showed up with an idea. She found Alex in the library, reading one of his zillions of books. Before she could lose her nerve, she took out a folded flyer and handed it to him.

"What's this?" he asked, adjusting his glasses.

With great solemnity, she indicated the flyer. "Just read it."

"'Locks for Love,'" he read. "'A non-profit organization that provides hairpieces at no charge to patients across the U.S. suffering from long-term medical hair loss.' And there's a donation form." He touched his pale hair. "Who would want this?"

She sniffed. "Very funny. Get the scissors."

He eyed her thick, curly hair, which swung clear down to her waist. "Are you sure?"

She nodded, thinking of her mother, the baby-bird baldness that had afflicted her after the chemo kicked in. She'd worn scarves and hats, and someone at the hospital gave her a wig, but she said it didn't look like real hair and never wore it. If only Rosa had known about Locks for Love then, she could have given Mamma her hair.

"Do it, Alex." She blew upward at the springy curls that fell down over her forehead. Her hair was always a mess. There was never a hair tie or barrette to be found in the house. Pop never thought to buy them, and she never remembered to tell him.

She looked up to see Alex watching her. "What?"

"You really want me to cut off your hair?"

"I need a haircut, anyway."

He grew solemn. "There are salons. My mother takes me to Ritchie's in the city."

"I don't think I would like a salon. Mamma used to cut my hair when I was little." Suddenly it was there again in her throat, that hurtful feeling of wanting. She blinked fast and tried to swallow, but it wouldn't go away. That was another thing about this girl-into-woman business. Sometimes she cried like a baby. Her emotions were as unpredictable as the weather.

Alex watched her for a moment longer. He pushed his
glasses up the bridge of his nose—a nervous habit. She
looked him straight in the eye and conquered her tears.
"Go get the scissors. And a hair tie."

"A what?"

She rolled her eyes. "You know, like a rubber band
with cloth on it for making a ponytail. Or just a rubber
band will do. The instructions say I have to send my hair
in a ponytail. Do it, Alex."

"Can't we maybe get Mrs. Carmichael to—"

"Alex."

Like a condemned man walking to the gallows, he
went upstairs, where she could hear him rummaging
around. Then he returned with a rubber band and a pair
of scissors. That was the thing about Alex. As her best
friend, he did what she wanted him to do, even when he
didn't agree with her.

It felt like another adventure. She grabbed a towel and
they went outside, Alex grumbling the whole way.

"Wait a minute," she said. "I have to brush my hair and
make a ponytail."

He shook his head. "Have at it."

Her thick, coarse hair was hopelessly tangled. She'd
washed it that morning in anticipation of the shearing,
but during the bike ride over, the wind had whipped it
into a snarled mass. Alex watched her struggle for a few
minutes. Finally he said, "Give me the brush."

She felt that funny wave of bashfulness again as she
handed it over. "Have at it," she said, echoing him.

"Turn around." His strokes were tentative at first,
barely touching. "Jeez, you've got a lot of hair."

"So sue me."

"I'm just saying— Hold still. And be quiet for once."

She decided to cooperate, since he hadn't wanted to

do this in the first place. She stood very still, and all on his own Alex figured out how to brush through the tangles without tugging or hurting. He started at the bottom and worked upward until the brush glided easily through her hair. His patience and the gentleness of his touch did something to her. Something strange and wonderful. When his fingers brushed her nape, she shut her eyes and bit her lip to stifle a startled gasp.

She could hear him breathing, and he sounded all right. She was always leery of setting off an asthma attack. But he was on some new medication that controlled his condition better than ever.

"Okay," he said softly. "I think that's got it pretty good." He smoothed both hands down the length of her hair, gathering it into a ponytail. Then he stepped out from behind her. "Rosa."

Her eyes flew open. "What?"

"You look weird. Are you sure you want me to do this?"

"Absolutely."

"Your funeral." A moment later he stood behind her, snipping away. It was nothing like the way Mamma used to do this, but she didn't care. She was happy to get rid of all the long, thick hair. It took a mother to look after hair like this, and without one she might as well get rid of it. Besides, there was someone out there who needed it more than Rosa did.

She felt lighter with each decisive snip. The fat ponytail fell to the ground and Alex stared down at it. "I'm not too good at this," he said.

She fluffed her hand at her bare neck. Her head felt absolutely weightless. "How does it look?"

He regarded her with solemn contemplation. "I don't know."

"Of course you know. You're looking right at me."

"You just look…like Rosa. But with less hair."

What did a boy know, anyway? With the exception of her friend Vince, no boy ever had a clue about hair and clothes. She'd have to get Vince and Linda to tell her.

She picked up the long ponytail and held it out at arm's length. Alex stepped back, as though it were roadkill.

"Well," she said. "They ought to be able to make a wig out of this."

"A really good wig," he said, edging closer. "Maybe two."

She put the hair into a large Ziploc bag, like the instructions said to do. At that moment, Pop rolled a wheelbarrow around the corner from the front yard. He was whistling a tune, but it turned to a strangled gasp when he saw Rosa.

"Che cosa nel nome del dio stai facendo?" he yelled, dropping the handles of the barrow and rushing to her side. Then he rounded on Alex, spotted the scissors in his hand and raised a fist in the air. "You. *Raggazzo stupid.* What in the name of God have you done?"

Alex turned even paler than usual and dropped the scissors into the grass. "I… I… I…"

"I made him do it," Rosa piped up.

"Do what?" Mrs. Montgomery came out to see what all the ruckus was about. She took one look at Rosa and said, "Dear God."

"It is the boy's fault," Pop sputtered. "He—he—"

"I said, I made him do it," Rosa repeated, more loudly. She held out the clear plastic bag. "I'm donating my hair to…" Suddenly it was all too much—Alex's sheepish expression, the horror on Pop's face, Mrs. Montgomery's disapproval, the bag of roadkill hair. The explanation that had made such perfect sense a few minutes ago suddenly stuck in her throat.

And then she did the unthinkable. Right in front of them all, she burst into tears. Her only thought was to get away as fast as possible, so she dropped the bag and ran, all but blinded by tears. She raced as though they were chasing her, but of course they weren't. They were probably standing around shaking their heads saying, Poor Rosa and What would her mother think.

She ran instinctively toward the ocean, where she could be alone on the empty beach. Breathless, she flopped down and leaned against the weatherbeaten sand fence and hugged her knees up to her chest. Then she lost it for good, the sobs ripping from a place deep inside her she had foolishly thought had healed over. It would never heal, she knew that now. She would always be broken inside, a motherless daughter, a girl forced to raise herself all on her own, with no one to stop her from doing stupid things, or to tell her everything was going to be okay after she did them.

Her chest hurt with violent sobs, yet once she started, she couldn't stop. It was as if she had to get out all the sadness she usually kept bottled up inside. The crashing surf eclipsed her voice, which was a good thing, because she was gasping and hiccupping like a drowning victim. After a few minutes of this, she felt weak and drained. The wind blew her chopped-off hair, and she brushed at it impatiently.

"Are…you okay?" asked a voice nearby.

Startled, Rosa crabwalked backward, mortified that he'd seen her lose it. "What are you doing here, Alex?"

He offered a half smile—half friendly, half scared she might explode. And he held up a manila-colored padded envelope. On the front, he'd carefully printed the address.

"I told our parents about your project and they understood. It's okay, Rosa. It's perfectly fine. Your dad got all proud of you and my mom said you did the right thing. You don't need to worry about getting in trouble."

She used her shirttail to wipe her face. She should probably feel mortified, but she didn't. She just felt… emptied out. Sitting back on her heels, she looked up at Alex. "I didn't think things through, and I'm so embarrassed," she confessed. "I look like a freak."

He dropped to his knees beside her. "Naw. You look good. Honest."

And then somehow everything shifted and changed in the blink of an eye. He set down the thick envelope and put his arms around her, awkwardly but with absolutely no hesitation. Rosa had no idea how to react, she was so surprised, and so…something. She didn't know what. She didn't even feel like herself, but like a different person, sitting here with his arms around her and his face so close she could hear every breath he took.

"It'll be okay, Rosa," he said. "I swear."

And then it happened. He kissed her. His lips touched down, first lightly and then pressing a little harder. She kissed him back, knowing she had never felt anything quite like this. She was engulfed, and for the first time she understood that a kiss wasn't something you did with your lips but with your whole self. It was a kind of surrender, a promise, and she couldn't believe how wonderful it made her feel.

They came apart slowly. He was red to the tips of his ears, and Rosa figured she probably was, too.

"Well," he said, adjusting his glasses, "I guess you're my girlfriend now."

"You?" She burst out laughing and jumped to her feet, grabbing the envelope. "Dream on, Alex Montgomery."

"You know you want to be," he said. His eyes crinkled when he grinned at her. He chased her halfway down the beach before she started to worry about his breathing and slowed down. And then they sort of fell together, shoulders touching, their hands caught, and they walked slowly back toward the house, talking like they always did, the best of friends. The coolness of the breeze on Rosa's neck made her smile.

PART THREE

Minestra

We never tired of being asked, "What makes Joe Louis win all his fights?" because we loved to shout the answer: "He eats pasta fazool, morning and night." This simple dish is almost too hearty to be termed a "minestra" (soup), but it's served in thick bowls rather than on plates, and eaten with a spoon. During Lent, this meatless dish is always on the menu.

Pasta Fazool, from the region of Puglia

Warm 4 Tablespoons of fruity extra-virgin olive oil in a large saucepan and gently sauté 1/2 onion, chopped, a peeled and chopped carrot, a rib of chopped celery and some minced garlic. Open a can of cannelini or Jackson Wonder beans and drain, then add to the vegetables along with 4 chopped plum tomatoes, a pinch of fresh rosemary and 2 cups boiling water. Bring back to a boil, then reduce heat and simmer for thirty minutes. Transfer about half of the beans and their liquid to a food processor and process to a thick purée.

Stir the purée back into the beans. Add 1/4 pound of ziti (or other pasta) and another 1-2 cups of boiling water to the beans in the pot. Cook, stirring constantly, until the pasta is tender, about 10-15 minutes. Remove from heat. Add salt and lots of black pepper to taste.

Serve in warm bowls, garnished with a drizzle of olive oil, a sprinkle of chopped flat-leaf parsley and some parmigiana.

Ten

Alex Montgomery awoke with the rumble of an eighteen-wheeler pounding through his head. His eyelids felt glued shut, and his mouth was so dry that for a moment he panicked, fighting for breath. Then, slowly, bit by bit, he peeled his eyes open to a painful squint and propped himself up on his elbows.

It wasn't a rumbling eighteen-wheeler he heard, but the roar of the surf outside his bedroom window. And he wasn't sick, but hung over.

Same difference.

With a groan, he pushed the covers away and sat up. In college, he used to consider head-banging debauchery liberating. Amusing, even.

Not anymore.

He groped for his glasses, found a pair of frayed, cutoff blue jeans and put them on, then staggered to the bathroom to brush his teeth before his mouth was declared a biohazard.

The picture in the mirror of the medicine cabinet made him groan. Beard stubble, bloodshot eyes, a mouth that had forgotten how to smile. He shuddered and opened the cabinet to make the reflection go away.

Brick-red water sputtered from the choking faucet. He turned the spigot another notch, and the spurt turned to a stream, and the stream turned—well, not quite clear but good enough for brushing his teeth. He studied the contents of the cabinet. Baby aspirin, its expiration date marked 1992. A bottle of iodine, its cap fused by rust. And of course, one of the ever-present syringes of his youth. He scooped it all up and threw it into the trash can.

Having second thoughts, he took out the baby aspirin and stuffed the bottle in his pocket.

Then he splashed water on his face and hair, scrubbed the towel over his head and put his glasses back on. He couldn't face shaving yet, and refused to think about putting in his contact lenses. "Coffee," he murmured, slinging the towel around his neck and shuffling down the stairs to the kitchen.

Here in this house, his mother was everywhere, as he'd known she would be, even though she had stopped coming here a dozen years ago. The house and grounds had been kept up, because God forbid it should look shabby.

As he passed the master bedroom, he imagined catching a whiff of her trademark scent—Chanel No. 5 and Dunhill cigarettes. He recognized her tasteful eye in the white painted frames of the photos on the wall of the stairwell, in the careful arrangements of dishes in the kitchen cupboards. He opened the pantry to find a few rusting cans of tuna and anchovies, baked beans, Campbell's soup and, of course, a lifetime's supply of martini olives—but no coffee.

The fridge held only the six-pack of Narragansett he'd stashed there yesterday when he arrived. He looked at the beer for a long time. Then he looked at the clock on the stove—10:30 a.m. The refrigerator motor kicked on as if prodding him to make up his mind.

"Screw it," Alex muttered. He grabbed a can of beer, opened it and took a slug. It was clean and cold—good enough.

Scratching his bare chest, he walked out to the veranda facing the ocean and sat in a half-rotten wicker chair. The cushions hadn't been put out in years. Maybe now they never would be again. In the past, before Memorial Day, his mother had ordered the house to be opened, the pantry stocked and the furniture uncovered.

Not this year. Not next. Never again.

Yesterday he'd sought solace from his friends, people who had known him for years, people who were supposed to care about him. The liquid sympathy they'd offered had barely scratched the surface of his grief. Numbness, that was all he felt. That, and annoyance because Natalie Jacobson had chosen last night to come on to him.

Mindless sex was always welcome, he conceded, even right after your mother dies. But when he looked into Natalie's hungry eyes, even the wine he'd drunk couldn't keep him from feeling a faint self-loathing.

Besides, by that point, his thoughts had been consumed by Rosa Capoletti. He'd actually believed the sight of her would make the old feelings go away. Fuzzy logic at best, but it had made perfect sense after partying with his friends all evening.

He should have known it wouldn't work like that. Rosa was special to him in ways he didn't even understand, and seeing her again only confirmed it. The moment he'd laid eyes on her, he'd known. The sight of the nautilus shell, in a place of honor and with its own special lighting behind the bar, underscored his certainty.

The shell was the first gift he'd ever given her, and discovering she'd kept it gave him food for thought.

He took another swig of beer and peeled the towel from around his neck. The day was already hot, but here on the shady veranda, the temperature felt perfect. Through stinging eyes, he surveyed the ancient property, once a place of family gatherings and elegant parties, a place where he used to run free with the best person he knew.

Even though the grass was cut and the hedges pruned, the garden had a neglected air. Lilypads choked the pond, probably fertilized by carcasses of koi.

On the far edge of the property was a huge stump, freshly cut and partially uprooted like a giant compound fracture. In a recent windstorm, the fallen tree had crushed the front section of the carriage house, crashing through the single-story garage while leaving the living quarters intact. Live electrical wires were involved, so the local authorities had ordered the tree removed. Power company workers had sectioned and stacked the logs and fed the branches to the chipper.

Other than structural damage to the building, which would be covered by insurance, the only casualty was his mother's old car, a blue Ford that hadn't been driven in twelve years or more. Each year his mother claimed she'd send someone to clean out the shed and have the old furniture, tools and car hauled away, and each year, she never got around to it.

Mother Nature put an end to the procrastination, and the local sheriff took care of having the car towed to the junkyard.

It was strange, being here at the beach house, a place haunted by cobwebs and memories. As he sat drinking and looking out over the yard toward the sea, he could hear echoes of his mother's voice as she talked on the phone to this designer or that decorator, to his doctors and women she called "school chums" no matter how old they got. He could feel her hand stroking his forehead at night when he was sick, which was pretty much every night.

And there, where the property sloped down toward the beach, was the place he'd first seen Rosa Capoletti. The friendship they'd started that day had been touched by the bright, ephemeral magic of summer. In time their friendship had flared briefly, painfully, to passion and then finally disintegrated in an eruption of tears and recriminations.

He hadn't thought it would hurt so much to see her again. He wasn't prepared for that. He should have realized that what was between them had never died. It just lay dormant until the sunshine of Rosa's smile and the moisture of old tears brought it back to life.

The beer imparted a faint buzz in his head. The need to sort out everything that had happened pulsed hard inside him, insistent, unexpected.

Unfortunately, if last night was any indication, she didn't feel the same way at all. She'd regarded him like an uninvited wedding guest. Too damn bad. He was back, this was a small town and it was long past time that they figured things out between them. Of course, he could and maybe should simply deal with the property and take off again, but that didn't feel right. His mother's passing had shaken him in ways he hadn't expected. There was something so achingly tragic about her death, because she'd never really lived.

It was probably a mistake to move back here, Alex reflected, yet it didn't seem wrong. He'd made the decision impulsively, walking away from an apartment, friends, a whole life in New York City. In addition to leaving the city, he had committed to taking the summer off for the first time in his professional career. His assistant, Gina Colombo, would manage things for a few months. He only hoped he could do so without going stir-crazy.

His decision was fast morphing into something crazy and real. He'd come to a point in his life where he didn't much like himself. He'd neglected the invisible, essential things, favoring a lifestyle over a life. He needed to figure out who he was when he wasn't in the company of air- kissing friends and the strangers he called family. He needed the vibrance and fulfillment he'd found only once before—with Rosa.

A seagull circled and then hung suspended above the shallows as though tethered by an invisible kite string. The first time he'd ever flown a kite, he had been with Rosa. She was there for a lot of firsts: the first time he caught a striped bass, fishing in the surf. The first time he'd sailed a Laser all by himself, skimming like a guillemot over the waves at a speed that stole his breath away. She was the first girl he'd ever kissed.

He could only wish she'd been the first woman he'd made love to, that he'd come to her as pure and full of joy and apprehension as she'd come to him, but it wasn't so. Even then, when he was gathering her into the deepest reaches of his heart, another part of him was running from her.

After leaving Rosa, he'd spent a few years trying to forget her. He did a good job of it, drinking and partying his way through college and business school, pretending he didn't notice when a small, dark-haired woman walked past or when he heard a certain kind of laugh or a distinctive Rhode Island accent. Now, seeing her again, he understood that even after all these years, she still lived inside him the way no other person ever had. She was part of his blood and bone. From the first day they met, it had been that way for him.

Leaving her, when all his heart wanted him to do was love her, was the hardest thing he'd ever done—harder than understanding the mysteries of his family, harder than growing an investment fund when the market sank, harder than convincing his father he had his own path to follow.

A lobster boat, with bony arms extended out over the hull, chugged past, and then a small sailboat skimmed by in the other direction. It was a funny thing about this place by the sea. From this perspective, it seemed as though time stood still and nothing changed. With the exception of the ruined carriage house, everything here was exactly the same as it had been when he left, awash in pain and rage, vowing never to return.

Now a new kind of pain forced him to come back, against his will.

A decade had passed since he'd seen this view, felt this breeze, tasted the tang of salt in the air. Two years after the accident, once Pete recovered, Alex came back to explain everything, but by then it was too late. He hadn't expected Rosa to wait for him and she hadn't. She'd made a life for herself, and that included a boyfriend who happened to be a sheriff's deputy.

From that point onward, Alex welcomed all the myriad distractions of his chosen profession, even cultivated them to pretend his busy life was fulfilling. With dogged determination, he avoided making a fool of himself over a woman he couldn't have.

He cultivated a God-given talent in finance and joined the family firm, becoming a player in the great American investment game. As it turned out, he excelled at it. Clients who signed over their capital were rewarded with returns that exceeded all expectations. Within two years of joining the family firm, Alex earned his reputation of rainmaker.

And it was funny, really, when he thought about it. All he did was put two and two together. He might hear that adding a certain protein to baby formula had been proven to make babies smarter. The rest of the world would be surprised when the stock shot off the charts, but not Alex. He did his research and trusted his gut. He remembered arguing with his father about the IPO of an obscure little Internet start-up called Amazon.com. No one had heard of it. Three years later, when that and similar equities soared 3800%, his father gave him his own fund to manage.

Some in the business believed Alex had an uncanny knack for timing. He knew it wasn't so. He read obsessively and knew how to interpret the signs of a company's rise or fall. He didn't do anything special. He just made sure he did it better than anyone else.

Among the funds he managed now was his life's work—The Medical Assistance Private Trust. Its revenues were used to fund health care for the indigent. He'd argued long and hard with his father to found the trust, and only when he threatened to leave the firm did his father agree to it. Alex didn't explain why the fund was so important. It was the one area of his life in which he was unequivocally doing good in addition to doing well, but of course, his father would argue with that.

Even more important was the Access Fund, another he'd created. It was consistently the least productive of the firm's products because he had deliberately created it for people who rarely had money to spare. Unlike all other Montgomery funds, this one had no minimum investment. Some of his clients had given him twenty dollars to start with. His father and colleagues thought he was nuts, that he was wasting his time and the firm's resources. Alex didn't see it that way. He saw it as giving a chance to people who deserved a shot.

His head throbbed.

He dug into the pocket of his cutoffs and fished out the baby aspirin. He shook the tiny pills into the palm of his hand. How much bigger was he than a baby? It didn't matter, he decided. The pills were so old, they had probably lost their kick. He tossed them into his mouth, tasting Sweet TARTS with a slightly bitter edge. He washed them down with a slug of beer. After a few minutes, his headache dulled to an aching thud. The hard blue lines of sea and sky gently melded and blurred. Nothing like a little beer and aspirin to buzz away annoying reality. Hell, in his family, it was a time-honored tradition.

He heard the crunch of tires on gravel. The slam of a car door made him wince. Maybe the expired aspirin wasn't working so well after all.

He stood up too quickly, and images flipped in front of his eyes like a shuffled deck of cards. Then he set down his beer and went to see who it was.

He came around to the front of the house just as Rosa Capoletti raised her fist to knock at the door.

Before she noticed him, he took a moment to savor the sight of her. He half-hoped that last night's attack of lust and longing had been caused by his drunken state. But no. In the stark light of day, she still had the power to stir his blood. She was earthy and colorful. She wore her dark, curly hair caught back in a ponytail. Even without makeup, her face was a study in vivid color—red lips and large brown eyes, darkly lashed, olive-toned skin that looked soft to the touch.

I suppose she's pretty enough, his roommate at

Phillips Exeter used to say as he studied the photograph Alex always kept with him, *in a grape-stomping Old-World sort of way.* Alex couldn't remember whether or not he'd hit him for that remark. He hoped he had.

"Hey, Rosa," he said as she raised her fist to knock again.

She turned quickly. "Alex. You startled me."

He motioned behind him. "I was around back," he said. "Join me?"

She eyed his bare chest, and her stare was so dubious, he thought she might walk away. But then she nodded once and headed for the porch steps. When she grasped the railing, the rotting finial broke off. She lost her balance and pitched forward.

Alex moved swiftly, in spite of his hangover, and grabbed her arm to steady her. "Hey," he said, getting high on the smell of her hair, "are you all right?"

"I'm fine." Flustered, she disengaged herself from him and stepped back. "You ought to do something about that railing."

"I intend to." He half expected her to flee. Instead she followed him around to the veranda. He couldn't get over how good she looked to him. She wasn't just beautiful, but mature and confident in a way that made him wonder about the lost years between them. Even as a child, a motherless child, she had never been needy. But as an adult, she seemed completely self-possessed. She had transformed herself into an A-list restaurateur whose reputation for fun, food and fashion was unparalleled.

He caught himself checking out her tits. Her smooth skin deepened to shadowy cleavage where a tiny gold cross lay nestled.

"Would you like something to drink?"

Her glance flicked to the beer can parked on the arm of the wicker chair. "No, thanks."

"I couldn't find any coffee in the house." Like that explained it. "I just got here and haven't had time to stock up."

She lowered herself cautiously to the bottom step, clearly hoping it wouldn't collapse. When she turned to look up at him, there was a moment—maybe caused by the slant of light that fell across her face, or perhaps it was the beer and aspirin. But in that moment he saw Rosa as he had always known her. She was a laughing tomboy leading him on wild adventures, a shy teenager looking for her first kiss, a young woman glowing with the power of her big dreams.

Then the moment shifted, and she was a complete stranger again. A stranger who had a hot car, expensive clothes and a look of distrust in her eyes.

You made this happen, he told himself. You have only yourself to blame.

The thought prodded his temper. He was mad at himself, mostly, for being here in a place filled with ghosts and no coffee or food. He was supposed to be a respected businessman, established in his field. He didn't like finding himself at a disadvantage.

He sat on the opposite side of the steps from her. Long ago, complete silence used to be comfortable between them. But that wasn't the case now. He watched her fold her hands, open them, fold them again. She didn't feel safe in his world. Maybe she never had.

"I heard about your mother this morning," she said. "Alex, I'm so sorry."

Ah, a sympathy call. He balanced his wrists on his knees and stared out to sea. "So now you know why I'm here."

"Last night, you let me think it was because of me."

"Last night, I had too much to drink."

"Do you do that often?" she asked.

"If I did, I'd be better at it."

"Don't ever get good at something like that."

He looked over at her, searching her face for some hint that she knew more than she was saying. Because, of course, there was so much more to the story than the papers reported. So much more to his magnificent, miserable mother's life. And to her death.

Rosa's expression gave no hint that she knew anything more than she'd read in the papers. "So do you have plans?" she asked.

Last night, before he'd seen her again, he would have sworn he was staying in the big old house for practical reasons. He planned to sell his apartment in New York City and open a branch office of the Montgomery Financial Group just across the Newport/Pell bridge. For now, he needed a place to live. But the moment he laid eyes on Rosa again, he knew his need to be here was much more complicated than that.

However, in his present condition, he was in no shape to explain himself. "The place needs fixing up," he said.

She looked over at the carriage house. "Storm damage?"

"That's right. The house could use some work, too."

"Maybe it's none of my business, but why aren't you with your father?"

She hadn't changed. She'd always been a family-first type of girl, which was one of many reasons they'd been such a mismatch. "I'll be going up to Providence this afternoon to…help with the arrangements." He knew he hadn't answered her question, but that was all he had in him at the moment.

"I take it the two of you never grew any closer," she said, reading between the lines.

Alex's headache kept trying to come back. "I wasn't the kind of son a man like my father knew what to do with." He knew she understood that. She had seen him at his worst with his father.

She held him in that soft, steady regard, the way she used to look at him long ago, never taking his measure, never judging him. And in that moment, she wasn't a stranger at all. She was Rosa, the best part of his boyhood summers.

As a kid, Rosa Capoletti had been more fun than a Ferris wheel ride. As a teenager, she'd set his hormones on fire. Now, as an adult woman, she was lethally attractive.

Alex supposed he'd known women who were more beautiful than Rosa, women who were smarter and more cultured. But none of them—not runway models, Rhodes scholars or concert pianists—affected him the way Rosa did.

"Alex," she said, "you still haven't explained your plans."

His true reasons for coming back to Winslow were rapidly emerging. It was nuts, completely nuts, but she'd nailed him. Again. Always. He had it worse than ever.

Maybe he was wrong about reconnecting with her. Maybe it was a mistake. Except that it wasn't. It was rare that he knew the truth in his heart; he hadn't felt the rightness of something in a long time but he felt it now. It was time. Events converged as though the universe was telling him to go for it.

"I'm opening an office in Newport." It sounded so sensible, spoken aloud. But the fact was, he would not have come near this place if his mother had lived.

He flashed a grin to hide his pain. "Enough about me. Let's talk about you," he said.

"Alex, you just lost your mother."

"All the more reason to avoid the extremely depressing topic of me." He didn't want to talk about his plans, his problems. He was sick of himself. He leaned back and gave her a long look. "So you're Rhode Island's premier restaurateur. That's what they say in the papers."

She smiled, and her whole being glowed with pride. Most people were too reserved to show the world who they really were, but not Rosa. If she felt it, she wore it on her sleeve without apology. She was living, breathing proof that the hard things of life didn't have to defeat you—or even define you.

"You're really something, Rosa," he said. And before he could censor himself, he added, "You always were."

He recognized the question in her eyes, the same question that had been there twelve years before, when he told her it was over.

What happened to us?

Now, as then, he kept the truth hidden. Years ago, he had lacked the emotional hardware to be the person she needed, the one she deserved. She wanted nothing less than everything from him, and he didn't believe even that was enough for her.

Her penetrating stare was taking him apart. She was so different now; he couldn't figure out what was going on behind those darkly-lashed brown eyes. "What?" he asked.

"God, we were so young. I was just thinking about how young we were."

"And now we're old," he said.

"Speak for yourself." She picked a blade of grass, wrapped it around her finger. "Did you know a child laughs an average of three hundred times a day, and an adult just three?"

"No, I didn't."

"I read that somewhere." She uncurled the blade of grass and let it drop.

They sat in silence for a while, watching the waves in the distance, listening to the timeless rhythm of the surf. A seagull landed on the stump of the fallen tree, perched on one leg. Alex started to worry that Rosa would get bored and take off, so he tried to start up the conversation again.

"Celesta's-by-the-Sea," he said. "I like that. You named it for your mother."

"Her cooking inspired the whole concept. Good thing her name wasn't Brunhilde or Prudence."

He lifted his beer can. "To Celesta's." He took a long drink, then noticed her watching him. "What?"

"It's not even noon yet."

"The lady tells time."

"Ah, hostile sarcasm. I don't remember that about you."

"I've been practicing. Anyway, don't worry about me. I'm merely observing tradition. When there's grieving to do, we drink. It's the Montgomery way."

"You call that grieving?" she asked softly. "You haven't even begun to grieve." She watched him with those large, unwavering eyes. It was like looking into a magical mirror, giving him an unsettling glimpse of himself. The truth was there, somehow, in her eyes, the most honest eyes he had ever known. He saw the real Alex, hardened and discontented and immeasurably disappointed in himself. It was an image he ordinarily tried to hide, but this morning he was failing.

"I'm so very sorry about your mother, Alex," Rosa said again. "What I remember about her was that here in the summer house, you were her whole world."

Brand-new grief, as bright and sharp as a fresh knife wound, was taking over, slashing through his control. He felt a squeezing sensation in his chest, and it took him by surprise. People tended to offer their most tender memories of the deceased, and Rosa was no different. The difference was, she understood the dynamics of his boyhood better than anyone he knew. He nodded and looked away, hoping she'd move on to a different subject. In the distance, the horizon line between the sea and sky blurred and pulsed.

"Now that I look back at it," Rosa went on, "making you her whole world was a lot to put on a kid, but I don't think she realized that. I remember how protective she was, how careful of your health. She absolutely adored you."

Rosa didn't understand, he realized. The way his mother adored him was a burden, not a gift. He looked down at his hand and saw that he'd completely crushed the beer can. He had no memory of doing so.

Rosa was looking at him, too. "It's normal to be angry."

He flung the can into the bushes. "I'm not angry."

She smiled at him as though the past twelve years had never happened. "I'm Italian, remember? I'm okay with emotion. The bigger, the better."

The tension in his chest eased like a tight coil unfurling. He didn't have to pretend for her. He didn't have to behave in a certain way. The sweet relief spread through him, more potent than beer and baby aspirin.

He heard another car approach and stood up. "I'd better see who that is."

She stood up, too. "Maybe you should put on a shirt, Alex," she said.

He touched his bare chest. "You're right."

"And I should go," she added.

"No, don't." He blurted out the words. "Please stay." He held open the back door.

She stood there for a moment, then walked to the door

and stepped inside. He couldn't read her expression, yet he came to an unexpected realization. The minute Rosa showed up, his headache had disappeared.

He grabbed a sweatshirt from a hook by the door, yanked it over his head and went to the front, stepping out onto the porch just as a car door slammed. He instantly wished he had not insisted that Rosa stay.

"Hello, Dad," he said. "I wasn't expecting you."

"Clearly not." His father looked perfectly tailored and groomed, as though for a board meeting. "That would have meant you were checking your voice mail. I left at least a half dozen messages."

Checking messages had been the last thing on Alex's mind, but of course, his father wouldn't understand that. "I don't get good reception out here."

The passenger side door opened and his sister got out. She shot him a poisonous look. "You should have called," she said. "The medical examiner's report is in. Mother killed herself. We just thought you might want to know."

Eleven

Madison's words hammered at Alex, and his headache came pounding back. Oddly, he felt no surprise at the news; in the back of his mind, he'd already known. He looked at them both: his family. They were supposed to be helping each other through this, yet instead they were like three icebergs bumping up against each other, awkward and disconnected.

"Come inside," he said to his father and sister. Even as he spoke, he was aware of Rosa's presence behind him. He held open the door. One look at Rosa's face told him she'd heard. The shock and horror in her expression made that crystal clear.

Alex noticed the same look on his sister's face when she stepped into the musty foyer and spied Rosa. He could see Madison wishing she had kept her mouth shut.

His father masked whatever he was thinking behind his customary icy politeness. "We didn't realize you had company."

He decided not to point out that they might have guessed from seeing the red sports car parked in the front.

"I was just leaving," Rosa said. She headed for the door, paused there and turned back. "I'm very sorry for your loss."

And then she was gone, the door banging shut behind her. Alex's headache roared like a locomotive. Madison glared at him; his father stood as stiff as a suit of armor.

"You didn't waste any time finding someone to comfort you," Madison said. "God, you just dumped Portia van Deusen last week, wasn't it?"

"Last month." Alex massaged his temples. "And she dumped me." He should never have gotten mixed up with her. At first, she'd been a pleasant enough diversion. Their families were close, she was beautiful, convenient and apparently crazy about him. They'd had a few laughs—a few too many—and ended up sleeping together several times. He thought that was the end of it. Portia had other ideas.

"You want everybody to think she dumped you. But the truth is—"

"Enough." Their father's voice brought them up short the way it always had, cleaving like a steel blade through their argument. "We're here about your mother, not Alexander's behavior."

Alex gritted his teeth in frustration. They were a family, for Christ's sake. They should treat each other better, particularly now. Just because they'd never learned how was no excuse. In a neutral tone, he said, "Come and sit down, okay? Please."

He led the way to the parlor, an airy, high-ceilinged room with a bay window framing a view of the sea. There, he peeled back the sheets draping the wing chairs and settee, and motioned for them to sit down.

Alex studied them both for a moment, and a strange notion came over him. He didn't really know these people. Madison was his sister; she'd known him all the days of his life. Yet she had always been a distant figure, tucked away at boarding school, at camp during each summer, then college, followed immediately by a society marriage and a swift conversion to A-list hostess. She was married to Prescott Cheadle, a partner in a Boston law firm. She had two kids Alex liked a lot, Trevor and Penelope. But he didn't know their mother—this strong, attractive woman—and somehow that felt like a loss. He suddenly found himself wishing they all knew each other better. No one had ever told them they might need each other one day, and for some reason, they hadn't figured that out themselves.

And his father… Alex couldn't begin to figure him out. On the surface, he was the epitome of success; the heir to a fortune who had grown the empire beyond all expectations, a respected and influential figure. Now he was a man whose wife had killed herself.

"Dad, I'm sorry," Alex said, stumbling over the hopelessly inadequate words.

"I'm sorry, too."

The three of them lapsed into an uncomfortable silence. Madison got up and plucked at some of the sheeting that covered the furniture, peeking underneath. "So who was that woman?"

She hadn't recognized Rosa. Madison, like his parents, had never realized the significance of Rosa. She was the gardener's girl, and like every other child of the domestic help, she was invisible as wallpaper. Madison had no idea what Rosa meant to him. She'd never known how profoundly the gardener's daughter had changed him, long ago.

But then again, he didn't know much about his sister's heart, either.

"Rosa Capoletti," he said.

Madison had no reaction.

"Pete Capoletti's daughter," their father said, like a game show host offering a clue.

Alex was surprised his father remembered. Madison still didn't recognize the name. Could she really not remember what had happened all those years ago? He glanced at his father and realized he seemed to.

"Mr. Capoletti takes care of the property," their father offered.

"Oh, that guy. Now I remember him. Nice Italian man, wore a flat cap and sang while he worked. Didn't you used to play with his daughter?"

"Yeah, that's right," Alex said, nearly choking on the irony of it. He didn't want to explain Rosa; he couldn't. "She stopped by to pay her condolences. Now, why don't you tell me about Mother?"

Madison looked like a model in a luxury hotel ad, sitting there. Her makeup was perfect, her nails done, every golden hair in place.

Their father cleared his throat and handed him a thick padded envelope.

Alex's heart squeezed as he looked over the papers. The state seal crowned the top sheet, and there were two notarized signatures on the bottom. In between lay an official-looking death investigation report and certifier's forms, the sort you never think you'll see. He scanned the reports, and his gut churned as he read the contents of his own mother's stomach, the levels of toxins in her system, even the placement of objects on the nightstand.

His hands shook as he replaced the papers in the envelope. "Didn't you know she was hurting?" he asked his father. He raked a hand through his hair in frustration. "Couldn't you have done anything?"

"One can always do something," his father stated.

His infuriating calmness caused Alex to snap. "Where the hell were you while she was swallowing all the pills and booze?"

His father gestured at the envelope. "It's all documented. I was in the study."

"You might as well have been on the moon."

"Do you want me to feel guilty?" his father demanded.

"I just want you to *feel*," Alex shot back.

"I feel terrible," his father said. "I am utterly dismayed."

Madison let out a humorless laugh, edged with hysteria. "*Dismayed*, for Christ's sake. Dismayed, as in, 'my stock portfolio dipped.' Or 'I just can't seem to correct that slice in my golf swing.' Or 'my wife just killed herself.' *Dismayed*."

"Madison," said their father, "that's enough."

"I haven't even gotten started," she said, her eyes bright with tears. "I need to know how to feel about this, and you're not giving me a single clue. You either, Alex."

"Don't you have a therapist for that?"

"Not funny, little brother."

"I'm serious. This is no small thing, and I'm as clueless as you are." Almost, he thought. He actually did have a clue, but he wasn't ready to say anything.

"We're pathetic." She stood and wandered to the kitchen, looking around slowly, as though seeking out ghosts. "Anything to drink?"

"Just beer." He sent a questioning look at his father.

"No, thank you."

"A beer sounds perfect," said Madison.

He heard the fridge open and close, heard the unmistakable crack of a can tab. She returned to the parlor and sat down, then drank what seemed like half the can. She held out her right hand. "I broke a nail opening that."

"It'll grow back." He sat in silence while she took a few more sips.

"So is your girlfriend going to blab?" she asked.

"What?"

"Roseanne Rosannadanna," she said, jerking her head toward the front.

"Jesus, Maddy—"

"I'm serious. Dad and I haven't told a soul."

"I wanted it that way," their father explained. "It's best for all of us. No need to air this tragedy."

What was best, thought Alex with a new flash of rage, would have been for this not to have happened at all. But that was life for you. *You never know what you're gonna get,* he thought in Roseanne Rosannadanna's accent.

"I don't want anyone to know, either," said Madison. "God, I hope that woman won't say anything."

Alex wanted to reassure her, to guarantee her privacy would be guarded, but the fact was, he didn't know. "If she's the same kind of person she was when I used to know her, she won't tell anyone."

"I swear, you are so naive. Everybody changes, Alex. You of all people should know that."

"What do you mean, me of all people?"

Carrying her beer, Madison got up and went over to the mantel, unveiling the objects there with a flourish— vases and framed photographs, a hobnail glass candy dish. "Ah, just as I thought. Pictorial evidence right here. See? If that's not naive, I don't know what is." She selected an old photo in a tarnished silver frame and handed it to him.

Alex felt as though he was looking at a stranger. But he wasn't. On the back of the frame was a label with his mother's tight, neat handwriting: Alexander IV, Summer 1983. The picture itself showed an undersized, pallid boy. He hadn't known at the time how sick he was, of course. His mother never would have allowed him to know. But he could see the ravages of illness now, like a shadow lurking in the background of the photograph.

He was standing in the library of this very house, which had been his favorite place when he wasn't allowed to go anywhere else. He was dressed all in white; his mother had probably been inspired by the Great Gatsby, which was the first video movie she had ever bought, and watched constantly. But on ten-year-old Alex, the effect was ghostlike. He had hair so pale it seemed translucent, legs so thin they resembled fragile bird bones. The eyes and cheeks were sunken in a refugee motif. His oxygen-starved skin was pale, his eyes almost unnaturally bright.

Alex put the picture aside, mystified as to why his mother had kept it all these years.

Madison sucked down the rest of her beer and got up to pace the room, stopping in front of a picture of their mother seated in one of the wicker chairs, looking out to sea. Given what had happened, the image seemed to have a haunted quality now.

"I need to know why she did it," Madison said to her father. "Please, tell us why."

The stark desperation in her voice touched Alex, though their father sat motionless. Alex went over to his sister and gave her an awkward hug. His father watched, expressionless; theirs was not a demonstrative family, and neither of them had mastered the proper way to hug.

"I don't know," their father said quietly. "We'll never know. I wish I could give you more than that, Madison, but I can't."

For the first time, Alex felt a flicker of unity with his father as they attempted to console Madison. "She kept things to herself when she was alive," he said.

"What do you mean, things?"

Oops. "She was a private person all her life. You know that."

"Too private," Maddy agreed, "and now this. *Why?*"

"She was unhappy," their father said.

"Who's that unhappy?"

Someone who lived a lie all her life, Alex thought.

"If she was always unhappy, then why would she kill herself on that particular day?" Madison asked. "What was special about it?"

Alex rubbed a weary hand over his unshaven face. "Anything we say would be pure speculation. What's the point of that?"

Madison sank down on a draped ottoman. "What's the point of anything?"

He frowned, worried by the bleak question. He and his father exchanged a glance. "How are you, Maddy?"

She looked startled by the question. "I just lost my mother. I'm a wreck."

"How did the kids take it?"

"They were devastated, of course. They adored Mother. Penelope has slept in bed with me the past two nights."

With me, she said. Not with me and Prescott. But Alex didn't go there.

"I pray I'll never have to tell them about..." She nodded toward the medical examiner's report. "My God, I have no idea how I'd explain that."

As he watched the anguish on his sister's face, Alex felt a fresh surge of fury. Their mother had been fully aware of the impact her suicide would have, especially on Maddy and her two kids. Yet she'd done it anyway.

Somehow, they managed to discuss "arrangements." It seemed surreal to be doing so. Surprisingly, Madison took over. His sister wanted the burden. She was one of the youngest and best hostesses around, and planning events—even her own mother's funeral—was second nature to her. She had very definite ideas on flowers and music. Alex wondered how she could even begin to think about those things. Maybe it kept her from thinking about the harder stuff.

Their father agreed to everything without discussion. Every time Madison asked if he had a preference, he would simply say, "Whatever you decide is fine."

Alex felt queasy. At the end of a thirty-six-year marriage, you'd think there would be more to say.

"What should we do with this file?" Madison asked.

"I don't know. Do we need it?"

"I certainly don't. Did she have life insurance? I'm sure they'll reject the claim after the ruling."

"She never had life insurance," their father said.

Madison looked intrigued. "She didn't?"

"She used to say, 'Dead or alive, I'm worth a fortune, and I can pay my own claim.'"

Madison looked bereft. "I suppose I never really knew her. I wonder if any of us did."

It was a strange and sadly true thing to say. Alex patted her on the shoulder awkwardly. "Not me. Father?"

"This is not productive. It's completely speculative." His cell phone rang, and he looked at the display. "It's the funeral home. I need to take this." He strode outside.

"I'm never going to be a mystery to my kids," Madison declared, dabbing at her face. "I swear that right now. No secrets. No mysteries."

"Good plan. Now. Can I get a lift with you and Dad back to Providence? I'll help you with the funeral. Then I need to pick up my car and bring some things back here for the summer."

She balled up the Kleenex in her hands. "Don't you have a car here?"

"Friends from Newport drove me." He didn't explain that he'd been in no condition to drive.

"And then just left you? Some friends. Isn't Mother's old car in the garage?"

"Apparently you haven't seen the garage." They walked out back and he showed her the storm damage.

"Oh," she said, examining the caved-in roof, the crushed window frames and split timbers. "So what are you going to do about this mess? God, the whole place is a project." She spread her hands and looked around the vast gardens, the plant-choked pond.

"Alexander, I want you to reconsider this move," their father said in a tone Alex recognized from a hundred childhood lectures. "The house is barely livable. Find a condo in Newport. I can have my secretary find you a place by the end of the day."

"No, thank you. I'll be fine here. There's work to do, and I've got a whole summer to do it."

His father shook his head. "You're going to need more than a summer."

"We'll see." Alex backed away from a full-blown argument. That was one thing his family was good at, so they didn't need any practice.

The three of them left the place together, and oddly, Alex felt eager to head for the city, to get through the ordeal of the funeral. Sometimes he thought his plan was as crazy as his father kept telling him it was. Coming back here was insanity. The entire property was haunted by memories.

Now, finally sober for the first time in a couple of days, Alex discovered something. He wanted to explore the ghosts of memory that drifted through the old, empty house, because a large part of who he was still resided here.

Twelve

~~~~~

Down at the Galilee docks, the air was thick with the reek of the day's catch—lobster and bluefish, mussels and quahogs, mounds of striped bass, scrod and tuna. Rosa strolled along with Butch, who marked things on an order sheet attached to a clipboard.

As owner and general manager of the restaurant, she could—and probably should—leave the buying to her employees, but the fact was, she liked coming here. It was a place where nostalgia hung thick in the atmosphere of ice-cooled warehouses. This was her world, and a sense of belonging folded around her felt like a hand-crocheted afghan. She watched the birds congregating on the corrugated rooftops of the icehouses and warehouses, and listened to the chug of ships' engines.

"I love the smell of seafood in the morning," Butch said, inhaling dramatically.

"Me, too." She stepped over a drying net buzzing with flies.

"Come on."

"It's true. I used to come here with my mother." She smiled, picturing her mother in a crisp cotton dress, her pocketbook strap looped over one tanned arm, her shopping bag over the other. "Her cioppino was legendary. Guys here fell all over themselves, trying to wait on her."

"Hey, *my* cioppino is legendary," he said.

Chefs, she thought. The good ones all seemed to be made of equal parts talent and ego.

"As a twenty-seven-dollar menu item, it had better be."

"It's the saffron." He wandered off to place his orders.

Rosa waved to Lenny Carmichael, a second-generation lobsterman she'd known since grade school. In his hip-high yellow boots and Red Sox baseball cap, he looked exactly like his father. She owed a large part of the restaurant's success to the fishermen of Galilee, who supplied her with the very best of local seafood. According to one of her myriad psychology textbooks, Rosa was trying to use the restaurant to recreate aspects of her late mother. After she read that conclusion, she shook her head. "Well, *duh.* I know exactly what I'm doing and why. Does that make me a nutcase?"

So she had idealized her mother in her mind. So what? Motherless for twenty years, she felt entitled to declare Celesta Capoletti the most perfect mother a girl had ever had.

She wondered what the self-help books would say about Alex's return. Most experts seemed to believe in confronting unresolved issues of the past. So did her best friend, Linda. Rosa wasn't sure she liked the idea of hauling herself through the old hurt and heartbreak.

The sound of Butch tapping his foot in exaggerated fashion brought her back to the present. "I'll just wait while you collect your thoughts, then."

"What?" She fell in step with him, passing mounds of chipped ice covered with fish.

"You aren't even listening to me."

"I am, too."

"Bullshit, Rosa."

"You just said—" She scowled at him. "I'm not ignoring you. I'm just preoccupied."

"About what?"

"Maybe this summer I'll hire a general manager."

"You say that every summer. That's nothing. You're thinking about Alex Montgomery."

"I am not." They both knew she was lying. She couldn't get him out of her mind—Alex Montgomery with his haunted blue eyes, who had lost his mother in the worst possible way. Even his facade of cool Montgomery reserve couldn't mask a terrible, raw anger. He had some serious grieving to do, yet he was resisting it; she could tell. She couldn't understand that. Why not let it all out?

She pretended to give her full attention to a huge cod laid out on a bed of chipped ice, its mouth open wide, its glassy eyes staring. But that made her think of death, and then she thought of Emily Montgomery and the fact that she had killed herself. Losing a mother was painful enough. Learning it was a suicide added a twist of the knife.

The appearance of his father and sister had been singularly uncomfortable; Rosa couldn't get out of there fast enough. Though she'd known Alex for many years, his family remained a mystery to her. Given what had happened, she wished she'd seen them comfort each other, not bicker. They were supposed to be each other's safe place to fall. That was what a family was for. She'd never seen the Montgomerys do that. Not even now.

"He's back from the city, you know," Butch pointed out.

She tried to act nonchalant, even though her heart

skipped a beat. He'd been gone two weeks, three days, an hour and twenty minutes, not that she was counting. "Actually, I didn't. It doesn't matter to me."

"It was in the papers. They buried Mrs. Montgomery in Providence a week and a half, two weeks ago," Butch persisted, watching her like a hawk.

"Yeah?" she said, elaborately uninterested. "So?"

"Must be freaky, knowing your mother killed herself."

A cold weight dropped inside Rosa. *"What?"*

"A suicide. It was in the papers today."

She stared at him. "Can you finish up here by yourself? I need to go."

He looked furious. "Where's your pride, Rosa? Why go crawling back to that guy?"

"I'm not crawling. I'm running."

A flock of seagulls burst skyward as she rushed to the parking lot and got into her car. She needed to find Alex, and fast.

Cioppino

A lot of people think making homemade tomato sauce is too much of a bother. It's not, really. You're ahead in the game if you have some fresh herbs growing in pots on the windowsill. If you get really good seafood, the shells add their flavor to the broth. Just pass around plenty of napkins. Robert and Sal used to get in trouble for practicing ventriloquism with the mussel shells at the dinner table.

Broth: 1/4 cup olive oil
about 6 anchovies, chopped
4 cloves garlic, chopped
2 bay leaves
1 stalk of celery, diced
1 onion, chopped
1 roasted red bell pepper, chopped
1 cup Chianti + 2 Tablespoons red wine vinegar
1 quart fish or shrimp stock
6-8 diced fresh tomatoes (use canned if you don't have fresh)
chopped fresh basil a good pinch of saffron threads
2 Tablespoons Worcestershire sauce
1/2 cup chopped Italian flat-leaf parsley
2-3 tablespoons fresh lemon juice
salt to taste
1 teaspoon red pepper flakes
2 tablespoons dried oregano, or twice that amount if using fresh

*1 teaspoon fennel seeds, crushed with the flat of
a knife
1 sprig of rosemary*

Seafood: Use whatever is fresh that day, 1/4 pound or more of each variety: prawns (save the shells for making stock), crab, scallops, mussels, firm fish cut in 1 inch pieces (cod, halibut, scrod, bass), fresh clams, fresh oysters (shucked), calamari for the adventurous.

Warm the olive oil and anchovies in a big pot. Add garlic and stir, then add the bay leaves, onion, celery and bell pepper, plus 1/2 of the herbs. Pour in wine, vinegar and Worcestershire and let half the liquid bubble away. Then add tomatoes, basil and the rest of the herbs. Simmer, then add the fish stock and lemon juice, bringing it all to a boil. Finally, toss in the seafood, cover and cook 7-10 minutes. Remove any mussels and clams that haven't opened. Ladle the stew into wide, shallow dishes and sprinkle with parsley. Serve with warm bread.

Thirteen

Alex wasn't at the house on Ocean Road, though Rosa knocked long and loud. She left a note wedged in the crack of the front door—*Call me, Rosa*—along with her cell phone number.

Frustrated, she got back in her car and started the engine. She had a hundred things to do today, but couldn't concentrate on anything except the fact that Alex was back, and the press had invaded his family's most private business. She drove past the long string of beaches where candy-colored umbrellas and floppy hats blurred together, creating a colorful lei along the shoreline.

On a hunch, she pulled off the coast road and headed for a part of the beach she rarely visited anymore. Alex knew this place; perhaps he was here.

She clambered past an abandoned stone house whose half-crumbled walls had stood sentinel for years, a silent monument to someone's foolish notion that it was safe to live this close to the sea. Safe indeed. Perhaps it was in the summer when the weather was fine. Whoever had built the place had probably never seen the way a winter storm skirled in from the Atlantic, its winds toppling stout stone walls and dragging trees out by the roots.

Another hundred yards of the beach led to an estuary overgrown with cattails and reeds. And beyond that was a cove as private now as it had been twenty years ago. Back then, when she was an adventurous tomboy and he a lonely invalid, they had discovered this place together. It held more memories than a sentimental girl's diary. But no Alex.

Rosa shaded her eyes and scanned from north to south. A ship's horn sounded in the distance. A group of sea kayakers paddled offshore. Sailboats breezed across the sound.

Suddenly she knew exactly where he'd gone. "Oh, man," she muttered under her breath as she hurried back to her car. "Why there?"

As she drove down an old, tree-lined avenue and passed through the auspicious stone gates of the Rosemoor Country Club, an ancient, bone-deep lump of discomfort took hold of her. She tried to deny it, but the leaden feeling in her gut didn't lie. This place was the scene of one of the most humiliating moments of her adolescence, the sort that haunted her at odd moments even twelve years later. She didn't belong here and never would, no matter how much time passed, no matter how successful she became. This was a bastion of tradition for people whose fortunes had been made many generations ago, preferably by someone who had just stepped off the *Mayflower*.

Wishing she had on something other than a denim miniskirt and a sunflower-yellow top, she crossed the parking lot. A curious, elegant hush surrounded this place; even the seagulls seemed to mute their cries and the *thwok* of tennis balls sounded decidedly genteel. The Tudor-style clubhouse, covered with twining old roses, was nestled between the manicured first teebox and the eighteenth green. The private dock in front of it provided moorage for gloriously restored wooden yachts and sleek racing boats. On the deck overlooking the water, attractive people in breezy tennis whites and visors chatted and laughed together.

Wishing she could be anyplace else, she walked past the Members Only sign and stepped inside. Soft music drifted from hidden speakers. At his podium, the host greeted her. He was polite enough, but she could sense him checking her out, categorizing her as an interloper. A *nonmember*.

"I'm looking for Alexander Montgomery," she said. "Is he here?"

"I believe Mr. Montgomery is on the deck, Miss…?"

"Capoletti." She nodded toward a stairway. "Is that the way to the deck?"

"Yes, but—"

"Thanks for your help." She didn't have to turn around and look at him to know he was staring after her, that he'd probably send someone up to make sure she behaved herself. Fine, she thought. Let him.

She emerged onto the deck and scanned the lunch crowd there, a sea of golf, tennis and sailing togs. All the umbrella tables were occupied. And there was Marcia Brady, regarding her with cool inquisitiveness.

Rosa offered no more than a tight smile. "I'm here to see Alex."

"Is he expecting you?"

"What, do I have to make an appointment?"

One of the guys jerked his head toward the end of the deck. "He went to see if he could get the bar to open early."

Rosa pivoted on her platform sandal and walked away without another word. She hated that she always felt self-conscious around these people. She imagined them regarding her as though she was semiliterate, fresh off the sardine boat. It wasn't true, of course. People like that simply didn't think of her at all.

She found Alex leaning against the bar, arms crossed over his chest, jaw set as he contemplated the rows of liquor bottles. The late-morning sun glinted off his hair and picked out the perfectly sinewed muscles of his arms and legs. There was no bartender in sight.

Alex didn't look at Rosa, but she saw him stiffen at her approach, as though bracing himself.

"Touché, Capoletti," he said when she was within earshot.

"It wasn't me," she said.

He wheeled on her, seeming to grow larger with fury. Lord, but he was something, she thought. Yet when she really looked at his eyes, she saw loneliness and desperation, perhaps a shadow of the boy who had once been her friend.

"You were the only one outside the family who knew," he stated, his voice low and taut.

"Obviously not."

"My sister's got young kids. This is hurting them, too, or didn't you think of that?"

She felt every ear straining to hear them. "We might not know each other anymore, Alex. But I swear I haven't become the sort of person who would do such a thing."

"I have no idea what sort of person you've become."

"Likewise," she said, holding her temper in check. *And whose fault is that?* She didn't say it aloud. Another time, she might, but not now, not when he was ravaged by fury and indignation on his family's behalf.

"Alex," she said, slowly and solemnly. "On the soul of my own mother, I never said a word."

He pushed back from the bar and stared at her for a long moment. The sea breeze rattled through the reeds along the shore and plucked at his hair. Sunlight glinted in his eyes, and she saw the fury subside.

There were things he would always know about her, no matter how much time had passed, no matter the distance between them. He knew she would never, ever swear by her mother unless she had absolute faith in what she was saying.

"I have no idea who leaked the story, Alex," she said quietly, "but it wasn't me. I would never want the death of your mother to hurt you and your family any worse than it already has."

He flexed and unflexed his hand as though he had a cramped muscle. Then he heaved a sigh. "It would be so much simpler if I could blame you. It's so nice and neat. You knew, and you have a grudge against me—simple."

"It wasn't me."

"Yes, damn it, I know that."

"Why are you so angry?"

"Because if you'd blabbed to the press, I'd have someone to be pissed at."

"Why do you need to be pissed at someone?"

"Because it's easier than being pissed at myself."

The stark honesty that rang in his words reverberated in the air between them. In that moment, she saw him as someone who had lost his mother in a terrible way. Rage was common in relatives of suicide victims. So was guilt. She wondered how he was dealing with it all. He'd led a charmed life that probably did little to prepare him for shock and tragedy.

"How did you know I'd be at the club?"

She stifled a snort of amusement. Summer people had always flocked to places reserved for members only. It was almost instinctual, like salmon swimming upstream to spawn. "Call it a hunch."

She felt for him now. She hadn't forgiven him, not by a long shot, but she felt for him. "Do you think we could go somewhere else?" she asked. "Your friends have had their share of live entertainment today."

"Don't mind them. Let's go for a walk," he said.

She let out the breath she'd been painfully holding in. "All right."

He headed for a flight of exterior stairs that led down to the dock. She could feel his friends glaring holes in her back. They didn't need a reason to dislike her; they simply did. It had always been that way, and her friends had always reciprocated, disliking Alex on principle.

She stole a glance at him, not knowing what she'd see next, but she'd lost the ability to read his mood.

Still, the silence between them was charged. She pretended she hadn't noticed—for a while, at least. They didn't touch but walked side by side along a pebble-strewn path that was probably as old as the more famous walkway along Bailey's Beach.

In the wrack line of washed-up debris that lay along the beach, Rosa didn't see any treasures, just the occasional tangle of translucent fishing line and shimmering heap of brown kelp. Alex used to be good at finding things on the beach—a bit of sea glass or a rare shell.

"What are you thinking?" she asked him. Spoken aloud, it was a strangely intimate question, though she didn't mean it that way.

"I don't know. I wasn't thinking. Just looking at the way the sand blows up against the fence."

"In the winter, it goes in the opposite direction."

"I've never been here in winter."

"I know."

More silence, only the sounds of the sea around them: the muffled boom of the rollers, the hiss of rocks being thrown up on the shore and then rattling down as they were drawn back into the depths. The wind was light, a balmy caress, tousling their hair.

"My father wasn't sure whether or not to send something," she blurted out. "You know, flowers or—"

"There's no need."

"It's not a question of need," she said. "He took care of the property for years, so I guess he—"

"Just drop it, okay?"

The edge in his voice made her frown. It was probably the trauma of the sudden tragic loss, she thought, making him short-tempered. At one time, she would've known. She used to be able to read his face as easily as her own, and he could do the same for her. Those days seemed so long ago.

She felt him checking her out, and she deepened her scowl. "Do I have something on my face?" she asked.

"What?"

"On my face. The way you're staring at me, I thought maybe I had something on my face."

"Sorry. I didn't mean to make you uncomfortable."

"You didn't," she said quickly.

Silence again. She felt something pressing from the inside, straining to get out. She tried to deny that she felt anything, but she did. Here she was with the man who had once broken her heart, and she was consumed with curiosity about him. She couldn't indulge it, not now. He wasn't ready to answer questions. He'd just lost his mother and the world knew it was a suicide.

"Now you're too quiet," he pointed out. "*That* makes me uncomfortable."

"I'm trying to figure out what to say to you. I'm trying

to decide if there's anything I can possibly say." She felt an almost overwhelming urge to touch him, and even lifted her hand toward his arm. Then, feeling a shimmer of heat, she dropped her hand, instantly regretting the impulse. "When I lost my mother, I was in a different place than you are. But there are some losses that are always going to be devastating, and this is one of them." She bit her lip and wondered how it might have made her feel to know her mother had wanted to die, had done so by her own hand. It would be all the more horrible to have the world find out, to be the object of gossip and speculation.

She stopped walking. "What are you going to do?"

"I'm not sure."

"Do you have any other theories about who leaked the story?"

"Maybe it was someone from the medical examiner's office. I'm sure we'll have it checked out."

"We?"

"My father and I."

"But if the paper quoted an anonymous source, they won't divulge anyone's name."

"We'll see."

His certainty intrigued her. She didn't want this. Didn't want to be fascinated by him. "Alex, how much does it matter?"

"What, that my mother killed herself, or that the story's in the papers?"

"Both, I suppose."

"Personally, I don't give a shit whether the way she died stays private or it's broadcast on the evening news, but my father's bugged by it. My sister, too. She's going to have to explain it to her kids. That's the part I hate the most."

Rosa noticed he hadn't addressed the first part of her question. And she was a little shocked to feel a deep sense of resentment on his behalf. In general, she regarded the press as her ally, helping her publicize the restaurant. Thanks to syndicated articles by travel writers from all over, her place had been mentioned in papers as far-flung as Miami, London, LA. Still, she knew how destructive bad press could be.

"I hate it, too," she said. "I'm sorry, Alex." She felt so cautious around him, so awkward. He was just a guy, she kept telling herself. Just a guy she used to know. She tried to remember that he wasn't special.

Even so, she kept sneaking glances at him, wishing he didn't seem so…sexy. She couldn't deny that he captivated her. She could picture him as a boy, and then a teenager. He had excelled at sports—tennis, rowing, cycling, sailing. Having been deprived of anything resembling a life when he was very young, he'd made up for lost time after his health improved. At thirty, he was tall and athletic, with that square-jawed all-American look which he wore as naturally as the sun on his hair.

"Tell me about your life, Rosa," he said out of the blue.

"Why?"

"Because I want to know what you've been up to."

Getting over you, she thought. Even after all this time, I'm still working on it. "There's nothing to tell. After Pop's accident, I stayed in Winslow. There was no way I'd leave him, not in the shape he was in."

"Rosa. I'm sorry—"

"Don't say it. I know you felt bad for me." *But not bad enough to stick around.*

She wondered how much he knew about the situation. An anonymous party, through a blind trust administered by the Newport law firm Claggett, Banks, Saunders &

Lefkowitz, had paid for her father's long-term care and rehabilitation, which had taken nearly two years. She assumed the angel was one of Pop's loyal clients. And every night, she thanked God for the favor.

"So after your father got better," Alex said, "then what? What about the cop?"

"He's the county—"

"—sheriff now. So you said. That's not what I'm asking, and you know it."

She decided to ignore the question. "And then…I got a raise at Mario's."

"The pizza joint that used to be where your restaurant is."

"Good memory." She tried not to feel defensive. "I moved up to general manager. And Mario was looking to get out of the business. It was tricky, though. The building is the last one standing on the protected waterfront. The property's small, its footprint can never be expanded and the parking lot can never be paved. Still, I wanted it. I wanted to start a restaurant, a really good one. I leased the place from Mario, and five years ago, I launched Celesta's-by-the-Sea." She folded her arms across her chest. "So if I'd gone off to college, I never would have started the restaurant."

Rosa suspected she sounded quite different from the dreamy teenager he had once known. That girl had glowed with shining ideals and high-minded convictions. She was going to be a philosopher, a diplomat, a rocket scientist. She would have scoffed at the idea of running a restaurant. Since then, she'd learned a few things about life and work.

His stare made her wonder what he was thinking. And the accelerated beating of her heart made her question her own motives for coming here.

"Come back to the club with me," he said. "I'll buy you lunch."

"God, you are clueless. Do you know how excruciating that would be for me?"

"Okay, wrong move. Let's get lunch at Aunt Carrie's."

She looked away, trying to hide her vivid memories of the outdoor café. She and Alex had gone there as kids, sunburnt, their hair stiff with salt and their feet bare, to eat clam cakes and blueberry pie.

"What do you say?" He didn't touch her, but she felt his gaze like a caress.

"I say this conversation is over."

"Rosa," he added, "we're not finished."

She burst out laughing, then tossed back her hair and looked him in the eye. "Yes," she said, "we are. You made sure of that a long time ago."

"I made a mistake a long time ago."

It was rare to hear a man admit he was wrong. To hear a Montgomery man admit it was…astounding. "And this just came to you," she said.

"No. I've thought about it a lot over the years." His frankness disarmed her.

"It's too late," she said in a low, rough voice. "We can't just go back to…we can't."

"True," he agreed. "We can do better."

"Alex, for Pete's sake, I don't know what you think I've been doing—waiting, pining away? We had a summer romance. I made the mistake of taking it too seriously. Girls generally do. After you left, I regained my perspective, and I assume you did, too." She felt herself getting overheated and took a deep breath. In spite of everything, she felt vulnerable to him, to his searching blue eyes and his gentle smile, and to her own tender memories of how she'd once felt with him, safe and adored. Along with her yearning and nostalgia came another sensation—fear. She was afraid. She hated that about herself. She wished she could play this for laughs, maybe have some fun with him and then walk away, like Linda said she should do. That was what Rosa usually did with men she dated. But with Alex, it would be impossible.

She said, "Listen. I feel horrible about your mother, and even worse now that it's in the papers. That's why I came looking for you, not to have lunch and reminisce about the past, which is completely pointless since it's over, and…" She forced herself to stop babbling. "I'm going. I have to be at the restaurant. Okay?"

"No, it's not okay. Damn it, Rosa. It's just lunch."

"And it's not going to happen."

As she walked away, she heard him give an ironic laugh. "Chicken," he said softly.

Don't stop, she told herself. Don't look back.

Fourteen

~~~

Rosa did a great job not thinking of Alex for whole minutes at a time. A few days after their encounter, she managed to convince herself that she'd only imagined the sincerity in his eyes when he'd asked her to come to lunch with him.

Her heart was not so easily fooled, and she felt an odd stumble in her chest at unexpected moments. She had often hoped to feel that half-sick, half-delicious lurch with regard to other men, but it never worked. Over the years, she'd dated almost too enthusiastically, only to be disappointed, or to disappoint.

Her best defense was to keep busy. Fortunately for her, she had plenty to do. The restaurant consumed half the day and most of the night, and her friends and father filled in the rest. Linda's wedding plans were moving ahead at warp speed, and Rosa found herself delightfully swept away by all the fuss.

After stopping at Linda's to drop off some sample menus for the reception, she went to her father's house, blinking the hall lights to announce her presence.

"In here," yelled Pop.

She followed the sound of his voice to the den off the kitchen, where Pop sat in front of the computer monitor. Behind him, the TV was on, closed-captioning words flickering across the screen of a Red Sox-Cardinals game. The TV was turned up too loud, which didn't bother Pop in the least.

The den, like the rest of the house, was cluttered with old mail, lottery ticket stubs, expired coupons and things her father never bothered to throw away. A stack of newspapers filled the plastic recycling bin nearly to the top. Pop had always been an obsessive news junkie. Online, his browser was bookmarked with a dozen news sites— the *International Herald Tribune,* Rome's *il Mondo*, the *Washington Post*.

Rosa found the TV remote control wedged between the couch cushions and hit the mute button.

"Hey, Pop." She kissed him on the cheek. "You left the front door unlocked. I could have been an intruder."

"An intruder wouldn't flash the lights."

"Pop—"

"Okay, okay," he said, waving his arms to fend her off. "I'll be more careful."

Sure he would. She didn't feel like arguing with him. "Checking your e-mail?"

"I got news from Rob and Gloria." He steepled his fingers together and leaned back in his chair. He had blunt hands, strong and callused from years of hard work, ill-suited to typing at a keyboard. Yet he was remarkably adept at it, and because of his hearing loss, he had embraced the technology of communicating by text message, e-mail and instant messages.

To Rosa, it was a godsend. She could text message his vibrating cell phone or zap him a quick IM to see if he was online, and stay in touch as closely as other people did with their hearing parents.

"So what's up with Rob?" she asked.

"Your brother and his wife are both gonna be deployed to Diego Garcia over the summer. Joey's coming to stay with me."

Rosa was surprised. Normally Rob and Gloria, both career NCOs, alternated deployments and shore duty so one or the other would be at home. They had four kids, though they weren't kids anymore. Their eldest had enlisted in the navy and was stationed in Bremerton, Washington. The twins, Mary-Celesta and Teresa-Celesta, were spending the summer in Costa Rica in a program sponsored by Youth International. The youngest, Joey, would be fourteen now. She hadn't seen him in more than two years, since the whole family had been stationed in Guam.

"I wonder how they both managed to get sea duty at the same time," she said.

"They're patriots, serving their country."

"I bet our country doesn't really need Joey's mother and father at the same time."

"Look at the world we live in." He gestured at the newspapers spread a week thick across the coffee table. "The least we can do is take care of their boy."

It didn't escape her that he said *we.* "Is that all right with you, Pop?" she asked. "Keeping Joey for the summer?"

"Sure, it's okay. He's my own flesh and blood."

"In the past, Gloria's folks have always kept the kids," she pointed out.

"Yeah. Well, they couldn't. They got some kind of conflict," said Pop.

Some kind of conflict, thought Rosa, like not wanting to look after a teenage boy all summer.

"Gloria's mother had to have female surgery," said Pop. "I didn't ask for details."

She instantly felt guilty for the thought. The Espositos were perfectly fine people as far as she could tell. They lived in Chicago and she didn't know them very well.

"When's he coming?" she asked her father.

"Day after tomorrow."

Way to give us advance notice, Rob, she thought. "I'll go with you to pick him up at the airport."

"You don't have to."

"Pop. I'm going." She had learned not to argue with him. It saved time to simply dictate.

He had learned to save time, too. He turned his hands palms up and looked at the ceiling. "You're a bossy girl. Just like your mother, you are."

Rosa loved being likened to her mother, which Pop knew very well. "I'll have the restaurant's cleaning service help you get the house ready."

"What, ready? He's fourteen. He's a guy. He doesn't care what the place looks like."

"I care." Rosa shook her head. "Fourteen…and he was just eleven the last time we saw him." She remembered an apple-cheeked boy with chocolate-brown eyes and a shy smile, nervous and excited about moving overseas. It would be fun to have him here for the summer, she decided. Still, she didn't know if her father was up to having a half-grown boy living with him. On the other hand, it might be good for them both.

"So anyway," she said, "we should get started. I'll help you."

Pop scowled. "What help? I don't need any help."

She eyed the cluttered room, the cardboard boxes stacked on the stairway as they had been for weeks, waiting to be taken up. She stood and pushed in her chair. When she was certain he was looking at her, she said, "I'm going to get the boys' room ready for Joey."

He didn't object as she seized one of the boxes and headed upstairs. She hadn't been up here in ages, and neither had Pop, judging by the cobwebs in the stairwell.

A curious sensation came over her. She was not just walking up a flight of stairs in the house where she'd grown up. She was ascending to a place where old memories shimmered like dust motes in the air around her. The boys' room, as it was still called even though the "boys" hadn't lived here in twenty years, was frozen in time, a snapshot of their world the day they had both left for basic training.

Robert had been eighteen, the ink barely dry on his high school diploma. Sal was a year older, though he'd stayed home the year after high school. Rosa had been too little to understand why he had stuck around while all his friends were heading out into the world to find their lives. Now, as an adult, she knew exactly why.

He had stayed home because that was Mamma's last year on earth. He, Rob and Pop had known. Mamma had known. But no one had told Rosa.

Sal had spent more time than anyone else with their mother. Along with the nuns and a visiting nurse sent by their church and funded by St. Vincent de Paul, Sal became Mamma's primary caretaker. Rosa could still picture him smiling gently as he spooned lime Jell-O into her mouth when she was too weak to feed herself. He had unflinchingly emptied and cleaned the tubes and bags that had become her prison in the end. Sometimes he would go to another room and sit down and cry in rough, jagged sobs that made his whole body shudder. But he never cried in front of Mamma.

Mostly, he sat by her side, held her hand and read to her, everything from the Bible to James Herriot books to a new novel called *The Color Purple*. Those times, Rosa believed, had brought him to a state of grace. At the side of his dying mother, he discovered the path his life was to follow. He found the strength of his convictions, and he made her a promise. He would be a priest. And he'd done it, attending seminary courtesy of the United States Navy, because they needed men of faith. Now he was a chaplain, and as good a priest as he was a warrior.

Rosa's brothers had left on a clear morning in June. She and Pop had driven them to the train station in Kingston, had stood numbly on the platform, waving goodbye. They'd returned to a house that was eerily quiet and diminished by loss, the same way it had been when Mamma died.

That afternoon, Rosa had gone to work with Pop because she was too young to stay home alone. It had been that same afternoon, she recalled, that she met Alex Montgomery for the first time.

The boys' room stood virtually untouched, as though Rob and Sal had just walked out of it five minutes before. There was a Winslow Spartans pennant on the wall, a shelf of baseball and Greco-Roman wrestling trophies, a dresser covered with photos yellowing in their frames. There were shots of Rosa at six, dressed like a miniature bride for her first communion, and at eight, proudly holding aloft a bluefish she'd caught while out on the Carmichaels' boat. The photos of her mother formed something of a shrine, and the faded quality of the prints seemed to enhance the deep, ethereal beauty of Celesta, haloing her with a look of untouchable grace.

Rosa cleared out the closet—Levi's and Chuck Taylor sneakers and shirts with pointy collars—and threw everything into plastic sacks for the dump. She was not about to burden the Salvation Army or Catholic Charities with old gym socks and Dukes of Hazzard T-shirts.

Eventually some combination of curiosity and guilt brought her father to the room with a dust mop, a can of Pledge and a roll of paper towels. He said nothing, but started on the floor in desultory fashion. They worked together in companionable silence until Rosa stripped the bunk beds and bundled up the sheets to take to the basement for washing.

"What are you doing that for?" asked Pop. "Those are clean sheets."

"They need freshening up." He didn't seem to catch "freshening" so she signed it.

"Suit yourself," he muttered, moving the things off the dresser to squirt it with Pledge. He wiped down the surface and then dusted each photo with care, smiling a little at the images.

She waved to get his attention. "What are you thinking about?"

He set aside a photo of Rob and Sal in their Little League pinstripes. His face was creased by lines of sentiment. "Thanking God for all of this, thanking God that it happened to me."

She ached for him, knowing he could recall a time when his hearing was keen and the house rang with laughter, when disease and disaster were things you read about in the newspaper. The accident twelve years ago had changed him, darkened his spirit.

She helped him arrange the pictures. "There are plenty of good times ahead, Pop."

He patted her hand. "You bet." Then he studied her face, and she could feel him reading her; he'd always been able to guess at her thoughts. "You are going to start seeing him again, eh? The Montgomery boy."

"I'm not sure. Maybe." She had no idea why she said that. She kept telling herself it was long over; she didn't want to see Alex again. But Pop had a way of getting her mouth to speak up before her brain could censor her.

"Rosa. This is a boy who hurt you. He did a terrible thing and the heartbreak nearly—" He stopped himself, she could see, with sheer force of will.

She knew he was thinking about her extreme reaction to the accident and Alex's departure. "I was a kid," she said. "I didn't have good coping skills."

"Well, now you got a perfectly fine life. Don't go messing with a boy like that. He'll do you no good at all."

Alex would always be a boy to Pop, a spoiled rich boy.

"Everybody changes," she pointed out, wondering even as she spoke why she was taking Alex's part. Probably because Pop took the opposite side, and the two of them loved to argue.

"His wedding got called off and he's just lost his mother. He's looking for a shoulder to cry on."

She paused, Windex bottle in hand. "Sounds like you've been keeping up with all the gossip."

"I read the papers."

"Then maybe you've read that he manages a trust to provide health care for the needy."

"Montgomerys are good at making money. They can't help it."

"You say that like it's a bad thing."

"Never mind that boy, Rosina. You got better things to do with your time."

She went downstairs and got some new lightbulbs; most seemed to be burned out in here. As she unscrewed a corroded bulb from the ceiling fixture, sparks shot from the socket. She nearly fell off the chair she was standing on.

"The wiring's terrible in here, Pop," she said. "This place is a firetrap."

"I'll get Rudy to come take a look at it." Rudy was a retired electrician who lived down the block.

"You do that, Pop. Tomorrow."

Fifteen

The main street of Winslow was lined with shops that catered to summer visitors and well-heeled browsers. The hardware store hummed this time of year, peak season for gardening and home improvement. Business was always brisk for Eagle Harbor Books, the Twisted Scissors Salon, the Stop & Shop and Seaside Silversmith. At the end of Winslow Way was a beach-access parking lot bordered by summer-only stands called "She Sells Sea Shells" and "I Scream For Ice Cream."

There were three dress shops, one that attracted the matronly golf set, one for tourists and trends, and a bridal boutique owned by a local woman named Ariel Cole. Her mother, a Portuguese immigrant, had started a tailor shop decades before, and Ariel still did a decent trade in alterations, but the larger part of her business was Wedding Belles, the bridal shop.

Linda's bridesmaids gathered at the boutique to try the three options Ariel had selected for them. Wearing strapless A-line gowns in aqua silk shantung, Rosa and Linda's sister, Rachel, stared at their reflection in the boutique mirror while Linda and Ariel stood back, examining them with a critical eye.

"This can't be right, Ariel," said Rosa. "This is a great dress. It actually looks good on us."

"And your point is…?"

"Bridesmaid gowns are supposed to be ugly so they don't outshine the bride. Isn't that a rule or something?"

"Not in my shop, it isn't," Ariel said with a sniff. She had always taken pride in her exquisite taste. She turned to the other bridesmaids, Linda's sister Rachel, and Sandra Malloy, a local writer who had become fast friends with Linda. "Well?"

"We love it." Sandra, who hadn't tried on the dress, patted her hugely rounded stomach. "This is our favorite. Now all I have to do is make sure the baby comes before the wedding. No idea what size I'll be, though."

"I'm doing the alterations myself," Ariel said.

"You look like a fertility goddess," said Linda, holding the gorgeous fabric against Sandra's pregnant belly.

Rosa was blindsided by a swift, sharp pang of yearning. Oh, she wanted to feel the way Sandra must be feeling now, as a contented wife with her first baby on the way. She wanted that with all her heart. She had for a long time, but the distance from the wish to the deed was vast.

"Earth to Rosa," Linda said, nudging her. "Last chance to cast your vote."

"I don't know," said Rosa, shoving away the painful thoughts. "It seems too easy. We're not objective enough. I want to go show Twyla." She went outside and headed for the Twisted Scissors Salon a few doors down. Rosa had always given Twyla full credit for rescuing her from the world's worst haircut when she was thirteen, and she'd been Rosa's stylist ever since.

As she hurried down the sidewalk, she noticed a tall man in painter's pants and a paint-spattered T-shirt and cap, carrying a five-gallon bucket out of the hardware store. Rosa slowed her pace. She was not in so much of a hurry that she couldn't stop for a moment to enjoy the view. She'd always been a sucker for a guy in work clothes.

She was thinking seriously about having her condo repainted when she realized who she was staring at with such lust. As he lowered the tailgate of a white SUV and loaded the paint in the back, she knew that perfect male butt could only belong to one man.

Rosa ducked her head and started walking again. But being inconspicuous on the street while wearing a strapless turquoise gown was impossible. A wolf whistle from the direction of the truck alerted her that she'd been spotted. She stopped before he could do it again, drawing even more attention to her. He closed the tailgate of the truck and walked over to her.

"Rosa." Alex's gaze slipped down and up, twice. "Nice dress."

His look alone gave her goose bumps, which she tried desperately to will away before he noticed. "Thank you. So anyway…if you'll excuse me…" She edged toward the salon.

He stepped in her path. "I've been thinking about our conversation…at the club last week."

The club. He had no idea how that sounded. "I'm sort of in a hurry here."

"I meant what I said about seeing you."

"Look your fill." She spread her arms and faced him with reckless confidence, goose bumps and all, even though she knew he'd dated women far more beautiful than she. Pictures of his glossy public life sometimes ran in the "Evening Hours" column of the *Times.* He always favored a "type." Patrician, fair and WASPy, his dates were as tall and thin as uncooked spaghetti.

Judging by the expression on his face now, Rosa suspected he might be willing to keep an open mind about his type. His eyes didn't just look, they touched. She felt a swift phantom caress on her lips, her throat, her breasts, as his gaze slipped over her.

"That's not enough," he said.

"That's all I'm offering." She brushed past him. "I have to go."

He took her by the arm and pulled her back to face him. "Not so fast."

Rosa hated herself for feeling that touch all the way through her, like a jolt of electrical current.

"It's not a lot to ask," he urged her. "I need to see you again."

As always, this was about his needs, not hers. He hadn't changed one bit. In spite of herself, Rosa remembered how she had ached with missing him, how she'd grieved for the future they'd never have together. To her horror, all those feelings came rushing back at her now, swirling around and engulfing her like a powerful undertow, pulling her feet out from under her.

How could this not have changed? she wondered in a panic. We're different people now. Why do I still feel this way?

Neurolinguistic implantation, she thought, dredging up something she'd learned in a cognitive science course. An event in the present evokes past sensations. But science couldn't explain how a foolish heart had the power to overrule common sense. Run, Rosa, run, she urged herself, yet somehow she stayed planted right in front of him. Maybe if he wasn't touching her, she'd be able to think straight.

"Let go of me, Alex."

He didn't, but rubbed his thumb along the inside of her elbow until she felt the heated sting of temptation.

"I don't want to."

She caught her breath and asked, "What about what I want? You don't even know whether or not I'm spoken for."

"You're not. I checked."

She pulled her arm away. "You've been checking on me?"

"Not really. I was bluffing, and you just told me what I want to know."

Oops. "I don't need you—or anyone—in my life. I'm perfectly happy with the way things are," she snapped.

He met her furious glare with a calm smile. "Remind me not to piss you off."

"Too late," she said with a small laugh. "I believe your exact words to me were 'We're not going to happen.' I think that still holds true, don't you?"

The expression on his face told her that he recalled the conversation, probably as clearly as she did. They both still remembered exactly what he'd said the night he had told her goodbye forever.

"Don't you believe in second chances, Rosa?"

Refusing to answer that, she studied him for a moment, subjecting him to the same scrutiny he gave her. There was a time when she had known every thought in his head, every wish in his heart. Where was that brilliant, lonely boy who had opened himself to her, who'd been the keeper of her deepest dreams and secrets? For a second, she thought she saw the boy's yearning and desperation in the man's blue eyes, but that was probably just a trick of the light.

"What?" he asked her.

"You're getting too skinny," she said, and that was

true, judging by the gaunt shadows under his eyes. He clearly wasn't treating himself well, all alone at the beach house. She tried to imagine what it was like for him, grieving alone, wondering what had driven his mother to take her own life. The bleakness of that image touched her in spite of herself. "You should eat."

"So feed me."

"Book a table at the restaurant, and I'll feed you."

"Your friends there are overprotective."

"There are other restaurants in town," she said. "Or—here's a concept—you could learn to cook."

He shook his head and gestured at the buckets in the back of the truck. "I have other projects going on."

"Why are you painting your own house? Couldn't you hire someone to do it?"

"Stop by and I'll explain it."

Rosa realized they were garnering stares from passersby. "I have to go." She turned and fled to the salon. He wouldn't dare follow her there.

She was wrong. She stepped inside, and just as she began to think she'd made a clean getaway, the bell over the door jingled lightly. Even before turning around, she knew it was him.

"Look, Alex—"

"I'm looking." He took off his painter's cap and offered everyone a friendly grin, stirring up a flurry of female sighs among Twyla and her customers. "Pardon me, ladies. I was just trying to make a date here—"

"I already told you no," Rosa snapped in frustration.

"What are you, nuts?" asked a woman whose head was covered in strips of foil. "The guy's asking you out."

"So you go out with him," Rosa said.

"I'm asking you, Rosa," Alex said. "And not for the first time."

"Then you should know you're wasting your breath. I won't change my mind."

He stood very still with his cap held over his heart, and she thought that at last she'd gotten through to him. For a second, she felt the tiniest twinge of regret.

Then he grinned again, put his hat back on and headed for the door. "Sure you will, honey," he said, loud enough for everyone to hear. "Sure you will."

Sixteen

"My God, Alex," said Gina Colombo, getting out of her rental car and goggling up at the place. "You live in a frigging ark."

Alex came down the porch steps to greet his most trusted colleague at the firm. "But you don't have to come aboard two-by-two."

She gave a happy little yell and hugged him with unabashed affection. "It's good to see you. How are you doing?"

"I live in an ark. I'm drifting."

"That's what you're supposed to do when you take time off. Oh, that's right. You wouldn't know what that's like."

"I'm not so sure I'm cut out for a life of leisure," he said, wondering if he should admit that he'd spent the past eight hours painting the fascia boards with nothing but a transistor radio for company. Since joining the family firm six years before, he had never taken time off. He wasn't sure why this was the case. There were plenty of places for him to go. In addition to the beach house, the Montgomerys had a ski lodge in Killington and a cabin in the Catskills. He could travel to Monte Carlo or Rome or anywhere in the world if he felt like it.

He didn't ever feel like it. Usually he just worked. When he worked, he was in his right place, doing something that mattered. "How is Don?" he asked.

"Fine. We're both fine. I can't wait to get him to Newport. I'm so glad we're making this move, Alex."

His associate was as capable and trusted as Alex's own left brain. It was coincidence, pure coincidence, that she happened to have a name like Gina Colombo, dark curly hair and olive-toned skin, and that she was short and compact, with perfect breasts and a sexy mouth. The attitude was all her own, however. As was her degree from the Wharton School of Business.

Alex's mother had called her the Bride of Frankenstein when she first met her, "Because you're trying to build a substitute Rosa."

The memory made him wince. His mother had always seen him too clearly; he only wished he'd understood her heart half as well.

Despite his mother's skepticism, he forged a deeply intimate partnership with Gina. She knew what he thought, could anticipate his desires in any situation. In practically every way, she was the perfect woman for him. Except she happened to be in love with her husband, a freelance photographer.

Gina embraced the challenge of opening the Newport office. She was on track to earning a promotion to partner in the fall.

"Tidying up an abandoned ark after your mother passes away hardly qualifies as a leisure activity," Gina pointed out with her typical bluntness. "You've lost weight. You look like shit, by the way."

"I feel like shit. How would you expect me to feel after

my mother's death? Which I'm not ready to talk about, so don't even start."

"All right," she said easily, heading for the front door. "Let's talk business instead. I'll take equity risk premiums and p/e ratios over depression and suicide any day."

Alex thought it was curious that she had thrown in depression. No one else had mentioned it, but that was Gina. There were no roadblocks between her heart and her mouth. She was only voicing something Alex had been thinking about ever since the phone had rung that morning. If his mother was in treatment for depression, why wasn't it working? And why that particular day of all days?

"So," Gina said, stepping through the door and heading straight for the parlor, "this is the Montgomery family compound."

"Once upon a time. Would you like something to drink?"

"No, thanks." She sighed, gazing out the bay window. She made a leisurely stroll through the downstairs, oohing and ahhing at the tall Carpenter Gothic windows, the antique woodwork. "I could live forever on this view. Boy, Alex. This is some place."

In the kitchen, she laid a thick legal-sized envelope on the window seat. "Earnings reports, forecasts, meeting minutes. Nothing urgent. I was feeling nosy, so I used this as an excuse to spy on you." She folded her arms across her middle and stared at him.

"What?"

"You look different as well as skinny."

He grazed his fingers through his hair. "I need a haircut."

She frowned and tilted her head to one side. "It's not that. It's—"

"Alex? It's me, Rosa," called a voice from the porch.
Gina raised one eyebrow.

Great, thought Alex, excusing himself and heading for
the door. The two of them together should be interesting.
Ever since making that scene in the beauty parlor, he'd
been hoping Rosa would break down and stop by, and
finally something had prodded her to come. But her
timing was unfortunate. Still, Rosa at the wrong time
was better than no Rosa at all.

He opened the door and she stepped inside, holding
a foil-wrapped parcel like a holy offering.

"I brought you something to eat," she announced.

Aha, he thought. This was the key to Rosa—she
couldn't resist a starving man. He couldn't help it; he
laughed. "You really want to feed me?"

She sniffed at the question and headed for the
kitchen. Alex felt like a deer in the headlights, but she
didn't seem to notice as she breezed through the house.
"You're clearly not doing it for yourself. You have to
promise to eat this while the sun is still up. My mother
used to say a well-made lasagne keeps away regrets and
bad dreams if—oh." She stopped in the doorway and
stared at Gina. "Hello."

Standing across from each other, they looked eerily
similar—dark, rounded, so very female. The two of them
together were a men's magazine fantasy.

"Rosa, this is Gina Colombo, my associate at the firm.
Gina, Rosa Capoletti. She runs—"

"Celesta's-by-the-Sea," Gina finished for him. "I read
that profile of you in *Entrepreneur*."

"Really?" Rosa's smile shone with pride. "Thanks.
You have a good memory." She indicated her parcel. "So
I'll just drop this off and—"

"I was on my way out," said Gina, swishing past Rosa.

"I need to get over to Newport to look at the rentals. It was nice to meet you, Rosa. I hope to see you again sometime."

Alex escorted Gina outside, saying to Rosa over his shoulder, "Be right back."

As he held open Gina's car door, he tried to avoid her gaze, but couldn't. "All right," she said. "Spill."

"Go away, Gina. Go to Newport. Call me next week."

"I want to know—"

"There's nothing to know, okay?"

"Oh, right. She's wearing red, she's bringing lasagne, she can't take her eyes off you…I wouldn't call that nothing."

"What would you call it?"

"Hello?" She playfully knocked on his head. "I might even approve of this one, Al." She twitched her skirt out of the way of the door. Lowering her voice an octave, she said, "I'll be back."

"You're not invited."

"Like that's going to stop me." She gave him a quick hug and got into the car. With the stereo blaring an Eva Cassidy tune, she pulled out of the driveway.

When he went back inside, Rosa was in the kitchen. She stood in the pale light of the sun, looking out the window at the lawn her father had cultivated and groomed over the course of decades. *Her father.* Alex considered asking her how Pete was doing. He didn't, of course.

Rosa turned to face him, hands on hips, and he could picture her in this house years ago, a dark, wiry little girl with bright eyes and a brighter smile. There had been magic in their friendship, but he couldn't sense it now. She was no more than a lovely stranger, standing in his mother's empty house.

"Gina really was just leaving," he said.

"Look, I came because I thought you might need something decent to eat," she explained. "And I suppose because, under the circumstances, I thought you should-n't be alone. Both times, you weren't."

"Yeah, sorry."

"Don't be. Never apologize for having friends and family around when you need them."

He searched for hidden meaning in her words. Did she intend to remind him of how alone she'd been at the end of their last summer together? He could still taste his guilt over that even now, all these years later. "Look, about Gina—"

"I don't need an explanation."

"Just so you know. She works with me. That's all."

"Fine. I really don't… It's none of my business, Alex." She indicated the covered dish on the counter. "All I'm doing is bringing you a lasagne."

She turned on her heel and headed out through the nearest exit—the back door. He followed her out into the yard and noticed the way she studied the pond, the lawn, the big gnarled tree where she'd once hung a rope swing. He wondered if she, too, felt that bittersweet pang of memory. Their lives—their love—had been so simple then.

"Thank you for bringing the lasagne." He didn't know what else to say. "I promise I'll eat every bite."

"It's a lot of food."

"Then stay and help me eat it." He stood in her way, blocking the path to the front drive. They stood very close, staring at each other. The rose-tinted sheen on her lips would give him something to think about for the rest of the day, he thought.

He caught her scent and was shocked to discover that he recognized it even after all these years. It was some kind of fruity shampoo or skin cream, and on Rosa it was as heady as a shot of whiskey. He could feel the warmth of her even though they weren't touching, and he imagined the smoothness of her skin under his hands. For a moment, the urge to touch her crackled like lightning between them. Recognition flashed in her eyes, and he knew she felt that unseen current of heat, too.

"Rosa," he said.

"I have to go."

"It's kind of inconsistent for you to show up and then say you don't want to see me." He risked pointing out the obvious. "You came to my house, not the other way around. The casserole's nice, but it's just an excuse. You do want to see me."

"I wanted to make sure you're okay," she insisted. "You've had a terrible loss and you're all alone out here. In that sense, I suppose I came to see you, but not in the way you mean."

Out here at night, lit only by the stars and the moon, with the wind soughing through the reeds and the waves swishing up from the sea, he discovered the true meaning of being alone. And each night, he searched for some way to make sense of what his mother had done, but the answers eluded him. The only thing that made sense was what he was feeling for Rosa.

"You want to stay." He took another chance and said it.

"That's bull—"

"Then why are you still here?"

That ticked her off. She shook back her curls and glared up at him. "Because you won't stop talking. Ah, but now you have. So if you'll excuse me…"

"I'll call you," he said. "You can handle that, can't you?"

She yanked a cluster of keys from her purse. "I'm busy."

"I know. At the restaurant, surrounded by guys who want to break my kneecaps."

"That's the one."

"Look, all I want to do is talk."

"About what?"

"About everything." Then he told the truth. "About our last summer together." He'd tried that once before. It hadn't worked then; why would it work now?

Her cheeks turned bright red, and he should have felt gratified that she remembered. Instead he felt like a heel. "I shouldn't have left you like that, Rosa," he said. "I was young and stupid, and I handled it badly. I didn't know what else to do. I've always wanted to explain it to you."

"We were both young," she said, pointedly not calling herself stupid right along with him. "Everybody knows that relationships like that never work out."

"Everybody but the young." A silence, heightened by the sound of the wind and the waves, rolled out between them. "Anyway," he said, "we're different people now."

"So?"

"So, we should get to know each other again—as adults."

"Why?"

"Because…we might be good together, Rosa."

"We might be a disaster."

"Are you afraid of that?"

She studied his face for a long moment. "Yes," she admitted. "Maybe I am."

Lasagne Magro

In the old country, if you can afford meat, you don't hide it in a lasagne. The original recipe is meatless. This delicious lasagne is commonly found in southern Italy.

Ingredients:
At least a quart of good tomato sauce,
*   preferably homemade*
1 large carton full-fat ricotta cheese
1 cup grated parmesano reggiano cheese
1 cup shredded mozzarella cheese
1 large fresh egg
1/2 onion, chopped
1/4 cup chopped parsley
1/4 cup chopped fresh basil
1/2 pound chopped fresh spinach
8 ounces additional mozzarella cheese,
*   sliced thin*
4 ounces additional grated parmesan cheese
1 package dry lasagne noodles

Mix the ricotta and grated cheeses together with egg, onion, spinach and herbs. Cover the bottom of a large lasagne pan with olive oil and then sauce. Add a little water and mix. Make an overlapping layer of the dry noodles across the bottom of the pan. Spread sauce on top, making sure the pasta is covered. Add a layer of the ricotta mixture and mozzarella slices. Continue in this manner until you run out of pasta. Top with sauce, add another layer of mozzarella, then sprinkle on the parmesan. Cover with foil and bake at 375° F for about forty minutes. Check occasionally, and add boiling water around the edges if the pasta seems too dry. Remove the foil and cook another 10 minutes. Let rest an additional 10 minutes. Serve in squares, topped with a basil sprig.

Seventeen

━━━◦◦◦◦━━━

Rosa fumed as she drove over to her father's house. What kind of idiot was she, anyway? *Are you afraid? Maybe I am.* What in God's name was she thinking, talking to him like that?

"I was being honest," she said, taking the turn onto Prospect Street a little too fast. "As if that ever did me any good. I don't know any other way to be. I never should have taken him that stupid lasagne."

She let herself in, flicking the lights to alert her father. "Let's go, Pop," she yelled, mainly for her own benefit. After seeing Alex, she definitely needed to yell. "Come on." She paced back and forth, eyeing the ancient school photographs that hadn't been changed in years, the boot tray with her father's mud-encrusted boots and a tiny holy water font with a frieze of St. Francis installed by the door.

The moment her father appeared in the front hall, she felt guilty about her impatience. Eager to see his grandson, Pop had dressed up in his good Cordovan leather shoes and his one perfectly tailored suit. The white shirt was as clean and crisp as newfallen snow. His salt-and-pepper hair bore the furrows of aggressive combing, and he'd done a precision job trimming his mustache.

"You look wonderful, Pop," she said, signing as she spoke, for emphasis.

"I'm gonna get all messed up in your convertible," he grumbled.

"We're not taking the convertible. It's only got two seats."

"I knew that." He took his hat from a peg by the door. "I borrowed Vince's Camry."

At Green Airport in the baggage claim area, they sat on a padded bench, nervously flipping through Rosa's purse-sized photo album, something she always carried. The pictures of Rob's kids had come enclosed in Christmas cards over the years. Her nephew, Joseph Peter Capoletti, had started out with that special angelic quality small children seemed to possess in abundance. As the youngest of four, he had been an adored little boy with a charming smile.

Around Joey's twelfth year, it seemed the novelty of him had worn off, because the pictures dwindled. Rob and Gloria had both been promoted and were busier than ever, living overseas. Rosa remembered Joey's shy smile, dreamy brown eyes with lashes so long they were wasted on a boy, and an acute fear of spiders.

The flight from Detroit, where he'd connected from L.A., landed. A wave of passengers emerged from the concourse. Rosa sensed her father tensing up as he scanned the crowd. There were business people with sleek luggage, young families juggling strollers and diaper bags, students and foreigners. She saw a couple reunited, radiating happiness and oblivious to the world as they embraced. From where she sat, Rosa could see the woman's eyes close as though to keep in the joy. Rosa looked away, burying a pang of sentiment.

The flood of passengers became a trickle, and she consulted Joey's hellacious-looking trans-Pacific itinerary. With a feeling of foreboding, she turned to her father. "He didn't make the flight."

Pop merely sat there, unmoving, watching the exit at the end of the concourse. His face betrayed nothing, and she looked again. The only passenger walking toward them was a lanky stranger with a pink Mohawk, dark glasses and a variety of uncomfortable-looking facial piercings. Under his breath, Pop emitted a string of curses in Italian, and Rosa nudged him to get him to behave. Really, she didn't blame her father. His adorable young grandson had morphed into a stranger.

Rosa prayed he hadn't seen her quickly rearrange her face from shock to delight. "Joey! You're a foot taller!" She opened her arms. He permitted her a hug that was brief and awkward, nothing like the exuberant embraces of his youth when he'd clung, monkeylike, as if he would never let her go.

"Hey, Aunt Rosa," he muttered, keeping his head down as though he'd dropped something. "Hey, Grandpop."

"Pop doesn't know what you're saying unless he can read your lips," she reminded him.

Joey tossed back his head and slowly, deliberately peeled off his shades. "Hiya, Grandpop," he said.

Rosa was grateful her father couldn't hear the sarcastic inflection in Joey's voice. Pop grabbed the boy by the shoulders and stood on tiptoe to give him two resounding kisses, one on each cheek, Italian style. Then he said, "You look like a freak."

Joey glared at him, his face burning with a blush from the kisses. "You got a problem with that?"

"Not as long as you don't act like a freak. Let's go get your bags."

His luggage consisted of a camouflage duffel bag patched here and there with duct tape. Aw, Rob, thought Rosa. You couldn't get the poor kid a decent bag?

As they walked to the car, Pop touched the stiff spikes of the Mohawk. "I bet your parents didn't see this."

Joey's ears and cheeks turned red. "That's right."

"They're gonna tan your hide when they see you."

"I'll risk it."

In spite of herself, Rosa felt a grudging admiration for the kid. "I'm glad you're here, Joey," she said. "It's going to be a great summer."

Eighteen

Alex wasn't much for shopping, but Rosa's lasagne, which he still dreamed about, was long gone. If he was going to spend the summer in a house by the sea, without a deli around the corner or a pizza delivery service, he would have to pay an occasional visit to the Winslow Stop & Shop.

In search of shaving cream, he stumbled into the wrong aisle and was confronted by a frightening display of feminine products. Eager to escape the panty liner zone, he tried walking briskly away—too briskly. At the end of the aisle, he took a corner fast and sharp, T-boning an unsuspecting cart with his own, causing bottles and cans to rattle and roll.

"Sorry," he said, but when he recognized his victim, he grinned in delight. "Hey, Rosa."

"Hey, yourself." Her smile, in contrast, was merely polite.

"Imagine running into you here," he said lamely. He had a reputation as a smooth talker, but he couldn't think straight when she was around. She wore a black top with skinny straps, low-slung jeans that showed a perfect olive-toned inch of skin above the waistband. And, God love her, she had a navel ring. Alex was a goner for them, and had actually seen very few up close and personal. The women in his world didn't self-mutilate, as they liked to call it. A tiny golden ring in a gorgeous female belly button was high art as far as he was concerned.

He felt like an idiot, standing there while an invisible hormone rush bathed him in painful lust. He distracted himself by checking out the contents of her cart. Tomatoes and grapes, a lot of leafy green bunches, cartons of ricotta and yogurt, three paperback romance novels. A bag of Chee•tos—"Dangerously Cheesy"— seemed out of place, as did the two gallons of milk and the package of Oreos.

She noticed his inquisitive stare. "I bet you're thinking I'm a closet junk-food junkie and romance novel addict."

"Are you?"

"Yes and no. I'll pass on the junk food, but don't get between a girl and her romance novels."

"Yeah?" He picked one. "*Cattleman's Courtship* by Lois Faye Dyer. 'Will a sophisticated city slicker find love with a rugged rancher?'" he read from the back cover. Tossing the book back into her cart, he said, "Bet not."

She sniffed. "Shows how much you know. They'll work it out."

"Why read it if you know the ending?"

She fixed him with a you're-too-dumb-to-live stare. "Because it's wonderful, every time."

Okay, so maybe she was in love with falling in love. Alex supposed he could understand that. It was all heady stuff—the blast of emotion so intense it made you light-headed, the physical burn of passion, the yearning so strong and sweet it made your heart ache. Alex was familiar with the symptoms. He'd experienced them all.

But only once.

"So the junk food's for…?" he asked. "You have a pet on a strange diet or something?"

"Nosy, aren't you? Actually I'm—" She broke off as a lanky, half-grown boy emerged from the magazine aisle. "There you are, Joey," she said, then turned to Alex. "Alex, this is Joey Capoletti."

Holy crap, he thought. Her son? He panicked as his mind raced through a swift calculation. Could this giant, spike-haired, nose-ringed kid be…no way. Alex rejected the notion. The kid was thirteen if he was a day.

Relieved, he reached out to shake hands. "Alexander Montgomery. Nice to meet you."

"Hello, sir."

"Joey's my nephew," Rosa said, and her wickedly amused smile indicated that she'd seen Alex's momentary panic. "He's spending the summer with my dad."

Joey was a punk, Alex saw, his sagging black jeans hung with chains from pocket to pocket, his T-shirt emblazoned with some sort of tribal symbol. He'd apparently inherited his aunt's penchant for piercing, only on Joey it had run amok. There was enough metal attached to him to set off alarms at airports.

But Alex knew appearances could be deceiving. For Rosa's sake, he hoped that was the case with this character. He suspected he was right when he saw the magazine Joey held—*Scientific American.*

"So, what do you think of Winslow?" Alex asked him.

"It's okay." The boy's gaze wandered to a blond girl shopping the aisle with her mother. She looked to be about his age and had the sort of long-legged, flowerlike beauty of a girl in the mysterious process of becoming a woman. They made eye contact, a message passing between them. "It's pretty nice here."

Rosa nudged him. "You're liking it better and better, huh?"

His ears turned red and Alex felt sorry for him. He thought he recognized the girl's mother from the club—somebody Brooks. But the moment to introduce them was past, so he changed the subject. "When I was a kid, I spent every summer here. I've known your aunt since she was nine years old."

"Uh-huh."

"I'm working on our family's old house," Alex went on, trying to figure out how to engage the boy's interest. This was his first real break with Rosa. If he could make friends with the kid, maybe she'd give him the time of day. He glanced again at the magazine. The cover story was something about planetary transits. "You know, I used to have an old telescope." It had been stashed in a window seat of the parlor, and as far as he knew, it was still there. "I was going to see if someone at the high school wanted it, but if you're interested—"

"That'd be great," said Joey.

"I don't think so," said Rosa.

Alex ignored her. He had an ally now. "Why don't you come by this afternoon and I'll show you what I've got?" He sensed Rosa winding up for a protest, and quickly added, "You're not busy this afternoon, are you?"

"Nope," said Joey, also ignoring Rosa. "I've got a job at the ice-cream place, but I'm off today. What time?"

"Will two o'clock work?"

"Sure."

"Your aunt knows where I live. She won't mind giving you a lift." Alex didn't want to give her a chance to back out, so he said, "I'd better get going. See you this afternoon, Joey. You, too, Rosa."

"Bye, Alex." She aimed her cart and sped toward the baking aisle.

Pretending great interest in a display of bagels in cellophane, he furtively watched her go. Then he threw a few frozen dinners and bags of pretzels into the cart, followed by milk and cereal, juice and beer. His major food groups covered, he checked out and started loading his purchases into the back of his Ford Explorer. On the far side of the parking lot, he saw Rosa and Joey getting into her red convertible. She wore sunglasses and a long polka dot scarf to protect her hair from the wind, and she was using the rearview mirror to put on a stroke of red lipstick.

That was too much. Alex grabbed his cell phone and dialed her number—the one she'd left stuck to his door the day the papers reported his mother's suicide. He'd immediately programmed it into his phone.

"Rosa Capoletti," she said in a businesslike tone. Alex could see her holding the tiny phone to her ear with one hand and clipping on her seat belt with the other.

"Have dinner with me," he said.

There was a beat of shocked silence. Then she cleared her throat. "I'm afraid that won't be possible."

"What's your schedule like?"

"It's full. Forever."

She was pissed that he'd invited Joey over, Alex thought. Too bad. "I won't accept that."

"Then I suppose," she said as she put the car in gear, "you'll have to find a way to deal with it."

"Stalking," he said with a laugh. "Would stalking work for you?"

"I have to go," she said, steering toward the parking lot exit.

"All right. But you might want to fix your scarf," he said. "It's caught in the door."

Her brake lights flared as she hung up and craned her neck around. She didn't spot him, though he stood in plain sight, leaning easily against the back door of the Explorer. She opened her car door, liberated the scarf and sped off.

Okay, thought Alex. Time for Plan B.

Nineteen

The minute they pulled into the driveway of Alex Montgomery's house, Joey felt like he'd entered a different cosmos. The place looked like it could be haunted, a classic old New England house with tall, narrow windows and peaked gables, a porch wrapping around three sides and a huge garden with a pond. About fifty yards beyond that was a beach.

The guy called Alex, who had been hitting on his aunt, came hurrying out of the house like he couldn't wait to see Joey. But of course, his face fell when he saw it was Grandpop, not Aunt Rosa, who had driven Joey over. Clearly Alex had been counting on seeing her. He totally dug her. You could tell that a mile off.

"Hey, Joey." He was acting cool now, like he didn't even mind that Rosa hadn't shown up.

Then when Grandpop got out of the car, it was like the hot summer day turned winter-cold. "Hello, Alexander," said Grandpop.

"Mr. Capoletti."

"I'm sorry for the loss of your mother."

Aw, jeez, thought Joey. He'd hoped the subject

wouldn't come up. Now everything was going to be all awkward.

"I appreciate that," said Alex.

Grandpop nodded and then said, "I will wait out here, Joey."

Joey figured Alex would insist that Grandpop come in, sit down, have a drink, whatever, but Alex just headed for the house. Must be some bad blood between the two, Joey figured.

"I've got the telescope right here," said Alex, walking over to a giant bay window. The lid of the window seat was propped up with an old fishing pole. Alex shone the beam of a flashlight into the cobwebby depths of the storage space. When he straightened up, he was holding an old telescope by the optical tube.

Joey felt a little beat of excitement, but he was careful not to let it show. Once you show how much you want something, it could get taken away. Joey was the youngest of four kids, and he'd learned that the hard way.

"Could I...see that?"

"Sure." Alex handed it over. "There are some other pieces and accessories in here. I'll just see if I can find them...." He turned and started rummaging in the window seat.

Joey checked out the telescope, rubbing his thumb over the tarnished brass latitude scale on the equatorial mount. It was a Warner & Swinburne, and he didn't know that much about it except that it was a valuable antique.

"So there's this," Alex said, handing him a tripod and brass finderscope. "And I found these lens boxes...."

"Are you sure you want to let me use this?" Joey asked.

"No." Alex spoke over his shoulder as he kept rummaging.

Joey's heart sank. "Then—"

"I want to let you *have* this." He pulled out a long black case. "For keeps."

"Uh-uh." Joey shook his head. "You don't want to do that. You don't know what you have here."

"A Warner & Swinburne refracting telescope, made in Boston in the 1890s," Alex said. "It's worth a few hundred bucks to collectors. I'd rather give it to someone who might use it and maybe even learn something. It's nowhere near as good as a modern scope, but Maria Mitchell used one like this at her observatory in Nantucket. It's all yours. The best place for viewing is Watch Hill. It's about a mile north of town."

"Why me? You don't even know me." Just then, Joey got it. "Oh, I see. You're being nice to me because you have the hots for my aunt."

"Did Rosa tell you that?"

"Nope."

"Then how—"

"Duh." Joey shook his head.

"What did she say about me?" Alex asked.

Joey snorted. "I thought I was finished with junior high."

Instead of being offended, Alex laughed. "When it comes to women, you're never finished with junior high. Hang on a second while I make sure I gave you everything." He pulled a bunch of old stuff out of the window seat—flat vinyl records by groups like The Byrds and the Herb Alpert Band, clothes someone probably should have thrown away decades ago, a stack of old piano music, copies of *Life* and *Time* filled with past history.

"Check this out." Alex handed him a clear plastic bag

filled with political buttons with slogans like Nixon. Now More Than Ever. and Goldwater in '64. Joey wondered who the heck they were. Old failed candidates, probably.

Joey picked up a framed picture of some woman and dusted it off. She had long red hair, and she was leaning against a blue car and laughing into the camera. "Who's this?"

Alex's face changed. Not a lot, but it hardened as if he'd just gone into the deep freeze. He took the photo and stared at it for a few seconds. "My mother, about twenty years ago."

"I'm sorry she died." Grandpop had explained the situation to him on the way over and it was a total bummer. The woman had killed herself. "It sucks," he added, and then he made himself shut up. Every word in the English language was lame in a situation like this.

"It does suck," Alex agreed. "I suck at dealing with it, too. I try not to think about it, and then all I do is think about it."

"So you should think about it," Joey said. "Maybe you're supposed to."

Alex grinned a little. "Maybe." He quickly dumped the old papers back into the box. "Anyway, I think you've got everything, Joey. Go see if you can get the thing to work."

Rosa was keyed up and distracted at the restaurant that evening, but she tried not to let it show. She greeted customers, monitored the kitchen and generally conducted herself as though this were any other night. No one could tell how rattled she was about Alex Montgomery.

Or so she thought.

Vince cornered her in the prep area of the kitchen. "All night you've been acting like you got a bug up your ass."

"How would you know how I'd act if I had a bug up my ass?" she asked. "For your information, I've never had one, so even I don't know how I'd behave."

"Just like you are now," he said without missing a beat. "Testy and maybe a tad distracted. I know I would be."

"Sicko." She brushed past him and headed toward the insulated double doors to the dining room. But before going out, she glanced at the monitor, which panned over the dining room, foyer, deck and parking lot. She squinted at the parking lot view and jumped back. "Oh, shit."

"I thought you were done with this conversation," Vince said. He glanced at the video monitor. "My, my," he said. "Miss Rosa has a suitor." He planted his hands on his hips. "Leave this to me. I'll make him go away."

Rosa cursed herself for not keeping a poker face when she'd spotted Alex. She was terrible at playing it cool. She always wore her emotions with the flash of the latest fashion accessory. "That's okay, Vince. I'll deal with him."

Vince kept watching the monitor. "No need. Teddy beat you to it."

She looked up to see Teddy and Alex in the parking lot, nose to nose, chest to chest, like an umpire and an irate player. Teddy was a large, formidable man. Most people knew better than to mess with him. His thick finger jabbed at Alex's face, but Alex didn't back down.

"Shit," Rosa said again, and rushed for the back door. She burst out into the breezy summer night. Her work clothes—a formfitting black dress and spike heels—were not designed for sprinting. Scurrying, maybe, if she was careful.

She scurried as fast as she could to the front parking lot, arriving in time to see Alex trying to push past Teddy toward the restaurant. He didn't get far. Even as Rosa called out "No…" and lunged toward them, Teddy cold-cocked Alex. She watched helplessly as Alex toppled like a heap of unmortared brick, and a puff of dust rose around him.

"For Pete's sake," Rosa yelled, "what are you doing, Teddy?"

"Guy wouldn't take no for an answer," he said, glaring at the groaning, groggy man on the ground. "He upsets you."

She started to say, "He does not…" but that would be a lie. Alex Montgomery upset her in the most fundamental way, making her body tremble and her palms sweat. But that was her fault, not his.

"Help him up," she said.

Teddy held out a hand to Alex, who looked dazed as he tentatively shifted his jaw from side to side. When he saw Teddy's beefy paw outstretched, he leaned away.

"He won't hit you again," Rosa promised.

"He doesn't need to." Alex eyed Teddy ruefully. "He got me the first time." He stood up and dusted sand and gravel from his tailored beige slacks.

Rosa turned to Teddy. "Why don't you go back inside?"

"But—"

"I'm fine, Teddy. Promise."

He ambled away, casting glances over his shoulder, and she knew he and all the others would be glued to the security monitors. It was stupid, she told herself, yet she felt like some sort of damsel in a joust.

"Are you all right?" she asked Alex.

"Just peachy." He rubbed his jaw, wincing at his own touch.

"I can't believe you came here and picked a fight with Teddy."

"He picked one with me."

"He wouldn't have if you hadn't shown up."

Alex leaned against a lamppost. "I didn't come here to make trouble," he said. "I'm sorry this happened." He touched his jaw again. "Real sorry. I should have walked away."

"Yes. You should have."

"Now it's too late." His eyes were hooded by the night shadows. "I'm not going to hurt you, Rosa."

She prayed he couldn't see that he already was. His very presence opened old painful places inside her, places she used to believe had healed. "I'll pass that message along," she said.

"Thank you." His gaze flickered around the parking lot until he found a security camera mounted on the center light pole. "Think he'll believe you?"

"I'll make sure he does." She glanced over her shoulder. "So…are you here for dinner?"

"I'm here for you, Rosa."

A chill that had nothing to do with the evening breeze slipped over her skin. She had a hundred reasons not to be with him; she'd lain awake at night dreaming them up. At the moment, she couldn't think of a single one. Best not to let him know that, though.

She laughed as if he'd made a joke. "Oh, I'd nearly forgotten. You're stalking me."

He offered a lopsided grin, favoring his injured jaw. "If that's what it takes."

She ignored the extra beat of her heart. "You're wasting your time. We don't belong together, and you were smart enough to figure that out years ago. Let's leave well enough alone. That's what *I* want—to live my life and run my restaurant."

"You don't want to live happily ever after?"

"It is *after.* And I'm happy," she retorted.

"So you've said before. I'd hate to see you when you're mad."

"Look, Alex. We're not kids anymore. Whatever happened in the past…it doesn't matter now."

Without warning, he cradled her cheeks in his hands. "My thoughts exactly."

She nearly melted right then and there, her whole body warming to his touch. "This is a bad idea."

Keeping his hands in place, he glared up at the security camera. "I'm going to have a seat at the bar—"

"I'm working. I don't have time to have a drink with you."

"That's not what I'm asking. I need to have a chat with your friends Vince and Teddy."

She stepped back. "No way."

"I'm not going to spend the summer sneaking around like teenagers."

"There's no need to sneak, Alex. Just walk away in plain sight."

"That's not going to happen." He started toward the entrance.

Her heart tripped over the possibility he held out. To be with him again, after all this time. She loved the idea; she hated it. She had made herself into a pillar of female strength, and now he was back, chipping away at her. "Are you crazy?"

"Maybe. I'll be in the bar if you need me." He paused and looked back at her. "It'll be all right, Rosa, I swear it."

She glared up at the camera and then went inside. When she stepped into the steaming, clattering kitchen, everyone was hard at work, as though they had not just been glued to the monitors, spying on her for the past ten minutes.

"If he decides to come inside," she said tersely to anyone who would listen, "let him."

Unable to resist, she kept an eye on the video system and noticed that Alex had indeed gone into the bar. He was not alone. Somehow he had persuaded Vince and Teddy to join him. Alex held a plastic bag of chipped ice against his jaw. The other two were both talking at once, leaning across the table, occasionally making a point with the pounding of a fist.

Rosa could still feel Alex's hands cupping her cheeks. She felt dizzy with the sensation of it. He was back, and willing—perhaps foolishly willing—to fight for her.

This was not the Alex Montgomery who had stolen her heart long ago, then walked away with it like a thief, leaving her empty. This was a different person.

Twenty

——❧❧❧——

"Thanks for meeting with me," Alex said to the two formidable, skeptical men. He knew he looked ridiculous holding the bag of ice on his face, chilly drops streaming down his arm. Plan B had seemed like a good idea at the time, but maybe he should have worked it out in a little more detail.

"We don't like what you have to say, we'll kick your ass," Teddy warned.

Christ, where did Rosa find these characters? Alex wondered. *The Sopranos?*

"You already did that," he said genially, "but I'm not changing my mind about seeing Rosa again. It's that simple. That's why I'm here."

"No, you're here because Rosa said to let you in," said Vince.

Alex remembered him as a skinny, pimply-faced punk. He'd turned into a fashion plate in an Italian suit. There was a fierce affection in his eyes when he spoke of Rosa.

"Okay," he said, "so she's lucky to have friends like you. But I have to ask, do all the guys she goes out with get the same kind of royal treatment?"

"No, of course not," Vince said with a wave of his hand.

"What's so special about me?"

Vince's glare was an arctic blast.

"We were young," Alex said. "Kids break each other's hearts every day. It happens, okay?"

"Not like that."

"Like what?"

Teddy and Vince shared a look. "This was not your ordinary broken heart," said Teddy.

"It's not like she took to her bed and ate a pound of chocolate," Vince added.

"Didn't eat anything, more like," Teddy added.

"Slow down," said Alex. "You've lost me." He tried to piece together the shattered memories of that time. Clearly these two thought they knew something he didn't. "You're saying she went on some sort of hunger strike and it's my fault?"

"She could have died," Teddy said, ignoring his question, "but you wouldn't know that. You were long gone."

A sick lump formed in Alex's gut. Running away from responsibilities—wasn't that what his father used to accuse him of? Was that what he'd done?

Vince folded his hands on the tabletop. "She was all alone after her father's accident. Her brothers tried to help, but they were in the service and couldn't stay. She stuck around while Pete learned to walk and talk again. It took two years, and he got better eventually. Except for his hearing."

"His hearing?"

"He's totally deaf. Does fine, but Rosa worries like crazy about him."

Alex reeled from the news. When Pete had brought Joey over the other day, Alex hadn't noticed a thing. Deaf. Pete Capoletti, who adored opera and jazz, had lost his hearing. One night. So many lives were changed by that one night.

"But the thing is," Vince went on, "she worked herself into exhaustion, all alone, trying to do everything on her own. She never admitted there was anything wrong until she collapsed at work one day. Someone called 911 and she had to go to the hospital."

He set down the bag of ice. His jaw was completely numb. "So where the hell were you guys while this was going on?" He could tell they felt guilty, too. Maybe that was why they were so protective now.

"At first, nobody noticed," Vince said. "Nobody realized she was staying at work until after midnight, getting up at dawn to go to the hospital, working weekends and trying to manage on her own."

He felt sick. Everything had gone so wrong for her. That wasn't supposed to happen. With only good intentions, he'd walked away from the love of his life. He thought it was the right thing to do under the circumstances. But when he considered what had happened in the aftermath, he wondered if he should've done something differently. But what? he wondered. What?

"She got better," he said, desperate to know her suffering had been brief.

"Hell, yes, she got better," Vince said. "She scared herself into getting well. She realized her father would be completely alone if something happened to her. But she's different now."

He tried not to crane his neck around, looking for her. He longed to see her through new eyes, with this new knowledge. "What do you mean, different?"

"You can't go through all that and not be changed by it. Her father was nearly killed by a hit-and-run driver. She lost out on her chance to go to college. You walked out when she needed you most, and she almost didn't survive. A few life-altering events, I'd say."

Alex crushed a cocktail napkin in his fist. She never knew he had thought about her constantly. From a distance, he'd followed Pete's recovery progress much as he was able. Clearly, he'd missed a few things. No wonder she was so bitter when he came back the last time. No wonder she'd sent him away.

"So," Vince said, "we don't like people coming to town and upsetting her."

Alex's jaw felt hot now, as the numbness tingled to life. "She's a grown woman who can take care of herself. So how about you let her make up her own mind about whether or not she wants to see me again?"

"She doesn't," Vince said quickly.

"Have you asked her?" Alex shot back.

Vince's hesitation and the glance he exchanged with Teddy indicated that he hadn't. "Just what are your intentions?" he asked.

Alex burst out laughing, then winced in pain. "I'll answer that question when it comes from Rosa."

"We don't trust you," said Teddy. "What the hell are you doing back here? You're rebounding. Your fiancée just dumped you."

Yet another charming aspect of being a Montgomery. Your personal life made the gossip columns. "That has nothing to do with Rosa and me," he said. "And frankly, neither do you guys. So back off."

Teddy glowered at him. "We'll do whatever Rosa wants us to do."

They sat in silence for a few minutes. Alex picked up the ice pack again and held it to his jaw. He was starting to question his own sanity now. *Sanity.* He hadn't even begun to deal with his mother's suicide. He and his father were like cordial strangers, willingly engaging in a conspiracy of denial. The Montgomery way, he thought. Sometimes it was probably better to haul off and punch someone.

"You want a beer or something?" Teddy offered in a conciliatory tone.

"No, thanks." Alex intended to stay sober. He didn't want to be poured home, as he had his first night here.

Rosa appeared in the bar. Her black dress was probably meant to be conservative. On Rosa, it looked like a Victoria's Secret ad. Alex had a swift, almost brutally carnal reaction. He hoped it didn't show as he stood to greet her.

"You're just in time to rescue me."

She looked bemused. "Do you need rescuing?"

Alex eyed Vince and Teddy. "They say they'll do whatever you want."

Her eyebrows went up. "Excellent. I want you guys to get back to work. How's that?"

They exchanged a glance, then subjected Alex to a final threatening glare and went to their stations. He held a chair for her. "What can I get you to drink?"

"A nice little espresso," she said, although she didn't sit down. She paused and looked him straight in the eye, her expression both frank and mysterious.

"At my place," she added.

Twenty-One

~∞~

Every bit of Rosa's common sense shrieked Danger as she drove toward her condo with Alex's headlights beaming in the rearview mirror. Everyone kept telling her she should deal with him so she could move on, once and for all. She was going to do her best to accomplish that tonight.

She had never been nervous about bringing a man home before. But Alex was different in every possible way—and *she* was different when she was with him.

They had started this meeting—date, rendezvous, whatever it was—with a debate about the cars. He wanted to drive her, but she wasn't about to leave her Alfa behind at the restaurant parking lot, thus informing the entire staff as to exactly how much time she was spending with Alexander Harrison Montgomery.

"At my place," she muttered under her breath, mimicking herself. "I've had better ideas."

Still, anything was preferable to being with him at the restaurant with everyone hovering.

She tried to remember how much of a mess she'd left her place in. If he didn't go near the bedroom or closet, she was safe. And she wasn't about to let him get anywhere near the bedroom, she told herself firmly, no matter how incredible he looked or how much she hyperventilated at the sight of him.

"Big deal, so he's coming up for coffee," she said, slowing down as she turned on to her street and into the parking alley. He pulled into a Visitor spot and they both got out at the same time.

The condos in her building had a commanding view of the bay. On a clear day, she could see the ferry steaming back and forth between the mainland and Block Island and the fishing fleet from the port of Galilee heading out to the banks. At night, the lighthouse beam swung out over dark water dotted with tiny lights from the fishing vessels.

"I bought this place three years ago," she said, trying to be smooth as she unlocked the front door. The historic building, once a Victorian resort, was now a beautifully refurbished condo complex. "It's small, but…" She forced herself to quit babbling. No need to explain or excuse anything.

She stepped inside and flipped on a light switch. Her place had a view of the sea and was filled with the things she loved. Unfortunately the things she loved were a haphazard collection, and a perpetually work-in-progress air hung over the apartment. The restaurant consumed her, and she'd never gotten around to serious decorating.

She did have a motif, at least. She'd created it around her favorite item—a tablecloth Mamma used in the kitchen for everyday. Its colorful design of flowers and roosters had influenced the other choices—painted vases, chintz curtains and white bead board trim everywhere. One of these days, she told herself, she'd get around to pulling it all together.

Still, even in this state, it was all terribly personal. Her house was…her home. It revealed so much about her. It would be like standing before him naked.

Although she suspected it would be less of a turn-on.

"Make yourself at home," she said. "I'll fix us an espresso."

"Thanks." He stepped inside and looked around. From the kitchen, she watched him as she took out the coffee and got to work. She used the same coffee served at Celesta's—estate-grown organic beans from the Galapagos Islands. The La Pavoni Romantica espresso maker had been one of her few extravagances for the apartment—a classic lever-style machine with polished brass and hardwood handles.

Alex wandered into the tall-ceilinged main room. She saw him looking around, but couldn't read his expression. She wanted him to see that she'd done fine for herself, that she had a great job, friends and family around her.

The furniture consisted of an overstuffed chintz sofa, a matching chair and ottoman. At present, the ottoman was occupied by a pair of cats who eyed Alex with blasé effeteness. He stuck his hands in his pockets and eyed them back.

"Romeo and Juliet," she told him. "They used to be lovers, but since that visit to the vet they're just friends."

"Are they friendly?" he asked, stretching out a hand to Romeo's funny pushed-in face.

"They're cats," she said, grinning as Romeo turned up his nose at the outstretched hand. Juliet wasn't interested, either. They poured themselves off the furniture, then minced away.

"I think they've been talking to your friends at the restaurant," Alex said.

"They don't talk to anyone." She saw him glance at

the terrarium on the windowsill. "The turtles are Tristan and Isolde, and their offspring are Heloise and Abelard."

"So where are Cleopatra and Mark Antony?" he asked.

"In a tomb in Egypt, I imagine. But you can look in the fish tank and see Bonnie and Clyde, Napoleon and Josephine, and Jane and Guildford."

He bent and peered into the lighted tank. "Fun couples. Is it a coincidence that they all ended tragically?"

"Not a coincidence, just poor judgment."

"Isn't it bad karma, naming your pets after doomed lovers?"

"I don't think they care."

"Do you mind if I put on some music?" he asked, picking up the remote control to the stereo.

"That's fine." She racked her brain, trying to remember which CD she had left in the slot. He hit Play, and it was worse than she'd feared—Andrea Bocelli at his most achingly sentimental.

So big deal, she thought. I like mawkish Italian music. So sue me.

Rosa refused to allow herself to cringe as she watched Alex peruse her bookshelf, crammed with paperback romance novels. She couldn't bear to part with her favorites, and her collection filled the space from floor to ceiling.

He moved on to another shelf, this one filled with books that were decidedly not romance novels. He turned to her. "Textbooks?"

"That's right." The grinder whirred as she ground the beans.

"You're going to school?" he asked when it was quiet again.

"Constantly." She put the ground coffee in the porta-filter and assembled everything.

"Where?" he asked.

"Where what?"

"Where are you constantly going to school?"

"Any place that'll have me." She laughed at his expression. "I'm not enrolled anywhere. I monitor courses that interest me. In the fall I'll be checking out Georgetown and the University of Milano. It's just something I do."

"You're kidding."

"Would I make this up?"

"No one would make this up. You're really something, Rosa."

She pulled the lever to force the water through the heat exchanger, and a loud hiss of steam interrupted the conversation. The espresso trickled into two white demitasses; then she added a bit of Frangelico to give the coffee a hint of hazelnut. Lord knows, after getting socked in the jaw, he'd earned it. She put the cups on a tray, laid a crescent-shaped pignoli cookie on each saucer and joined him in the living room. The couch or the chair? she wondered with a sudden flutter of nerves. The simple matter seemed a critical decision.

Alex took the tray from her and set it on the white-painted coffee table. Then he took her hand and brought her to the sofa, smoothing over the awkward moment with ease.

"Thank you." He smiled, though not without pain. His jaw was visibly swollen.

"You're welcome. How's your face?"

"I'll live." He sampled the coffee and a look of delight came over him. "This is fantastic."

Relax, she told herself. It's just coffee. "Thanks," she said. "I wanted to thank you for loaning Joey that telescope."

"It's not a loan. I want him to have it."

"It's a valuable antique."

"How can something have value if it's not being used for its purpose? He found his passion and it's a good one. Nurture it."

"He's also a kid. What if he breaks it, pawns it, sells it on Ebay?"

"It's up to him. No strings attached."

"Thank you. Pop says he's got it all taken apart with the parts labeled. It'll be a good summer project."

A comfortable silence settled over them. Surprisingly comfortable. So his next question caught her unawares. "What's on your mind, Rosa?"

She could lie, but she'd never been good at deception. "That I feel comfortable with you. For the moment, that is."

"There's a reason for that. We've known each other twenty years."

She took a deep breath and reminded herself that she'd invited him here. It was all her brilliant idea. She shut her eyes and felt an old hurt start to throb. He had once held her heart in his hands. Perhaps that was why she'd felt so betrayed by him in the end.

Bocelli's voice swelled dramatically into the silence. She opened her eyes and watched Alex over the rim of her cup. He seemed to be listening to "Con te partiro" with deep appreciation. You never knew.

"Did you study Italian, too?" he asked her. "In your course work, I mean."

"Sure."

"'Time to say goodbye,'" he translated the song on the stereo.

She raised an eyebrow. "You speak Italian?"

"No," he said. "I have this album, too."

Maybe that was when she started to be afraid. Because she felt herself starting to love him again.

Panic set in. Love him? Loving this man was the emotional equivalent of stepping off a cliff in the dark. No rational woman would do it.

But she couldn't help herself.

Like a lab rat in one of those horrid experiments, she kept going back to the source of her hurt.

"Are you all right?" Alex asked her.

"No." With unsteady hands, she set her cup and saucer on the table.

"What's the matter?"

"I shouldn't have invited you over. I'm sorry, but I think you should go. You know, *con te partiro* and all that."

"Hey, this was your idea."

"It was a bad one. I made a mistake."

He took her hand, and his eyes turned soft. "I'm here, and the world hasn't come to an end."

She knew it would look foolish and petty to snatch her hand away. Besides, she didn't want to. In that moment, she felt utterly mesmerized, still falling off that cliff into the unknown. He was not the one who could save her. Quite the contrary, he was the one who had pushed her.

With one hand, he gently tipped up her chin so that their lips were nearly touching. Her heart sped up and chills rushed over her.

Kiss me, she thought wildly. Kiss me. Kiss me. Kiss me.

He didn't. He couldn't hear her yearning thoughts and she was too afraid and vulnerable to speak them aloud.

Sometimes, she thought, a freefall was fun—until she hit the ground.

She reminded herself of all the reasons that this was impossible. He probably saw nothing wrong with killing a summer pursuing an old girlfriend. He was on the rebound from a broken engagement, grieving for his mother, sorting through a house that had stood unchanged for a decade. Flirting with her was probably a diversion for him.

"You can stay until we finish our coffee," she heard herself say.

"I'm a slow drinker."

She looked down at their joined hands. "I simply don't understand why you think this is a good idea."

"Maybe it's not. But then again, maybe it is." He let go of her hand and then did something worse. He slid both arms around her. "I have something to tell you, Rosa. I never had a chance the last time we were together."

Caffe Frangelico

Frangelico is a liqueur made from hazelnuts grown in the orchards of Lombardy. It's clear and sweet and so delicious, it's said to cause the teeth to sing.

2 parts Frangelico
5 parts hot coffee
Top with whipped cream and crushed hazelnuts.

PART FOUR

Pasta

There once was a time in Italy when a traitorous
poet named Marinetti claimed that pasta
"…induces scepticism, sloth, and pessimism
and…its nutritive qualities are deceptive." In the
ensuing pandemonium, one fact rang clear:
Italians love their pasta for all its best qualities as
a food. It's abundant, simple to store, delicious to
eat and, with no regard for Marinetti's opinion,
nutritious and adaptable. In the summer, use the
freshest ingredients in nature and see for
yourself.

Penne Pasta With Fresh Arugula, Tomato and Mozzarella

Success depends on fresh tomatoes and arugula and basil. And don't even think about using anything but the freshest mozzarella. You don't need much, so go ahead and splurge on the good stuff.

1/2 pound penne pasta
4 ripe tomatoes, diced
about 10 ounces fresh mozzarella, drained
  and diced
5 ounces arugula, torn into bite-sized pieces
a few fresh basil leaves
1/2 cup extra virgin olive oil
salt and red pepper flakes to taste

Cook the pasta. Put the tomatoes, arugula, basil, mozzarella, olive oil, salt and pepper in a large bowl. When the pasta is ready, toss it with the tomato mixture and serve.

Twenty-Two

⤮

Summer 1992

"So how'd the interview go, kiddo?" asked Mario Costa. "Did you get the scholarship?"

Rosa tied on her apron, emblazoned with a whimsical winged pizza, the Mario's logo. "All right, I guess," she said. "It's up to the committee now." The mere thought of the whole intimidating process made her queasy with nerves. She was on the brink of going to college. And not just any college. Brown University in Providence, that three-hundred-year-old, ivy-covered bastion of higher learning. She'd been accepted and offered a financial aid package that was adequate, though not generous. If she won the coveted Charlotte Boyle Prize, a large grant for which she'd just interviewed, the burden would be lightened considerably. All through spring she'd dreamed of going away to college, wondering which classes she would take, which professors would teach and guide her.

Her brothers had urged her to join the navy as they

had. Rob was married with two boys and twin daughters, Sal was a chaplain, and their lives were filled with adventure. But Rosa couldn't see herself in the service. She intended to fight for her education, too, but she was no warrior. Still, it would be wonderful, she thought, not to saddle Pop with more bills than he already had.

He'd hidden his financial situation from her for years. As she grew older and took on more responsibility, she traced the problem to its source, and the source did not surprise her. Her mother's three-year ordeal, with all the attendant surgeries and treatments, had wiped him out when Rosa was nine. Lacking medical insurance, he was obliged to pay for every penny of her treatment.

Rosa had discovered all that and more when she took over the bookkeeping for her father. She'd come across records of three clients who never paid a cent for the work Pop did. At first, he had resisted her questioning. But finally, he admitted the clients were Mamma's doctors—an oncologist, an anesthesiologist and a surgeon. He repaid them by maintaining their property and would probably do so for many years to come.

She wondered if it made Pop bitter to keep working for them long after Mamma was gone.

In the spring when the college letters had arrived, she'd offered to attend the state college in Kingston to save money, but Pop wouldn't hear of it. He proudly insisted that she attend Brown, that it would be worth the sacrifices they'd both make.

She scrubbed her hands at the big stainless steel sink and pushed her nerve-racked doubts away. Then she stood before a small mirror and checked her hair, which was pulled ruthlessly into a bun and covered with a regulation net. Since that summer five years ago, when Alex

Montgomery had cut it all off, she'd let her untamable curls grow down to the middle of her back.

"You ready for the lunch rush?" Mario asked her.

"You bet."

They still had a half-hour before the place opened. The ovens were roaring, the giant steel mixers churning out smooth, pale mounds of pizza dough.

"I wanted to show you this," she said, reaching into her pocket. "Two things, actually."

Mario put on his reading glasses. "What's that?"

"A new seating grid for summer. If you arrange the tables in this layout, you'll increase your capacity by eighteen. Twenty-four, if you add two tables to the deck. It will help move the summer crowds faster, not to mention increase the till."

He studied the sheet of graph paper with deep absorption. Rosa had stayed up late last night, figuring out the arrangement. Mario always encouraged her to make suggestions for improvements around the place. Over the years, she offered her opinion here and there, ways to improve efficiency or cut costs, maybe save on expenses or overage. A glass front for the self-serve soft drink case had increased sales by fifty percent. The addition of a salad bar raised the average tab by three dollars. Plastic number tents for each table increased accurate orders.

The minor adjustments were all obvious to Rosa, but Mario always acted as though they were revelations. He was, she had come to realize, a wonderful person but a mediocre businessman.

Fortunately, because of the summer crowds and the prime location of the restaurant, mediocre was good enough for Mario.

"Perfect," he said. "I'll tell Vince and Leo to come in after closing time tonight and do a reset."

"Vince hates doing resets," she said. "Don't tell him it was my idea."

Mario tacked the grid to the bulletin board over the clock. "Rosina, *cara ragazza*," he said. "Don't be so modest about being good at this. It's a gift."

Big deal. Who wanted to be good at running a hot, greasy kitchen and feeding people who were often rude to you? What the heck kind of a gift was that? She longed to be good at calculus or philosophy or nuclear physics, not feeding people.

She handed him a computer printout. "Take a look at this. I was talking to one of the vendors about our paper goods order. If we increase our quantity of pizza boxes by just two hundred, they'll give you a price break."

He gestured at the already busy, overheated kitchen. Stainless steel shelves were stuffed to the ceiling with supplies, some of them years old. "I got no more space."

"I'll make space. I promise." Rosa knew she was creating extra work for herself, but inefficiency drove her nuts. "And also, if you order the supplies on the Internet, they'll ship from out of state and you won't owe sales tax."

"The Inter-what?" Mario frowned.

"The Internet. It's…an electronic network." Rosa had no clue how to explain it. "Sort of like ordering from a catalog, but it's through the computer."

"And this is legal?"

"As far as I know."

Mario beamed at her. "Such a smart girl. That scholarship committee will give you anything you want. You'll see. Did you show them my letter of reference, eh?"

"If I was five years dead, they'd think you were trying to canonize me."

"Nah. I just told the truth."

Rosa smiled, but her stomach was churning. She had prepared carefully for the interview. She'd borrowed a perfect outfit from her friend Ariel, whose mother had an alterations shop. She had reviewed her qualifications and practiced in front of a mirror, trying to figure out the proper way to sit. She wrote a list of talking points on index cards and memorized each one.

Despite all the preparations, the interview had been singularly intimidating, particularly since Mrs. Emily Montgomery sat on the committee. Both Mr. and Mrs. Montgomery were alumni of Brown. It was strange to see her sitting there, judging Rosa, knowing all she knew. Not that she knew anything bad about Rosa, or good for that matter. It would have been nice if Mrs. Montgomery would vouch for her, but that would be the day.

Maybe she honestly didn't know the first thing about the gardener's daughter. The two of them were linked by a single tenuous common thread. Alex. And Rosa hadn't seen him in ages.

Alex didn't come to Winslow in the summer anymore. Not since junior high, although she thought of him more often than she probably should. After the first time he'd kissed her, they had done a lot more kissing that summer. Then he had gone away to boarding school, because the doctor said his asthma was so much better that he could live in a school dorm.

Rosa thought it surprising that Mrs. Montgomery would let him out of her sight. She was normally so overprotective. Maybe he'd rebelled, told her to quit hovering. Rosa could picture that. Alex was a scrawny kid, but when he made up his mind, he could be really stubborn.

He'd written to her a couple of times in the beginning. He liked school, but more than that, he loved the freedom of being away from home. She wrote back that she'd started a part-time job at Mario's and was saving her money for college. Despite their best intentions, the correspondence quickly dwindled along with the autumn leaves that year. And Alex never again came back to the beach house.

After her fourteenth summer had come and gone, Rosa made herself stop hoping he'd return. Still, whenever she saw Mrs. Montgomery, who came to Winslow by herself and had garden parties and cocktail hour for her friends, Rosa couldn't resist asking from time to time: *Is Alex coming this summer?*

He had other things to do, his mother reported. There was summer camp, one that seemed to last for three whole months. He stayed with friends from boarding school. One year he went on a trip to Europe—a study trip, Mrs. Montgomery called it, but Rosa pictured Alex goofing off on a train or drinking pastis and smoking Gauloises somewhere on the Riviera. Then there was a Wall Street internship, which sounded really important, though Rosa imagined him standing around a Xerox machine, bored out of his gourd. Finally she forced herself to stop asking. She didn't want to seem too transparent or, God forbid, pathetic.

She wondered if he was enjoying all the travel, the summer camp, the visits with friends. She wished he'd send just one or two postcards from places like the Isle of Man or Mykonos, but that was dumb. What would he say to her on a postcard? What would she say to him?

As kids, when they were together, they never ran out of things to talk about. Even their silences were filled with wordless exchanges and shared feelings they both understood.

But that, she reasoned, was the nature of summer friendships. Now that she was older, she understood. A summer friendship flourished lavishly but temporarily under the extravagant brightness of the summer sun. At the season's end, the relationship simply stopped. Like a beach umbrella, it was folded up and stored away until the next summer returned.

She smiled a little at her own thoughts as she inventoried the supply of takeout boxes. Maybe she'd study things like this in college—the psychology of friendship. There was probably a course on that alone. If she was honest with herself, she'd admit she was pretty daunted by the phone-book-sized course catalog. College was going to be hard, that was for sure. Still, it was necessary to her success. She didn't want to spend the rest of her days hanging around Winslow.

Humming along with the radio while she worked, she reorganized the supply shelves. The phone started ringing as requests for deliveries came in. Mario's wood-burning oven, which he'd built himself brick by brick, was modeled after the one in his father's trattoria in Naples. It exuded a fragrant heat that would, by midafternoon, make the kitchen an unbearable hell. The two cooks, Vince and Leo, would take turns stepping out back to cool off with a wet towel and a Newport cigarette, littering the ground around the Dumpster with butts.

Note to self, she thought. Put out a bucket of sand for an ashtray. She kept meaning to do that.

As the first pizzas of the day went into the ovens, she shut her eyes and inhaled. This, she thought, was why she worked at Mario's year after year. Lots of local girls worked in boutiques or as lifeguards at Town Beach. Some went all the way to Newport to be waitresses or hotel clerks. Rosa, with her reliable reputation, could have landed a more challenging job, maybe even an internship at a radio station.

She was comfortable right here in the clattering, over-crowded, overheated kitchen with Tony Bennett crooning on the radio, the smells of baking dough and marinara sauce spicing the air.

There was a spring in her step as she went to the counter to power up the register and credit card machine. Through the front window, its glass painted with—what else?—a winged pizza, she could see the first customers of the day gathered on the sidewalk outside.

She went to flip the sign on the door from Sorry, We're Closed to Come In, We're Open, turned on the neon lights and opened the door. A crowd of half-grown boys, all in green YMCA Day Camp T-shirts, pushed inside, each straining to be first. The kids were all shapes, sizes and colors, probably on a field trip to the shore for the day.

They were shepherded inside by a tall, broad shoul-dered camp counselor who wore a baseball cap over his sandy hair. The surging pack of hungry boys streamed toward the counter, and Rosa hurried after them.

Taking an order pad and pencil from her apron pocket, she said, "Welcome to Mario's Flying Pizza. What can I get for you?"

"Man, it smells good in here," said a boy wearing a stick-on name tag that read Cedric.

"I could eat a bear," said another.

"You look like a bear," his friend teased.

"Do not."

"Do so."

"Got any bear pizza?"

The conversation disintegrated into boyish banter, and Rosa looked to their camp counselor for help. He took off his baseball cap, and their eyes locked. His were ocean-blue, and they crinkled when he grinned at her.

She blinked to break the spell, but he was still there. *Alex.*

A smile started deep inside her somewhere. She felt it rise up through her slowly like a rainbow-colored soap bubble on a breeze and then unfurl on her lips.

Alex Montgomery. Alex was back, at last. He looked so…different.

"Hi," she said.

"Hi," he said, and his voice nearly laid her out flat. It was a deep, almost musical baritone, the voice of a stranger. "I heard you worked here."

"You heard right." She sounded like a dork.

The natives were getting restless. And noisy. Clearly this was not the moment to ply each other with questions.

She burned with curiosity as he ordered four extra-large pizzas, two cheese, one pepperoni, one sausage. Soft drinks all around.

"For here or to go?" she asked Alex, then waited as though he was about to reveal the meaning of life.

"Here." He gestured. "I'll take them out on the deck."

Mario's deck was set with a few picnic tables shaded by Campari umbrellas. The place didn't have a beverage license, but Mario's cousin Rocky had a distributorship which kept him well-supplied with umbrellas and lighted clocks.

"What do I owe you?" asked Alex.

An explanation, she thought as she punched buttons. Where have you been for the past four summers?

She gave him the total and he reached for his wallet.

"Oh, man," said one of the kids, "Alex is making googly eyes at the waitress."

"Get on outside," Alex said. "And don't feed the seagulls."

They pushed and shoved toward the side door leading to the deck, and Tony Bennett sang into the ensuing silence.

"I am, you know," Alex said as she counted out his change.

"What?"

"Making googly eyes at you."

God, he was flirting. In a baritone voice. She tried to be cool, hoped he couldn't tell she was blushing.

"Where are your glasses?" she asked. "You might be mistaking me for someone else."

He winked. "Contact lenses. Now, what time do you get off work?"

"Seven o'clock."

"That's forever. I'll be done with the hooligans by five. I'll come by then."

Don't give in too easy. That was her friend Linda's motto. "I'll still be working."

"Take off early."

Oh, she was tempted. Mario would let her take off if she asked him. But she wouldn't. Not even for Alex.

"Seven o'clock," she reiterated.

Twenty-Three

The day dragged, each minute longer than the last. When the hour lurched to 5:00 p.m., she called herself an idiot for not getting off sooner. It was a weeknight, still early in the season, and business was slow.

During the long periods when no one was around, she took a paperback novel from her purse, perched behind the counter and indulged herself. If anyone came, she slipped the book under the counter and hoped no one noticed the hot-pink cover emblazoned with an embracing couple. Someone who was going to Brown couldn't possibly be reading romance novels.

Several times she reached for the phone, intending to tell her best friend Linda who was back in town. But she wasn't ready to share Alex's reappearance with anyone just yet. Instead, she phoned home and left a message on the answering machine, letting her father know she would be late.

If only she had a mother or a sister, she thought wistfully. There were certain things for which a girl needed her mother. Getting your period or shopping for your first bra, for example. Those just weren't the sort of issues you wanted to discuss with the nuns at school or your dad.

And sometimes you were bursting to tell her everything inside you, like when Alex Montgomery came back to town, having transformed himself from a geek to a Greek god.

She served a noisy family who had just taken a beach rental on Pocono Road. Then a skinny woman with complicated special instructions about anchovies arrived. Rosa chatted with the retired guy who delivered the Chamber of Commerce papers for the rack by the door, but her mind kept wandering to Alex. She couldn't believe how much he'd changed. She wondered if he knew he looked like a guy on the cover of a romance novel. Probably not. He was reading Bulfinch's Mythology at age ten. He was probably reading Proust now. In French.

The clock somehow dragged toward evening. From her station at the counter, she watched the beachgoers pick up their straw bags and ice chests and head for their cars. In the slanting rays of the setting sun, the water turned to flickering gold. Far down the coast, the lighthouse blinked its signal—two long and two short, nine seconds in between.

And finally seven o'clock rolled around. A girl named Keisha came on duty to take Rosa's place because, in the summer, Mario's was open until midnight, seven days a week.

"Slow tonight, huh?" asked Keisha.

"Yes." Rosa tried not to look hurried as she peeled off her apron and hair net.

Technically, Keisha was a summer person; her family lived in Hartford during the school year. Her grandfather had been a Black Panther, a fact that seemed to embarrass Keisha. Then he wrote a memoir and got himself elected to Congress, and suddenly they were a middle-class family. Her parents were both lawyers, and, fiercely intellectual, she was headed for Amherst College. Still, she never acted like the summer people who strolled around in their tennis whites. She fit in with the townies just fine.

"See you tomorrow," Rosa said.

"Bye." Keisha settled herself on a stool behind the counter. It was then that Rosa remembered that she'd left her book under the counter. To her dismay, the girl found it and studied the cover, flipped a few pages and said, "Cool." Then she settled down to reading it.

You never knew, thought Rosa. She stepped outside and was hit by sea breeze and salt air. A bonfire burned on the beach, illuminating tall girls with tanned legs and sleek ponytails. They were roasting marshmallows and talking nonstop. A few shirtless boys tossed a football back and forth. Summer people, oblivious to the locals heading home from work.

Alex was nowhere in sight. She scanned the parking lot and saw only a few cars. A couple strolled past, holding hands and leaning on each other in a way that made her feel wistful.

Still no Alex. Maybe he'd been a figment of her imagination. The guy who'd come into Mario's did not look or sound anything like the Alex she remembered.

The Alex she remembered was skinny, awkward and funny. He had a high-pitched voice and an infectious laugh. This Alex was—

"Sorry I'm late," he said, breathless as he jogged across the parking lot toward her. "One of the kids' mothers never showed up, and I ended up driving him to Pawtucket."

"That's okay." It was all she could do not to stare. Burnished a deep red-gold by the sunset, he seemed like a figure out of a dream.

Then she realized something. He was studying her as intently as she was studying him. She felt self-conscious as his gaze touched her hair and eyes and lips, then slipped downward even though he clearly seemed to be trying to play it cool.

"You're staring," she said softly.

"So are you."

She blushed. "You've changed a lot."

"So have you."

The last time they'd been together, he was undersized, pale, often bright-eyed with medication and oxygen deprivation. She had been small and dark, her hair wild, her tomboy physique stick-straight. Now he looked like an Olympic athlete, and she had the kind of figure that drew rude sounds from boys on the beach. She liked it, and she didn't like it. Sometimes she lay awake at night wondering how to deal with her ultra feminine body. Should she hide it or accentuate it? Feel pride or shame?

"Well," he said, "what would you like to do? Do you need to go home first, or…?"

"No. I called my father and said I was going out after work." She smiled uncertainly. "So I'm out."

"My car's over here." He gestured at a shiny two-seater MG convertible. "Unless, um, you have a car you need to—"

"No." She gestured at a much-used Schwinn La Tour leaning against the side of the building. "I ride my bike to work. I drive my father's truck sometimes, but we share it." Rosa made herself stop babbling. She hated the feeling of embarrassment that crept through her. She didn't have her own car. With her going away to college, she and Pop had to be careful with money. "Anyway, you can just bring me back here after we…after our…" What? She didn't dare call it a date.

"No problem." He grinned at her.

She smiled back, feeling a curious sort of relief. She had seen a glimpse of the old Alex, the boy who had been her best friend each summer. He might look like a hunk, but he was still Alex.

Then, with an unexpected air of gallantry, he held open the passenger side door for her. As she climbed in, she faintly regretted not treating this like a real date. Maybe she should have gone home to primp and try on different outfits and do her hair. Here she was, in her jeans and white shirt with Mario's stitched on the pocket, the smell of pizza sauce infusing her hair and even the pores of her skin.

He pulled out of the parking lot and drove along the coast road. It was a clear night, and the breeze felt heavenly as it rippled over her, sweeping away the last vestiges of the pizza joint.

They both reached for the knob of the radio at the same time and their hands bumped awkwardly.

"Sorry," she said, drawing her hand back.

"It's okay. Do you have a station you like?" He turned on the radio and The Heights, singing "How Do You Talk to an Angel?" drifted out.

"I think that's probably it—92 Pro out of Newport."

They drove along, listening to music and feeling the warm summer breeze. She wondered if he was as lost in memories and as full of questions as she was.

As they headed away from town, he asked, "What's North Beach like these days?"

"Exactly the same."

"Deserted, you mean."

"Usually."

"You want to go check it out?"

She knew then exactly what he was asking. It wasn't

about the beach but about them. He wanted to know if it was time to go back to the past, back to the friendship they'd once shared, and then maybe go forward from there.

"Yes," she said. "We should definitely check it out."

He drove by his family's house, and Rosa saw the porch light glowing and lamps brightening the upstairs windows.

"Your family's here?" she asked.

"Just my mother. My father's in the city and my sister got married in May. She lives in Massachusetts now."

"One of my brothers is married, too. Rob married a fellow officer in the navy. I have two nephews and two nieces. A set of twins and two boys."

"All in the last four years?"

"His wife's Italian, too."

He took his eyes off the road for a second to glance at her. "You're an aunt."

"Aunt Rosa. Pretty wild, isn't it? My other brother Sal is a priest. A navy chaplain."

"Tell me where to turn," he said. "I haven't been here in a while."

"I know." She cringed, hoping he hadn't caught the note of wistfulness in her voice. She directed him to the gravel pull-out by the side of the road. On rare occasions she came here to walk and think, sometimes to rake quahogs to surprise Pop with his favorite meal of spaghetti alle vongole.

The sun was nearly gone as they got out of the car. The tall marsh grasses were painted in deepest black against the fire-colored sky. Out over the water, darkness gathered and melded with the horizon line.

He led the way along the sandy footpath. Beach grasses nodded as they passed, and wild rose branches snatched at their shirts. Then the path widened, opening to the beach, which spread out before them in splendid isolation.

A sense of wonder welled up in her the way it always did when she came here. All her life she'd found solace down by the sea where its power and vastness diminished everything. It was a place where the will surrendered. Here was a force that would not—could not—be controlled. She found a strange comfort in that.

"First time I ever flew a kite was right here," Alex said.

"I know," Rosa said, startled that he would mention it. "I was there."

"First time I went wakeboarding, too, and you were there."

"And scared to death."

"That didn't stop you from doing it," he pointed out.

"Being scared never does," she said. Then she felt him staring at her, and his look made her blush. "Let's walk," she suggested. Her legs were tired from the day's work, but being with Alex filled her with nervous energy. They headed down to the water's edge and took off their shoes.

She sneaked a glance at him and caught him still staring. She gave an embarrassed laugh and tried to smooth down her hair, hopelessly tangled by the ride in the convertible.

"What?" he asked.

"This is just so weird, seeing you again."

"Good weird or bad weird?"

"Good. Definitely good." She moved a little closer to him so their shoulders were nearly touching. "So why haven't you been back here?"

"Once I started high school, I finally got to have a life."

"What, you didn't before?"

"My mother never used to let me out of her sight."

"I remember that."

"She backed off when my asthma got better."

"Better. You mean it went away?"

"Not exactly. The symptoms went away. The doc said that's pretty common during a growth spurt. He was hoping for it all through my childhood. I'm still an asthmatic, but I outgrew my asthma. In three years I've had just two attacks. I'm on an experimental drug that's working, so I'm not planning on having any more."

"Alex, that's fantastic." She was amazed and thrilled for him. A miracle had transformed a sickly little boy into…into Brad Pitt.

"I can't explain how it felt to suddenly be able to do things like a normal kid," he said. "I played sports, didn't have to lug around a breathing apparatus. It was like getting out of jail, finally. I wasn't keen on spending summers under my mother's thumb."

"It's great that you're better, Alex." She was on the verge of admitting that she'd missed him, that summer wasn't the same without him, but she kept quiet. Too much information.

He slowed his pace as though he wanted to prolong their walk. "How about you?" he said. "You've changed, too. I mean, I can't help noticing it."

"I haven't been to Europe or Costa Rica or Egypt," she said, then blushed because she'd all but admitted she'd been asking about him. "I haven't been anywhere. Just here."

"Here's fine."

She nearly told him about Brown, but changed her mind. Not yet.

They stopped to look at the water, reflecting the last

colors of the sunset. A long way down the beach, the lighthouse beacon swung its beam out into the night. There was no sound except the waves hissing up to their feet, rattling over rocks.

"I sure missed coming here," Alex said. "I just didn't miss my mom watching me like I was a lab rat."

"So what did you do with all that freedom?"

"I went to a very boring high school. Phillips Exeter Academy in New Hampshire. My father went there, and his father, and so on, right down to old John Phillips himself, as far as I know."

"It's supposed to be a terrific school," she said. "I can't believe you were bored." He was extremely smart, she remembered. Maybe classes moved too slowly for him.

"All right, I wasn't that bored. I was so ready to get out of the house, I would have gone practically anywhere."

Rosa could certainly understand that. "Because of being sick?"

"Yeah. I needed a different life." He met her gaze and held it steady. "But there was something I missed about spending the summer here."

Goose bumps rose and spread over her skin. "Yeah?"

He grinned. "Definitely."

"Are you staying until fall?" Great, Rosa, she thought. Way to sound eager.

"That's the plan. I'm working full-time at the Y."

She shut her eyes and suppressed a shudder of delight. Then she had to ask: "You're going to college?"

"That's right. You?"

"Yes." She folded her arms across her middle. "I'm going up to Providence. To Brown."

Even in the dark, she could see his grin, and she knew then that he was going there, too. "No kidding."

"No kidding." Once or twice, Rosa had asked herself why she'd chosen Brown. Was it because it was the best school in the state? Because she'd been given a good financial aid package? Or because somewhere in the back of her mind, she knew Alex would end up there? It was where his mother had gone, his father and grandfather. It was where all Montgomerys went. There was a photo in the library of Alex's house of his parents, sitting on the chiseled stone steps of Emery Hall.

Suddenly her future, which had seemed unbearably exciting ever since the coveted acceptance packet had arrived in the mail, felt real. For the first time, she could actually picture herself there, walking across a quad, sitting in a lecture or lab. And now Alex was part of the picture.

"Remember this place?" he asked, clearly not as excited as she was. He probably wasn't, because it was so…expected.

"No," she said. "What about it?" Inside, she was dying. She remembered this with every cell of her body. She dreamed about it, thought of it with the frequency of obsession. Here. It had been here. With the sunlight warm on their faces and the breath of the wind in their ears, her relationship with Alex had turned from friendship to something else. Something more.

Then he was right in front of her, very close, and she caught her breath at the full impact of his height.

"Liar," he said. "You do so remember."

She felt her cheeks grow warm. "We were a couple of dumb junior high kids," she said. "That's what I remember."

"Don't tell me you don't remember your first kiss."

"What makes you think you were the first? You weren't, you know."

"Was so."

"Were not." But she was lying, and he knew it. In seventh grade, Paulie diCarlo had tried to steal a kiss at a school dance, but she hadn't let him succeed, and after that she didn't speak to him the rest of the school year.

"It's kind of cool that I was first," Alex whispered.

"I could say the same." Rosa never used to ask him much about his school in the city, but she was pretty sure he was a loner. The one time she'd asked him, he had dismissed the question with a wave of his hand. "I don't have any friends there," he said. "Everybody calls me a freak." Now, she knew without asking that the situation had changed for him.

"Rosa, do you have a boyfriend?"

"If I did, I wouldn't be here."

"That's good." He took her in his arms and pulled her close. She felt the surprising strength of his body, the hardness of his muscled limbs. Her senses filled up with him, and she felt strangely helpless, strange because she was usually in control of herself.

She looked up at him as he bent to close the distance between them, and felt a sudden ripple of apprehension. "I'm not looking for a boyfriend, Alex."

"Not anymore, you aren't," he said, just before he kissed her.

Spaghetti alle Vongole

4 dozen littleneck clams in their shells, the
    smaller the better. (If you use quahogs, you
    only need a dozen; just chop the clam meat
    fine.)
2 Tablespoons of sea salt
1 pound dry spaghetti
1/2 cup olive oil
4-8 garlic cloves, minced
1/2 cup white wine (Principessa Gavia is
    preferred)
2 Tablespoons chopped flat-leaf parsley

Scrub the clam shells under cold running water.
Cook the spaghetti until al dente. In a heavy pan
with a lid, heat the olive oil and sauté the garlic. Add
the clams in their shells and the white wine, bring
to a boil, cover the pan and cook until the clams
open. This should take a few minutes, and feel free
to add more wine. Discard clams that do not open;
you'll find a few rejects in every bunch. Remove
the clams with a slotted spoon. Add the cooked
spaghetti to the sauté pan, stirring it into the sauce.
Add the parsley. Serve in individual bowls, topped
with the clams.

Twenty-Four

Rosa floated. She was lighter than the clouds of the marine layer that drifted in with the morning sunshine. She was lighter than the pink cotton candy spun in big silver pans at a booth at Town Beach, lighter even than the tunes played by the Cranberries floating out of the kitchen radio.

Pop was already gone for the day. He'd had to leave his truck at the mechanic's, and today he was commuting on his familiar old yellow bicycle. That bike was such a powerful reminder of the past. He used to ring the bell when he got home from work, and Mamma would go flying out the back door to greet him.

Maybe he'd be working at the Montgomerys' house today.

"Alex is back," she said to the photo of her mother propped on the windowsill. "Alex Montgomery is back for the summer."

They had arranged to meet at the beach, which would be busy and crowded today. Their work schedules conflicted, but they discovered they could see each other in the morning if they got up early enough. She had promised to be there by eight, and said she would bring something to eat.

As she fixed breakfast, she relived last night's kiss over and over again, and it was wonderful, the pleasure and the dizzy burn of his lips against hers. She probed each moment, each heartbeat, on a molecular level, trying to figure out why it was so magical. Their kiss had been familiar enough to feel safe—this was Alex, after all—yet new enough to tantalize her with a fine sharp edge of risk. She felt something brand new for an old friend. Until now, she hadn't realized such a thing was possible.

She hummed along with the radio while cutting thick slices from the ring of ciambellone bread she'd made earlier. It didn't taste exactly like the ciambellone she remembered from her childhood, but it was close. She fixed the sweet, lemony bread the way she always did, the slices spread with mascarpone and sprinkled with cinnamon and sugar.

"You're a natural in the kitchen," Pop always said.

Being good at cooking was nothing special. She wanted to be good at Latin, at vector analysis, at Jungian psychology. Not cooking.

Yet she always seemed to be feeding people in spite of herself. In high school, she was the one who brought snacks to study tables or booster meetings. By senior year, she had football players eating cicchetti and the student council debating the merits of different types of olive oil.

She took along some fresh berries to eat with the bread, added two round, squat bottles of Orangina, loaded everything into the basket of her bike and took off. She floated all the way there. It was amazing how Alex filled her mind. Simply amazing. Only yesterday, thoughts of moving away and getting an education had consumed her. Now she could think of nothing and no one but Alex.

He wasn't exactly waiting for her, she observed as she glided under the stone archway leading to the beach. But he was there, already engaged in a game of volleyball on a team of visitors against a team of locals. Unnoticed, Rosa watched them. Or rather, she watched Alex. He looked incredible with his shirt off, hanging from the waistband of his shorts. It was hard to believe skinny, pale, wheezing Alex had turned out this way. She felt a strange shiver of heat as she studied his muscular chest and flat middle and the way his golden hair fell over his brow. On long, strong legs and bare feet, he moved with an assurance that was nearly a swagger.

No matter where they were from, all guys tended to turn a simple volleyball game into a life-or-death struggle. The locals were boys she knew from school or work—Vince, Paulie, Leo and Teddy. They wore cutoffs and muscle shirts, and some of them sported tattoos and mustaches or goatees. They talked and jeered in loud voices, and Rosa found herself wishing their differences from the visitors were not so noticeable.

The other team was made up of summer people, instantly recognizable by their patrician looks, their casual clothes that cost a fortune, their shiny hair. Three other girls also watched from the sidelines. Rosa didn't know them, but she knew their type. They would have names like Brooke or Tiffany, and they probably attended schools with zero church affiliation. Their silky pale hair, caught back by hairbands, swung as they moved. They wore khaki shorts and oxford blue shirts rolled back to the elbows. Their negligent sense of style set them apart from Rosa and her friends, who studied every issue of

Glamour and *Cosmopolitan* and hopped on each passing trend like short-haul truckers.

"Hey, Rosa," yelled Vince, all but beating his chest.

Finally, she thought. It was about time someone noticed. She waved at him.

"I'll be through in a minute," Alex said.

The volleyball match turned into an all-out battle. You'd think the state championship was at stake, the way they went at it.

Linda Lipschitz, Rosa's best friend, arrived and sat down beside her, and they dangled their bare legs against the concrete wall. Linda was eating a banana and drinking a Diet Dr Pepper. This was her latest fad weight-loss scheme. Yet as hard as she tried, Linda never changed. She was born round and seemed destined to stay round. And she was cute that way, with a bright smile that made her endearing no matter what.

"How was that interview?" she asked.

"Fine."

"I can't believe you're leaving us to go away to college."

"I'm not leaving you." But it occurred to Rosa that she might be lying.

"That's what they all say. You'll probably wind up in Europe or California and I'll never see you again."

"Why would I go to Europe or California?"

"That's where people go with a fancy schmancy education." Linda watched the game for a while. "Someday, years from now, you'll be on their team." She jerked her head toward the summer people.

Rosa laughed. "They'd never have me."

"True. You would need to bleach your hair. Oh, and grow taller and flatten your boobs," she added.

"That's Alex Montgomery." Rosa pointed him out and savored Linda's look of astonishment.

"No way. You mean that geek you used to hang around with in the summer?"

"The very same."

Linda put her hand to her heart. "Oh, my God."

Rosa leaned back on the heels of her hands. She thought she was being nonchalant, but the expression on her face must have given her away.

"Holy cow," Linda said in a stage whisper. "You hooked up with him."

Rosa stared straight ahead. "Whatever gave you that idea?"

"Come on, Rosa. Spill."

"There's nothing to spill." She couldn't keep the grin from her face. "Yet."

"Holy cow," Linda said again, elbowing her playfully.

Alex spiked the ball to score, punching it down right next to Paulie diCarlo's head. "Game point," a boy shouted as he prepared to serve.

Paulie ripped off his muscle shirt and hurled it at the ground. "Screw it."

"No, thanks," Alex muttered.

With a roar of fury, Paulie charged the net, ducking under and bearing down on Alex.

Laughing, Alex sidestepped him and started to run, but Paulie dove, grabbing hold of his ankle and yanking his foot upward. Alex came down hard on his back, and even from where she sat some distance away, Rosa could hear the air rush out of him.

"Oh, no," she said, instantly fearing an asthma attack. She could see the panic and confusion bright in his eyes, and she was terrified for him. But even before she jumped down to the sandy volleyball court, he'd regained his breath without the aid of an inhaler. He moved so fast it was a blur, but through the cloud of dust, she could see

that he had flipped Paulie to his back and held him
pinned.

"You lose," he said. "Again."

"Big mistake," Linda murmured. "He should apologize."

"Oh, like that's going to happen."

"Come on, Paulie," said Teddy. "It's time for work,
anyway." They were on the beach patrol for the parks department. They drove a county truck and wore uniforms,
cleaning up the beaches and roadsides and parks. But
they strutted around as though they were extras on
Baywatch.

The girls watched them, whispering among themselves. Rosa didn't miss the looks they shot at Alex—
adoring, possessive looks. She felt an awkward moment
coming on.

"Hey, Alexander," said the prettiest, blondest one of
all, "let's go over to my place. My parents are gone for the
day."

He looked at them, then over at Rosa. She wanted to
die, completely die. She never should have come here,
never should have agreed to meet him in town. They
were from two different worlds, and unless they were
alone, they made no sense together.

"Thanks, Portia, but I can't," he said with a grin. "I'm
busy." With that, he brushed the sand off his arms and
chest and walked over to Rosa. "Ready?" he said.

Behind her, Linda sighed audibly.

"Completely," Rosa said.

Twenty-Five

One Saturday morning, Rosa heard the mail drop through the slot and went to get it. She'd been on pins and needles, waiting to hear about her scholarship. She shuffled through the usual junk mail and bills, then caught her breath when she came across an elegant envelope of cream stock, hand addressed. It was from the Charlotte Boyle Center.

The rest of the mail drifted to the floor. She tore open the envelope, trembling as she read the committee's decision.

Oh, no, she thought.

She found her father in the driveway, putting a new chain on his bicycle. "I need to talk to you, Pop," she said.

He wiped his hands on a red handkerchief. "What's the matter?"

"Everything's fine, but…I heard from the scholarship committee. I didn't get it, Pop. I didn't get the scholarship." She stared at the cracked concrete driveway. She felt terrible. The generous prize would have taken a burden off her father.

She told herself that there were many other girls more

qualified and probably just as needy. Still, a tiny voice inside her whispered that perhaps Emily Montgomery's influence had affected the decision. Mrs. Montgomery had never liked her.

"Anyway," she continued, "I was thinking I…could wait a year." She tried to sound upbeat as she said it. It was the most practical course of action. "I could stay here and work full-time."

"What, wait?" He shook his head, and when he looked at her, there was a gleam in his eye. "You're not gonna change your plans now. You go to college, Rosina."

"Really? Really and truly?"

"It is what my Rosa wants, it is what you worked so hard for, of course you are going."

She flung her arms around him, inhaling his familiar, comforting scent. "Thank you, Pop. Thank you so much."

"You're gonna get all dirty," he said.

The summer days sped by far too quickly, and Alex and Rosa found too little time to be together. Most days, he was busy with his boys at the Y. Most nights she was at Mario's, earning every penny she could for college.

One hot July day, Alex and Rosa both managed to get the whole day and evening off, a rare occurrence given their busy work schedules. They met for coffee, and she was thrilled that he remembered how she took hers, with lots of cream and sugar. Alex borrowed a sleek Club 420 sailboat from the Rosemoor and they sailed clear out to Block Island. Rosa was happy to lean back, clasp her hands behind her head and let Alex do the work.

The sky was an endless arch of brilliant light over the small, fast-moving boat. Rosa could think of nowhere else she would rather be than out here in the blue Atlantic, where the water was veined with the white whorls of undercurrents. The craggy island was cloaked in a mantle of wildflowers and blueberry shrubs, and the sweep of scenery dazzled Rosa. They moored in a sunny cove and went ashore for a picnic by Settlers Rock, which was engraved with names from the seventeenth century. They collected jingle shells and bits of sea glass, and Rosa found a rare mermaid's purse.

Alex scrutinized it. "That's the egg case of a skate."

"Huh. It's a mermaid's purse. It has magical powers." She handed it over. "Here, you keep it."

He put it in his pocket. "I need all the magic I can get."

She considered telling him she still had the nautilus shell he'd given her the first day they met, but decided against it. He would think her hopelessly sentimental. Especially if she admitted that not only had she kept it, but she'd put it in a special place on a glass shelf in her bedroom window, where the sunlight shone through it from behind.

"It's nice, getting away for a day," she said. Here, walking the Mohegan Bluffs among tourists and strangers, she didn't feel like a misfit at all as she held hands with Alex. She just felt like…Alex's girl.

He had no idea about the scholarship prize. Maybe he didn't even realize his mother was on the committee. She pushed the thought from her mind and hid her thoughts behind a bright smile. Just for today, she wasn't going to let herself worry about it.

In the afternoon, they headed back to the mainland. "You're good at this," she told him as he turned into the wind.

"You're just saying that because you want me to do all the work."

She leaned back and trailed her hand in the cool water. "I'm saying that because it's true." He'd never been much of an athlete as a sickly boy, but clearly he'd made up for lost time. He maneuvered them expertly out onto open water, the sun glittering over the surface. Yet for all of nature's beauty around them, Alex seemed distracted. His attention kept returning to one spot in particular.

He was staring at her boobs, she was sure of it. So maybe her white shirt, blowing open to reveal her tomato-red bikini top, needed buttoning. But she didn't button up or even buckle her life vest. Because if she was completely honest with herself, she liked the way he looked at her. That was the whole idea behind wearing a red bikini in the first place.

She liked staring at him, too. With the passage of summer, his coloring deepened, and the contrast of his light hair against his skin was striking. His mouth was perfectly chiseled, like a Donatello masterpiece. She loved the way his lips felt and tasted when he kissed her, which he didn't do nearly enough as far as Rosa was concerned.

"What are you thinking?" he asked.

The unexpected question drew a blush to her cheeks. She was trapped, and she was an incredibly bad liar. "Actually, I was thinking about you." Maybe he wouldn't make her elaborate.

"What about me?"

"I'm just glad you're spending the summer here."

She wished they had more time to laze around in the boat, but the light had deepened to a fiery golden glow and evening was coming on. It was a bad idea to sail at night without proper equipment. Working together, they sailed into the channel at Galilee and tied up at the dock of the Rosemoor.

They stopped in Winslow at the ice-cream parlor. Rosa was so busy perusing the huge buckets of mocha almond and caramel fudge that she scarcely heard the bell of the door jingle.

In walked two of the summer girls who clearly recognized Alex. One of them had three small dogs attached to a single leash. It probably violated some health code, but the guy behind the counter didn't object.

"Hi, Alexander," said the girl with the dogs, beaming at him and showing off a set of freshly lasered teeth. She looked perfect in a denim skirt and Weejuns, a cotton sweater slung around her shoulders. They were both so incredibly stylish. How did they do that, making it look so simple? Rosa wondered. She herself was at a hideous disadvantage here. In addition to cutoffs, bikini top and flip-flops, she wore the sweat and brine of a long day out on the water. Her hair looked like a troll doll's.

"Hey." Alex stepped back to include everyone. "Rosa, this is Hollis Underwood and Portia…"

"Van Deusen," said the taller girl, sending Alex a moue of chagrin. "Don't tell me you forgot, Alexander. Our fathers are best friends."

"Right," said Alex, clearly not on the same page as Portia.

"You work at that pizza place, right?" the girl named Hollis asked Rosa.

She nodded, wondering what that had to do with anything. "Are those your dogs?" she asked, hoping to change the subject.

"Temporarily. These are rescue dogs. I'm socializing them so they can be adopted." She bent down and petted each one. "Aren't I, Wizzy Kizzy," she said in a baby voice that made Rosa want to cringe. Then she straightened up. "Would you like to adopt one?"

"I would, but I'm going to college at the end of the summer." Yet as she looked at the furry little herd, Rosa felt an unexpected softness. They had never had a dog in their family. Pop said they were expensive and too much trouble.

"You are?" asked Portia. "Which college?"

"Brown," Rosa informed them, trying not to sound smug. But she didn't even bother concealing her satisfaction at the expressions on their faces.

Alex turned back to placing his order. Despite his dismissal, Portia leaned on the glass case, blocking his view of the ice cream. "So are you planning on going to that charity formal at the club?"

Portia, thought Rosa. Portia Schmortia. She called it "the club."

"I'll be there," Alex said, taking out his wallet to pay for the ice cream.

Rosa hid her surprise. He hadn't said anything about a formal at his country club. Not to her, anyway.

Portia glanced at Hollis, then back at Alex. "Do you have a date?"

"Yeah. I do."

Rosa tried not to choke as he handed her an embarrassingly large cone of maple nut crunch. All right, she told herself. Don't panic. It's not like we're a couple or anything. If he's got a date, I'm fine with that.

As she left the ice-cream shop, she felt about an inch tall. She was as insignificant as a house fly, an ant. An ant with boobs.

But the feeling of insignificance vanished as Alex opened the car door for her. When she was with him, she felt like the most important person on earth.

"Friends of yours?" she asked, licking her ice cream and acting nonchalant.

"I know them from school."

She was burning up with curiosity about the charity event. Even worse, she was dying to hear about this date Alex supposedly had.

She savored her ice cream and acted like it didn't matter, but she was about to explode. Finally she couldn't stand it anymore. "So do you really have a date to that thing?" she blurted out.

"Depends," he said, then took an infuriatingly long time to finish his ice cream, crunching the last of the waffle cone with a satisfied look on his face.

"Depends on what?" she asked, a slow burn of frustration rising through her.

"On whether or not you say yes." He looked at her for a moment and then burst out laughing.

"You rat," she said, punching his shoulder, but she couldn't contain her grin. She smiled all the way through town. A formal dance. Not a prom, either, but an actual event with a purpose. And she was going. He explained that his mother was chairman this year and the goal was ambitious. They wanted to raise a hundred thousand dollars for the Sandoval Art Museum.

Glancing at the clock on the dashboard, she said, "I promised my father I'd be home early tonight."

"I'll drive you," he said.

Rosa hesitated. She hated that hesitation, that moment of thinking *I don't want you to see where I live.* That impulse to say lightly, *That's okay, I can walk.* There wasn't one thing wrong with her house. It was just different from what Alex was used to.

"Thanks," she said. "That'd be great."

"You're going to have to give me directions," Alex said as they left the main drag.

"Right at the stoplight." Nerves jumped inside her. In

all the summers they'd spent together, Alex had never seen where she lived. As the road wound away from the shoreline, the neighborhoods grew weedier, the houses smaller. "Take a left here, on Prospect Street."

The street where she'd grown up was lined with clapboard houses with fading paint, overgrown yards with toys left out, driveways with too many nonworking cars.

"Up there?" he asked. "Isn't that your dad's truck?"

"That's the one."

He pulled alongside the curb and opened the door for her. Across the way, a curtain stirred in the window. Mrs. Fortenski was at her post.

"Thanks for the lift," she said.

"You're welcome."

Okay, she thought. In for a penny, in for a pound. "Would you like to come in?"

"Sure."

She adored him for not even hesitating.

Her father, bless him, was a world class gardener. The front yard and walkways were as beautiful and neat as the neighbors' were untidy. She wished she could say the same about the inside of the house, but the fact was, Pop was kind of a slob. Rosa kept the kitchen and her own room clean, and she did her best with the rest of the place, but Pop had a habit of leaving a trail of litter behind him—old newspapers, empty glasses, effluvia from his pockets.

Rosa knew a moment of wistfulness. If her mother were alive, she'd go bursting in, full of her news about the formal, and Mamma would be just as excited as she was. Pop was a guy. He wouldn't get it.

She took a deep breath, made sure her blouse was buttoned over the bikini and opened the front door. "Pop, I'm home," she yelled.

"There you are," said Pop, coming from the den. "How did—oh." He stopped when he saw Alex.

"Hello, Mr. Capoletti."

"Is everything all right?" asked Pop. Clearly he misunderstood Alex's presence.

"Everything is fine, sir."

"Alex gave me a ride home. We went sailing today."

Pop took his measure in that fearsome way of his. There was something about Pop's thick eyebrows, his sharp eyes, his compact, muscular build, that was designed to intimidate. But Alex didn't flinch.

"Come in and have a seat," Pop ordered, and led the way to the den.

"I'll get us something to drink," said Rosa.

In the kitchen, she went into what Linda called her Martha Stewart mode, putting crescent-shaped pignoli cookies on a plate and little sprigs of rosemary in the lemonade glasses. Actually, Rosa secretly admired Martha Stewart, who had her own magazine. According to *People* magazine, some publisher had turned her into a media figure, whatever that was.

When Rosa arrived at the doorway to the den and saw Alex sitting with her father, a strange and powerful feeling came over her. It was an extraordinary emotion, so strong that she scarcely remembered to breathe. For a few seconds, she didn't bother trying to put a name or a value on the feelings rising inside her. She just watched Alex for a moment, knowing the world was changing in some silent, secret way.

There he sat with her father, in a dingy living room littered with old newspapers, and he was completely, utterly at home. He was as comfortable and nonjudgmental as a parish priest or a really good doctor. This boy, whose family had homes and villas all over the world, who dined on fine china every night, whose family had more money than some third-world nations, looked utterly content in the company of Rosa's father. Alex was, she reflected, the most sincere and unpretentious boy she'd ever brought home.

Finally she understood the feeling that struck her with such force. In that moment, with all the power of her young, yearning heart, Rosa fell in love with Alex Montgomery.

Rosemary Lemonade

In the Old Country version of "Sleeping Beauty," the princess was awakened from her enchanted slumber with a whiff of rosemary-scented water. The prince was probably miles away, lost.

2 cups water
2 cups sugar
2 cups lemon juice
Grated rind of one lemon
Two sprigs of rosemary
Ice cubes
Cold water or club soda

Combine the water and sugar in a pan and bring the mixture to a strong boil. After three minutes, remove the pan from the heat and stir in lemon juice, lemon rind and rosemary. Cover and steep for an hour. Strain the mixture into a jar. To fix a glass of lemonade, fill a drinking glass about a third full with the lemon syrup, add ice and water or club soda to the top of the glass, and stir. Makes about 4 cups.

Twenty-Six

~~~~~

"This boy," Pop said the night of the dance at the country club, "he's got to have you home by midnight."

"You bet, Pop. Otherwise I'll turn into a pumpkin." Rosa paced up and down in front of the hall mirror as she waited. She wasn't nervous, but excited. She'd never even seen the inside of the Rosemoor Country Club, much less danced on its hundred-year-old parquet floor.

She patted her hair, which she wore swept up and held in place with spangled pins. The dress was a dramatic strapless red sheath she and her friend Ariel had found in a church thrift shop. Ariel swore that, after alterations, the dress would look as though it had been tailor-made for Rosa. The bright cherry-red was delicious, the open-toed ruby and rhinestone sandals made her look taller and she felt wonderful.

She turned to her father. "I guess I'm as ready as I'll ever be."

"You look very beautiful. That boy, he better treat you like a lady."

"Of course, Pop. It's Alex, for heaven's sake. We've known him for years."

"Makes no difference. Something happens to a boy when he is with a beautiful girl. His brains, they quit working. They run right out of his ears or something."

"Alex is a perfect gentleman," she said. "Oh, Pop. He's just as smart and kind and funny as he was as a kid. And, I don't know, he seems to have no idea how incredible he is. I've seen girls fall all over themselves to get his attention, and he doesn't even notice."

"You don't need to be falling all over anything," he said. "This boy, he—"

"We're just friends," she said quickly. She didn't know why she said it. Alex was so much more than a friend. But she didn't want her father to know. Not yet, anyway. What she felt for Alex was as fragile and elusive as spindrift. She felt the need to protect it, to keep it to herself and nurture it in the privacy of her own heart, at least for a while.

The sound of a car door slamming ended the discussion. Alex came up the walk, resplendent in a black suit with a crisp white shirt, gleaming shoes and a glorious smile that shone even brighter when he saw Rosa.

"Wow," he said. "You look great."

"So do you."

He shook hands with her father. "Hello, sir."

"Alexander." Pop smiled, but there was something in his eyes, a concern Rosa didn't quite fathom. "You wait a minute. I'll get the camera."

He took a picture of them at the foot of the carpeted stairway, and then one in front of the roses in the yard, and finally a shot of them standing beside Alex's car. Rosa was happy and excited about her evening. Yet between her father and Alex she sensed a curious disconnect as though they lived on different planets.

Alex kept glancing over at her as he drove. "You are really something," he said.

"Yeah? Maybe you are, too."

"You used to be all skinny and messy."

"I was not messy," she said with a laugh.

"You had scraped knees and dirt on your face. Your hair was always wild."

She studied the French manicure Linda had given her. "I guess I clean up pretty good."

He drove in silence, the smile lingering on his lips. He pulled the car under the porte cochere of the venerable old country club.

A valet opened the door for her, and she smiled up at him. He looked sweaty and uncomfortable in his black suit and white gloves, but his eyes lit when he saw her. "Good evening, miss." Then he did a double-take. "Rosa?"

She felt hideously awkward as she offered a lame smile. "Hey, Teddy," she said. It felt weird to have a guy she knew from school waiting on her.

Alex came around the car, offering her his arm, and they entered through the tall glass and brass doors. She felt like she was stepping onto a luxury liner, into a world so beautiful and rich that it seemed made out of spun gold and fairy-tale dreams. The sound of a swing band blared from the main ballroom. Rosa's heart fluttered with excitement as she entered on Alex's arm. Tonight, she promised herself. Tonight she would tell him that she loved him. He didn't need to say it back. She'd make sure he understood that. She wanted him to know what was in her heart.

She half expected to encounter the Great Gatsby and Daisy, but at the arched doorway of the ballroom the Montgomerys were waiting. They greeted guests, chatted, sipped martinis, shook hands and air-kissed. As chairman of the event, Mrs. Montgomery probably had plenty to do. Rosa and Alex waited their turn. She had not seen much of Alex's father over the years. He was a financier who always seemed to be busy with meetings. He almost never went to the house by the sea, and when he did, he tended to work in the study with his briefcase open on the desk and a phone held to his ear.

She took the opportunity to study him now, and she could see that he was younger than her own father and quite handsome. Like Alex, he had light hair and eyes, broad shoulders and strong, squarish hands. Unlike Alex, he held himself with stiff dignity and his smile seemed forced, as though his shoes were too tight.

She wondered what he was like, this man whose son was so important to her. Later, perhaps, she would ask Alex. He never said much about his parents, although he'd once told her there was no pleasing them. She was mystified by that; he seemed like the perfect son.

They moved to the head of the line. Alex presented her to his parents, sounding formal and old-fashioned. His parents were equally formal, his father clearly unaware of who she was. His mother recognized her, of course.

"Well," she said. "Rosa Capoletti. What a surprise."

And not a pleasant one, Rosa suspected. Mrs. Montgomery held her smile in place as she turned to a linen-draped tray, picked up a martini and took a drink.

Rosa felt a wicked urge to mention the scholarship, but she held her tongue. It was already decided, and speaking up was not going to change anything. Besides, it was a big night for them all.

"Straighten your tie, son," murmured Alex's father.

Alex glared at him and jerked the knot in place. "How's that, sir? Good enough?"

The tension crackled between them, and Rosa couldn't stand it. She wished he had the easy trust and intimacy she'd always shared with Pop. Life was simple when you knew you could count on someone.

She slipped her arm into Alex's and said, "Why don't you show me around?"

As they entered the glittering ballroom, she was burning up with self-consciousness. She felt as though everyone in the whole room was staring at her. "You might have warned your parents that I was your date."

"What, and spoil the surprise?"

Blazing anger stung her. "Is that all I am? A prank you're pulling on your parents?"

"Aw, come on, Rosa. These days, everything I do gets at them. I can't please them."

She noticed he didn't deny it. "You set me up, Alex," she said between gritted teeth. "I don't belong here, and you knew it all along."

"That's bull," he said, his eyes narrowing. "You have every right to be here. I don't know why you're so paranoid about being at a stupid party."

Before she could reply, two girls approached them. Hollis Underwood, Rosa remembered, and Portia Van Deusen. The dog trainer and the one with the hots for Alex. Hollis looked chic in a gown patterned with stylized black poodles around the hem. Portia was in pure white, debutante style.

"Hello, Alexander," Hollis said, then turned to Rosa. "I don't remember your name."

"That's Rosa," Portia informed her. "You know, the pizza girl."

"Excuse us." In the blink of an eye, Alex managed to slip his arm behind her waist, send a dismissive smile to the girls and steer Rosa out on the dance floor.

She should have been grateful, but instead she felt a dull thud of panic knocking in her gut as she looked around the ballroom. Dancing with him was only a reprieve. The whole evening was going to be a series of awkward encounters and veiled insults. Even her red strapless gown, which had seemed so perfect just a short time ago, branded her with bad taste. She wanted to sink out of existence. She wanted to melt down between the cracks in the parquet floor.

"What's the matter?" asked Alex, gazing down at her.

"I look like a painted fire hydrant."

"You look hot."

"You're such an idiot. If you need to thumb your nose at your parents, that's your business. You shouldn't have used me to do it."

"I didn't use you. I have no idea why you'd think that."

"Now you're treating *me* like an idiot. You knew, Alex. You wanted to see your mom have a cow at her event, so you brought a townie as your date. Is that why you're dating me?" Rosa felt the icy burn of tears in her eyes, but she blinked fast and conquered them. "Is that what you've been doing all summer?"

He stopped dancing, right there in the middle of the floor. He tightened his grip on her, perhaps sensing she was inches from running away. He pinned her with his stare. "Where the hell is all this coming from?"

"From the fact that you didn't tell your parents I was coming and you didn't tell me not to go strapless and you—"

He touched his fingers to her lips. "My God, Rosa. I had no idea you were so insecure."

Neither did I.

"And you have no reason to be," he said. "You belong here. Right here with me."

She shut her eyes briefly, then looked up at him.

"Do you want to leave?" he asked.

"Are you kidding?" Somehow she managed to summon up a smile. "Let's keep dancing."

And they did. And for a few seconds Rosa forgot herself and had a wonderful time. But mostly, she felt so awkward she wanted to scream. A boy named Brandon Davis danced with her, grinning as he said, "I heard there was some local talent around here."

"Talent?"

"You got any girlfriends?" His hand slipped downward. Rosa pushed him away so hard that he stumbled.

"You creep," she said.

He laughed, but there was an edge in his voice. "Ooh. Boobs *and* a mouth."

At that, it was Rosa's turn to laugh, and that was how Alex found her.

"Having a good time?" he asked.

She laughed harder and hoped the tears of mirth wouldn't ruin her makeup. "Oh, yeah," she said. "Just dandy."

After that, things improved. Brandon Davis had done her a huge favor. He had made her realize that there was nothing special about this crowd. Like any other roomful of people, they were everything: Petty, generous, insecure, gregarious, mean, kind…and in spite of her misfit status, she liked it. She liked the elegant setting and the discreet waitstaff, the heaviness of a crystal glass in her hand and even the congregation of valets outside, smoking cigarettes and telling jokes to pass the time. She took in everything around her, right down to the smallest detail. She noticed the quality of linens on the tables, the sound system, the enormous vases of flowers, even the arrangement of canapés on the platters of servers circulating through the crowd.

She sampled several bites and kept her expression bland. But Alex knew her too well.

"You hate the food," he said.

"No, it's really—"

"That's okay. I hate the food, too."

"I thought it was just me."

He slipped his arm around her waist. She noticed his mother watching them with laser-beam eyes, the ever-present martini in hand. Next to her stood a stout, balding man. "Who's that man with your mother?" she asked.

"Some lawyer. I think his name's Milton Banks."

"Is she in trouble?"

Alex frowned. "What?"

"People don't have lawyers unless they're in trouble."

"Sure, they do. My folks have lots of lawyers. So does the company. I think their job is to keep us *out* of trouble." His mother polished off her drink and took another from the tray of a passing waiter.

"Let's get some air," said Alex. He led the way through the French doors to a flagstone patio surrounded by a low stone wall.

Groups of people congregated here, and their conversation floated gently on the breeze. Lights glittered from boats moored at the yacht club marina, casting a glow upon the water lapping up against the shore.

Rosa discreetly wrapped a paper napkin around her canapé—a dry affair of puff pastry and greasy smoked salmon—and deposited it in a wastebasket. She wasn't discreet enough; Alex noticed.

"Too bad about the food."

"I bet it cost an arm and a leg, too. Boy, these people would probably kill for a piece of pizza right now." Before any important gathering or holiday, her mother used to work on the food for days. Rosa would stand on a stepstool at the counter beside her, shaping meatballs or cutting dough. In the summer, she and Mamma would wrap paper-thin slices of prosciutto around melon balls and serve them on toothpicks. There was nothing wrong with keeping food simple.

"What do you say we get out of here?" asked Alex.

"Won't your parents expect you to stick around?"

"This is for their crowd, not mine." He looked around the patio area at the elegant people, sipping drinks and making small talk. "Once we're at Brown, I'm thinking the parties will get better."

At Brown. An invisible thrill went through her. In the fall they would be in a whole new world. On that venerable, leaf-strewn campus, the sense that they came from two different places would simply melt away. How amazing that was to her. To be in a place where it made no difference if you were rich or poor, an immigrant's daughter or a descendant of the founding fathers.

"If the parties don't get better," she said, "I'm going to have to rethink college."

Before leaving, she sought out the Montgomerys and thanked them. Mrs. M's disdain was nothing new to Rosa. She had always been disapproving, only tolerating Rosa at Alex's firm insistence. When Rosa and Alex were little, his mother used to worry that he would be lured into doing something dangerous to his health. Now that they were college-bound, she looked just as worried.

Get over it, lady, Rosa wanted to say. Instead she said, "Congratulations on this event. I know the art museum is going to be so grateful."

Mrs. Montgomery looked startled by the comment. "A thriving art collection is gratitude enough."

Rosa smiled, but deep down she couldn't help but think about how much all this money could benefit cancer research. The world needed art, too, she supposed.

"Thank you for having me," Rosa said.

"You're welcome, my dear."

I'm so sure, thought Rosa.

She wanted to thank Mr. Montgomery, too, but he was surrounded by well-dressed people who all seemed to be vying for his attention.

"Your dad sure has a lot of friends," said Rosa.

"He makes them ungodly amounts of money."

"He must be really smart."

Alex's eyes narrowed as he watched his father, so smooth and impeccable in his tuxedo, with his martini. "His clients were rich to start with. What would really be smart is if he could make a poor man rich."

"If there was an easy way to do that, everyone would be wealthy." She regarded him thoughtfully. The tension between Alex and his father was a tangible force. "Which is definitely not a bad thing."

"Just because something's hard doesn't mean it shouldn't be tried."

She looped her arm through his. "I think that was a triple negative. Let's go."

Alex escorted her outside and sent for the car. "Well," he said under his breath. "That sucked."

She bit the inside of her cheek to keep in a giggle. With a curiously adult smoothness, he tipped the valet and slid into the driver's seat. Once the doors were closed, he said, "I can't stand valet parking."

"Why not?"

"It's stupid unless you're disabled or something, which I'm not."

Guys didn't like other guys being in charge of their cars, she reflected.

"Where are we going, Alex?"

"I haven't decided yet."

"You don't have to entertain me," she said.

"I know. But you're too pretty to take home."

She nearly melted into a puddle on the floor. In high school, she'd never had a steady boyfriend and her friends often asked her why. She didn't really know the answer until now. She was waiting for Alex.

He headed into Newport, where Thames Street teemed with tourists and glittering restaurants and shop windows. The whole area was filled with strolling couples, and jazz music drifted from clubs or open air decks. He found a parking spot and hurried to open the door for her. "You're even too pretty for this," he said, "but it's the best I can do."

"I love you," she said, before she lost her nerve. She stood up and faced him, her back pressed against the car. "I really do, Alex. I love you."

For a moment he just stared at her. She couldn't quite decipher the expression on his face. He looked either like someone who had been kneed in the groin, or who had just won the lottery.

"Is it that shocking?" she asked, beginning to regret her admission.

"Yes," he said. "Yes, it is."

"Well, I can't help it. I wanted to tell you. You don't have to…" Her voice trailed off. She was at a complete loss.

"Don't have to what?"

Now she was in trouble. Me and my big mouth, she thought. Suddenly she was fighting tears. Oh, that's swell, she scolded herself. First throw your love at him and then burst into tears. That's got to be every guy's dream.

He was looking at her with that endearing crooked grin that reminded her so much of the young Alex. But she still didn't know what he was thinking.

"You don't have to do anything," she managed to say

in a husky voice. "I mean, just because I said that doesn't mean you have to say it back to me."

"No, I don't have to say it back." He cradled her cheek in the palm of his hand, caught a renegade tear with his thumb. "I wish to God I'd been the one to say it first."

And just like that, all of Rosa's fears and insecurities slid away on a warm tide. "Really?"

"I've always loved you, Rosa, from the very first moment I met you. I think I knew it back then, even though I had no idea what to do about it. But now…" He bent down and kissed her long and deeply. Then he came up for air and added, "Now, I do."

Twenty-Seven

On Labor Day weekend, Rosa invited Alex to the annual picnic of Mario's Flying Pizza, which Mario hosted for his workers, friends, family and guests. Employees took turns keeping the restaurant open that Monday, but Rosa had the entire day off. Mario seemed to understand that this was a special period for her. In a week, she would set off for Providence and college.

The event took place at Roger Wheeler State Beach, and it had grown to accommodate well over a hundred people. Rosa promised Alex he would not have the same problems with the food that they'd experienced at his country club.

She found her father in the garage, working on his truck. "Hey, Pop," she said to the propped-up hood.

He emerged from beneath the hood. "I hope you're not gonna need the truck today," he said, wiping his hands on a rag. "The clutch keeps going out."

"Alex is driving me to the picnic."

Pop scowled as he sprayed the rag with solvent. "What's he want to go to Mario's picnic for? It's not his crowd."

"Alex doesn't have a crowd." Rosa was instinctively cautious when discussing Alex with her father. She wasn't quite sure why. "He gets along with everyone."

Despite that assurance, her first glimpse of him when he showed up made her uneasy. He was dressed as though he'd stepped from a J. Crew catalog, in khaki shorts and a crisp blue shirt with the cuffs rolled back. He looked so…WASPy.

"What?" he asked.

"People wear really casual clothes to this picnic, Alex." She gestured at her shorts and Flying Pizza T-shirt.

"Who cares? You make such a big deal about stuff like this, Rosa. Why is that?"

She flushed. "I have no idea. Come and help me finish up the ciabatta bruschetta."

As they put sprigs of basil on the appetizers, he stole one from the tray. "That's about the best thing I ever ate."

"Really?"

"Pretty much."

"Then you're in for a treat today." She hugged him hard. Her father chose that moment to walk through the back door. She practically jumped away from Alex as she spun around. "Hi, Pop."

"Hello, Mr. Capoletti." Alex's ears turned bright red.

Pop nodded. "Alexander."

The phone rang and Pop picked up the handset. "I'll see you there," he said and then answered the phone. "Yes, ma'am," he said and turned away.

One of his clients, Rosa thought. "We should go," she said hastily, wrapping the tray with plastic. "Are you ready?"

As they drove to the state park, she wished she could find a way to make Pop and Alex like each other. It was important to her. *They* were important to her. And so were the people who jammed the picnic area, she realized as Alex parked in one of the few remaining spots.

On the smooth, tree-shaded lawn donated by the Winslow Knights of Columbus, a group of older men played a serious match of bocce balls. Working together under the oblong picnic shelter, women laid out the feast while their husbands grilled Italian sausages so spicy the aroma made Rosa's mouth water at a hundred paces. Children raced through the surf while their parents watched.

Rosa felt a rush of love for this world, this rich place of grandmothers who spoke only Italian, women who lived to feed people and men who grew loud and boisterous and competitive for no apparent reason except that they were men. For the first time, she actually felt a pang of apprehension about leaving.

"You ready?" she said brightly to Alex.

"Sure."

Pop arrived on his bicycle and leaned it against a tree. He probably hadn't finished fixing the truck, then. He waved to Rosa, then headed over to the bocce ball court and was greeted loudly and heartily.

Alex stuck out like a white-bandaged sore thumb amid the guys in their black jeans and muscle shirts. It was the Sharks versus the Jets, but Alex had only one on his side. As Rosa led the way to the pavilion, she pretended not to see a group of her school friends eyeing them.

"Hey, Rosa," said Paulie diCarlo, refusing to be ignored. "We're having a game of flag football."

Rosa put her hand on Alex's arm. "You don't need to—"

"I don't mind," said Alex, then turned to Rosa. "How about you?"

"Okay," she said, sending Paulie a look of defiance. "Let's go."

"One team takes their shirts off, the other leaves them on," said Paulie. "I vote Rosa is on the shirts-off team."

"In your dreams," she said.

His gaze gave her the once-over. "You guessed it."

"Go shampoo your brain, Paulie," she said, then lowered her voice to warn Alex. "You know they'll play target practice with you."

He grinned. "They're going to need some luck."

Alex played as hard as he'd promised. And true to Rosa's warning, the ball drilled right at him time and time again. He managed to catch most of the passes, giving the opposing team multiple opportunities to attack. Even from a distance, Rosa could hear their grunts on impact as Alex was tackled, the whoosh of wind being knocked out of his lungs. The third time it happened, she decided to say something.

"Paulie, this is supposed to be flag football."

"It's fine." Alex peeled himself up off the ground and shoved his flag back into the waistband of his shorts. He gave as good as he got, elbowing and shouldering a tortuous path toward the goal line, earning a small measure of grudging respect from some of Rosa's friends.

The game didn't end; it was declared over by Nona Fiore, calling everyone to eat. There was a stampede to the food—panzanella with tomatoes and bread, every conceivable variety of pasta, grilled sausages, fresh fish roasted in foil, Napoleon pastries and reginatta made with creamy half-melted ice cream. The older people drank Chianti from juice glasses and spoke Italian among themselves. Every once in a while, Rosa heard them mention *quel ragazzo;* Alex was being discussed. She wondered what was so wrong, that he couldn't simply be welcomed and accepted by the people she loved.

"Here, you eat that, you're too skinny," said Nona Fiore, Mario's elderly mother-in-law. Rosa turned to see her give Alex a big piece of *trippa marinata* on a toothpick. Before Rosa could warn him, he thanked the old lady and ate it.

"It's delicious," he said, holding a napkin to his mouth because he was still chewing. He would be chewing for a very long time, Rosa knew. When Nona smiled, then nodded and moved away, he asked Rosa, "What am I eating?"

"Pickled tripe. Made from cow's stomach."

He swayed a little and chewed faster, his eyes bugging out.

"Chewing doesn't help," she explained. "You chew and chew and chew, but it doesn't get you anywhere. Just swallow."

He made a loud gulping sound. "Let's go get something to drink."

He went to an ice-filled chest and pulled out two Cokes. Mario and his brother-in-law Theo tried to include them in a conversation. Alex seemed stiff and unnatural as he spoke with them, and he ducked away as soon as he could. There were lots of moments like that throughout the day. Rosa didn't want it to be so, but as the day progressed, the truth emerged like a storm cloud. He didn't fit in with the people she loved any more than she fit into his world. He sampled the hot, rich food, laughed politely at incomprehensible jokes, gave his undivided attention to grandmothers who barely spoke English. The harder he tried, the more foreign he seemed. And the more she loved him for trying.

She loved him for accepting a plate of pasta so big it took two hands to hold it, for pushing child after child on the swings, for trying to win her father's approval even though Pop made it clear he didn't approve of anything about Alex. Rosa could think of only one reason for Alex's efforts—her.

Afternoon stretched into evening, and fireflies spangled the darkness while someone gathered the kids to roast marshmallows over the grill. Rosa looked at the glow upon the faces of her friends and neighbors and then at Alex beside her, and she felt another wave of contentment, shutting her eyes to keep it in. To be surrounded by such things, she thought, boldly leaning her shoulder against Alex's, was the very essence of happiness.

Mamma would love this, she thought, listening to the women chatting in Italian. Then it occurred to her that perhaps her mother wouldn't be thrilled with Rosa falling in love with a rich Protestant boy from the city.

"Let's get out of here," Alex whispered to her.

"All right."

Parents trundled their sleepy little ones into station wagons. Men dumped the ice from coolers while women packed away empty Pyrex dishes and pasta bowls. Rosa and Alex found Pop smoking his pipe and gossiping with the older men.

"Good night, sir," Alex said. "Thank you for including me."

"That was Rosa's idea," Pop said.

Rosa bridled. "What my father means is you're welcome," she said. "You're very, very welcome. Right, Pop?"

The darkness masked his features, but his posture was stiff, formal. Anything but welcoming. "Yeah, okay," he said. "You be careful driving."

Rosa and Alex exchanged a glance. "We're going to the movies in Wakefield."

"Now?" asked her father. "It's late."

"No, it isn't. It's not even nine o'clock." She didn't want to fight with him about it, not now. Not in front of Alex. But the expression on Pop's face tore at her heart. She was leaving home and her father would soon be completely by himself. The prospect sat uneasily inside her.

Don't do this, an inner voice whispered. And yet she must. She had to go out into the world and find her life, and leaving Pop was part of the process. People did it every day. They left home and they were fine, and their families were fine, and that was exactly how it would be—fine.

Twenty-Eight

Rosa and Alex escaped the picnic, exiting through a gauntlet of people before making it to his car.

"That was awful for you," she said. "I'm sorry."

"It was fine."

"Liar. You're a terrible liar, you know," she pointed out.

"I know. That's why I always tell you the truth, Rosa. I was going to say today was no picnic, but it was. Just not my kind of picnic."

It was my kind, she thought.

"I'm sorry about Paulie diCarlo," she said.

"Don't be. Open hostility I can handle. Just…" He turned up the radio, which was playing "Walking on Broken Glass."

"Just what?"

He pulled slowly out of the parking lot. "I can't wait until we're away from both our families."

Again that wave of unease rolled over her. He probably wasn't used to the intimacy and openness of the familial atmosphere at the picnic; maybe it made him uncomfortable. She wasn't sure she felt the same way, but she said, "Yeah. Me, too."

She leaned back against the headrest and watched the night flow past. She saw the long, thoughtful wink of the lighthouse beacon and wondered what it would be like to live surrounded by city lights. She'd never spent a single night away from this place, and though she knew she wanted to, the idea still unsettled her.

"What?" asked Alex.

She looked over at him and smiled. He was so good at reading her moods. "I'm not like you," she confessed. "I've never been anywhere."

"Are you saying you don't want to leave here?" He sounded incredulous as he turned the volume down on the radio.

She winced. "What's so bad about this place?"

"Nothing, except that there's a whole world out there."

There's a whole world right here, she thought, watching shadows flicker in and out of the big salt marsh as they passed. "It's different for you," she said. "After you're gone, your parents will still have each other, but my father will be all alone."

He stared straight ahead, his wrist balanced on the top of the steering wheel. "That's not exactly right, about my parents."

"What do you mean?"

"They won't have each other. They never have."

A chill licked down her spine. Were they getting a divorce? Plenty of her friends' parents got divorced. Everyone always said it was for the best, and maybe they were right. But things were never the same, no matter what. Vince, whose parents had divorced a few years earlier, said it was like trying to rebuild a house after a fire. In a way, the family was as disrupted as Rosa's own had been after her mother died.

"Are they splitting up?" she asked.

"No way. She'd never leave him, not in a million years." He pulled off the road at a gravel turnout and cut the engine.

"Then that's good, right?"

He shifted sideways to face her. "It's not good or bad. It's just…it's the way things are."

"So they're not happy together," she said.

"They're happy apart. My father spent one weekend here this summer. He came down for the Rosemoor ball."

"I assumed he stayed in the city because he had to work."

Alex gave a short, unamused laugh. "Ha ha." He rubbed his chest in an unconscious gesture, the way he'd done when he was little and felt an asthma attack coming on. "I used to think their marriage was normal. Every kid thinks his situation at home is normal. They're incredibly civil, but they don't really have conversations. Just planning sessions about business or travel or my mother's charity work."

"Why did they marry in the first place?"

"No one ever said anything, but Madison was born seven months after they got married."

It sounded so bleak that she ached for him. Rosa wished he'd had parents like hers, who were utterly at ease with one another, laughing or simply sitting together in the garden in the evening. "I'm sorry, Alex." She leaned across the seat and kissed him. "They did something right," she added. "Somebody must have taught you about love."

He held her by the shoulders and looked deep into her eyes. "You did that."

She felt a shiver of emotion. "My mother used to always say we only get one shot at life, and it's a shame to spend it being unhappy."

"I guess my father gets his kicks from the family firm,

and my mother from doing her good works. And from drinking. Mustn't forget that."

It was the closest he'd ever come to talking about the fact that his mother was probably an alcoholic. She sensed his mood darkening like a cloud moving in front of the moon. "What is it, Alex? You're really down on your mother."

"It's not…ah, shit. Right before I picked you up, she and I kind of had words."

"Words about me," Rosa said, knowing it in the pit of her stomach. She pulled away and stared straight out the windshield. "About us."

He made a fist around the steering wheel. "She'd had a few too many mint juleps or whatever was being served on the lawn today. Sometimes when she drinks, she says stuff…."

"Stuff she doesn't mean?"

He shook his head. "No, but things she wouldn't ordinarily say."

Finally she said it aloud. "Like the fact that your mother doesn't think we should be together." Rosa thought about the phone call to Pop earlier. Maybe it didn't have anything to do with gardening.

"It's all such bullshit," he said. "And I told her so. I'm tired of her nagging me."

Rosa suspected it was a bigger fight than Alex was admitting, and that it had been going on all summer long. She also suspected he would never tell her everything, like the precise details of his mother's opinion of her.

She hated the idea of them fighting because of her. "You should apologize."

"No way. She's completely wrong about us. She doesn't understand. Rosa, I told her I'm in love with you, and I told her I wasn't ever going to stop. And she freaked, completely freaked."

His fierce declaration was both thrilling and vaguely frightening. "I still think you should apologize for upsetting her. It's horrible having your mother mad at you."

He got out of the car and went around to open her door for her. "I am officially changing the subject."

She stepped out of the car. "To what?"

He slipped his arms around her and leaned down to whisper in her ear. "Let's not go to the movies tonight."

She pressed her cheek against his chest. "Let's not. Let's just be together." When she was alone with him like this the whole world fell away. Their rival groups of friends, their totally different families, ceased to matter.

She pulled back momentarily to study the deserted road, a black ribbon that disappeared into the night. Then she looked up at Alex and saw the moon reflected in his eyes. And finally, she opened the trunk of the car and took out the thick Tattersall blanket she knew he always kept there. "Let's go," she said, and led the way to the beach.

They didn't speak as they walked along the moonlit path, but Rosa suspected they were each thinking about the same thing. Their hands were clasped tight—in desperation, anticipation—and their footfalls barely made a sound on the sandy track.

The deserted beach welcomed them. The Montgomery house was within shouting distance but lay around the curve and out of sight. Stars created a thin, misty sweep of light across the sky, and the waves held the glow of the moon in their restless, foamy crests.

Rosa stopped walking. "Right here is fine."

"Are you sure?" he asked her.

"Yes, absolutely. One hundred percent." She pushed

every misgiving from her mind as she turned to look at him. How tall he was. Limned by moonlight, he was as handsome and sincere as a prince in a fairy tale.

He cupped her cheek in his hand and leaned down to kiss her lips. She felt…peculiar, feverish, as though he had somehow magically slipped inside her and turned up the heat.

She couldn't bear it. She needed him, all of him. She needed the mysteries and dreams and fantasies she had woven about him, about them both. Making a wordless sound of yearning, she stepped back and disengaged herself from his arms.

"Rosa?" He stood still, though she could see the rapid pulse in his neck and the quick rise and fall of his chest.

"It's okay." She studied his face and detected a flicker of uncertainty in his eyes. Then, before she could change her mind, she unbuttoned her sleeveless blouse and let it slip to the ground.

His eyes widened briefly as he recognized the blatant invitation. In one swift movement, he took off his shirt. But when she reached behind to unhook her bra, he said, "Don't."

Rosa froze, mortified. Had she made a mistake then? Read him wrong?

He smiled gently at her confusion. "I've always wanted to do this." His arms slipped around her. She felt his fingers unhooking the bra, and even that light touch caused a wild leap of fire inside her. She shut her eyes and pressed her lips to his bare skin, and slowly, deliciously, her hesitation slipped away. She was a woman now; this was what she was made for. She trusted Alex, and this felt right. She was exactly where she was supposed to be, safe in his arms.

He stepped back a little and looked at her, and the expression on his face gave her a keen sense of...she wasn't sure what. Power and gratification, perhaps.

He drew her down on the blanket and lay beside her. She trailed her fingers over his chest. A shiver passed through her because he was so different from the Alex she had once known, and those differences were never more apparent. In childhood, he had been open and funny and fragile. He cherished their friendship and made no secret of it. The new Alex was still funny, but sometimes he was completely unfathomable and not fragile at all.

Yet when she looked up at him and saw him gazing in awe at her, she recognized the Alex she knew, even though his frank stare made her blush.

When he realized he'd been caught staring, he seemed to blush, too, though in the dark she couldn't be sure. With slow deliberation, he took a condom from his pocket and set the packet on the blanket, a wordless declaration of intent. There in the moonlight they shed the rest of their clothes and came together in a fierce clash of wanting. They kissed again, long and hungrily, and she felt his hands on her everywhere. A storm swept through her body.

All the times she had daydreamed about this could not have prepared her for what it was really like. It was awkward and wonderful and mysterious. She surrendered her free will, and gladly. She disappeared into the moment and lost herself. She made a sound in her throat as though she was about to explode. A pounding surge, a force she didn't want to resist, pushed her toward him. She touched him in ways no one had ever taught her, but she seemed to know with mysterious instinct, and so did he. She felt pressure build and then a flash of pain and then nothing but the exhilarating upsweep of intensity.

She heard herself cry out, and then at last Alex went rigid, let out his breath in a long, groaning rush and held her so close she could scarcely breathe.

Everything slowed down—their breathing and heartbeats, the sigh of the night wind and maybe even the shush of the waves licking up on the sand. She wished she could freeze this moment forever. She wanted to hold it in her heart, to cherish this feeling of wonder and joy, to savor this burn of love so pure and true that it changed the very color of the world.

She had no idea what was going through Alex's head. He sat up and handed Rosa her shirt, then tugged on his shorts. "Are you all right?" he whispered.

"Yes," she said. "Shouldn't I be?"

"Well, sure, but…I thought I should ask."

"I'm fine," she said. "What about you?"

He laughed.

"What's funny?"

"I've been asked that before but never in this situation."

She bit her lip. "Meaning…you've been in this situation before."

"I went to boarding school. Well, but not like—wait a minute." He pulled back and the night breeze chilled her skin. "You mean you haven't—you've never—"

"No." She rescued him from having to complete the question.

He pulled the edge of the blanket over them. "God, Rosa. I swear I didn't know."

She turned and lay sideways to face him. "Does that mean you assumed I wasn't a virgin?"

"Nobody is." He brushed his hand in the sand. "You should have told me. Are you sure you're all right?"

"Shouldn't I be?"

"I don't know. God, I'm sorry." A worried frown creased his brow.

"Sorry for what?"

"Well, that I…you know." He held her closer, stroked her hair.

She smiled at his awkward tenderness toward her. "Don't apologize. I'm glad you were the first."

"Honest?"

"I'm always honest with you. And I thought you were with me, but apparently that's not the case."

He looked away, resting on his elbows and staring at the open water.

"Come on, Alex," she said. "I can't believe you didn't tell me."

"It's private."

"I thought we told each other everything."

"Maybe you did."

She pushed away from him and hurried into her clothes, suddenly eager to cover up. "No maybe about it. I just never considered the idea that you've kept secrets from me."

He sat up and pulled his shirt on. "We've only ever been together in the summer. I have a whole life separate from you."

That was true. He knew everything about her because he came to her world. She had never been to his. Still, that didn't mean he was right to conceal something as important as this. "All right," she said, "spill."

"I just did."

"Very funny."

"Was it?"

"No." She shivered. "It was…" *Wonderful.* But she felt cautious now. How could she tell him anything if she didn't know how he felt? He claimed he loved her, that he had always loved her, yet he was a stranger still, in so many ways. Their differences hung between them like poison ivy on a wall.

"It was what?" he prompted her.

"My first time," she said. "I don't know why I assumed it was yours. I have two brothers. I should know it's different for a guy. So do you have a girlfriend somewhere?" She braced herself, waiting for his answer.

"Of course not. Come on, Rosa. There was just a couple of times, back in school and one time at summer camp…I wish you wouldn't think that it matters. It was special with you." He stroked her hair and scooted toward her on the blanket. "I knew it would be."

"I knew it, too," she admitted, trusting the tenderness she saw in his eyes. "I'm glad I waited for you."

He opened his arms and she leaned back against his chest, lifted her gaze up to the stars. "It's going to be perfect once we're at school."

She swallowed hard. It all seemed so surreal, heading off to the strange new world of college. "I guess," she said.

Somewhere in the distance, a siren wailed. Labor Day partying had probably gotten out of hand.

"What do you mean, you guess?" he asked. "You can't change your mind now."

"I'm not. I'll probably go up to Providence a few days early to get a job."

"Get a job where?"

"I don't know yet. Waitressing. Or something at night." She smiled at his groan of disappointment. "What?" she teased. "I can hardly hear what you're saying around that silver spoon in your mouth."

He didn't take offense. How could he, when he knew it was true?

"It's going to be hard, working and going to school."

"Beats joining the navy. I've been working since I was fourteen," she said, to herself as much as to him. "It's no big deal."

"It sucks."

"It's reality." She couldn't keep in a sigh of frustration.

"What?"

He seemed to read her mood even in the dark, perhaps from the way she felt in his arms. "Nothing. I'll be all right. I feel lucky just to be going."

That was certainly true. The town of Winslow didn't offer a lot of escape hatches. Her best friend Linda would be working for a bookkeeping firm. Ariel was helping out at her mother's alterations shop. Vince would be heading to Newport to bus tables at a high-end restaurant. Paulie diCarlo was joining his uncle's waste management business. Some of her friends were getting married—a mistake, in Rosa's estimation, but when people were in love, you couldn't tell them anything. Only a few graduates of her high school were headed for college. Rosa was grateful for the shot, and moonlighting was a small price to pay.

She turned in his arms. "Tell you what. Let's change the subject again."

"Good plan." He gave her a long, slow kiss and she ran her hands up under his shirt. He started searching his pockets for another condom, but she had the presence of mind to check her watch. "I have to get home."

"Stay with me," he whispered, and tightened his arms around her.

"I promised my father I'd be back by eleven," she said. "It's eleven o'clock now."

He grumbled in frustration but didn't argue further. At

the front door of her father's house they kissed goodbye, its sweetness unexpectedly piercing. She felt a sting of tears in her eyes as she lifted up on tiptoe and said, "I love you, Alex."

He kissed her again, longer, harder. "Bye, Rosa."

She floated into the house. "Pop! I'm home!"

He didn't answer, but that wasn't unusual. He went to bed early and was a heavy sleeper. All the same, she headed to his room to nudge him so he'd know she was home.

His bed was empty. She frowned, not overly concerned. He'd probably gone to the Fiores' after the picnic and was still talking and smoking his pipe on their back porch, late into the night.

So she'd cut her date with Alex short for no reason, she reflected, scowling. The minutes with him were precious, but at least they had college to look forward to. Finally their lives were about to converge. They could be together without having to deal with their families and friends. Maybe it would last forever. Judging by the way she felt tonight, that was exactly where it was headed.

She stood in front of the hall mirror and contemplated her reflection for a long time. It was so strange that she looked the same even though her whole world had changed. She'd made love for the very first time and it was unexpected and bumbling but completely wonderful. So what if he wasn't a virgin, too? There was no sense in trying to change the past.

She was filled up with love for him. She had given him everything she had, all of her heart. She hoped that was enough.

I love you, Rosa. I always have.

She clasped the invisible gift of his words to her heart. Then, too dizzy with elation to sleep, she went to the kitchen and poured a small glass of Mosto d'Uva. She took a sip of the intensely flavored grape juice, then went to the den to watch TV and wait for Pop. There were things she would never share with him, but happiness burst from her, and she could certainly share that. She was brimming with excitement about school, about her future. She knew Pop worried about her leaving home, probably even more than she worried about leaving him.

Tonight she finally knew for certain that everything would be all right, and she couldn't wait to tell him.

She flipped through a few channels. There were probably things in this world more boring than a telethon, but for the life of her she couldn't think what those things were. The first time she nodded off, she caught herself and tried to follow the telethon totals, but the second time she gave in and stretched out full-length on the sofa.

Alex was everywhere, surrounding her, whispering *I love you* into her ear, and she was annoyed when an insistent ringing sound awakened her.

The phone. She lurched up off the sofa and stumbled to the nearest extension in the front hall. "All right, all right," she muttered. "I'm coming." It was probably one of her brothers calling from overseas. Or better yet, it might be Alex, who was still thinking about her.

She grabbed the black receiver in the middle of a ring. "Hello?"

"Is this the home of…Pietro Capoletti?" asked a voice she didn't recognize.

The official tone was an icy spike, poking her awake.

"This is his daughter, Rosina. Who's speaking? What's the matter?" Even before he replied, her body instinctively braced itself for a shock. She had her feet planted firmly on the floor, her arm against the wall.

"Miss Capoletti, your father is here in the emergency ward of South County Hospital. I'm afraid there's been an accident…."

Twenty-Nine

The ensuing days melded into a blur. There was the rush to the hospital with Mrs. Fortenski, whom Rosa had to awaken by pounding at the door. Under the glaring, unkind lights of the emergency ward, the grim news was delivered to her alone. Her father, the victim of a hit-and-run, had suffered massive injuries including severe head trauma. He was in a coma.

She made frantic phone calls, summoning her brothers, informing family friends and phoning Mrs. Montgomery in the wee hours of the morning, asking to speak to Alex.

Mrs. Montgomery informed her tersely that she would relay the message when Alex awoke. Then she hung up on Rosa.

People arrived in a steady stream from church, the neighborhood, Mario's restaurant. It was an outpouring Rosa had not seen since her mother had taken ill. There were prayers and tears and whispered questions about why he had been out so late, but no one had an answer.

The next day, her brothers arrived and the consultations began. The doctors said Pop's condition was grave, but he might improve with intensive therapy. That meant a lengthy stay in a private care facility providing extensive, round-the-clock rehab. Sheffield House, a facility in Newport, was such a place.

Then someone from hospital administration sat down with Rosa and her brothers. An indefinite stay at Sheffield House was something only a heavily insured private patient could afford. And of course, with no insurance at all, their father wasn't likely to have that option. Lacking any means to pay for his long-term care, he would be moved to a public facility.

Rob put his fist through the wall of the consultation room. Sal stopped him from doing further damage and then went straight to the church to see what could be done.

There were more meetings, of course. Discussions with the church, with the bank, with friends. But the bottom line was, Pop's destiny was a state facility with little hope of recovery. Rosa was so terrified for her father and so confused by all the meetings that she had no time to stop and wonder where Alex was or why he hadn't called.

A few days later, Father Dominic had news. On behalf of an anonymous benefactor, a Newport law firm was going to pay every penny of Pop's medical bills, including his private care treatment.

People speculated about the identity of the benefactor, but Rosa and her brothers didn't dare question a miracle.

And Rosa didn't allow herself to wish for more than she'd already been granted. That fall, instead of going to Brown, she stayed alone in the house on Prospect Street and continued working for Mario. Her brothers both took extended leave, but once Pop was settled in Newport,

Rosa assured them that she was fine, and they both shipped out again.

She had a hard time letting go of the dream. She contacted the professors of the classes she wanted to take. Without exception, each one gave her a course outline and reading list and expressed the hope that she'd arrive the following semester. She kept herself from going insane from boredom by practicing Latin, studying invertebrate anatomy or reading opera libretti. She fully intended to go her own way once Pop was on his feet again.

But in the process of taking care of business, she made a disturbing discovery. Her father had taken a high interest loan and was about to default; he was on the brink of destitution. How could she think of going to school when her father was in such trouble?

That moment, plugging numbers into the cheap discount-store calculator, had marked her transition from childhood to adulthood. The change was invisible and no one witnessed it, but that didn't matter. When she got up from the table, she was a different person. She closed the door on being someone she'd always dreamed of being—a college girl, living in a dorm, working toward a fabulous future. The door she forced open that day led to long hours, hard labor, aching feet. And a paycheck every Friday.

Adding to her heartache was the fact that Alex never called, not once. Hurt and mystified by his silence, she phoned the college and got his number. Several times she dialed it but hung up before anyone answered. Finally, late one night, her anger fueled by loneliness, she called him. A strange voice answered.

"I'm looking for Alex Montgomery," she said.

"Hey, Montgomery! Some chick for you...."

When Alex came on the line, she coldly asked, "Were you ever planning to call me?"

"No, I…no. I do want you to know how sorry I am about your father's accident—"

"In order for me to know, you would have had to call."

"If there was something else I could do, I'd've done it, Rosa. It's complicated."

"What, speaking to me?"

He paused. "I don't really have anything to say for myself. I screwed up, okay, by not calling and then by making you think I…we… Listen, we had fun this summer, but everything's different now. We have separate lives. And anyway, I…I wish you all the best in the world," he said with a regretful finality. "But this— us—we're not going to happen. I hope you understand…"

"Actually, I don't. What made you change your mind? Did your mother finally convince you not to associate with a beach mongrel?"

"This was my decision," he said tonelessly.

Through a haze of shock, she managed to mumble, "Then there's nothing more to say," and hung up.

She still couldn't believe what was happening. The night of the accident had started out as the best of her life. With that phone call, it deteriorated to the worst. Worse even than losing Mamma, because she had faced Pop's ordeal alone. And now this—another blow, another loss. All the joy she'd found in Alex's arms was shattered by one phone call.

No one returned to the Montgomery place after that year, not Mrs. Montgomery and not Alex. Rosa considered this a small mercy. She didn't think she could stand it if he and his college pals showed up at Mario's Flying Pizza, to be waited on by Rosa Capoletti in an apron and hair net, a romance novel stashed under the counter.

She rationalized the loss in hopes of making it easier to bear. On one hand, she knew they were impossibly young and belonged in different worlds. But on the other hand, she had always felt a certain magic shimmering between them, invisible but very real. She'd believed in the power of that magic, so deeply that she couldn't let go.

As the weeks and months dragged on, she slept poorly, in short naps, and often forgot to eat. She worked full-time for Mario, and filled in as a sub every chance she got, willing to do anything to stay away from the empty house on Prospect Street and from memories of Alex.

Maybe he already understood what she was discovering for herself. It was easier to forget when you stayed miles apart.

Thirty

∽∾∽

Summer 1994

Rosa rubbed her aching back as she labored over a secret project. She was working on a business plan. Mario was talking about retiring. He wanted to hand the business over to his son, but Michael wanted nothing to do with it.

Rosa did, though. She was only twenty, but she had six years' experience in the business and she had a vision. Her plan would take years to complete, but at the end of it all, she would have something of her own. She wanted to turn Mario's into a fine restaurant. So far, she had only the germ of an idea, but she knew Mario would support and encourage her. With Pop laid up, Mario took it upon himself to look after her.

The phone rang, startling her out of her daydream. She grabbed it and answered.

"Rosa? Hi, it's Dr. Ainsley at Sheffield House."

Her heart dropped the way it did every time they called about Pop. "Is my father all right?"

"Better than all right," said the doctor with a smile in her voice. "He's coming home."

Immediately tears washed down Rosa's face. She shook all over. The staff had been promising her for weeks that once he reached certain benchmarks, he'd be discharged, finally.

She sobbed as she carefully took down all the information the doctor gave her. A social worker would come to the house and help her prepare for her father's return. Her brothers, currently stationed in Pensacola and Virginia Beach, would fly back for the homecoming.

Two years, she thought. What a long journey it had been. Pop was getting better, too. He would never hear again, but he'd regained the ability to walk and talk, to function just like anyone else. She had been praying for a long time that he'd be able to come home.

As he walked out of the hospital, his familiar flat cap in place, leaning on a cane, she saw that he was a different man, an old man, and it broke her heart to see how thin and weak he was. But his smile was filled with love for her.

She cooked for him and scolded him to eat like the most vigorous Strega Nona, and he grew stronger every day. Once assured her father was going to be well, she let down the invisible wall she'd built around her heart. She could breathe again. She could be young.

One of the first things Rosa did after Pop came home was to say yes to Sean Costello, a young sheriff's deputy she had met during the accident investigation. He'd worked longer and harder than anyone else, gathering clues from the vacant roadside field where a passing semi had spotted Pop and called in the accident. Sean had combed the scene inch by inch, seeking clues as to who had mowed her father down. Despite his best efforts, the

hit-and-run incident was never solved. People speculated that it was someone passing through, a stranger who
would never be apprehended.

As for Sean, he ordered pizza at least three times a
week, trying to get Rosa to go out with him. He was
steady and good-looking, reliable and gentle. And he
had a large, affectionate Irish Catholic family. Even
Mario approved of him. Now, with Pop at home and
getting better, she had run out of excuses. It was time to
join the living again.

All through that summer, she went to the movies with
Sean, and sometimes he took her dancing in Newport.
She saw him in church every Sunday and invited him to
dinner at her house with Pop. Everything about the courtship proceeded as planned. It was perfect, right down to
the roses he brought her at work every once in a while.

Except that no matter how hard she tried, she couldn't
fall in love with him. And she did try. She wanted to feel
that sweet burn in her chest. She wanted to float around
thinking of him at all hours of the day. She wanted to picture
herself in the future with him and their babies. However,
the wish was a long stretch from reality. Love, like time,
would not be forced, no matter how much she wanted it.

By summer's end, she came to grips with the truth and
decided it was only right to tell him. Sean was a good
man. He deserved a girl who would adore him because
she couldn't help herself, not because she felt indebted
to him. As they stood together on her front porch, she
searched for a way to explain her heart to him. It was
nothing he had done. The failure was hers. She had given
everything in her heart to someone else, and she didn't
know how to get it back.

It was late afternoon. Sean was on the night shift and
impeccably dressed for work in his crisp khaki uniform

and dimpled hat. His boots and gun holster shone so brightly she could see reflections in them. Rosa was torn between telling him now and waiting until morning, when he got off work.

Now, she thought. Afterward he could go to the station, be with the guys, unload on them if he needed to. "Sean," she said, reminding herself to maintain eye contact, not to chicken out. "I need to be honest with you. I'm not going to see you anymore."

"Come on, Rosa. What's this about?"

"It's about letting you find someone who deserves you," she said. "Someone who can love you. I can't be that person." She took his hands in hers, gripping hard. "I mean it, Sean. I'm so sorry I'm not the one."

"Damn, Rosa…" He kept hold of her hands, but his shoulders sagged a little. "All right, I wasn't feeling it from you, but I thought, in time…"

"I thought that, too. But it's not happening, and I can't force it. I'm sorry. I wish there was something else to say."

A late-model Mustang pulled up at the curb and a tall, broad-shouldered man stepped out. Rosa wasn't quite sure how she managed to stay standing, but she did. She even managed to send a look of icy disapproval to Alex Montgomery.

"Who the hell is that?" asked Sean.

"His name is Alex Montgomery." She let go of Sean. "Excuse me. I'll just be a minute." She stepped down to the curb and faced Alex. "You're not welcome here," she said. Her heart was nearly hammering its way out of her chest.

"I didn't think I would be." He looked different. Even taller, maybe, his hair longer. The all-American college man. "Rosa, could we talk?" He glanced at Sean. "In private?"

She laughed at his audacity. Two years of silence and now he wanted to talk. "Absolutely not."

At the hostility in her voice, Sean started to move toward Alex. She held him back, grabbing his hand again.

"I heard your father's better," Alex said. "I swear, I don't expect anything from you. I just want to explain why I left."

"I know why you left, Alex."

"You do?"

"Because you were a dumb kid. You couldn't handle anything more than a summer girlfriend. You didn't want to be in it for the long haul. Especially my long haul, given what I was going through. I understand. But I don't forgive you. I never will." She was appalled by his audacity and by the rage it inspired. She'd needed him when her father's life hung in the balance; where was he then? "You should go, Alex."

"You heard her," Sean said, posturing, his fingers brushing his holster. "Hit the road, pal."

Alex hesitated, but not for long. He looked at Rosa, then at Sean, then at their clasped hands. He yanked open the car door, got in and sped off.

"Sorry about that," Rosa said, trying hard not to shake. Her cheeks felt like they were on fire. "I can't believe he just showed up like that. He's nobody. Just some guy I used to know."

"He's the reason you're breaking up with me," Sean said. It wasn't a question.

PART FIVE

Entrata

Mamma never did approve of stealing, and she
never did explain why a perfectly good fish
recipe would be named for San Nicola. He's
been the patron saint of Bari, in Puglia, since
Barese merchants stole his saintly relics from
Myra on the Aegean coast of Turkey in 1087.
Maybe he didn't care what they did with him
after he was dead, but that wouldn't be very
Catholic of him.

Pesce alla San Nicola

Traditionally, individual fish are dressed inside and out with olive oil, garlic, herbs and lemon slices, then wrapped in parchment for roasting, which is a handsome thing to send to the table. But it all works fine with fish steaks or fillets in foil instead of parchment. Halibut, tuna steaks and cod are good choices, or if you live by the sea, try a small, perfectly fresh tinker mackerel (whole) or a small bluefish, sometimes called blue snapper, in season.

Preheat the oven to 400°F, or fire up the gas grill. For each portion, dress the fish with 2 teaspoons extra virgin olive oil, sea salt and freshly ground black pepper, 1 teaspoon minced flat-leaf parsley, 1 sprig oregano, 3 pitted black olives, 2 lemon slices, garlic slivers and 2 teaspoons fresh lemon juice.

Wrap each portion in foil or parchment. Place each packet on a baking sheet and slide into the oven or place on the grill and cover. Bake for 20 minutes, or until the fish just begins to flake.

Thirty-One

~⧫⧫⧫~

While Andrea Bocelli crooned in the background, Rosa stared at Alex, who sat next to her on the couch. Her couch, in her home. Drinking her hazelnut coffee while his bruised jaw swelled visibly. The whole situation seemed completely surreal—except that it wasn't.

"Wait a minute," she said. "You have something to tell me about that night?"

"Yes," he said, "yes, I do."

"You had information about Pop's accident and you never told me?"

"Not the accident."

"Then what?"

He looked down at his hands, flexed and unflexed them. Rosa was startled by his obvious discomfort. "What do you mean?" she persisted. Seeing the deep sadness in Alex's eyes, she felt an echo of that pain and confusion. A single moment had changed so many lives. Her father had struggled for two years to recover, and she completely changed the direction of her dreams. Alex followed the path that was expected of him, college and business school, a position in the family firm.

"When I heard your father was hurt," he said, "I didn't know how to comfort you."

"You knew where to find me. You could have picked up the phone, or, better yet, you could have gotten in your cute little MG and come to see me."

"No," he said quietly. "I couldn't."

She studied his face to see if he was pulling her leg. He regarded her with utter solemnity. She forced a small laugh. "What, were you held hostage by the Brown radical underground?"

"No. By a promise I made." He rested his lanky wrists on his knees and steepled his fingers. It was a gesture she recognized from long ago; he did it when he was thinking hard. "To my mother," he said at last, and looked up at her.

As she studied his troubled blue eyes, the deepening bruise on his jaw, she remembered something she had discovered early on in their friendship. Alex didn't lie. He never had.

"So let me recap this very strange conversation. You promised your mother you'd dump me."

"Yes."

Rosa got up from the sofa and went to the window, glimpsing her anguished face in the reflection. She composed herself and turned back to him. "Why, Alex?"

"I thought it was my only option. My mother and I made a deal."

"What kind of deal?"

"She took care of your father's medical bills."

Rosa went completely still. It took a moment to find her voice. "Come again?"

"She paid for his treatment, right up until the day he was discharged."

Rosa felt dizzy with wonderment. "When? How?"

"I went to the hospital as soon as I heard. You were with your family, but the priest, Father Dominic, explained what was happening. He was calling all your father's clients to let them know. The next day, my mother had everything arranged."

"I had no idea. None of us did, ever."

"That was the idea."

"My God, what was she thinking? It was wonderful of her." Rosa's thoughts were spinning. Finally the mysterious benefactor, the person who had given her father a second chance at life, was unmasked. "We tried and tried to find out," she said, "but the administrator at the law firm insisted we were never to know. I wish I'd known," she said. "She made a miracle happen. I wish I'd had a chance to thank her. And if we'd known, my family would have paid her back—"

"That's not what she wanted." His gaze tracked her as she paced back and forth. "She didn't want gratitude, either."

Rosa stopped and turned to him. Although she thought she knew the answer, she needed to hear him say it. "What did she want?"

"For me to stop seeing you."

So that was the deal. Rosa crossed her arms over her chest and shuddered. "What was she thinking? Did you ever ask her?"

"Of course I asked her. She always wanted me to have a certain kind of life," he said.

Like the life she'd had? Rosa wondered. A loveless marriage, suicide? Rosa felt furious, manipulated, nauseated. Yet the object of her frustration was gone forever. She'd never get the whole story. "I wonder if she believed it was worth everything she spent."

He steepled his fingers again. "That, I can't tell you.

She was clearly unhappy about something. Maybe everything."

Rosa's heart lurched at the anguish in his voice. He almost never spoke of what had happened with his mother. He did such a good job hiding his feelings that she often forgot what he was dealing with.

He looked at a picture of a seascape leaning against the wall, one she'd never gotten around to hanging, as though searching for answers there.

"So you thought walking away rather than explaining this was the honorable thing to do."

"She didn't want it known. Then, after your father was better, I came back to explain everything to you." He turned to look at her for a moment. "I could tell it was too late. You were with someone else and everything had changed."

"I didn't want to hear any explanations from you."

"So I gathered. I drove straight to the airport that day. I went abroad to study at the London School of Economics. Then I finished my degree and went to business school and, after that, everything—all this—seemed so distant. Like it had happened to other people, in another life." He got up from the couch. "I told myself it was for the best, Rosa. I was a kid from a screwed-up family. I didn't know how to make a relationship work. And I sure as hell couldn't see how our lives could ever fit together. So I left you alone."

He crossed the room and took her hand. "Everything's different now." He smiled with the undamaged side of his face. "Now I see exactly how we can fit together."

She was dumbstruck as she pulled her hand away. "Why, because we were so successful last time?"

"Because we can get it right this time," he said.

She escaped him and sat down, absently massaging her bare foot. She felt like crying, or flying into a rage.

"You went to your mother for help. Why not your father?"

"That wasn't an option." He cut his eyes away. "There's nothing more to say."

His quick, evasive shift unsettled her. "There is, Alex. You're not a liar. You want to try again yet you start by keeping things from me. How is that going to work? I tell you everything, like before, and you hold back. I suppose that's always been our pattern, only I didn't see it then." She realized that she had revealed her heart. Not just to him, but to herself. She went to the sofa and sat down. "Finish the story, Alex. Or we don't have anything more to say to each other."

Moving like a man in pain, he sat down next to her. Then he turned and touched her cheek, gently, perhaps regretfully. "Our parents were screwing around," he said. "I nearly walked in on them the night of the Labor Day picnic."

Rosa's first reaction was utter confusion. It took her a moment to grasp whom he meant by "our parents." Then she wanted to laugh at the patent absurdity of the statement, but all that came out of her was a harsh sound of disgust and impatience. "You should have said something long ago. I would've assured you that you were wrong."

"I wish I was. I'm sorry, Rosa."

He sounded so sure of himself, but he couldn't be. Still, this was Alex. He didn't lie. He believed it was true. She folded her hands carefully in her lap. "What do you think you saw?"

"That night, after we…after I dropped you off, I came straight home. I was thinking about what you'd said, that I should apologize to my mother for fighting with her. I went looking for her. That's when I heard them…in my mother's bedroom."

Rosa's temples pounded. No. No. No. "But you didn't see them."

"Come on, Rosa. I was a dumb kid, but I wasn't that ignorant."

She felt hollowed out, a little queasy. Her father and Mrs. Montgomery? Impossible. Although, she reflected, there had always been a part of her father that was like an undiscovered country, one she had no inclination to explore. Her mind didn't go there, even though he was a widower. She'd been willfully ignorant of his needs as a man. People could go on indefinitely without sex. Lord knew, she was proof of that.

"I don't believe this," she said. "It's insane."

"I know what was going on, Rosa. I didn't tell you because I figured you'd freak out, too. And you are."

"So now that your mother's gone, you can suddenly stand the sight of me," she said, not bothering to temper her resentment.

"That was never the issue," he said.

"God, you're crazy, Alex."

She put together the events of that terrible night, adding this new twist. That had always been an unanswered question in the investigation. What was her father doing, out on his bicycle so late at night?

Weeks later, when he regained consciousness, he had no memory of that night, but for the first time she wondered if he might just be saying that.

And by wondering that, she was forced to entertain the idea that her father had had a mistress. And not just any mistress, but Emily Montgomery. Rosa was appalled at the idea, but deep down a tiny part of her opened the door to listen. Emily was an attractive, lonely woman trapped in a loveless marriage. Rosa's father had been widowed terribly young. Perhaps…

She looked at Alex. "Does anyone else know?"

He hesitated, and she knew that by asking the question, she was buying the story. "No," he said. "I don't think so. I sure as hell didn't say anything."

How it must have hurt Alex to carry the knowledge around, to see his parents together, knowing what he knew.

"Do you think your father…?"

Alex looked out the window. "If he had any suspicion, he was as silent about it as I was." He flexed his hands, studying them as though they belonged to someone else.

Chills skittered over her skin. "It's so…tawdry. They should have known nothing good could come of it. Didn't they read *Lady Chatterley's Lover?*" She looked at him. "What? Don't you dare laugh, Alex."

"I'm not. I swear." He reached behind her and gently massaged the back of her neck. She nearly groaned from the pleasure, but instead, shifted away from him on the couch.

"My dad's part of the package," she said. "You know that, right?"

"Why do you need to shape your life around your father?" he asked.

"Because that's who I am," she said. "It's what I do." She looked at him steadily. "My father's not going anywhere. I've even toyed with the idea of moving back to the house to help him now that he's getting older." She shifted her glance away. "For what it's worth, he doesn't seem to like you any more than you like him."

He dropped his hand from her neck. "I never did a damned thing to him except keep his sleazy secret and leave his daughter alone, just like he wanted."

"He didn't want—" Rosa stopped. He did. Pop had barely tolerated Alex. He used to take every opportunity to enumerate all the reasons they didn't belong together. Agitated, she got up and paced aimlessly. She felt like an accident victim herself, numb with shock, battered and dazed. "I think you should go, Alex."

"I'm not leaving."

"Why not? You're good at it."

He glared at her. "I suppose I deserved that."

"I deserve some peace and quiet. It's late, and I have some thinking to do. I mean it, Alex. Please."

He studied her face and she struggled to appear impassive.

Finally he stood up. "I'll call you."

Alex was in his office in Providence, cleaning out his desk. Everything else had been transported to Newport. All that was left were the personal items in his sleek Danish maple desk: an antique wooden slide rule that had belonged to his grandfather, a framed photo of Madison with her kids. In the pencil tray of the top drawer lay the egg case of a skate, a treasure Rosa insisted was a mermaid's purse, a lucky charm. He picked it up. The small dark pod weighed nothing.

"Alexander?" His father stepped into the office. He was dressed as always in a tailored suit, every hair in place, every line of his face arranged to convey disapproval.

Alex slipped the object into his pocket. "I was just finishing up here."

"There's no rush, you know." His father picked up a box and moved it into the hallway.

"I've got this," said Alex.

"I don't mind giving you a hand." When his father picked up the next box, the bottom dropped out of it and its contents spilled on the floor. Both of them bent to retrieve the papers.

"What's all this?" his father asked, picking up letters, cards and notes in all different shapes and sizes, mostly handwritten, a few typed.

"Just some business correspondence." Alex grabbed a roll of packing tape to reinforce the bottom of the box. He saw that he was too late; his father was already reading some of the notes.

"This is about the Access Fund," he said, then read aloud from one of the letters: "'Thank you for this opportunity…'" And from another in the tremulous writing of an elderly person. "'You've given me a future I never thought I'd have.'" Some of the notes included photographs of clients' homes, their children or grandchildren, young people holding college diplomas.

Alex watched his father's face as he sorted through the notes. Surprise gave way to a perplexed frown.

Alex was chagrined. This was something he needed but didn't flaunt. His Access Fund clients earned the firm next to nothing, but he considered them his most important investors. He braced himself, expecting sarcasm from his father, who had always been critical of the unproductive fund.

Yet unexpected sentiment showed on his face as he put the papers back in the box. "And all I get from my clients is a bottle of Glenfiddich at Christmas," he muttered, carefully sealing the box for transport.

Then, as quickly as it had come, the moment passed. "Are you acquainted with a Sean Costello?" asked Alex's father. "South County Sheriff?"

Alex's gut churned. "Not personally. Why do you ask?"

"I've had a message to call him. Wonder what he wants."

"It could be something to do with the storm damage on the property." Alex turned away and busied himself with the last of the packing. He had no opinion of Costello. At one time he'd wanted to believe the guy was a good match for Rosa. Alex had gone straight to the airport that day, driving too fast, the image of Rosa and Costello burned into his mind. He'd tried to be happy for them. She was young and beautiful and all alone in the world except for her scoundrel father. No way should Alex have expected her to wait around for him.

As he wrapped a framed photo of his mother, he was touched by a twinge of pain. Had that sadness always haunted her eyes, or did he notice it now because of what had happened? Before, he'd seen only coldness in her face and felt only anger at the lengths she'd gone to in order to keep him and Rosa apart.

He shoved the picture into a box. "Did you and mother ever…?" He wasn't sure what he was asking. "Were you happy together?"

"We were married for thirty-six years."

"That doesn't answer the question," Alex pointed out.

"Of course it does."

Thirty-Two

On the day Rosa got up enough nerve to talk to her father about the things Alex had told her, he wasn't home. She let herself in and blinked the lights, but he didn't call out. There was no sign of him in the back. She noticed, though, that the side door of the garage was ajar.

"Hello," she called, stepping into the dim workshop adjacent to the garage. "Joey, are you in here?"

He started, dropping something on the floor. "Hey, Aunt Rosa."

"Hey, yourself." She eyed the objects laid out on the workbench. "What are you up to?"

"Fixing something on this telescope," he said. "Alex found the original booklet that goes with it." He held up a slim pamphlet of yellowed paper.

"You went to Alex's?"

He rolled his eyes. "Not the junior high stuff again. Jeez."

"He gave you those, too?" She jerked her head toward two large banker's boxes, each labeled Montgomery Financial Group.

Joey's gaze flicked away. "It's just some stuff he was

throwing out. He's fixing his house, and he has a whole Dumpster full of trash."

There was something furtive in Joey's manner. "Is everything all right?" she asked him. "You're not in any trouble, are you?"

He snorted. "Not hardly. There's nobody to get in trouble *with*."

She studied him for a moment. The Mohawk was gone; he'd probably tired of the daily ordeal with stiff gel. The pink color had faded somewhat, and the only piercing she could see was a stud in his right earlobe. He really was a good-looking kid, she reflected, when he wasn't trying so hard to look bad. "Haven't you met any kids at work?"

"Sure, but what am I going to do, take off my apron and go hang out with them?"

"I don't know. How about that cute girl who keeps coming in for Jamoca Almond Fudge?" Rosa asked, re-membering a tidbit someone at the restaurant had passed on to her. "The one who looks like Keira Knightley. I doubt Jamoca Almond Fudge is her only reason for stopping by." She saw a flush rising in his cheeks. "Hazard of living in a small town," she said. "Everyone knows your business. Now, where's your grandfather?"

"He went to do someone's yard. The…Chiltons. Does that ring a bell?"

"Yep. I'll try to catch him there. Stay out of trouble, kiddo."

"Of course."

She drove a little too fast, eager to get this over with. Her father's truck was parked at the side of a New England saltbox style house facing the sound. She found him in the back, raking clippings into a pile, and waved to get his attention.

He turned and waved back, then removed his gloves. "Hiya, Pop." She kissed his cheek. "You got a minute?"

"Of course. I have an hour, if that's what you need."

She took a deep breath. What she was about to say would change their relationship. It might do irreparable damage. But she had to know.

"Are the Chiltons at home?" she asked.

"They come on weekends only. Rosa, what's the matter?"

She took another breath and stood in front of him, signing as she spoke. She didn't want him to miss anything. "Pop, after your accident, Mrs. Montgomery paid your hospital bills. Did you know that?"

His face registered a succession of reactions—shock, disbelief, suspicion and, finally, wonder. But no guilt. Nothing to indicate he'd known.

"It's true," she said. "She never wanted anyone to know, but Alex told me. He also told me the reason she did it."

"And why would this be?"

"You were with Emily Montgomery the night of the accident. In her bedroom."

Now she saw it—the guilt. The expression on his face confirmed her worst fears.

"It's awful, Pop. I mean, I know you must have been lonely, but a married woman?"

His face darkened a shade. "Alexander Montgomery told you that? Told you I seduced his mother?"

"He didn't say seduced."

He took a bandanna from his back pocket and wiped the sweat from his face. "How can you think I would do such a thing? That boy dishonors the memory of his mother."

"Does he? Are you denying this a hundred percent?"

"He sends you here with this terrible accusation. What kind of person is he, eh?"

"He's confused. If you can set the record straight for him, then I think you should."

He made a slashing motion with his hand. "No more, Rosina. Do not start up with him again. He is as bad for you now as he was as a boy, and this is proof."

She could tell he was trying to turn the subject away from him, but she could be stubborn, too. "Tell me about that night, Pop. I need to know."

"There was no love affair with Mrs. Montgomery." His gaze was unwavering as he spoke. "That is all you need to know."

"If it wasn't an affair, then what was it?"

He shoulders sloped downward. "A misunderstanding."

She refused to soften. "Tell me."

He nodded, steadying himself with his rake as he sat down on a rock wall. "When I came home that night, she called me. She was very upset about her son."

"Because of me."

He nodded. "She was…not well, Rosa. I went to see her because I was worried."

Not well. "She'd been drinking?"

Another nod. "She was all alone and quite ill. I took her to her room, tried to calm her down so she would go to sleep. She wouldn't listen, though. She carried on…for hours, it seemed. Whatever Alex thinks he heard…I was trying to help a hysterical woman. It was nearly midnight when I left her. And that, my Rosina, is what happened. I am sorry I said I didn't remember, but that was the only lie I told."

She wished she felt more satisfied with his assertion, more vindicated. But she didn't. "Maybe things would have turned out differently for us if you and Mrs. Montgomery had left us both alone. You wanted us apart as much as she did."

"You missed out on nothing but heartache. Alexander was a boy, not a man. He would have been careless with your heart, not because he's a bad person but because he wasn't ready. I don't think he will ever be ready."

"You took away any chance we might have had to find out."

"No, Rosina. Your chances were over when he walked away."

Rosa was at the restaurant at closing time, supervising the nightly wrap-up when her cell phone chirped with her father's ring. It was close to midnight; Pop was always asleep by ten. She was already worrying when she retrieved the text message: *Joey missing.*

Just that, and nothing more.

Her hands shook as she sent a message back. "I'm out of here," she called to Vince. "I need to go check on my father."

Vince straightened up from wheeling a canvas-sided laundry cart between tables. "Is he all right?"

"I think so." She tugged her purse strap up her shoulder, then dug inside for her keys. "Don't forget to clean the tap lines in the bar. And padlock the Dumpster, don't just latch it. The raccoons are bad this—"

"Hello? It's me, Vince," he reminded her, making a shooing motion with his hands. "I've got this, all right? Just go."

She bit her lip, nodded once and dashed for the door. As she drove through the summer night with the top down, she scarcely noticed the canopy of stars or the coolness of the air. She was speeding and thinking about Joey. Where in the world had he gone?

Kids tended to hang out at the drive-in theater on White Rock Road, which hadn't actually played a movie since 1989. The abandoned parking lot became the scene of impromptu parties, and the enormous screen a target for hurled stones, beer bottles, the occasional can of paint. It was not the most wholesome place for Joey, but he was unlikely to come to any harm there. Then there was the video store, the state park and other kids' houses. She racked her brain trying to decide where to begin, but she could think of nothing. She didn't know the kid, she thought with a pang of guilt. She needed to spend more time with him, but she was always busy at the restaurant.

She pulled into her father's driveway and parked. He was waiting for her by the front door, looking lost and quite possibly ten years older.

"I got up in the middle of the night," he said. "For the bathroom. I decided to check on Joey, you know, like I did when you and your brothers were small."

She nodded, remembering the secure feeling she used to get when Pop would open the door to her room, make a satisfied sound in his throat and shuffle off to bed.

"You looked everywhere?"

"All over the house. His jacket's gone. And the bike. I'm gonna call the sheriff."

"In a minute." She rushed upstairs to Joey's room. There was something absolutely chilling about the sight of a child's empty bed, the covers thrown back, in the middle of the night. Pop had obviously already gone through it, and she cursed her nephew under her breath.

"He didn't run away for good," she told her father, who had followed her upstairs. She gestured at the laptop computer, which sat open on the dresser, a Starship Enterprise screensaver drifting across the screen. "He'd never go anywhere without his—" She stopped as an idea hit her. "Is that old telescope he was working on still in the shop?"

Pop hurried for the stairs, hope shining in his eyes. "I checked the garage for the bike but I didn't think about the telescope." He led the way through the one-car garage that had always been too cluttered to actually house a car, flipped on a light and headed into the workshop. It smelled of ancient motor oil, lawn fertilizer and disuse, and held the detritus of years. There were old motor parts lying about, spools of fishing line, plant food and snail bait, bicycle chains hanging from nails on the walls.

"It's gone," said Pop. "The little *parte di merda* went out to look at the stars. Why would he sneak? Why wouldn't he tell me?"

Rosa tapped her foot. "Beats me. So what do you want to do? Wait for him to come home, or should I go out looking?"

"I don't feel like waiting up all night, worrying my heart out."

Rosa didn't blame Pop. He wouldn't rest until he knew Joey was safe. "So where do you suppose he went with that thing?" She drummed her fingers on the work bench. Somewhere within biking distance, she thought. Somewhere high and dark. She could think of a dozen places like that. It was going to be a long night. She and her father returned to the house.

"Wait here," she said, gesturing for emphasis. "If he gets home first, make him call me before you kill him."

"Yeah, okay. And you send me a text message if you find him first."

"I will. He's fine, I'm sure. But he won't be after I beat the snot out of him."

She went to her car and got in. Now what? Point

Judith? The Singing Bluffs? It would take a genius to figure out the best place to see the stars.

She snatched her phone from her purse and punched in the number. "It's me," she said when he answered. "I hope I didn't wake you…"

Thirty-Three

"You have to understand," Joey said to the girl beside him, "it's my first time."

"Mine, too," whispered Whitney Brooks, even though they were completely alone at the top of Watch Hill and there was no need to whisper. "Just do the best you can."

"Yeah, all right." He smiled in the darkness. She was unlike any girl he'd ever known. Maybe she did look a bit like Keira Knightley. And there was a wildness about her. She liked extreme rock climbing and kiteboarding. She knew how to make kamikazes with Rosa's lime juice and vodka, and she had a fake ID, which she'd used to get a real tattoo of a phoenix at the small of her back. She was hot, but that wasn't even the best thing about her. She was also incredibly smart, and she wanted the same thing he wanted.

He couldn't see her face as he said, "Here goes nothing," and bent his head. Work, please work, he thought. Then the most incredible sensation came over him—blinding bright elation, a sense of triumph so powerful he thought he might burst. "Wow," he said in a raspy whisper.

She moved against him, her compact, sinewy body brushing his. "Here, let me—" she reached out for him "—it's my turn, after all."

"Be careful," he said, then cringed. What a dweeb, talking like a baby.

"Don't worry," she said. "I know what I'm doing."

"I thought you said this was your first time."

"Shows how much you know." She bent forward and emitted a long, slow sound of pleasure. "This is incredible, Joey. It's perfect. Just perfect."

Joey caught his breath and felt a soaring delight, sharing her pleasure.

Watching her look through the telescope, he beamed with pride. The transit of Mercury was so rare that, after tonight, the celestial event would not be seen for years. The telescopes of professionals and amateurs alike were trained on it tonight, but not here. He and Whitney were all alone. They took turns looking at the colorful, pulsing beauty of the planet transiting the moon.

"You're quiet. What are you thinking?" she asked him without looking up from the eyepiece.

"That I'm glad I met you." It was easy to be totally honest in the dark.

"I'm glad we met, too. If it hadn't been for my insatiable appetite for Jamoca Almond Fudge, we might still be strangers."

He grinned. "That's true." The minute she'd appeared in the ice-cream shop, he'd felt something special in the air. Maybe she had, too, because she'd lingered through two helpings of Jamoca Almond Fudge and three free glasses of water. After that, she came in every day, and by the end of the first week, he learned her name. By the third week, he learned that she went to a school called Marymount in New York and that her family had a summer house on Ocean Road. It was probably like Alex Montgomery's place, huge and fancy. She and Joey didn't seem to have much in common, but when he mentioned the telescope, she became his new best friend.

Before long, they were trading instant messages and e-mail, and even though they didn't call tonight their first date, they both knew it was. And nature had cooperated by providing a rare celestial event and a crystal clear night.

She, too, loved the stars and the planets. Joey dreamed of being an astronaut while she had always been fascinated by astronomy. Between them, they had a virtual encyclopedia of knowledge.

"This is the best night ever," she said.

Maybe he was only imagining it, but she seemed to be leaning closer to him. He could smell the shampoo she'd used on her hair, could feel her warmth as she brushed up against him. Maybe if he leaned a little closer, it might seem almost like an accident when he put his arm around her. Joey wasn't usually shy around girls, but Whitney was different. Other girls he'd gone out with—all two of them—giggled at nothing and talked about their favorite boy bands. Whitney was quiet and patient, and even though she didn't say much, he knew there was plenty going on in her head.

Finally she spoke. "You should probably kiss me now."

Oh, man, thought Joey. "Why do you say that?"

"You want to, and I want you to, so we should do it."

He shook his head. "We'll feel all weird if we sit here and talk about it and plan every move."

She laughed and shifted closer to him. "That's what I've been doing ever since I met you—planning this."

He broke out in a sweat. She sure as hell was different, with her disarming frankness and direct gaze. With a jolt of panic, he realized he didn't know what to do. Where should he put his hands, his mouth?

Calm down, he told himself. Here was this girl he was crazy about, and she wanted to kiss him. Who was he to hold back?

He cupped his hands around her shoulders and she scooted even closer. He was glad Grandpop had made him lose the tongue stud and nose ring, refusing to feed him unless he took them out. This, he decided, was going to be the best kiss ever. Because he wasn't going to worry about doing it right. He was just going to kiss her and hope for the best.

He took a deep breath and went for it.

"Hold it right there." The blinding beam of a nightstick sliced between them like a light saber.

Whitney gave a little scream. Joey crab-walked backward, his heart hammering "Nearer My God to Thee."

"You must be Miss Brooks," said the sheriff. "Your parents are very worried about you, young lady." He flashed the beam toward the road below. "Come with me, please."

The sheriff. Jeez, didn't he have anything better to do?

"We weren't doing anything wrong," Joey said, finding his voice at last. "We came up here to look at the transit of Mercury."

"I don't care if you're looking at the man in the moon, kid. Mr. and Mrs. Brooks sent me to find their daughter who, it turns out, is absent without leave."

"How did you find me?" Whitney demanded in a superior, rich-girl voice Joey had never heard before.

"You left your IM box open, so they figured out where you'd gone as soon as they checked your computer."

Joey suppressed a groan. You'd think she'd have the

smarts to shut down her messages before leaving the house. He exchanged a glance with her but could tell nothing by her grim expression. Nothing good, anyway. He picked up the telescope and tripod.

The sheriff went for his gun. "You," he barked. "Drop it."

"It's a telescope, okay?" Joey said. "It doesn't belong to me. I don't want to break it."

"I said, drop it."

"But—"

"Are you deaf?" the sheriff demanded.

That sparked Joey's temper. "No," he said, setting it down gently instead of dropping it. "No, I'm not." Maybe the deputy was, though. "All I want to do is put it in its case."

"Please," Whitney added.

"Yeah, please," Joey agreed.

The guy hesitated, then nodded once. Joey knelt down to lay the pieces in the antique velvet-lined case. Then they were led down the rocky path.

At least, Joey thought, he wasn't in trouble. He'd told Grandpop after dinner that he was going out, and Grandpop had offered a vague nod which Joey took as assent. And even if he didn't have permission, Grandpop slept like, well, like a guy who couldn't hear. All summer long, Joey had been coming and going as he pleased.

Tonight, he decided, he'd just make nice with Officer Friendly and sneak back home, no harm done.

The fantasy sustained him until he reached the bottom of the path. Next to the squad car sat a small, gleaming convertible. Two people stood next to it.

Aunt Rosa stepped forward. "You are in such trouble."

Joey swallowed with an audible gulp.

It was worse than he could imagine. His aunt text-messaged Grandpop that he was fine. Alex made him lock the bikes together; he'd have to come back for them in the morning.

"I'll take that," the sheriff said, reaching for the telescope.

"I've got it." Alex Montgomery stepped forward. "It was mine, and I gave it to the kid."

That's all Joey was in that moment. A kid. A punk. Just a few minutes before, he'd been on top of the world, with a view of the stars, about to kiss a girl.

Alex took the scope away and shut it in the trunk. Joey doubted he'd ever see it again.

But that wasn't the worst moment Joey would suffer. The worst was when they made him get in the back of the squad car with Whitney. Behind the cage. There were no handles or locks on the rear doors of the squad car. Joey had never realized that until tonight.

"Thanks, Sean," Aunt Rosa said.

Great, thought Joey. She's on a first name basis with the law.

"Not a problem. I still pull night duty sometimes. Keeps me in touch with the nonvoters."

It was decided that the sheriff would drive both Joey and Whitney to the Brooks' house, where he would apologize. From there, his aunt would drive him back to town.

"You're gonna behave, all right?"

"Yes, sir." Joey wanted to protest that they hadn't done anything, but he knew better. Being absent without leave made grown-ups freak. He'd seen it in his own household many a time. His parents went ape-shit when the twins went missing, which they did a lot. His sisters liked to party.

And he didn't. It was so unfair.

He turned to Whitney, who sat quietly, staring straight ahead. "You okay?" he asked softly.

"Don't say anything, kid."

"I was just asking if she's all right."

"What'd you do to her, kid?"

"*Nothing,* okay?" Whitney said with that superior tone. She pursed her lips and continued staring straight ahead. Joey prayed she wouldn't cry. He couldn't stand it when girls cried; he felt totally helpless. His sister Edie was a crier. The whole house shook when she sobbed about a bad grade, a boyfriend, a broken nail. But maybe crying helped, he reflected, counting the squares of the grid that imprisoned him. Not crying was actually painful, an ache of pressure in his chest. Maybe girls cried because it let off the pressure.

To his relief, Whitney didn't cry. She just sat there until they pulled through the gate of her parents' house. It was one of those summer places that got featured in magazines, a historic house with historic gardens and historic statues everywhere. Probably Roger-effing-Williams had taken a pee right on the grounds. Whitney had told him there was a gun emplacement somewhere that had figured in the Battle of Rhode Island a zillion years ago. Whitney's mother thought it made the Brooks family better than regular people. Whitney didn't, though; she tended to scoff at her mother's snobbery.

Waiting in front of the house, her parents looked as grim as the couple in that famous *American Gothic* painting, only they wore better clothes, even at one in the morning.

The squad car door opened and Whitney slid out. Joey followed, eager to escape.

Whitney's mother broke out of the frozen pose and hurried across the cobblestone drive. "Where in heaven's name have you been, young lady?" she said. Whitney looked over at Joey and mouthed along with her mother's next words: "We were worried sick about you."

Joey almost lost it, but he managed to stand up straight, shoulders back, chin tucked, eyes ahead, stiff as a new recruit. "Mrs. Brooks, ma'am, I'm sorry about tonight. It was my idea."

"I found them at Watch Hill," the sheriff reported. "They claimed they were looking at stars."

"We were," Joey asserted. "A planet, actually. The transit of Mercury was tonight and we both wanted to see it."

As he spoke, the Alfa pulled up beside the squad car. Whitney's mother flared her nostrils as Aunt Rosa got out of the car. She was still in her work clothes, a black dress and high heels.

Whitney's father spoke up for the first time. "And you are…?" He looked at Aunt Rosa's boobs, even though he pretended not to. Joey disliked him and his patronizing tone immediately.

He stepped forward. "Sir, my name is Joseph Capoletti, and this is my aunt, Rosa Capoletti."

Mr. Brooks gave him the once-over, taking in Joey's hair, the earrings, the clothes. "Wait inside, Whitney," he said, still glaring at Joey. "Go to your room."

"But—"

"Now, Whitney." As she marched toward the house, Mr. Brooks turned to the sheriff's deputy. "Thank you for bringing our daughter home. You've done a good night's work."

The cop didn't say anything. He was probably pissed at Brooks's attitude, patting him on the head like a birddog. He got back in his car and spoke into the radio, then pulled out of the driveway.

Meanwhile, Alex got out of the Alfa. The Brookses were glaring at Rosa as though trying to freeze her with their eyes. "We'd appreciate it, Miss Cappellini—"

"That's Capoletti," she corrected. Joey could see her getting ticked off. It wasn't anything physical, just a certain energy that seem to zap around her like an invisible force field.

"Yes, well, we'd appreciate it if you would support us in keeping Joseph away from Whitney."

"Oh, I'm sure you would," said Aunt Rosa.

Clearly they didn't hear the sarcasm in her voice.

"I'm glad we agree. Whitney is a very sheltered child. She's not accustomed to boys like your nephew."

Joey held in a snort of disbelief. Whitney was the go-to girl when you needed a fake ID or booze. And judging by the way she'd come on to him tonight, he figured she'd had plenty of practice. But her parents didn't want to hear that.

"Joey will be held accountable for his actions," said Aunt Rosa, her temper still seething just below the surface. "However, it's a free country, and unless you lock your daughter up, she might make friends with boys like Joey, so get used to it."

"Look, Ms. Cap…" Mr. Brooks cleared his throat. "We don't want to press charges—"

"Hey, maybe *I* want to," she said, snapping like a dry twig. "Did you ever think of that, *asino sporco?*"

Joey bit the inside of his cheek to keep from laughing when Alex stepped forward.

"Excuse me," he said, nodding at the Brookses. "Alex Montgomery," he explained. "I live down the road—"

"Alexander, of course." Mrs. Brooks shifted effortlessly into social mode as though she was at a cocktail party. "Our mothers went to Brown together. Mine was older, of course, so she was terribly shocked to hear of your loss."

"Oh, for heaven's sake," Rosa said under her breath.

"Get in the car, Joey. I'm taking you home." She turned to Alex. "I assume you can find your own way home?" She didn't wait for an answer but got in the car and gunned the engine.

Joey kept holding in laughter as she peeled out, leaving Alex looking like a doofus while the Brookses fawned over him. "You shouldn't have ditched him," said Joey.

"He lives a quarter-mile down the road, and this car only seats two."

"What was he doing here tonight, anyway?"

She went screaming around the turnoff to Winslow. "He was the one who figured out where you'd be." She clicked her red fingernails on the steering wheel. "I guess maybe I shouldn't have ditched him with those people. Me and my temper."

Joey tried to shrink down in the seat of the Alfa. Maybe she'd stay off track and forget to tear him a new one. "He probably doesn't mind," he suggested. "He might have needed a nightcap anyway."

Mistake. He should have kept his mouth shut. "What he needs," Rosa snapped, "is to be sound asleep in bed. That's what we all need. But you and your little girlfriend weren't thinking about that, were you?"

"She's not my girlfriend."

"And I'm not my mother's daughter. I wasn't born yesterday, Joey. I know a pair of revved-up teenagers when I see it. Look, this is for your own good. Don't give your heart to a girl like that."

"Like what?"

"Summer people."

"I'm summer people."

"You are not. You're just here for the summer. There's a difference."

"I have no idea what you're talking about. Anyway, nothing happened. Nobody gave anyone's heart away. That's your issue, not mine."

"What?"

Joey wished the car had an escape hatch. He should learn to keep his big mouth shut. Oh, well. In for a penny, in for a pound. "You know what. You and Alex, that's what."

"There is no me and Alex."

"And I'm not my father's son."

"You're not funny," she said, accelerating through the last stoplight before home. "And quit trying to change the subject. You sneaked out, you were groping some girl—"

"Like I said." He exaggerated the enunciation of each word, figuring his best defense was to distract her with snottiness. "We just wanted to use the telescope."

"If it was so innocent, why didn't you get permission?"

"Grandpop said it was okay."

Rosa slowed the car a bit and glanced over at him. "He didn't tell me that."

"He probably forgot," Joey blurted out, "like he forgets everything else."

She slammed on the brakes right in the middle of a deserted street. "What the hell is that supposed to mean?"

In the yellowish glare of a street lamp, Joey could see something flickering in and out of her anger. He thought maybe it was fear. He would need to choose his words carefully, he realized a little late. It would freak him out if someone told him his own dad was losing it. He'd better remember that. This was Rosa's father.

"Joey?" she said over the burble of the engine.

He cleared his throat. "Grandpop forgets stuff," he said as gently as he could.

"So does everybody," she said. "I forgot your mother's birthday last month and I still haven't sent her a card."

He felt a little sorry for her; she was so desperate to believe this was nothing. He'd tried that, too, when he first moved in. Grandpop was a deaf guy. That made him more likely to forget to turn off the water in the sink, or to leave his electric razor on, or to ignore the mail when it dropped through the slot on the front door. He wondered how much of this Aunt Rosa knew.

"I'm not talking about that kind of forgetting," Joey said. "I'm talking about almost everything. Every day it's something. He left the truck running until it ran out of gas. He left a pot of beans boiling on the stove. The house reeked for hours and now there's a huge black circle on the ceiling from the smoke. When I tell him anything, I usually have to repeat it about a zillion times. Half the time, he calls me Roberto, and when I correct him, he gets all mad."

Rosa blinked fast, like she was batting away tears. Oh, man, thought Joey. Not another one. Fortunately she didn't cry. "Have you…talked to Grandpop about this?"

"Constantly, but he blows me off. Alex said—"

"Whoa, Bubba." Any possibility of tears disappeared, probably boiled away by her temper. "You mentioned this to Alex?"

"Maybe," Joey said quietly. "I didn't think it was any big secret. Besides, the smell from the burned beans was all over me, so when I went to Alex's and he asked—"

"You went to Alex's?"

This was going from bad to worse. "He had some astronomy books to loan me, okay? It's a free country."

"So you said something to Alex, but not to me," Aunt Rosa observed. "Maybe you should just write a press release. Have you discussed this with your parents?"

"No. My dad would probably have the same reaction as you."

"What reaction? How am I reacting?"

"Loudly," Joey said.

Across the road, a light went on and curtains stirred in a window. Rosa shifted gears and drove on in complete silence to the house on Prospect Street.

Thirty-Four

Linda snapped on a pair of rubber gloves. "Okay, let's get started."

Rosa looked around her father's house and grimaced. "Now I know how Hercules felt when he saw the Augean stables."

"Aw, it's not that bad."

"It is. I can't believe you volunteered for this."

"Hey, what are friends for?" Linda grabbed a bottle of Windex.

"Probably not degreasing my father's kitchen ceiling, but I love you for being here."

"It's all right, Rosa," Linda assured her. "You've helped me out of many a jam. Were you able to get an appointment at the doctor for him?"

"They worked us in at eleven o'clock." To cover her unease, Rosa turned away and switched on an ancient radio that had sat on the same shelf for decades. After a rumble of static, she found a local station playing Belle and Sebastian, and then got to work.

Rosa went into the den and surveyed the area. She visited her father all the time. She'd stepped over piles

of clutter, but it had never occurred to her that Pop was
having serious problems. As time went by, his careless-
ness had increased, but Rosa hadn't thought anything of
it. She wanted to cry but refused to allow herself the
luxury. She didn't deserve to cry. She was a Bad
Daughter.

In the past twenty-four hours, since Joey had
declared the Emperor naked and forced her out of her
cocoon of denial, she had faced facts. Her father was
in trouble and she hadn't allowed herself to admit it.
She'd been so wrapped up in the restaurant and her
own life that she'd ignored what was going on right
under her nose.

She hadn't said anything to him. Yet. This morning,
she let herself into the house and announced that she was
going to do some cleaning and sorting. He'd waved her
in, completely indifferent. Linda insisted on joining her
and tackling the more obvious things. Rosa knew she
could have engaged the restaurant's cleaning service,
but thought better of it; this was her penance.

She had arranged to take off an entire day and night
from the restaurant, leaving Vince in charge. It was
perhaps the third time she'd been absent from Celesta's.
Joey was at work, and Pop was out puttering in his
garden, where the tomato bushes were heavy with fruit
starting to ripen and the dahlias were bursting into bloom.
From time to time, Rosa would glance out the window.
The sight of him, bent over a plant or snipping a flower
to tuck into the brim of his hat, filled her heart. He was
everything to her, and she was eaten alive by guilt.

She spent a solid hour putting things in the trash—
junk mail, wrappers, used plastic bags he'd saved for no
apparent purpose, rusty paper clips and thumb tacks,
empty mason jars. The desk was covered with papers—

more circulars and junk mail, mostly, but she also found packets of unopened bank statements, personal correspondence and…bills. The power company, the gas company, subscription services. Some were stamped Final Notice.

Her first inclination was to sit down and pay the bills. That wouldn't solve the problem, though. The issue was deeper than that. She went out back, noticing as she passed through the kitchen that Linda had it gleaming already and was applying primer to the ring on the ceiling. Rosa caught her father's attention and showed him the envelopes. "Pop," she said, "you've been forgetting to pay your bills."

He glanced at one of them, postmarked six weeks before. "Put them on the desk. I'll take care of them tonight."

"They were on the desk. Pop, you're worrying me. You seem to be forgetting a lot of things."

"What, forgetting?" He waved a hand in annoyance. "I've been busy."

"But, Pop—" Rosa stopped herself and glanced at her watch. "There's no time to argue. We need to get to your appointment."

"What appointment? I don't have any appointment."

"Yes, you do. As of eleven o'clock this morning. Dr. Chandler says you haven't been in to see him in three years. Three years, Pop. That's nuts."

"He charges a hundred fifty for a lousy office visit. I feel fine. I don't need to see any doctor."

"But I need you to." She took his arm. "*Please.* For me. Just to shut me up."

He glared at her, and for a moment she was afraid he'd refuse. Then his gaze softened. "You worry too much." He smiled and placed a kiss on the top of her head. "I'll go, then. Just to shut you up."

* * *

Dr. Chandler's office was adjacent to South County Hospital, and Rosa perfectly understood her father's reluctance. This was where they'd brought Mamma for her treatments, and they would forever associate this place with gloomy, excruciating futility. Years later, Pop had been taken to the emergency ward here after his accident, and Rosa's memories of that time were streaked with the violent horror of nightmares.

Today's appointment took much longer than it should have. She read *Rhode Island* magazine, *Newsweek* and *Women's Day*. She was trying to decide between *Parents* and *Highlights for Children* when she realized she couldn't remember a single thing she'd read. The wait was too nerve-racking. She stood and went to the window, looking out across the tree-shaded hospital lawn, the busy parking lot.

Everything was such a mess. A few times, she took out her cell phone to call Sal or Rob, but resisted. No sense worrying them, too, until she knew exactly what they were dealing with. She didn't allow herself to call the restaurant, either. Vince always got ticked off when she tried to micromanage while he was supposed to be in charge.

There was always Alex, of course. She could call him. Since he'd told her his suspicions about their parents, she'd only seen him once, last night when she needed help finding Joey. Alex needed to know he was completely wrong about her father. Best to tell him in person, she decided, tucking the phone away.

By the time Pop came shuffling back to the waiting room, Rosa was frantic. "What?" she demanded.

"We're supposed to wait."

"Wait for what?"

"He sent samples to the hospital lab and put a rush on them. He wants us to wait here for the results."

Rosa's heart pounded with dread. Lab tests usually took a few days. She wondered why there was such a rush. It couldn't mean anything good. The last thing Pop needed was to see her fall apart, though. She sat down and patted the seat beside her. "How do you feel?"

"Fine. I was fine when you dragged me here," he grumbled. "I swear, when you got nothing to worry about, you think of something." There was a twinkle in his eye as he patted her knee. "Your mother was always worrying. You're just like her."

She put her hand over his. "I hope so." Impulsively she asked him something others had asked him many times before, but for Rosa, it was a first. "Pop, why didn't you ever marry again?"

He didn't answer right away, but stared across the waiting room, out the window. A courier came in and dropped off a box with the receptionist.

"I was a good husband to your mother," Pop said. "I would not be a good husband to another woman. It would not be fair, because I gave everything I had to my first marriage. Love is like that for some people."

It was a lovely, mournful sentiment, Rosa thought. Maybe it was true for her, too. Maybe that was why she'd never really gotten over Alex.

Dr. Chandler came to the door, a file folder in hand. "Mr. Capoletti? Would you and your daughter step into my office, please?"

She nearly hyperventilated on the short walk down the hall. The office was contrived to look homey and warm, with mahogany shelves and plush chairs, but to Rosa, it felt like a prison cell. Dr. Chandler motioned for them to sit down.

"I'm glad you came in," he said. "The reason I rushed the lab was that I hoped we might be dealing with a fairly simple matter here." He leaned back in his chair and smiled. "Turns out we are. It's a pretty severe vitamin deficiency, completely treatable."

Rosa slumped with relief. "A vitamin deficiency?" She turned to her father. "Did you catch that?"

He nodded, his eyes bright with tears. For the first time, Rosa realized he'd been as petrified as she.

"Your neurological changes—the numbness and tingling in your hands and feet, difficulty maintaining balance, digestive upsets—are classic symptoms of vitamin B-12 deficiency. You've had some other symptoms, too, the fatigue, confusion and poor memory."

Rosa dug herself even deeper into guilt. How could she not have noticed all those symptoms? "My father doesn't have a poor diet," she said. Then she turned to him. "Do you, Pop?"

"My diet's fine," he stated.

"That could well be," said the doctor, "but you have a helicobacter infection. It blocks B-12 absorption. Fortunately the treatment's simple—a course of antibiotics. Once we eliminate the infection, the symptoms will go away."

Rosa looked at her father to make sure he understood. He nodded. "You'll write me a prescription, then."

"Right away. This infection can lead to ulcers, so you'll want to take the whole course. In ten days, you'll be good as new."

In the now-immaculate kitchen, Linda greeted them. "I got a huge shock changing a lightbulb upstairs," she said.

Rosa nudged her father. "I thought you were going to get the wiring checked. You promised."

"I'm gonna do that next week, all right?"

"Pop—" She heard a car in the driveway. "Someone's here."

She and Pop went around the side of the house to see a silver Miata and a white Explorer parked at the curb. Alex Montgomery and a strange woman with a small dog both arrived at the same time. She watched her father's face and caught the exact moment he spotted Alex.

"Son of a bitch," he said under his breath.

Given what Alex believed about her father, she couldn't figure out why he would come here. The short, heavyset woman looked vaguely familiar, but Rosa couldn't place her. The woman set the little dog down and it ran straight for Pop. It was a terrier mix, brown and white with a clownish face. Pop regarded it in confusion.

"Hello, Rosa," Alex said with a slightly formal air. "Mr. Capoletti," he said, nodding to her father. "This is Hollis Underwood and Jake. Hollis is with Paws for Ability."

Rosa got it right away. She looked at her father to see if he realized what Alex had brought. Pop was glaring at Alex with deep dislike. Hollis scooped up the prancing dog and stepped in front of Pop so he didn't miss what she was saying. "I'm a friend of the Montgomerys from way back," she said. "Alex thought you might want to see what an assistance dog can offer."

"I don't need any dog," Pop said stolidly, watching the squirming, exuberant terrier, which strained toward him, licking frantically.

"Jake is a rescue dog," Hollis said, then set him down again so she could sign as she spoke. "We found him when he was a puppy, and he's just completed his training as a signal dog. He's ready for adoption if we can find the right home for him." Without asking permission, she headed for the back door, then turned to address him. "Let's go inside and I'll show you some of the things he's trained to do."

To Rosa's amazement, Pop went along with her. She could hear Linda greeting them and exclaiming over the dog. Stunned, she turned to Alex at last. "What the hell is going on?"

"How about 'Hello, Alex'? Or 'How are you, Alex?' Or 'Thanks for helping me find Joey last night'? Or, here's a thought, 'Sorry I ditched you after dragging you out of bed'?"

"Are you finished?"

He laughed. "I'm just getting started."

"What are you doing here? What's up with the dog lady?"

"Joey said your dad might be able to use some help," he said simply.

Offended pride rose up inside her. Joey had a big mouth. "It wasn't his job to tell you."

"No. He decided to do that on his own."

"It's none of your damned business."

"Maybe not." He jerked his head in the direction of the house across the way, where Mrs. Fortinski just happened to be watering her plants in an open window. "Is it the neighbors'?"

Rosa lowered her voice. "You have a terrible opinion of my father. Why would you try to help him?"

"This is for you. If training with an assistance dog helps your father out, then it helps you out."

She hated that logic. She hated any logic that worked against her. "He won't go for it. He's never had a dog, or even a cat or goldfish. It's not his style." She realized they were talking around the real issue. "I told him what you said, Alex. He categorically denies what you said about him and your mother."

"Of course he does."

"He said she called him that night, and he went to see her because she seemed…upset."

"Drunk, you mean."

"I'm sorry, Alex."

"Sorry? Sorry for what?"

"The thing you should remember and hold on to is that she didn't do…what you've thought all these years. I'm sure she believed she was doing what's best for you. And if you want to change your mind and take that dog home, I'll understand."

"I won't change my mind. And thank you for…what you just said."

That night in her apartment, he'd told her plenty about the past. Yet now it occurred to Rosa that the biggest thing he was holding back was the way he felt about his mother's suicide.

Which was probably the most important thing for her to know. "Alex—"

"I need to go. I've got some papers to file at the court-house." Then he did the unthinkable. He bent down, kissed her lightly on the cheek and said, "See you, sweetheart."

She felt like she was on fire as she followed him out to the truck. "Just a doggone minute."

He stopped on the front sidewalk, keys in hand. "Now what?"

"You kissed me and I wasn't ready."

"You are now." Without warning, he kissed her again, this time full on the mouth.

Across the way, there was a splat as Mrs. Fortenski misfired with her watering can.

"And that's just for starters," Alex said, releasing her.

Then he strolled to his truck, waving as he pulled away from the curb.

"Well, well, well," said Linda, bringing a black plastic bag out to the curb for garbage day. "Alex the wonder boy strikes again."

"He kissed me," she said, wondering if the neighbor got a snapshot.

"You don't say. Should I dial 911?"

"Come on, Linda."

"Come where? The guy is crazy about you, Rosa. Why not relax and enjoy it?"

"Because I don't trust him," she blurted out.

"And you don't trust yourself with him."

Rosa bit her lip. "I simply don't see the point of getting involved with Alex Montgomery."

"Why does there have to be a point? Just be with him. See where it goes."

"I'm not letting it go anywhere."

"Then you're an idiot."

"No, I'm protecting myself."

"You've been doing that for years. Don't you think it's time to let him in?"

"For what?"

"Rosa, if nothing else, for the sex. You don't get laid nearly enough."

"How do you know how often I get laid?"

"Maybe you should lower your voice," Linda said, nodding toward the neighbors' window.

Rosa threw up her hands and headed for the house. She and Linda stepped inside just in time to see Jake sniffing the mail on the floor under the slot.

Linda frowned. "What the—"

"Hush," said Rosa. "Watch him."

The dog paused to look at them for a moment, then

went back to the mail. He managed to pick up a mouthful of envelopes along with a grocery circular and a catalog; then he trotted off with them.

Rosa and Linda followed the dog to the den, where Pop sat in his easy chair. Hollis sat quietly observing. She said nothing when Rosa and Linda showed up, but motioned for them to wait and watch. The dog dropped the mail and went back for more, twice. After three trips, all the mail lay beside Pop's chair. The dog gently lifted up on his hind legs and brushed his front paws with gentle insistence against the cuff of Pop's pants.

He picked up his mail and said to Hollis, "He did good."

"Remember what I said—reward him."

Pop bent and patted the dog on the head. "Good boy," he murmured. "Good Jake."

Hollis nodded approvingly. "Well done, both of you."

"Now, how can I get him to pay the bills for me?"

She laughed. "That's not in his job description, but there's a lot more to learn. Jake knows forty commands. He can alert you to bells, alarms and timers, dropped objects. And if your computer makes a sound when you get mail, he can tell you about that, too."

"No kidding."

Rosa was amazed. Pop readily claimed he didn't like dogs. Too many of his clients had ill-behaved pets that ruined gardens and soiled yards. She stepped into the room. "So you like that dog, Pop?" she asked.

"Yeah. A dog's a big responsibility, though."

"You don't have to make a commitment right away," Hollis said. "We need to be sure you and Jake are compatible. There are forms to fill out, a visit from a social worker. Then the training begins." She paused, and Jake did, too. He tilted his head to one side, watching Pop with total absorption. "So what do you say, Mr. Capoletti? You up for it?"

He looked right back at Jake. "How else am I going to learn?"

"This is how it works?" Rosa asked Hollis.

"Yes," said Hollis, watching as Jake sprang into Pop's lap and settled into the crook of his arm. "That's how it works."

Thirty-Five

Alex awakened to the crunch of car tires on gravel. Damn, he thought. What time was it? According to the antique clock on the wall, 6:30 a.m.

Then he remembered with a groan of misery. Portia van Deusen had called to say she was on her way to the Newport Jazz Festival; she planned to drop off some of his stuff. But why would she do it herself rather than sending someone? And why at this hour?

Two things came to mind. She was best friends with Hollis Underwood, who had probably filled her in about Rosa. And Portia must still be mad at him about the broken engagement. Let her be, he thought. She'd brought it on herself, even though he'd agreed to let everyone believe she had dumped him and not the other way around. Only Gina Colombo, his assistant, knew what had really happened.

Yawning and scratching his chest, he went to the window, squinting at the white sunlight streaming in.

He paused in mid-yawn and mid-scratch when he recognized his visitor, and his scowl changed to a smile. Rosa was rummaging in the trunk of her car, and emerged with a large wicker basket covered with a red-and-white checkered cloth. She wore a red polka dot halter top, red clamdiggers, gold hoop earrings, big sunglasses and ruby- colored finger- and toenails. The adult-entertainment version of Red Riding Hood.

"Oh, man," he said and ducked into the bathroom. There, he stuck a toothbrush in his mouth and rolled it around while simultaneously splashing water on his face. No time to shave. Then he stepped into the nearest presentable clothes—a pair of swim trunks. He finished brushing, grabbed his Red Sox T-shirt from a hook behind the door and sniffed. Not too bad. He tugged it on over his head, then finger-combed his hair as he went downstairs to answer the door.

Rosa looked as fresh as a flower, standing there, smiling up at him. "I hope I didn't wake you," she said.

He stifled another yawn. "Not at all." He held open the door for her. "I make it a point to get up at 6:30 in the morning when I'm on vacation."

"Liar," she said, marching past him with the basket. Something inside it smelled incredible, and he followed the fragrance into the kitchen.

"Wow," she said, "you've been busy." She checked out the paint job on the wainscoting, the newly sanded and sealed floors, the painted cabinets.

"Until 1:00 a.m. every day," he said.

"I would have called first," she said, "but it was too early and I didn't want to wake you."

He didn't even try sorting out her logic. "Rosa, what's going on?"

"A picnic," she announced, putting a handful of napkins into the basket. "A breakfast picnic, to be exact. We used to do this when we were kids, remember?"

Hell, yes, he remembered.

In the basket, he spotted a thermos of coffee and some rolls that were still steaming hot. "Couldn't we just eat it here?"

"Then it wouldn't be a picnic."

"But it would be breakfast." He had worked like a dog yesterday, and now that he was awake, he was starving.

"That's not the point," she said and looked up at him brightly. "Ready?"

He was physically incapable of saying no to this woman, or to food on any terms. Besides, he wanted to know what she was up to. The presence of food was a good sign. Maybe this was a peace offering. He offered a sleepy smile and picked up the basket. "Yeah. Lead on, McDuff."

They went out the back and across the yard, which over the years had lost its spectacular lushness. Alex couldn't help noticing the way Rosa's tight red pants, cropped off just below the knee, hugged the finest ass he'd ever seen. Jennifer Lopez only aspired to have a butt like this.

"You're awfully quiet," she remarked.

He cleared his throat. "Still waking up. Do you do this often?"

"Nearly every day. I get up early, I mean. If I don't, the day is shot by midmorning. That's when I head over to the restaurant."

His gaze lingered on her a moment longer. "Sleep deprivation agrees with you."

She slowed her pace and looked over her shoulder at him. "You think?"

"No question."

They walked along the ancient path, which was overgrown by brambles and beach roses. "No one ever comes here," she said. "No one ever has except—" She broke off and brushed a branch out of her way.

"Except us," he finished for her.

People flocked to the beaches that had parking and easy access. But he had always preferred this all but inaccessible piece of paradise. This was remote, a world apart, the dunes bordered by an ancient, half-collapsed wooden fence with sand blown up against its base. There was no gate but a gap where the fence was down, and Rosa stepped through and along the slope toward the beach. The newly risen sun spread a glow of benediction across the water.

Alex loved the feeling of privacy and privilege it gave him. He'd been a lot of places but none had ever quite matched the beach of his boyhood. There was a feeling of serenity here, of belonging. He wondered if Rosa understood how much she was a part of that, how important she'd been to the person he had become. He had never told her that, but he suspected he would one of these days, soon.

"How about here?" She indicated a spot on the sand.

"I've got a better idea," he said, walking past the spot and moving closer to the water's edge in the shadow of a huge rock. It was, he believed, the exact spot where they'd made love the first and only time. "How about here?"

She looked him straight in the eye. "Here is fine."

They spread out the checked tablecloth and he opened the basket. Rosa set out the feast she'd brought—mascarpone and hot rolls whose fragrance had been teasing him all during the walk, a wedge of melon and something in a plastic container.

"Coffee?" She held up the thermos.

"Bless you. I take it black."

"I know. That's how you ordered it at the restaurant." He took a sip. "You have a good memory."

She smiled at him over the rim of her coffee cup. "Hungry?"

"Starved."

"You'll like this," she said, setting out two plates. She served a frittata, a savory egg dish with herbs and cheese.

Alex ate in silent ecstasy, plowing through two helpings of frittata, three rolls slathered with creamy mascarpone and half the melon. "You're incredible," he said.

"I know," she said, sitting back and admiring the sunrise. "It's a gift." She lifted her cup in his direction. "Aren't you going to ask me why I went to all this trouble?"

"Because you're trying to seduce me," he said with a grin. "And congratulations, it's working."

"Dream on."

"Believe me, I do. Actually, I was curious, but I didn't want you to change your mind and take it all away."

"I've never taken food away from a person in my life," she said. "It's to thank you for the dog." Her voice trembled with emotion. "You see, my father never will."

Nor did Alex want his thanks. Ever. But Rosa's gratitude he would take, any day of the week. "So it's working out?"

"Yes. Your friend Hollis is truly a miracle worker."

"She's pretty incredible."

"She was such a snot when she was younger," Rosa said.

"People change," he reminded her.

She pulled her knees up to her chest. "In just a few days, that dog changed his life. I feel guilty for not coming up with this on my own long ago."

"He probably wouldn't have agreed to it long ago."

"I was pretty upset when I found out Joey told you about my father's troubles."

"I wish someone would have spoken up about my

mother's troubles," he blurted out before he could stop himself.

"Oh, Alex." Her hand trembled a little as she touched his face. Rosa had the unique power to coax emotion from him. He didn't know why he sought it out, except that it felt so real, unlike so many other things in his life.

She took off her sunglasses and watched his face. "In a horrible way," she said softly, "I was lucky to lose Mamma when I did. I'm sure she was a flawed human being, just like everyone else, but I was too little to see her flaws. Now when I remember her, she's a saint."

"Your point being, of course, that I had the misfortune to know my mother's flaws."

"Go ahead and get defensive. I'm not backing down. And that wasn't misfortune. It was life. I suppose, if I'd known my mother longer, I would have known a more realistic picture. God, what I wouldn't give to have her right here with me now, warts and all. You had thirty years with your mother. I envy that."

"And you had a mother you regard as a saint. I envy *that*."

She paused. He felt the tension straining between them.

"I wonder, Alex… Have you thought about seeing someone…a psychologist?"

"It's a waste of time. I know damned well what my issues are." He forced a smile. "This day started out so well."

"I didn't come here intending to bring up your mother, but she's always there. She always will be so long as you refuse to deal with what happened."

"Spare me the New Age homilies," he said, then added, "please. I'm desperate here, Rosa. We need to change the subject."

A smile flickered across her mouth and he felt the

tension ease. "This is not turning out the way I'd planned," she said.

"How is it supposed to turn out?"

"I wanted to bring you a delicious breakfast and sincerely thank you for helping my father, not upset you."

"I'm not upset," he said. "I swear it." To prove his point, he ate a third helping of frittata and finished off the orange juice. "Honestly," he said, "this is the most pleasant breakfast I've ever had. Ever."

"Really?"

"A beautiful sunrise, a beautiful woman, a meal fit for the gods." If he could do this every day, he would never want another thing in life. And he hadn't even had sex with her. Yet.

He covered her hand with his. "Could you please pass the melon?"

She got a little skittish then and took her hand away. "Sure."

Though he wasn't really hungry anymore, he ate some and smiled at her. "When you feed me," he said, "it's like you're coming on to me."

"Oh, please. I feed a hundred forty seatings a night." But she blushed. He could see that immediately.

"Not like this," he said, leaning back on his elbows and crossing his legs at the ankles. He patted his now-supremely-satisfied belly.

"Alex," she said.

"Mmm?"

"What are you thinking about?"

He put his hand on her thigh. "Having sex with you."

She scooted away from him on the blanket. "That's asking for trouble."

"Come on, Rosa. It's asking for the next natural step. There's nothing standing in our way."

"Except ourselves. Oh, not to mention our friends, families and lives. It can't work out for the same reason it didn't work out the first time. The world won't go away and leave us alone, Alex."

He edged closer to her. "Fine with me. Then let's go away and leave the world behind."

"That's just it. I'm not a jet-setter. I don't want to be anywhere but here."

"You know, just because it isn't easy doesn't mean we shouldn't be in love."

"You need more coffee." She refilled his cup, her hand unsteady. "Now, run that by me again. It's too early in the morning to decipher triple negatives."

"I want a second chance with you, Rosa. That's all I'm saying." He set aside the cup, then touched her cheek and let his fingers wander into her hair.

"I thought you were saying something about sex."

"Well, that, too," he admitted. "That comes with the second chance."

She took a cube of melon, closing her lips around it provocatively before popping it in her mouth. "You're saying you want to have sex with me."

"Of course I do. Who wouldn't?"

"Alex!"

"Sorry. I mean that as a compliment. You're hot."

"And you want me because I'm hot?"

"Actually, I'd want you even if you looked like a ling cod," he said, then quickly backpedaled. "I mean, you don't, but even if you did—ah, shit." He abandoned talk, grabbed her and pulled her against him. Before she could push him away, he kissed her long and hard, the way he'd been wanting to ever since finding her again.

Kisses had been invented for moments like this, when words failed but there was still so much to say. Her mouth was cool and sweet from the watermelon, and she felt perfect in his arms.

When he pulled back, she looked a little dazed, her eyes unfocused and her mouth slightly puckered. Another good sign. "I guess," she whispered, "I'm on board with the idea."

"With what idea?"

"Sex. Isn't that what we're talking about?"

"Oh, yeah," he said, pressing her back on the blanket.

She twisted away from him. "I didn't mean here. It's broad daylight."

"I thought all that changed with Vatican II."

She glared at him. "Not funny, Alex."

"Well, I don't think it's funny to offer me sex and then change your mind."

"I didn't offer," she said. "You asked."

"And you said okay."

"Did I?"

"No, actually you said 'I'm on board with the idea,' which sounded like okay to me, until you started making it conditional—"

"Of course it's conditional," she said. "All sex is." She put the picnic things away in the basket. "Everything about this is complicated. After all that's happened, I just don't see how this can work."

"It's simple, Rosa, but maybe you're scared to try."

"We're from two different worlds. Our friends don't get along. Our families can't stand each other. They never have and never will."

"I don't want to have sex with them. Just you."

He was rewarded with an amused twitch of her mouth, which he probably wasn't supposed to see.

"Well?" he said.

"We're both adults now. We know how to set limits."

We know how to get past them, he thought.

"Whatever the lady wants," he said, and got up to help her fold the tablecloth.

It was a start, at least. She really believed she could keep her emotional distance, even now. Alex grinned as he led the way back to the house by the sea. In some ways, he knew her better than she knew herself.

Savory Frittata

Always use naturally nested eggs laid by uncaged chickens. The eggs taste better, and the chickens will thank you.

4 medium potatoes, scrubbed and diced fine
6 large, fresh eggs
1/4 cup cream
3/4 cup chopped tomatoes
1 small zucchini, grated
1/4 sweet onion, chopped
1 Tablespoon minced herbs, including oregano, thyme, flat-leaf parsley, red pepper flakes, garlic
2 Tablespoons olive oil + 1 Tablespoon sweet butter
salt and pepper to taste
1 cup shredded cheese

In a wide ovenproof skillet, grill the potatoes in olive oil and butter until browned. Add zucchini and onions, then tomatoes and herbs. Season with salt and pepper. Whisk the eggs together with cream and pour the mixture over potatoes. Sprinkle on the cheese. Bake at 400°F degrees for 25 minutes or until top is firm. Serve in wedges warm, or at room temperature.

Thirty-Six

―⤜⧓⤛―

Alex had become a fast walker, Rosa reflected as she followed him back to his house, taking two steps for every one of his. He seemed to be in a particular hurry this morning.

In the kitchen, he set the basket on the counter. She went to the sink to start washing things but he stopped her, trapping her between him and the counter and turning her to face him.

"Alex, I—"

He interrupted her with a kiss, and it was like the one on the beach, the one that had melted her bones. When he came up for air, it was all she could do to keep her wits about her. "I'd better go," she said.

"Let's go upstairs," he whispered.

She pushed against his chest but it was like a warm, immovable wall. "I don't think so."

"You just said we were going to have sex."

Oh, God. She had, hadn't she?

"I meant…maybe at some unspecified point in the future…after we discuss it some more."

"I like this point." He smiled down at her.

He took her breath away—ocean-blue eyes, aristocratic features, lips she dreamed about, even though she'd never admit it. Everything inside her leaped up to say no, but when she was finally able to speak, what came out of her was "All right."

Upstairs in the big house, she stood face-to-face with him in an expansive, sun-flooded room with gleaming plank floors and a high antique bed, its linens looking deliciously rumpled, as though they still held his scent. She had the urge to dive headfirst into the bed. He kissed her again, backing her up against a bedpost and cupping her hips in both hands.

She turned her head to whisper, "This isn't what I came here for."

"Sometimes—" he touched her chin and brought her mouth back to his "—you just get a bonus."

His kisses made her lose track of time, of herself, of everything. He unhooked her top and undid the tie behind her neck. The look on his face made her feel like a goddess, and in that moment, she was a goner. And he was right. She *had* come here for this. With a sigh of surrender, she kissed him hard, hungrily, finally giving in to an urge that had been building all summer long. They left their clothes tangled together in a heap on the floor. He pressed her down on the bed and her hair fanned out on the pillow. She arched upward, reaching to pull him against her. She felt light-headed, barely able to think except for one thing that rang clear in her head. There were some things that simply didn't change and never would. And one of them was that each time Alex Montgomery held her in his arms and kissed her, it was like coming home.

Rosa didn't sleep or dream, but she drifted, there in his arms in the rumpled bed with the sun streaming over their entwined bodies. With her cheek pressed to his chest, she listened to the heavy thud of his heart. She didn't want to think or talk or plan anything, and that was so unlike her. Somewhere a vintage clock clicked quietly, but she lost track of time and didn't stir until she sensed a subtle twitching in his chest and raised her head to look at him.

"It's nothing," he said, leaning over to rifle in the drawer of the bedside table. He took out an inhaler and put it to his mouth. Three deep breaths and a smile.

"You're sure?" she said.

"Absolutely." He curled a lock of her hair around his finger. "Any more questions?"

"Mmm-mmm." She stretched like a cat, her gaze drifting lazily around the room at the beautiful wainscoting, richly detailed and dark with a patina of age. The windowpanes had the wavy, brittle quality of old glass. This was such a fine house. She couldn't believe he was getting rid of it. If this place was hers, she would stay here forever, filling the rooms with cut flowers, working in the kitchen with its view of the sea.

Rosa realized that they were already starting to relate to one another in silence, in the way of lovers, with their own nonverbal signals. They spoke without words, read each other's moods. Whether she admitted it aloud or not, they were acting like a couple. A very intimate couple.

A cell phone rang and Alex groaned. "Ignore it."

"It might be my father," she said, sitting up and grabbing her handbag.

Alex reached for the bedside table. "Or mine," he said and scowled into the display. "Hello, Dad."

Rosa tugged the sheet up under her armpits. Nothing like a call from a parent to dampen the mood.

"I understand," Alex said. His face was completely neutral. "Maybe another time, Dad."

Jerk, thought Rosa, wishing Alex's father could see the disappointment in his son's eyes.

"I haven't heard from Maddie, either," he said into the phone. "Last week, there was an e-mail from Taipei. I'm sure she'll check in with you when they get to a place that has cell phone service…. Yes, all right. Bye." He set down the phone and immediately slipped his arms around Rosa. "Sorry about that. Change of dinner plans tonight."

"Your sister's in Taipei?"

"Was. I think she might be in Mongolia now. She decided to show her kids the Far East. Her way of dealing with the tragedy," he explained, "in true Montgomery style. My father would probably do the same, except that the firm seems to be a more satisfactory distraction."

"I wish the two of you were closer," Rosa said.

"Yeah? Why?"

"There's such a…I don't quite know how to put it. A richness in being close, such a sense of security. That's how it's been for me, anyway."

"You're lucky, then. It's different between my father and me. I don't know how to explain our relationship, but 'sense of security' doesn't really fit the situation."

"It should."

"He always considered me a disappointment. When I was little, I was too sick for him to bother with, and when I got older, I distanced myself from him on purpose."

"Yet you went to work for his firm." She studied his eyes, troubled and hurting, and knew there was more to this relationship than mutual disregard. "You should fix things with him, Alex. I mean it. It's important. Things aren't as bad as you think. Have you ever asked him what he thinks of you, your relationship?"

He laughed. "It would never occur to either of us to talk about our relationship."

"And that's funny?"

"It's just not something we would ever do."

"Well, I bet what he truly thinks would surprise you."

"Then why is it such a secret?"

"Maybe because he doesn't really know how to show his feelings for you."

"It's never been hard for him to show disapproval. That's a feeling."

"I bet he thinks the world of you and just doesn't know how to express it."

He smiled and kissed her temple. "You're always ready to believe the best in people."

"You should, too, when it comes to your own father. You believed something terrible about your mother and it turned out not to be true." She studied his face but couldn't tell if he believed it or not. The distant clock chimed, and after the ninth ring, Rosa sat straight up, clutching the sheets against her chest. "Damn it!"

"What?" Alex propped himself on his elbows.

"I have to go." She jumped up and started getting dressed. "I scheduled a meeting fifteen minutes from now."

"Aw, come on. Skip it."

"Can't. We're doing the final menu for Linda's wedding. Her mother-in-law-to-be made a special trip just for this."

"God, what I wouldn't give to steal you away," he said, wrapping his arms around her. "Far, far away."

Rosa reveled in his embrace. She wondered if he knew

she'd follow him anywhere. If he asked her to move to New York, to London, to Hong Kong or Taipei or Mongolia, she would do it. She would walk away from everything she knew and everything she loved, because she loved Alex more.

Frightened and exhilarated by the thought, she grabbed her purse and rummaged for a hairbrush, managing to dump her wallet, PDA, cell phone and sunglasses in the process. "Damn it," she said again.

"Hang on," Alex said with resignation. "I'll help you." He pulled on his shorts and took the brush from her hand. "The world won't come to an end just because you're late to a meeting." With slow, rhythmic strokes, he brushed her hair for her.

She shut her eyes and dropped her head back, reveling in the searing intimacy of his touch. "That feels good."

"This whole morning has felt good."

"Remember the time you cut off my hair?"

He finished brushing, then bent and kissed her neck. "I remember everything."

She wanted to linger, but she broke away and began stuffing things back into her purse. "I really have to go."

The sound of a car door slamming came from below. She frowned. "Are you expecting someone?"

He looked a bit sick. Maybe an asthma attack was coming on. "Actually…"

"You need to sit down," she said. "I'll go tell whoever it is you're not feeling well." She hurried down the stairs.

He followed, yanking on his T-shirt and saying, "I'm okay, Rosa, but there's something—"

The front door opened and a tall, slender woman walked in carrying a large cardboard box. "Alex," she yelled, "Alex, I need some help with—oh." She set down the box with a thud.

It was Portia van Deusen, Alex's ex-fiancée. She recognized her from photographs—imposing and self-confident, with patrician features and designer clothes.

Portia's cool gray-eyed glare locked on Rosa as Alex made hasty introductions. "Portia is dropping off some things of mine," he explained.

"He left them in my apartment," Portia said. "We were engaged."

"I know," Rosa managed to admit. She had never suffered such a hideously awkward moment.

"We're not anymore," Alex pointed out.

"The rest of the stuff is in the back of the Land Rover," Portia said.

Grumbling, he headed outside.

"I was just on my way out," said Rosa. "I've got a meeting at work." This was too weird. She went to the door, eager to get out of there.

"Did he tell you why?" Portia asked suddenly.

Rosa froze with her hand on the doorknob. "Pardon me?"

"Why we broke up. Did he tell you?"

"Actually he's never mentioned you at all." Rosa felt evil as soon as the words were out of her mouth. Portia didn't deserve that.

She flipped back her silky hair. "He'd probably lie anyway. The truth is, he dumped me when I was pregnant with his child, and I miscarried."

Rosa nearly lost her frittata. "Oh, God…I'm terribly sorry." She looked across the driveway at Alex, who was pulling cardboard boxes out of the Land Rover. Dear Lord, was he capable of that? "I don't know what else to say. Please, excuse me," she said to Portia, and all but ran to her car.

Alex put aside the box he was carrying. "Rosa, I'm

sorry. I knew she was coming, but I didn't think she'd get here so early." He studied her face. "Damn it. What did she say to you?"

Rosa couldn't even find the words. "I'm late, Alex."

He held open her car door. "I'll call you later."

"I really need to go." She bit her lip, trying to think of what else to say, but there was no time to sort things out. Besides, she wasn't sure she wanted to. If she sorted things out with him, she might have to deal with the truth—that she was falling in love with him, all over again.

She turned the key in the ignition and took off.

Thirty-Seven

Alex watched the love of his life take off, the top down on her red sports car, a white scarf covering her dark hair. She *was* the love of his life, and if there had ever been any doubt about that, there was not now. He knew with perfect clarity that they were meant to be together.

He wished she'd stuck around so he could explain about Portia. He vowed not to let the sun go down on this issue.

Swearing under his breath, he picked up a cardboard box of odds and ends—a basketball, some paperback novels, old CDs. "You should have thrown this stuff away," he said to Portia, setting the box on the porch. "You didn't have to go to this trouble."

"I wanted to see you."

He spread his arms wide and echoed something Rosa had once said to him. "Look your fill." He retrieved the last box from her Land Rover. "Thanks for bringing my stuff. Now, I've got work to do."

"The least you could do is offer me a cup of coffee."

"No, the least I could do is tell you I'm busy and so long."

Her eyes glittered with tears. "I miss you, Alex. Can't we just talk about getting back together?"

He felt a twinge in his chest. She was a piece of work, but he didn't enjoy hurting her. "No. We can't. Drive carefully."

She wiped the tears away with the back of her hand. "You won't be happy with that woman," she snapped. "Yes, Hollis told me all about her."

Great, he thought. Portia was like a bad fairy come to put a curse on his new connection with Rosa.

"She's not for you, Alex, and you'll find that out for yourself soon enough."

Like I found out about you? He didn't let himself say it aloud. He wasn't blameless in their fiasco of a relationship. He'd drifted into it thoughtlessly and hadn't bothered to figure out whether or not they were right for each other. His mother had been ecstatic, of course; she adored the van Deusens and couldn't wait for the nuptials. Neither, it seemed, could Portia. Alex had escaped by the skin of his teeth.

She stalked to her car and peeled out, spraying up gravel and crushed shells in her wake.

Alex went inside and shut the door, feeling a distinct twitchiness in his lungs. He took another puff on his inhaler and ran a hot shower. His docs put no store in the effects of warm steam, but it made him feel better.

As he was drying off, his cell phone chirped. Except that it wasn't his phone; the sound came from somewhere else. He followed it to the bed and found Rosa's phone in the tangle of bedclothes. The incoming call was from *Costello, Sean.* Alex frowned. The guy she'd dated, now the sheriff of South County. He didn't answer. It was none of his business, but it pointed up the fact that in so many ways, he and Rosa were still strangers.

At least, he thought, pulling on a golf shirt and clean shorts, he had an excuse to pay her a visit. He needed to see Rosa, to explain about Portia, to tell her it was going to be all right. *They* were going to be all right.

He would make sure of it, he thought as he sent a text message to her father. *We need to talk. Coming right over. Alex M.*

He loaded his pockets, then grabbed his inhaler, hesitated and stuck that in his pocket, too. Eager as he was to get to her, he had a stop to make on the way. Things wouldn't be right with her until he dealt with her father, one on one. Pete and Rosa were a package deal, and Alex intended to find a way to be all right with that.

Outside, the contractor's crew was just arriving. Repair and restoration on the carriage house seemed to be going well. He greeted the foreman, who was drinking Pegasus Coffee from a paper cup. "Good news, Mr. M," said the foreman. "We're going to finish on schedule. Just a few more weeks and we're done."

"That's great," said Alex. He got in his truck and headed inland, toward Pete's house. He felt like an awkward kid, vying for his girlfriend's dad's approval. But it had to happen, or he and Rosa didn't stand a chance.

When he turned the corner onto Prospect Street, Alex sensed something was amiss. He couldn't place it immediately. Then he looked up and his blood froze. There was black smoke streaming from a second-story window of Pete's house.

Even before his truck screeched to a stop by the curb he was thumbing 9-1-1 into his phone. There was an older lady standing on the sidewalk in front of the house.

"I called the fire department already," she said. "They're on their way."

Alex repeated the call and was told the ETA was

three minutes. And sure enough, in the distance, he heard sirens. "Is he at home?" he asked the neighbor. "Is anyone in there?"

"I don't know. I didn't want…I was afraid—"

He took the front steps two at a time, tried the door and found it unlocked. Smoke alarms shrilled and blinked uselessly into the dense gray air. A wave of heat and acrid smoke hit him.

"Pete!" he yelled. "Pete!" Pete couldn't hear him, of course, but the dog could; a distant barking sounded from somewhere upstairs.

Blinded, gagging on smoke, he checked the downstairs rooms and then made his way upstairs. The middle room, the one that had been Rosa's, was ablaze, blasting him with light and heat. Pete knelt in the hallway, beating the roaring flames with a towel. His face was red in the firelight, his eyes terrified.

"Jesus, Pete!" Alex grabbed the old man's sleeve. "I've got you," he yelled, holding on. "Where's Joey? Is he home? Joey," he repeated.

"At work," Pete yelled.

Alex gave him a tug. "Let's go."

"Jake," Pete protested, pulling back. "Still in there."

Oh, Jesus, thought Alex, hearing ominous pops and hisses as the fire gathered momentum. "Get out," he said. He grabbed Pete's face between his hands and added, "I'll get the dog."

"No—"

"Go!" Out of patience, Alex half shoved him down the stairs. He thought he heard the sound of sirens drawing close. Hurry up, he thought. Hurry the hell up.

The terrified dog had scampered to a corner of the burning room and was barking at the flames. His eyes streaming and his lungs convulsing, Alex plunged after him. "I've got you," he said. "Come to Papa." He grabbed the dog and held it like a football, whirling toward the exit. Flames surrounded the doorway now, and the hallway outside was a river of fire.

Alex couldn't remember the last time he'd taken a breath. He staggered toward the window. Through the curtain of flames, he saw Rosa's photographs, books, a shell collection on a shelf. The source of the fire was a ceiling fixture, now a flaming hole.

He couldn't open the window one-handed, and he refused to set down the squirming dog, so he stepped back and put his foot through the glass. Maybe the noise would alert the firefighters.

The infusion of fresh air fed the fire, and it roared like a dragon behind him. He kicked most of the glass from the frame. Just a few feet below the window was the porch roof. He ducked out the window and stood in the light, the graveled roof seeming to undulate beneath him, swaying as he fought for breath. Something trickled down his back; he'd probably cut himself getting out.

When he opened his eyes, he saw a ladder touching the eaves. A firefighter in full bunker gear appeared, his face masked, his hands gloved. Jake growled in fear.

"Boy, am I glad to see you," Alex gasped, moving toward the ladder. He was dizzy and wheezing. He felt himself sway and stumble on the slanted roof.

"Easy, fella," the firefighter said. "We'll get you down."

"Take the dog," Alex said, handing it to him. "I don't feel so good."

As soon as the dog was nestled securely in the firefighter's arms, Alex felt an invisible wave slam into him.

His eyes rolled up in his head, his bones collapsed and he felt himself falling.

Thirty-Eight

Somewhere in town, sirens and truck horns sounded, but Rosa barely noticed. All through the meeting, she had felt Linda's stare taking her apart, piece by piece. Vince seemed equally curious, but when she glared across the table at him, he rolled his eyes to the ceiling, all innocence. It was disconcerting to say the least, and she tried to ignore them during the meeting.

They were seated around a table in the bar, and the beautiful nautilus shell was directly in her line of vision. Morning sunlight caused its delicate inner whorls to glow as though lit from within, and the sight of it made her think of Alex and the way they had been together this morning…until Portia showed up.

Portia, she thought. Portia Schmortia.

Rosa could barely sit still. She was relieved at the conclusion when everyone seemed thrilled with the menu for the reception: tinker mackerel alla Santa Nicola, penne pasta with tomato, arugula and mozzarella, arancini, pizette, egg pasta with lobster and asparagus, Guinea hen stuffed with vegetables and a towering Italian cream cake. As the gathering broke up and people wandered toward the coffee, Rosa walked Mrs. Aspoll and Mrs. Lipschitz to the door.

"You don't know how much fun this is for me," Rosa told them, "being a part of Linda's wedding. It's just like we planned when we were kids."

Mrs. Lipschitz beamed at her. "I remember the two of you in my nightgowns, parading up and down the stairs with flowers from your father's garden. I hope you know Linda has instructions to toss the bouquet directly at you."

Rosa gave a nervous laugh. "Honestly, if I got engaged every time I caught a bouquet, I'd be J-Lo. It doesn't work on me."

"It will at Linda's wedding, and it's about time. I'm so happy for you, dear." Mrs. Lipschitz gave her a hug and left the restaurant.

Rosa was seriously ticked off as she went in search of Linda and found her with Vince, leaning in close as Linda spoke rapidly.

"What's going on?" Rosa demanded.

The conversation stopped. Gazes lowered and feet shuffled.

"What?" she asked.

Vince said, "We were just discussing your sex life."

Her cheeks began to burn. "I see. And what, may I ask, is the nature of this incredibly high-minded discussion of my…sex life?"

"Well, mainly that you finally have one again."

She swallowed hard. No wonder people tended to leave their home towns. If you stayed too long, privacy went out the window. "And how would you know that?"

"Hel*lo*," said Linda. "You practically rolled out of bed to get to this meeting. Even my mom could tell."

Unconsciously, Rosa touched her hair and wondered

feverishly if Alex had somehow marked or branded her in some visible way. "How is this your business?"

"We love you, Rosa, and we want to be sure you're not making a mistake."

"Whether or not I'm making a mistake is…" Rosa hesitated while stinging tears welled in her eyes. "It's too late. I've already made it." She covered her face with her hands. They pressed close, a human cocoon, murmuring with sympathy.

"What is it, honey?" Vince asked. "You can tell us. Don't keep it in."

"I ran into his ex," she said miserably, accepting a Kleenex from Linda. "She wanted me to know that he dumped her when she got pregnant with his child."

Linda gasped. "There's a child?"

"She miscarried."

"She's lying," said Vince. "I can smell it."

"Did you ask him?" Linda handed her another Kleenex.

"Yes. Well, no, not yet. It's not just that. We have bigger issues. Our values are so different. People like Alex and Portia van Deusen, they're a breed apart. They try on relationships like trendy outfits and discard them when they don't seem to fit anymore."

"And people like us don't do stuff like that?"

"*I* don't," said Rosa. "You should see that woman, Portia van Deusen. She's…perfect. Absolutely perfect. Beautiful, educated, stylish. She's everything a man like Alex needs, and he lost interest in her completely. When she was pregnant, no less. It makes me wonder how long he'd keep someone like me around."

"You're not her," said Vince.

"No. I'm shorter. Louder."

Linda burst out laughing. "And that matters?"

"Come on, Linda, you know better than that."

"Listen, don't judge his relationship with you by his relationships in the past."

"According to the most basic principles of psychology, past behavior is the single best indicator of future behavior."

"Well, according to me and everyone else here, you're not asking the key question."

"And what's that?"

"Do you love him, Rosa?"

She crushed the Kleenex in her fist. "I've always loved him. I probably always will."

"Then—"

"That doesn't mean I can be with him. How can I trust him with my heart?"

Linda handed her another tissue. "You have to ask yourself what is the bigger fear, that you'll get hurt again or that you'll walk away before you ever find out what could have been."

"Thanks, Dr. Lipschitz, but I don't like either of those options. I like my life just the way it is. I wish you guys would understand that."

"Ah, Rosa." Linda's eyes were damp, too. "You've already started to change. You think you have it all, but you're missing the only thing that really matters."

She looked from Linda to Vince. "You never liked him. And now you're trying to push me into this?"

"You said the magic words," Vince pointed out with a smile. "You said you love him. And he's not so bad. He's ready, Rosa. He's finally good enough for you."

A cell phone rang, and several people checked theirs. Rosa looked in her purse and frowned. Odd. It wasn't there. Maybe she'd set it down in her office, or in her car. As it turned out, Teddy's phone was the culprit. He took the call, retreating to a corner of the bar and lowering his voice.

Rosa stared long and hard at the nautilus shell behind the bar. She heaved a sigh. "Whatever happened to happily ever after?"

"It's still an option," Linda assured her. "But you'll never get there if you don't take a risk."

"You could say the same about disaster."

"That's why it's a risk."

"I just can't—"

"Rosa, we've got to go." Teddy crossed the room in two strides and yanked open the door. "There's a fire at your father's place."

She raced Teddy out to his Jeep. They jumped in, and he peeled out of the parking lot. The ride to Prospect Street was the longest in all eternity. She hardened her spine against the back of the seat so she wouldn't collapse. She used Teddy's phone to try her father's cell, but got no answer. That could mean anything, she realized with a shudder.

"You're sure he's okay?" she asked Teddy.

"That's what I heard from the dispatcher."

"What happened?" she demanded.

"I didn't get much information. Started upstairs, I think he said."

"Oh, God. *Joey.*"

"The kid's at work. You know that."

"Maybe it was bad wiring. Damn. I warned him about that. I should have taken care of it myself. But Pop's all right. You're sure you heard right."

"That's what I heard."

Things didn't look okay as they turned on to Prospect Street. A ladder truck blocked the way and a crew swarmed over the house. Flames licked from the upstairs windows. Neighbors gathered on the sidewalk across the way.

The most chilling sight of all was a red and white EMS vehicle, its lights rotating ominously, its rear doors wide-open.

Rosa gasped. "He's hurt."

"They're probably just here as a precaution," Teddy said.

She spotted a white Ford Explorer parked in the driveway. "That's Alex's truck. What the hell…?" She jumped out before Teddy came to a complete stop and jostled her way through the crowd. "Pop!" she yelled, wishing he could hear her. "Pop."

Then she saw him next to the rig, haggard but standing on his own, holding Jake in his arms, a bag valve mask against his face.

Rosa gave a cry of relief and ran to him. "Thank God you're all right." She hugged him and kissed the dog on the head. "What happened?"

When she stepped back to sign the question, she saw that something was wrong. Pop didn't look hurt, but his eyes were filled with sadness.

"It's just a house," she told him, knowing it was so much more. "We'll replace everything—"

"Rosa, I don't worry about the house," he said. "It's not that. It's—"

"Make way," someone yelled. "Step aside, please."

"Rosina," said Pop. "I am so sorry…"

"I don't understand…" She looked at Alex's car. It couldn't be him on that stretcher, strapped to a backboard and cervical collar, buried in fireproof blankets. It couldn't be.

She must have swayed or staggered a little, because Pop took her hand and held on tightly. Through a fog of dawning comprehension, she watched the EMS crew navigating a path toward the open rear doors of the ambulance. An EMT ran alongside the stretcher holding an IV bag high in the air. Someone else barked coded language into a radio. Another worked an automatic external defibrillator similar to the one they had at the restaurant.

Screaming, Rosa wrenched away from her father and lunged toward the ambulance. They wouldn't let her near. Still, she managed to catch a glimpse of the victim. Just barely, but enough to confirm what she already knew in the pit of her stomach.

Thirty-Nine

~~~

They wouldn't let Rosa in to see Alex because she wasn't immediate family. However, lacking any other source of information, the EMTs relied on her. As she stumbled through details in a flat, incredulous voice—age, weight, allergies, medical conditions, insurance coverage—it struck her how little she knew about him, this man who had just saved her father's life, this man she was afraid to love.

She felt numb with terror as she entered the hospital. She'd made this trip before, after a midnight phone call. This time, her father walked in on his own, submitting to tests as a precaution.

"I'm looking for Alex Montgomery," Rosa said to a nurse. "He was just brought in."

"I'll send someone."

Another nurse, this one harried-looking and studying reports on a clipboard, approached her. "You're with Mr. Montgomery?" she asked.

"Yes, I…we… Is he all right?"

"The doctors are evaluating him right now, ma'am." She flipped a page of the chart. "What was he doing prior to the fire?"

A trap door of guilt gaped open, and Rosa teetered on the edge. Just a short time ago, he had held her in his arms. She leaned forward and told the nurse, "He ate…a normal breakfast, eggs and fruit and coffee." She refused to hold anything back, so she added, "We were together, you know?"

The nurse's expression conveyed that she did.

"He seemed perfectly fine, but he did use his inhaler at least once. He's a chronic asthmatic, and this morning his lungs were twitchy," she added. "I told the EMTs about it."

"What time?"

"Early. I left him around nine-fifteen. Can I see him? Please?"

"I'll keep you informed, ma'am." The nurse made a note and went through the heavy double doors to consult with the doctor.

Rosa's father sat on a bed in a curtained area, still holding Jake. Pop looked grim, his face ashen with regrets as he gave a statement to a man with a notebook. "It was an accident," he said, "but it shouldn't have happened. I knew the wiring was bad. I got a neighbor, Rudy, who's an electrician. I was supposed to have him check it out. It completely slipped my mind."

Rosa clutched at the curtain frame. She thought about the night Joey had told her about Pop's forgetfulness. Just getting him a dog wasn't enough; she should have known that.

"It didn't seem so bad at first," Pop went on. "I tried putting it out myself, didn't know it would spread so quick. When the curtains caught fire, I called 9-1-1. And Jake, he panicked and ran off. I could not leave the house without him. If Alexander had not arrived, both Jake and I might not have made it out."

Rosa shut her eyes as her father finished making his statement.

"There was a great cheer when we saw them both on the roof," he went on. "Alexander gave Jake to a fire-fighter and then…"

Rosa opened her eyes to see that her father was weeping again.

"Then something happened. He fell. It was like somebody shot him. He collapsed and went off the roof. I'm sorry. So sorry."

Her father wanted to stay and wait for word about Alex, but Rosa put Teddy in charge of him, sending them to pick up Joey from work. They'd have to salvage what they could from Pop's house. After that they'd be staying with her until they figured out what to do.

"And you?" asked Pop, watching her with a terrible worry in his eyes.

"I'm staying here."

He nodded. "Of course." With those two words, he indicated his changed opinion of Alex. Rosa could see it in his expression.

"I'll let you know when I hear something."

"Yes. And Rosina—" He hesitated, then said, "It is… We will talk about it later."

"About what?"

But he didn't hear her. He was already heading for the door.

No one would give her a report on Alex's condition.

The charge nurse flicked a glance at the closed door of the exam room, a resuscitation bay surrounded by wire mesh glass. The area was so crowded with doctors and technicians that Alex couldn't be seen. "They're still working on him. I promise, they're doing the best they can."

Rosa wondered if the nurse had any idea how unsettling her words and manner were. "Can you tell me if you managed to get hold of his father?" she demanded. "Can you at least tell me that?"

"I understand someone's on the way."

Rosa paced. She got a drink of water and paced some more. Then she searched her handbag for her phone and remembered it was missing. The nurse had said someone was on the way. She could only assume that meant Alex's father. His sister, Madison, was somewhere in Asia, and he didn't have any other family. Portia? Maybe she should be contacted. An ex-fiancée might qualify as family if she kept quiet about the "ex" part.

He needed *someone*. If she were in his position, she knew she'd draw strength from the presence of friends. Friends and family, surrounding her, supporting her, willing her to get better. She wanted that for Alex but she didn't know how to give it to him. His whole world was an alien planet to her.

As the minutes crawled by, more people showed up. Slowly, in small groups, they all came to see her, much as they had the night her father was hurt. Shelly and the guys from the restaurant. Mario and his family. Linda and Jason. They came because they loved her, and they wanted to be there for the man who had walked through fire for her father. She realized with a deep gratitude that these people were her whole world. They had propped her up through the bad times and celebrated the good.

She found herself remembering her vow this morning, which seemed an eternity ago. Only this morning, she'd believed she would follow Alex to the ends of the earth.

Now she wondered how she could even think of leaving. This was the only place where life made sense.

Vince came to sit with her. Although she was grateful for his presence, the whole situation felt ghoulish, like a death watch. She and Vince were clutching each other in terror when the automatic doors swished open and a tall, elegantly dressed man hurried across the foyer, followed by Gina Colombo, Alex's assistant. Neither of them seemed to notice Rosa as they were whisked into the exam room.

Through the glass wall, she could only see Alex's father from behind. He was broad-shouldered and athletic-looking. At first glance, he seemed to possess the graceful, emotionless demeanor of an android. She quickly realized it wasn't true. Those big shoulders were very expressive. As she watched, they drooped and then shook violently.

It took a minute for her to find her voice. "That's his father," she told Vince.

His arm slid around her. He didn't say anything, didn't try to assure her that everything would be all right. He knew she'd stood right here in the same waiting room twelve years before, not knowing if her father would live or die and then learning that he would exist in some shadowland between the two, perhaps forever. So Vince knew better than to offer reassurances before they had all the facts.

Mr. Montgomery was signing papers on a clipboard when Gina came out. In a business suit with a short skirt, she looked crisp and professional, but her face was ashen, her eyes troubled.

"They said you came in with him."

"Yes," said Rosa. "How is he?"

"Going up to ICU, that's how he is."

"Hey," said Vince.

Rosa waved her hand to settle him down. She could see the terror in Gina's eyes. Her anger was just a mask for an abject fear Rosa understood all too well. "Please, what's his condition?"

Gina seem to soften slightly. "The burns are minor but…they need to do more tests for possible brain trauma. They're worried about intracranial hemorrhage. He's been intubated and hasn't been conscious since he was brought in."

Icy terror closed around Rosa. Her father had suffered brain trauma. It had taken him two years to get better. "I want to see him."

"You can't," said Gina.

Rosa walked away to peer through the glass. There was a screen around the gurney so she couldn't see much. She stood watching the team getting ready to move Alex. His father hovered, looking helpless. Then someone pushed the screen out of the way, and she could see Alex at last, but only a little. She caught a glimpse of soot on his forehead, like an Ash Wednesday benediction. The top of the laryngoscope and the Ambu-bag obscured the rest of his face. He was missing one tennis shoe. There was a cut on his cheekbone right where she had kissed him this morning.

Only this morning, but so long ago.

She leaned her head against the glass, tormented, feeling Mr. Montgomery's eyes on her but physically unable to move. Then he turned away from her and she saw him, that inattentive husband, that cold unfeeling father, bend and press a kiss on Alex's soot-smudged forehead, then squeeze his son's hand. When he straightened up, his lips were moving rapidly in what could only be a feverish, desperate prayer.

Behind her, Vince and Gina were conferring like thieves.

Rosa watched the room empty out as a pair of orderlies angled the gurney through a wide door and down a gleaming hallway. Nurses and technicians wheeled the accompanying bags and monitors alongside the gurney. Speaking rapidly, a doctor directed traffic. Mr. Montgomery followed, his head bowed. The empty room looked ransacked, like a crime scene, with tubes left hanging, blue and white packaging on the floor, trays of instruments everywhere.

Vince touched her on the shoulder. "Honey, Gina needs to tell you something."

Rosa nodded, resigned to whatever the snappy, defensive woman might have to say to her. It was clear that Gina was devoted to Alex. Rosa was glad he had people in his life who loved him. She found herself wishing he had more.

"There's something you should know about Alex and Portia van Deusen," Gina said without preamble.

That. It seemed like an eternity had passed since Portia had told her about the pregnancy. Rosa whipped a glance at Vince. The big mouth. But it was too late now; Gina obviously knew something. Rosa folded her hands and waited.

"Whatever happens with Alex," said Gina, "I don't want you believing what Portia told you."

Rosa flicked another glance at Vince. "You shouldn't have—"

"Yes, he should. Because Portia lied. I'm not supposed to know anything about this, but… What can I say? I'm his closest friend." She looked around the waiting area, which was deserted except for the three of them. "Portia was never pregnant. She lied and said she was so Alex would marry her."

Rosa took a moment to catch her breath. "That's the oldest trick in the book."

"It's old because it works," said Gina. "Especially on an honorable man who wants to believe the best of people. When they were dating, Alex didn't have the first thought about marrying her, but the minute she said she was carrying his child, he offered."

"It's diabolical, really," Vince said. "Once she gets a ring on her finger, there's a miscarriage, but she's still got her rich husband. I saw that once on *Dynasty*."

"When Alex figured out what Portia was up to," said Gina, "he ended the engagement. He let her act like she broke it off, you know, to save face."

"How did he figure out she was lying?"

"I figured it out. You could ask me how," Gina said, "but there's a gentleman present."

"I guess we saw the same episode of *Dynasty*," said Vince.

"Gina, why are you telling me this?" asked Rosa.

"Because he's the best man I know. I don't ever want his integrity questioned. If something happens to him...if he doesn't—" Gina's voice broke and she stared at the floor, pinching the bridge of her nose. "I just think he'd want you to know the truth about that situation, but he's too much of a gentleman to tell you himself."

Hours later, most people had left. That was when Rosa noticed Mr. Montgomery across the hall in the gift shop, staring unseeingly at the last remaining copy of *Investors Business Daily*. She squared her shoulders and went over to him.

"Mr. Montgomery?" She was surprised by the hesitation in her own voice.

He replaced the newspaper in the rack and turned to her stiffly. "Yes?"

"I'm Rosa—"

"I know who you are," he said.

She took a deep breath. In all the years she'd known Alex, she had never actually had a conversation with Mr. Montgomery. Now she knew why. He was formidable. "Sir, I want you to know how grateful my family is to Alex for what he did."

"I'm sure they're extremely grateful."

"And I've been waiting all day to find out how he is. I know I'm not his family, but I…" She took another breath, this one deeper than before. "I'm not leaving."

He studied her as though she was a lab specimen with an unusual growth. She could see Alex in his face, in the sharp cut of his jawbone, the blue eyes, the abundant sandy-colored hair, the broad shoulders. Yet the expression on his face was that of a stranger, a disapproving stranger. She found herself wishing she wasn't wearing the tight red pants, the polka dot halter top, the red high-heeled sandals.

Without taking his eyes off her, he reached down for his briefcase and stalked toward the main exit. "Come with me," he said.

He led the way outside, taking out a cigar in a yellow-and-red tube. She followed him past a sand-filled ashtray where a few people stood around, smoking cigarettes with a slightly shamefaced air. Mr. Montgomery was unapologetic as he lit his cigar.

"He had a severe asthma attack, probably induced by smoke inhalation. That caused him to lose consciousness while on the roof, and at that point, he fell and went into cardiac arrest. There are some broken ribs. What the doctors are most worried about is the intracranial hemorrhage. If he doesn't regain consciousness…"

The briefcase dropped from his fingers as though he'd suddenly gone weak. It popped open and manila file folders fanned across the walkway, but he didn't seem to notice. She squatted down to put all the spilled files back.

"I'll get that," he said quickly, and with the speed of a man half his age, he scooped up the strewn papers and photographs.

In those few seconds, Rosa had seen…something. A notice on letterhead from the South County Sheriff's Office. Some grainy eight-by-ten color photographs, close-ups. She burned with curiosity but there was no way to ask him anything without seeming hopelessly nosy.

He shut the case with a decisive snap. "They advised me to contact the rest of the family. That can't mean anything good."

He sank down on the heavy cedar bench and dropped his head into his hands. The cigar seemed forgotten between his fingers.

"What can I do?" Rosa asked, trying not to feel panicked by his despair. "Is Gina still here?"

"No. I told her I'd be in touch."

"Can I call your daughter for you?"

"She's overseas and her cell phone is useless. I left her a message and sent her e-mail."

Rosa had a strange urge to reach out to him, maybe pat him on the shoulder. She didn't dare. Here was a man who was all alone, his wife gone, his daughter away, his son on life support, his friends weirdly absent.

She sat down on the bench, took the barely smoked cigar from him and stuck it in the sand ashtray. Then she drummed up her courage and put her hand on his arm. "I'm not leaving you. I'm going to stay here until Alex gets better."

"I certainly can't stop you."

Rosa gritted her teeth. "Listen, I don't need for you

to like me, just to understand that I love him every bit as much as you do."

Mr. Montgomery hung his head. "I never should have let him come here after his mother—" His voice broke and he cleared his throat.

"He's a grown man," she reminded him. "It wasn't a question of you letting him do anything. It was his choice."

"I've never understood the appeal this place has for him, why it keeps drawing him back, again and again, even though he could go anywhere in the world."

"Don't you have a place like that?"

He lowered his hands and looked at her as though she'd spoken in a foreign tongue. "I'm not a sentimental man, Miss Capoletti."

"This is not about being sentimental," she said. "It's about finding your home, the place where you belong."

"Alexander is a Montgomery. He doesn't belong in some backwater resort town. If he had stayed where he belongs, none of this would have happened." He gestured angrily at the looming facade of the hospital building.

Rosa sniffed. "If you stay in bed every morning and never get up, nothing will ever happen to you. But that's no way to live."

He glared at her. She braced herself, thinking he would lash out again. He didn't. His expression remained fierce as he said, "I can see why my son likes you."

She didn't know what to say to that; it sounded more like an accusation than a compliment.

Forty

——◦◦◦——

Pretty much everything Grandpop owned was in the back of the old pickup truck, lumbering toward the other side of town, where Aunt Rosa lived. Joey adjusted the passenger side mirror and looked at the depressingly small load, mainly from the garage, which had survived the fire and subsequent dousing with water and foam. Jake perched on the seat between them, checking out each car as it passed.

Joey had lost everything, too, but fortunately that didn't amount to much, though he'd miss his clothes and laptop computer. The telescope, which Alex had returned to him after the night at Watch Hill, had been in the garage. Still, it was the creepiest feeling in the world to come home for lunch and find the street blocked by emergency vehicles, the upper story of the house stark against the sky, like a black skeleton.

His cell phone rang and he looked at the display. He leaned forward so Grandpop, who was driving, could see him. "It's my folks," he said. "Again." Then he took the call. "Hello?"

"Is everything all right?" his dad asked.

"Same as it was five minutes ago when you called," said Joey. Since the fire, he'd talked to his parents at least five times.

"I won't apologize, sport," said his dad. "This is serious stuff. How does Grandpop seem to you?"

"He's still all right. I swear it, Dad. He's got his dog and his pipe to smoke, and we're taking some stuff over to Aunt Rosa's place. We're going to stop at the hospital to see how Alex is doing, and then we're having dinner at Celesta's." Sheesh, thought Joey. How many times did he have to go through this?

"I requested leave," said Dad. "Tell Grandpop I'll be there this weekend. And I just got through to Uncle Sal. He's going to be there too."

"Great. Have you seen Aunt Rosa's apartment?" Joey said. "It's got, like, four rooms, total."

"We'll work things out when we get there."

"Fine. I have to go, Dad. We just pulled into the hospital."

"Okay, sport. Listen, you tell Alex I said thank you a million times."

"Got it, Dad. You bet."

Grandpop parked and put Jake on his leash.

"If they let you in to see him," Joey said, "you should tell him thank you."

"He knows he has my gratitude."

Joey glared at him. Alex was a good guy, but Grandpop never wanted to see that. The old man's scowl deepened. Joey didn't flinch. Then Grandpop said, "You have *la vecchia anima,* Giuseppe. You are wise beyond your years."

"Well, somebody in this family has to be."

They found Aunt Rosa on the covered walkway in front of the hospital, talking to some tall guy in a business suit. She got all nervous when she saw them, and introduced the guy as Alexander Montgomery, Alex's father.

"I hope your son is well," Grandpop said.

"He's in intensive care," said Mr. Montgomery, who looked like a cold fish. "We're waiting to hear."

Like most people, Mr. Montgomery wasn't used to talking to a deaf guy, and Joey could tell Grandpop hadn't caught what he said. He nudged Grandpop and mouthed "waiting to hear."

"Well," Mr. Montgomery said in a clipped, sort of distracted way. He glanced down at the briefcase in his hand. "Well, I certainly don't know what to say at this point, but there is something else you should—"

"Mr. Montgomery?" A woman in pink scrubs hurried toward him.

"Yes?" He had the look of a man facing a firing squad.

"Could you come with me, please? You're needed in the ICU right away."

Forty-One

~~~~~~~

Sirens and glaring lights. The hiss and roar of water rushing through hoses, the crackle of flames, blazing heat… Alex lay helpless under the bombardment. He felt strangely immobile, his limbs encased in concrete, his throat rigid.

"…hear me, Alexander? Squeeze my hand if you can hear me."

Why would I do that? He spoke but no sound came out. His whole throat was intensely sore. He tried to claw at it, but someone held both his hands.

"Open your eyes." The stranger's voice sounded painfully loud.

He tried to drag his eyes open, but when he did, a piercing glint of fiery white light drilled straight into his head, and he ducked for cover.

"Alexander, do you know where you are?"

Enough, already. With a supreme effort of will, he opened his eyes and glared at his tormentor. Actually, there were four of them, maybe more.

What the hell…

"You're at the hospital, Alexander," said the woman

with the grating voice. "There's a tube in your throat to help you breathe. Now that you're awake, we want you to breathe on your own." She spread a plastic sheet like a dropcloth over him and placed an enameled basin on his chest. Someone's hands clamped around either side of his head. "When I say three, we'll get that tube out. One, two, three…"

Alex gagged, feeling something in his throat that shouldn't be there. The something moved, slowly and sickeningly at first, then was ripped from his throat with startling violence.

He gagged some more and then puked. The nurse seemed unperturbed as she took away the basin. She swabbed his face and removed the plastic sheeting. He lay back, gasping, and lifted his hand in supplication. There were strips of white Velcro on his fingers and a clear tube going into the top of his hand. *I feel like shit,* he wanted to say, but no words came out.

He took a deep breath and felt himself cracking in two. A moan of pain escaped him.

"I'm Dr. Turabian," said the woman. "We're glad you decided to join the party. You've got some cracked ribs. That's the pain you're feeling. You went into cardiac arrest and you've got a head injury, but you were pretty darned lucky. You won't be able to talk for a day or two."

I don't feel lucky. She was right; he had no voice at all.

She handed him a white marker board with a marker on a string and a cloth. "Now, there might be some short term memory loss. After we get you cleaned up, we'll be asking you some questions."

She did something with a monitor while the nurse swabbed salve on his lips. "The EMTs said you were quite a hero. You were the only one hurt in the fire. The older gentleman and his dog are fine."

Thank God, thought Alex. Thank God. Pete was all right. The dog made it. Sweet relief poured through him.

The nurse finished cleaning up and they both left, leaving the door slightly ajar. Time passed. Alex didn't know how much. He studied the monitors, but for all their buzzing and humming, he couldn't find a clock on any of them. He wondered what day it was. The same day he had made love to Rosa?

"Alexander?" His father's bulk filled the doorway of the cramped white room. He approached the bed and loomed over Alex, obliterating the glare of the high-powered overhead lights. "Son, thank God you're all right."

Alex took a moment to assimilate everything. It felt surreal to have his father here, holding his hand, no less. Maybe Alex was on drugs. Hallucinogens.

Just in case it wasn't a weird vision, Alex scribbled "Thx 4 coming."

Then something even weirder happened. At first Alex thought his father was choking or gagging. Then he was stunned to realize he was crying. To Alex's knowledge, his father had never cried. Not even when they laid his wife to rest.

Are you… Alex grimaced in frustration at his inability to talk. He wrote "U OK?" and tapped the white board.

"Yes." His father took the ornamental silk handkerchief from his breast pocket and scrubbed his face with it. "You gave me a scare, son. I didn't think I'd lose it like that. This kind of took me back, you know, maybe that's it."

Alex sent him a questioning look.

"To when you were little. We were in and out of the emergency room so many times."

"Felt routine to me," Alex wrote.

"Not to your mother and me. Each time, we were terrified they wouldn't get you breathing again. And each time, it killed me a little. Just now, it all came back. The incredible fear of losing you."

Stunned, Alex thought he'd heard wrong. His dry lips cracked and stung with the effort to offer a reassuring smile. "Not going anywhere."

They sat together for a while. Alex could not remember such a comfortable silence between himself and his father. It was a strange finish to a strange day. Contrary to the doctor's warning, he had no trouble remembering every detail. Things had started out pretty damned great, he recalled, thinking of Rosa. After making love to her, he knew the day couldn't possibly get better. But it got worse in a hurry.

His father handed him a plastic water bottle with a straw. "Dr. Turabian says you're moving to a regular room in the morning if all your vitals check out. You can have visitors once you're moved. There are some people waiting to see you."

Alex frowned.

"Rosa Capoletti, for one. She's charming. I expect you've always known that. And there's a young man with pink hair and Gina's here, as well. And Pete Capoletti, of course. But they can't visit you in the ICU. Once you're moved to a private room, you can have visitors if you feel up to it."

"Of course I feel up 2 seeing Rosa," he scrawled.

"I hope you look better in the morning," his father said bluntly. "And you smell like an incinerator."

Now, that's the dad I know and love, Alex thought, his lips cracking as he smiled.

"I could bring you some things. Clean clothes, a razor and toothbrush."

Alex took a sip of water and nodded as much as he was able. Then he wrote, "Rosa?"

"I spoke to her at length. Delightful girl. I always thought so."

"BS," Alex wrote.

"I did." He seemed agitated and restless in the small room. "It was your mother who objected to her. And speaking of your mother, we have several things to discuss."

"M…? She has nothing to do with today."

"On the contrary, she has everything to do with it." Alex's father stopped and stared down at his hands, turning them palms up in his lap, looking bewildered.

Alex tapped on the word "Mother" again.

His expression grim, his father took a thick file folder from his attaché case.

Forty-Two

~~~

"**W**hoa, wait a minute, slow down," said Rosa, alone with Alex in his flower-filled private room. Sunshine flooded through the slats of the venetian blinds. No one but his father had been allowed to visit him the previous night; ICU visiting rules were strictly enforced. "You lost me after the storm damage."

Alex smiled at her from the bed. He was sitting up, wearing a pajama top printed, disconcertingly, with the Playboy bunny symbol. Furnished, he claimed, by his father. A singed right eyebrow gave him a perpetually quizzical look.

"When that tree fell on the shed on our property and took out a power line, they had to tow my mother's old car—the blue Ford that had been parked there forever." His voice was raspy and whisper-soft from a throat damaged by the breathing tube. "Your friend Sean Costello noticed something about the car."

He handed her a glossy photograph of a right front fender with a long yellow scratch. "Sheriff Costello has a good memory. He was a rookie deputy the night your father was hit, but he remembered Pete rode a yellow bicycle. The tire treads match the marks, too." He indicated a manila file folder. "Costello expects everything to be verified by the state crime lab, but it's not a priority case since it…since she…"

Finally, with a queasy sense of certainty, Rosa understood. "Oh, no. Sean thinks…?" She couldn't even finish the thought.

"It was a hunch. He paid a visit to my mother in Providence. She claimed she didn't know a thing. Then the next day, she took her own life."

"Oh, Alex. Oh, my God." Rosa sank down on the swivel chair beside the hospital bed. She shut her eyes as anguish welled up. Mrs. Montgomery had been drinking that night; Pop had been trying to help her. She must have followed him, though Rosa could not fathom why. She was hysterical, her father had said. Who knew what she was thinking? She'd hit him by accident, surely. Rosa couldn't help but wonder what Mrs. Montgomery had been feeling that night, knowing she was responsible for such a terrible thing. What was it like, Rosa wondered, to live with that kind of guilt for so many years?

Judging by the way Emily Montgomery had ended her life, it had been torture. "Alex," she said, "I had no idea."

"No one did. That was what she wanted. Appearances at any cost. Even if it meant living in hell for the rest of her life."

Rosa let out a soft gasp. "You can't let yourself be angry at her anymore, Alex. Everything she did was out of love for you. She made terrible choices, but she had the best of intentions."

"She ruined your father's life and destroyed herself, and you want me to forgive that?"

He was trying to put her off with his fury; Rosa could

see that now. Along with the flash of rage in his eyes, she saw a glint of tears. That's good, she thought. Finally.

With slow deliberation, she took his hand between hers. "Yes," she said, "I do."

Alex felt her sympathy like blows from a hammer, and the pain took him by surprise. He wrenched his hand away, unable to bear her touch. Still, her words, uttered with calm deliberation, cracked straight through to his heart, and his grief burst wide-open. For the first time since that blood-freezing early-morning phone call at the beginning of the summer, Alex came apart. All the rage and devastation inside him welled up and erupted, and his body convulsed with shuddering sobs.

His mother was gone. She'd driven him crazy all his life, and the way she had died would torture him forever. He shook with a violent, angry grief, the harsh sobs clawing at his throat. He wept for his mother and all the ways he'd failed her. He wept for the happiness that had slipped through her fingers, and he wept because he'd never been able to change that.

He had the presence of mind to turn away. "Shit," he said when he could finally talk. "I didn't mean to do that. God, that's embarrassing."

Rosa sat quietly by, waiting. She didn't reach out to him, but she didn't leave either. "Are you all right?"

He used the bedsheet to wipe his face. "That's the first time I've cried for my mother," he said. "It's the only time."

"You should have done that long ago." She seemed completely unperturbed by his breakdown.

Alex lay back against the pillow. His head throbbed. He felt drained and exhausted, but for the first time since his mother's death, he felt a certain quiet in his heart.

"I'm so, so sorry." She put her hand over his again, and this time he didn't take it away.

"Yeah," he said. "Me, too. I need to talk to your father. I don't know what I'm going to say to him, though." His mother had left him and his father to deal with the broken pieces she had left behind. He had no idea how to begin doing that.

Knowing the true nature of the issue between his mother and her father hadn't put his guilt at ease. He felt weak and shaken as he put away the photographs and paperwork. "I need to tell your father I'm sorry. God, that's so inadequate. I was there that night. I heard them, and I thought the worst. Then I turned around and took off. If I'd stuck around, they never would have—"

"Don't, Alex. It's over. It's in the past and we can't change it."

He brought her hand up and pressed it briefly, fiercely, against his lips. "Then let's talk about something else. Let's talk about the future."

She tried to pull her hand away. "Not now," she said. "You need to get better. Alex—"

He kept hold of her hand. He had broken down and cried in front of her, and she had watched him with a sense of awe. And in that moment, he could see everything in her eyes—regret and pain and hope and…love.

"Just listen, okay?" he said. "I need to ask you something."

PART SIX

Dolci

Dolce is Italian for sweet, and it applies not just
to music and food, but also to life itself. Just as
every meal should end with something sweet, so
should every life be filled with il dolce.

Torta Crema (Italian Cream Cake)

1 stick unsalted butter, softened
1/2 cup shortening
2 cups sugar
5 eggs, separated
2 cups flour
1 teaspoon soda
1 cup buttermilk
1 teaspoon vanilla
1 cup flaked coconut
1 cup chopped pecans

Cream the butter and shortening, add the sugar and beat some more. Add egg yolks and beat. Mix flour and baking soda, and add alternately with buttermilk. Stir in vanilla, coconut, and pecans. Fold in stiffly beaten egg whites. Pour batter into three well-greased round cake pans or a 13 x 9 x 2-inch baking pan. Bake at 350°F for 40 to 45 minutes, until a stick of dry spaghetti inserted in the middle comes out clean. Cool before frosting.

Cream Cheese Icing

1 package cream cheese, softened
1/2 cup pure unsalted butter, softened
1 box powdered sugar
1 teaspoon vanilla
Chopped pecans and coconut

Beat cream cheese until smooth. Add butter and sugar, then stir in vanilla and beat until smooth. Frost cooled cake in pan or in layers. Top with chopped pecans and coconut. Serve with good strong coffee, or espresso if you have the equipment.

Forty-Three

꩜

The groom was going to faint; Rosa was sure of it. As she gazed into his endearingly nervous face, she saw that he was sweating a little, and his eyes darted with barely-suppressed trepidation. She could tell he wanted to get this right.

She knew he was wondering—*Should I smile as I say my vows? Say something original, or is that too hokey?*

Go for it, she wanted to urge him. Don't be afraid. Nothing's too hokey when it's true love.

Rosa held her breath while he struggled with a moment of panic. His hand shook a little as he took the ring from the satin pillow.

Silly man, thought Rosa. He had no reason to be nervous. Didn't he know their love would last forever and a day?

She sneaked a glance around, even though she was supposed to be paying attention. There was nothing, she thought, quite like the feeling of being with everyone you love on the most perfect day that had ever dawned. Rob and Gloria were present, both resplendent in full dress uniform. Pop and Joey stood between them, beaming at her and then at Alex. Sal was officiating, his deep voice reverberating through the church.

Come on, she thought, her heart pounding with anticipation. Go for it. Just say the words. Just say it. *I do*.

Such a simple phrase, but so filled with mystery and magic, faith and uncertainty. For a second, a heartbeat, she was terrified that he'd chicken out. Then she saw his mouth form the words. *I do*. He spoke with all the depth of love she could see in his eyes. Wedding guests shifted in their chairs to look on fondly.

Beside Rosa, the bride's sister let out a loud sob.

"Rachel, for Pete's sake," Rosa whispered out of the side of her mouth. "Not so loud. We want to hear them—"

"…pronounce you husband and wife," said Sal in a triumphant voice. The music swelled and the happy couple turned to face the world as a married couple. Rosa saw the joyous love in their eyes and felt a flood of affection for them both. That and the sense that, finally, everything was as it should be.

At that point Rosa lost it, too, weeping with happiness for her best friend, Linda, and for Jason, who looked as though he'd just won the lottery. She mustered her courage, if not her dignity, and handed Linda the bridal bouquet for the recessional. Then Rosa took the proffered arm of Jason's brother to follow them down the aisle while the music swelled romantically. As she walked past Alex, she knew her whole heart was in her eyes.

Two weeks after the fire, he looked wonderful, the cut on his cheek nearly healed and his right eyebrow growing in nicely. She still couldn't believe what he'd asked her, right there in the hospital, only a day after he'd been brought back from the dead, literally. He'd asked her if her father's home had been insured, and when she told him it wasn't, he'd made an incredibly generous offer.

He wanted Pop to live in the rebuilt quarters on his property.

"Isn't that a little ghoulish?" Rob had asked. "After all, it's where she left the car she was driving the night she creamed him."

Sal had a different take on it. He had listened to the story from Rosa, from Pop and even from Alex. "Let Pop decide," he'd said. "They've both got some mending to do."

Under the August sun, there was a glorious shower of bird seed, a lengthy pause for photos, then a limousine cavalcade to the reception. After the short ride, Rosa stepped out of the limo and felt a thrill of anticipation. The deck of Celesta's-by-the-Sea was festooned with white net bunting and satin ribbons. The weathered sign by the entrance had a special notice: Closed For Private Event.

"This is our first, you know," she said to Alex. "Our first wedding reception."

"It's going to be perfect," Vince said with confidence. "The 'Best Place to Propose' is good for other things, too."

She felt Alex looking at her, and when she saw the pride in his eyes, she nearly wept again with happiness. This, she thought as she took his hand and led the way inside, this was what she'd been missing all her life. She used to believe she had it all, but that was just a smoke-screen. She needed more. *Deserved* more.

She stopped in the foyer of the restaurant, which had been decorated with swags of white silk roses. The portrait of her mother by the podium had its own little garland over the top of the frame. Hi, Mamma, she thought. It's a new day.

Rosa turned to Alex. "I love you," she said. "You know that, right?"

"Yes," he said, "absolutely. And, Rosa—"

"There you are," said Leo, emerging from the kitchen, the thick doors flapping behind him. "We just ran out of polenta, and none of the table candles have been lit. Butch is fit to be tied."

Rosa gritted her teeth in frustration, but held it in. If she freaked out, everyone would follow her lead. She let go of Alex's hand. "I'll just be a few minutes."

"Sure."

Arriving guests soon filled the deck, the bar and the dining room, and Rosa headed for the kitchen. Tying an apron over her bridesmaid's dress, she ordered someone to light the candles, then pitched in, finding a sack of cornmeal and setting it on to simmer herself. Within a relatively short time, things were under control, and she peeled off the apron.

The party was in full swing in the dining room, the ensemble playing, guests sitting down to a wedding feast they'd tell their grandchildren about. Rosa sat with the wedding party, but she scarcely ate as she scanned each table, making sure the salad was perfect, the entrée impeccable, the champagne flowing. People raised their glasses in toast after toast, and Linda and Jason looked ready to burst with joy.

Alex looked surprisingly at ease, seated with her father and brothers and Joey, whose hair was now back to its normal shade and length. Jake the dog slept under the table near Pop's feet. At Linda's insistence, Gina Colombo, Hollis Underwood and Mr. Montgomery had come to the reception. Only a few weeks ago, the combination of personalities at that table would have seemed bizarre, but now, everything was as it should be.

And then the simple truth dawned on her. She finally acknowledged that it didn't matter who you were or where you came from. Love and respect put everyone on equal footing.

After dinner and countless toasts, couples crowded the dance floor. The best man claimed Rosa for a dance, and she was swept into the festivities. The next hour was filled with laughter and dancing, with greeting people and making introductions. She caught a glimpse of Alex a time or two, but never quite managed to connect with him. Every time they started across the room toward each other, one of them would be waylaid en route. Finally, after another hour had passed, she felt a pair of strong, familiar arms around her.

"I haven't had this much trouble catching something since my father took me fly fishing in Vermont," said Alex, smiling down at her.

"You never told me your father took you fly fishing."

"I'll put it on the list. May I *finally* have this dance?"

She laughed. "My feet are killing me."

"I could always take you straight to bed."

The laughter stopped, but the smile remained. "That's tempting, but I'll tough it out. They're playing 'Fly Me to the Moon.' We can't miss out on that." She felt his hands skim over her bare shoulders and sighed with happiness as they moved onto the floor.

His arms tightened around her. "I feel like I need to make an appointment to talk to you."

"What would you like to talk about?" she asked, inhaling his scent, practically floating. Her feet didn't hurt at all anymore.

"Sweetheart, I think you know."

She hid a smile against his chest. Please, let her instincts be right this time. She sensed her whole life had been leading up to this moment, that everything that had happened to them had brought them here, finally. "You definitely don't need an appointment."

The piece ended, but before they could steal away somewhere, Ariel grabbed Rosa's arm. "It's time," she said, pulling her away from Alex.

"Time for what?"

Rosa didn't hear the answer as squeals went up from the female guests. The throwing of the bride's bouquet, of course. She aimed a helpless look over her shoulder at Alex as Ariel tugged her toward the stage. He grinned good-naturedly and stepped back to watch.

"I warn you, I have a wild pitch," Linda was saying to the women gathered around her. Then she beamed. "I wish for every one of you what Jason and I found today." She brought the beautiful pink and white bouquet to her face, then turned around and flung it up and over her back.

Rosa did not consider herself a superstitious person, but nothing—not one blessed thing—was going to get between her and those flowers. With a leap and a reach that nearly made her pop out of her bodice, she shot up in the air and snatched the bouquet. Amid hoots and whistles, she waved it in triumph.

Then she waved it again in the direction of Celesta's portrait. *How am I doing now, Mamma?*

Linda rushed down to give her a hug. "You did it, Rosa. Oh, I wanted it to be you. See?" she said to Vince and Teddy and anyone else who would listen. "Didn't I tell you?"

"We all told you," Vince added. "And we were right, weren't we?"

"Yes," said Rosa, holding the fragile bouquet against

her heart. When she turned, she saw Alex coming toward her, weaving his way between the tables. In that moment, she didn't see anything but him. "Yes, absolutely."

* * * * *

Dear Reader,

I hope you enjoyed this visit to the fictional seaside town of Winslow. I confess, I gained a few pounds while creating and testing the original recipes here. They are adapted from many sources, and Deborah Mele's enchanting Web site, www.italianfoodforever.com was particularly inspirational. Some truly excellent recipes didn't make the final cut into the book, so you'll find those on my Web site. In doing this delightful research, I was reminded of something Rosa has always known. One of life's simplest pleasures is preparing delicious, fresh food, which needs no special garnish other than the company of friends and family.

Happy reading (and eating),

Susan Wiggs

www.susanwiggs.com

#1 *NEW YORK TIMES* BESTSELLING AUTHOR
USA TODAY BESTSELLING AUTHOR

SUSAN WIGGS

Never get attached—Private nurse and protected witness
Claire Turner lives by this motto. Fleeing a treacherous past,
she knows no other way.

Never give up—In the twilight of his life, George Bellamy's final wish
is to reconcile with an estranged brother. He and Claire journey to
Willow Lake—where it all went wrong for him fifty years ago.

Never let go—George's grandson Ross is ruled by devotion to family
and mistrust of the mysterious Claire…yet sparks fly whenever
she's near. Faced with a wrenching loss, amid the enchantment of
Willow Lake, Ross and Claire risk everything for love.

The *Summer* Hideaway

Available wherever books are sold.

#1 *New York Times* bestselling author

SUSAN WIGGS

portrays the intrigue and majesty of
King Henry VIII's court in her classic
Tudor Rose trilogy.

Available wherever books are sold!

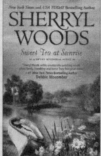

REQUEST YOUR FREE BOOKS!

2 FREE NOVELS
FROM THE ROMANCE COLLECTION
PLUS 2 FREE GIFTS!

YES! Please send me 2 FREE novels from the Romance Collection and my 2 FREE gifts (gifts are worth about $10). After receiving them, if I don't wish to receive any more books, I can return the shipping statement marked "cancel." If I don't cancel, I will receive 4 brand-new novels every month and be billed just $5.74 per book in the U.S. or $6.24 per book in Canada. That's a saving of at least 28% off the cover price. It's quite a bargain! Shipping and handling is just 50¢ per book in the U.S. and 75¢ per book in Canada.* I understand that accepting the 2 free books and gifts places me under no obligation to buy anything. I can always return a shipment and cancel at any time. Even if I never buy another book, the two free books and gifts are mine to keep forever.

194 MDN E4LY   394 MDN E4MC

Name	(PLEASE PRINT)
Address	Apt. #
City	State/Prov.	Zip/Postal Code

Signature (if under 18, a parent or guardian must sign)

Mail to **The Reader Service:**
IN U.S.A.: P.O. Box 1867, Buffalo, NY 14240-1867
IN CANADA: P.O. Box 609, Fort Erie, Ontario L2A 5X3

Not valid for current subscribers to the Romance Collection
or the Romance/Suspense Collection.

Want to try two free books from another line?
Call 1-800-873-8635 or visit www.morefreebooks.com.

* Terms and prices subject to change without notice. Prices do not include applicable taxes. N.Y. residents add applicable sales tax. Canadian residents will be charged applicable provincial taxes and GST. Offer not valid in Quebec. This offer is limited to one order per household. All orders subject to approval. Credit or debit balances in a customer's account(s) may be offset by any other outstanding balance owed by or to the customer. Please allow 4 to 6 weeks for delivery. Offer available while quantities last.

Your Privacy: Harlequin Books is committed to protecting your privacy. Our Privacy Policy is available online at www.eHarlequin.com or upon request from the Reader Service. From time to time we make our lists of customers available to reputable third parties who may have a product or service of interest to you. If you would prefer we not share your name and address, please check here. ☐

Help us get it right—We strive for accurate, respectful and relevant communications. To clarify or modify your communication preferences, visit us at www.ReaderService.com/consumerschoice.

"Forgive me, *mon Père*, for I have sinned—" She stopped, her throat closing. She wanted to weep, for she could never confess all that she had done, and surely no penance would erase the curse of what she was.

"Yes, my child?"

"*Mon Père*, the revolutionaries have murdered my family. . . ." She heard the rustle of cloth, a whispered prayer, as he crossed himself. And then she told him; it seemed forever, her body and her voice shaking. She could not stop her voice or her shaking.

"Stop, my child. It is enough. You have committed a grave sin. But these men would have committed more horrors if you had not stopped them; the laws are gone that we have relied on for so long. These sort of men are the law now." He paused, and she heard him take in a deep breath. "You must be strong to have killed so many by yourself. Go out and save those whom evil men wish to kill. And do not kill again, unless it be in self-defense. That is your penance."

"*Merci, mon Père*." She waited for his blessing, and when he gave it, she rose and left.

There was not much time left now; the sun would be rising soon. Simone ran into the woods again, running with feet now light with hope. She would do it; she would save those marked for death.

Night Fires

Karen
Harbaugh

A Dell Book

NIGHT FIRES

A Dell Book / December 2003
Dell mass market special edition / August 2004

Published by Bantam Dell
A Division of Random House, Inc.
New York, New York

This novel is a work of fiction. Names, characters, places, and
incidents either are the product of the author's imagination or are
used fictitiously. Any resemblance to actual persons, living or dead,
events, or locales is entirely coincidental.

ISBN 0-440-24251-7

Manufactured in the United States of America
Published simultaneously in Canada

OPM   10 9 8 7 6 5 4 3 2 1

Acknowledgments

The conception of this book is all Mary Jo Putney's fault, bless her heart. If she hadn't planted the idea of creating a vampire heroine in my brain, I wouldn't have been tortured with it for years afterward and been forced by my muse to write it and send it out.

In truth, fellow writers and friends are always the spur to greater growth and greater joy in creativity, and for this I'm thankful. Many blessings to my critique group; to my agent, who persisted in sending it out and who put up with my fears and worries; to my editor, Wendy McCurdy, who took a chance and bought the book; to Kathy Carmichael, who figured out where the action was mere running in place; and to my dear husband and best friend, John, who believed the completion of the book was more important than finding yet another full-time technical writing job.

Night Fires

Prologue

1793, Normandy, France

SHE MADE ALMOST NO NOISE AS SHE slipped through the forest, and the brush of ferns against her skirts sounded like the cold wind through the trees. It was her way, traveling swift and silent as a ghost. The light of the gibbous moon glinted on metal gates in the distance; she could see no movement near them, or hear any sign of the living. The heat of fear burned her feet; her steps quickened.

"Marthe!" she whispered. "Marthe!" But she was not close enough yet for the old nursemaid to hear; the name was a prayer, the first in many winters. There was blood in the air, and she was afraid. Her fingers touched metal at last, and she controlled the tightening of her throat.

"Marthe!" she cried, still afraid.

A sigh and a whimper, a soft weeping, and then a gray shape in the moonlight, a wisp of mist arising from the ground. Almost she thought it was a spirit, but she put her hand beyond the gate and her hand touched cloth as the shape came near.

"Mademoiselle Simone?" The voice shook with age and grief.

"I am not too late, Marthe. Tell me I am not too late."

Grief and shadows furrowed the old woman's uplifted face. She sighed. "At least you are left, my little one, my little one." She began to sing a lullaby.

Simone clutched the woman's cloak. *"Tell me I am not too late!"*

Marthe's face crumpled. "Ah, mademoiselle, mademoiselle! They took them, and there are none left."

"You lie!" Simone clutched the cloak more tightly, and it tore in her hand, as hope and fear began to tear her heart. The old nursemaid had become senile, her memory disordered. She tried not to remember that Marthe had always had a sharp mind, up to last week when she last saw her.

The old woman shrank from her. "Your face—Simone, *mon infant,* you are ill to be so pale."

Simone drew in a deep breath and stilled the weeping that threatened to rise up from her belly. "No, Marthe, I am . . . well. My family—they are living, yes? They have not been taken?"

A cunning look smoothed out the wrinkles on the old woman's face. "No, not all. Look you, mademoiselle, I have saved one." She held out in her arms a ragged swaddled shape, silent, too silent.

Simone gently opened the gate. Marie's child, perhaps? Or perhaps Antoine's? She took the bundle from Marthe.

It was light, too light to be what she hoped. She pushed aside the blankets and moaned.

It was a doll, its ivory face painted with a knowing smile. She remembered it; it had been hers when she was a child, almost too long ago to remember. She looked at Marthe and did not scream the anger and the sorrow that hammered for release behind her teeth.

"Is this all, Marthe?" Simone asked at last.

"All? But this is the heir, mademoiselle!" The old woman shook her head and began to sob. "I have saved the heir of the de la Fers! If I had not, there would only be Simon de la Fer left, and defenseless . . . defenseless as I, alas. She may be dead now, without children, for I would have heard if she had married, poor lady."

Simone pulled up her shoulders, as if she felt a chill, though she rarely felt heat or cold, or the passing of seasons. "She is not dead, Marthe. I have seen her myself."

Marthe's expression turned eager. "Then give her what I have saved, mademoiselle. Give her the heir until the Terror has passed."

Simone de la Fer lifted her head as the breeze increased in speed and moved the trees to rustle. The blood in the air sharpened her senses so that she could feel at last the cold of late autumn, and the promise of a colder winter. "I will take this—this to the lady, Marthe." Simone drew her shawl from around her neck and tied it around her shoulder and back in a sling. "The others, Marthe. Where are they?"

Marthe's voice became a whisper. "I do not know. I fled with the heir, you see. I did well, did I not?"

Simone drew in her breath, holding back her impatience. She touched Marthe's face briefly, and the woman flinched. She dropped her hand and sighed. "Yes, of course. Go, now, Marthe." She lowered her voice and made it soothing and soft, though her heart hammered in grief. "Go to your son's house—he is a good citizen of the Republic—and do not ever mention the de la Fer family again. You do not know them; you have never known them." The old woman's eyes became glazed in the moonlight and she blinked slowly, then nodded. "Go now."

"Yes, mademoiselle." The woman turned and shuffled

away. Simone stared at the retreating figure until Marthe's shape became mistlike and faded into the night.

The wind pulled at Simone's skirts and the blood rose again upon the air. It called to her, and her stomach churned with need. Simone clenched her teeth together. She knew from whence the blood came; it came from the home of the de la Fer family, her home. She closed her eyes. Marthe must be wrong; perhaps it was from their enemies; perhaps the de la Fers had fled.

It had been many years since she had stepped within the gates of the de la Fer estate. She hesitated from habit before she pulled the gate open further and began to run toward the château. It had been so many years, but her feet flew over the grass and earth as if she had never left. Simone closed her eyes briefly against the familiar rise and fall of the land, the familiar trees and gardens.

It hurt her to remember. Best to think of her family. Marthe had spoken nothing but nonsense; what Simone feared could not be true. And look, there were lights in the windows—the drawing room, in fact, where her mother had once entertained brilliantly dressed lords and ladies, and where Simone herself had met—

No. No memories. No memories.

The windows were closed, but they were large, and bright candles shone through them, as if a ball were in progress. She braced herself against the sound of music she wanted desperately to hear—the one thing she had left to her was music, and it was a knife-thrust through her soul whenever she heard it.

There was no sound, just the sound of the blood-laden wind, just the light of candles through the windows.

She reached the door of the house; it was ajar. The scent of blood made her gasp and the cold wind bit into her suddenly hypersensitive flesh. She pushed open the door until it stopped halfway from some obstacle. She slipped within, and saw what had kept the door from opening all the way.

She should be used to such by now; she had seen death in many guises. But this was her home, and the man—the butler, it must have been, by his livery—was dead from a slit in his throat, no more than a few hours dead perhaps. Simone closed her eyes and crossed herself—an automatic gesture of which she could not rid herself. It did not matter. She did not know what she believed any more.

No sound, of course, for there would be no ball—the thought of it almost made her laugh hysterically. She stilled. Yes, sound. Her hearing was keen now. The sound of voices, laughing, drunken. She ran through the house, ignoring the torn wallpaper where paintings had obviously been pulled from the wall. She remembered rich draperies at the windows; they, too, had been torn down.

Rage and grief, sudden and hot, rose up from her belly; her hands shook with it. She stilled them, stilled the shaking inside as well. The tears would not come—they were forbidden her—but the rage turned as cold as the autumn chill that pierced her flesh like knives. Her feet became quiet; she walked like a cat in the night, hunting mice, though her spirit wailed in protest.

The drawing room. The candlelight blaring through the open door like the noise of brass trumpets upon her eyes. The drunken voices of living men inside. The smell of blood, thick and heavy, the smell of spent lust.

She tenderly laid down the bundle within the shawl, and then entered the room. She dropped the cloak from her shoulders, and her flesh gleamed white.

The black-clothed men were drunk with wine stolen from her family's cellars. They were drunk with the lust they had spent upon serving maids and ladies now dead, they were drunk with the power of killing men they envied. Simone's glance took in the age-scored, knife-scored faces of brothers, sisters, parents; grief filled her heart with poison. The bodies still strewn about the drawing room showed that the murderers had not spared terror on their victims, her family.

She turned to ice.

She smiled her cold rage at them, her smile a sensuous thing they should have feared, but none ever had. She moved toward them on cat feet, with a serpent's seduction in her body.

She was prey, she was predator, she was light, she was dark. The fire in her belly moved onto her mouth and lips and became the hunger she feared so many times. But this time rage obliterated all fear. Her sharp teeth pricked the flesh of her lips as she smiled at them. The men's eyes filled with lust and violent power as they looked at her and came at her with knives.

She allowed the first one to put his lips upon her and lay his knife against her neck before she tore the life from his throat—easily, quickly, and more mercifully than he deserved. She was the handmaiden of Death; they fell without knowing what had come upon them. The alchemy of rage and grief turned her into fire; her mind burned with vengeance, vengeance.

Then it was still and dark. The candles guttered in the chandeliers and in the sconces against the wall, and the only sound in the drawing room was the crackling of the embers in the hearth.

The murderers for the Republic were dead now, and her rage and thirst were sated. But sorrow and horror lay leaden in her stomach, and though she was filled with the power of the blood she had taken from the killers, she lifted her moon-pale face to the sky and moaned, grief and shame biting deep.

She was the last of the de la Fers. There were no others. She, Simone de la Fer: she who was outcast and stained, and cursed to live forever young when her family—who had wept when they turned their backs upon her—were now all dead.

Dead. Death. She was the embodiment of it, for she was as deathless as Death itself, and she dealt it swiftly, unstoppable as stormwinds. Her breath sobbed in her throat. *Mon Dieu.* She had not wished for the blood-thirst, she had resisted it, but it took just one taste of rage and despair and she had loosed it upon these men. Would she never be rid of it?

She worked until almost dawn, cleaning the drawing room and the hall of blood and bodies. She was strong and tireless and could do this until the light of morning made her weak. And then she washed herself, tied the doll upon her back, and walked aimlessly inside the house and then outside, groaning her grief, until she reached the abbey nearby, where the good Abbé Dumont was already awake and done with his matins.

She paused before the church, hesitating. She did not deserve to be here. And yet, she entered, and stepped into the confessional and crossed herself, ignoring the sizzling pain that crept across her skin at being in a holy place. If she stayed here long, she would surely die, as she had seen others of . . . of her kind do. It did not matter, and perhaps be a blessed relief. At the very least, she would make sure the priest would say prayers for her family's souls and attend properly to their burial. She could hear a suppressed yawn from the other side of the screen.

"How may I help you, my child?" The abbé's voice was warm and soothing, and she wished the warmth of it were tangible so that she could wrap herself in it, and cease shaking with blood-power, soul-deep cold, and the angry dance of fire on her skin in this holy place.

"Forgive me, *mon Père,* for I have sinned—" She stopped, her throat closing. She wanted to weep, for she could never confess all that she had done, and surely no penance would erase the curse of what she was.

"Yes, my child?"

"I cannot . . ."

"Is it that you are afraid? No sin is so great that it cannot be forgiven."

Forgiven. Could she be forgiven? She listened to the abbé's warm voice, and remembered when she had come to this confessional, when he first arrived at the abbey perhaps as long as fifteen years ago. He had not been the de la Fers' father confessor then, of course. She sighed. A long time ago, when her father and mother were alive, and her brothers and sisters—not dead, as they were now. Abbé Dumont's voice was warm back then, too, as it was now.

"*Mon Père,* the revolutionaries have murdered my family. . . ." She heard the rustle of cloth, a whispered prayer, as he crossed himself. And then she told him, it seemed forever, her body and her voice shaking. She could not stop her voice or her shaking.

"Stop, my child. It is enough." His voice trembled with grief or anger, and she knew them as she knew her own heart. He would cast her out now, as her family had cast her out, for she was no better than an animal, her hands wreaking death as if they were the claws of a wild beast. She put her hands over her face and drew in a breath. She should leave. Surely it was an abomination that one such as she should be here.

"I have seen atrocities," the abbé said slowly, and his voice made her stay. "Not even the priesthood is exempt from the madness."

He had not told her to leave. Her body shook harder with the pain of being in a holy place, with the power of blood, and with the painful hope of acceptance.

"You have committed a grave sin. But these men would have committed more horrors if you had not stopped them; the laws are gone that we have relied on for so long. These sort of men are the law, now."

"What should I do?" she whispered.

"Penance, boy."

Boy . . . He thought her a youth. Of course. The abbé could not see through the screen. Her voice was deep for a woman, and how could a mere woman avenge herself upon so many men? She opened her mouth to correct him, then closed it again. What did it matter?

"That is all?" she said instead.

He laughed dryly. "You have not heard your penance, my child." He paused, and she heard him take in a deep breath. "You must be strong to have killed so many by yourself. Go out and save those whom evil men wish to kill. And do not kill again, unless it be in self-defense. That is your penance. And if that is not enough for you, you are to say ten Paternosters and Marias as well."

"Merci, mon Père." She waited for his blessing, and when he gave it, she rose and left, mindful of the doll she carried, and careful to run quickly so that the abbé would not see her.

There was not much time left now; the sun would be rising soon. Simone ran into the woods again, running with feet now light with hope. She would do it; she would save those marked for death. Perhaps the penance would erase the curse upon her. Perhaps saving lives would erase the sin of having taken lives.

Her steps slowed for a moment as the shaking overtook her again. She took in a deep breath, and the autumn air bit into her lungs. She ran faster, and now she was in the depths of the wood, the dry leaves thick upon the ground, rustling around her ankles. Yes, she would even look through her family's belongings and find a rosary; perhaps she would find the one her mother used to wear.

Such holy things hurt her hands when she touched them. She did not mind pain so very much. She knew she was still alive when she felt pain.

At last the dry leaves at her feet came almost to her knees; the wood was thick with trees and fern here. Here was a hollow in which she burrowed for a bed, a shallow cave of stone, oak roots, and dirt. She laid herself down against the deep side of the hollow where she could feel the wood of the oak, and dug deep into the leaves she had gathered there. They would cover her and protect her from the light; the ferns were a curtain against intruders.

Simone sighed and closed her eyes. Tomorrow night she would begin her penance. She would save those marked for death, she who knew death like a lover. She would strike swiftly for life, she who could see life only in darkness.

She took the bundle Marthe had given her and pulled it close to her. She would even say her prayers.

And perhaps . . . perhaps, she would cease to be a vampire some day, and see the blessed sun at last.

Chapter 1

London, 1793

HE PUT HIS FINGERS—SPLAYED, AS IF PLAYing a harpsichord—on the chill library window, and watched the fine mist collect upon the glass around each fingertip. He could see it clearly against the dark dawn sky. Then he removed his hand, and blew upon the marks he made. His breath obliterated the fingertip mist in a large, round circle of gray, then the winter chill outside the window permeated, and made it all disappear.

The glass clear again, he stared out of it, watching the city awaken with a shivering, hesitant movement. Bakery boys' feet slipped on the wet cobblestones, and the voices of tradesmen shook or groaned while hawking their wares. How very *active* of them, the man thought. And so very ordinary. A thought that ordinariness would be welcome at some time in his life strayed into his mind, but he shook it off, as well as the accompanying fatigue. A day of rest, and he would be ready for another assignment.

His lips twisted. There was no rest for one such as himself. Rest meant time to contemplate life and other ordinary things, and contemplation was only for fools. It was no use contemplating his life. He'd done enough of that already.

A closer sound, the tread of firm footsteps, came from behind him, but he did not turn around. It was, no doubt, Sir Robert Smith; a worthy and solid soul, as solid as the sound of his footsteps.

The steps hesitated for a moment, perhaps because the library was dim, lit only by the fire in the hearth and a brace of candles. The man by the window allowed himself a smile. Sir Robert was also wise. One did not walk boldly into dark places.

"I am here, Sir Robert." The man could hear Sir Robert walk toward him, and at last he turned around.

There was no hesitation in Sir Robert's steps as he came closer, but certainly there was in his eyes. *My reputation, oh, my reputation,* the man thought, amused.

"About Marat," Sir Robert said, still watching him. The name was a statement, not a question.

A pause, then a small shrug as the man glanced out the window at the lightening sky. "You have access to the papers," he said. "You know whatever you need to know about me and my assignments—and Marat." He walked to the window again, placing his fingers on the glass as he did before and blowing on the finger marks.

"Except what I am to call you." Sir Robert moved to the desk and brought out a packet of papers from his coat pocket. His eyes held curiosity.

The man almost smiled. He had carried out Sir Robert's orders for almost a year now, and it amused him not to reveal his name. It was safer that way; the less anyone knew of him, the less hold on him they had. He had even rented this town house under an assumed name through a third party, and he had entered it unnoticed. He turned. "You may call me whatever you wish."

Sir Robert frowned, irritated. "Yes, and since I know all

I 'need' to know about you, I also know you like playing games with your name, Mr. Whoever-you-are."

This time the man laughed, a soft sound. "You must allow me some amusement, Sir Robert," he said. He rested his chin on his hand, and tapped his index finger on his lip, as if in profound thought. "You may call me Corday."

Sir Robert's hands paused in the straightening of the papers before him. "Corday." He gazed sternly at the man. "As in Charlotte Corday. I do not find the use of that name amusing."

"Try to see it as a tribute to a job well done," Corday replied flippantly.

"We do not pay you to have someone else complete the assignment."

"Ah, but I did complete it." Corday's voice cooled. "Your papers will tell you I have been very successful." He almost sighed. He did not regret what he had done; it was his occupation, and he did it well. He did regret that Mademoiselle had been such a zealot that she went eagerly to her death to prove her point, rather than leave with him. But she had fancied herself a martyr, and there was nothing one could do to convince such people into prudence.

Sir Robert stared at him, pursing his lips thoughtfully. "Usually," he said. "When it pleases you to be successful."

"True," he replied. He leaned next to the window with a negligent air.

"Hmph." But a small smile crossed Sir Robert's lips before he drew his brows together, looking at the papers before him. He glanced at Corday. "This time, however, you *will* be successful, whether it pleases you or not."

Corday said nothing and looked out the window, allowing a long silence between them.

"These are serious affairs," Sir Robert said at last, his voice grave and perhaps a little rebuking.

Corday did not move. "My assignments always are," he

said. "I have never thought differently. I deal out death, do I not? And death is always serious."

Silence hung between them again, and Corday smiled to himself. Perhaps he had shocked the respectable Sir Robert with his bluntness. Corday wondered if Sir Robert would protest, or bluster, as his predecessors had done.

"Yes," Sir Robert said instead, his voice holding a certain pity. "Yes, you do."

Quick irritation shot through Corday, surprising him, and he turned, his feet making only a whisper against the carpet. He stared at Sir Robert, who regarded him calmly, his expression unafraid. Either his new superior was a fool, or had no regard for his life or his loved ones. Corday could kill him here, now, and no one would be the wiser about who had done it. He could cause the death or ruination of Sir Robert's wife. Sir Robert should know by now with whom he was dealing.

They watched each other, unmoving, tension stretching between them. Sir Robert also knew much about Corday; how much, Corday was not sure. But Sir Robert gave a small nod, almost a bow, as if acknowledging the danger inherent in both their positions.

"And this is another time we wish you to 'deal death,' " Sir Robert said. He sighed as if he was reluctant to give this assignment; perhaps he was, for Sir Robert, by all accounts, was a decent man. But Corday never assumed anyone was decent, or could not be corrupted. This assumption, after all, was the soul of espionage. Sir Robert glanced at the papers before him on the table, and shifted them apart with his hand. "There is a man, someone we wish you to eliminate," he said.

"Kill, you mean," Corday said pleasantly.

"Kill," said Sir Robert, and his lips twisted in a wry smile. Corday began to like him, reluctantly, for he admired anyone who was frank with him, and this was not the first time Sir Robert had been so. "Although in truth, if you could eliminate the man without killing him, I would be just as pleased. However"—his smile disappeared—"this man is too dangerous for us to consider anything but the most extreme measures."

"Meaning myself." Corday began to feel bored. While there had been some difficulties in his assignments, they had been overcome. He smiled inwardly. Indeed, he had more difficulties overcoming his whims than any challenges his enemies had decided to throw his way.

"He killed Johnson and Bramley," Sir Robert continued.

Bramley . . . Johnson. Two highly skilled men. Even Corday had come to respect them, for they, at the beginning of his career, had helped train him. They were even comrades of a sort; he and they had traded jokes both practical and verbal—the former could be dangerous and was frowned upon, but their superiors in their branch of government intelligence had little humor, after all.

No humor now. Corday looked at Sir Robert. "How?"

His superior shook his head. "Knifed and mauled, both of them."

"Impossible."

"No. There is no mistake."

"Someone they knew." It was a statement. No one could have come that close to the two men else, Corday thought.

Sir Robert's brows drew together, and his eyes showed worry. "It's possible. The Revolution in France grows apace, and they'd spread it to England if they could, if only to chase down the aristocrats who escaped. There is no law but the agents of the revolution now." He pressed his lips together and his eyes met Corday's.

Infiltration. Sir Robert didn't have to say it; it was necessary at least to consider the possibility. Corday managed not to show the irritation he felt. Some idiot bureaucrat probably got himself in a wedge and had no choice but to put his head through a spy's collar and leash.

"Shall I search out the corrupted one for you, Sir Robert?" Corday asked, watching him again.

Sir Robert grimaced, showing distaste. "I would prefer it, but I want you to find the man behind it. I'm not as good as you are, and the man in France is far more dangerous."

"Flattering me, Sir Robert?" Corday grew still, watching for minute changes in his superior's expression.

"Yes." Sir Robert grinned suddenly. "I don't want to leave my very comfortable wife and home, thank you very much. Besides, you know the French tongue better than I do, and that's a fact." He gave Corday a curious look.

Corday gazed at his superior, and wondered if it was he. Perhaps. He almost chuckled. No doubt Sir Robert wondered the same thing about him. Such fearful insanity, this game of espionage. Corday would have his contacts watch Sir Robert's activities nevertheless. A man on a leash would bite where he was told, although it would be a pity if it were his superior, he thought. He had begun to like Sir Robert, and it would be disappointing to have to eliminate him, too, if he were ordered to do it some day.

"Very well, then," he said.

His superior raised his brows, and Corday repressed a smile. Did he think the agreement came too quickly? Sir Robert had little choice but to send him, Corday, after all. There were few others who could do the job.

Sir Robert glanced at the papers before him again, and for a brief moment tapped his fingers on the table, as if in thought. He sighed as if he had come to some reluctant conclusion and gazed again at Corday. "The last communication we had from Johnson located our target's base." He grimaced. "Paris, of course. Where would such a man as he have more influence? None of it is overt. A word here, a rumor there, a discreet killing or accusation—it amounts to the same thing. But a pattern, nevertheless."

"Where in Paris?"

Sir Robert gave him an apologetic look. "The docks on the Seine, or close to them. That is all we know."

"That's hardly 'located,' Sir Robert."

A shrug. "It's the best we've been able to do. We thought your contacts—"

"Will have to do more work, and therefore it will take more time and more risk," Corday said.

"You will be compensated, of course, half in advance," Sir Robert replied cordially. "Deposited at the usual place."

"Excellent." It was easy to deal with Sir Robert in these matters, Corday thought. He hoped the man was not an infiltrator; it would mean a change of management if Sir Robert's superiors determined it was necessary for him to be eliminated, and that in turn usually meant having to deal with someone new and unfamiliar. An inconvenience, and Corday disliked inconvenience in his dealings.

"We will need you to leave soon, tomorrow morning," Sir Robert said. "I imagine you will leave for Margate." He raised a questioning brow.

Corday smiled at last. "Imagine nothing, my dear sir. I will arrange my own transport, as usual."

Sir Robert shook his head, lips pursed in disapproval. "As usual. For your own safety, we should know where you are."

"You implied an infiltrator." Corday gazed at him coolly. "For my own safety, no one should know where I am."

His supervisor grimaced. "True." He sighed, and rubbed his brow with his hand. "I will be glad when this is over."

I, too, Corday thought, as he rose and left, after a short bow in Sir Robert's direction. Fatigue touched him again.

A little sleep, and he would begin the assignment. It was all he required, until the ultimate rest all men slipped into at the end. He was familiar with that kind of rest, and sometimes envied the men he aided to it. It was, after all, a tiring thing to be an assassin, and it would be pleasant, for once, not to be one.

But there was only one kind of true rest for assassins, and that was death. And he was not quite ready for that, yet.

The small yacht that left from a hidden shore was sturdy and slim, and cut through the water like a knife. Corday watched as the dim white shores faded into gray in the night. He closed his eyes for a moment, breathing in the dank salt air. The cold wind scored the skin of his face with icy fingers and lifted his hair from his scalp. He should go belowdecks and stay as warm as he could, but he always stood on deck when leaving England. Pulling his coat closer around him, he shrugged his shoulders, then thrust his hands in his pockets. How sentimental. But he supposed, after all these years of leaving, he should be allowed some sentimentality.

He watched the faint gray in the distance turn dark at last, then walked across the deck to the stairs that led to his chambers below. As he entered his room, he could hear the *shush-shush* of the water against the creaking hull, and the footsteps of sailors above; oddly soothing sounds. Perhaps it was because he was relatively safe here; it was a small reprieve before pulling on the cloak of wariness and sensitivity to danger once he went ashore. Safe . . . He must be getting on in years, to be thinking of such things. Better to think of the assignment before him.

Opening a small chest, he pulled out the papers Sir Robert had given him, as well as notes collected from his various sources. He brought near the lantern he had left lit in his room, then examined the papers.

Sir Robert had been very thorough, which Corday appreciated; his supervisor had detailed each movement, each incident thought to relate to the man Corday was to seek, as reported by Johnson and Bramley. He read on, and his shoulders tensed as he noted the condition of these agents' bodies. Bloodied, broken, and the faces so scarred as to be nearly unrecognizable. Luckily, the clothes had been easily identified as belonging to the two men, and though it looked as if the murderer had tried to cut off Johnson's finger so as to dislodge his signet ring, the ring still remained, and it was, indeed, Johnson's. Corday massaged the back of his neck and shrugged his shoulders to release the tension that had gathered there. He should try to sleep as well as he could before the yacht landed. Being tired at the start of his mission was not a good way to begin.

Corday tapped his fingers against the wooden table as he thought over the man's movements, the course of the Revolution, and areas of unrest. Every right had been suspended since the summer, and even the powerful Church was in fear. He smiled cynically. The leaders of the Revolution were said to be the most intelligent and educated of men, and yet they worshiped slogans and let empty words do the thinking for them. Of all people, the intelligent were among the most easily manipulated, for they often thought they were beyond manipulation.

The man he sought was a master manipulator; he seemed to have his fingers in every pie, both social and political, and certainly criminal. He went by different names, and even sometimes seemed to have a different appearance from time to time, but Corday shrugged at that. It was a simple thing to fool people regarding one's appearance. But the man's influence was weblike, with strands connecting him here and there to people of authority. And yet, Corday doubted that those very people the man manipulated knew exactly who he was.

How very spiderlike, Corday thought, then smiled. Who knew which of the names he called himself was his own? *So much like yourself,* said a little part of his mind. His smile turned wry. But of course. It was the very nature of gathering information, was it not? He had half contemplated not going on this mission; he could be entering into a trap. Sir Robert had mentioned an infiltrator, after all. But would he have mentioned it to him if he himself was the infiltrator, and intended to trap him? Probably not. It would have been simpler not to have mentioned it at all, and have let Corday himself find out about Johnson's and Bramley's deaths when it was too late to turn back.

And so, he was going. It did not take long for his contacts to give him the information he needed. They were efficient and careful, and did their job well. Indeed, he even had some inkling as to who the infiltrator might be. Should he inform Sir Robert? Perhaps. It depended on whether he could get the information to his superior without anyone knowing about it. He would have to see.

Corday shuffled through the papers again, reading them once more, and frowned. There was something familiar about the way the bodies had been treated, but he could not recall what it was that pricked his memory. He made a mental note to think on it later.

He had been in Paris before, but had not dealt much with the docks, or with those involved in the French side of smuggling. That would be his weakness. It might be possible to find help in this. He had heard of aristocrats—trying to escape the guillotine—being smuggled out of France . . . perhaps a trade of services. He had a few contacts who could lead him to those smugglers of humanity, and had even heard of some himself. Corday grimaced. There was no counting on such a thing, however. He might have to rely on bribery or threats, but those ways of dealing with informants were uncertain at best. . . .

The watch above decks, calling out the hour, made him aware that his eyes were closing. He rubbed his face with his hands. He was getting old to be so tired. No, not so old; he was only thirty-two. But he felt old—ancient, even. He sighed. It was a warning to him. He needed to be wary, more watchful, especially of himself. He would sleep, and then be ready for what was before him. Slowly, he tore up the papers, burned them bit by bit with the candle in his room, then brushed away the ashes. He checked his weapons and put his dagger under his pillow before he settled himself for sleep.

A light jolt woke him; the setting of the anchor, he supposed. It was time. He gathered together his belongings into his bag, then hung the bag from his shoulder. He would go about as a common man, an itinerant storyteller and scribe, and—Corday smiled slightly—a very harmless individual. If he needed more, then he had his resources, though he preferred not to use them. He had, also, a dagger strapped to his leg and another to his arm, and a pistol—very plain, and purposely crude-looking, but of German make and very well balanced and straight-shooting. One could never be too careful in this lawless land, after all.

He nodded to the captain as he stepped down into the small rowboat that eventually took him to shore. The captain had nodded back, but did not address him—it was better this way. There was no need for names. He was sure the captain was involved in smuggling goods, and would prefer no questions.

When his feet touched the shore, it was still dark, near dawn. The cold humid wind promised wet misery, though Corday could still see the moon's fugitive light through passing clouds. He hurried his steps; he did not want to appear to have arrived from the ship, but from some distance down. A mile, perhaps, and along the shore, and the tide would wash away his footsteps before the sun rose. Then he could turn to the woods, and find some slight shelter there if he could not find a suitable hedge tavern or inn.

And then a sound: a creaking, a rustling from ahead—the stomp of hooves, the sound of a wagon. Not, Corday thought, an enemy. The sleepy cry of a child quickly hushed spoke of farmers, perhaps, or fishermen, although he had been told he'd be far away from any such. He frowned at first, then grinned. Perhaps the ship he had just left had another sort of smuggling career in addition to French brandy—he had suspected as much, but it was rare that a man involved in smuggling goods would also be smuggling for humanitarian reasons.

Perhaps the captain was well paid to do it. In which case, Corday thought, it was possible that the organizer of this effort was not only well moneyed, but was even very knowledgeable and had useful resources. Corday sank down behind a small hillock near the woods, then took out his pistol. He would watch, and perhaps cultivate this person's acquaintance once his task was done.

A large wagon came close to the shore and trundled near him; a cloaked figure sat atop it. The wind wafted the smell of stale, dirty straw to him; it seemed the wagon was filled with it. Then it stopped, and the hay moved.

"*Allez-vous! Vite, vite!*" The voice was low and husky; a boy, it seemed, drove the wagon—or no, perhaps a woman. Clearly the French side of this smuggling scheme. A sob, then a hushing sound came from the wagon, and the mound upon it rustled and moved furiously as a man leaped down, and gave his hand to a woman clutching a bundle—a baby, from the way it moved. Two more people climbed from it, one an elderly, bent shape, one a child.

"Quickly! You must go, hurry, down to the ship—do you see it?"

The man bowed before the figure on the wagon. "*Merci, merci*, our rescuer—"

The cloaked one waved an impatient hand. "No time! Go, quickly! I will have your thanks later, if we meet, if *le bon Dieu* so wills. Go now!"

The man stumbled back, then got his footing, and hurried the family beside him down the shore.

Too late.

A shout from near the woods, and gunfire, and the man fell.

"Henri!" His wife beside him sank to her knees and pulled at his arm. The cloaked figure at the wagon was gone.

"Damn," Corday muttered, and settled his pistol on his arm. The Revolution's Public Safety corps, no doubt, and eager to catch aristocratic prey. He glanced at the couple huddled together, and at the old man who shielded the boy with his body. Corday ignored the screams of the bucking horse; the animal would bolt in a minute, and it and the wagon would be out of the way. The man next to the woman groaned, and made a staggering step upward. Not dead yet. Good. One of the agents came forward, swaggering. Corday took careful aim.

At nothing. He blinked.

A high keening wail rose in the air, raising the hair on his neck, and then the thump of a body sounded near the hillock he sat behind. The old man sank to his knees and crossed himself. "*La Flamme!*" he cried. "*Ah, Dieu merci!*"

What the devil?

A dark shape whirled in front of him, and then away into the woods. A cut-off cry of mixed terror and pain, and then the cloaked figure emerged again, crouched low, a hunter's stance, searching, searching.

Good. She hadn't run away.

The flicker of moonlight on metal caught Corday's eye—another agent—and he turned his pistol and pulled the trigger. Another cry, and the bushes crashed. Three. He slid the dagger down from his sleeve, then primed his pistol again—not easy in the dark, but he could do it. There could be others; he had heard the agents rarely came in small numbers when there was a fugitive family to arrest. Perhaps one or two more.

Another man came at the cloaked one, but the cape swirled again and the man fell. Four. Perhaps another—? One more agent leaped at the smuggler from behind, and Corday shot. The man fell upon his prey, a dead weight. Five. Corday smiled.

Silence.

He primed his pistol once more and waited. A low noise came from under one agent's body and it heaved. Corday tensed, then relaxed, remembering that it was the last one he had shot. The noise grew louder, and he grinned, recognizing French curses.

The body turned over, and the cloaked one rose from beneath it. "Idiots!" she said. "So stupid they shoot themselves in their haste to catch us." The dark figure looked to the family huddled on the shore and strode toward them. "Can he walk?"

"Yes, monsieur," replied the man. "The bleeding is not bad. My good wife has bound the wound." *Monsieur?* Was the cloaked one a youth after all? Corday pursed his lips in thought. Her—or his—voice was just in the range that could belong to a boy in the midst of adolescence, or to a woman with a deep contralto voice.

The figure paused, gazing toward the east, then said, "Nevertheless, I will help you. Come, take my hand."

Corday wondered if he should accompany them, perhaps even offer help. But the cloaked one took the weight of the injured man as if he weighed less than a feather, and the group trudged forward. No, he would let the youth, or woman, take the family, and follow at a discreet distance. There was no need to let the refugees know of his presence—better if they did not, in fact.

He skirted close to the woods, so that his form would blend against the shadows of the trees and small rises here and there, and watched the group carefully. The injured man seemed not too hurt; he managed a limping walk after a while.

It was indeed the boat he had just left that took in the refugees. He watched as the family was transported to the yacht while their rescuer stood silent on the shore, the only movement a brief flapping of the cloak in the breeze. At last, the ship lifted anchor and glided out to sea.

Corday moved behind a tree before the figure turned and walked back along the beach, then pulled out his pistol. The cloaked one was quick, and if he, or she—*it*—needed persuading, it was best if the pistol was ready.

The figure stopped.

"If you were going to shoot me, monsieur, I think you would have done so by now."

Corday raised his brows; he thought he had been very quiet, very discreet. The cloaked one must be quick-witted as well. He stepped out from the shadows. "True. However, one can never be too careful," he replied.

"Your accent is very good, but not from . . . Normandy, I believe?" The dark figure before him turned slowly, seeming to look at him.

"You may believe what you will."

The figure gave a shrug. "It matters not. I have things to do, so if you will excuse me, monsieur . . ." La Flamme bowed, and walked away.

Corday's pistol cocked with an audible click. The cloaked one stopped again.

"If you think to shoot me, do it now, unless you want

something of me. Money? You would have done better to have shot me earlier and given me to the Committee of Public Safety." The figure bent its head, apparently in thought. "Therefore, it is something else. Let me see. . . . Perhaps you are a desperate man, in need of some aid. Perhaps you think I can give you some information." Its hands came up to its waist. "In either case, I tell you I will not be persuaded at gunpoint."

Perhaps it was the cloaked one's mocking voice or posture of seeming unconcern and defiance, but something about him—surely male because of that defiance—made Corday want to laugh; the youth in front of him was a mouse compared to what he faced, and yet he acted as if he were a lion. Corday suppressed his brimming chuckle. "You might be persuaded by pain, however," he said instead.

The figure cast a hurried glance at the eastern horizon again, where the merest brush of light appeared. "So I might," he conceded. "But if you shoot me, who is to say that I would not be so overcome by pain, that I would be incapable of giving you what you want?" He stamped his foot—the cloaked one must be young, Corday thought. "I have no time for this. I must leave, and so must you. When these agents do not return with those they sought, they will seek both of us, which I am sure you do not want."

Corday's brows drew together in a frown. "What, are the agents not all dead?"

"You may have killed some—and yes, I know you must have been the one who shot them, though I said differently—but I did my best not to, only injure them enough to put them out until the day dawns . . . which is soon, too soon."

Irritation shot through Corday, but he uncocked his gun and put it away. "You should have killed them."

"I will not have more blood on my hands." The cloaked one spat out the words.

"Very noble, but very impractical." *More blood.* So the

cloaked one had killed before. Male, then, and one whose voice had not yet turned; few women had the stomach to kill at all. Of course, the youth could kill again. Good, if it meant that they would have to join forces for a while. Bad, if it meant that the youth would be inclined sometime in the future to kill *him*. However, the latter was not so bothersome; the cloaked one was a youth, and Corday was a man who had killed since youth. And he was, as always, watchful.

"I have no time to talk to you. I must go." The cloaked one turned and walked swiftly away.

Corday hesitated for a moment, then followed, catching up with a few quick steps. "Very well, then: I believe you might be the one who could give me the aid I require."

"And you sought to persuade me with your *so* elegant manners!" the cloaked one replied sarcastically.

This time Corday did chuckle. "You are a dangerous one, *mon petit*. It was the only way I believed I could get your attention."

A reluctant laugh emerged from the youth. "Should I be flattered?"

"Yes."

The hood of the cloak flicked upward for a moment, as if the youth gave him a sharp glance. "As you, too, are dangerous."

"Not I. I am merely a scribe and itinerant storyteller."

A disbelieving snort burst from beneath the hood. "You are no more a scribe and storyteller than I am a v—violet."

"Violet, you would be surprised at how good my hand is, and what stories I can tell."

"No, I would not be surprised, since you are bent on telling me a story now, but you are neither."

Corday shrugged and grinned. "I will not convince you, I see."

"What do you want of me?"

"Company . . . to Paris, if that is where you are going."

"And?"

Corday's grin grew wider. The cloaked one was no fool. "Information, of course, which I will request of you later, if you agree."

"I work alone, monsieur."

"As do I, so I appreciate the sentiment. However, there comes a time when company is useful . . . such as in accomplishing a complicated goal."

The sky was lightening now, but though the path before them grew more clear, the cloaked one's quick steps slowed, and his breath grew more labored.

"Think, boy. Much of your work seems best done at night. What would you say if we traveled together, both day and night? You say you work alone—I am sure the authorities know it. They would not be looking for a pair. Throwing them off the scent would accomplish your goal all the faster."

The cloaked one had turned from the path, and into the woods. Corday followed, and almost bumped into the youth when he stopped abruptly.

"There is something in what you say," the youth said. His voice was not much above a whisper, muffled perhaps by the hood.

"And you must know by now that if I meant you harm, I would have killed you at the start, instead of helping you." Corday paused, then said: "I have no love for your Revolution, after all."

A tired chuckle floated out of the hood, and then a large sigh. "English, then, if you are not a Royalist from Normandy." The figure seemed to waver for a moment. "Very well. There is an inn some ways from here, loyal to our poor king, though they hide it well, called La Liberté. You may meet me there tonight, at nightfall. You will arrive there near noon—ask them for a lamp to light your room, and they will know I sent you."

"That is all very well, but how do I know you will meet me, and what is more, how will I recognize you?"

"I have told you of the loyalty of the inn, and this is a danger to them if you prove to be false. That should be enough of a guarantee."

"And how will I know you?"

"You will know me by this." The cloaked one stood straight, and thrust out his hands from beneath his sleeves.

Corday froze.

Each arm was wrapped in rags from fingertip to elbow, with not one bit of flesh showing, as if bandaged over some loathsome disease.

"And this." The hands pushed back the hood.

The cloaked one had no face.

Simone de la Fer summoned one last burst of strength that allowed her to sprint into the woods away from the man who had helped her and who badgered her so. She smiled wearily. Covering her head and face with rags and gauze gave the impression of ghostly facelessness—a good disguise, in that it at once hid who she was and usually scared away those who did look at her. It did not fail her this time, either: Her rag-wrapped hands and face had managed to shock the man, enough so that he did not react fast enough to follow her.

Her feet knew the woods well; the trees were her protection against the light, and small hills and caves under overhanging roots and tall ferns gave blessed dark relief. She had not intended to stay out so close to dawn, but the family she had transported included both an old man and little children, slowing their progress. Then, too, the agents of the Committee of Public Safety had somehow followed her. Simone grimaced. She should be more careful with her plans.

An old oak towered above her, the branches now a silhouette against the lightening sky. She could feel the sharp tingling of her skin in response to the light, even through the rags wrapped around her body. She could bear sunlight if she were well wrapped, but it wearied her, and her strength faded with the rising of the sun. Thrusting aside the thick ferns that surrounded the large, deep hole under the roots of the old oak, she climbed inside, then settled into the blankets she had hidden there.

Simone sighed. She would much prefer a comfortable bed, but she was too far from her home. Better here, anyway; the stranger would no doubt ask about her here and there, and would find she had disappeared. Very few followed her into the woods at night. She could see like a cat even on a new-moon night, and even through the gauze over her eyes, so she could escape easily.

An uncomfortable bulge at her back made her shake her head at herself. She had forgotten about the doll. Unstrapping the doll from her back, she turned it over and looked at it in the darkness. Its white face still wore its little pout, and its hair was still intact, if messed. Simone smoothed back the hair into a semblance of its old coiffure. It was a little more battered than it had been when Marthe had first given it to her, but still in good shape. She could not throw it away even in her rage and grief, but had for some reason kept it, and then it had become part of her disguise. It gave her a hunched back under her cloak, which she hadn't realized until the broadsheets calling for her capture described her as such. And somehow, it gave her an odd comfort, and it reminded her of her purpose.

She sighed again, put the doll beside her, and closed her eyes. No more thinking. She would sleep, and see the stranger tonight.

Chapter 2

FOR THE SECOND TIME THIS MORNING, Corday blinked. The figure was gone, with only the swaying of low branches to show there had been anyone at all. He debated going after the youth, but it seemed the cloaked one knew the woods well, and Corday was sure that, if he followed, he would lose his way.

He stood staring into the forest's darkness, letting the cold breeze nip at his face. But the wind rose and touched his face with trailing mist until he pulled up his collar and wrapped his muffler close around his neck and over his mouth. He turned away from the woods to the road. He would seek this inn the cloaked one spoke of; if the youth appeared there, they could talk further. If not, then he would go on his way and accomplish the mission on his own. But it would be good to have company.

Corday's stride slowed. Where had that thought come from? He had not ever wished for company before on his missions. It was an inconvenience, and he was best working alone. He cast a last look at the woods he had left—no movement now, only a few winter birds chirping frailly in the echoing silence between the trees. Perhaps it was because the cloaked one had made him want to laugh . . . and he realized he had not laughed in a very long time. Laughed, perhaps, out of cynicism, but not out of sheer amusement. He shook his head. Yes, he was no doubt getting old for his career. His eyes closed. Dangerous thoughts. After his mission, perhaps, he could think them. But not now.

It took him more than a few hours to walk there, but the inn was as the cloaked one said it would be. It was large, and looked as if it had originally started as a cottage, then had bits and pieces built onto it. If a few buckled shingles on the roof were any indication, Corday expected it leaked from time to time. It was clean, and as well cared for as the owner could make it, he supposed. He glanced at the sky again, and a spit of rain hit his face. It would not at all hurt to stop at the inn for a while, at least until the threatened downpour ended.

The inn had the flag of the Revolution set in front of it. There was a stable to one side; he could hear the occasional snorting of horses and the rustling of hay. A rooster crowed behind it and as he approached the door, the muffled bustling movements of people within sounded through it.

It was, in all, a fairly prosperous inn. As Corday stepped inside, he glanced around at the neat curtains and the faint scent of bread baking from somewhere in the back of the inn. Suspiciously prosperous. Flour had become expensive, for all the French government's restrictions, yet it seemed this inn could still produce some for its guests. No doubt it received its income from more than one place.

The plump innkeeper greeted him with a wary smile and slight bow. "May I be of service, mon—*citoyen*?"

"A room, if you please, and breakfast; I've traveled far,

and wish to rest a day before I continue." *Citizen.* Corday hid a smile. Obviously, the innkeeper was still not used to the revolutionary Republic's title for their people.

"Your name, citoyen?"

Corday raised his brows. It was said with suspicion, not the casual welcome he was used to. "Robert Thibaut," he replied.

This time the innkeeper raised *his* brows. Corday laughed at his skepticism. "I assure you it is my name, as ordinary as it is. Indeed, I have been burdened with it the whole of my life."

A reluctant grin formed on the innkeeper's face. "*Eh bien,* Citoyen Thibaut. We do not want aristos, after all, in this place." He looked defiantly around the room and then at Corday, as if expecting some listener to accuse him of precisely the opposite. Perhaps there might be; the guests around him avoided each other's eyes. One could never be sure, after all, Corday thought, and this area of Normandy was known to be restless under the Revolution's new laws. "A room and food we have, citoyen," the innkeeper continued. "I am Pierre Titon, at your service. A meal in your room, or would you prefer in the taproom?"

"The taproom, *s'il vous plaît,*" Corday replied. It would be better than hiding away. A stranger ensconced in his room would be more suspect than one out in the open.

"Dumont!" Monsieur—rather, Citoyen—Titon called out, as he led the way to the taproom. "A cider!" An elderly man stood behind the counter and poured the cider, while Corday gazed at him carefully. His face was ascetic looking, his clothes very plain, even poor, his blue eyes at once innocent and sad. For an old man, his hair was thick except at the top, where it seemed new hair grew, as if he had once been tonsured. Corday wondered if the man was one of the priests who had refused to take a loyalty oath to the supremacy of the government. If so, the man was lucky to be alive, never mind having an occupation.

Titon asked a price for the cider that made Corday raise his brows. Prices had risen higher even during the few months since he had been in France last. He pushed a newly minted revolutionary livre over the counter and noticed Titon's slight grimace as the innkeeper took the money and left to attend his other guests. Little love of the Revolution here.

Corday sipped his cider, and watched other guests descend from the rooms above, moving sluggishly to the taproom. A mix of people; some poor, some well-off. A hard-eyed man in well-tailored black showed himself to be one of the Third Estate: a man of the middle class. Another man's blue coat could have indicated an aristocrat, but his face was thin, his coat worn, and his hands callused. Corday shrugged and took another drink of cider. What their stations had been before the Revolution, there was little way of telling. The middle class were often more rich than the nobles, while a nobleman might be so poor as to pull a plow next to the donkeys he owned in the countryside away from Paris and Versailles. The French nobleman's estate would be no different now than it had been then. The man would be poorer, perhaps, because of the famine, if not dead from the unfortunate fact of his noble birth. A strange, mad country, this France. Mad with slogans and bloodlust.

A tug of nostalgia for England made Corday grimace. He was half inclined to leave, and let France go its course with its self-cannibalism. But Sir Robert and his superiors feared the French government's offer to fund revolutions in other countries, and so here he was. Duty calls.

"Is the cider not to your liking, citoyen?"

Corday looked up. It was the old man, looking anxious.

"I fear your master has watered it," Corday replied, watching him carefully.

The old man cast a quick look around him. "Alas, we must make do with what we have, mon—citoyen."

Corday lowered his voice, staring hard at the man. "And yet, you have bread."

The old man's expression grew frightened. "It is little that we offer our guests; we wish to give them the best."

"Who gives it to you?"

"Our hard work and the generosity of our guests." The old man's eyes slid away from Corday's. So, there was some other source of income. He filed the information in the back of his mind: He would find out what it was later; it might be useful.

"Is there something more you wish, citoyen?" Corday looked up to see Titon, who had stepped behind the old man and put a comforting hand on his shoulder. The innkeeper's eyes were hard, challenging. Corday glanced out of the window at the light of the midday sky.

"Yes. I wish a meal . . . and a lamp to light my way to my room, if you please."

It was almost comical to see the relief in both Titon's and the old man's eyes. The innkeeper bowed. "Of course, of course." He leaned toward Corday and said in an undertone, "The horse in the stable is yours as well, and the next inn you may procure one will be Le Maison Bleu. Say to the innkeeper there what you have told me, and you will be given it." He moved away from him, then said, "Some bread and cheese as well, citoyen?"

"How much, in addition to a room?" Corday returned, and they haggled over the price. But before Titon could turn away, Corday held his arm. "Tell me," he said, his voice low. "Who is this La Flamme?"

Titon glanced around the common room for a moment, and his gaze seemed to catch on something behind

Corday before the innkeeper gave a long look at him. Corday resisted the temptation to turn around to see what it was that had caught the man's eye. Titon's lips pressed together before he said in a louder voice, "I do not know, citoyen. Some say La Flamme is a ghost, some say *le Diable* himself. Me, I have not seen him." The man's hand came up, almost as if to cross himself, but he pressed it down on the table instead.

"La Flamme is an enemy of the Revolution," came a sure and confident voice behind Corday. "No more than a man who uses the superstitions of others to flout the orders of the Republic." He turned slowly around.

The man wore the colors of the Third Estate, but unlike others of that class Corday had seen, wore clothes that did not speak of ill-gotten wealth. His clothes were plain, even worn. The man himself was no more than average height, and he had a pleasant, good-featured face. But he radiated a vibrant energy, and though he looked like a man who might laugh easily, his eyes were intensely intelligent, his lips were pressed together in a thin, bitter line of disapproval.

"You have seen this La Flamme, then?" Corday asked.

The man turned to Corday. "My duty is the high honor of finding this outlaw and bringing him to justice." His lips twisted in a bitter smile. "Seen him? Yes. La Flamme is a clever one, and like all criminals works best at night." The man threw a scornful look at the innkeeper, who quickly became busy wiping a table. "I know better than to subscribe to superstitious nonsense. *Le Diable*— pah! There is no devil but the aristos who burden the backs and feed on the hearts of the people."

How very noble and idealistic and very amusing, Corday thought. He put on a serious expression. "Indeed, citoyen, I hope you catch this criminal. Better for the Republic that all such outlaws are dealt with, and superstitions wiped clean from this land." He hoped his voice sounded earnest enough.

Apparently it did. The man bent an approving look at him after an initial suspicious one. Corday gazed at him steadily. "A loyal citizen, I see," the man said after a moment. He pulled out a sheaf of papers and gave one to Corday. "This is the description of the outlaw and his habits. I would appreciate it if you—" he shot a sharp look at Citoyen Titon, "—and anyone else who has information about La Flamme report it to me immediately."

Corday gave a small bow from where he was sitting. "Robert Thibaut at your service, citoyen. And to what name should I refer to, if I find such information?" Always useful to know one's obstacles, he thought.

The man gave him a surprised look, then chuckled. "Jacques du Maurier, agent, Committee of Public Safety." He smiled ruefully and shook his head. "There, my responsibilities have gone to my head. My mission for our Revolution is so important to me I assume it must be so for everyone; I forget not everyone knows of the danger to our State. You are obviously from Normandy, and I have only been here three months, of course."

The man's words were plainly sincere, his humor at himself genuine. Corday half wished du Maurier was not an obstacle. The French agent reminded him of Sir Robert Smith: solid men who took their responsibilities seriously. He wondered if du Maurier had a family like Sir Robert's.

Irrelevant to your own mission. Remember that. It did not matter. He would look out for this agent in case he became troublesome, and if so, he would be eliminated.

Corday grinned at him. "Citoyen, I am new as well, having come from the farthest reaches of that good province. Every village is its own kingdom and is reluctant to take in newcomers even from the next village down the road, yes?"

Du Maurier's lips turned up briefly before his expression became solemn. "True. But we will be united under the Republic, and it will be the people's will that rules this country, not corrupt aristocrats."

Monsieur Titon brought a platter of cheese and bread to Corday's table, and gave him a warning look from behind du Maurier's back before setting down the food. Corday gazed at the innkeeper blandly while he gestured to du Maurier to sit. He pushed the plate of food toward the agent, inviting him to eat. Titon frowned before shrugging and going back to his duties.

A pleased expression came over the agent's face. "*Merci*, good citoyen," he said, and sat in the chair opposite Corday. "It is not often I see a friendly face, I tell you! What I do is for the good of all; it is necessary for wrongdoers to be brought to justice, after all."

"Indeed," Corday said cordially.

Du Maurier sighed and shook his head, then placed a slice of cheese on a small chunk of bread. "It is not easy. Conspirators are all around us, citoyen." He jerked his head at the innkeeper, who had turned to other customers. "One such as he, for example. I have no evidence, but I suspect he would be pleased to see me fail in catching this La Flamme."

Corday paused before he picked up his fork and wondered if he should mention to Titon that he was under suspicion; it mattered not whether there was any proof or not of a man's guilt these days. Suspicion of antirevolutionary sentiment was enough to send anyone to prison. On the other hand, he was never his brother's keeper—Titon would have to take care of himself.

Besides, there was the issue of hiding his own mission. He paused, contemplating his meal—should he show himself to be a finicky sort or one who ate robustly? He glanced at du Maurier, noticing that the man ate robustly himself. No, he would be finicky. It would make du Maurier think he was inconsequential, and inconsequential people were easily dismissed. Corday raised his brows delicately and poked at his food with a knife. "But you have not arrested him."

Du Maurier frowned. "By rights I should. But I prefer that I have more than suspicion before I arrest anyone. The law is not an arbitrary thing, and must be obeyed."

A law, thought Corday, that changed daily to meet the whims of the revolutionary government. Perhaps his thought showed on his face, for du Maurier's expression was half frustrated, half defensive.

"Our government is new, of course, and grave matters of state and loyalty are not decided overnight," the agent said. "And education comes slowly. Even now many are not aware of the oppression they themselves have suffered under the aristos, nor how France has been the victim of foreigners." Corday opened his mouth to murmur something sympathetic, but a burst of impatient air erupted over his head.

"Oppression!" Monsieur Titon growled, as he came into view. "I had enough money to repair my roof two years ago, but with these—these paper assignats, which I have not been able to exchange for livres, as we have been promised—I see nothing but leaks in my future." He laughed bitterly. "Nights of rain under a leaky roof are more oppression than I have had before." He shoved a plate of sliced ham on the table.

Bold and foolish words, Corday thought, and wondered if du Maurier would arrest the innkeeper on the spot. But the agent only looked at Titon gravely. "There are people in our country who would have been glad of any roof at all, leaky or not."

Titon's face turned red. "And if you had not done away

with our convents and abbeys they would have had a place—"

"Be careful of what you say, citoyen." A soft voice came from behind Corday. "I am certain you would not cooperate with outlaws, but your words might make you suspect. I am sure you would not want that, yes?"

Corday watched Titon's mouth close tightly as he eyed the newcomer with reluctant respect. He nodded tersely. "As you say, citoyen. I am no friend of outlaws, after all." Corday wondered whether Titon's definition of "outlaw" was different from du Maurier's. Probably. He watched as the innkeeper turned and greeted other customers who had just entered the inn.

"Ah! Hervé!" du Maurier exclaimed, his voice sounding pleased. "I was wondering where you had gone." He stood, and Corday stood also and turned around.

The man was perhaps just above medium height. He wore clothes similar in style to du Maurier's, and just as unassuming. His hair was between mouse brown and gray; Corday calculated his age to be perhaps around sixty. His face was also ordinary: even-featured and pleasant, his skin neither dark nor light, with no distinguishing marks. A man who looked like anyone and everyone, one who might seem familiar, but was also eminently forgettable, Corday thought. He would do his best *not* to forget.

Hervé bowed slightly. "I was making sure our coach was ready and our bags packed, monsieur."

"*Citoyen*, Hervé! *Citoyen*. We are equals, even though you may have started as my servant," du Maurier chided. "Are we not both agents of the Revolution?"

Hervé bowed again. "Of course, citoyen. However, you still outrank me as an agent, so I must follow your orders."

"True," du Maurier replied, frowning, then his face cleared. "However, I imagine one day your loyalty shall be rewarded, and you will be a leader of agents soon, especially when we catch the outlaw La Flamme."

"Especially," Corday agreed, gesturing Hervé to sit at the table with them. The man might, after all, have some information about the outlaw. "A dangerous one, I assume?"

"Very dangerous," du Maurier said, "and formidable." He sat back on his chair, and his brows drew together in thought. "I try not to underestimate or overestimate an enemy, citoyen, for that way lies folly and mismanagement. It is necessary to see him clearly—his virtues and his faults." Du Maurier smiled slightly as he glanced at Corday. "You seem surprised. Yes, it is rare that a man, however evil, does not have some virtues. And to discount them is to fail in the hunt, for it can lead to overlooking the very detail that will lead to capture."

Corday leaned back in his chair as well, relaxing himself, but his mind grew more alert. Du Maurier was not to be underestimated, it seemed.

"I will say that La Flamme tries to avoid killing," du Maurier continued. "It was not apparent at first, but the reports time after time have shown it. And yet, he continues to escape, and continues to do so with the enemies of the Revolution. That he can do both is a testament to his cunning and strength. That he refrains when he can from killing tells me he has reserves we cannot underestimate."

Corday nodded. Most definitely du Maurier was not to be underestimated. He could even be dangerous to the mission. Corday toyed with the idea of eliminating du Maurier and his assistant while they stayed at the inn—an easy thing to do. He was decidedly quieter and more practiced at entering bedchambers at night than La Flamme, and his dagger had quietly dispatched more than a few obstacles to his past missions.

No. It would bring suspicion to his presence at this

inn, and disposing of bodies was always awkward. Besides, he might have need to find shelter at this inn again, and it would be inconvenient if the Committee of Public Safety razed it to the ground in punishment for two dead agents. "Have you any knowledge of this dangerous man's direction?" he asked.

Du Maurier smiled triumphantly. "Be assured I do. He has transported the last of the criminal aristos, citoyen. We have secured the last place at which he smuggled them. He will most likely return to Paris for more. We will return as well."

Corday made himself grimace and shudder. "Good citoyen, I thank you for the warning. I, too, am going to Paris to find more work, but I do not relish encountering this villain." He wondered if La Flamme knew of this man yet, and if he knew of his reputation. Perhaps. He would need to find out.

The agent gave him an indulgent look. "We follow on the man's heels, Citoyen Thibaut. It will not be dangerous until we catch up with him—if you wish, you may accompany us for a while."

"You are too generous, Citoyen du Maurier," Corday replied. "I might take advantage of your offer—if I did not think it more dangerous than I like." He gave a rueful smile. "Only tell me what route this villain will take, and I will content myself with avoiding it."

The agent's chuckle was laced with pity for Corday's apparent cowardice. "I suspect La Flamme will take the most direct and speedy route. We have found that foreign agents have infiltrated the Abbeye prison; once we isolate them, we will deal with them and their conspirators. I suspect all will be done by the end of next week. Two days after that, we will no doubt have the trial, and in the next few days, they will be dealt with."

Corday pretended to shudder again. "Perhaps I will

not go to Paris after all. I have no stomach for these things." He made himself yawn and grimace apologetically. "Many pardons, citoyens," he said, "but I am weary. I am afraid I stayed up much too late last night."

"Your occupation keeps you from your bed, citoyen?" said Hervé. His voice was soft and unassuming, but Corday was sure the question itself was not. This man was subtle, he thought. He glanced at Hervé's unrevealing eyes, and thought perhaps the assistant could be more dangerous than du Maurier. He should find out more about this man.

He smiled. "Too often, alas. I am a storyteller and scribe for the unlettered." He winked and gave the agents a knowing look. "And am I to blame if my stories weave a spell on certain softhearted mademoiselles? They are demanding, these sweet ones, and plead so prettily. How can I not . . . tell them another story?"

Du Maurier laughed. "You are a rogue, I see! Well, keep to the scribing—it's an honorable profession, and has served the Revolution well." He nodded at the near-empty plates before them. "My thanks, good citoyen, for your hospitality. I shall be sure to return the favor when we meet again."

Corday rose and bowed, then gathered up the rest of the cheese, bread, and a boiled egg in a napkin. "It was my pleasure," he replied, and after an additional bow toward Hervé, took the lamp Titon held out to him. The innkeeper gave him another warning look, then turned away with an audible sigh as Corday walked to the stairs and to the bedchamber he had reserved.

There was no real need for the lamp; a small window at the end of the hallway upstairs let in enough light. He entered the room and saw it was small and plain but well kept, with a firm bed at one corner. A sturdy writing table and chair sat against one wall, and Corday opened the drawer, examining the contents and surfaces for anything hidden he might be able to use. Nothing; just paper, ink, and pen.

Across from the foot of the bed a fire crawled fitfully over a log in the fireplace. The bed beckoned to him. He had dozed only a little on board ship, and Corday suspected if he were to work with the cloaked one, he would be traveling at least partly at night. It would be wise to have all his wits about him.

He would set the chair near the door. Should anyone come through it, the door would hit the chair, and the noise would wake him. He put his pack down near the head of his bed, and took two daggers from it and slipped one knife under his pillow. His pistol . . . yes, he would prime it and also have it ready, although he preferred to do any killing in silence if possible. He smiled wryly. It wouldn't do to have gunfire disturb any citizens loyal to the revolutionary Republic.

Now for the bed. Corday sighed and gazed at it appreciatively. It was a very good bed; the good Titon must be getting funds from another source than his innkeeping. He pressed his hand on the mattress. The eiderdown fluffed around his fingers, and when he removed his hand, it left a brief imprint. Yes, very good, and no doubt a last comfort for someone who might have his throat cut if he were not wary.

It would not hurt to sleep in it, however, if he were careful. Corday stared at the large wardrobe on the wall opposite the door. He frowned, then strode to the window and looked out of it to one side. He had noticed that the windows of the inn seemed more than the usual distance from one side of the wall, and this was also true of this window. It was possible that the room had a false wall.

Corday tapped the wall, listening for hollow sounds, but there was no more or less noise than if it were a normal wall with studs and wood over stone. He looked again at the wardrobe.

It would not come away from the wall when he pushed it. No doubt the wardrobe had a false back that opened to admit or let escape whoever wished to use the room for secret purposes. The wardrobe door opened silently when he pulled at the handles. He grinned. The good Titon also kept it well oiled.

The back of the wardrobe looked no different from any other large wardrobe—of cedar, and smoothly sanded to keep away moths. It seemed to be made of one piece; no seams revealed any kind of opening at all.

The lantern. Corday took the lamp Titon had given him and peered closely at the wood—yes. He ran his hand over what seemed to be a part of the grain of the wood, and the back parted without a sound. Clever. No sound to indicate entrance or egress, whether the wardrobe door or the back panel opened. Nothing would warn anyone sleeping in this room of an intruder.

He sat back on his haunches and considered the problem. Being taken unawares meant risking death, but he did want to rest as much as possible to shore up his strength, for he often received little sleep on his missions. And yet, he had only one chair and that he used for the chamber door. All he needed was something that would make a noise. . . .

Taking the dagger from under the pillow, he put on his coat and slipped the knife up his sleeve, then left the room after shoving his bag under the mattress. Nodding to the innkeeper as he passed him in the common room, he gazed idly at the various pictures on the wall before wandering out to the inn's stables.

The inn did have a serviceable stable around at the back. A flapping of a paper nailed to a post that formed the corner of the stable attracted Corday's attention. A broadsheet, it seemed, with a picture on it. He spread it out with one hand. It was a good idea to see what news the local authorities broadcast. He never knew when it could be used to his advantage. "La Flamme, enemy of the Revolution," it said above the picture of the outlaw.

There was not much to identify La Flamme in this picture—it showed a caped figure, with a hunched back, rag-wrapped hands, and a male face with heavy dark eyebrows and deep-set, evil-looking eyes. He supposed any poor hunchback with a cape might be suspect. He wondered if La Flamme had seen the broadsheets, and whether he—or she—had been amused or offended at its depiction. Offended, probably. The little one had pride, certainly. He suppressed a grin and turned to the stable.

Falsely complimenting the groom there on the mediocre specimens of horseflesh languishing in the stalls, Corday eyed one of the more fit horses, and it eyed him back in suspicion. That one probably had more spirit than the rest; it belonged to some citizen who paid to have it stabled here, the groom had said, but rarely came to ride it. Corday nodded, keeping the horse in mind for possible future use, and picked up a handful of clean straw.

"Citoyenne Titon would be displeased at muddy boots, I think," he said in reply to the groom's questioning look.

The groom nodded. "*Mais oui,* she is insane with neatness, that woman, I tell you!" He leaned toward Corday in a confidential manner. "Wipe your boots where she can see you, and she will give you an egg for your breakfast—I have done so these three months, and have become fat with it." He patted his nonexistent stomach with satisfaction.

Corday grinned. "I thank you for the information."

Leaving the stables, he carelessly kicked a few stones as he wandered back to the inn and picked up a few pebbles on the way. He smiled a little as he carefully wiped his shoes with some of the straw where Madame Titon might see him, then went up the stairs to his room again, the rest of the straw in one of his coat pockets. The straw rustled as he pulled it out and spread it on the floor of the wardrobe, and the pebbles rattled loudly in the silence of the room as he scattered them among the straw. He nodded in satisfaction, then brushed off his hands, once again slipping his dagger under his pillow and checking his pistol. He turned and gazed pensively at the wardrobe.

There should be little trouble waking when the cloaked one entered, for the door would make a noise against the chair, and the pebbles and straw should rattle and rustle enough to wake him if that was the entrance chosen. The wardrobe was cleverly made; he had to give the cloaked one his due. It had to be the youth, not the innkeeper, for only good money could have crafted such a neatly made piece of furniture, and his ears were keen enough to note a cultured voice behind the rags the cloaked one wore.

An interesting disguise . . . to keep from being recognized, of course, but why not paint his face, if he—or she— could not wear a beard or mustache? Corday opened the napkin he had brought up and took a bite of bread he had saved, then turned his gaze to the fireplace.

"La Flamme." He smiled, amused. His own reaction to the white-swathed facelessness was the answer: To be shocking, of course. To put one's enemies off guard. Such a typically French and very youthful flamboyance.

He'd have none of it, of course. There was no room for flamboyance or disguises unless it served a purpose, and the less attention brought to his mission, the better. The cloaked one must be quite knowledgeable to have gained a reputation and to have smuggled people successfully away from under the noses of the agents of the Committee of Public Safety. But if he was to use La Flamme's knowledge of the underworld to fill out his own, then the youth would pay heed or be disposed of.

He frowned. Boy or woman? In any other circumstance, he would avoid working with either. But the way the cloaked one eliminated his enemies proved he—she—had both strength and swiftness, more than anyone would suppose one so young—or female—would possess. Woman, perhaps, especially with such a name, and yet he had never known of a woman who had enough strength to dispatch more than a few men.

Puzzling. He did not care for puzzles, especially if they might get in his way. Therefore, it would be best to eliminate the puzzle, one way or another.

Corday ate a bite of cheese as well and wrapped the leftover food in a large handkerchief, put them in his bag, then tied it tightly to keep out any rats. It never hurt to keep a few provisions for another day.

He glanced at the bed again. A few hours of rest until nightfall would be welcome, certainly, and the linens seemed fresh enough not to contain bedbugs. Pondering over how comfortable he should let himself become, he decided on not dirtying Madame Titon's freshly cleaned bedclothes, and removed his clothes.

His muscles ached as he relaxed into the eiderdown. Yes, a good decision to be as comfortable as possible. He closed his eyes. Might as well, since he was certain he'd not be as comfortable after this night. . . .

The rustling of straw and the click of pebbles woke him. Corday kept his eyes closed and moved restlessly, let out a loud snore, then reached under his pillow for his pistol. No other sound. He moved restlessly again, sighed, then slipped his dagger into his right hand. The moon gleamed through his window, throwing a crosslike shadow across the floor from the window's panes. Another shadow moved from the deeper ones near the wardrobe, and Corday cocked his pistol. The shadow froze.

"I thought you must have heard me," the shadow said in a conversational tone. "You are a very suspicious man."

"But of course. One must be, to stay alive, Monsieur La Flamme." Corday shifted himself up from the pillows. Monsieur or mademoiselle? The voice was more muffled this evening than it was last night.

The shadow chuckled. "I would not have killed you."

"I don't know that."

La Flamme shrugged. "*Oui*. You have nothing but my word, but I assure you, my word is good."

Corday felt inclined to believe him, but it was never safe to believe anyone completely. However, he had his pistol cocked and ready to shoot. A man could be believed a little more if he had a pistol aimed at him.

"Besides," La Flamme continued, "if my word was false, I would not be here. I could have neglected to meet you at all."

"Perhaps you wished to kill me now rather than before."

"If I wished to kill you, I could have done so when we first met." La Flamme shook his head. "*Par Dieu*, you are a *very* suspicious man! But look, you—you ask me these things, and you are pointing your pistol at me. Perhaps *you* wish to kill *me*, or give me to the revolutionary authorities."

"If I had wanted to do that, I would have—"

"Done it when you first met me." La Flamme said it in unison with him. "We are at an impasse, *oui*?"

Corday grinned and lowered his pistol. "Very well." He nodded toward the chair by the door. "Please sit, and I'll be grateful if you light those candles at the table."

La Flamme hesitated. "Having you light the candles would be better, monsieur. My rags—a good disguise, but not around fire."

"A pity you didn't think of that before you acquired it." Corday uncocked his pistol but carried it with him as he threw off the bedcovers, then rose to light the tapers from the still-burning fire.

"It serves my purposes."

Corday brought the brace of candles to the table. "Let me see you," he said as he sat on the edge of his bed.

The youth drew back the hood from his face, and Corday tried to ignore the prickling at the back of his neck.

The impression of facelessness was still there, but behind a veil of gauze the candlelight showed small glimmers of reflected light where the eyes would be. Both wide and narrow strips crisscrossed around La Flamme's head and neck, making it weirdly shapeless, flattening the nose and obscuring the jaw. He could not tell if there were ears—of course there must be, for the youth could obviously hear well enough. Knots protruded from various places where the strips were tied together, and a piece of gauze moved over where the mouth and nose would be: the only sign of life in the pale expanse of cloth. La Flamme leaned against the table, putting his arm on the surface, and Corday saw that the hand was also carefully wrapped. He—she—took a breath, and the firelight caught a glimmer on the rags over the chest. A crucifix. It marked La Flamme as an outlaw.

"Why do you use such a disguise? You look like a leper."

Another chuckle. "How do you know I am not?"

"Because a leper would be too ill to do what you have done."

"Well, perhaps it is because I desire to look like one—or a ghost. Most people do not wish to inquire in either case."

Corday nodded. "Convenient. However, I do wish to inquire, since we are to be partners."

"Are we?" The youth began to tap his fingers on the table, clearly impatient. "I do not recall agreeing to it. *En fait*, I do not even know your name."

"Yet, here you are, at least curious about my proposal, or else you would not be here."

"*Eh bien,* I am curious. Tell me where you are going and what you plan to do." La Flamme's voice was sharp.

The least amount of information, the better, Corday thought. "Paris—the docks of the Seine. I am looking for a man who furthers the Revolution." The youth's tapping fingers stilled. "And no, not to aid him," Corday continued.

"Who is this man?"

"He goes by many names. Perhaps you might recognize one: Buteau, Fichet, Ranier, Letour. . . . It is important I find him." He watched the youth carefully—much good it did him, for the damned rags on his face showed nothing. There was not even a tension about the cloaked one's body to reveal any sort of recognition of the names he mentioned. A disadvantage. But Corday would make sure that disadvantage disappeared soon.

La Flamme—Simone—gazed at him through the light gauze over her eyes. The candlelight touched the lean planes of the man's cheek and chin with red and gold, but his face was impassive, his body relaxed against the bed. Clearly, he was going to reveal as little as possible. She shrugged impatiently. "Common names. What does he look like?"

"Uncertain," he replied. "He has appeared in different guises. However, I understand he is about my height."

"And when you reach Paris, no doubt you will find him in an instant with such a description," Simone said sarcastically. She arose from the chair. "My apologies, monsieur, but if you are not more forthcoming, I cannot help you."

She heard the click of his pistol being cocked, and her impatience grew. "You are too ready with your weapons. If it did not convince me before, why should it now?"

He gazed at her, suddenly expressionless. "But *I* am not convinced."

Simone's irritation flared into anger and she hurled

herself at him, toppling him backward onto the bed. She seized his pistol before he could move, slipping her thumb between hammer and flash. Wrenching it from his grasp, she uncocked it and flung it away. The pistol rattled on the floor. Her hand went to his throat and squeezed.

She could feel his chest rise quickly against her, and his breath rasped in his throat. His blood pulsed strongly under her fingers, making her blood-thirst rise.

No. She clenched her teeth, forcing down the urge to drink.

For one moment his body stilled beneath her, then his breathing slowed. He stared at her, a curious expression—almost of understanding—in his eyes, and she wondered wildly if he might somehow know she had wanted to drink of him. But no, of course not. No one, except the Abbé Dumont, knew what she was.

She kept her hand tight at his throat. "As you see, monsieur, I am not at all afraid of your pistol."

"So I do indeed see," the man replied, his voice bland. She felt a sharp prickle through the rags over her neck. "If not a pistol, perhaps a dagger?"

Merde. She looked carefully down. The knife was wickedly slim; the candlelight gleamed on one edge. She could feel his other hand tight around her back, pressing her against him. Though she could break away from him, it would take a moment to pull away, and a moment would be all it took for the knife to slice through her rags and sever a vein. The injury would incapacitate her until daylight, for it would take that long to recover. Inconvenient, this, and potentially dangerous. She gazed at him again; his eyes were coolly amused. Six inches lower, a thrust through her ribs into her heart . . . Another glance at him showed a smile hovering around his mouth.

"An impasse, yes?" he said.

"You first," Simone replied, nodding her head slowly.

He removed the dagger from her throat and she withdrew her hand from his neck. "What is your name?"

He sat up on the bed, and cocked his head to one side. "Mmm. Corday."

"I think that is not your name—and neither is Robert Thibaut."

He shrugged. "What should it matter to you?"

Simone let out an exasperated breath. "It matters so that I know you will come when I call!"

"Woof."

She bit back a laugh. "Even dogs need names."

"Corday will do."

"That is not a wise choice of name these days."

He shrugged again. "I will change it when convenient." He leaned back in the bed against the headboard. "Neither force nor humor will move you, it seems." He gazed at her thoughtfully. "Money? I expect not."

Simone sneered. "You expect correctly."

"A trade of services, then. I am efficient about removing . . . obstacles, as you know. If you help me find the man I seek, I will aid you in your mission. At the very least, you owe it to me for helping you."

"And if I do not?"

"Then I will have to do what I can by myself."

Simone gazed at him a moment, assessing him. Somehow, she doubted she would be rid of him, whatever he might say. "Very well, though I must be mad to consider it. I have no guarantee you will keep your word."

"True," he replied. "However, I have one great failing—"

"Only one?"

"One failing," he continued smoothly. "Curiosity." One corner of his mouth lifted in a faint smile. "I have a great desire to discover who you are, and I will persist until I do."

"Consider that desire hopeless," Simone said.

Corday's smile widened. "I think not . . . *mademoiselle*."

Chapter 3

SILENCE REIGNED FOR A FEW HEART-beats, then Simone crossed her arms, jutting her chin forward aggressively. "A woman? You insult me, monsieur! Would a weak woman be able to dispatch as many men as I have?"

"No," Corday said, and Simone gave a mental sigh of relief. He tapped his bottom lip with his finger, then looked her up and down in a thoughtful manner. "Not a *weak* woman. Then, too, very few men cross their arms as you are now doing—low, toward your waist, as if you were avoiding crossing them over your breasts."

Simone adjusted her arms higher. "I have no breasts, monsieur." *Merde*, that was a stupid answer, but she had not thought he would discern her gender. It had startled her, for no one had guessed anything about her before this.

Perhaps she could convince him otherwise. But she had to be careful. It might be preferable to allow him to know she was a woman, and let his curiosity be satisfied in that respect. With any luck, it would be enough so he would probe no further.

"No?" He shook his head mournfully. "And to think I believed myself well acquainted with the female form. Despite your attempt at flattening your breasts with your wrappings, I distinctly felt a feminine figure pressed against me when we were on the bed." His hand ran over the bedclothes, a sensuous movement, and Simone could not help looking at the rumpled sheets beside him and remembering how she had flung herself upon him when she had seized his throat. She had been pressed close enough to feel the beat of his heart against her chest; of course he would have been aware of her, as well. It had been a long time since she had been that near a man . . . she had forgotten. . . .

Stupid! She had let her anger get the best of her, and had not thought she would be revealing anything of her identity reacting in that way.

She shrugged. "You said you are a storyteller and a scribe; your imagination is no doubt wild enough to make up anything you please." She made her voice mocking. "Perhaps you have been without a woman for so long, you imagine anything pressed against you is female." There, that would put him off, perhaps even make him angry enough to leave. She grimaced, then was glad he could not see her face. He would then know her statement for a lie; he had undressed for sleep, and she could see his lean upper body was all muscle, with not one speck of fat on him. His face was also lean, the cheekbones slanting down from piercing dark eyes to a wide and sensual mouth. His dark hair was pulled severely back in a queue away from his face, the clean sharp hairline giving an impression of austerity. He would have looked as ascetic as a priest if it were not for that mouth; it gave him a fallen look. If Corday was not Lucifer himself, he must have been *le Diable's* own brother, for the faint smile on his face made his eyes look seductively wicked, as if he had seen heaven and rejected it for all the secrets of hell.

Simone shifted uneasily on the chair, suppressing the urge to cross herself at the thought. Idiot! To be tempted by his seductive appearance would be a mistake. She had had her experience with those who sought the netherworld; she did not want to repeat it. Even if he were not in league with the devil, he must be mad to waste whatever seductive powers he might have on someone wrapped as repulsively as herself.

Or, he was trying to manipulate her. That was likely.

"Perhaps I do have an active imagination." His smile grew wider. "But then, imagination always enhances one's curiosity, I have found. Why would a woman wrap herself about with rags?"

"This is a stupid conversation, and nothing to the point," Simone replied, rising from the chair. She turned away from him. "I am going. If you wish to come with me, you will have to persuade me better than you are doing now." A pistol cocked again, and her temper flared. "Another pistol! You will find it does not persuade me at all. If you shoot me, the good Titon will come and, being a *good* citizen of the Republic, will turn you over to the Committee of Public Safety." Her voice mocked him again. "Their agents often sleep in this inn, and you will not get away with it, no, for I am indeed stronger than you think, and not a weak woman." She moved to the wardrobe.

"But I might reveal you for the enemy of the state as well," Corday said, his voice easy, almost lazy. "Then, too, with you dead or disabled, think—how many more people will not escape the prisons and will surely face the guillotine? I understand the Abbeye prison is most . . . unpleasant."

Bile rose in Simone's throat and her feet froze. The

ghostly faces of the men, women, and children there sometimes haunted her dreams, their eyes sunken in their heads
from the lack of food, their movements alternately frantic
and sluggish, like starving dogs trapped in a pit. She had
taken as many as she could out of the prisons, but there
were so many . . . so many.

"Then, too . . ." He hesitated, and she turned, gazing
keenly at him. Indecision seemed to cross his face, but it
was only a flicker of an expression; another look at his eyes
made her doubt he was ever indecisive. "Would it persuade
you if I said my mission would at least keep more of your
countrymen from entering those prisons?"

Hope almost choked her and she closed her eyes. To
not enter the blood-soaked streets of Paris and have to
fight the blood-thirst that burned her stomach every time
she walked there. To stop the madness, both against the
innocents and within herself. She drew in a deep breath,
and looked at Corday again. His smile was gone now, but
the candlelight shone on his lean cheek and outlined his
lips.

What if he lied? He was a wickedly handsome man. It
was said that the Devil could put on a beautiful face and
tempt with sweet words. She could not afford to go down
that path; she had spent so much of her resources fighting it.

A vision of her dead family came to her again, and the
faces of the children in the prisons. Infants, some of them.
Simone looked at Corday—not one flicker of a smile, but
he was watching her still, as if he could see beneath the
gauze she had put over her face.

She stared at the man on the bed and grasped the
small crucifix that hung around her neck even though it
stung her hand like thorns though her rags. *Sainte Marie*,
she prayed. *Show me the true path.*

For one moment, the stinging seemed to lessen, and

the tiny pearl and ruby on it seemed to glisten. She released the crucifix, hoping it was truly a sign and not her imagination. Faith. She had to have faith that she would not be led wrongly.

"I will go with you," she said. "But if you betray me or those I care for, I will kill you." She hoped she wouldn't have to—it would barely be self-defense, closer to revenge, coming too close to the sin of murder. But this Corday was a man of threats, and she supposed he would only respond to threats.

Corday nodded. "Fair enough." He stared at her, and though he smiled once more, his eyes were cold. "And if you betray me, you will most certainly die." He uncocked his pistol. "My associates will make sure of that, if I do not."

Her eyes did not waver, and she did not flinch. "But of course," Simone said. "I would expect nothing else."

He did not know why he had exerted so much effort in persuading La Flamme into accompanying him. Corday kept the woman in view as he moved from the bed and put his pistol in a pocket of his coat. She sat there, relaxed, as if she meant to stay for a while; it was an insult in a way, as if she believed, despite his threats, that he was no threat at all.

The firelight glittered on her crucifix, the chain moving with her breath and the impatient tapping of her fingers on the table beside her. Perhaps it was her idealism that made him persuade her. He remembered being idealistic once. Perhaps it was because her cause was something that saved lives. He remembered he had thought the same thing once.

There was no use in speculating on it. His mission was a game, nothing more. The stakes were life and death, the rise and fall of rulers and governments, but it was just a game, played over the millennia—or so history showed—with different players. Corday suppressed a smile. And now he had another player, whether she knew it, or liked it, or not.

"The horse in the stables below—yours, I presume?" he asked.

Her tapping fingers paused and flattened on the table. "Who told you?"

"Good," he said, ignoring her question. "We will need it."

"You have not answered my question, nor have I given you my permission."

"Irrelevant." He took his shirt from the table on which he had placed it, then pulled it on. He had spent too much time here as it was, seeking out La Flamme; it was time to go. "It is necessary that we leave soon. Your government—"

A snort of disgust came from La Flamme. "It is not *my* government—"

"*The* government of the new Republic has offered money to whoever wishes to overturn his own government. A tempting prize. Eliminate—"

"Kill, you mean."

"—eliminate the source of the funds, and the danger to my own government is lessened. We have enough people in our own land who would find this quite a temptation. Your traveling seems to be done mostly at night; mine is done during the day. A light wagon will do for both of us if we can't find a coach. I will drive it during the day, you will drive it during the night. We'll arrive in Paris in half the time."

Protesting noises issued from behind the rags over La Flamme's face. "Who has said you will take my horse? Not I!" she said at last.

He grinned, deliberately provocative. "I will pay, of course, and for any other horses as well."

"I will not be beholden to you, monsieur!"

"Don't be stupid." He pulled out his bag from under the mattress. "What is more important, the lives you save or whether I pay for our mode of traveling?"

She answered as he intended she would. "Lives, of course." She drew in an audible breath. "It would be faster," she admitted.

"Good." Corday nodded at her rags and her cloak. "You will need to dispense with those clothes, and the wrappings." He put on his coat and slid his dagger up his sleeve.

"No, monsieur, I will not."

"Why not?"

"It is much, much safer if I do not."

There was a serious, even deadly note in her voice. He remembered La Flamme's unnatural swiftness in attacking him, how she had taken the pistol from him. *Seeming* unnaturalness. He had been taken unawares, perhaps because he'd still been drowsy from sleep. Best not to let that happen again. His hand paused in checking his weapons. Yet, there was her swiftness in dispatching the agents of the Committee for Public Safety, also unnatural in the dark of the night.

Corday looked at her costume again. Unnatural indeed. The costume was repulsive. A draft of air made the candles flicker, and for a moment her figure was cast into shadow. That was it, of course—the black cloak and light wrappings made her seem to appear and disappear in the night, giving an illusion of swiftness. He was a realist: If a costume was good enough to take him unawares, then it was an effective one.

"Very well," he said. "You may keep it."

"You are soooo gracious." Her voice contained a sneer.

"Yes, I am." He smiled, gazing at her from head to toe. "You may find your rags stripped from you one day. Remember it."

La Flamme rose suddenly from her chair, the tension clear in her body. Her hands turned into fists. Well, thought Corday. This little one has a temper. But then her hands opened, and she let out a harsh breath.

"I have no reason to go with you, other than the possibility that if I help you, you will find this man who is behind the horrors inflicted on my people." *My people*. She said it with almost a royal air. Her voice, Corday noted again, had a cultured accent. An aristocrat, then.

"But if you show yourself to be false, then you will certainly regret it," she continued, her voice grim.

"Saint-Claire, the Durant family, Mont Michelle, de la Fer." Corday held up a finger for each name. "Do you know them?"

The tension in La Flamme's body changed—she became stiff as stone. The fire in the grate crackled; that and the sudden harsh breath that left her were the only sounds in the room.

"They are all dead. Fathers, mothers, children." Her head bent, as if in silent prayer, but her voice was flat, purposely brutal, perhaps to shock him.

It did nothing; he was beyond being shocked. "The man I seek sold them to the Committee of Public Safety," he said. "Those families, and others."

The echoing hoot of a distant owl made the silence between them stretch long and cold. La Flamme raised her head at last, and though Corday could not see her eyes, he felt her gaze, and he wondered if she looked at him with contempt.

"I will go with you and help you if I can."

"Do you give your word?"

She hesitated. "*Oui*. However, I will not kill this man— it is a sin. But I will not stop you if you do, and I will pray for your soul, and for mine."

Corday smiled, but it turned crooked. "You may try, mademoiselle, but my soul is long lost."

Her rag-wrapped hand clasped her crucifix. "Then I will pray that it will find its way to you again." He thought, almost, that he could hear a smile in her voice.

An odd pressure built under his breastbone; if he did not know any better, he would almost call it hope. Perhaps if he did not die during this mission there might be a chance he could persuade—coerce or threaten, more likely—Sir Robert to forget that he, Corday, existed.

He was a fool. He shrugged. It mattered not that he was becoming tired of this game called espionage. He would complete his mission, and then, for a time, he would rest. Then there would be another mission, and another, and more men would die. Was there a time when this was not so? He was intimately associated with death, and knew nothing of a normal life: It was a foreign land, beyond a deadly sea. No doubt he would die before he ever achieved it.

"It is too late, mademoiselle. Much too late," he said, buttoning up his coat. He gathered his bag and strode to the wardrobe. He opened its door, then bowed and gestured for her to go first. "After you, mademoiselle."

La Flamme hesitated, her rag-wrapped face turned toward him. Then she nodded, and climbed into the wardrobe.

Simone had gone through the wardrobe and down the hidden stairs before many times and by now did not need to light her way to navigate through it. She'd led fugitives through it, hidden in it, while pursuers searched the room for her and the royalists she protected. The stairway was narrow, but it was cleverly made during the time of the Huguenot wars so that it was not cramped.

But this time, the walls seemed to press down upon her. Her neck prickled with the way Corday stepped softly close behind, with the way his breath whispered close to her in this cold, windless place so that it felt like a summer breeze touching her ear. It disturbed her. She should not be so acutely sensitive. Perhaps it was the blood-thirst she had experienced earlier that made her so. She pulled her hood over her head. There. His breath would not bother her now.

She stopped to slide back the bolt that locked the door at the end of the passageway. Corday, however, did not stop, and her breath exploded out of her as his body squashed her against the door.

"Imbécile!" she rasped. The pressure against her back eased, and she took in a deep breath. "Do not follow so closely, *s'il vous plaît*!" She remembered in time to keep her voice low.

"My apologies," he murmured. He did not retreat, however, and irritation made her teeth clench.

"Move!" She abruptly jerked, pushing at him with her back.

A mistake. His hands came up, apparently to steady himself, and grasped her waist. She drew her breath in sharply.

His hands fell away immediately, but an image of his fallen angel lips flashed before her. Simone closed her eyes, forcing herself not to shiver. She stepped away from him.

"Do not touch me," she hissed through gritted teeth.

"Definitely a woman," Corday whispered, and she could hear amusement in his voice.

"Touch me again, and I will kill you."

"An impractical command, don't you think?" He stepped away from her, however, and she sighed in relief. She shoved the door bolt to one side, more forcefully than usual, but it was well oiled and muffled by the cotton stuffed at both ends, so made no noise. "If we are to work effectively together, at some time I must know what and who you are," he continued. "There will also be times when I will need to touch you, and you, me."

"You have surely been without a woman too long, if you are trying to seduce one such as I." Simone pushed open the door, then strode through the yard, attempting to put some distance between her and Corday. "There will be no time when I will need to touch you, monsieur."

"Call me Corday," he said. He sounded as if he were introducing himself in a drawing room, his voice cordial. He is mad, surely, Simone thought. "And how was I trying to seduce you?" he continued. "I was merely referring to the fact that we might be reduced to gestures should there be need for silence."

Simone's hands clenched with mixed embarrassment and anger. Then a twinge of guilt made her grimace. He had not touched her on purpose; each time had been accidental, or not from his own actions. To be honest, it was her own weakness that betrayed her in thinking otherwise, enough to react irrationally. Dangerous, this reaction.

A momentary weakness, however. No doubt it was from the shock of hearing her family's name in the list of people who had been betrayed by the man Corday sought. The sound of the de la Fer name on the man's tongue had been a knife twisting through her chest. She had not heard the name for a long time, only in her own mind, her own heart, for they were gone now, all gone. . . .

Old grief rose and shook her, but she thrust it away. There was no time for grieving, and no sense in it. All the grieving in the world would not bring her family back to life, nor would it bring her back into their arms if it did so. She was alone and had no family, and nothing would change this. All she could do was pray for their unshriven souls, though she did not know how effective prayers were from a cursed one like herself.

And she had promised Corday she would help him rid France of the man who caused the murders of those families—and her family. If the man Corday sought was so dangerous as to destroy so many people and to threaten other countries, stopping the man was imperative. She had never gone back on her word, and would not do so now.

Simone pointed to the stables. "Go, take the horse, and if the stable boy wakes, tell him the owner wishes it. I cannot go in without frightening him. There is a small wagon there as well, and I would be pleased if you would hitch it to the horse."

The moonlight frosted the stable yard, and touched Corday's bared head with silver light as he bowed elegantly to her. "As you wish, mademoiselle."

She watched him enter the stables, then glanced toward the inn. The good Abbé Dumont was probably still awake, even after being done with his duties in the common room. Monsieur Titon was a devout man, and housed the priest when the revolutionaries had taken over the abbey, and though the priest had insisted on earning his keep, Titon kept the old man's duties light. Abbé Dumont was no doubt at his devotionals at this moment.

Simone hesitated, then turned and ran light-footed back to the inn, making no noise as she pulled her hood over her face and crept up the short stone steps. She would ask a blessing of the priest on this journey, as she had in the past. Her lips twisted wryly. She would need it on this journey with Corday.

The faint, guilty thought that she was avoiding, just for a moment, Corday's unsettling presence occurred to her, but she shrugged. Perhaps he would become impatient, or perhaps he would think she had abandoned him.

In which case, he would leave, and there would be her excuse to go about her business as usual.

Simone tapped lightly on Père Dumont's door, glad that his hearing was still good for an old man. Carefully, she untied one strip of rag that held the gauze in place over her face, and her shoulders relaxed. This was one person, at least, with whom she could be herself.

After a moment, the door opened, and the priest blinked at the darkness before she stepped forward. He smiled. "Ah, mademoiselle! Welcome, welcome!"

Taking her hand in his, he led her to a small, rickety chair near the fireplace. Simone glanced at the flames in the hearth and moved the chair a little away from it before she sat. It was a spare, austere room, and in Père Dumont's case spoke of his poverty and his unworldliness. The firelight and single candle cast a warm yellow light on the room, turning it into a dark toast-colored nest, and adding a sheen to the dull colors of the priest's shirt and trousers. Mme. Titon had donated heavy curtains to cover the small windows, and a thick coverlet for the bed on cold winter nights. For all its plainness, it felt safe and warm to Simone, much like its owner.

"What can I do for you, my child?" the abbé asked. He sat on another chair next to the table at which he'd been working. Books and papers were piled on it, and a small trunk containing his robe and vestments and more books sat open close by.

"Mon Père, I go on another mission, and wish your blessing," she said, then grinned at his grimace of worry. "And you know I must, for you yourself said it was my penance."

"That was before I knew you were a woman, and not a boy." He shook his head. "I would not have given it to you had I known."

Simone's grin turned wry. "And a vampire, which changes everything; admit it, mon Père."

His lips turned up briefly before they pursed in disapproval. "You are impertinent, mademoiselle." He sighed and restlessly pushed the papers about on his desk. "But it is true, your ... unusualness has sent me to my books more than once, so that I may know how to deal with you." His smile returned. "You would be difficult regardless of your state, I believe."

"Even more reason for me to go on my mission, and complete my penance," she said, and smiled.

Père Dumont chuckled. "As you say."

She hesitated, then said, "Have you any word ... from the cardinal ... ?"

The priest sighed again. "Not yet, and I do not know how long it will take; my letter—and any reply—would have difficulty crossing our land since our government has seen fit to make war."

"It has been three months ..." Simone tried to keep the pleading from her voice.

He leaned forward and patted her shoulder, deep sympathy in his eyes. "I sent another letter last month, in case the first one has gone astray—another week, perhaps."

Mixed hope and despair curled around her heart, and she bit her lip, tamping down the despair. "It would be good to know if I can ever ... if I can ever become human again."

Abbé Dumont took both her hands in his own and pressed them tightly. "There is no sinner who cannot be redeemed if he has hope." His hands looked fragile in the dim light, but Simone looked into his kind eyes and felt a certain strength flow from him into her heart. "I am sure there is a way. You have already repented of the sin that made you a vampire, and your sins since coming to me after the death of your family have been small at most, or certainly excusable. You work now to save innocents from death; if that does not make you regain your humanity, it must contribute to it."

"It does not hurt as much as it used to when I enter a church," Simone said, releasing a trembling breath, and the reminder was a comfort. "And sometimes it does not sting my hand to hold my cross."

"Surely these are signs that you are on the right path," Père Dumont said encouragingly. "And soon we shall receive notice from the cardinal as to the particulars." His eyes lighted mischievously. "At least, from the exorcism I performed, we know that you are not possessed of a devil."

Simone laughed. "And very disappointed you were when you found I was not! I believe you would have been delighted if you had caused a devil to flee in your very first exorcism."

"No, no, of course I was happy that you were not possessed," Abbé Dumont protested. "But it would have been very interesting had you been, you must admit, for the few exorcisms I have seen were done upon poor deluded or insane souls, who would have done better if treated with kindness instead of being frightened out of their wits with cruelty." He sighed. "There is much work to be done there, as well, and I would be glad to continue it."

"As would I," Simone replied. "And I do wish you had had removed a devil from me, for then I would be cured of my malady and never feel the thirst for blood again." She sighed, and knelt before him. "Bless me, Father, for I fear the curse is strong about me, and I need all the blessings you can give for those I hope to save and for my soul."

The abbé sighed once more, took up his cross, and put his hand upon her head. "Bless you, my child, in the name of the Father, the Son, and the Holy Spirit, and may His Mother keep you safe and in the cloak of her grace. Go in peace and in faith, and may your hand strike for justice instead of vengeance."

Guilt tweaked her at the thought of vengeance, but the thought was cut off as a sharp sizzling pain from where his hand lay on her head shot through her. Then it dissipated and a soothing waft of air seemed to touch her, as if someone had put a salve of cool mint over her face.

His look questioned her.

"It hurts still when you bless me," she said.

"But does it hurt less than before?"

She hesitated. "It is hard to say. But the pain leaves quickly, and now there is a . . . soothing relief of a kind."

Abbé Dumont smiled. "Good, good! There is hope, as I said. You had no relief when I first blessed you."

Simone rose to her feet, hope rising within her heart at the same time, and fear also. She was afraid to hope, she knew. But that was all she had now, until the cardinal's letter returned to Abbé Dumont, and told him how she might be rid of the curse of vampirism. There must be a way, she prayed. There must be.

With one last smile at the priest, she tied the gauze over her face again and left silently down the small steps and back to the stables.

Corday was waiting for her, and her heart sank. She had half hoped that he would go without her, for he had seemed an impatient man. But he was there, with the horse and a small straw-filled wagon hitched to it, lazily twirling the reins around in one hand. He said nothing as he watched her approach, but leaned against the wagon.

"I went to see a priest," she blurted. "For a blessing on our journey." Stupid! She owed him no explanation.

"I see," he said, and pushed himself away from the wagon. "I suppose it can't hurt."

A short, hysterical laugh escaped her. "It should not, yes," Simone replied. She glanced up at the sky; it was clear, and the stars shone starkly against the black cloak of the night, the gibbous moon farther down in the sky than it was some minutes ago. It would be another seven hours until dawn at this time of year. "I will drive first, since it is night, and you may take what sleep you can in the wagon. I have made sure there are blankets there, and the straw should help keep you warm as well."

Corday seemed about to protest, then he nodded and gave her the reins. "Very well," he said, and climbed into the wagon, stretching his lean body out in it as much as he could.

A brief image of his bare chest and shoulders flashed before her eyes, and she dismissed it hastily from her thoughts. Quickly, she leapt up into the wagon seat, and managed not to disturb the horse much when she did. It could sense her predatory nature, she was sure; horses were uneasy around her. She glanced back at Corday as she nickered to the horse to go forward. Perhaps it was just as well that Corday accompanied her. He disturbed her, for certain. But at least he would not disturb the horse.

Chapter 4

"I DO BELIEVE I AM UNCOMMONLY FOND of eggs," Corday said conversationally in the wagon behind her. Simone heard a crack and the crisp sound of an egg peeling. "However, I am willing to give you half if you wish."

"No, I thank you," Simone replied, then gritted her teeth. She had hoped Corday would fall asleep immediately, but instead, he had kept up a stream of chatter that would almost make her think him the storyteller and scribe he claimed to be.

But then there was his pistol, his knife, and his search for the man in Paris. He was, of course, a spy or some sort of emissary sent to negotiate—or more likely kill. No one would send a man with such accuracy of pistol and knife, else. A man used to killing, obviously. . . .

And remarkably careless of that information. He could have pretended more convincingly to be something other than he was. But his assertion of being a storyteller was only that, and his later insistence only a token one. He did not, therefore, care that she knew he was on such a mission. Either he trusted her—which she was sure he did not—or he had some plan to keep her silent.

"It's a very good egg from what I can tell," he continued.

Simone closed her eyes for a moment, tamping down her impatience. "I care not whether it is good or bad. I do not want it." She heard a sigh behind her.

"Very well, I shall have it all."

"Do." She bit off the word, and then smiled to herself when a thought occurred to her. "So," she said, just as conversationally, "when were you planning to kill me—before you eliminated the man you seek, or after?" A sudden, confrontative question. Perhaps he would choke on his egg in surprise.

To her disappointment, he did not.

"Mmph," he said.

"What?"

"Mmph uf fwl."

"What?"

A pause, then: "The problem with eggs is that they can be difficult to swallow if one's mouth is dry. Would you happen to have a sack of water or wine with you?"

Tiens, this man was difficult! She pressed her lips together in an attempt to press down her irritation. She reached beside her on the wagon seat and picked up a leather bottle of wine. "Here," she said, and threw the bottle behind her, hoping it would hit his head.

It did not. "Thank you," Corday said, and emitted a satisfied sigh after a few gulps. "Not the best vintage I have had, but it will do for washing down an egg. The wine is not, I assume, from your estate?"

"Of course n—" Simone stopped. "I have no estate."

"You did—unless it was taken from you."

"How can one such as I have anything like that?" She made her voice sound scornful.

"Come, now. Whatever you look like, your voice is that

of a lady, not a peasant." The straw in the wagon rustled and his voice sounded closer—and amused. "You must have been well educated. You would hardly be one of the Third Estate, or else you would not be trying to ship royalist refugees to England, so your education did not come from there. Unless you are dedicated to a convent—which I doubt, considering your present occupation—you must have received your education there or at home. So, yours is an aristocratic heritage, if your taste in furniture is any indication, for I doubt the wardrobe at the inn was within the range of Mme. Titon's purse."

She turned and looked at him and her hands tightened on the reins. The wagon stopped. Corday sat closer to her perch on the wagon seat, and he had turned his coat collar up around his ears so that the moonlight shone only partly on his face, leaving the rest in darkness. He rose slowly, and leaned against the rails of the wagon.

"Give it up, monsieur," she said. "You will not distract me, however much you try. Whether you meant to or not, you have revealed to me that you have been sent here as a spy from, most probably, England. You are well versed with pistol and dagger; therefore, you have a great capacity to kill, which you have displayed already."

Corday did not move; he seemed to be watching her from the shadows of his coat collar.

"It seems you wish to go about in disguise, but you are careless with your apparent identity around me," Simone continued. She took a deep breath, then let it out again. "Therefore, since I see you are not a stupid man—"

A chuckle emerged from him, and he bowed.

"—I can only assume you do not care if I know who you are and what you are. This means you either trust me, which I doubt, or you mean to kill me once you get what you want."

"I have always liked intelligent women, and I see you

are one such," Corday replied, his voice admiring. "It will be a pleasure working with you."

"You have not answered my question, monsieur."

"Since there is no guarantee I will get what I want, there is no guarantee I will kill you, is there?" Corday said. He moved closer. Simone gauged the short distance between them; she was swifter than he. Should he decide to kill her now, she could kill him before his knife left its sheath. Or disable him. The latter, of course. She had vowed to do her best not to kill.

"There is also no guarantee you will not," she replied tartly.

"You do not trust me," he said. His sigh sounded morose.

"And you have given me a reason to do so?"

Corday shook his head and sighed again. "My sweet, did I not kill those bad men for you? I assure you, I wouldn't do that for just any woman."

"I am not your sweet, and you did not know I was a woman when you did so," Simon said, her annoyance growing. "If you think to manipulate me, you are failing miserably. On one hand you talk of killing me, and then you call me 'sweet.' Even if you did not talk of killing, I cannot be your sweet when you do not even know what I look like."

"But I have always loved a mystery, mademoiselle, and you are very much a mystery. I can imagine you to be anything I like: blond, brunette, red-haired—"

"Ugly, bald, or scarred." Simone cut him off. "You love your own imaginings and the sound of your own words."

"And then there is your voice," Corday continued, as if she had not interrupted. "Low, rich, and provocative to the ear. I could feast on the sound—"

"If you stopped talking long enough to listen," Simone retorted. A sudden bubble of laughter tried to force itself out of her, but she let her exasperation squash it. Surely he must know she would not be moved by such words—especially when she was not at all certain if he would try to kill her at the end of his mission.

And yet, she realized, she did not think he would. She felt wary, of course. But it was not a wariness that waited for possible death. Strange that she should feel this. He was, absolutely, a deadly man. "Hmph," she said. "Well, you may not kill me now, but be warned that I will be watchful once we reach Paris." The horse tossed its head restlessly. She jiggled the reins again, and the wagon moved forward.

A chuckle emitted from the man behind her, and another rustle of the straw indicated that he sat once more. "Did I not say I love a mystery? You are a mystery and a challenge, mademoiselle. It would not be amusing if you died before I discovered who you are. Indeed, more amusing still would be if you revealed yourself to me willingly."

"Be assured, I will not. Why should I, if death be my reward?"

"Did I say you would die once discovered?"

"You said—" She frowned. He had not precisely said he would kill her at the end of his mission.

"I said I would kill you if you tried to kill me—self-defense—or if you tried to stop me from accomplishing my very important mission."

"Very well," Simone said. "But you have been very careless of your identity. Yet, one such as you would not survive long if you were careless."

"True. But you know very little of me. All you have is a name to hang upon."

She smiled slightly. "I know you are an English spy, no doubt sent to assassinate someone the English government believes is dangerous."

"Well."

Simone measured the tone of his voice: neutral . . . almost. Was there humor just at the edge of it? She wondered if she should challenge him further. Again she thought of the distance between them, then smiled slightly.

"Well?" she returned, her voice mocking.

A short pause, then: "Perhaps I find you trustworthy."

She made a rude noise. "You flatter me. Or if you do not, you are a liar. In either case, you are a fool for thinking I would believe you."

A chuckle sounded behind her, and the straw rustled some more. "Alas, you are right. I am very much a fool." His voice came lower within the wagon this time; perhaps he was preparing to sleep. "And yet, here you are, traveling with me."

"I, too, am a fool," Simone said. "By rights I should leave you."

"Why do you stay?"

Why, indeed. Simone's hands clutched the reins again, then loosened them as the horse began to slow. *Saint-Claire, Durant, Mont Michelle, de la Fer.* All the people she had known as a child, and her family. Dead, all of them. She turned to look at him down in the wagon. She could not see his face; he was all in shadow, curled up against the side of the wagon, his head upon a mound of straw.

"I have already said I am a fool, monsieur."

"Ah."

The soft sound faded into the dark. She waited for more words from him, but there was only silence and the slowing rise and fall of his chest. Turning back to the horse, she shook the reins and the wagon moved faster.

The night crawled to the small hours of the morning. It made Simone restless. She usually found the regular rumble of wagon wheels a soothing sound, making her lax body roll with the bumps and lurches on the road, but this time, it did not. Occasionally, she glanced at the moon slipping in and out of thin clouds and between the web of bare tree branches against the sky. It was her clock, and told her how soon she would have to hide herself against the sun.

Rumble, bump, creak, rumble. She tried to focus on the sound, pulling down her shoulders to relax, but found she was still listening, listening . . . to the whisper of the wind, the rattle of dry leaves against bark, the occasional snort of the horse, the clip-clop of its hooves . . . listening. . . .

For his breath. Yes, it was there: regular, slow, deep. Corday was asleep. She let out a deep breath of her own and her shoulders finally fell loose with relief and comfort. Comfort. She shook her head. There was little reason why she should feel comfortable—the opposite would be wise. He slept, that was all, as had many of the people who had traveled with her. At most, his sleeping made him vulnerable to her. She shook her head again. He was a fool to make himself so open to attack.

Or, he trusted her. Simone glanced back at his sleeping form. In truth, she doubted he was as foolish as she had claimed. Spies did not live long if they were fools, and this man must be at least thirty. He probably did not think she was a fool, either—men such as he knew better than to trust one.

She let out an impatient breath. She wasted too much thought on this Corday. They would travel together until they accomplished their missions, and that would be the end of their partnership—if not before. Indeed, if she could find a way to honorably end it soon, she would.

A cock crowed in the distance, and she looked to the eastern horizon. No light yet. But the moon had sunk low in the sky and she would need to find cover soon. She was near her family's estate; it was less than an hour away. She would go there, and catch up with Corday on foot at night; easily done, for she could run swiftly and tirelessly until the dawn. Simone smiled wryly to herself. Her curse had certain advantages; she could not deny it, and if she were to be honest with herself, she enjoyed her strength and her swiftness. She had other abilities as well. She could see like a cat in the night, and hear slight sounds from far away, or discern whispers among louder noises.

And when her blood-thirst was upon her, all of these abilities rose to a high, unbearable pitch. Sometimes, it almost drove her mad. She was thankful for the dullness of the senses that enfolded her after the thirst had run its course.

No, she should not think of enjoying anything about her curse. She wanted to be rid of it.

The faint crow of a rooster caught her ear again. Soon, the sun would rise. She needed to leave now. Once more she glanced at Corday. Should she leave him now, or wake him? Wake him, then leave swiftly. There was no need to hand him the reins; the horse needed rest, anyway. She would tie the reins to a low-hanging branch, wake the man, then run to the de la Fer estate. It was too dark for him to follow her, and even if he could see as well in the dark as she, she knew well how to step so that her movements were noiseless.

Simone slowed the horse and the wagon rumbled to a stop. The rooster crowed once more. She needed to leave now. "Corday."

The straw rustled, and she turned to look at him. He stood, and the moon low on the horizon shone on his watchful, emotionless face, making him look like a silver statue.

"I must leave," she said. His chin rose slightly, and she wondered if he would speak, but he said nothing. "Take this wagon a mile, and you will find another inn—the one

Monsieur Titon mentioned to you—that has taken my coin from time to time. You may trade this poor horse for another, more fresh one there. Take it, and tell the innkeeper you wish a candle for your journey before you do. He will understand." The wind suddenly blew through the trees, rattling the leaves in the forest.

Silence, then: "You will return." His voice gave no clue whether it was a question or command.

Irritation pricked her. "I have given my word, and that is all you need to know. You will see me again once the sun sets, depend upon it."

He moved suddenly, his hand rising in a gesture surely meant to seize her arm. But Simone leapt from the wagon seat to the ground, and another leap took her to the soft earth and dry leaves of the woods. She smiled, and a chuckle escaped her as she gave one last glance behind her where he stood, his hand still outstretched, staring where she had disappeared. No, he would not catch her. She was too quick, too fast, too silent. Monsieur Corday the spy knew less of her than he thought. Her smile turned grim. And the less he knew, the better.

She had disappeared as quickly as a flame in the wind, and just as silently. Corday let his hand drop to his side. He hadn't caught her because he'd just been wakened and it was still dark. He grimaced. Bad. Very bad. There was no room for a mistake like that. It could get him killed.

If La Flamme had chosen, she could have killed him when he was sleeping in the wagon. . . . She hadn't, however. In that, then, her word was good.

Should he go after her? He stared at the darkness between the trees; he doubted he could find her. He would have to trust that she would come back.

Irritation itched at him. He was not used to trusting. It

went against everything he had learned in his life. A man could trust another for a short while, perhaps, as long as self-interest held the person he trusted. But as soon as it disappeared, he knew enough that a knife—figurative or real—would be ready for his back.

And yet . . . He felt La Flamme would return. He smiled slightly to himself. She had principles, that little one. It would kill her some day, but for now it meant the chances were good she would return.

His smile fell from him. However, he would not allow her to run off the next time. If it meant he would have to chain her to the wagon, so be it. She had information he needed. He would make sure she was here when he needed it.

There was not much time, either, if what Citoyen du Maurier said was true—and Corday was sure the man thought it. That a foreign agent might be fomenting revolt from within the Abbeye prison instead of outside of it was nonsense. He might not know about another agent, however. Doubtful; if Sir Robert with his very good connections had not caught a whiff of it, then he, Corday, would have known of it. If there was not another agent . . . it could be that someone had got wind of his arrival.

This was possible. Sir Robert had talked of an infiltrator, an informant, one who had killed Johnson and Bramley. If this infiltrator knew of his presence in France, it was possible he—or she—had let the agents know as well.

In which case, the sooner he arrived in Paris and dispatched his mission, the better.

Impatience seized him. He should leave for Paris now. Unfortunately, he had not as intimate knowledge of the city as La Flamme obviously did; otherwise, she would not have been so successful in escaping the net of the Committee of Public Safety. She had resources he needed.

He would be quick, then, and persuade her. The

persuasion should be easy; he need only tell her of du Maurier's suspicions of foreign agents within the Abbeye. She would know it meant death for whatever innocents the Committee decided were guilty; she would be moved to save the innocents.

It would mean, of course, that he would need to find her before her usual arrival time. He has allowed her to disappear the first time he met her. He had not minded it too much beyond a little irritation, especially when he thought to indulge in a little more rest than he usually gave himself on his journeys, but he could not afford it now. Neither could she.

He could also ill afford her masquerade. He thought he'd tease her identity from her over the course of their travels, but he needed to be sure she was not some part of the infiltration.

It should not take very long to find her, for he was practiced in tracking prey through the woods. He would tell her of the threat to the prisoners in the Abbeye, and no doubt she would cease her annoying disappearances and do at last what she was told. He grinned. He wondered how furious she would be when he found her. It would be most amusing to find out.

He climbed onto the wagon seat and took up the reins. He would go to the inn, deposit the wagon at it, and follow her. The sooner he discovered the identity of La Flamme, the better.

Chapter 5

THE WAY BACK TO THE PLACE WHERE LA Flamme had disappeared into the woods was thankfully faster without the burden of the wagon, and Corday entered the wood once he found the mark he had made earlier, leading his horse onto what looked like a small deer path.

Gray sunlight filtered its way through the tree limbs and faintly illuminated the shrubbery before him. Corday slowed a little, gazing around him. Yes, there—a bent elder tree branch, more bracken pointing in one direction than not . . . she must have gone to the west.

He watched for the signs of passage carefully—a small piece of rag hanging from a shrub, a fresh footprint in the mud—picking up the pace when the path grew wider, slowing when it narrowed. Finally, the path widened, the trees cleared, and he found himself in front of an iron gate.

It had been a long time since anyone had lived within these gates, he was sure; anyone who cared for the estate, that is. The iron was rusted, the walls on either side clothed in ivy, and the wide path beyond was only that: a road that had shrunk to half its size for the grass and brush that had overgrown it. Beyond the gate, he could see a mansion of gray stone; he thought he could see Norman influence in the part of the building that peeked through the ivy that had overgrown nearly a quarter of it. Old, then, and the family who owned it—or had owned it—no doubt equally old.

He touched the gate, and it opened with only a whisper. Corday grinned. Yes, she must be here, despite the air of age and neglect the grounds and mansion suggested. It would be in her best interests to pass through here without a sound. He mounted the horse, and moved forward through the gate into the fog that rose in wisps before him.

He half expected to be challenged on his way toward the mansion, but no sound came to him except the small breeze that fitfully rustled the dry grass and dead leaves strewn across the field to the house. No servants appeared to ask his business when he took the horse to a stable in the back of the house; no movement or light showed through any of the windows as he followed the traces of his quarry to a side door. It was as if the house slept in a blanket of mist and ancient oblivion. He shivered, then pulled his coat more closely around him. He hoped the house would be warmer.

It was not. He opened the door, dislodging a few spiders that had made themselves comfortable along the top of the threshold, and peered into the interior, dim with the ivy overhanging the windows. At least no breeze flowed through it to make it any colder, Corday thought. The shapes before him came into focus as his eyes grew used to the dimness and he made out a chair, then a table, and a large fire pit of a hearth—it seemed he had entered the kitchen. He blew on his gloved hands and pressed them together. If this was La Flamme's hiding place, it would be best not to light a fire and alert the Public Safety agents of anyone's presence. However—his gaze fell on a few dusty candles tucked in a corner of the kitchen—something to light his way would be helpful.

It took a few minutes for the tinder in his tinderbox to catch fire and then light the candle, for the tinder had taken in the dampness in the air, and the cold room didn't help. But the shavings took fire at last, and he carefully lit then settled the candle in a small glass-paned lamp before he left the kitchen to follow the small, clear path through the dust that led from the kitchen to the rest of the house.

She must have taken the way from the kitchen to the hall often, since it was the least dusty. But from there the neglect of the house and the different ways she apparently went through the rooms made it less easy to follow. It was, however, little different from and easier than tracking her through the wood; less dust in one direction, the pushed-away sheet that had covered one chair less dusty than another, the faint, still damp footsteps that led up a long staircase from the main hall all pointed to where she might be.

It led to a closed door not far from where the servants' quarters might have been. Carefully, he tried the door. Locked, of course. Corday gazed thoughtfully at the keyhole, and pulled a small metal pick from his sleeve. A few moments passed before a satisfying click told him the door was no longer locked. He pressed the door latch and went into the room, tucking the lock pick back into a tiny pocket in his sleeve.

Darkness. His lamp seemed hardly to pierce it, and he paused just past the doorway before his eyes made out a few shadowy drapes. No sound, not even a slight whisper of breath he might expect to hear from someone who slept. He sensed a presence nevertheless, perhaps because of some sound he might have heard when he entered.

He held his lamp a little higher. More drapes—bed

drapes, he noted as he drew closer to the dark shape before him—heavy ones by the feel of them. He drew away from the bed, going around it toward where the windows would be, and found more heavy cloth, completely blocking any light that might be let in. If La Flamme was in this house, she would surely be here in this room, perhaps in this bed. He raised his hand and pulled back the bed drapes.

A woman lay there, asleep. Corday frowned. Was this La Flamme? She seemed too delicate to be someone who could exhibit such strength as he had seen. Perhaps it was the dark and the dim light of the candle that made her seem so pale, but this certainly could not be someone of robust health as the outlaw must certainly be. He pushed back the drapes more completely, and bent closer to shine the lamp on her face.

She was lovely. He chuckled softly. So much for ugly, bald, or scarred. Her face was unmarked except for slight shadows under her eyes, and the dark hair strewn across her pillow shone thick in the candlelight. Long lashes lay on high cheeks that tapered down to a stubborn chin. Her skin was translucently pale, and her lips full and very kiss-able.

He wondered if she would awake if he kissed her, and his grin widened. For all the fairy tales he had told on his travels, he had never thought he would play the prince to a sleeping beauty. His grin turned wry. He was no prince, and no doubt she knew it from their first meeting. Corday put his hand on her shoulder and shook it.

No response. Her skin was cool, more than he would expect from a living person. Damn. Had she become ill and died? He put his hand over her mouth: a slight breath, and her chest rose and lowered slightly. No, she slept, slept heavily. He brought the lamp closer, and his gaze went to her lips again—they were deep pink, not the blue-gray of someone near death.

Corday rose, leaned against a bedpost, and gazed at the young woman. A very interesting dilemma. He could take advantage of the moment and kiss her—he was, after all, curious to see whether her lips were as kissable as they appeared. He doubted she would awaken; she did not awake when he had shaken her shoulder.

He suppressed a sudden laugh. No, he would not kiss her—for now. He would much rather she be awake—or better, not so deeply asleep so that he could awaken her with a kiss. It would, after all, be far more entertaining to see her reaction then. She would be furious, of course, and he would then see if her eyes flashed or her cheeks grew red. Yes, he would wait for that opportunity—it would be much more amusing that way.

Now, however, he needed to attend to business. Some people were more easily awakened by sunlight. Obviously, she was one such, since the room's curtains and the bed drapes were so tightly closed. Corday pushed the bed drapes farther apart, then moved to the window and thrust aside the curtains.

A high, agonized scream made him freeze, and he turned swiftly toward the bed. She was gone.

He had not heard the door open; she could not have left the room. Therefore, she was still here. He remembered her swiftness and the strength of her hands just the night before: She was also quite dangerous. Carefully, he put the candle on a small table and listened.

Panting came from beneath the bed, the sound edged with a harsh wheeze, as if some animal in pain hid there.

Corday frowned. She could not be in pain unless she had suffered some injury in their fight with the Public Safety agents. Yet, she had shown no signs of injury since that time, and certainly not when she had attacked him. It could be that she had somehow been injured after she had left him.

Unfortunate, if it were severe. He hoped it was not; it would mean he would have to dispense with her knowledge of Paris, increasing the time it would take to find the man he sought, and this would hamper his mission. He walked softly to where the breathing was loudest.

"Mademoiselle, you may come out. I will not hurt you." He squatted next to the bed and raised the bed-clothes that had slid off the mattress.

A sudden movement made him scramble back, and a brief flash of steel sliced the air where he had been. He rose slowly from the floor.

"Ah," he said cordially. "You are clearly one who does not have the best of dispositions in the morning. I sympathize; normally I prefer not to rise before ten o'clock, and rising at dawn usually puts me out of temper for at least an hour." The breathing under the bed stopped then started again, this time coming more slowly, and the harsh edge was gone.

"Quelle bonne chance." Her voice managed a sarcastic tone through its trembling. "I have fallen in with a madman."

"Good luck indeed," Corday replied. "And I would remind you that I am not the one hiding under the bed."

A small, frustrated growl emitted from under the bed. "Close the curtain, then I will come out."

"I have already seen what you look like, mademoiselle, so hiding yourself is useless."

"Close the curtain. Then I will come out," she repeated.

"I will drag you out if I have to," he said.

"You will not. I have a dagger."

"And I have a pistol."

"Always the stupid pistol," she muttered. Silence, then: "Close the curtain. Let no sunlight show through. Then I will come out." A pause. "Please."

Corday suppressed a smile at her grudging civility. He would indulge her—this time. "Show me your dagger."

Metal clattered on the wooden floor, and he picked up the knife—a fine Italian stiletto, he noted—and closed the room's curtains. Darkness fell again, save for the candle he had set on the side table. He lifted the candle.

The bedclothes draped over the other side of the bed rustled, and the woman slowly rose from the floor, cradling her left arm. Corday frowned and walked around the bed to her. She stepped back, watching him warily.

He let out an exasperated breath. "I have told you that if I had wished to kill you, I would have done so already." He held out his hand. "You have injured your arm. Let me see it."

She continued to stare at him. "It will heal quickly."

"Don't be stupid," he said, and grasped her arm.

She gasped, and as he turned her arm, she let out a soft grunt of pain.

An angry streak of red scored her skin from wrist to elbow, and blisters rose even as he watched. He released her arm and held her chin in his hand, looking into her eyes.

"What happened to you?"

She pulled away. "Nothing," she said, and her eyes slid from his gaze.

"You are a poor liar. You were burned, and I know a cry of pain when I hear it. For all I know, you may be injured elsewhere."

She looked at him steadily this time. "I am not, I assure you," she replied. "*En fait*, my burn is almost gone." She lifted her arm toward him, but she flinched away from the flame as he brought the candle closer to her. Her jaw clenched, as if she steeled herself against pain. She clearly lied; such a reaction to a small candle flame showed that someone had burned her, and badly. He grasped her wrist and pulled her toward him.

Her skin was smooth, and only a light streak of redness marked her arm.

He blinked, then took her other arm and brought it into the candlelight. It, too, was smooth and pale, with no sign of any injury. He looked at the other again; this time, the red was but a small pink line. He frowned and looked at her. "It was blistered."

"You must be mistaken." Her voice had stopped trembling, sounding firm and sure now, but her eyes flickered away from his for a moment before staring at him again. She was a bad liar . . . yet another glance at her arm showed only smooth, pale skin. She must have seen his hesitation, for her lips lifted in a faint smile and she nodded at the candle. "You only have one candle—it is difficult to see such a thing in the dark."

He stared at her in silence for a moment, then moved toward the curtained windows again. "Very well," he said, and his voice took on a speculative cast. "I will use better than candlelight." He put his hand on the curtains.

"No!" With her last ounce of energy, she leapt at him across the bed, pushing him away.

A foolish move. Light streamed in and struck her arm again. White-hot pain seared her hand, her arm, her shoulder. She clamped her teeth down on the agony. *Get away. Hide.*

She opened her eyes. Pain, still, but not as bad. She was under the bed again; she must have managed to crawl underneath somehow. The pain lessened a little more, and she grew conscious of her own breath, coming out in short, shallow grunts. She swallowed, and forced her breath to slow.

"You may come out," came Corday's voice from above the bed. "I will not open the curtains again."

Simone closed her eyes again. She wanted to rest, not move. The pain lessened and she tried to flex her fingers.

They felt numb. It would take a night and possibly part of another for her to gain full feeling again.

"You have my word on it."

"I should trust your word?" she managed to say.

"Yes."

That was all: just "yes" and nothing else, no justification or evidence of trustworthiness. Simply "yes."

She rolled over, barely biting back a groan as her arm hit the floor. She cradled her arm in the other, and pushed herself out into the room again.

She caught sight of him, watching her, his face half obscured in the dark. She wanted, badly, simply to sleep away the pain. But no, she would not lie at his feet. She was Simone de la Fer, the last of her ancient family. She would never be at anyone's feet.

She pushed herself up, leaning against the wall as she did so, for her legs trembled. She watched him, and for a moment he swayed toward her, as if he were about to assist her. But he grew still again, watching her in return. A wise decision, she thought, if he had decided to refrain; she did not want his help, and would have pushed him away.

And fallen again in the attempt, no doubt.

Simone bit back a grimace and closed her eyes again. If she could imagine him away, she would, but she had no such powers. Besides, he was clearly a persistent man, and would follow her even into hell if he so wished.

"What do you want of me?" she asked. She opened her eyes and stared up at him. Up. She had slid down a little. She pushed herself standing again.

"Who you are. What you know."

"Why should I tell you?"

"Because I need to know if you have revealed my purpose and my presence to anyone."

She needed more time to recover; arguing with him would give her that time. "Why should I tell you?" she said again. "If I did, I would not be such a fool to reveal it to you. If I have and did not know it, I would still have nothing to tell you."

He strode around the bed and seized her arm with one hand, while the other took her chin. He stared into her eyes, his expression cold and measuring. "You will tell me because if you do not, most assuredly you will die—along with the prisoners in the Abbeye."

Simone stared at him for a long moment, looking for some emotion in his eyes. There was none. "What do you mean, the prisoners in the Abbeye? Will you give me up to the Committee of Public Safety?" Fear and anger flamed within her, sudden and hot. So, he was one of them after all. *Eh bien.* She curled her lip and spat at him. "Try it, and you will be dead before you succeed."

His smile was ironic as he stared into her eyes and slowly wiped the spittle from his face. His eyes were no longer cold; angry heat burned there. "I doubt it, my lady fire-eater. You can barely stand as it is." His hand closed over her neck. "If you think you can kill me, do it now." His voice dared her, and she stared back at him, her heart beating faster now, for it seemed almost as if he wanted her to try. No, he could not be so mad as to want such a thing. No, he was trying to exert power over her, force her to his will.

Never. She gritted her teeth and seized his wrists, digging her thumbs into the soft spot just above the palms of his hands, and pulled hard.

His hands loosened for a moment, and his eyes widened in surprise. His hands grasped her again, and her arms trembled with effort—almost, almost she could feel him release her, but she had not yet regained her strength. She dug her thumbnails into his wrists, harder, and the faint scent of blood came to her nose.

Blood-lust flared. *No!*

She released him.

Harsh breathing sounded loud in her ears: It was her own. Another sound came to her: the light quick breath of the man before her. His hand was still around her neck—it had never moved, she realized, never tightened more than it originally had, and in fact had held her no tighter than a necklace she might have put on herself. He had only held fast against her hands, nothing more. He was very strong, she realized, and used to control—over others perhaps, but most certainly over himself.

"What do you want of me?" she asked.

"I want to know if you have betrayed me."

She stared into his eyes; they were no longer cold or full of anger, but watchful. "You are mad," she said. "I have done nothing to suggest it."

"No? Let me see. You refuse to tell me who you are. You disappear during the day and I have no idea what you are doing or who you meet. This is a land where you cannot trust anyone, a time when your neighbor might turn you in as an enemy of the state. You know this, and yet you give not one token that you can be trusted."

"And you do?" Simone retorted.

Corday smiled slightly. "Touché. But at least you know where I am at any time. I have consistently gone to the inns to which you have directed me—I have given you that much trust. You may ask M. Titon. He will tell you I have caused no trouble for him, and indeed have even managed to elicit information from an agent of the Public Safety Committee."

An agent. She looked at him sharply. "Where?"

"At Titon's inn."

Merde. Reinforcements had come faster this time. But they were in general an incompetent lot, and she had had little trouble evading them in the past. It would not take much to evade them now, she was sure. "It is nothing," she said. "I will elude them."

"I would not be so confident," Corday replied. "There is one—du Maurier—who should not be underestimated."

"Him!" Simone sneered. "I have slipped from under his nose before."

"And with each escape, I suspect he has come to understand your movements better," Corday said. "He is not stupid." He gazed at her, his expression assessing. "I would not underestimate his assistant Hervé, either."

"Guillaume Hervé?" She frowned at a vague memory. "I do not recall . . ."

"I am not surprised. He is a forgettable man, which makes him all the more dangerous. A man who draws no attention to himself can go anywhere and be anyone."

She stared at him; his words made sense. She hadn't thought someone so inconsequential as an unmemorable agent's assistant could be dangerous, but she had to admit that to assume anything else was foolishness. She grimaced. She did not like to admit she had been foolish, but she had not the luxury to be vain of her own perceptions.

She nodded. "Very well. I thank you for your advice." She smiled slightly at the fleeting surprise that flashed across his face. "What, did you think me so caught up in my own opinion of myself that I cannot take good advice?"

His brows drew together for a moment, as if he had met a puzzle difficult to solve, then his expression became smooth again. "People commonly refuse it."

She felt his hand slide from her neck to touch her cheek briefly before it fell away. He looked toward the covered windows before he gazed at her again.

"I will not give you away," he said. "You have my word on it—for what that is worth." His mouth lifted in a small, cynical smile. "In truth, I do not think you might have betrayed me intentionally." He moved away from her and leaned against a bedpost. "Du Maurier mentioned that the Committee for Public Safety suspects that a foreign agent is fomenting revolt from within the Abbeye—" He held up his hand when she opened her mouth to protest. "Nonsense, I know. But his claim gives rise to the possibility that someone knows of my arrival. My first thought was that you had revealed my origins to one of your associates who might be less than discreet."

"No, of course not. I said nothing of you to any of those loyal to our king, and I stay away from any I suspect are loyal citizens of the Republic."

"How do you know? You did not consider Hervé, after all."

Simone tamped down her rising irritation. "Except for one man at Titon's inn, I have not talked to anyone except you."

"And you assume that one man will not talk to any agent of the Revolution?"

"He is a priest; my words were said in the confessional. His holy vows forbid him to reveal anything I say. Besides, I did not mention you at all to him; he assumes I travel alone."

"He did not see you from a window as you left?"

"If he did, he would not have seen you, since the stables are not within sight of his room." Her hand cut the air in an impatient, dismissive gesture. "He is a priest and a friend, and has no love for the Republic. *En vais,* that I tell you he is a priest, and so one of the hunted, should tell you I trust you more than I should."

"I have only your word on that."

Anger forced a cry from her, and she thumped her fist against the wall. "We go around and around, and never come to the point. You do not trust me, I do not trust you. Where does that lead, eh? We have no reason to work together. I do not even know why you even proposed it, or why I agreed."

Corday stared at her for a moment. "The prisoners in the Abbeye—if they are hiding the foreign agent, they will be punished," he said.

Dread crept over her. "There are no foreign agents in the Abbeye."

Corday continued to gaze at her, and she thought that a faint pity showed in his eyes. "You know what the Committee of Public Safety is like. They were born of the Jacobins and the Girondins, and both parties think conspirators are behind every corner and cobblestone. If they choose to find a foreign agent in the Abbeye, I am sure they will search, in their characteristic way, until they find one. Or two. Or three."

Simone swallowed. "They would not—they would not—" The words stuck in her throat.

He said nothing.

"You are lying," she said. He must be. He wanted her to accompany him to Paris. Perhaps that is why he told her this.

"Ask M. Titon."

"He knows?"

"He heard."

She could easily verify it, if she chose, but she looked into his eyes and believed him. He could be a very fine actor, she thought, and she was sure he would not hesitate to lie if he thought it expedient. "When will the committee . . . begin their investigations?"

"In a few days, to finish in perhaps a week and a half."

She almost groaned. She would have to hurry. There was barely any time to spare. She could not travel by day, and would have to start as soon as twilight descended.

"If we started now, we would be there ahead of the agents."

She looked at him. How could she explain to him that she could not travel now? It was one thing to pretend that her work at night made hiding her refugees easier. It was another altogether to reveal that she could not do anything but work at night, and that exposing herself to the sunlight tired her at best when she was well wrapped.

"Well?" he said.

"I . . . it will be difficult."

"Why?"

"I . . . I am not used to traveling during the day."

"Then become used to it. We need to travel quickly."

"The light hurts me."

"What?" He gazed at her, his brows drawn together in a frown.

She moistened her suddenly dry lips. "The light hurts me. That is why I cried out when you opened the curtains."

"I have never heard of such a thing."

"It is true—you saw it yourself." She gazed steadily at him. "I lied when I said my arm was not hurt. It did have the blisters you saw." She grimaced. "That, in truth, is why I travel at night."

"Is it a disease?" he asked, although he did not draw away.

She smiled wryly. "It is not. I wish it were as simple as that. It is not catching, I assure you."

His lips pressed together in clear frustration. "Perhaps I should go alone, after all. I do not wish to be hampered in my travels."

Fear crept through her: If the Committee of Public Safety was intent on seeking out insurrectionists within the Abbeye, she would need help to get as many people out as possible. Even with her strength and abilities, she could not release that many. She stared at him as he shook his head.

"No. I think it better that I travel alone after all."

His words stung, and she curled her lip. "I shall not be a hindrance, monsieur. Indeed, I can easily outpace you, yes, even if you were riding *ventre à terre* to Paris, and I traveled only at night."

"I doubt it. If you have such a debilitating condition that you cannot stand the light of day without injury, then you would be a hindrance, not an asset. If it is not true that the light affects you so, then you are a liar, and I have no use for you." He said it with no heat, no anger, no discernible intent to insult; she could see it was merely the truth as he saw it. She ground her teeth in frustration. Of course that would be the way it appeared. How was she to convince him differently? He turned, as if to leave, and she caught his arm.

"Don't go," she said. "I will come to you, later, when it is dark."

"A most attractive offer, my dear, but I am afraid not." His teeth flashed in a sudden wide smile. "However, since I dislike disappointing a lady, I will, at least, give you a token of my regard." His movement was swift, and she was still too weak from the exposure to sunlight to react as quickly as she normally would, and then . . . and then, it was too late.

He pulled her into his arms and kissed her.

His arms did not crush her, but held her against him firmly. His lips did not push with a bruising force against hers, but brushed them gently then pressed her mouth open with a sweet insistence. The faint scent of blood came to her—faint because the cut she had given his wrist was now healing, but not enough to bring her to full blood-thirst.

But it was enough to bring her senses to a wild, sharp, hunting peak, enough to make his hands feel hot upon the skin of her hips and waist and breast through the thin shift she wore. His scent came to her: the fresh scent of the woods he had passed through, the light scent of his skin and hair. He must have taken some wine, for his mouth tasted of it, and suddenly she wanted more.

She made a small sound, and when he drew back, she threaded her hands through his hair and pulled him to her again.

A soft laugh came from him, and he kissed her more deeply, moving her body hard against his. Heat flared everywhere he touched her, and her senses came to a high, agonizing peak as her hunting senses gained strength.

She could feel the pulse beneath her fingertips, and ran them down the sides of his neck, where his blood beat with an incipient excitement. She pushed aside the collar of his shirt and put her tongue against his neck. His pulse beat faster.

She excited him; it gave her power over him, she knew. She could do anything to him now, and he would obey. She could seduce him with her body, and make him stay with her and make him wait for her. She could even take his blood—

A sudden soft, triumphant laugh—loud in her now sensitive ears—pulled the haze of the blood-hunt away from her, and she gazed, startled, at him.

He gazed back, and holding her chin in his hand, kissed her quickly then pushed her away. "Alas," he said. "It seems I will have to disappoint you after all, my sweet. Duty calls, and I must be gone. However, if you are patient, I will try to return so that we can . . ." He grinned widely and nodded toward the bed. "Finish what we started." He chucked her under her chin. "Do be a good girl and keep it warm for me."

His words slapped cold sense into her, and she forced sensual haze of the blood-hunt from her mind. Anger took its place: anger at him for taking advantage of her, anger at herself for almost losing control and putting a compulsion on him. Anger that she had so easily given in to his kiss.

"Don't." Her voice sounded low and harsh in her own ears. "Don't do this again, for I will surely kill you." If he had not broken away at that point and had not spoken, she would have given into the hunt, to the sensual pull of flesh and blood.

He flicked a finger against her cheek. "You will have to convince me better than that, sweet one." He went to the door and opened it. "And do leave off the rags." He looked her up and down. "You look much better without them." He tossed her stiletto to her, and she caught it, awkwardly, then he blew her a kiss and closed the door behind him.

Thunk! The doorjamb sprouted the dagger, and she growled.

Le cochon! The pig! It would have served him right had she given in and drained him of every drop of blood in his body.

Chapter 6

CORDAY SMILED SLIGHTLY AS HE CLOSED the door, strolled down the stairs, and stepped out of the house. He had almost, almost tumbled the chit, and who would have blamed him? It had needed just a brush of her lips to make him want more, and she had given it. He could have taken her.

He found his horse where he had left it, cropping grass, and mounted it. His smile faded. But then she had looked at him, her eyes wild and openly vulnerable, and he had stopped. Duty called, after all—

Damned, damned duty. It wasn't enough that he had to hurry his journey to Paris, but he had to leave behind what could have been a most useful ally and potential bed partner.

Haste, however, was of the essence. Whether she truly had a condition that prohibited her from traveling in the sunlight or whether it was some strange aberration of her mind, she clearly would not travel during the day. He could not afford any handicap. He would have to find his own way around the Parisian underground; it was not as if he had not been thrown on his own resources before, after all.

He wondered if she would follow him. Probably. She was a stubborn creature. The thought that he would like to see her again drifted into his mind, and an image of her lovely form reclining in a bed brought back the heat he felt when he kissed her. That was something to regret! He doubted she would wait for him as he teasingly requested; more likely she would kill him instead. He chuckled. At least he was reasonably sure she had not betrayed him. Her face too transparently showed her emotion of astonishment and anger, and she had revealed nothing of his presence to the one man she had talked to.

Which left open the question of whether someone else had alerted the Committee of Public Safety to his presence. He could not dismiss the notion; Sir Robert had told him of some infiltrator, a traitor to the British crown. This infiltrator had apparently caused the deaths of Johnson and Bramley; it was not above possibility that he would try to cause Corday's.

The horse wended its way through the wood again, and the path opened to the road, but Corday did not urge a faster pace. It would do no good to tire the horse, and he needed to think through the events of the past few days.

He was fairly sure the traitor was in England, perhaps high in the organization's hierarchy. There could be no other way for the movements of Johnson and Bramley to be so well known to the killer. The information must have passed to a killer-collaborator here, in France. The transmittal of the information concerned him little; there were more than a few ways information could travel unnoticed in this chaotic land, and even if it were of concern to him, he would waste too much time tracking down the path. It was not, after all, his mission to trace the flow of information. It was his mission to kill the killer, the one Sir Robert said was likely to move the Revolution to England's shores.

Information, however, was always valuable to such a creature, and who would have more information than the Committee of Public Safety? It made sense, then, that the man he looked for was intimately tied to the committee. Perhaps he was an official, or perhaps an agent himself. Hmm. Official or agent? Not an official. Agents had mobility, and mobility and information often went hand in hand.

Corday twisted his lips wryly. It seemed he needed to cultivate the acquaintance of du Maurier and his very innocuous assistant, Guillaume Hervé.

Very well. He would feign nervousness at the apparent presence of La Flamme, and beg to travel with them. They would no doubt be scornful but indulgent; what agent would not be? It mattered not. All that mattered was that he could milk them of whatever information they might have.

La Flamme. Corday blinked, then grimaced. He still did not know who she was. A bad slip, that. He should have forced the information from her, or better yet, seduced it from her. Now, that he did regret; it would have been very pleasant to have seduced it from her, and from her response, it would not have been that difficult.

Corday's grimace became a frown. He needed to watch himself. He could not afford to make such a mistake again. Luckily, it did not matter at this time, and should he accomplish this mission successfully, he could try to seek her out and seduce it from her after all.

His smile returned. That was most certainly an incentive to finish this mission quickly. And if she were to follow him, perhaps he could do it sooner than that.

Corday looked at the road ahead of him. If he hurried, he might just catch up with the agents within a few hours.

He pressed his heels against the horse's side, and the horse moved into an easy canter. He sighed. It was a pity he would have to associate with the agents from now on. He doubted La Flamme would venture near them, and he had hoped he might have an opportunity to try a bit of seduction. Ah, well. Duty called.

Simone pulled her dagger from the doorjamb and thrust it into its sheath. Twilight had wakened her, and she dressed quickly—but not in her rags. No, she had a plan, one that no one looking for La Flamme would associate with that outlaw. She chuckled to herself. In a way, she had Corday to thank for it; he had said she should leave off her rags, and the words had stuck in her mind. The night never hurt her, and so she could easily travel this way. She would take a horse; though horses disliked her riding them, she could still control them and bend them to her will. She would catch up with Corday, and her appearance would very definitely disconcert him. Oh, she would have her revenge on him. It would not be in a way he would foresee; oh, no. But it would be revenge, nevertheless.

Simone pondered over two overskirts: one red and the other blue. The blue was more worn, suitable for a woman of the lower middle class, slightly educated. It was necessary to be of this class; any lower and her gloves would be out of character. A large fichu was also necessary; it could serve as a cover against the light and add some modesty to her dress. She gazed at the mirror and her lips twisted. She should have tied the corset tightly, but she had to choose between flexibility and neatness. Flexibility was far more useful than neatness.

In all, however, she looked as she wished to look: like a woman who survived well enough in society if she was careful of her funds, her pale appearance hinting that she had a little less than she needed. She strapped her dagger's sheath to the calf of her leg, and thought suddenly of Corday's pistols. She did not care to use pistols, for she did well enough with her dagger and the strength and swiftness of her body. But she would need to free as many prisoners as she could, and it would be helpful if she could arm some of them. She had not many pistols, and she could not carry them if she had, but two, she thought, should do for now.

She went to the wardrobe in one corner of her room, and pushed aside the clothes. She had hidden the pistol case there that had belonged to her brother. The pistols were not new, but she had made sure to take care of them, and had learned over the years how to use them. A small bag of shot and another of dry powder lay under the case, and she pocketed them, thankful for the large pouches hidden in the skirts of her dress.

As for the pistols themselves . . . should she carry one? Yes, one; the other she would stow in her shoulder bag along with her rags, her boy's clothes, and a change of clothing. Another search into the wardrobe brought forth a jewelry case. She opened it, and pulled out half a string of pearls—what was left of her mother's pearl set.

Simone sighed. Although she still had a good store of de la Fer jewelry, each piece that she sold gave her less of family to hold on to. She had to be practical: The pearls would do for trade. The Revolution's paper money was near worthless, but no one doubted the worth of pearls.

As for provisions, as soon as she reached Petit's inn, she would buy food. It would not do to let herself become hungry for long—it turned too easily to the blood-hunger, and she tried not to give in to it. Occasionally, she did. Père Dumont believed it could not be helped if she wished to stay alive, and purposely refraining would be the same as suicide, which was a grave sin. She still felt ashamed she had not the strength to resist it, however. The good priest suggested that she keep to taking blood only from those who offered it freely, and failing that, from those who were clearly of a low moral nature.

Well, there were few who would offer it freely, and even then they did not so much give it freely but were seduced into it when the blood-hunt overtook her. She doubted anyone, knowing what she was, would willingly give their blood for her sustenance. As a result, when she felt weak from the lack of blood, or when she had stayed up too long into the light over a succession of days, she went once again into Paris, and sought those who would kill or torture for pleasure.

Simone grimaced. It had not been difficult to find these sorts of men since the beginning of the Revolution. Indeed, it had been difficult to resist finding them. She had, however, kept herself chaste during her blood-taking. She would not make herself a whore to men she detested. Simone pulled her cloak on and turned to leave.

She stopped. The doll—she had almost forgotten her doll. That, more than anything, made her remember her purpose. She remembered when her old nurse, half mad from the terror of that night, had given it to her. It was the night all her family had been destroyed, the night that she had exacted her revenge, the night that she had vowed to save those condemned to death by the Committee of Public Safety, as many as she could.

She picked up the doll—rumpled, but remarkably undamaged from all her activities—and tucked it tenderly in her bag. She could not leave it behind; it reminded her of her purpose, and it was part of her disguise. . . . She sighed. It reminded her, too, of simpler times, when she was a child and did not think of anything but bright sun that did not hurt and flower gardens whose varied colors defied any artist's palette. Sometimes she would gaze and gaze at the doll, then close her eyes. The afterimage of the doll would merge with her memories, and sometimes she almost felt she could touch the innocence of long ago once again.

Long ago ... before she had left her family, before they had died. She shook her head, dispelling memories, and brought her mind to the present again.

Simone took one last glance around her room and sighed. She would be glad if it had felt like a home, but for all its memories and the fact that it was the home of her family, she had been away from it too long, and the memories were too painful for her to wish to live here. But it was the only place she felt safe, and the rumors and the frights she had set about the countryside made sure that people avoided it, even the Public Safety agents. She supposed she would live here forever; there was nowhere else for her, after all.

She sighed, and pushed away thoughts of the past and of the future. For now, she had an important task; all her energies were needed to accomplish it. With a last look around her chamber, she stepped through the threshold and closed the door.

Corday made sure he stayed away from du Maurier and his assistant until he arrived at his destination: an inn where he was certain the two would stay for the evening, not the one at which La Flamme had advised him to stay. He entered and saw to his satisfaction that the agents had not arrived, and procured a room for himself. He would have his dinner in the common room, the better to catch sight of the agents. It had been a simple thing to determine where the agents would stay. A few discreet questions—with, of course, the right political slant—and he had determined the most probable stopping place for the agents.

This particular inn was a bustling place, no doubt because it was on the main road to Paris, and its prosperity showed in the neatly laid-out common room and clean, well-made window curtains. The plump and kind-faced innkeeper's wife put a heavily laden plate in front of him, and the wink that accompanied his thanks made her blush and offer him their best wine. He contemplated it, then shook his head, asking for their second best wine instead.

When the agents appeared in the inn's doorway, he hid a smile. How obliging of them to do as he wished!

Du Maurier's face showed impatience, while his assistant's showed boredom, but du Maurier's expression lightened as he caught sight of Corday.

"Ah, Citoyen Thibaut! We meet again. It seems we are going in the same direction, *oui?*"

Corday put a relieved smile on his face and gestured to the agent and his assistant to sit at his table. He pushed his plate of meat and cheese toward them. "Indeed," he said. "It seems work is scarce here in the country, and my pockets grow slim. I would have better work in Paris, I think, than here."

Du Maurier nodded, then shot him an amused look. "So, you are willing to brave the possibility of meeting an outlaw on your journey?"

Corday grimaced and pretended to shudder. "I do what I must, citoyen, I do what I must. Besides, I may as easily encounter La Flamme here as in Paris, and you must admit, I would come to his notice far less in such a populous city as in a humble country inn."

Du Maurier chuckled. "You are right, of course, citoyen. Well, if you are still afraid, you may join us—I doubt we will encounter the villain on our way to Paris, for it is out here in the country that we meet him most. But I am willing to offer you our official protection." He picked up a slice of bread and bit into it. "Indeed, it would only be fair in return for your sharing of your supper with us."

Corday almost laughed at how easy it had been to get du Maurier to agree to accompany him. He let himself smile widely instead and said, "You honor me, citoyen! I admit I would be greatly relieved to have company. Very well, then! I shall join you." He pretended to hesitate, then said, "I hope I will not be a hindrance to your mission?"

Du Maurier frowned, then shook his head. "No. No, I doubt it. The investigation of the Abbeye will not start before I arrive. They will need what I know of the smuggling I have seen along the coast before they begin." He raised his eyebrows at Corday. "Did you wish to travel slowly?"

"No, not at all," Corday replied. "In fact, the faster I arrive in Paris—"

The inn door opened, then slammed shut. A slight caped figure stood framed in front of the door, looked swiftly about the room, then caught sight of him. The cape's hood whipped back and the owner pointed a finger at him.

"You!" cried the woman. "How dare you!"

It was La Flamme. She was not wrapped in her rags, but dressed in the clothes of a woman of the middle class. Her hair glinted in the candlelight, and her chest heaved in apparent indignation. The noise of the common room faded as the occupants turned to look at her.

She strode up to Corday and poked her finger at his chest. "You!" she said again. "You said you would not leave! You promised me—" Her voice faltered and her lower lip trembled, but she lifted her chin as if steeling herself against a terrible grief. "You promised me the world if I—if I—" She turned her head away, as if shame overcame her. She apparently caught sight of the agents at the table, and gasped. "Oh, I am sorry, citoyen—I did not mean—but this man, this betrayer, this—"

Corday bit the inside of his cheek to keep himself from laughing; he could see where this superb bit of acting was leading. Should he play along, or not?

Du Maurier glanced from him to the woman, looking decidedly uncomfortable, and Hervé looked less bored. It could not hurt to find some entertainment, Corday thought.

"Marie!" Corday cried.

"Aaiiee!" cried La Flamme. "He does not even remember my name! Oh, it was only three months ago that he cried out my name and begged me with sweet words to give in to his demands, and now, now—" She put her hand to her brow and covered her eyes. "Betrayer!"

"Citoyenne—" Du Maurier said hesitantly, "if I could—"

"It is Simone!" the woman cried, dashing apparent tears from her eyes, and stared at Corday. "Simone! As if you did not say it daily, no, every hour I was in your arms!"

"Surely not every day?"

She bent a gimlet eye on him. "Every day," she said firmly.

"I thought your name was Marie. . . ."

Corday put a downcast look on his face and watched La Flamme bite her bottom lip to suppress a smile before she said, "No, it is not, and it is clear that you have played me false! You said I could come with you—you said you would, you would—" Her voice faltered, and she turned away from him, and spread her hands toward du Maurier. "Citoyen, you are clearly a man of importance, and his friend—can you not convince him not to leave me? He promised me he would care for me, that I could accompany him in his travels—"

Du Maurier looked decidedly uncomfortable. "Citoyenne, my association with this man has not been of long duration—I could hardly persuade him in personal matters—"

La Flamme looked about to weep. "Ah, citoyen, I had thought you were a man of morals. A man dedicated to the principles under which our great Revolution was founded—*en effet*, an agent for the Committee of Public Safety . . . but I see I was mistaken." The woman put her hand to her eyes again, and her shoulders heaved.

Du Maurier shot a half-pleading, half-accusing look at Corday, and leaned toward him, whispering, "Citoyen, you put me in a difficult position with your way with women, and yet you say nothing. Do right by this woman, Thibaut; it is clear she is an innocent, and not in the best of health, by her color."

Corday put on an apologetic expression. "My sins have caught up with me, I'm afraid. However, my memory of this woman is weak at best, and she could merely be looking for a man to—"

"Weak!" cried La Flamme, who had obviously heard him. "No, you meant only to take advantage of me, and if you forswear me, I . . . I do not know what to do . . ." She heaved another large, sorrowful sigh, and hesitated. Corday thought perhaps there was a decision made behind the hesitation, and waited with a sense of combined dread and amusement to see what she would say next.

"I do not know what I"—she put her hand over her belly—"or my child will do."

Good God. She was incorrigible. He wondered if he could slip out of this situation. He glanced around the inn room and noted condemning looks cast his way, and sympathetic ones sent to La Flamme. Still, if he argued his case well enough—

"Ah! Pauvre petite!" cried the innkeeper's wife, and she put her arm around La Flamme's slight form. She shook a finger in Corday's face. "For shame! For shame! How can you abandon such an innocent, monsieur? Eh, did I not see your wink and your sweet ways for myself when I served you your supper?" She turned to the rest of the inn's guests. "Look at him! Can you doubt a woman might succumb to his wiles?" Nods and an assenting murmur rose among the female guests, and their husbands began to look troubled at their reaction. They turned accusing eyes toward Corday, as if he had tried to seduce their wives as well.

This was not good. Corday cast what he was sure was an exasperated look at La Flamme—under the circumstances, some relief for his real feelings should be given him. She had put him in an awkward position, and he was sure she knew it, and did it deliberately. If he refused to acknowledge her, he knew the tale would be repeated over and over again in this inn, and then spread beyond it. She had imbued her performance with too much drama for it to be forgotten, and if the look in the inn-wife's eye was any indication, that good woman would repeat it to every traveler who stopped for a night or a drop of refreshment. She would no doubt describe his dastardly looks to everyone who came along, fueled by righteous indignation. This was definitely not what he wanted. His mission would be better accomplished if he remained as innocuous and drew as little attention to himself as possible.

And La Flamme was doing everything in her power to make it impossible. He sighed and pretended to look keenly at the young woman in front of him. Then he shook his head and turned to the innkeeper's wife. "My dear citoyenne," he said apologetically. "This young woman does look familiar, and I did have a fiancée, but I have traveled long, and have been busy . . . if you could kindly let us have a room where we can talk privately, I am sure we can clear any misunderstanding there might be."

The inn-wife looked uncertain, then nodded firmly.

"*Mais oui,* I have a parlor newly cleaned. You may have it for a quarter hour only, for I will not let this poor little one be taken advantage of again." She turned away, beckoning to Corday. "This way, citoyen."

The inn-wife took a lamp hung from the wall and led the way to a small room, neatly apportioned and decorated. Four chairs sat around an oak table, and the inn-wife lit the three candles at the table with the light from the lantern. A lively fire crackled in the fireplace, and lit the room with a warm light.

"There," she said. "You may sit here, and come to the right decision." She gazed sternly at Corday as she spoke, then turned to La Flamme and smiled kindly. "I will return in ten minutes with hot milk for the little one, for you need to keep up your strength." She patted the younger woman's cheek. "We cannot have you so pale, eh? It is not good for the baby." With a last admonishing look at Corday, she closed the door.

A slow, triumphant smile spread over La Flamme's face. "I told you I would catch up with you even though I will not travel during the day," she said. "Leave me, and the story of your libertine behavior will spread from inn to inn. I am sure you will not want that."

Corday's lips twisted wryly. "No, indeed, I do not." He pulled out a chair, and gestured toward it. "Do sit. I think we have a few things to discuss."

"What is there to discuss?" La Flamme crossed her arms and stared defiantly at him. "I will now accompany you to Paris. I will help you to find your way around the city, and you will help me free the prisoners in the Abbeye." He remained standing, his hand on the chair that he had pulled out, and she shrugged and sat.

"But I am already traveling with du Maurier and Hervé," he said, and sat in the chair opposite her.

"Them!" she said, and her lip curled. "We will travel faster without them."

"Perhaps," he replied. "But the trials will occur after he returns with his evidence, and I suspect we shall travel in relative comfort if we travel with them, most likely by coach. Further, it would be useful to know what kind of evidence he has to present, and other pieces of information that might help my—and your—goals."

La Flamme hesitated, then nodded slowly. "You are right. It would be useful to know what he knows, and it might lead to the freeing of more prisoners."

Again, Corday felt a faint surprise at her acknowledgment. As contrary and stubborn as she was, it was clear she was not like the rest of her sex, prone to illogic, excessive displays of emotion, and a disinclination to admitting wrong. Or, to be fair, people he encountered in general. She clearly had a strong, practical streak, an attribute he appreciated, for he was also practical.

"Very well," she said. "I will go with you and the agents."

Corday bit back a sigh. Perhaps he could still dissuade her from accompanying him. He raised his brows. "I thought you could not travel by day."

La Flamme shrugged. "I have thought of a way. You have said they will most likely travel by coach. It will of course be enclosed, and I will be sure to be well covered against the light, and wear a heavy veil and gloves. In the evening, it will matter not."

"And yet, you were most definitely weak when you were exposed to the light. How do I know you will be well enough to travel? And how will the agents be convinced to keep us with them if you are?"

La Flamme smiled slightly. "I am clearly fully recovered since I caught up with you here, *oui?* As for my weakness during the day—" Her smile turned into a grin. "Why, monsieur, have you never heard of morning sickness? Many women of good health have morning sickness all day."

Corday gave a mock shudder. "I pity our poor agents; not only will they be stripped of whatever information they may have, but they will have to contend with a pregnant woman with morning sickness." He gazed at her hopeful face, and admiration for her cleverness sparked again, making him smile reluctantly. He should not let her accompany them, for her reaction to daylight could be a hindrance, whatever she may say. However, he could not deny she had caught up with him in a very short time, and seemed to be quite well, with no sign of any weakness at all. He also could not deny that her knowledge of the Paris underground would be very helpful. "Very well," he said. "You may accompany me." He almost smiled when she gave a little hop and beamed her triumph.

"I thank you, monsieur," she said, and bowed her head in a courtly manner. "You will not regret it."

He let himself smile, and chucked her under her chin with his finger. "My dear, if we are to be affianced, you must stop calling me monsieur."

La Flamme nodded. "Of course, citoyen."

He grinned. "No, you must call me Michael—Michel, if you wish."

She looked startled, then a speculative expression crossed her face. "I thought your first name was Robert?"

"No, that is my second name. You should call me Michael, since it is my first; one would expect one's lover to know it."

"I will not be your lover." She leveled a hard look at him.

"No," he said, "but it is what they think since you are having my child." He smiled slightly. "What they expect is all that matters, yes?"

She stared at him suspiciously, then nodded. "That is true. You may call me Simone."

"And is that your real name? I should know it, for I assume you would not want me to call you 'sweet one,' 'my love,' and other endearments of that sort all the time."

She gave him a cool look. "*C'est vrai*, I would not," she said. A knock at the door made her turn and look at the innkeeper's wife, who entered with a mug of steaming milk.

She looked at them sternly. "Well? Have you come to an agreement?" She gave an especially censorious glance at Corday, then turned to La Flamme and held out the mug to her. "Drink, citoyenne; it will do the little one good, eh?"

Simone took the mug and sipped it gingerly, while she looked at Corday, one of her eyebrows raised as a prompt.

"But of course, citoyenne," Corday said smoothly. "It was a terrible misunderstanding. She was a plump little darling when I first met her, as pink as a fresh peach. But you see how she is now! I did not recognize her at all, for she has gone pale and thin, and not at all as I remembered her." He went to Simone's side, took her mug from her hands, and raised them to his lips, kissing them lingeringly. The inn-wife sighed sentimentally. "I understand a woman with child can change in appearance, and so it was with my poor Simone-Marie!"

Simone made herself sigh, and lift his hand to her cheek, then picked up her mug again. "So true, citoyenne! As you see, my clothes do not fit me nearly as well as they used to." She sipped her milk again, and patted her belly for emphasis. The inn-wife's look of pity told her that her and Corday's act was very convincing.

"It is clear that I must take care of my poor little one," Corday continued. "And as a result, I will need to find a magistrate so that we may marry right away."

Chapter 7

SIMONE CHOKED ON THE MILK AND BE-
gan to cough violently. The inn-wife hurriedly patted
her on her back until Simone was able to breathe again,
and brushed away the milk drops that had splattered on
her dress.

"Marry—?" Simone gasped. *Mon Dieu*, what was he
thinking? She cast a warning look at him, but he merely
gazed at her blandly.

"We must marry with all haste," he said. "The child
must have a name, after all, and it is best if I am to take care
of you, *ma petite*."

The inn-wife bent an approving eye on him at last. "You
are a sensible man, citoyen!" She smiled kindly at Simone.
"He is right, of course, and though every girl dreams of a
great wedding, we must think of the child, yes?"

"But . . ." Simone gazed at the inn-wife's kind but firm
expression, then at Corday's amused one. She gave him a
brief, grim look as the inn-wife glanced once again at him in
approval. He wished to have revenge on her, it was clear. Well,
she would show who would be the most uncomfortable with

this arrangement. "Of course, you are right, citoyenne," she replied, and sighed. "I had thought of a grand wedding, but it is not possible." If he thought to scare her away from traveling with him, he was quite mistaken. She would not be married to him, but she would agree to it for now, and make sure it did not happen. She gazed at him steadily, and thought she saw a flicker of unease in his eyes when he smiled in return. Good.

The inn-wife sighed again, clearly thinking she watched true love before her. Simone itched to disabuse her of this idea, but it was important to keep up pretenses. She turned to the woman, ducking her head and putting a shy expression on her face. "Citoyenne, there are a few things I wish to discuss with my fiancé. If we could have a few more minutes . . . ?"

The inn-wife beamed at them. "Of course!" she exclaimed happily. "Let me know if you need anything else—I will be near!"

Simone was sure she would, no doubt listening at the door. She pitched her voice low when the door closed.

"Monsieur—"

"Michael. Call me Michael."

Simone bit back a curse. "*Monsieur*. This had better be part of our plan. Any attempt at frightening me off by proposing marriage will not work."

One corner of his mouth lifted, and he pulled her suddenly to him. "Afraid, are you?" He still held her, and she could feel the beat of his heart against her chest.

"No. I am not," she said coolly. She stiffened her spine, making no movement toward him or away; she forced herself to think of him as nothing more than a block of wood, despite the warmth of his body and the breath she could feel smoothing over her skin. "I will not marry—you or anyone else."

His smile turned into a grin. "You are the one who

pleaded your belly, my dear, and claimed I was the father. You should suffer the consequences. Besides, lately I have had a fancy to marry—why not you?"

Simone pushed him away, ignoring the flicker of surprise on his face at the strength she used. She kept her eyes on him nevertheless, watching his expression for his intentions. His eyes showed nothing more than bland interest. A fleeting thought that he might be serious flickered across her mind, but she dismissed it. Regret also surfaced, surprising her. She had given up all thought of marriage, long ago— No. Useless to think of it even now. Men such as he did not marry, or if they did, they would be a trial to their wives, she was sure. He was already being a trial to *her*, for that matter.

She gave him a cynical smile. "Because I am not so easily persuaded into committing my life to someone in whose character I have little faith." There, that should stop this nonsense.

He put his hand on his chest and heaved a long sigh. "You wound me, *ma petite*. Am I that repugnant to you?"

She turned away, forcing her movement to appear impatient, but she closed her eyes for a painful moment. *No. No, dear heaven, he was not repugnant.* Another surge of regret made her wish he were, that he was the ugliest man she had ever seen, instead of a handsome, hell-sent temptation. Her body near wept with want, even as she mentally cursed him.

She made her lips curl in a sneer. "Still you think I'm no more than a stupid girl just out of a convent. You only wish revenge on me because I put you in a difficult situation—admit it. If you wish to marry me at all, it is only to put me in my place for thwarting you."

The grin dropped from his face, and his expression cooled. "Or, it could be I have decided that it would be convenient for our mission."

Of course. Regret rose once more, and shame followed on its heels. Simone bit her lip in vexation. It made sense; what better way of hiding that she was La Flamme, and he a British spy?

"It would be a civil ceremony, after all, and divorce is easily done later," he continued.

Simone made herself look at him steadily. "Yes, you are right. It would not be a true marriage, but appropriate for our mission." It was against the law for priests to conduct marriages. She could not even be married in a church, for if the altars had not been profaned with idols and symbols worshiping the Revolution, they had been turned into meeting rooms for government officials. She allowed herself a rueful smile. His intentions were simply expedient. She should have more discipline over her thoughts than this, and not let useless regrets overcome her reason. It was, in fact, an equal bargain; each of them would use the other for the sake of their missions. It was nothing else. Nothing else.

"Very well," she said. "If need be, we can go through with it. As it is, I doubt we can find a magistrate to perform the marriage until we reach Paris."

Corday shrugged, his lips lifting in a slight smile, and she could not help feeling relieved that his chill expression had vanished. "We will do it when convenient. It matters not. It is enough that we appear married—or at least soon to be so—for now."

Simone nodded, and suddenly felt pleased with herself. In truth, a small rage at his behavior had moved her to act more outrageously than she normally would have, but she had done it with the intent of forcing him to accompany her to Paris. The situation had taken an unexpected turn, uncomfortable at first, but she had to admit that no one would expect la Flamme to be a weak and sickly mother-to-be.

She could travel fairly openly, and she had to admit that she could bear Corday's company if it meant she could doff her disguise from time to time. Perhaps she could even convince the agents that they had scared away their enemy for a while. Her actions had not been so ill-advised, after all, and had she not accomplished her aim? Yes, she was very pleased with the way it had all turned out. Confidence filled her once again. "It will turn out very well. No one will suspect either of us of any kind of subversive activity, especially if I show myself to be very, very ill." She nodded decisively.

He stared at her for a moment, then a slight smile touched his lips. "No doubt you are right." He gestured to the door. "Shall we go? I am sure our agents are eager to continue on their journey."

She smiled and nodded, and opened the door.

The inn-wife must have been waiting on pins and needles for their exit, for she appeared immediately as soon as the door creaked on its hinges.

"Well?" she demanded. "What have you decided?"

"To marry immediately, of course," Corday said.

The inn-wife beamed, and gave a little clap of delight. "Eh, I knew you would do what is right. And look you, the magistrate is in this very inn, and may perform the ceremony."

Alarm shot through Simone, and she opened her mouth to protest. But she felt Corday's hand press a warning on her shoulder.

"Excellent, citoyenne. Let it be done," he said. The inn-wife bustled off, calling out into the common room the name of a Citoyen Broussard.

Simone paused before turning to look at Corday, suddenly unnerved. For all that their pretense was a good idea, he had taken control of the situation once again, pushing this sham marriage when he could have made some excuse to marry later. For all her brave words, she wondered how their association would turn out. He was clearly used to taking control, she thought. But then, so was she.

For one moment, it seemed his expression softened as he gazed at her, then he chucked her under her chin and leaned close, his breath brushing her ear. "Do not worry, *ma petite*," he whispered. "All will be well. We will both accomplish our missions and then we will part ways. It is a good disguise; what is more ordinary than a man traveling with his pregnant wife? No one will suspect us. After a while, we will leave these agents, claiming the need for you to see a doctor. We will go on ahead, and be in Paris before them." He took her hand and led her to the common room.

A firm step came toward them, and before Simone could turn, Corday pulled her to him and pressed his lips to hers. "Pretend you like it," he whispered against her mouth, and kissed her again.

Simone let herself lean into him, and put her arms around his neck. It is pretense, she told herself; it means nothing. But it was an easy pretense, and if there was nothing behind his kisses, she could not tell, for his lips parted hers easily, expertly, as if they had kissed often. She heard a sigh behind her, and she pushed away from Corday at last, pressing her hands against her cheeks as if she were pressing down a blush.

The inn-wife shook her finger at them but smiled. "No, no, not until after the marriage, *hein?*"

Simone made herself look away as if in shyness and heard Corday chuckle. "Very well, citoyenne, not until after the marriage."

Simone brought her gaze to his face, and his smile was most definitely amused. Irritation made her frown at him briefly before she turned to the man behind the inn-wife.

It was the magistrate the inn-wife had called for, for he

carried his rotund body with obvious self-importance and wore the Revolution's tricolor cockade prominently on his shoulder. He hooked his thumbs under the edges of his vest, looked at both Corday and herself, then winked before he grinned widely.

She detested the magistrate, even more now that she knew he was a winker. People who winked like that usually thought themselves clever, when at most they were only sly. To be married by this man! Simone bit back a grimace. It was no less than appropriate, however—a sham marriage presided over by an appointee of a sham government.

Broussard brought out a marriage certificate, and laid it on the table before them.

"Read it carefully, citoyen, citoyenne," he said. "Even though I know you would prefer to rush through it." He winked at them again and Simone stifled a sneer. "It is an important document, a document sanctioned by our revolutionary government. It recognizes the importance of marriage as a unity that reflects the ideals of our state."

Unity exemplified by the constant squabbles of the Jacobins and Girondins, Simone thought sarcastically. Broussard motioned to the inn-wife, and she brought forth a bottle of ink and a quill. He pushed the marriage license on the table toward Corday. "Please sign," he said.

Simone watched as Corday signed his name. *Michael Robert Thibaut,* he wrote, in a fine, precise hand. She wondered if his given name was false; she was sure his last name was. She looked at the paper in front of her, and she thought quickly of the name she would write and smiled slightly. *Simone Marie Normande.* That would do. It was a common enough name. It mattered not that she used her first name, and she would give a reason why Corday had thought her name was Marie. Using her middle name would give some veracity to their pretense. She would be more likely to react naturally to her real name than a false one, and it was important for her to pay attention to even the smallest detail. With a sigh, she put down the quill.

The magistrate peered at the signatures, and with a satisfied nod, signed his own name at the bottom of the license. He winked at them again.

"By the power invested in me by our glorious Revolution and the rights it preserves for us, I announce in front of these good witnesses that you are man and wife." He held out his hand to Corday. "That will be five livres, citoyen." Corday raised his brows, then pulled out a small bag from his pocket. Simone noticed that the bag was not plump; even though he did not hesitate as he presented the money to Broussard, she was certain his pocket contained no more than was necessary to complete his mission. She would make sure to reimburse him.

Broussard winked once more. "Now you may kiss the bride," he said.

Simone drew in a resolute breath and let it out again. One more time, she thought. He had kissed her more than she had ever been kissed in years, and she was not used to it. It was difficult to steel herself against the feel of his lips, but this time she would. She felt his hand under her chin and she gazed up at him.

"Try not to be such a martyr, *ma petite,*" he whispered, his breath brushing her cheek. He pressed his lips against hers, softly, and drew away before she could react. She turned away, feeling discomposed, but hoped she looked as if she were embarrassed, kissing in front of the onlookers in the inn. Simone made herself smile slightly when a cheer went up from the crowd. She glanced at the people who cheered her, and a true smile reached her lips. It was only a civil marriage ceremony, but the faces of the inn's guests had lightened, regardless of their station. If it did not accomplish anything else, at least the ceremony brought better spirits to them for a while.

She suppressed a grimace, however—she had prepared herself against another onslaught of the blood-hunt, and there had been no need for it this time. It made her feel unsettled, and she knew she would have to either feed on blood soon or sleep deeply through the day. She glanced at Corday—Michael—talking to du Maurier and saw the agent glance at her, then smile and nod in amusement. No doubt they were talking of the vagaries of women, perhaps even of the fits and starts of pregnant ones. If so, good. It would help lay the foundation for their association—and her subsequent "illness"—with the agents. There would be little sleep for her during this journey. She would have to do as best she could.

Simone assessed the room and the crowd. Everyone had gone back to their business, although with a lighter air than before. She caught the glance of the magistrate Broussard, and he gave her another wink. She refrained from sneering at him, and managed a slight smile before she turned and sat at the far end of the table from Corday and du Maurier. A tightness across her shoulders told her that she had been on alert for a long time, and she shrugged them, letting herself relax.

"Madame . . . ?" came a tentative voice. Simone looked into the thin, wide-eyed face of one of the inn's maids. "Mme. Proust wishes to know if you would like another cup of milk?"

Simone thought of the milk she had drunk earlier; it was not something she, since her change into a vampire, cared for. She saw another maid with a platter of beef pass by to another table—the meat was not fully cooked, and she could smell the blood. She swallowed. It would not hurt, perhaps, to ask for a bit of that meat and take some blood from the rarest part of it. She had enough money to afford it, and it would not be hard to exchange some pearls for more later. The blood-hunt moved in her gut, and she pressed her lips together briefly before looking at the maid again.

"A bit of that beef, *s'il vous plaît*, from the middle of the roast, the rarest part, citoyenne." Simone emphasized the last word, and a frightened look entered the maid's eyes.

"Yes, yes, citoyenne, of course. I will get it quickly." The maid gave a hasty curtsy and hurried away to the kitchen. Simone regretted the maid's fear, but it was necessary for the girl to use the right words these days. The wrong ones could get a person in trouble. She turned her attention to Corday and du Maurier.

"It is a sorry state of affairs when a counterrevolutionary can infiltrate our prisons and cause discontent from within," du Maurier was saying. Corday—she must remember to call him Michael from now on—made a sympathetic noise. Clearly her new "husband" was eliciting information from the agent. Good. She leaned closer to *Michael* to hear more.

A shuffling to Simone's other side made her turn: Broussard. He winked at her and she suppressed another grimace. He had finished the ceremony and Corday had paid him; surely Broussard had other business?

Apparently he did not; he sat down beside her and shifted his large derriere about on the bench until he had settled himself comfortably. Broussard nodded toward Corday, who had turned more toward du Maurier, apparently deeply interested in what the agent had to say.

"I have presided over many marriages," Broussard said, sighing. "You are, of course, doing the right thing, citoyenne, for the good of your child, but I would not trust one such as he."

Annoyance and indignation made Simone's back stiffen again, and she pressed her lips to keep heated words from erupting. She let out a breath—*control, Simone, control.*

The man is not worth hasty words. She gave him a small smile instead.

"I am sure you are mistaken, citoyen. Did not my Michael agree to wed me immediately when he recognized me? My confidence in him is fully restored, I assure you." There, that should shut his mouth.

It did not. Broussard shook his head and gave her an ingratiating smile. "Me, I would not leave such a lovely one as you. But then, it seems your husband is one who needs to travel for his living." He eyed Corday's back, his gaze resting on the slightly worn collar with clear contempt. "Some men must do so; I count myself lucky that I do not." He ran his hand over his embroidered waistcoat in a satisfied manner, and winked again at Simone. "I understand you are to travel with him?"

"Yes." Simone barely kept herself from snapping at him; it would do no good to be less than civil. He was a magistrate, after all, and it would be awkward should he draw any sort of official attention to her.

Broussard shook his head. "Not for long, citoyenne." He gestured toward her belly. "When the child comes, you will not wish to travel, mark my words, and I am sure for the month before it is due."

Simone lowered her eyes to prevent him from seeing her irritation, and hoped he would think it shyness. "My husband will provide for me."

Broussard bent his head closer to her and lowered his voice. "Your faith is touching, *ma chou,* but you would be better off with another man."

"I am not your '*chou,*' Citoyen Broussard," Simone said, and let him see the anger she was sure showed on her face.

The little maid arrived, bringing a plate of sliced beef. She set it before Simone, and glad for the blessing of a break in the conversation, Simone gave the girl a grateful smile. She looked at the plate, and frowned slightly. "Citoyenne, I did not ask for a sausage with my meal."

The maid looked nervously at Simone and at Broussard. "Madam—Citoyenne Proust said you were to have a sausage as well as the beef, to make sure the little one"—the maid blushed—"the little one is well fed, too."

Simone smiled, although she did not care for sausage. "Give Citoyenne Proust my thanks." She reached into a pocket of her dress and pressed a coin into the maid's hand. The girl smiled, turning her plain face pretty, before giving one more curtsy and walking quickly away to the call of another customer.

Simone took up knife and fork and sliced a piece of rare roast. She popped it into her mouth and sucked on the undone juices. Food did little to revive her without blood, and though there was not enough in the beef to help her recover completely, there was enough for a while. Human blood always brought her quickly to full strength, but she tried to avoid it as much as possible. She closed her eyes as a spurt of energy trickled through her limbs, then swallowed down the meat.

"He left you with little, I see," Broussard said.

Simone opened her eyes and stared at him. "I do well enough."

The magistrate looked at her up and down, his gaze resting briefly on her breasts before meeting her eyes. "You are thin, citoyenne. I cannot think you did well since you last met your husband."

"I am as *well* as anyone can expect," Simone replied, managing not to grit her teeth as she spoke. "I understand some pregnant women become thin at first." Especially with the continued mismanagement of food prices and government economy, she thought. Clearly Broussard did not suffer from it. Even in the candlelight she could see that his clothes were beautifully made, and the flickering flames illuminated the fine embroidery on his waistcoat. She wondered from what aristocrat's or church's treasures he had stolen to have enough to afford such finery.

"I see you have noticed that I am quite able to provide for any woman I choose," he said, passing a caressing hand over his waistcoat's embroidery. "Indeed, should a woman decide to cast her lot with me, she would never want for food, clothing . . . or attention." He winked at her again.

Simone managed, after a moment, to erase the astonishment she was sure showed on her face. Was this man born an idiot, or had his mother dropped him on his head and made him so? Surely he must have heard from the innwife that she had searched for Corday until she found him at this inn? Even if he had not, did he not conduct the marriage ceremony himself? How could he even believe that she would think of an alliance with anyone other than the man she just married?

Anger burned suddenly, and she gripped the knife in her hand. Broussard was close enough that it would take only a moment to thrust the knife through his richly embroidered clothes. Her blood-hunt rose—

She raised her hand and thrust her fork into the sausage instead. The fork scraped hard against the plate, giving out a scratchy squeal. She stared into Broussard's eyes. "Citoyen Broussard," she said, blood-hunt and anger forcing her words out in a low growl. "I thank you for your offer of protection."

Simone raised her knife and, still staring at him, jabbed the point through the sausage. "However, I am sure my husband is more than capable of giving me all the *attention* I need." She smiled grimly at the magistrate, and with a jerk of her wrist, sliced the sausage in two.

Broussard's complacent smile became uncertain, and his eyes flicked toward the sausage she had just cut. She methodically continued slicing the sausage into pieces with small, forceful jerks of the knife as she continued to stare at the man. "You are so kind to think of my future, Citoyen Broussard," she said. "But I assure you, I am well able to take care of myself, whether my husband is present or not." She gave what she hoped looked like a fond glance toward Corday, and found that du Maurier had left, and that he—Michael—was watching her, an amused look in his eyes. Had he been listening to their conversation? She turned back to Broussard. "But I am sure that my dear husband will do all he can to ensure my well-being and fulfill my every wish."

She felt Michael's hand on her shoulder as the other went possessively around her waist. "Rest assured, Citoyen Broussard," he said, so close that his breath brushed her ear. "I took your words in the marriage ceremony most seriously."

The uneasiness in Broussard's smile grew, and he shifted away from them. Imbecile or not, he had clearly received the message this time that his presence was no longer wanted. He cleared his throat and managed to revive his smile.

"I am glad, Citoyen Thibaut," he replied, and rose from the bench beside Simone. "It is always well to heed the words sanctioned by our glorious Revolution."

"Indeed, citoyen," said Michael. "Indeed." His voice sounded serious. Simone felt him shift beside her in a slight bow.

Perhaps there must have been something more than mere civility in Michael's look, for Broussard took a hasty, stumbling step backward before he gave a quick bow in return and left.

Simone turned to look at Michael. "Thank you," she said.

He nodded. "I thought I should come to the rescue."

"Although I needed no rescue—I was well on my way to

taking care of his impertinence myself," Simone continued, nettled.

Michael raised his brows. "Did I say I was coming to *your* rescue? No, no, my dear. I was coming to poor *Broussard's* rescue." He nodded at the scattered slices of sausages on her plate. "I saw a certain ferocity in your movements and thought I should intervene before you turned that ferocity toward, er, him. Indeed, I begin to fear for myself when I think of our marriage bed upstairs."

She eyed him grimly. "Since there will be no marriage bed, you need not fear at all," she said, her voice low.

Michael nodded toward the inn-wife busily attending to her customers. "However, *she* expects it, and it would cause her to wonder and comment—loudly, I am sure—if we did not at least appear to be, ah, intimate." He gave her an ironic look. "You were the one who instigated this masquerade, *ma petite*. I think it only just that you abide by it now that we are set on this course."

Frustration made her growl; then she pressed her lips together briefly. "Very well. But I will not tolerate any attempts at seduction."

Corday raised his brows again. "Of course." She could discern no emotion on his face; from his expression it seemed he was indifferent to the idea. She suppressed the touch of disappointment, then smiled a little, for she had to admit: For all that she was dedicated to remaining as virtuous as possible to speed her return to humanity, she was woman enough still to wish for the attention of an attractive man.

She gazed at him, at his devilishly handsome face and his coolly assessing eyes. He *was* attractive, dangerously so. Any ordinary woman would have succumbed to his teasing and his kisses long before this.

But she was no ordinary woman. She was strong, stronger than any man. She could kill with the strength of one hand, drain the life of a man in less than an hour. Her smile faded. Even if she allowed him to make love to her, he would not want to, not if he knew what she was.

He took her hand. "Come, my dear, it is late. The least we can do is make an appearance of going to our chamber together."

She nodded and stood up from the bench, and he rose as well. They passed the inn-wife on their way up to the stairs, and she beamed at them and patted Simone's cheek.

"He will be good to you," Mme. Proust said. "Is he not a fine figure of a man? He will protect you, I am sure."

Simone merely smiled, tamping down the irritation that rose at the idea of Corday protecting her. She pressed the good woman's hand in instead.

"I think you, Citoyenne Proust," she said. "You have been very good to me."

The inn-wife blushed lightly, and shook her head. "No, no, it is only what any good citizen of the Republic might do," she said. "These are hard times, yes? We must do all we can to help each other. It is why our Revolution began, to help us better each other."

Simone saw clear sincerity in the woman's eyes, and with a slight shock understood that this woman was a true believer in the Republic. She had been so used to thinking of revolutionaries as her enemy that she had difficulty thinking positively of any of them. But this one, this good woman, had been kind to her.

"Come, *ma petite*," Corday murmured, and took her hand. The inn-wife smiled and bustled away to her next customer. Simone nodded, and went up the stairs with him. She gazed at him as they went down the hall to his room, watching the flickering lights of the sconced candles play with the shadows of his profile. The inn-wife was not as she, Simone, had assumed. Simone knew Corday was a dangerous man, a British spy and used to killing. But if there was more to a simple inn-wife than she had first thought, surely there would be more to this man.

She smiled to herself. But of course there was; if he would not reveal his true name, heaven only knew what else there was that he would not reveal. She glanced at him, and wondered if she would ever find out. The thought intrigued her. She had never taken the time to truly *know* a person, she realized suddenly. She had not the time, nor the opportunity. In reality, she had not done so for fear that she would be found out herself. Would it be possible to know someone without revealing something of oneself? Perhaps.

Perhaps she would try. It was important, for she might have to trust him with her life, and more important, the lives of others. Indeed, it was just as important to know his true nature, in case she needed to defend herself against him some day, or at least predict his actions.

Corday's steps slowed and he stopped; they were at his—their—room. He opened the door, and held it for her, and she stepped in. Perhaps he thought the same thing, that it was important for him to know her as well.

Simone glanced at him again, and found him watching her, his face inscrutable. She sighed. She did not think it would be at all easy to know him. No, not easy at all.

Chapter 8

MME. PROUST'S KINDNESS WAS EVEN more evident in the warm, cheerful fire in the hearth, and the cozily-made bed. A plate of cheese, a bottle of wine, and wrapped sweets sat on a minute side table, and the draperies on the bed and the windows were—thankfully—not only fresh but thick.

Corday went to the bed and pressed his hand on it. "Very good, and sure to give a comfortable night." He put his hand on the bed curtains and tugged on them. He grinned. "And obviously made for privacy."

"For which I am grateful," Simone said repressively. "As you know, I am susceptible to light, so will need to have the curtains totally drawn against the morning light."

His grin grew wider. "Of course."

"Remove your grin, *s'il vous plaît*," Simone said. "If you think you will sleep with me, you are quite mistaken."

His grin remained. "I doubt I would sleep at all."

Simone swallowed the retort that came to her lips and continued: "For as you know, I am a creature of the night, and sleep during the day." She jerked her chin toward the bed. "Therefore, you may take the bed first." She stared at him defiantly.

He stared back, and began unbuttoning his waistcoat. "You are too kind, *ma petite*. I promise to keep the bed warm for you."

"You are too kind," she echoed mockingly. "As for me, I will look about the inn to see what I can learn." She turned back toward the chamber door.

"That is unwise."

She turned to him again. "Do you think I am easily caught?"

"No," he said. "But it would look most peculiar."

"If I am seen, I will make a believable excuse."

"Still difficult if you are found outside."

"I will be careful not to be found."

Corday stared at her. "You are persistent," he said. "I wonder why it is so important for you to wander about this inn?"

To avoid you, Simone thought. Truth to tell, she was not sure whether she could stay with him a whole night without being lured into kissing him again . . . and more.

She was afraid of the "more." It had been a long time since she had allowed a man to touch her intimately, and she was not sure what would happen if she let him. She was no virgin, not since she had become a vampire. But she had found it difficult to separate the blood-thirst from bodily pleasure, and it was too, too easy to take blood by force during the peak of the act. She watched Corday as he continued to unbutton his waistcoat and then his shirt, and she could not look away from him, for his eyes stared into hers, his mouth turning up in a small, intimate smile.

She wanted him.

Simone turned away, shuddering with the force of her wanting, feeling ill at the thought that she could not tell if she lusted for the touch of his body or the taste of his blood.

"It is not important," she replied. "There is nothing but boredom if I stay here in this room all night."

"It need not be boring," he said, and his voice held the promise of heat and pleasure.

It had been so long since she had been held as he had held her these two days. She turned and looked at him, this time capturing his gaze. "No," she said. "I am sure it would not. But I dare not." She shrugged her shoulders. "Should I be caught below stairs, I will say I have come down for more of the good Citoyenne Proust's warm milk."

He said nothing for a moment, merely watching her, his expression unreadable. "I suppose it would do no good to lock you in this room," he said.

"No." She smiled. "And it would do you no good to watch me, for you will need your sleep." She rose and went to the door.

"Stay, mademoiselle," he said. "I would like to know more of you. Your name, your family."

She looked at him, trying to discern his meaning from his expression. She could not tell much from it—his smile was gone, and he had turned half away from the hearth. The candlelight threw flickering shadows across his brow and cheek, hiding whatever expression there might be in his eyes.

"The night is still new," he said. "There can be no harm in talking."

Simone hesitated. Talking. She had not truly talked with anyone except for Père Dumont. The conversations she had had with the innkeepers along her route and the people she smuggled out of France had been brusque, short, and instructional.

"You wish to talk?" she asked.

"Yes." He smiled. "Is that so hard to believe? I think

you mentioned not long ago that I liked the sound of my own words. How much better it would be if there was someone else to appreciate them."

Relief caused a bubble of laughter to burst from her, and she nodded. "Very well," she said.

He was half undressed now, and she made herself look at him, as if she were indifferent to him. "Put on your shirt again—you will be cold," she said. "I will stay, for a little while."

He gave a polite smile, as he pulled his shirt on over his shoulders, and it reminded her of times past, when she saw such smiles on the faces of courtiers. She wondered if he had ever been to court, and if he had dressed in fine silks. Well. He wished to talk. Perhaps she would find out.

He patted the mattress beside him. "Come, sit." She raised an eyebrow at him and he laughed. "Sweet one, I promise not to assault you."

Simone snorted. "With every evidence to the contrary," she retorted.

"I promise you, I will not," he said solemnly, but she could hear amusement in his voice. "On my honor, I swear it."

"Assuming you have any honor," Simone said, but sat gingerly on the bed.

He put a hand over his heart. "You wound me, *ma petite*. Have I not kept my promises?"

Simone shook her head, smiling ruefully. "I suppose you might, but I do not recall that you have made any promises, monsieur."

"Michael, my dear. *Michael*. You must remember to call me by my given name." He moved off the bed to the table on which there were the food and the bottle of wine. He picked up the bottle and pried open the cork, then turned his head and looked a question at her, lifting the bottle.

Simone nodded and hid a smile. If he thought to get

her tipsy and thus seduce her, he would be very mistaken. Wine had little effect on her, other than to put her into a relaxed and sense-heightened state; it did not otherwise affect her mind at all. Indeed, it would prepare her better for seeking out any additional information regarding the agents or movements of the revolutionary government.

"That is a beginning," Simone said instead. "Your name. What is your real name?"

"Michael Robert Thibaut," he said promptly, and poured the wine into the glasses.

"I doubt it, monsieur, and I doubt Corday is your last name, either." She looked thoughtfully at him. "Although I must say Corday fits you better than Thibaut."

"I think it does as well, although I was never as zealous as poor Charlotte," he replied, handing a glass to her.

A small shock went through Simone. "Charlotte Corday? You knew her?"

The fire in the hearth flared and cast a brief grim shadow on his expression. Silence reigned for a moment, then he said: "At least, the first two names are mine. I have found it easier in long-term associations to use one's true given name; you are more likely to respond to your real name than a false one."

He did not wish to speak of Charlotte Corday, it was clear. Simone wondered about his association with the woman. Did he have anything to do with Mlle. Corday's assassination of Marat? She sipped her wine in contemplation—it was a white wine, slightly sweet with a hint of apple, and would go well with the cheese—and decided not to pursue the topic, for now. She nodded. "I agree. One is not likely to forget and thereby make a mistake."

"Am I to assume that your name, then, is indeed Simone Marie?" He leaned against the table and sipped his wine.

She smiled. "Yes."

"But Normande is not your last name." It was a statement, not a question; he had read the document carefully.

"Of course not," she said. "I would hardly put my true name on a marriage license neither of us will honor. Besides, I am sure you did not put *your* real name on it, either."

"True. Although I would not be adverse to honoring some of it."

She ignored his comment and the wicked look that accompanied it. "If you would be so kind as to pass the plate of cheese to me, I would be most grateful."

He picked up the plate and brought it to her, but when she moved to take it, he sat on the bed beside her and put the plate on the other side of him, away from her.

He looked into her eyes. "Say please, Simone."

She gazed sternly at him. "Please give me the cheese, monsieur."

He shook his head, smiling slightly. "We have some practice to do, *ma petite*. We hardly sound like a newly married pair, and if we do not, I am sure we will rouse the suspicions of those we meet, not to mention those of the agents with whom we will travel. So, repeat after me: 'Please pass the cheese to me, my love.' "

Business again. Simone suppressed her disappointment at his words. "What nonsense," she said. "I will remember when the occasion calls for it."

"But it will not come from you naturally. We would be more convincing if it did." Taking a piece of cheese from the plate, he pushed the plate farther away on the bed. He waved the cheese in front of her face. "Say it, Simone."

She rolled her eyes. "Oh, very well. Please pass the cheese to me, Michael." She held out her hand.

He gave her the cheese. "Better, but not what I said. Say it again: 'Please pass the cheese to me, *my love*.' "

"This is a silly game."

"Say it."

"Hmph! Please pass the cheese to me, *my love*. There! I hope you are satisfied."

He moved closer to her and held out the slice of cheese, but jerked it away when she raised her hand to take it. He grinned. "No, I am not satisfied. Say it again, as if you meant it."

She sighed. He was clearly not going to reveal anything of himself at this time. But perhaps if she went along with his game, he might in a little while. It might be worth the attempt. She made herself smile sweetly and looked deep into his eyes. "Please pass me the cheese, my love."

His grin grew wider. "Better." He avoided her hand and brought the cheese to her lips. She raised an eyebrow as she took it.

"I am not a dog, monsieur."

He shook his head. "Not 'monsieur.' It is 'Michael' or 'my dear' or 'my love.' And of course you are not a dog, but do not lovers play at feeding each other? Our marriage may be a fraud, but we must act as if it were not if we are to be convincing." He took another slice of cheese. "Come, try again."

Simone drew in a breath, shaking her head slightly, not sure whether to be exasperated or amused. Well, she had said she wished not to be bored; he promised he would not bore her, and thus, no doubt, this game. Amusement grew. Very well!

She leaned toward him, gazing deeply into his eyes. "My love, please . . . the cheese . . . I must have it. Now!" She made her voice breathy and low, as if on the edge of passion.

His hand paused midway to her lips, then fell as he burst into laughter. "Excellent! But not at the breakfast table, or else I am sure you will make poor du Maurier blush." He lifted the piece of cheese to her lips and she took it. His fingers lingered for a moment as she licked the tips of them, then fell away as he turned to the plate again for another piece. "Once more—with a little *less* feeling."

Simone took another sip of wine and put it down on a table to the side of the bed, swallowing down a laugh at the same time. He wanted her to act the lover—and so she would! She would pretend so well, he would regret his request in a few minutes. She leaned toward him, her face close enough so that she could see his eyes clearly though he was still in the shadows, close enough so that she was sure he could see her breasts if he looked down. "Michael," she said, making her voice low and husky. "Feed me. Please."

He stared at her, saying nothing, doing nothing, and then he leaned toward her as if he were going to kiss her.

She ducked, slipping quickly from in front of him, and ran to the door. She picked up her shawl and put it over her head and neck. "It is late now. I think you should get some sleep. I will go out and see if Mme. Proust has more of her excellent cheese." Simone grinned, opened the door, and stepped out.

Corday stared at the shut door through which la Flamme—Simone—had just left. This time, it had not been an illusion, and he was not that tired. She had moved very, very fast, faster than he had seen any human move. He had thought her speed had been an illusion made up of her disguise and the darkness of night. But she had not worn any disguise this time, and the room was fairly well lit with candles and the fire in the hearth. One moment she had been in front of him, her eyes and lips inviting kisses, and the next, she was at the door, her shawl neatly tied under her chin.

He rose, taking the plate of cheese and putting it on

the table to the side of the bed. He gazed at the bed and then to the door again. For all that he had jested with Simone about their mutual insanity in working together, he had still all his wits about him, and had never been prone to seeing visions, even on those rare occasions in his younger years when he had managed to drink himself into a stupor. He was also not so tired that he had fallen asleep in the midst of their lover's play. His groin tightened at the memory of it and he smiled ruefully; no, he had been very much awake.

Therefore, she did indeed move faster than he had seen any human move.

It added up to a very interesting picture. A woman who worked alone, at night, for whom exposure to the sun meant becoming ill, but who also moved inhumanly fast. It could be that she had been lying about feeling ill, but he was sure he had seen the wounds on her arms, which she had at first denied were there and then admitted. There was no mistaking she had a fear of sunlight, and he could not see the need to pretend to such a handicap.

It meant one of three things: that he himself was mad, that she was mad, or that she was something he had not encountered before.

The first he dismissed. There was no madness in his family that he knew of, and he had never been prone to fantasy. The second was possible, but the woman showed no signs of the kind of insanity that would give her such inhuman swiftness and strength. She was intelligent, clever, and more rational than most people he had encountered. That left the third notion: that she was something he had not ever encountered.

Corday let the idea settle in his mind for a moment. Something different. Something not quite . . . human. Something that was swift, strong, and worked best at night.

Impossible. She was no ghost. He smiled briefly. Her body was too real and responsive for that, and he had seen enough death to know that nothing came of it except a most definite end. If not a ghost, then something else.

". . . A creature of the night." She had described herself so just a little while ago. It was an odd description, an odd way of describing her susceptibility to sunlight. Most people described their illnesses or disabilities as something not tied to themselves. He would himself have phrased it as something along the lines of "I am susceptible to light," or "I feel strongest at night." But she had described herself as a creature of the night, as if she were other than human, and had said it easily, as if she had long thought herself so.

What was she, then? His mind flickered toward old legends and fantasies he had told past audiences under his guise as scribe and storyteller, but he smiled and shook his head. Nonsense. Those were only fairy tales and fantasies. This was an age of science and new ideas, not one of phantasms or old superstitions. Had not the Americans captured lightning through Mr. Franklin's experiments? Had not he himself seen men flying aloft in great balloons? Men had captured heaven itself, disproving any supernatural force.

He shook his head at his momentary fancy. No, there was nothing supernatural about La Flamme—Simone. If there was some kind of condition about her that seemed beyond human, then it would be easily explained. He needed only to find out.

He frowned. Well, he had failed to do that just now, hadn't he? He had thought to seduce information from Simone, but had been distracted by the game he had created. There was no doubt about it; she was a tempting wench. But he had at least kept her for a few moments before she had slipped away, and it was clearly out of curiosity about him. Indeed, she had a strong streak of curiosity. That, if nothing else, would keep her at his side.

Very well. He would reveal a little here, a little there, and that would keep her near him and make her reveal her true identity.

Corday went to his coat and pulled out a watch. It was well into the evening, and if he was to discover more about Simone, he should go after her. Indeed, it would be good to see exactly why she felt it necessary to leave this room.

He replaced the watch and put on his coat. He would most definitely find her and bring her back. The night was early yet, and the sooner he brought her back, the better. He grinned. As she said, he needed his sleep, after all.

Simone went swiftly, quietly down the stairs. The inn's noise had settled into a quiet murmur of conversation among the few guests who had not yet gone to their beds, the crackling of the fire in the large hearth, and the faint clink and clatter of kitchenware at the back of the inn. She tugged the hood of her cloak over her head and looked quickly around. No one that she recognized, and she clearly heard Mme. Proust's voice from the kitchen, admonishing a kitchen servant.

Good. She needed to leave the inn for a short while. The blood from the beef had given her some energy, but not enough to sate her need, and the taste was enough to make her want more. She would need to feed on something, preferably some animal of the woods—better than beef, not as effective as humans. She grimaced. She should not have taken the beef. Better to have gone without than to endanger the inhabitants of this inn.

She slipped out the door as she heard the sound of an approaching carriage. More guests. Good. That would occupy the good inn-wife and her husband, and make it less likely they would notice her movements.

A coach had indeed stopped in front of the inn.

Simone moved away into the shadows. She wondered if it were anyone important.

Two men stepped out, and while one paid the coachman, the other walked toward the inn, looking briefly about him. Simone moved further into the shadows. The man hesitated, as if he had heard her move, but then the other one walked over and bent his head toward him.

"Do you think he might be here?"

The first man shook his head. "It's possible, but as usual he left no trace of his movements. We'll talk to this du Maurier and his man, and see what they've discovered."

English. Simone raised her brows, glad that her blood-hunt had heightened her senses so that she could hear them clearly. English was a dangerous thing to be. Perhaps they were trying to leave the country. If so, then this inn would not be a good place to stay, if they were not fluent in French. She watched as the men approached the inn and opened the door. She heard them call for the innkeeper in a barely accented French that could be mistaken for a provincial one.

Were they spies, then? She thought of Michael and wondered if he knew them. If so, did he come to this inn specifically to meet them? He had not told her this, of course. Perhaps she should find out.

Simone moved from the shadows toward the inn again, but a sharp cry from the stables behind her made her turn swiftly. "Please, monsieur, I am not like that—I am a virtuous girl, and saving myself for marriage."

It was the voice of the little maid who had served her the beef, clearly shaking with fear. A low husky voice answered her. "Please, monsieur, don't!" the maid cried again.

Simone hesitated, looking toward the inn where the English gentlemen had gone. She should find out what these men were about—

"No, please, monsieur!" The maid's voice was frantic now.

Simone ran to the stables. She could hear the rustling of straw, the sobbing breath of the maid.

"*Monsieur.* Citoyenne, are you then a Royalist, and not a loyal follower of the Revolution?" The man's voice was low, rough, and triumphant: Broussard's.

"A mistake, mon—citoyen! I did not mean—I am not used to the words—" The maid's voice was high with fear.

"You will be punished for such disloyalty, citoyenne . . . but I am a merciful man, *ma petite.* No one need find out . . . if you do not tell."

Rage and disgust poured into Simone, fusing with the blood-hunt, and her senses came to a fine, painful point. Broussard—the hypocrite! He was abusing the helpless as if he were the dissolute aristocrat he was supposed to despise, using his position to justify his intimidation and rape. She entered the stable. The mustiness of straw and horse came to her, and underneath it the incipient sweat of lust and the sharp tang of fear. There—that stall. More rustles, loud now in her ears, and a high, despairing, whimpering sob.

She seized the stall door and flung it open with a bang. "Get away from her, Broussard, or you shall be sorry for it."

The man turned, half raising himself from the maid. The girl pushed herself away from him and, scrambling to a corner of the stall, covered her face and wept softly.

Broussard peered at her. "Ah. Citoyenne Thibaut." He smiled expectantly. "Dare I hope you changed your mind?"

Simone stared at him, suspended between rage and amazement at his arrogant idiocy.

"Please, please, I *am* loyal to the Revolution," whimpered the maid in her corner. "Please don't report me."

Simone looked from the girl to Broussard. So. That

explained his rich clothes and his assumption of power. Men such as he were indeed the law now. Anyone could be accused of disloyalty to the Revolution and be sentenced to death on the spot, on nothing more than the accusation. She had even seen women sent to their deaths for weeping over their guillotined husbands. No doubt Broussard was one such accuser, who used his position to coerce women out of their virtue, or people of their money.

Rage shook her, and she stepped closer to Broussard, staring into his eyes. She could kill him now, before he drew his next breath. Her blood-hunger grew. She could drink from him and be sated.

No. The faint protest uncurled in Simone's heart.

"No," the girl said, still sobbing, as if she were Simone, long ago as a girl the same age, suffering the same pain.

Simone pulled her gaze from Broussard, and he fell back on the straw in the stall, momentarily released from the spell of her blood-hunt. "Go," she said to the maid, her voice husky. "Go now, and tell no one of this." She returned her gaze to Broussard, willing him to be still, willing him to give up his blood to her. She noticed the maid's frantic departure as little as she would notice the movements of a fly.

Broussard stared at her, unmoving, slumped upon the straw, his smile vacant, his eyes still full of lust.

The pig, Simone thought, and rage flooded her again. He should die, as he had sent others to die. She would seize his throat and tear the life from him as she drank of his blood, as the guillotine had cut the life from his victims. She lifted her hand, her fingers curling, and she smiled, her sharp teeth pricking her lower lip.

"Simone, stop!"

Her hand shot forward and clamped around Broussard's throat. The man's eyes bulged and he wheezed. She squeezed harder, and bent to put her teeth on the vein that pulsed at his neck.

"Stop, damn you, woman!"

Her head jerked back—an arm around her neck—and a voice hissed in her ear. "What the *devil* do you think you are doing?"

Chapter 9

CORDAY. MICHAEL. THE SCENT OF HIM—like a breeze through an autumn forest—came to her. Simone stared at Broussard before her, looking confused in the trance she had imposed on him. She saw her hand on his throat.

No . . . no. She should stop.

She released him, and the man took in a deep breath, wheezing, then coughed in deep spasms.

A breath brushed her ear. "What the hell are you doing?" Corday whispered. His arm around her neck did not move.

"I . . . I . . ." Simone shook her head. "I was angry. He tried to rape the girl."

"You fool. Now he will do all he can to turn you in to the authorities—did you not think of that?"

"No. I only thought . . . I wanted to drink . . ." Simone stared at Broussard, and as the fog of the blood-hunt faded from her mind, a growing dread took over. *The mission. Her purpose.* She had forgotten, and had thought only of the blood-hunt. Michael's arm released her neck and he spun her around. She let out a low moan and covered her face with her hands.

He seized her shoulders, drew her close, and whispered in her ear. "We will have to kill him to prevent him from reporting us, and then we will have to do what we can to show we have nothing to do with it."

Simone looked up at him. The moonlight cast a harsh shadow on his face. "No!" she said. "I won't kill him."

"No matter." His face grew cold, and his eyes glinted ice. She heard the soft sound of a knife released from its sheath.

"No!" She seized his wrist, squeezing hard, and shook her head. His eyes widened. "There is another way. I can make him forget."

His arm relaxed. She thought relief flashed across his face, but the expression quickly disappeared. "How?" he asked.

"I can put him in a trance and tell him to forget everything, and he will forget."

"Mesmerism."

"Yes."

He let out a breath. "I have seen it done. Do it. It is the best way, and will leave no evidence of this night's doings."

Simone turned to Broussard and took his jaw in her hand. "Look at me," she commanded. The magistrate stared at her, still under the trance she had set on him while in her blood-hunt. Good.

"Listen to me. All will be well. You are feeling relaxed, and you are ready for your sleep. You will remember nothing of being in this stable or in this stall this night. You will not remember me, the maid, or this man beside me. We were not here. Your throat is sore because you have a bad cold. If anyone asks what you have been doing this night, you will say you were restless and decided to walk off your restlessness before you settled to sleep. Now you feel very sleepy. You will go to your room and sleep in the soft sweet bed. Go now."

She released Broussard's chin and moved to the side of the stall. The magistrate rose and yawned, pressing his palms against his eyes. He rubbed his throat and coughed, then sniffed experimentally. "Eh, it seems I have a cold," he muttered. He shook his head, and shuffled past Corday, out of the stable.

Simone leaned against the side of the stall and groaned. She had almost let her rage and her blood-thirst take over. She had almost killed a man. She would have done it if it hadn't been for—

The stall door closed with a click. She opened her eyes. Michael. He stood in front of her and took her chin in his hand.

"Why did you come here?" he asked, his face set in hard lines. "Was it to see Broussard?"

"Don't be stupid," she said. "I almost killed him."

"Why?"

"Because he was about to rape the girl."

"Why did you come close enough to the stables so that you discovered it?"

"I wanted to see if du Maurier or Hervé might be awake and if they might be up to anything."

"They are asleep," Corday said, and his expression relaxed. "I made sure of it." Simone wondered if he might have used some kind of sleeping potion to be so sure. A soft chuckle came from him. "I thought you might be inclined to wander the inn, so yes, I did ensure they would have a good night's sleep and be fresh for our journey in the morning." His hand released her chin, and his fingers moved over her jaw and then behind her ear, gently massaging the back of her neck. She closed her eyes at the soothing sensation, and let her head drop slowly back. "But I did not think Broussard might be inclined to nocturnal activity outside of his room. Tell me—" His fingers caressed the back of her head, and down to her neck again. "—did you purposely come here to meet Broussard?" His body was warm against hers and his breath brushed her ear.

Her eyes flew open and her head snapped upright, indignation filling her. "Broussard? The thought of him makes me want to vomit. He disgusts me. How can you think—"

"Good," Corday said, and kissed her. The kiss was slow and sweet, moving softly over her lips, then pressing more firmly, then away, teasing.

It was torture. Simone moaned and seized his face with her hands, kissing him with all the heat that rose from her belly. Corday—*Michael*—pulled away for a moment with a laughing breath, and brought his lips to her throat. His hands moved from her shoulders to the fichu around her neck and pulled the cloth away. His fingers brushed the revealed skin, softly like feathers. She moaned. The blood-hunt had not faded entirely, and intensified the feeling of his hands on her, heating her skin and her secret places until she felt afire. He pressed her against the side of the stall, the wood slats hard on her back. Something poked her spine, enough to rouse her from the sensation of his hands on her and her hunger for it. Hunger.

"No." She pushed at him, but he held her fast. "I can't." The faint residue of the blood-hunt was still there— or was it a sensual haze?

"I won't hurt you," he said. He kissed her again, and she let him for a moment, then pushed him away.

"I am afraid *I* will hurt *you*," she blurted.

He laughed. "I promise you I will bear it with fortitude." He splayed his hand over her breast, dipping a finger under the edge of her bodice. She moaned again, wanting him, hating that she could not tell whether or not it was the blood-hunt. She seized his hand and held it.

"No, you don't understand," she said desperately. "I almost killed Broussard. I might also kill you."

"Yes, but you *wanted* to kill him, because he was very, very, very bad," Corday said, kissing the corner of her mouth, under her chin, and at the hollow of her throat with each "very." "You will not want to kill me, for I promise to be very, very good."

I am a vampire. She gave a despairing groan. He would not understand. He was not the type of man to believe such things. "I might still do it" was all she could say.

He laughed and kissed her again, then suddenly lifted her in his arms. "You are right. This stable had dangerous implements. You might accidentally stab me with a pitchfork at the height of our lovemaking. Let us go elsewhere." He kissed her again as she tried to protest, then explored the rest of her mouth. The heat and the hunger within her rose higher, and she pressed herself against him. She heard a dull thud as he kicked open the stall door; the sound was loud in her ears, jolting her out of her sensual haze. But his lips were upon her again, the haze returned, and she was hardly conscious of their return to the inn, the chuckles of a few guests, and Mme. Proust's gasp and hurried explanation that they were newly married.

She cared for none of that; only Corday's lips on hers, only his arms holding her close as he ascended the stairs, only the darkness and heat that closed around them as he tugged the curtains around the bed and began to pull off her clothes.

He was slow, agonizingly slow. A kiss followed each tug of the laces that held her bodice together. A kiss followed each movement of his hand as he pushed away the cloth of her gown. A kiss followed the cool air that brushed her skin as he pulled apart her corset.

He did nothing then, but let his fingers and the back of his hand slide across her skin as he kissed her, pausing at her breasts and caressing them gently.

It was maddening. She could not let him do this; it was dangerous; but she wanted him. Her hands reached for him, intending to push him away, and met cloth. He had not even taken off his coat. The heat within her made her cry out in confusion and frustration, and she sat up and pushed him upright, fumbling at the buttons of his waistcoat. A husky chuckle brushed her ear, and his hand covered hers.

"No," he said. "Not yet."

Her skirts came up suddenly, and then they were up and over her head. The fabric rustled as it slid over the side of the bed, falling to the floor. A sudden jerk, and her unlaced corset followed the skirt. He pushed her down on the bed, untied the petticoat from her waist, and pulled it off, leaving only her shift.

"Better," Corday said, and put his mouth on hers. Simone felt his hand on her shoulder, pushing down her shift, smoothing over the shoulder and circling down to her breast. He did not touch it, however, merely going to the side, below, and between until she ached with wanting him to touch her there.

"Please," she whispered against his mouth. "Please."

His lips left hers, and followed the same route that his hand had followed, and then . . . and then, he took the tip of her breast in his mouth.

She gasped, then took in a harder breath as his hand slowly pushed up the hem of her shift, fingers brushing the inside of her legs. The heat that had grown in the pit of her stomach flared, and followed the path of his hand until it found the true source of the heat between her thighs.

She moaned, clutching his shirt, and a loud rip sliced the silence of the room. Another chuckle brushed her cheek, and she felt him move over her, the wool of his knee breeches harsh against her skin after the gentleness of his hands. She pulled at his clothes once more.

"Not yet," he said again, but she felt his hand move below, parting her legs, then unbuttoning the cloth between them. She moved against him, urgently, as he bent to kiss her breast again. She closed her eyes.

Then there was no cloth rubbing against her legs, but skin, and a hardness that pushed against the apex of her thighs. It slid, slowly, back and forth, and her eyes flew open with the gasp that the sensation forced from her.

He was looking at her, watching her as he moved slowly, pausing as if he were about to enter her, but he did not. The familiar hunger burned higher, and a faint alarm sounded in the back of her mind and gave voice.

"I can't—"

"I think you can," he said, and kissed her deeply before withdrawing and watching again as he moved upon her.

"We don't know each other—" She broke off in mingled lust and frustration. Another stupid thing to say—she had been saying too many stupid things. The thought vanished as a burst of fire between her legs made her squeeze her eyes shut and cry out.

A burst of air came from him, and she opened her eyes. He was smiling. "True. We should try to know each other better. And there is nothing like the present, yes?" And he pushed himself deep within her.

A groan tore from her throat, and she closed her eyes again. It was too much—it had been a long time—she was not used to this sensation, this feeling of a man above her and within her, this aching and wanting.

His weight rested lightly on her, and he kissed her, then withdrew below. "We could start with names," he whispered. She arched toward him, but he moved away slightly. "My name is Michael. Say it."

"Michael." He pushed into her again. "Michael!"

"Good," he said, and kissed her ear. "And your name is Simone, yes?"

"Yes."

He pulled out. "And the rest?"

She moved against him, but he would have none of it. "Marie," she said.

The hardness nudged at her but did not go in. "And?"

Her hands clutched his hips and her fingers dug holes into his breeches. "Take these off."

He nudged at her again. "No," he said, withdrawing further and resuming the rubbing he had done earlier.

Simone groaned. "Simone. I am Simone de la Fer."

His motions stopped—had one or more survived? "All the de la Fers are dead." He moved back and forth again, lazily, in excruciating slowness.

"Noooo. . . ." Simone clutched his hips, panting. "No, I am the last."

He poised himself at the entrance of her heat again. "How do I know you are telling the truth?"

"*Mon Dieu,* how can I not?" she cried out, and seizing his hips, forced him into her again.

Corday closed his eyes and bit the inside of his cheek to prevent himself from spilling into her. The pain was enough to keep him from thrusting over and over again— he had bitten hard. He gazed at her, her eyes closed, her lips parted and panting, and he lifted himself from her to gaze at the white skin of her breasts flushed with passion. He had pictured her this way in his dreams, even before he had discovered what she truly looked like behind her disguise of rags. Her voice alone had lured him into wild imaginings, and for all his jesting he had indeed feasted on it until the sound alone had not been enough.

Her response to his touch was more than he had imagined. She had kissed him with a clumsy ardor that had at first made him think she might be a virgin. But she was not, and he was glad. A virgin's pain would have suspended the pleasure he had intended for her, and he wanted her lost and helpless in her passion. It was working; she was more responsive than he had ever dreamed.

He closed his eyes and let himself thrust in a little, slowly, then out again, slowly drawing out the sensation. Her inner muscles closed hard on him, and made him draw in a long, deep breath. He would make this last. She said she was Simone de la Fer. He wanted more.

She shifted against him now, in short frantic movements. *God.* He clenched his teeth and withdrew. She wailed clear frustration.

"How can I know for sure?" he asked. He moved over her again, back and forth, watching how her head turned from side to side, how quick, frantic breaths parted her lips. He wanted to be in her, drive both of them to completion, for she was close, he could tell. He almost took back his question. If she were as close as he to the climax of passion, she could tell nothing but the truth.

"I am—I am Simone de la Fer. I am the last. The mansion I slept in—ah!" She clutched at him again, her hands unnaturally strong, even in passion. "It—it is my home." She convulsed against him as he pushed into her and stopped. "Please—ah! Please . . . my home. Château de la Fer is my home."

He moved rhythmically for a few moments—a reward for her answer, a reward for him. He closed his eyes, and buried his face in her hair that spread across the pillow. It felt like cool water on his skin, different from the smooth heat below, and a sudden impatience made him raise himself from her and pull off his coat, his half-untied cravat, then his waistcoat, throwing them to the side of the bed.

She opened her eyes and stared at him, then she reached out to him, slipping her hands beneath his shirt.

Her hands were hot, as if she had held them up to a fire. They traveled upward, moving over his stomach and chest, lingering as if memorizing their shape. The shirt traveled up with her hands, then he ducked his head through the collar and tossed the shirt away as well.

He had been still while removing his coat and shirt, and he remained so, holding himself up on his arms and watching her. She had come away from the peak he had almost taken her to again, but her body trembled beneath him. She looked at him, and it seemed she also watched as well. For a moment a sad, wise look entered her eyes, and he wondered what made her sad; then her lip trembled, and her eyes showed nothing but a vulnerable passion. A strange, almost forgotten sensation moved within him; an echo to the sadness that had been in her eyes. He touched her face, following the contour of her temple and cheek, down to her jaw. He ran a finger across her lips. She blinked slowly, then closed her mouth tightly shut. She stayed that way for a few moments, then sighed. "Do not be so tender, Michael. I could hurt you, and then you will not want to be near me."

Almost, he made a jest, as he had before, but the old, sad look came into her eyes as she spoke, and he knew that she wished to be near him. Not out of lust, not out of love, he was sure, but out of a deep loneliness.

He closed his eyes, shutting out the sight of the emotions he saw in her eyes, for an ache began to grow within him, an echo to what he feared was her heart's need. He moved within her then, not knowing how to respond, and he heard her sigh. He opened his eyes again, in time to see a relieved expression, as if she were glad of a distraction.

He stroked her cheek. "What is it?" He heard the words, then realized they had come from himself. He had not meant to say them.

"I am selfish, Michael. I could hurt you, but I want

this . . ." She pressed herself up into him. "I should stop now. I should make you go away."

He smiled slightly, still stroking her face. "How could you hurt me? You are a little thing."

"I am very strong."

She was; he had experienced it himself. But her eyes wavered a moment while she gazed at him, and he knew she concealed something. Obviously. Did he not just this evening ponder her nature?

"Something concerns you. Tell me." He said it haltingly—he was not used to saying such words.

"I—" She shook her head.

He wanted, suddenly, to know. He kissed her, and began to move in her. "Tell me," he said softly. "Tell me, Simone."

She moaned, her trembling increased, and he knew she was nearing her peak.

"I . . . I am Simone de la Fer. I am the daughter of the Comte de la Fer. The revolutionaries killed my family. I am the last of the de la Fers—ah!" She trembled more violently beneath him, and her hands clutched his hip and his back, her fingers digging into his flesh.

He pressed his lips on hers, and still did not quicken his movement within her. "What else, Simone? Tell me."

She shook her head, then she twisted beneath him, urging him to go faster.

Not yet. He took a deep breath and bit the inside of his cheek again.

"Tell me, Simone. Don't be afraid."

She gazed at him, her expression dazed. "I am Simone de la Fer," she said again. "But I am not as I was." She closed her eyes as her trembling increased, and he felt it—a spasm, a clutching of his member deep inside of her. She opened her eyes again, wide and lost. "The sheath of your dagger. You must give it to me," she said, panting.

"Why?"

"Not the knife. The sheath. I am not as I was."

Corday slowed his movements, and stopped. She groaned and pushed at him, whether to urge him on or to comply with her direction he did not know. It would not hurt to see what she was about. He shifted their bodies to their sides, and reached under the mattress for the dagger that he had placed there. He shook the knife out and it dropped to the floor, then he put the sheath in her hand. He moved her gently into position again.

And found himself on his back. He blinked and looked at her, straddling him. "Now," she said, her voice shaking. "Now you will be safe." She put the dagger's sheath between her teeth and plunged herself down on him.

God. The change was sudden and swift. Now she had the control, not he. A groan burst from him as she frantically rubbed against him, her breasts sliding across his chest, her hips rising and falling on his. She lifted herself up, clutching his shoulders, moving harder and faster. The thin leather sheath between her lips looked like a knife and the flickers of light from the fire caressed her body like a lover's hand. She looked like a pagan goddess, her rising rhythmic moans a chant of love and death. Her moans grew louder, faster, and her lips parted to reveal teeth, sharp and feral, buried in the leather of the sheath, as she moved faster, deeper, deeper. The sight of her—dangerous, yet helpless in passion—inflamed him.

A crying moan came from her, and she shook, hard. He could feel it, clutching him, and it was too much. He seized her wrists and rolled over, holding her hands above them as he plunged into her, hot as fire, as deep as death. She screamed and slammed her body hard against him, then sank back into the bed. He took the sheath from her lips and placed his mouth there instead, groaning into her mouth as he spilled his seed. A sudden pain lanced his lower lip—she had bitten him. But it was nothing, nothing compared to the searing pleasure that did not stop, that kept him thrusting and thrusting inside, as if seeking the core of her, as if he could not get enough. He felt her tongue on his lips, licking away the blood that he could taste there.

He sank down upon her at last, letting out a deep breath, then kissing her, licking her lips as she continued to lick and suck on his own. He did not move from her, and soon felt her hands on him again as she continued to kiss him. She caressed his back and buttocks, then slid her hand between them. He hardened again.

If she was indeed some unnatural creature of the night, then she must be a witch, for her hand and her body bewitched him to plunging into her again, listening to the music of her sighs and moans as he took her to her peak again.

At last they rested, and she lay with her head on his chest, her neck arching up so that she could gaze at him. She said nothing, merely tracing the contours of his face with her hand before she moved her hand downward to rest on his chest. Corday looked at her, at the expressions flitting across her face: satiety in her brief, soft smile, an odd mix of sadness and gratitude that faded into bleak loneliness as she closed her eyes.

He held her close against the feelings that suddenly twisted his gut, taking refuge in the sensation of her skin cooling where their bodies did not meet. He pulled the bedclothes up around them, then stopped his hand when he found himself gently stroking her face, her hair, and her back.

No. Touching her, at least, he could afford. She sighed, and relaxed into him. Certainly, he could allow a measure of comfort for himself from this woman. He—or she—might die during this mission, and even if neither of them did, he doubted their association would be of long duration. His occupation demanded it. It was necessary that he remember this, and ignore the strange emptiness that he felt at these thoughts. He had no time for such things, and his intent this night—aside from the pleasure of seduction—was to obtain information from this woman, Simone de la Fer.

He smiled ruefully at himself. He had made her reveal more about herself, but it had not been much more than her name. It had been worth it, however, for she had ridden him like a wild woman, and the intensity of her body upon him had resulted in a mindless explosion of pleasure he had not remembered receiving in a long, long time.

Still, that she claimed to be the last of the de la Fer family explained much. The place at which he had found her was clearly her home, and obviously her base of operations. The de la Fers were all dead; it made sense that she would react in a way that defied those who killed them. It was a vengeance of a sort, and a vengeance in truth if she had killed any of those who murdered her family. That she worked under disguise said she worked mostly alone. The fewer who knew her identity, the better. It was not surprising he had formed a liking for her; they were not so different, after all. He wondered if she, too, grew fatigued of her mission, wanting to rest.

He grunted. If he was fatigued, it was because of a long journey and a most satisfying session of lovemaking. He would be better for a night's sleep.

He looked down at her, and saw her watching him, a slight smile on her lips. He bent and kissed her, which she returned eagerly, and her hand moved downward. He seized her wrist and laughed.

"You flatter me, my dear. I would prefer to be well rested before we do this again. Indeed, I am surprised you do not wish to sleep yourself."

Her gaze slid away from his, and her smile faded. "I do not sleep during the night."

He flicked her chin with his finger. "Come, my dear, surely habits can change."

"It is not a habit," she said, her voice abrupt. "I told you, I am not as I was. I am not what you think me."

Stubborn woman! He would be inclined to irritation at her insistence, but he was too sated to emit more than a sigh. "You are not what I think you are," he repeated. "You have no idea what I think of you."

She smiled slightly. "Tell me what you think I am."

Did she want flattery, then? He smiled. Very well! He turned on his side and gazed at her, touching her cheek. "I think you are a beautiful woman. Your skin would be the envy of every woman in London. Your lips—" he kissed them gently, "—are full and red as ripe cherries." He lifted a strand of her hair and let it slip through his fingers. "Your hair, a dark silken draft of wine that makes me drunk to feel it." He let his hand drift over her shoulder to her breast. "Your breasts are—"

She closed her eyes briefly and shivered, then seized his hand, holding it tightly. "That is very flattering, monsieur, but I am not a catalogue of food."

He grinned. "Oh, I don't know . . . I could happily feast on your—"

"Stop!" She placed her hand on his mouth, though her eyes were dancing with suppressed laughter and a certain gratification. "*Who* and *what* do you think I am?"

He kissed the palm of her hand, and held it. "You are Simone de la Fer," he said softly, and caressed the hollow of her hand with his thumb. "You are the last of a murdered family, and they were murdered by the revolutionaries. If you have not killed out of vengeance, then you have at least killed out of self-defense. Perhaps your mission of smuggling those destined for death is a way of saving those who remind you of your family, or perhaps it is to spite those who killed them. You are fierce, you are intelligent, and you are clever. You work in disguise, you work alone, and because you are a woman who does these things, you have few, if any, friends. You have no true husband, no fiancée, and have not had a lover for a long time. You are also . . ." He hesitated, remembering her feral looks during their lovemaking, almost an illusion of firelight and wild imaginings, and remembering also her strength. "You have an aversion to sunlight, you sleep during the day, and you are very strong, and amazingly swift."

Her expression had initially been surprised at his recitation; and the emotions on her face flitted from alarm to a brief indignation, and finally, at his last words, to the sadness and gravity he had seen before.

There was silence as she took in his words, and then she sighed. "And this suggests nothing to you?"

He wondered what she was trying to say, and why she would not say it. He smiled. "It suggests that you are a beautiful, desirable, very unusual woman." He touched his lower lip and winced. "And highly passionate."

She shook her head and let out an impatient breath. "Do you see nothing else?"

"Is there anything else?" Corday watched the frustration grow on her face, and had made his voice deliberately flippant. She was clearly suspended between fear of revealing something, and a deep desire to reveal it. He had thought that seducing her might bring her to this point, and it had. Now his words irritated her more, and she was bursting to tell. Despair appeared on her face for a moment, and she hung her head on a deep groaning sigh.

He reached for her then and pulled her close to him, for he did not want to see her despair; it caused a fleeting thought that he understood what she felt, and to think that was impractical. He stroked her hair and her back, and felt her relax into him.

"Tell me, *ma petite*," he said softly, surprised to find he sounded very concerned. "What frightens you?"

"I—I am not frightened," she said, clearly trying to sound defiant.

"Very well, you are not frightened." He continued to stroke her, and her back lost its stiffness. "But something causes you sadness, and I would know why."

Her breath caught, and he almost thought the sound was a sob, but she looked at him, surprised. She looked startled. "Who told you this?"

He smiled. "It is not difficult to see your sorrow, *ma petite*. You as much as tell me, here and there, in the little things you say and do." He continued to rub the palm of her hand, for it had stiffened in his, and it slowly relaxed again.

"I should be more careful," she said ruefully.

"Yes, you should." But he shrugged. "You are, actually, but I am used to watching for these things. I doubt anyone else has noticed, nor do I think you associate yourself with anyone long enough for them to take note."

She nodded, and fell silent. He was sure there was more, but he felt too relaxed, too physically sated to pursue more at the moment. It did not matter. She would reveal herself to him and he would understand more over time. If he had any virtue at all it was patience; waiting for the right time to strike or elicit information was key to the success of any mission.

An odd dissatisfaction settled on him at the thought. He was on a mission to kill the man who funded and encouraged the spread of revolutionary terror to other countries. Simone was part of that mission. But the thought that she was, somehow, a mission as well or even part of this mission sat ill with him. An illogical feeling, of course.

Yet . . . he felt he needed to take his time with her, that it mattered not what she told of herself, that he would find it out at some time, and that what she revealed in the last few minutes was enough for now.

"Stay with me. Please." He was not sure why he said it—that is, he was; it was to ensure she would not venture out again.

"Yes," she said after a brief hesitation. She lifted herself to move closer to him, and for a moment he watched as the flickering firelight highlighted her form. It would be pleasant if she decided to sleep with him. Just to sleep. He pressed his hand against his temple again, pushing down the tired ache that had formed there. A warmth crept into the center of him, very near his heart as she shifted herself closer to him, and stroked his face. He closed his eyes and felt his body sink further into the bed. Her hand felt feather-light and cool. It reminded him of a time long ago, when his life was not filled with intrigue and death. When he had had a family, a mother and a father. His shoulders tensed; then he made himself relax, and was rewarded by her drawing closer to him. He sighed, and as he sank further into sleep, a thought flitted through his mind that all his questioning tonight had not brought her closer to him, but a simple request and the gathering of his arms around her had.

Simone relaxed against Michael, feeling his arms around her loosen, and his breath deepen into sleep. She would allow herself this feeling of comfort a little more before she left him for the confessional.

She did not want to go; a strange thing, for she had gone willingly to confession ever since she had begun her penance, even eager for it, so as to cleanse her soul of whatever might keep her from lifting the curse from her. She had gladly confessed every violence she had committed, every use of her unnatural speed and strength, every uncharitable thought.

But she did not want to confess her time with Michael, or what she had done with him. Michael. She did not think of him as Corday, for clearly it was a false name, but she held on to his name, Michael, held on to it with all her heart, for she was sure it was truly his. For the first time in a long time, she had let herself take comfort in the nearness of a man.

Seven years. That was the last time she had lain with a man in the aftermath of lovemaking, fitting her body to his, easily, naturally; she had believed herself in love with her first lover. All the other times had been quick, and she had not felt much but the laxity of a sated body. But now, even though they were on a hurried journey, she let herself burrow underneath the bedcovers, closer to Michael. She was not sure what the difference was. She searched her mind, her heart. . . . Safe. She felt safe with him. An odd thing to feel, for he was most certainly the most dangerous man she had ever met. It occurred to her that she had not truly felt safe with anyone for a long time.

Simone closed her eyes and sighed, listening to the far chime of a clock in the inn. It would be a few hours until matins, when the local priest would be up and at his duties. She would go then. Meanwhile . . . meanwhile, she would lie here and take comfort from Michael, from the warmth of his body, and what he had given her this night. She let herself doze a little, even though she was not accustomed to it. Her body felt lax and warm enough that she could almost fully sleep.

The clock chimed again, and pulled her out of her doze, and she found she had curled up against Michael's back. She smiled wryly to herself. Surely she had gone mad. She had known this man only a few days, and she had already been in his bed. Oh, she could blame it on her blood-hunt—it always made her susceptible to the touch of a man. But it had been more than that. She had been fully able to keep herself from lying with a man since the beginning of her mission, blood-hunt or no. This time, she had given but a token resistance, even though it was dangerous for him, even though she was capable of taking his blood to the point of disabling him, perhaps even to the point of death.

Dangerous for him. Dangerous for her. But, sweet heaven, she wanted him. Even now she felt the heat of her wanting moving within her.

And that was why she needed to go to confession, if only to clear her mind and bring it back to the purpose of her mission, instead of indulging in this quite hopeless, impractical *affaire*. Simone watched Michael for a few more moments, then gently moved from him. She halted for a space, for his body tensed, then relaxed again. She let out a breath and slipped quietly from the bed. Her gaze caught the slight bleeding on his lip, and guilt pierced her. She had restrained herself—barely. Even now, despite her guilt, the thrill of taking even that little bit of blood coursed through her body.

Quickly she gathered her clothes. A church stood but a mile from this inn, and the priest there was one who had pledged supreme loyalty to the Revolution, and so had escaped persecution, but the revolutionary agents suspected him nevertheless, for his praise of the new state had been lukewarm at best. Père Roucault knew her own Père Dumont, for they were both scholars, who had corresponded with each other regarding various church and historical texts. Père Dumont had disagreed with his fellow priest about paying lip service to the Revolution, but for all that, he had told her that Roucault could be trusted.

She had even agreed that they could discuss her vampirism, if it would help find a cure.

Simone pulled on her clothes, this time carefully wrapping the rags around her hands, legs, and head before she put on her dress and a heavily veiled hat. It would be best to take precautions should she be delayed and caught out too close to dawn.

Her hand fell on the doll she had carried with her in her journeys. Should she leave it here? No. If it was necessary to play the role of La Flamme, she would need it to act as the hump on her back. For now, she would carry it, and if she was seen by a passing villager, she could pretend she was a mother taking her sick child to the doctor. She made a sling of rags and tied the doll to the front of her body, then felt for the dagger she kept in her pocket. Yes. It was still there. It was likely that du Maurier had set out agents in the vicinity, but she had evaded them before. She cast a look at Michael, still sleeping. If he did not follow her, all would be well. She pursed her lips in indecision. Best to leave him a note and warn him not to come after her, and assure him that she would soon return. The memory of the Englishmen she had seen outside the inn earlier came to her; she would tell him of them, as well. Perhaps he would search them out instead of going after her.

She pulled out paper, ink, and pen, swiftly scratched out her note, and put it on the table. There, that would do. Simone pulled her cloak closely around her and walked quietly to the door. With one last look at Michael's sleeping form, she opened the door and left.

Chapter 10

JACQUES DU MAURIER GAZED INTO THE flames that lit the fireplace in his room. The bright yellow and red light reminded him of the hair of his dead wife, Gabrielle, and that of his little girl, Thérèse. It had been a while since he had allowed himself to think of them, but the marriage tonight at this inn made him remember. Citoyen Thibaut and his wife would soon have a family, and it made him think of his own that was no more.

He rubbed his hand over his face, feeling wearier than he had felt in a long time. He was tired of his hunt for La Flamme, as well as tired of looking for the aristocrat who had raped and killed his wife and child. It was Hervé who had brought him the news, who had brought their bodies to him. It was Hervé who had brought du Maurier back to sanity after he had cursed God and nearly killed himself out of rage and grief. He gave a wry laugh. Hervé had been right; it was no use cursing God when it was clear there was no God, none that would keep a good woman and innocent child from death.

Du Maurier took in a deep breath, controlling the rage

that threatened to overwhelm him again. No. Unreasoning rage was never the answer; cool logic and keen wit would bring justice to those who, like him, had suffered cruelty at the hands of the aristos.

But now he was summoned to Paris; he allowed himself a spark of pride, for the message from his superiors had required his services in the heart of the city itself. He had only been to the city twice, long ago when his wife and child had been alive. Now, he was to have more business in Paris, more responsibilities in addition to his duties in Normandy, and he would be given an office to which he could go. He sighed. If only Gabrielle were alive to see it!

But duty was duty, and he was grateful to have a chance to serve the Republic.

A slight knock sounded at the chamber door. "Enter!" he called out.

Du Maurier did not turn when Hervé entered their room. "So?" he asked. "What did he have to say?"

"We are to expect a spy, soon, perhaps here even now, to eliminate the funding of our revolution."

Du Maurier sighed and turned to his fellow agent. "It is not enough that we have to contend with the villain La Flamme, but now we have to deal with this threat as well."

"Our duty—"

"Yes, yes, our duty." Du Maurier waved his hand in a gesture both accepting and dismissive. "I am ever conscious of our duty, Hervé—how could I forget?" For a moment his mouth turned grim. "There is not a day I do not remember my own Gabrielle and Thérèse, though there are days I wish I could forget the horror of it."

Hervé made a sympathetic sound, and du Maurier lifted his head and smiled at his fellow agent. "But they are not the only ones who have suffered, I know." Hervé nodded gravely, and his smile held an understanding for which du Maurier was grateful. He did not like to speak of his loss, but it was a comfort nevertheless to have someone who understood.

He thought again of Citoyen Thibaut and his new wife, and frowned. If the wife had not demanded the man's acknowledgment of her as his fiancée, and if it had not been very clear that Thibaut had been born in Normandy or at least close by, he would almost suspect him of being the spy they sought. He fit the description that Hervé's sources had given him. Du Maurier wanted to be sure, however. It did not serve the Revolution to accuse unjustly.

He turned to Hervé. "This Citoyen Thibaut. He claims to be a scribe, and though he has not said where he hails from, I would suspect he is from Normandy, a troublesome province. Have we any scribes there registered by that name?"

"We have many by that name, Citoyen du Maurier," Hervé replied respectfully.

Du Maurier grinned. "Of course. It is a very common name." He twisted his lips wryly. "Eh, no doubt he is as he says he is . . . or maybe not?" He gazed at his assistant, wondering if the slight twitch of the man's lips indicated any sort of emotion. Although du Maurier had long admired Hervé's calm and resolution, they sometimes annoyed him, for he was used to reading the emotions of others for clues as to antirevolutionary sentiment. That he could rarely read his assistant's expression made him realize that his skills were not as sharply honed as he would like them to be. He gave a mental shrug. Ah, well! It was a minor thing, to be dismissed for the trivial vanity it was.

"It would be wise to watch him, I think," Hervé replied smoothly.

"Even if he is clearly a man trapped in a marriage he had not sought out?"

Hervé gave a slight bow of acknowledgment. "As you say, Citoyen du Maurier. But there is a foreign agent newly come to our shores, and we have not caught the outlaw La Flamme. I think no one can be beyond suspicion."

Du Maurier nodded. "This is true." He grinned suddenly. "And Citoyenne Thibaut's performance, for all that it was very convincing, was quite dramatic, yes?"

A slight smile appeared on Hervé's lips. "As you say, citoyen," he said again.

Du Maurier nodded. "It is just as well they travel with us, then. I will insist on it. If Thibaut is the spy, or knows anything of La Flamme—I doubt he is the outlaw himself, for he is too tall—then the longer he stays with us, the better."

"And his wife?"

Du Maurier shrugged. "If she is involved in any antirevolutionary action, then it will come out sooner or later. Women do not keep secrets well."

Hervé nodded. "I have made sure our men are on alert, not too close to this inn. Shall I have the men arrest either of them if they venture too far away?"

"No." Du Maurier looked into the hearth again, and after a moment, sighed. "If our men see either or both engaged in unlawful behavior, have them watch but do nothing, and report it to me. Let Citoyen Thibaut and his wife think they are safe." He sighed again. "It is time we rested. The journey will be long." He glanced at his assistant, his expression growing grim. "Be sure to procure the largest coach this inn has. I am sure we will want to accommodate our fellow travelers in as much comfort as possible . . . all the way to Paris." Hervé bowed once more, and left the room as unobtrusively as he had entered.

Simone was glad of her swiftness now as she entered the woods just beyond the inn, for her recent blood-thirst and subsequent lovemaking with Michael had brought her senses to an acute pitch. The blood-thirst had faded, as had her sensitivity, but the chill wind still bit into her flesh like knives as she ran to the Church of St. Elisabeth. A sliver of dread lay in her gut; if the wind cut into her as it did now, how much more severe would be the sting of a holy place?

She would not think of it. It was necessary that she go to the confessional now. She was not sure if she would have a chance after this to do so, and once she and Michael reached Paris, there would be little time to do anything else but complete their mission.

Michael. She closed her eyes briefly, then opened them, for the vision of him rose behind her eyelids and threatened to make her return to him. *Mon Dieu*. Even as she sought absolution, her thoughts returned again and again to him. She was afraid, very afraid, that she was losing her heart to him, and she could not.

The wind whipped the hood from her head, and laced her hair across her face as she ran, swiftly, silently through the woods. It was best this way, for she was sure the agents would watch for any movement on the road, not near the trees. She stopped for a moment at a dark movement to the left of her. Yes. She smiled. One of du Maurier's men, no doubt. He was looking toward the road, sitting but ten feet from her. She moved away, careful to match her movement with the rustling of the wind in the tree branches, as she had taught herself to do many years ago. He would not know that she passed by this way at all.

Once she was well past the agent, she ran, and her heart grew lighter despite all her worries. There was a certain freedom in running this swiftly, faster than any man or even horse. It was like flying. For a while she could pretend that she was not a vampire, but a bird, free to fly wherever she wished, as high as the sun, free of the intrigues of men and the dictates of an oppressive government.

Soon, though, the spires of St. Elisabeth's church grew before her, and clipped the wings of her rebellion. She should not be glad of any aspect of the curse laid upon her. Swift running was part and parcel of the very thing of which she wished to rid herself.

Simone easily opened the church's heavy door; it was unlocked, and the sounds she could hear with her still—sensitive ears told her that the priest's matins were nearly over. It was not the usual time for confession, but she could ask for it regardless; indeed, she wondered if Père Roucault had been allowed to keep his usual schedule for confession, and if his parishioners felt it wise to come to confession when they would be least noticed.

She looked cautiously about the narrow hallway of the vestibule. Good, there was no one about. She did not think she had been followed here; she had watched the way carefully, and had encountered no one other than the one agent who missed her entirely. No doubt there had been more agents along the road, but since she had not gone that way, she doubted any of them had seen her. She stood still and frowned. Something was different.

Her feet did not hurt upon entering the church, and the fiery pain that often flickered across her skin when entering a holy place was not there. She hesitated before she dipped her fingers in the cistern's holy water. It stung, but only for an instant before she made the sign of the cross. Only an instant, and not the fiery lance of pain that usually coursed down her arm. Simone swallowed. There was no reason for this; she had not yet given her confession. Perhaps . . . perhaps it was a sign that she was doing the right thing. Her thoughts flickered to Michael again. Even though she had lain with him? She shook her head. Surely not. Surely not. She put her hand to her head. She did not understand; before this night, even putting her foot on the steps of a church would cause a sizzling pain on the surface of her skin. Her heart felt suddenly light. It could be that she was nearly cured of her affliction. Perhaps she could even go into the sanctuary without much damage.

Her heightened hearing picked up the sound of steps within the sanctuary. No doubt Père Roucault was within. She would ask him to attend her in the confessional; she would not tell him that she was the vampire Père Dumont had discussed with him, for she trusted only Père Dumont to understand the curse under which she operated. She opened the door to the sanctuary.

Fire seized her limbs and burned away the hope that had flickered in her. Ah, *Mon Dieu!* She staggered for a moment at the onslaught of pain, then closed her eyes and forced herself to stand. She opened her eyes and focused on the cross that stood opposite her at the far side of the sanctuary above the altar. Her eyes fixed on the figure hung on the cross. *What I suffer is nothing compared to that*, she thought. She straightened her spine, and walked forward.

The cross and the altar began to blur in front of her eyes as she put one foot in front of the other; the prickling fire that coursed over her limbs cut deep until she gasped. A red haze filled her vision, turning bright like fire. A voice seemed to float around her ears: "Mademoiselle . . . mademoiselle, are you well?" Then another voice: "Mademoiselle de la Fer! What do you here?"

Then the fire turned suddenly into darkness.

Corday woke and reached out his hand for Simone. Nothing. He sat up and threw the bed curtains aside. He had heard something—a click, a scratching, a whisper. Seizing a candle, he went to the fireplace. The embers burned low in the hearth, but there was enough burning to blow upon and kindle a small fire to light the candlewick.

The candlelight fell on a piece of white paper on the table nearby, and on it a message written in a neat, educated hand. At least she had left a message. He picked it up, read it, and let out an exasperated breath. How very *considerate* of her to let him know where she had gone, and that she knew there were Public Safety agents about, but that she would of course evade them, and that he was not to come after her, for she would return shortly. And to tell him *now* about the Englishmen she had seen earlier.

He had thought perhaps the civil marriage ceremony and their lovemaking would keep her with him, cease her sudden disappearances. Women valued these commitments, however lightly a man might enter into them. It seemed this woman did not.

Idiot woman! Corday crushed the paper in his hand, then threw it into the fire. She would be well served if he let her be captured by the agents she knew were looking for her. He looked around the room. Her dress was gone; at least she had dressed as a woman, so if she were indeed caught, they would not think she was La Flamme. By rights he should leave her and go on this mission alone.

But of course he could not. They had agreed to go into this sham marriage, and now it would look suspicious if he suddenly left without her. It would look equally suspicious if she were hurt enough to be unable to travel. Since there was no guarantee that she would not be hurt—despite her supreme confidence in her abilities—he would have to go after her.

His gaze fell on a shiny glint on the floor, and he picked up his dagger that had fallen to the floor earlier. He could not help smiling slightly, thinking of how she had taken the sheath between her teeth near the height of her pleasure. He looked around the bed for the sheath—there, half beneath the coverlet. As he resheathed the dagger, he frowned, for it did not slip in as easily as it had before. He looked closer, and unease flowed through him.

There were marks of teeth on the leather, which he expected, for Simone had clearly bitten down hard during her climax. But if he did not know better, he would have thought some animal had bitten it, for the marks were not the same as he would expect a human's to be. Two deep indentations pierced the leather. He turned the sheath over. So deep that they had cut the leather and had indented the other side as well.

I am not as I was, she had said.

A stillness took him, and he stared at the door through which Simone had gone so quietly and quickly. Old legends and stories seeped up from his memory as he remembered her unnatural swiftness and strength. Well, he thought, as the pieces of Simone's puzzle clicked together in his mind, and an odd excitement grew in his gut at the possibility of discovering something . . . no. No, they were fairy tales only, and he had little proof.

He shoved the dagger deeper into the sheath, then felt underneath the mattress where he kept his pistols. There they were; he pulled them out. He had taken out the powder and shot, fairly sure he and Simone would be undisturbed, but perhaps it would be best if he loaded them again. If she did not come back soon, then he would need to look for her and risk being seen.

If the men she mentioned were spies, it might be necessary to have his pistols at hand, even if they might be English spies. There were more than a few of his countrymen who sympathized with the French revolutionaries; in fact, he had not long ago been sent to capture a group of Irishmen who had found the lure of French money and revolution too tempting to resist. It had been a ragtag group of hotheaded youths and embittered older men who took too easily to drink. He had contemplated ridding the British government of them all, but their half-starved and belligerent faces and his sense of humor had stayed his hand. Instead, he had blown up their munitions and taken the money, putting the funds into a bank with a provision that gave only their wives and mothers access to them, with a letter to each of those worthy women informing them of their men's shenanigans. He thought it might amuse him to see the men under their women's thumbs, but he had left before he could see them scolded within an inch of their lives. Pity. It would have been amusing indeed.

It had been curious how easily that money had crossed the channel, however. No doubt this was why he had been sent to find and remove the source . . . and he had hoped Simone would help him do so.

Simone . . . he thought again of the abilities she had revealed in the course of their travel together. Interesting. How many other useful qualities did she have? Despite their differences, she had made a good partner in more ways than one. He could use someone of her swiftness and strength, and if she could put others in a trance as easily as she had Broussard, it would more easily hide their movements. A clock chimed somewhere inside the inn. There was still quite a bit of time until the dawn.

Corday pulled on his clothes, shivering in the cold room. Damn the woman! If she had not left, he could still be in the bed, much warmer, preferably with her warming it. He had not enough time if he was to go in search of her *and* search out the Englishmen, but he would go insane if he did not find out how she fared. He emitted another curse as he saw the large rip in his shirt before he put it and his waistcoat on.

He should have gone alone on this mission. Partners were a nuisance, especially ones who tore one's clothes, even if it had been in the midst of extremely good love-making. Still, he needed to find her.

She had mentioned a church. He was somewhat familiar with this area, having passed through it once long ago, and knew the church of which she had written. He would have to take his horse, for it was perhaps a mile away. He did not relish walking to and from it, and possibly risk missing du Maurier's offer of a coach ride.

It was easy taking the horse from the stables. The stable boy snored loudly; nothing would pierce that sound, not even the creak of the stall door or the snort of the horse. Corday strapped on the saddle, mounted, and rode in the direction of the church.

Clearly Simone had not taken the most obvious route; if she had, he would have caught up with her . . . but no. He remembered her unnatural swiftness of the night before. She was, perhaps, already at the church.

And perhaps, this time, he would find out more about her. He grimaced. It had become an obsession with him, and it no longer had to do with his duties or his mission. She would not reveal herself to him, and he wanted to know, as he never had wanted to know about any woman before. He wanted to know everything about her, down to her soul, for the exploration of her body had not been enough. It would never be enough, damn her.

Damn him. He spurred the horse into a canter.

The moon shone low in the sky, but it was full enough to gild the road before him with silver. The church of St. Elisabeth loomed up before him, its Gothic spires black spears against the moonlit night. It sat in the middle of the village, a mile south of Mme. Proust's inn. Corday frowned. He had not noted any movement; all was silent so far.

Too silent. Even though it was near dawn, no winter birds sang in the trees as he passed the wood to the village.

No doubt agents waited there, watching. He wondered if du Maurier did indeed suspect Simone and himself, as he had told Simone. If so, du Maurier—or Hervé—must have told their subordinates to watch and gather evidence. If du Maurier wanted to take them to Paris for trial, then it would do no good to accuse him and Simone now, and risk their escape. Corday chuckled in spite of his irritation, feeling the rising excitement of the chase as he did whenever he was in the thick of a mission. Very well. If they wished to play cat and mouse, he would oblige them. Let them watch.

A faint bell sounded as he tied his horse to a post in front of the church. He paused on the steps as he looked up at the tall spires that seemed to touch the sky. It had been a long time since he had entered a church; he remembered he had gone to one as a child, and all he could remember was the long drone of the vicar's voice, the smells of candle wax and incense, and the colored light from the windows.

He shoved aside the memories. He was no longer a child sitting next to his mother, listening to catechisms. Far, far from that.

A soft murmur caught his ear. Following the faint echoes off to the left of the vestibule, he saw doors to the confessional. Corday smiled wryly. Was Simone, then, confessing her trivial sins? Or perhaps she was meeting with one of her associates? He stepped toward the confessional, an elegantly wrought wooden booth of antique design that spoke of wealthy patrons long in the past.

But a movement caught his eye. A man, a scarf muffling his face, peered around the room from the other end of the room. He was dressed in a black coat, but a stray breeze picked up one lapel and revealed a tricolor ribbon. Corday stepped behind a pillar. One of du Maurier's men.

He could hear the voices come closer—Simone's and

someone else's, not in the confessional. He glanced at the man from behind his pillar. If Simone was indeed talking to someone who helped her in her activities, then it would not do for one of du Maurier's men to catch her at it. It would also not do for him to reveal he knew the man was an agent. Therefore, he would play the jealous husband. He watched as the agent turned toward the sound of the voices, away from him.

Quickly, soundlessly, Corday slipped behind the man, at once clapping his hand over the man's mouth and twisting his arm behind his body.

"So. You have an assignation with my wife, eh?" Corday whispered. The man shook his head frantically. Corday could feel his pulse quicken at his wrist. "Don't lie to me," Corday hissed. He tightened his hold on the man's arm, and the agent grunted in pain. "She is a lovely woman. I saw how Broussard tried to seduce her. Perhaps he sent you to take her to him?" Corday was sure others had overheard the magistrate try to elicit her services. The thought of Broussard touching Simone made him twist the man's arm, resulting in another groan of pain. Corday relaxed his hold. This was not Broussard, of course, but that thought brought the idea of another possibility; it could be that Broussard thought to procure Simone for his whore and used this man to do it. Well, he would not. Simone was his wife. His grip on the man tightened.

But the man shook his head again, and Corday moved his hand from his mouth. "Speak softly. Tell me why you are here."

"I . . . I am to watch her. . . ." The man's voice was hoarse, and he swallowed.

"Broussard wants to bed her."

"No, no! I am not from Citoyen Broussard."

Corday could hear Simone's voice, closer now, and an answering, lower voice. He needed to rid himself of this man, quickly. He drew out his dagger. "Tell me!" he said harshly into the man's ear. "Were you after her yourself, then? Even as she goes to a priest to make her confession?" He could hear Simone's voice, her words discernible. "For shame, citoyen!" he said, and he could not help the smile that came to his lips. "Please remember from now on that I am a jealous husband, and no one but myself will touch my wife." He raised his dagger.

And knocked the man unconscious with the blunt pommel of the knife.

Chapter 11

SIMONE TRIED TO MOVE HER HEAD against the dizziness that had seized her. "Père Dumont?" Her voice sounded parched, even to herself. She forced her eyes to focus on the face that loomed above her. "Père Dumont?"

"Come, bring her out of here," she heard the abbé say. She felt arms come around her, lifting her up just before her knees gave out beneath her.

They must have taken her from the sanctuary, for the pain began to fade, turning into a light sizzle on her skin's surface.

"What has happened to her?" Another voice, different, rough, not a priest's. She laughed weakly. No, not a priest's. *Michael*.

"Who are you?" That was Père Dumont's voice.

She felt herself taken from the arms of the priests into stronger ones. She lifted her hand, feeling fine wool and muscles beneath. "Michael."

"Yes, *ma petite*, I am here." His muscles shifted, and he said, "Where may I put her?"

"This way, monsieur."

Michael. He held her close, and she rested her cheek on his shoulder, taking comfort in his warmth. The sizzling on her skin faded even more as he walked, and then a door opened, and she felt cushions at her back.

Warm fingers stroked her cheek. "What happened, *mon cœur*? Were you attacked?" His voice sounded strained, but his breath touched her face softly.

Mon cœur. My heart. He had not called her that before.

"No, Michael." She opened her eyes. His face was still, impassive but for the strained lines that surrounded his mouth, and the fire in his eyes. Was he angry with her? He stroked her cheek again. No, he was not angry with her. She closed her eyes and pressed her cheek against his hand.

"Then what happened?"

She heard the flutter of vestments. "Monsieur, she is ill."

"Why?" Michael's voice was sharp.

Père Dumont hesitated before he said, "That is not for you to know."

"You are mistaken."

"Monsieur, we are her friends, and will care for her. Who are you to her that her welfare is your concern?"

"I am her husband."

Simone's eyes flew open, and she stared at Michael. He stared back coolly and his lips were pressed together as if he had let the words slip from him involuntarily. A shocked silence let the sounds of the wind whipping the spires of the church into the room. "Her husband?" whispered Père Dumont.

She shook her head. "No, only in a civil ceremony. It was no true marriage."

The priests looked at each other, and Père Dumont nodded. "We will care for her, monsieur," he said to Michael.

"No, you will not."

Simone gazed at him. His expression had not changed—hard, still. What was his game? Surely he could see she was among friends? She shook her head again. "Michael, we are not truly wed. Surely you do not think it."

He grinned suddenly. "By all the laws of the Republic we are, *ma petite*."

"The laws of the Republic mean nothing to me."

His grin disappeared and he lifted his chin, suddenly haughty. "Do you say that you wish you had not wed me?"

Simone glanced at the two priests who gazed at her with interest, Père Dumont with a brow raised. She looked away from them, not wanting to lie. She was sure Michael was trying to exert control again—understandable this time, for he did not know these men—and the only reason she had agreed to the marriage was because she knew it was a sham, not countenanced by the church. *But you lay with him, as if it were not a sham at all,* said a small voice within. *But I was under the influence of the blood-thirst,* she argued with the voice. *And under his influence, and of your desire for him.*

"Do *you* wish you had not wed *me*?" she countered, hoping to challenge him.

His smile returned. "No." *He does not know what he is saying,* she thought, and her heart sank.

She heard Père Roucault chuckle. "It seems you agreed to more than you thought," he said.

Simone shook her head. "No, it is M. Corday who has agreed to more than he realized."

Michael's smile faded again, and he looked at her seriously. "You underestimate me, *ma petite*." He sat next to her, took her hand, and brought it to his lips. "I believe I know exactly what I am getting into. We would make a good pair, you and I. And—" He looked at the two priests before them. "How well do you know these men?"

"Very well, monsieur," replied Père Dumont. "I have known her family since she was a young— That is, fifty years." He nodded at Père Roucault after an assessing moment. "He also is to be trusted."

Simone looked at Michael. "It is as he says."

He nodded. "You know what we do is dangerous. Neither you nor I might survive it."

A shiver of dread shook her. "Yes."

"Would it hurt so much to enjoy each other's company before the end?"

"I . . ." She looked at him sternly. "We need not wed for that."

He looked up at the priests, and his smile turned mischievous. "I would make an honest woman of her, messieurs."

Père Dumont looked both hesitant and grave. "I—I do not know. It is not proper for her to travel alone with a man to whom she is not related."

"*Mon Père,* you know it is not the usual case for me!" Simone protested. "You know I am not as other women."

"You are, however, a woman, nevertheless," the priest said gently. "Both you and I know what you have experienced in your life." He paused, and an uncertain look grew in his eyes. "And yet . . . and yet . . ." He glanced at Michael. "Do you know her nature, monsieur?"

Michael said nothing, gazing at her for a long moment, then turned to Père Dumont. "I believe I do," he said calmly.

Simone's heart beat hard and fast. She wanted him to know, wanted him to understand and accept what she was . . . but no, no, he could not. She had not told him. Certainly, he could not guess; she was a creature from ancient tales, from an unreal world. He was not a man to believe in fanciful stories.

"You don't understand" was all she could say.

"I understand that you are ill. I understand that you are not as other women. I understand that if you do not go with me, it will go badly for both of us." He hesitated, then whispered, "I understand that if I do not do this now, I may never do so. We may die. Grant me this one thing."

Simone closed her eyes. His voice had held a hint of the deep loneliness she had often felt herself. But she could not give in to him. She could not agree, no matter how much she might want to weep at what she, too, may never have. "You are dreaming, telling yourself stories, monsieur."

"I have had few dreams, Simone. Allow me this one."

"You. Do. Not. Understand," she said fiercely, desperate and despairing. She seized his face, looking into his eyes. "I am a creature of the night. I cannot stand beneath the sun, and I am so evilly cursed that I cannot enter a church without risking my life, or at least becoming ill."

She drew in a deep breath. *Mon cœur*, he had said. *My heart*. She had seen this in his eyes. She could not bear it that he might want her, even love her, without knowing what she truly was, and then turn from her in disgust. She would tell him now, and be damned to him when he turned away. "I drink blood, Michael. I am a vampire."

The silence was broken only by Père Roucault's gasp and crossing of himself. Simone opened her eyes again, forcing herself to look at Michael.

A wry smile turned up his lips. "I know," he said.

Corday watched her staring at him, barely noticing Père Dumont's hasty escort of his fellow priest from the room. "You know?" she said, her voice disbelieving.

He stood, then drew up a chair near the sofa on which she lay and straddled the chair, resting his hands and chin on the low back, and gazing at her. She looked no different from how any lovely young woman might. Her skin was pale, her eyes dark and unlined, and her hair richly waving dark. Her lips were pale, more pale than they had been when they had made love, and he could well believe that she was ill from her appearance alone, if not from her still-shaking hands and trembling voice. She had been like this when he had discovered her in the château and exposed the room to sunlight. Then there had been her strength, her swiftness, and the very clear indentations on his dagger's scabbard that were definitely not made with human teeth. The old legends he had heard on his travels had come to him before when he had looked at the marks on his dagger's sheath, and he remembered them again now. Everything she displayed matched.

So his mind and logic told him. Belief . . . that was more difficult to come by. He pushed aside his emotions and focused on the information at hand. He shook his head. "I am not one to believe in anything, Simone. But what else is there to explain you, other than the tales I have heard from far lands?"

She gazed at him warily. "But I could be a madwoman. I could only *think* I am a vampire."

"Yes, I considered that," he said, then laughed when she looked offended. "Indeed, I considered the fact that I myself might be mad. Did I not say so from time to time?"

"I thought you were joking."

He sobered. "Only half joking, *ma petite*. Sometimes I think I must indeed be mad to do what I do, and the devil knows I come by it naturally." A wave of fatigue came over him at the thought of his occupation, and he looked at his hands that had killed so many men, he did not remember the number. But he had felt as a youth that he was fit for nothing else.

She said nothing, only watching him, listening. He became aware of her hand resting on his knee, as if she wished to give him comfort. He did not remember if anyone had listened to him in all of his life since he was a youth or given him comfort. His shoulders tensed, and he made them relax. He let her hand stay where it was.

"But I did not become what I am and survive without cataloguing the facts or by ignoring the most possible explanation for these facts, however improbable," he continued. "I therefore considered the possibility, and did not dismiss it, not entirely." Not entirely. The idea existed, and he wanted a natural explanation for it. There was no such thing as the supernatural, after all. . . .

"So you believe I am truly a vampire?" she said.

"It is a good description for your condition."

She made a face. "You make it sound like being a vampire is an illness. Believe me, monsieur, I am not ill."

"No, I believe, as you mentioned to me, that it is not a communicable disease."

She slapped his knee angrily and let out an impatient breath. "No, it is not catching, and it is not a disease. I was cursed with this, I tell you!"

He smiled indulgently. "So it may seem, *ma petite*. I grant you, it may not be a disease. Perhaps you were born with the condition."

Simone pushed herself upright on the sofa with still-trembling arms. "I was most certainly *not* born with this."

Corday paused, watching her breathing quicken, her mouth pressed together in indignation. She would tell him how she became a "vampire" in the next moment. A yearning ache almost made him open his mouth to spur her into telling him. He wanted to know everything about her, he wanted all of her. Their bedding had not been enough for him; he had been mistaken thinking that a mere tumble would ease his interest in her. He had always been intrigued with mysteries, and she was a mystery all in herself.

And yet, he could not. She looked at him with indignation, but underneath it was fear and a yearning too close to what he himself felt, had felt, he realized now, since he first met her. No, he would say nothing. Surely it did not matter. But she swung herself around so that she sat on the sofa, and put both her hands on his knees. She gazed at him intently, and the pain in her eyes shone clear.

"Listen to me, Michael. I will tell you something I have only told my confessor. I have told no one else." Simone closed her eyes for a moment, her shoulders stiffening, as if she warded herself against impending injury. When she opened her eyes again, she looked past him, and he thought he could almost see memories flickering across her face.

"Nine years ago, though it seems an age, I was a girl of sixteen. I had just come from the convent where I was raised to be a proper young lady to be wed to a highborn man of my family's choosing." She sat back and laid her hands loosely in her lap. "But I was rebellious, tired of the constant strictures of living with the Sisters of Our Lady's Mercy. I rebelled at the idea that my parents would choose my husband." She smiled slightly. "And what romantic young girl would not?

"Yet, my parents were not unkind. They acknowledged that a young noblewoman should be introduced at court, and so I was. But for all that they were of an ancient line, they were not courtiers, and thought I would be safe for a few years with my very fashionable aunt, the Marquise la Belleversé."

Simone's smile faded. "My aunt was indeed very fashionable, and in the court of Louis the Sixteenth, the fashionable were more decadent than an innocent from the country could comprehend. What I could discern in my innocence only fed my rebellion. How dull and countrified were my parents! I was determined to be all that was fashionable, and took any admonition to be otherwise as just as dull.

"And I was not an ignorant young girl, not at all! Did I not attend all my aunt's salons? Did I not converse with the most intelligent of philosophers and scientists? Did I not—" She paused, and her mouth grew grim. "Did I not come to believe all the Sisters of Mercy had taught me was mere superstition?" she whispered.

Pain appeared in her eyes again, and the urge to stop her confession and the urge to know all fought within Corday. But he sensed that she wanted to speak, and said nothing.

Simone looked at him, her expression bleak. "You wanted to know. I will tell you. It will be a relief, in a way."

She took in a deep breath. "I fell into bad company." She gave a short laugh. "That sounds like a line from a morality play, does it not?" She looked down at her hands and pressed them down on her lap. "But they were quite bad. They had secret ceremonies, and I was invited." She swallowed. "I had managed to remain a virgin until then. But I knew everything that went on between a man and a woman from whispers and stories and jokes I had heard from the courtiers that surrounded the king. And I had a lover—we had not . . . well, we had not. Until that night."

She looked at him directly, honestly. "It was all very secretive, delicious, and profane, and I felt very daring and sophisticated. It was all a play, I thought. My lover was . . . he was the first. He was very good, and I liked it very well. But then came the . . . the others."

She looked away then, and her profile paled to a translucent white. *Stop,* he wanted to say. *You need not tell me.* But she hurried on before he could speak. "They tied me up to the altar and they had me, one after another. They chanted profane things to *le Diable* himself as they did so. They thought my screams were screams of pleasure, or so they told me, over and over again."

Corday rose from his chair and pushed it away. He sat next to her and took her in his arms. "Stop. That is all I need to know. More than I need to know." He did not want to believe this. He wanted to believe it was the shock of the incident that had changed her. He had seen such a thing before; hysterical illnesses manifesting in a victim's body. *And yet, there is her strength, and her swiftness, and how else to explain the unhuman scoring on his dagger's sheath?*

She struggled away from him, and as he gazed into her eyes, he saw a desperate desire that he believe her. "No, Michael. That is not how I became a vampire." Her fingers dug into the fabric of the sofa. "The last one . . . the last one took my blood as they chanted, took it until I became unconscious. I was with child after that, and I did not know who the father was. How could I? I lost the child, but my aunt discovered my pregnancy, and she told my parents." She sighed. "They mourned me as if I were dead, and to them, I was, for I was no longer virtuous, no longer a fit wife for a noble. I had to earn my living then." Her brief smile was cynical, but she closed her eyes as if in pain. "I earned it holding fashionable salons to rival my aunt's, and I earned it on my back."

"I knew something had changed as soon as I lost the child. The sunlight hurt my eyes, and my skin burned easily. I grew afraid of fire. At first I thought it had something to do with the aftermath of the miscarriage. And then, my former lover came to me again, and I killed him. I killed him so swiftly that he did not know what had happened to him. But not before I found out why they had treated me so."

She said it simply, without emotion, as if she told a child's tale of long ago. But she lifted her eyes to his, and they were wide with anguish. "You see, they wished for eternal life. There are others like me—vampires. They had that vampire make me into one. And then each one of them would use me again in the hope that I would make them vampires as well.

"Fools." She closed her eyes wearily. "It only gives eternal youth and quick healing; a vampire might be killed by misadventure, or fire, or . . . or being confined in a holy place. I killed my lover out of the blood-thirst that grew from my rage. And when I found what I could do, I killed as many of those men as I could who had tied me up and used me, when they came to use me again. Each time I fed on their blood, I grew stronger.

"So you see, monsieur, I am a killer." Simone smiled bitterly. "And the irony of it is, I cannot tell the difference between the blood-lust and the lust of the body. One spurs the other. You see how impossible it is, this relationship you propose. I am death to whoever would use me so."

Michael sat at the other end of the sofa, various emotions flitting across his face. "How fitting," he said at last on a shaking laugh. "I have courted Death all my life. And here I am, courting you again, and have even bedded you." He grinned and rose from the sofa. "Now, that is something to boast about." His voice was firm now and he gave an elegant bow as if to an audience. " 'Attention, *mesdames et monsieurs*! Observe the amazing Michael Corday—he has made love with death itself, and has lived to tell the tale.' "

Anger flared hot and Simone felt her hands curl into fists. "You mock me."

"No, *ma petite*. I do not mock you. I am merely saying that it is a very dramatic story. Drink blood? I doubt it." He gazed at her assessingly. "Where is the proof?"

Simone rose from the sofa, unsteadily, but her feet became firm as she stepped toward him. She seized the lapels of his coat, hard, so that the sound of tearing cloth echoed in the room. "Remember this, Michael?" she said, fury underneath the seductive softness she put in her voice. She kissed him, then bit his lip, laughing quietly when he pulled away a hairsbreadth. She ran her finger across the welling cut, and licked away the blood. "Remember when I did this?" She kissed him again and sucked on his lower lip. He groaned and pulled her to him, deepening the kiss. Heat flared under her skin, her senses rose to an intense pitch, and the blood-thirst seared her mind, reducing her to the near-instinctive hunt.

No!

She pushed him away, panting, then slapped him. She wanted to make him angry, angry enough to go away and not be a temptation to her. Dear God, she wanted him, wanted everything he said to be true, that he was her husband, that he wanted her. But it was a stupid wish. She watched with anguished satisfaction when a matching anger grew in his eyes. "You fool. I could have killed you then. I was an inch away from it. I could kill you now," she whispered. "I want you to go away from me. I want you to leave me alone. It was foolish of both of us to think we could work together."

He seized her arm and then her chin, making her look at him. "Too late, madame. Yes: *madame*. Will you nill you, you will be my wife. You were the one who put me in the role of husband, and so we are set on this course, whether you are well or ill, vampire or no, I do not care. We have agreed that we have little choice in going to Paris together, to divert what suspicion we can from our identities. I will not explain it again to you, for you know full well what you agreed to." He laughed shortly. "So, you are a killer. Madame, we are well matched, indeed."

The pain of his grip on her sense-heightened skin banished the haze of blood-thirst from her mind. Simone swallowed. Of course. Of course what he said was right. She had agreed to it, on her honor, and as the only sensible way to accomplish their mission. She would have remembered it if entering the sanctuary had not disabled her so.

She moved from him, straightening her spine and lifting her chin. "My apologies, monsieur," she said. "My conduct was unworthy of a de la Fer. It was a momentary aberration and will not happen again."

"Ah, Simone . . ." He lifted his hand, as if to touch her cheek, then turned away. "Is your priest near?"

"He probably is." She frowned. "I wonder why Père Dumont is here? I had not heard that Père Roucault had called for him or needed his help."

"I am here." They turned toward the door, and the abbé entered.

"You were listening!" Simone exclaimed.

"Of course I was listening," Père Dumont said complacently. "I did not know this man, and you were in a weakened state. You seemed to, ah, be familiar with him, so I thought it wise to let you speak in relative privacy, but stayed close in case he should do you harm."

She nearly laughed in spite of herself. The slight, elderly man was no match for Michael, although she supposed he might serve as a momentary diversion.

"Monsieur, will you do us the honor of marrying us?"

Simone whirled to look at Michael. His face was again impassive, perhaps a little stern. "Do not listen to him, *mon Père*. He does not know what he asks."

The priest looked at them gravely. "I think he does, mademoiselle." His eyes suddenly twinkled. "And I think he is more than a match for you."

"How can you *say* that? *Mon Père*, you know above everyone else what I am!"

"Yes, and so, it seems, does he. If it does not bother him, why should it you?" the priest said reasonably.

Simone put her hand to her spinning head. "It is not

right—you know what I am capable of doing. What if I should kill him some day?"

Michael's smile was wry. "I would do my best to prevent it, I assure you. Besides, you restrained yourself quite well last night." The smile he turned on her was the most seductive she had ever seen on a man, and the retort she had gathered together was choked off by her sudden cough. A beseeching glance at Père Dumont elicited no response from the old man but a deep blush.

"Are you a Catholic, monsieur?" the priest asked instead.

Michael raised his brows. "No. But I am sure there is a way around that to a marriage, yes? Besides, it is important we be married . . . for the sake of her soul, of course."

Dumont coughed and Simone was sure he had suppressed a laugh. "It is most unusual, monsieur."

"These are unusual times, are they not?" Michael replied. "She considers herself cursed. Do you?"

The priest hesitated. "From what I have been able to determine, it seems she is."

"Can her condition improve if she lives in a state of sin?"

"No, of course not." Dumont's voice was firm.

"Would marriage improve the state of her soul?"

"Insofar as it is holy matrimony, yes."

"Therefore," Michael replied smoothly, "it seems best she marry me to improve it and improve her condition as well."

The priest opened his mouth and closed it, clearly feeling in a quandary. "Your logic is faultless," he said finally.

Simone looked from one to another. "You *agree* with him, Père Dumont?" Indignation rose as she turned to Michael. "And *you*! *You* dare speak of the state of my soul, as if *yours* was completely spotless?"

Michael grinned and moved to the sofa, sitting on it in

a leisurely way, as if he thought to stay there permanently. "No doubt holy matrimony would improve the state of my soul as well."

This time the priest definitely choked off a laugh, but he managed to bring a stern look to his expression. "No doubt, monsieur," he replied. "Very well. I agree, you should be married."

"What?" Simone cried. "Am I not to have a say in this?"

Both men turned to look at her, brows raised. "Of course," they said at the same time.

"Well, then, I shall not wed."

Père Dumont gazed at her gravely. "Is that what you wish? Do you wish not to be married and to live in sin, *ma fille*? Just when you have improved in your condition lately?"

"But he is not Catholic!" she protested.

The priest hesitated. "It can be done if he agrees to allow you to practice your faith, and if any, ah, children you have are raised in the faith." He looked a question at Michael.

"Of course," he said. "I will sign whatever you wish."

"With a false name, I am sure," Simone retorted.

Michael looked at her calmly. "No, I will sign my real name, and you will sign yours. It will be a true marriage according to your church."

"Why?" She gazed at him, not understanding. How could he wish to wed her knowing all that he knew now?

He smiled slightly. "Because I am tired of you leaving me every evening and not telling me where you have gone. Literally tired. It does my sleep no good, worrying over you, *ma petite*."

She looked away, not sure of his meaning. But his smile had been tender, not angry, not cold or calculating. "I don't know!" she cried out.

Michael looked at Père Dumont. "Perhaps she would

be best talking with you, monsieur, and not arguing with me. You have known her longer." He turned to Simone. "But be quick. Dawn comes, and we cannot be away from the inn for long before we are noticed. Indeed, I am afraid we already have been seen."

"No!"

"Yes. I am afraid I have . . . disabled one of du Maurier's men in the vestibule."

Alarm seized Simone's heart. "You have not killed him?"

Michael looked insulted. "No, of course not. I remembered that you did not like killing, and suspected that you would especially not like it done at a church. Since I wished to please you—and you must admit you would be less inclined to marry me had I killed him—I merely knocked him out." He nodded at Père Dumont. "You might have your friend take care of him."

"Monsieur!" the priest exclaimed. "I cannot have such a thing going on in this church! Père Roucault cannot afford to have such attention brought to him; he is in a precarious position already for harboring me here."

"Père Dumont," Michael said, his voice barely patient. "It was necessary, I assure you. Had I not disposed of him in that way, he would have seen you, and I suspect you would not have wanted that, since your presence here was not . . . expected, I assume?"

Dumont pressed his lips together disapprovingly. "It is as you say," he said after a moment, then moved to the door. "I will see that Père Roucault tends the man; then I will speak to Mlle. de la Fer." He closed the door firmly as he left.

Simone stared at Michael. "You wish to have a hold on me. That is why you want to marry me. The marriage itself means nothing to you." *I mean nothing to you,* she thought.

He smiled slightly. "You are wrong," he said. "It means a great deal."

"To the mission, of course."

"Among other things."

She twisted her hands together. Other things. She wondered what they were. "What do *I* mean to you?" she said at last.

Silence. He looked away from her, and the lamp that Père Dumont had brought made a silhouette of his profile, leaving his expression in shadows.

"Hope," he said softly, then gazed at her, his eyes dark and fiery. She could not look away. He glanced toward the door. "Your priest comes." Simone closed her lips. She would ask at another time what he meant.

Père Dumont entered again, and shot a reproving look at Michael. "Père Roucault is tending the man's wound. Your blow was quite disabling, monsieur. He is only just becoming conscious."

Michael nodded. "Good."

The priest shook his head. "I would almost counsel Mlle. de la Fer not to marry you, if I did not think it would be her chance to reconcile her soul to God." He pursed his lips in thought. "And if I did not also think you say these things merely to be outrageous."

Michael grinned and bowed.

"Père Roucault will conduct the marriage," Dumont continued. Simone opened her mouth to protest, but the priest held up a hand. "I cannot. In truth, if I were to sign my name to any document in this church, I would put him in danger."

Michael gave him a sharp look. "Two marriage documents, then," he said. "One true, one false, should du Maurier or any of his subordinates question your friend."

The priest nodded. "Yes, that is wise. We will keep the true one hidden." He held out a hand to Simone.

"Mademoiselle, it is time you gave your confession, whether you mean to wed or no."

Simone glanced at Michael, but he said nothing, merely giving her a challenging look. She shrugged, and turned to the priest, following him out the door.

A clock chimed somewhere in the church. It was indeed a few hours until dawn. Simone wet her lips anxiously. Whatever she decided, she needed to decide soon. Père Dumont motioned her to the confessional, and she entered it. It smelled of cedar and beeswax, sending her back to the days when she made her confession regularly at the usual time of the week during the day, not in surreptitious moments. She crossed herself as she heard the priest settle himself in the room next to her. "*Mon Père,* forgive me, for I have sinned . . ."

She made her confession, and accepted the penance, noting with relief and hope that holding her cross stung even less than a few days ago. She began to rise.

"Wait, mademoiselle," Père Dumont said. "Have you made your decision? Will you wed this man?"

"I am afraid, *mon Père.*"

"Of him, mademoiselle?"

Simone paused. No. She was not afraid of Michael, even though she knew he was indeed quite deadly. She had never been afraid of him. She frowned. "I am not afraid of him. I do not think he would hurt me. He has not done so, and I think he would sooner hurt himself than me." She tested what she said in her mind. It felt right. He had asserted . . . what? That he was dangerous, true. But as far as she was concerned, he had only mentioned self-defense. She laughed slightly. "Indeed, he has come after me, sometimes I think out of mistrust, but certainly out of fear for me." She shook her head. "I do not understand it."

"Do you think he loves you?"

She swallowed. "Surely not." She laughed again. "*En*

vrai, he does not like to be bested or contradicted, and since I contradict him at every turn, he wishes me to be with him to get the best of me."

Père Dumont chuckled, then his voice sobered. "Perhaps. But consider this, mademoiselle: He knows what you are and what you have been. Even so, he is willing to enter into holy matrimony with you. Both of us know what sins still lie on your soul, and who knows what his are. This would go a long way to reconciling you to God, and cleansing you of sins that still claim you. Perhaps it might be the saving of him, as well. How could this be wrong?"

He does not love me. "It might help me be rid of this curse," she said instead. "And I must be practical. It would certainly explain why both of us came to this church in the early morning."

"True." She could hear Père Dumont shift his robes on the other side of the screen. "I will be frank, mademoiselle. It would be of help to me, also." He sighed. "There is bad news. Titon's inn has been confiscated."

"No!" Anguish clutched at Simone's heart. "Did I— Was I the one who led the agents to them?"

"You may be at ease, mademoiselle; you did not. Titon spoke a little too freely of his sentiments when he thought no one was listening, alas. Luckily, the agents did not discover the hidden stairway, and Titon and his family escaped that way."

She breathed a sigh of relief. "*Le Dieu merci!* But what of you?"

"I go to Paris. There are lost souls and wounded bodies in need of me there, I think, and I am so old that no one can think me a threat—or even remember my existence." She could hear the smile in the priest's voice. "I have been a servant in Titon's inn for long enough that any who see me would remember me as that rather than a priest. And if any remember me as a renegade priest . . . well, I am old and tired, and have seen too many tragedies, mademoiselle. I would go without regret."

"But . . . but what will I do? Who will I go to? What of the cardinal's letter about my curse?"

"I have directed that any letters go to your home by secret courier, should anything happen to me. As for who you will go to . . . you will go to your husband, Mademoiselle de la Fer, and stay steadfast in your faith."

Simone drew her arms about her shoulders and shivered. If she had felt alone and abandoned before, it had not been to this extent. When she had been cast off from her family, she had at least friends for a while, and she still found a way to learn news of her family. Even when they died, she had an anchor in Père Dumont and in her faith. Now . . . now the good priest was leaving for Paris to minister to those who needed his services.

"We cannot travel together, of course," she said, glad there was only a slight tremble in her voice and not the weeping she felt. "But perhaps I will see you there once I am done with my mission with Mich— Corday."

"May it be so, mademoiselle." He sighed again, and she saw his shadow against the screen stand. She stood as well. "Let us go. Père Roucault will be done with his patient, and I will make sure that we have two marriage lines for you and your fiancé to sign."

She opened the door of the confessional, and managed to smile at the old priest. She took his hand. "I shall miss you, *mon Père*."

He smiled gently. "Our parting is not forever, Simone de la Fer. It is a change, and it is not as if you have not had to deal with change before, and very bad change at that."

She smiled wryly. "But I do not have to like it."

"Very few of us do, mademoiselle," Père Dumont said, and his eyes twinkled. "Very few of us do." He sighed. "Certainly not an old man like me." He motioned toward the room where she had been taken after she had fainted in the sanctuary. "Go back to your fiancé. Let him know your decision."

Simone nodded.

She hesitated, resting her hand on the door. It was near dawn. She had made her decision.

Michael sat at a table, turning the pages of a book. He looked up. "Hello, *ma petite*."

Simone gazed about the room before she spoke, not wanting to meet his eyes at first. She had been so focused on their discussion earlier that she had not taken in that they had been in a small library. Her doll lay on the table before Michael, and she took it up, smoothing down its hair.

He gave her a quizzical look. "It is yours, then?"

"Yes. It was mine when I was a little girl, and now forms part of my disguise." He raised his brows in question, and she could not help letting out a mischievous chuckle. "It's the hump on my back that the broadsheets describe." She sobered. "My very senile nurse brought it to me, saying she had saved the heir of the de la Fers." She shook her head. "Aside from my mother's jewels, it's the only thing I have left of my family."

"But the château—"

"Is mine only until I die and only if I defend it, and then, who knows? For all the government is concerned, it belongs to nobody but malicious ghosts who frighten away tenants within a fortnight." She glanced at the window, and noticed a faint lightening of the sky. "Père Dumont will bring the papers, Michael. His friend will perform the ceremony," she said.

He looked at her gravely. "Thank you," he said.

"I hope you will not regret this."

He smiled. "I have regretted many things, Simone. What is one more to all that? But I think I will not regret this one."

"But why?"

He rose from the chair and took her hand in his. "Hush," he said, and pulled her in his arms and kissed her. "Let us go. It will be light soon."

After the brief ceremony under Père Roucault's disapproving gaze, Simone's hand still shook from the effects of her fainting spell when she signed the papers. One showed the name she had given the magistrate, and one showed her true name: Simone Marie Bernadette de la Fer. She watched as Michael wrote the false name with a bold hand and then paused over the second. He glanced at her, an amused expression flitting across his face, wrote quickly, snatched up the paper, and gave it to the priest before Simone could see what he had written.

"It is best that you do not know," he said when he saw that she was about to protest. "If we are caught and interrogated, all you would be able to give is a false name, or say that I have given out so many different names that you do not know which one is the true one. They'll know you for an innocent then, and your chances of survival will be better."

The two priests nodded in agreement, and Père Roucault nodded in grudging approval. Père Dumont lifted his hand in blessing. "Go now, my children. Do good in the world."

Simone crossed herself and nodded, then glanced at Michael. He looked at the priests for a moment, and his gaze flickered to the cross that stood at one end of the library. He took her hand and kissed it. "Come, wife. Dawn draws near, and we do not want to keep our friend du Maurier waiting." She nodded, and after a quick kiss on the blushing cheek of Père Dumont, took Michael's hand and left the church.

Chapter 12

SIMONE AND CORDAY ENCOUNTERED NO more agents on the way back to the inn, though Corday was sure they were still there, watching. He thought of how he might approach whatever information du Maurier might have received from them the next morning. Taking the offense rather than the defense would be the best response, he thought. There was nothing like basing one's lies on the truth to convince others of their veracity.

There was still more than an hour before the dawn. Simone seemed to doze as she sat behind him on the horse, leaning her cheek against his back. She said nothing, but he could feel the rise and fall of her chest as she breathed.

He shook his head, wondering if he had fallen into a dream, or perhaps had succumbed to insanity at last. He touched the bite on his lip with his tongue and winced. That was very real, and since he was not one to have fantasies and since he had not ever had delusions, he could only conclude that he was not insane at all or in a dream, but that he had indeed married Simone and that she was a vampire. It was the only logical conclusion, and it was clear the very scholarly and intellectual priests believed the same. He had examined the books and the correspondence of the two men while they were away, and there was no hint of fantastical imaginings in any of their letters. Indeed, their discussion of Simone's condition was almost scientific in their tone.

He wanted a natural explanation for her condition, for he did not believe in the supernatural, or in the divine, for that matter. He had seen no evidence of either, and what he could not see or discern held little interest for him except perhaps as an intellectual exercise. Still, he had little doubt of her abilities or her sensitivities. Her sensitivities could be a liability, to be sure. However, he himself had seen her swiftness, her strength, and her potential for deadliness. She could have other gifts as well, all of which would be strategic assets in any mission, for no one would expect them of a woman, and a supposed pregnant woman with morning sickness, at that.

He heard a sigh from her, and she rubbed her cheek against his back as a trusting child might in sleep. A twisting sensation entered his heart, and he felt regret that he had forced her into what she considered a real marriage with him. He would have preferred that she had entered it wholeheartedly. But he could not afford that. He felt instinctively, intuitively, that this would be his last mission. He did not believe in the supernatural, but he did believe in instinct and intuition, for these things had saved his life more than a few times. If this would be his last mission, then at least he could pretend at living a man's normal life before the end.

He laughed. A normal life. What he had done—married a woman who called herself a vampire—was hardly normal. It was insane. He wondered if it were partly Simone's fault, something she had done to him, for he was not a man who easily gave in to impulse. It was typical of him, however, that he should choose the most strange and bizarre way of wedding, and a mate that most men would avoid. Still, though he did not know what to make of Simone, she would make what life he had yet to live more interesting.

Ah, Simone. She was, frankly, irresistible, whatever she was, and he could not have enough of her. Delusion or no, vampire or not, he had not ever met her like in sheer vividness and strength of personality. When he was a child, he had had a German nurse who had told him a story of a princess whose skin was white as snow, lips as red as blood, and hair as black as ebony. That could describe Simone, but she was no fearful woman-child who ran away from forest noises, but one who would run with wolves and fight as fiercely. He had never met a woman like her, passionate, brave, and sensual beyond imagining, who made him laugh and feel more alive than he had ever done before.

He closed his eyes and wet his suddenly dry lips. He had not felt this alive in a long time, not since he was a youth. There was no real reason why he should feel any different with her than without. He only knew he could not bear to have her leave him, and that old emotions— damnably soft emotions he had thought he had rid himself of—shifted their way to the surface of his heart when she looked at him with her large, dark, vulnerable eyes. She trusted him. Her actions showed it, whatever she may have said. She was fool enough to trust him . . . and he was fool enough to want to show he could be trusted.

His feelings made no sense to him. The emotions between a man and a woman—other than pure physical lust— had never made any sense to him when he had watched their manifestation in other men. They still did not, and he had no faith in such things as marriage, whether civil or religious. They were words said in front of witnesses only, easily reneged upon because of the quixotic emotions that brought a man and a woman together in the first place.

Very well, then. He would see how he fared with the marriage, and it would be better for him if he focused on the real, practical reason he had proposed it in the first place—to keep Simone from disappearing at unexpected moments. She had agreed to obey him when she had said her vows. She was clearly religious and had a sense of honor, so therefore would do her best to keep to her vows and stay at his side this time. And, she would have protested harder if she had been totally against marriage to him. He knew her that much, at least.

A cock crowed in the distance, and Simone's body jerked against Corday's back at the sound. She drew away from him and looked about her. The sky was still dark, but she could see the large, white bulk of the inn before them, the form of an ostler shaking and shivering himself out of his sleep from the stables into the cold dawn air, and the clanking sounds of kitchen servants starting hearth fires and breakfast.

She became conscious of her arm bent awkwardly around a lump resting on her hip, and breathed a sigh of relief. She had forgotten her doll, but it seemed Michael had remembered it and had someone—perhaps Père Dumont—tie it to her waist. She must have fallen into a doze as soon as she had mounted the horse.

Corday said nothing as he helped her from the horse, and dismounted after her. She was content to let the silence be, for too much had happened this night, too quickly, and she had not yet even begun to assess all of it. Dawn was coming, and because of her weakness, all she wished for was rest.

They entered the inn, and Corday called to a yawning

maid, asking her to wake them when Citoyen du Maurier awoke. Simone placed her foot on the first step to the chambers above, but a creak at the top of the stairs made her pause and look up. Alarm flared. She was glad of her night sight, for she was able to discern the face clearly, even though the dim light from the fire barely pierced the top of the stairs. It was the taller Englishman she had seen earlier. Quickly, she turned and pushed Corday back, then seized his arm, taking him to a near corner of the common room. She placed her back at the corner and pulled him to her, and looked into his startled face.

"Do not look around," she whispered. "It is one of the men I saw earlier."

He leaned toward her, and put a hand on the wall beside her. He bent his head a little, as if he were going to kiss her. "Tell me what he looks like," he said. He put his arm around her waist.

Simone sighed with relief; he was quick of wit, *le Dieu merci,* and did not question her command. "He is tall, with dark hair, straight and unpowdered," she whispered. "His nose is long and like an eagle's. His chin is square, and there is a small scar near the left side of his mouth. His eyebrows are thin and arched; his face is at repose, but he looks as if he were surprised." Michael's arms tightened around her.

"You can see all that, even in this light?"

She hesitated. "Yes."

"Interesting."

She rested her cheek against Corday's neck, watching the man cross the room to the back of the inn. The firelight glinted on his hand—a ring. "He wears a large ring on the middle finger of his right hand."

"Is there one on his index finger?"

"I cannot—" The man paused in the middle of the

room and turned toward them. "Kiss me, quickly!" she hissed.

His lips met hers, and she sighed. It was pleasant, but she sensed a preoccupation behind his kisses, and it dissatisfied her. *Keep your mind on the matter at hand,* she told herself sternly.

"You, girl!" the man called to her. "Cease your play and attend me."

Le Diable! She did not want to draw attention to them at all. She pushed Michael away from her slightly, and gazed long into his eyes. "Listen to what I say to him," she whispered. She turned to the man and put her hands to her cheeks, as if holding down a blush, then straightened herself haughtily. "You will not address me like that, citoyen. I am not a servant; I am merely fetching my drunken husband before he becomes too ill." She pointed toward the kitchen. "You will find your servant there." She heard Michael moan suddenly and watched him bend over, holding himself up by a trembling hand on one of the tables. "*Mon Dieu!* He drank too much last night. Ai!" she cried, as Michael made a retching sound. "Excuse me, citoyen, but I must get my husband upstairs." The man made a disgusted face and turned away toward the kitchen. She sighed with relief and seized Corday's arm, then pulled him to the stairs as soon as the man's back was to them.

They reached their room. Simone shut the door with a decided slam and turned to Corday. "You fool. You see what you almost caused to happen. We were almost discovered. You should not have followed me to the church. Had I discovered him alone when I came back, I could have engaged the man in conversation. But no, you could not keep away, and thus we have no information at all."

Corday said nothing for a moment, but the muscles in his jaw looked strained. He looked away, staring into the fire in the hearth, then sat on a chair nearby. "You are right, of course," he said. "It would have been better if I had stayed here." His admission startled her; it was not said jokingly, nor did he follow it with a quip. He pressed his hands briefly against his eyes, and for a moment Simone thought she saw a deep weariness in them when he brought his hands down to rest on his thighs. Then a slight smile came to his lips. "But you mentioned the Englishmen in your note to make me stay here, admit it. Did you not think I might not wish to be recognized?"

Simone frowned. She *had* thought her mention of the Englishmen would distract him from her, and that he would investigate them as part of his mission.

"Is there anything else you should tell me?" he asked, before she could reply. She quickly described them and told them they had sought out du Maurier and Hervé. He sat up straighter.

"Ah," he said, then sighed. "The dead have risen." He caught her questioning look. "The men, as you suspect, are indeed Englishmen. I recognized the voice of the one we encountered downstairs. He was supposed to be dead—as was the one the maid described."

She gazed at him warily. "Did you try to kill them?"

He raised his brows, and a humorous glint entered his eyes. "No, I try not to kill my compatriots, especially ones I know well. I was told they were dead."

"But they are not."

He nodded. "But they are not." He gazed at her with a rueful smile. "Which means I cannot make such a mistake again as I did below stairs. I . . . we cannot trust anyone, Simone. I wonder if we should go with du Maurier after all, since these men have talked with Hervé."

Simone frowned. "But if they are your compatriots, perhaps they are talking to Hervé to accomplish the same thing you are."

He shook his head. "I cannot assume that. My superior told me of their deaths. If they are not dead, then either he was mistaken, or he lied. If he lied, then their presence means nothing good to me. If he did not lie, then he was misled, and that does not bode well for this mission, for it means he was misled for a reason, and that these two men may have a part in the misdirection. It would also explain why there were so many revolutionary agents to greet you—and me—at the shore a few days ago. It is possible someone told them to expect a spy."

"Perhaps," Simone said. "Or it could be that they had followed me in some way."

"Have you encountered this many agents before?"

Simone hesitated. "No . . . although it would not be beyond reason." She smiled wryly. "I am a desperate outlaw, you know."

"I know." He fell silent, staring into the fire. Simone gazed at him, saying nothing, for he seemed deep in thought.

She thought over their situation; if these men were indeed traitors to their country, then it would be best to stay far away from them. It would mean parting ways with du Maurier and Hervé, and traveling without a coach, but perhaps she and Michael could use a wagon from the inn. She grimaced. A wagon would not be as swift as a coach. Perhaps it would be better if they traveled by horse. It would mean she would have to find a hiding place during the day, for she wouldn't have the cover of the coach to protect her. She sighed. "Should we, then, part ways with du Maurier?" she asked.

Michael turned toward her. "No . . ." he said slowly. "No, I think not. If we left after saying we wanted their company, any suspicion they have of us would be confirmed. Much better to continue as we have been, and keep our eyes and ears open." He smiled slightly. "And if they do suspect us, then how much easier it is for them to think they have trapped us, and have us travel with them to Paris, where we can be tried and convicted for the desperate outlaws we are."

"Let them think we are desperately stupid outlaws, then," Simone said. She gazed at his shadowed eyes and at how he bent his head and pressed the palm of his hand to his temple. "I, for one, shall be glad of the comfort of a coach instead of a rough wagon or horseback."

"Yes" was all he said, but it was almost a whisper. *He is fatigued,* Simone thought, and wondered how long he had been at this business of espionage. She looked at the lines between his eyebrows and thought perhaps he had been at it for a long time.

"We should rest," she said. "It will be a long journey, and we cannot afford to be tired. Perhaps we can find another coach, and travel separately. I could beg severe illness."

"No." Michael shook his head, smiling briefly. "Not until we near Paris. Their coach will be the fastest tomorrow." He gave her a searching look. "But we should indeed rest."

She smiled. "Sleep, then," she said, rose from her chair, and stepped toward the bed. She stumbled, and he caught her in his arms, then gently laid her on the bed.

"How are you feeling?" he asked.

"Better."

"How long will it take for you to recover totally?"

She grimaced. "It depends. A day or two, since we are to travel by daylight."

"Will anything shorten it?"

"Sleep, or— Sleep," she said, and her eyes slid away from his.

"You really should not lie, *ma petite,*" he said. "You are very bad at it."

She laughed weakly but said, "It is not a lie that I will improve with sleep."

"But there is something else, isn't there?" He sat on the edge of the bed and took her hand in his, kissing her knuckles and then the palm of her hand. "If you don't tell me, I could always seduce it from you." He grinned, letting her know he would do it if she wished.

Her breath left her, and she shivered as she looked at him. She would not be averse to it, he thought. Neither would he, for that matter, if it would be anything like their lovemaking last night.

"You would like that, wouldn't you?" He moved over her. She said nothing, but her eyes were wide now, her breath coming faster. "*I* would like it," he said. "I would like it very much." He pressed his lips to hers, gently. "But if you don't, you must tell me. I'll stop immediately."

He pulled the fichu from her dress and undid the rags that she had wrapped around her head, and her hair came loose, spilling over the pillows.

"You are doing this on purpose," she said breathlessly.

"Yes," he said. "Most of what I do is on purpose." He untied the laces at the front of her dress, parting the bodice.

"You know that lust and blood-thirst are twined within me, that I cannot separate the two." Her voice was desperate.

"I had forgotten it until now," he said. "Thank you for reminding me." He reached down and pulled his dagger and sheath from his boot, and the dagger clattered to the floor. He curled her fingers around the sheath. "Is that what you mean?" His hand slid over hers, rubbing her fingers into the indentations she had made in the leather earlier.

"Yes. No . . . yes." Her voice trembled.

He kissed the soft skin beneath her ear. "Are you

frightened? I will stop if you are." He slid his hand between the laces of her bodice and under her shift.

She raised her hands to his face. "No," she said, whispering fiercely. "Not for myself. For you. You should be." And she pulled him down and kissed him.

She pulled at his clothes, and he grasped her hands. "Gently, sweet one. I have run out of thread to repair my shirts." He rose and pulled off his coat, shirt, and boots. When she sat up to pull off her bodice, he gently pushed her down again. "I'll do it, *ma petite.*" Slowly he untied the already loosened bodice and corset and tugged them off her shoulders, so they lay open, a frame for her body. He untied the ribbon that held her skirt on, and pulled it off, slowly slipping off her clothes until she wore only her shift. She stared at him, still, her breath coming quickly. "There, now," he said, and lay next to her again. "Slowly." He gazed into her eyes, and touched her face with his fingers, stroking softly. She closed her eyes and moved so that her lips kissed the palm of his hand.

"Ah, Simone, what you do to me." He laughed quietly. "You say you could kill me, that you are a danger to me, but you have already been the death of me, for I am in constant danger of loving you."

Her eyes flew open, and the hope in the depths of them struck him hard and painfully. "Do you?" she whispered.

His hand drifted lower, stroking her neck and pushing her shift off one shoulder. His fingers curved around her breast, his thumb gently circling around the nipple. She drew in a sharp breath and her body trembled.

"I don't know, *ma petite,*" he said at last. He frowned contemplatively, his hand almost absently wending its way over her shift and down to her hip. "I only know I love this." He kissed her, deeply, tasting her lips and her mouth, feeling her body rise against his. "And this." He moved his kisses across her cheek and to the soft skin at her throat. His hand crept lower, gathering the cloth of her shift up until skin met skin. "And this," he breathed against her lips.

His fingers brushed the curling hair between her legs and she moaned and pressed her lips to his, frantically. "Very much this," he said, pulling away for a moment. He took in a deep breath, controlling his own response. He moved his hand away, and she cried out a protest, but he smothered it with another kiss. "Wait, *mon cœur*. It will be better for the waiting." He pushed her shift to her waist and kissed her there and lower, touching his lips and tongue to all the sensitive places he knew she had. She wailed, and her hips moved, her hands grasping the bedsheets frantically. "Please," she said, panting. "Please."

Corday took in another deep breath, willing control over himself. Quickly he grasped the hem of her shift and pulled it over and off her body. He undid his trousers, but her hand pushed his aside, and pulled apart the soft wool opening, grasping the hard length of him.

"God." The word burst from him, and he almost lost control. Her hand slipped up and down and her other hand came up behind his head and she pressed her mouth to his. "Now," she murmured. "Now."

"No. Not now." He moved a little aside and traced a line with his fingers from her belly to the dark curls lower down, and slipped his hand between her legs. "First this," he said, and touched her woman's bud with a finger. She made a choking sound. "And then this." He pushed his fingers inside, moving in and out, and she let out a harsh groan. "And then, and then, sweet one—" He moved on top of her and put himself at her entrance, and breathed deeply again. "And then this." He thrust deep.

She cried out and her legs came up, forcing him even deeper, and he almost spilled into her, but he took his hand between his teeth and bit down, letting the pain force down the ecstasy. He rested his forehead on her breast, easing his breath, and then slowly withdrew.

She opened her eyes, bleary with passion. "The sheath," she said, and groaned as he pushed in again.

"What if I didn't give it to you?"

"I would hurt you."

"How?"

She turned her face away, but her hips rose and her breathing came fast again as he moved within her. "How?" he said again.

"No," she murmured, and her lower lip trembled. She stopped her movements against him and held still.

He brushed his hand against her cheek. "Don't cry, sweet one. I would not hurt you."

She looked at him, and the old sorrow he saw not long ago was clear in her eyes. "Vampires cannot weep, Michael." She touched his face gently with her fingers, then let her hand drop to the bedsheets. "I would hurt you."

"How? Tell me. You are my wife now. What we do in this bed is no sin, by your beliefs."

A flare of anger replaced the sorrow. "Taking your blood would be a sin. By anyone's belief it would be." She twisted away from him, but he held her firm beneath him.

He placed his lips on hers, gently. "But not if it was given, yes?" he murmured.

She let out a hopeless laugh. "There is none that would give it freely, trust me."

"I would."

Simone stared at him. He had whispered it; surely he could not have said what she thought he said.

"What?" she asked.

"I would," he said. "Give it to you." He closed his eyes and moved within her and she shivered involuntarily, the heat mounting in her loins once again. "Sweet Simone," he murmured. "Sweet." He slowed his motion, sighing reluctantly. "I would give that and more for a lifetime of this." A thread of regret, as if he thought he had not a lifetime, wove beneath his words. He moved apart a little, to the side of the bed, reached down for something, then rose over her again. The firelight from the hearth glinted on the metal in his hand. "Where do you take it, *ma petite*?" he asked, folding Simone's fingers around the hilt. "From the throat, the wrist?"

"No!" She threw the dagger across the room, and struggled under him, but he held her firm. She cursed her weakness from the nearness of the dawn, from her exposure to the church sanctuary, and cursed the still-flaming heat in her body. She wanted desperately to weep. "Don't— don't! I don't—" She drew in a deep breath. "You think that is the way I take blood. You think to mock me." Anger flared as she looked at his face, his expression both curious and aloof. "You do not know what you are dealing with."

"That is often the case in my occupation, but I eventually learn what I need to know." He lifted his upper body away from her, but pressed more deeply within her. "Tell me, then, Simone. Tell me what I am dealing with." His voice held both a challenge and deep desire, and her body shook with hopeless anger and passion's fire in her belly. *He would not understand, he does not believe.* She closed her eyes, wishing she did not love the feel of him, for then she would have the strength to part from him and keep from taking what he offered. But he did not believe, and though it was too late to refuse marriage, she could at least offer him the truth of experience. Despair threatened to overcome her, but she forced it down, and let her anger flare.

"This," she said, and seized his wrist. Her teeth grazed his skin, and she barely kept herself from sinking them deeply into it. But it was enough to open the skin and let out some blood. She put her lips upon the cuts and sucked hard.

Michael let out a surprised grunt of pain, and she gazed at him to see the fear and disgust she was sure he would show. There was nothing but a brief confusion. Power surged into her as the blood seeped down her throat, and the power flowed to where she and Michael were joined. She bucked against him, and this time he voiced a groan. A red haze came over her vision, and she sank her teeth a little deeper, mindlessly taking in the power. Her senses heightened, and her skin grew acutely sensitive. She could hear his breath catch, and knew he was sinking into the sensual haze that overcame those whose blood she took. He grew inside of her, harder, and began to move. The rasp of the cloth of his trousers on her skin became a pleasure-pain, and she reached down and tugged them lower, smoothing her hand up to his back. He thrust harder.

"God, Simone!"

She could feel all of him inside, hot and heavy. She bit deeper, and the heat seized her muscles, shaking her. His other hand moved beneath her, and she raised her legs over him. "God, now, Simone!"

A burst of heat and light blazed across the red haze of her vision, and sanity returned. She forced herself to release his wrist, thrusting up to him again and again, crying out at the pleasure that cut into her like a knife. He lifted his head, arching his body to meet hers, let out a groaning sigh, and she felt warmth spill inside of her.

He let himself down on her slowly, his arms trembling. He kissed her neck, then her lips before she could pull away. He opened his eyes, staring at her, clearly startled.

"Blood." He touched his hand to his lips and gazed at the red that smudged his fingers.

She pressed her lips together, the sensual haze suddenly gone from her, and tried to push him off. She had to get away. He would curse her now, for how could he not now understand what she was and what she had done?

"It's true, then."

"Yes, it's true," she said. "Did I not tell you?" She put her hands over her face. "I told you! But you would not believe." She felt him shift from atop her, but he did not leave the bed. Instead, a loud ripping noise sounded in the room. She dropped her hands and looked at him.

He sat on the bed, wrapping the hem of her shift around his wrist.

"My shift!"

He gazed at her, a slight smile on his lips. "I think it's only fair, considering you caused the wound, *ma petite*."

She stared at him, open-mouthed. "You do not mind?"

"Of course I mind," he said. "I dislike bleeding all over the bedsheets."

"But I took your blood."

"I understand a little bloodletting is good for one's health," he replied, then secured the knot of cloth with his teeth. "Do dispense with the dramatics, love. It was just a little blood." But he did not look at her, and she could not discern his expression.

"It was more than a little," Simone whispered. Shame overcame her at her lack of control, at how she had let her anger bloom into blood-taking. She turned away, not wanting to look at him.

"Perhaps," he said, and she felt the bed sink next to her as he pulled her to him, her back against his chest. "I have let more blood than that, sweet one, with much less of a reward at the end." He stroked her belly, then held her breasts in his hands. She closed her eyes at the sensation.

"How do you feel now?" he whispered, his breath moving the hair around her ear.

"Good," she said. His hands moved lower.

"I know *that*," he said, chuckling. "I mean do you still feel weak?"

Her eyes flew open and she slapped his hands away, pulling the bedcovers over her breasts. "You are a bad man, Michael," she said severely, turning to look at him.

He laughed. "But you like it, admit it, *ma petite*."

She looked away, but then glanced at him again, her heart suddenly light. He was still smiling, and the only expression in his eyes was a curiosity as he gazed at her. Curiosity she could tolerate, for it was not the repugnance she feared. He still wanted to touch her, even after what she had done to him.

"I am strong now," she said. "*Merci*, Michael." She gazed at him, feeling oddly shy. No one had ever freely given her his blood. She had always taken it, and for Michael to have given it to her made her feel exposed, too vulnerable. She was not sure she liked the sensation.

His smile turned crooked. "No need to thank me, sweet one. I was curious after reading your priest's letters, and wanted to see if it were true."

"Ah," she said. Well, he was a man who liked to pierce mysteries, and that was all he had done. She should not have expected anything else.

A finger came up under her chin, making her look up at him. "Don't be despondent, *ma petite*." He grinned. "Curiosity was not my only motivation, and heaven knows I was well rewarded. You are strong again, and that helps our mission."

Somehow these words did not lighten her mood. She shrugged. "You are right, of course," she said. "We must be practical." She wished, however, that practicality was not his sole consideration.

He yawned and stretched out his arms, then shot her an amused look. "I would willingly do it again," he said. "Just let me know when you feel weak."

She looked at him, feeling uncertain of his meaning. Was he truly willing to make love with her again, for the sake of their mission? "I will not weaken that soon, unless I am exposed to a great deal of sunlight, or faint in a sanctuary again," she said.

He shook his head and pushed her down on the bed again. "Don't be so dense, my sweet. The letting of a little blood was well worth the rest of the experience." He let his hand trail down her breasts again. "And admit it, you like it as well."

She pushed him away, despite the return of desire. "It's still dangerous, Michael. I could take too much, even drain you."

"But you did not, this time."

"If I had taken blood from your neck, I could have."

He shrugged. "Then we shall be sure you take it from elsewhere." He stood up and then bent over to retrieve the dagger and its sheath from the floor. He pushed the dagger into the sheath, and put it on the small table next to the bed. He glanced at the window. "It's dawn. Dress well." He tossed her the dress, the shift, and the rags he had unwrapped from her. "I may be willing to make love to you again, but I have only so much blood, *ma petite*." He yawned again. "Meanwhile, I need more sleep. Let me know when the maid calls for us."

He got into bed, pulled up the covers to his chin, and closed his eyes. It was only a few minutes before Simone heard his breath deepen into the breathing of sleep.

She stared at him indignantly. She had bared her body and soul to him, had revealed a truth that should have shaken him down to the ground, and all he did was throw her clothes at her and fall asleep!

"Impossible man!" she muttered as she pulled on her clothes. "See if I will restrain myself the next time I take your blood."

But it was a false threat. She would do her utmost to save him from himself, for he had given her a gift no one else had given her: acceptance. Not even Père Dumont had given it to her totally; the priest asked that she change, and though she was more than willing to gain her humanity again, it was change nevertheless.

But Michael asked nothing of her but knowledge, knowledge of her own self, and her company on this mission, even when she revealed to him what she was. She sighed, and an unfamiliar warmth filled her heart. She felt, almost, as if she had come home and been enfolded in warm arms.

She dressed, then touched his face gently. She loved him. Even though their time together had been short so far, she knew this. Kind, dangerous, foolish Michael.

He murmured in his sleep, and moved so that his cheek fit her hand. "Simone," he whispered, but did not open his eyes.

"I love you," she whispered, so quietly that she was sure he did not hear.

A cock crowed in the distance, and she hastily drew up the rags around her face. She put a veil over her head, and pulled the cloak's hood over it. There, she was ready now. She looked at where Michael slept on the bed. It would be best if she did not lie there. The chair would do; then it would not be difficult for him to make her rise and go to the coach when it was time to go.

She pushed the chair near the fire, for she still felt the blood-thirst's sensitivity, and the room's damp cold air seeped into her clothes. She yawned. Perhaps a little nap would do her good. Just a little one . . .

Chapter 13

A KNOCK SOUNDED ON THE DOOR. "Citoyen Thibaut!" called the maid's voice. "You asked that you be wakened!" Wooden-clogged footsteps walked away from the other side of the door.

"Simone."

Corday groaned and turned over in the bed, feeling for her. He had had the wildest dream, that Simone had made love to him until he was mindless with lust and had pleasurably drained him down to his very bones. He felt hot, thinking of it, and his manhood stirred. "Simone," he murmured, and moved his hand over the bedsheets.

Nothing. He sat up and winced at the pain in his wrist.

A rag was wrapped around it, and blood stained the bed where he lay. No dream, then. He wet his suddenly dry lips.

A slight noise took his attention to the corner away from the window. A figure sat there, slumped, seeming asleep. It was clearly Simone—he recognized the cape around her shoulders. He looked again at his wrist, pressing on the inside of it, and grimaced. He had remembered it clearly after all. She *had* taken the blood he had half-seriously offered. He shook his head. His world seemed suddenly tilted, not what it was before. He looked from his wrist to Simone. She had taken his blood.

In all his years of soldiering and espionage, in all his travels, he had never seen her like. He shook his head. He must have dreamed . . . and yet, his wrist . . .

He left the bed, reaching for his trousers that had fallen to the floor. He pulled them and his stockings on, then walked to Simone. She breathed, but so slightly he could have taken her for dead if he had not seen her sleep so deeply before. Her head rested on one hand, her elbow resting in turn on the arm of the chair. He saw her hand was encased in a glove to the elbow, and the other that peeked from beneath her cape was also gloved. Her hood fell far over her face, and when he pushed it aside, he saw that she had once again wrapped her head in rags and that she wore a thick veil over her face. He circled around her, observing her stillness, the slow and shallow rise and fall of her body as she breathed. A creature of the night, she had said. He remembered her riding him on the bed, her eyes closed in passion, her breath coming short and fast.

Siren, succubus, queen of the night. She had brought him to *la petite mort*—the little death—with her body, and taken him to heaven with her sad eyes and pleas to possess her. He had bedded more than a few women in his life, but never like this.

Yet, here she was, dressed and covered like a common, modest woman of small means, sleeping as innocent as a babe.

He would not have believed all of it had it not been for the pain in his wrist and the rag—the hem of her shift, he remembered—wrapped around it. He circled around her again, as if she were a loaded weapon, ready to fire.

She was, at that. If everything he had perceived of her

were true—her speed, her strength, her fierceness—she would be an effective weapon against the revolutionary agents.

If, if, if. He shook his head. Part of him wanted it to be all an illusion, for if Simone had indeed supernatural powers, then it meant the supernatural was real. And if the supernatural was real . . . He thought of the church she had gone to and the priest, her confessor, and how she believed she would be done with her curse some day and return to humanity again.

No. All he knew was that she was not an illusion. His wrist ached. That was not an illusion, either. He thought over the night before, their trip to the church, their marriage. Their marriage. Good God. He was married to her, this woman who took blood.

This vampire.

The sun forced its way through the window curtains to cast knife-edged lines on the wood floor, lightening the dim room, and removing all vestiges of sleep and sense of illusion from his mind. He looked at Simone again. He had, indeed, married her. What was worse, he doubted she did cast a spell on him, and highly suspected that he had married her on his own volition. He would ask her, of course, if she had put a trance on him, and he would then know, for she was a poor liar.

In truth, he had no one to blame for his situation but himself. He let out an irritated breath. He had become impulsive of late, and his impulses centered around Simone.

Then, too, he did not really believe in the vows he had said, did he? He had gone through the ceremony only to ensure that Simone would be obliged to obey him. They had to go on with their mission, and he had married her so that she would not stray again. The man who had embroiled him in his mission and threatened England with the export of French terror awaited in Paris, and the sooner Corday found him and killed him, the better. Then, he would see what could be done about Simone.

Meanwhile . . . Corday remembered last night's lovemaking. There were certain advantages to being married. He smiled slightly. He would not want last night's experience to be a dream, for that would mean it could not happen again. His smile widened. He most definitely wanted it to happen again, and he would enjoy the challenge of making sure that she did not take his blood again—which was, frankly, not as much as the leeching and cuppings he had received on the battlefield in years past. He wondered if she had managed to restrain herself last night. Perhaps. His smile turned crooked. The possibility that she might not in the future would bring a certain edge to their lovemaking. But then, he was not averse to living on the knife's edge.

A clock chimed in the distance, and he realized they had slept longer than he had intended. They needed to leave. He touched her arm. "Simone," he said softly.

She did not rouse. He shook her arm harder. "Simone!" he said loudly. Still she did not move, and he frowned. "Devil take it!"

He contemplated her still form for a while, then shrugged and finished dressing. He packed his belongings in his knapsack, then turned to wake her.

He shook her once more, harder than before, but she merely shifted her position and moved no further. "Difficult," he murmured. He remembered what it took to wake her before, and hesitated. He would prefer not to hurt her or weaken her if he could avoid it. But she needed at least to walk to the coach that would be waiting for them; if she appeared too ill, he was sure du Maurier would object to her accompanying them, and it was necessary for them to do so for a while. Corday sighed.

He went to the windows, pushed back the curtains,

and peered out. Thick clouds covered the sky, and whatever bit of sunshine there might be. Perhaps it would not hurt much if she did not feel the direct sun upon her.

He left the curtain open, then walked to where Simone sat on her chair. He hesitated, then pushed back the cape that covered her arm. Slowly, he peeled down the glove that covered her elbow, exposing the pale skin beneath.

A start and a sharp gasp told him she had awakened. Her arm pulled in close to her body and her back stiffened.

"Don't," she whispered. Her voice sounded tired. He could not help smiling. If she felt as drained as he had last night, he would not be surprised. They had made love more times than he was accustomed to, even when he was not on a mission.

"I am sorry, *ma petite*," he said. "But I am afraid it was the only way I could wake you."

She lifted her head to look at him, and the expanse of white cloth in front of her face disconcerted him. It was as if her veil was more than just cloth; it seemed as if it were a rebuke. He wanted to see her face again, and his hand raised to move her veil, but her hand stopped him.

"No," she said. "I am awake."

He dropped his hand to his side, feeling oddly discontented. It mattered not whether he saw her face. "Good," he said, then smiled. "Though I regret to see you so well dressed, I am glad you are ready to go." He held out his hand. "Come. I am sure our coach awaits us."

She hesitated, then put her hand in his.

As they left the room and went down the stairs, she seemed to grasp his hand more tightly and leaned on his arm. Mme. Proust was in the common room, serving guests newly arrived, and a worried frown crossed her face. She bustled up to them and laid a hand on Corday's arm.

"Excuse me, citoyen, but is the little one well?"

He put an apologetic smile on his face. "Alas, citoyenne,"

he said. "My poor wife feels a little ill—the morning sickness, I believe."

The inn-wife nodded wisely. "Yes, that is the way with women in their early months. She will be over it soon."

A low moan emerged from beneath Simone's hood, and the inn-wife shook her head. "*Pauvre petite!* Look you, stay a moment, and I will fetch some food for you both, some bread and boiled eggs, which should not be so very harsh on the stomach. And if she cannot eat the eggs, you may save them for later. Some pregnant women cannot keep much more than bread and water in their stomachs in the morning."

Corday smiled. "I see you know much about such things."

Mme. Proust nodded proudly. "Eh, have I not had six healthy children of my own? They lived, all of them, and two of them have made me a grandmother. And I have attended twelve women this year and delivered them of their babes, and not one died in childbirth or of the fever." She nodded proudly, as she bustled to the kitchens. "Eh, I know a thing or two of mothers and their babes, if I may say so, citoyen," she called out before returning with the eggs and bread.

"I shall remember it," Corday said, "should we come this way again when my child is due to be born."

Mme. Proust beamed at him. "It is good that you acknowledged the girl and the little one, citoyen." Her face sobered, and she looked quickly over her shoulder. "The Revolution looks to the future for its people, but many husbands and sons have been given to its cause, and what are we women to do then?" Her voice faltered. "My own son left his wife behind for the cause. He was a good son and . . ." She looked at Corday and gave him a firm smile. "He was a good son."

Something moved Corday to pat her hand. "I am certain he is a son to be proud of, good Citoyenne Proust."

She beamed. "Yes, he is." She shooed him away with her hands. "Now, you must look to your wife and your child-to-be, and go before the coach leaves without you."

Corday nodded and smiled once more, before he took Simone's arm again and led her to the waiting coach outside.

My wife. My child. He rolled the words around in his mind, murmured them under his breath, tasting them as if they were some unfamiliar dish served up to him. The words sat oddly on his tongue, and he wondered if he had ever truly thought of such things in relation to himself. He could not remember if he ever had. These were things that had nothing to do with his career; he had seen more of life cut down than the creation of it. He wondered if his union with Simone would produce a child. The thought almost made him stop their progress to the coach. So far as he knew, his dalliances with women in the past had produced no children. But they were brief encounters with women who soon left for other men.

But Simone . . . despite the fact that she was not a virgin, she did not seem to be that kind of woman. She had not hidden her desire for him, but at the same time she had resisted it until he applied all the persuasion of his own desire on her, unlike the women he had encountered in the past. He remembered the cross she wore at her neck, and wondered if she confessed giving in to her desires as a sin. He grimaced. No doubt.

Awkward, but he would make sure she and the child would be well provided for, if one were created. It was the least he could do. He would write a message to Sir Robert Smith with directions for her welfare and give it to Simone to deliver should anything happen to him.

The coach before them was large and easily held four;

du Maurier and Hervé had already taken their places, and the former glanced at his watch as Corday helped Simone up into her seat. Hervé had a book open before him.

"My apologies, citoyens," Corday said. "My wife does not feel well, alas. It is the morning sickness, or so Citoyenne Proust has told me."

Du Maurier looked uncomfortable. "I am sorry to hear . . . she will not be ill on the way, will she?"

Corday shook his head. "I am sure she will recover quickly; indeed she has said that she needs only to sleep and she will feel better."

Du Maurier looked relieved. "Very well, then." He knocked on the roof of the coach and it jolted into movement.

The coach was well sprung and the seats comfortably cushioned. Corday sat next to Simone, and watched her as her head nodded and as she finally slid toward him. He sighed, and put his arm around her. She nestled against him and her breathing slowed until he almost wondered if she breathed at all.

He looked up to see du Maurier smiling. "So I see you do indeed remember her."

Corday grinned. "After that entrance, who could not?" He watched the agent carefully; du Maurier revealed neither in looks nor in manner whether his agents had reported any unusual activity. This would be a good time to take the offensive. If he had assessed du Maurier at all well, the agent valued directness. Corday made his face look grave. "Indeed, it seemed I was not the only one who noticed her." He hesitated, pretending to be reluctant to speak. "She is a virtuous woman, Citoyen du Maurier, for all her superstitious belief in the church." The agent raised his eyebrows, and his eyes grew sharp, but he nodded. "I do not like to make accusations, citoyen," Corday continued, "but Citoyen Broussard . . . well, let us just say that despite my wife's rebuffs of his attentions, he sent a man to abduct her while we were at the Church of St. Elisabeth."

Du Maurier pursed his lips in thought. He gave another sharp look at Corday. "I am surprised indeed."

"I would be, also, but the man was there at the church. I went with her—she insisted on a church marriage as well as a civil one—and caught the man spying on her." He put an apologetic expression on his face. "I fear I am a jealous husband, Citoyen du Maurier. I lost control of myself and . . . well, I knocked him unconscious." He gazed earnestly at du Maurier. "Do you think I should send a note of apology to Citoyen Broussard?"

Du Maurier gazed at him thoughtfully for a moment. "No," he said at last. "No, I think it would be best to forget the incident. If Broussard complains, I will deal with him."

Corday pretended to sigh in relief. "I thank you, citoyen. I would not want to cause more trouble than I already have, most particularly not when it concerns Citoyen Broussard." He grinned. "If I had not caught the man spying on her around the church, I would not have brought up the subject, for she seemed well enough able to take care of herself last night."

"She has much spirit, if I may say so, citoyen," du Maurier said, smiling. "I, however, prefer a quieter sort."

"You have one such a wife, then, Citoyen du Maurier?"

The smile faded from the agent's face, and something at once bleak and angry flared in his eyes. "Yes," he said softly after a while. "But she is dead."

"I am sorry to hear it," Corday said, and for a moment he felt a sympathy for the agent. "She must have been a good wife."

"She was." Du Maurier looked away, out the window. "I do my best to honor her memory." He looked again at Corday, and a smile touched his lips. "I fear I do not always do her justice, but I try." His lips pressed together in a brief line. "I *will* do justice by her."

Corday wondered what had happened to du Maurier's wife, how she had died. His eyes rested on the Revolution's tricolor cockade that decorated du Maurier's coat. The man was an idealist. He would not be surprised if Mme. du Maurier's death had to do with aristocrats, and that the man embraced the Revolution out of grief and hatred for those who had had a part in his wife's death. It was often so with men of good character, and he had no doubt that du Maurier was at one time a man of virtue.

"She must indeed have been a jewel of a woman."

"Yes," du Maurier said, glancing out of the window again. His eyes were not bleak now, but a determined glint remained. It was clear the agent did not want to talk of his wife, and the conversation died. Corday glanced at Hervé, who had listened with seeming disinterest to his superior's and Corday's conversation, and when the silence grew long, drew out a book from his pocket and began to read.

Corday looked out of the window, at the dripping wet that drew gray lines down the glass, and was glad he had not decided to go alone. He yawned and hastily covered his mouth. He caught du Maurier gazing at him, amused.

He grinned in return. "You must excuse me, citoyen. My wife and I, er, had little sleep last night. She may have morning sickness, but let us just say she shows no trace of it in the evening."

An amused glance came from over the edge of Hervé's book, and du Maurier's lips twitched upward. But he merely said, "It is a comfortable coach, Citoyen Thibaut. I have fallen asleep in it many times when traveling around this province."

"A good idea," Corday replied, and shifted himself more comfortably in his seat. "It would not hurt to doze for a while." He would, in truth. The more rest he could get on this mission, the better. He closed his eyes, and sleep came immediately.

Simone's dreams flitted into her mind and out again as the day grew stronger and sleep demanded her attention. Occasionally, when a slight burning sensation touched her consciousness, she would awaken—sometimes one of their fellow travelers opened the window of the coach.

But then the coach jolted to a stop; the noise and the fear of the light woke her. She hesitated at the door as Corday took her arm to help her out, but she gripped his hand and hurried out. She sighed with relief as he guided her into a dark corner of an inn room, where she sat, leaning up against the wall. She roused enough to sip tea, but wanted nothing else. Dear heaven, she was tired, but thankfully not as tired as she would have been had not Michael given her his blood. She had even a measure of strength, so much so that being out in the day was not as painful as it normally would have been.

He had given her his blood. He had *given* it. No one had ever done this, not willingly, not when she had not put them in a trance.

For she had not put him in a trance at all. She had tried her best to resist him, and even when she had given in to his seduction she was more intent on showing him how he would regret seducing her and making love with her.

But he did not seem to regret it. He had given her his blood, and even as she had taken it, he had continued to make love to her, treating her blood-taking as trivial.

She shook her head. She did not understand it, nor why he had insisted on marrying her in truth in the church.

Simone closed her eyes and dozed for a few moments, then opened her eyes and, through her gauze, and veil, watched Michael eat his luncheon. He ate heartily, and she smiled; she supposed he should after all they'd done last night. She shifted and turned her gaze toward the Public Safety agents.

Hervé and du Maurier did not seem to be in much of a hurry, for they lingered over their luncheon, talking of things that did not interest her. Even when they were done with their lunch, they did not arise, but stayed and continued talking—about nothing that she, and she supposed Michael, didn't already know, however. She watched Michael as he looked around the inn, seeming bored, until a small commotion caught his attention.

"I cannot help you, citoyenne," she heard the innkeeper say. "I can do accounts, but my handwriting leaves much to be desired." The innkeeper raised his voice. "Is there a scribe here, or one who can write a good hand?"

Hervé spoke up. "Here, innkeeper, we travel with a scribe. I am sure he would be glad of a few sous." The agent's voice was smooth, conversational in tone, and his gaze was nothing but bland when it lit upon Michael. But there was, nevertheless, something challenging in his voice. Simone tensed. The agent was clearly suspicious of Michael, as both of them had already discussed. This should be no test for her husband. He was an intelligent and educated man.

Michael ignored the agent. He rose. "Here, citoyen, I believe I can help."

A thin woman wearing worn clothes turned from the counter, hope in her eyes. "Mon—that is, citoyen, I cannot pay much, but I was hoping . . . My husband is in the army, you see, and my son and I have had to leave our home and . . ." She gave a large sigh, then lifted her chin. "If you could write a letter for me, I would be very grateful." She held the hand of a little boy and drew him forward.

Perhaps Simone had made a noise, for Michael turned

and look at her, as if trying to discern whether she was awake. She touched his arm briefly, and he turned back to the woman.

"Of course, citoyenne." He took out a small writing box from his pack and laid it on the table before him, taking out a piece of paper, a bottle of ink, and a quill. "What would you have me write?" he asked as he pared the quill with his knife.

The woman hesitated, then opened her mouth to speak, but the little boy tugged at her arm. "Maman, when will we go home?"

The woman bit her lip. "Not now, Pierre. I must have this man write a letter for us, and then we will go to Aunt Cecelie's house."

The boy pouted, and tugged his mother's arm again. "May I go outside to see the horses, Maman?"

The woman sighed, this time in exasperation. "No, Pierre, you are much too small and the horses are big. The horses will trample you, and then what shall I do?"

"But, Maman—"

"Perhaps if you are good, Citoyen Thibaut will tell you a story, boy." Simone turned to see du Maurier smile slightly and nod toward Michael. "I understand this man is a prodigious teller of tales."

Simone stiffened, all sleep fleeing at du Maurier's words. Now du Maurier was testing him. Writing and education were one thing, but could Michael spin a tale that would confirm that he was indeed both a scribe and a storyteller?

Michael turned back to the woman and ruffled the boy's hair. "Of course I will tell you a story, Pierre, but only if you are good, and only if you let your mother tell me what she wishes me to write to your papa."

"Will it have pirates in it, monsieur?" the boy asked

eagerly, ignoring his mother's whispered admonition to say "citoyen."

"Of course," Michael replied. "It will be a story of the dread pirate Pierre the—" Simone saw him glance at the boy's red, curling hair, "—Pierre the Red, called so because of his hair so red that his enemies feared that his bloody deeds showed forth in his hair."

The boy's eyes grew round and he nodded eagerly. "I will not say a word, monsieur, until Maman is done, I promise." He made a cross over his heart. "I swear it."

"Very good." Michael turned to the woman and smiled. "And now, citoyenne?"

The woman sighed, clearly in relief, and told him what she wished her husband to know, and where his regiment was stationed.

Michael wrote, and sanded the result. He folded the paper and gave it to her in exchange for a few sous.

"Thank you, citoyen," she said, and took her son's hand.

"But, Maman, he has not told me my story!" little Pierre cried.

She grimaced. "He was being very kind, my son. But I have not any more money to pay him for stories."

Du Maurier pushed a coin on the table toward Michael. "There is your money," the agent said, looking at him. Again Simone could hear the challenge in it. "Now Citoyen Thibaut may tell you a story."

Most definitely the agent suspected Michael, or at least meant to flush him out to see if he was what he claimed. Simone thought of Michael's cleverness and his quick wit. It only made sense that whatever skills he said he had, he possessed in truth. He could not afford to be exposed when on his mission. Therefore, he was no doubt a fine storyteller, as he had claimed when they first met. She drew in a breath, then put her hand on Michael's arm and turned to the woman. "Indeed, citoyenne, he is famous for his storytelling, are you not, *mon cœur*?"

He lifted her hand in his and brought it to his lips. "You flatter me, my dear." He turned to the woman and put the coin in her hand. "There, now you have the money to pay me." He lifted the boy and set him gently on his lap.

"Once upon a time, there was a boy named Pierre—"

"I thought you were going to tell me a story about a pirate," the boy said.

"I am, you'll see," Michael said, then continued. "This boy was very adventurous, and sometimes troubled his very patient and virtuous mother with his adventures." He cast a humorous glance at the boy's mother, who chuckled.

"One day, the boy became a youth, and he decided he would become a sailor. He was a brave young man, and did very well, so well that he was made a captain. But one day, a pirate ship came aside Pierre's ship, and fought a terrible battle with Pierre's crew. The captain's ship was destroyed."

"No!" cried the boy.

"Yes," Michael replied. "And who was the pirate who destroyed it? It was none other than Erik the Black."

Michael's voice lowered with portent as he said the name. The boy stared at him, open-mouthed. "No man had ever stood against this pirate, for he was a wicked man, who had made his first kill as a boy." Michael paused for a moment, and Simone thought something dark had passed over his expression, but then he spoke again. "Pierre fought him, but he was a youth, and Black Erik was a grown man and very strong. All that Pierre could do was disarm him long enough to jump over the side of the ship, and seize a broken piece of lumber and drift until he reached an island." Michael's voice was soft and distant, and he stared over the boy's head as if he could see the island in the far wall of the inn. "There, he was treated well, but alas, he grew ill, and the illness passed onto those natives who tended him, and they, too, died."

The mother spoke up, her voice sad and disapproving. "There is much dying in this story, citoyen," she said.

"Is it not the way of this world, citoyenne?" Michael replied.

She nodded and sighed. "Yes, alas."

"And such things may form a man, as it did the youth Pierre. For in his grief at the deaths of his crewmen, and the deaths of the natives who cared for him, he vowed revenge on Black Erik, for it was he who had caused such misfortune to all those for whom Pierre had cared, and who had cared for him."

Michael shook his head and smiled wryly. "The youth could think of no way of accomplishing his aim but to become a pirate himself." Simone leaned forward and gazed at Michael, drawn into the story in spite of herself. She could not help but wonder if this story had anything to do with his own life. Perhaps he had been at sea, or perhaps he had fought many battles. She did not know, and was sure he would not tell her, at least not now. He had revealed nothing of his life. Perhaps, when this mission was all over, he would tell her. She would ask.

The boy sighed with satisfaction. "I was wondering when he would become a pirate."

"And a very good one he was," Michael replied. "He landed in the Americas, just as the revolution there began, and learned how to smuggle goods for a living, and how to hunt like an Indian through the woods, stealthily and quietly as a wolf. He learned how to use a knife and a pistol, and he was already quite prodigiously good with a sword." He sighed, and shook his head. "And then he became the captain of his own ship once again, and his fights against various ships were so notorious that he became known as

Pierre the Red, for the decks of the ships he boarded were sure to flow with blood. But Captain Pierre was not content with his victories, for he wanted victory against one man: the dread pirate, Erik the Black."

"Did he find him, monsieur?" the boy asked, his eyes round.

Michael's face grew solemn. "He did indeed, and they fought a terrible battle."

"Was it very bloody, and was there blood all over Erik the Black's ship?" the boy asked eagerly.

"Pierre!" his mother cried. "That is a terrible thing to ask!"

Michael cast an apologetic look at the woman. "Not any more bloody than any other battle, boy," he said. "For Pierre found Black Erik, and fought a hard duel with him, and at last the dread pirate was dead."

The boy sighed with satisfaction.

His mother smiled. "Thank the good man, Pierre, because we must be leaving."

The boy sighed again, this time with reluctance. "Merci, mon—that is, citoyen," he said.

"I thank you, also," the mother said to Michael. "It was very good of you—" and she turned to du Maurier "—and you to let Pierre have his story." She took her son's hand and hefted her travel basket in the other. "Now, Pierre, we must go." With a last nod to Simone, she and the boy left.

There was silence for a moment, then du Maurier grinned. "Well, Citoyen Thibaut, that may have been a tale to satisfy a child, but I am afraid you may not be the storyteller your wife says you are."

Michael raised his eyebrows in mock hauteur. "How so?" he asked.

"Why, you never did say what happened to the pirate Pierre the Red."

"Ah." Michael's eyes grew distant again, though he

smiled. "I am afraid he remained a pirate. He had spent years honing his skills for the sole purpose of revenge. After he achieved it, he found he was fit for nothing else."

Simone drew in a slow breath and let it out again. She did what she did out of penance, not revenge. True, she would put no bar in front of bringing the man to justice who had killed her family, but she had vowed she would not kill unless in self-defense. However, she had not looked beyond the possible end of the Revolution, nor what she would do if she ever regained her humanity.

Silence remained, and she looked at du Maurier, who had asked about the future of Pierre the Red. Du Maurier's smile had fallen from him, and his lips turned white from being pressed hard together. His eyes looked at once angry and hopeless.

So, thought Simone. On whom did du Maurier wish to wreak vengeance, and whom did he want avenged? Did Michael know? She glanced at how his brows were raised as if in question, but the rest of him was still; perhaps he wanted to see if the agent would blurt out his motivations. If Michael did not know, he had no doubt guessed, and was subtly punishing du Maurier for trying to expose him. Sudden sympathy moved her; she could understand acting out that wish. Was she not still doing penance for hers? Still, it would not be convenient for the agent to be angry. She shook her head. "Michael, you have become rusty in your storytelling. You forgot poor Pierre's *maman*. No doubt he returned to her after his revenge and poured his riches in her hands, and set himself up as a wealthy man in their village. I am sure his mother would have found a good wife for him, and he ended his days in comfort, with a dozen children around him. Certainly, if Pierre the Red did not deserve such a good life, his *maman* did."

Du Maurier laughed, and the anger fled from his face. "And no doubt that is the way little Pierre's *maman* would prefer it." He nodded, his good humor apparently restored.

"But what if the pirate's mother was not alive?" said Hervé suddenly into the easing atmosphere. He stared intently at Michael.

Michael's gaze rested contemplatively on the agent's face. "Then it would be as I said, that Pierre the Red continued to be a pirate the rest of his days. There would be nothing to lure him home except perhaps sentimentality, and I would assume such a man would not be sentimental."

Simone looked from Hervé to Michael. An underlying current of . . . something seemed to go from one to the other. There seemed to be some kind of test between them. She glanced at du Maurier. He reclined in his chair, relaxed, his hands folded over his stomach, watching the other men with curiosity.

Hervé nodded. "Perhaps you are right," he said and suddenly seemed to lose interest.

An air of unease permeated their corner of the inn, and Simone thought it best disbursed. "I prefer my version of the ending," she said. "I have had enough of bad ones these days."

Du Maurier looked at his fellow agent for a moment and seemed about to speak, but turned and smiled at Simone at her words. "I too, citoyenne," he said softly.

A servant came up to their table and bowed. "Your coach is ready, citoyens," he said. Du Maurier nodded and paid the man, then stood.

Simone watched the agents as they prepared to leave. Most certainly they suspected Michael, if not herself, if the undercurrent of unease was any indication. She and Michael would have to be very careful. Very careful indeed. She looked at du Maurier's face, his expression grim. She rose from her chair, sudden pity and curiosity warring in her heart, even though he was her enemy. She turned to Michael. "Go, husband, and attend to our baggage." She smiled at du Maurier. "The good Citoyen du Maurier will help me into the coach." Michael raised his eyebrows at her, but nodded and left behind Hervé.

She touched du Maurier's arm and he looked at her. His face was still pale, his eyes haunted. "I am sorry, citoyen, that my husband's story upset you. He tells them quite vividly, for he is a fine storyteller, as you can see."

The agent gave her a stiff smile. "He is, indeed, citoyenne," he said politely. "I congratulate you; he will earn a good living with his stories."

He turned, then looked at her again, clearly barely remembering that he was to escort her to the coach, for it was a moment before he held out his arm. She pressed her fingers on it, holding him back when he took a step forward.

"Stay, for a moment, citoyen," she said. "I do not mean to pry, but I see you are in grief. So many people have died, indeed, in my family as well. . . ." She trailed off, hoping her concern would elicit the response she wanted.

His arm stiffened under her hand, then relaxed. His smile fell from him, and his lips turned down. "I—my wife and my child, citoyenne." His voice was barely a whisper. "They were killed. My Gabrielle, and my Thérèse. By the damned aristos. My little Thérèse." He sighed and cleared his throat, for his voice had thinned, sounding tight. "She was only five, citoyenne. She loved flowers so much, my— my wife and I called her *Thérèse des jardins*. Thérèse of the gardens. She was a flower herself, I tell you, madame. I will find who killed them some day, Citoyenne Thibaut. I and my faithful Hervé. It was he who found them, you see. He brought them to me."

Simone squeezed his arm, her heart melting for this father's sorrow. "I am so sorry, citoyen. So sorry. It is a terrible thing to lose one's family—" She swallowed and shook her head, remembering the rage and grief she had felt when her nurse had brought her the news. "My own family—" She broke off, and shook her head again.

Du Maurier drew in a deep breath, and patted her hand. "All will be made right some day, citoyenne." His voice grew stronger. "Our Revolution will make it so."

Compassion made Simone bite back her automatic reply, and she put her hand over his, her enemy's hand. Her enemy. She did not feel he was her enemy at this moment.

She moved forward toward the inn door, dreading a little the sting she would feel when the light would strike her. She hoped that du Maurier would walk quickly so that she could enter the coach soon. She glanced up at him through her veil, and saw that his eyes were alight with fiery resolution. Aristocrat or not, she hoped that whoever had killed his wife and daughter would be punished. The death of innocents could not be excused. She paused at the threshold of the inn, and with a determined breath, stepped into the light of day.

Chapter 14

"TELL ME WHAT REALLY HAPPENED TO Pierre the Red," Simone said.

She sat on the edge of the bed in the chamber at the inn they would stay in for the night. Their journey since the last stop had been quiet, the conversation desultory as they neared Paris. Michael did most of the talking, and even the inscrutable Hervé would grin from time to time at the stories Michael would spin. But those stories made her think of the one he had told to little Pierre, and the persistent thought that the story was based on Michael's life came to the surface of her mind.

She looked at him now, silhouetted by the flames in the fireplace. He was pulling off his coat and waistcoat, preparing for bed. He had maintained a certain distance from her since the morning after their marriage. He did not refrain from her touch; he never drew away when she leaned against him in the coach. He even kissed her hand in the presence of the agents. But . . . he kept his distance. It was as if he felt she was some wild animal he needed to watch.

She looked down at her hands. What else could she expect after she revealed to him that she was a vampire? And yet, he had married her even so. She glanced at him again, wondering if he had heard her request, for he remained silent, concentrating on folding his clothes in a neat pile on the chair as he took them off.

He slipped under the bedcovers and rested his back against the pillows he had propped against the head of the bed. Simone remembered the night she had come through the wardrobe in Titon's inn, and how she had thought Michael had looked like *le Diable*'s own brother, with the ascetic lines of his face and the decadent shape of his lips. He looked so now, his hair loosening from its queue so that it looked like a dark halo about his head, and the hearth's fire lighting his eyes.

"Why do you want to know?" he asked at last.

She shrugged. "You are a good storyteller, Michael, and I wished to know more."

He waved a dismissing hand. "It's but a child's story."

"I am perhaps nearly as old as you," she said. "But not so old that I cannot like a child's story." She turned and gathered her legs under her in the bed so that she faced him. "Tell me."

He was silent again, watching her, then said, "First, you must tell me something: did you put a spell on me, or mesmerize me into making love to you and marrying you?"

Quick anger flared through her, and she stumbled off the bed away from him. "You—you think I forced you to marry me? You think I forced you to make love to me?" *He regrets marrying me,* she thought with despair. *Perhaps he regrets even touching me.* She clenched her hands. "No, I did not cast a spell on you or put you in a trance. I told you, you should not have married me! I should never have agreed to it, and I was a fool to even think you wanted it."

She groped for the door, feeling suddenly suffocated. If she ran, she would feel free; she would not have to be here with him, her husband who regretted their marriage.

The bedsheets rustled and quick footsteps crossed the floor. Her hand met flesh instead of the door latch. She looked up. Michael stood, leaning against the door, staring at her. A half rueful smile turned up his lips.

"Such dramatics," he said, and touched her cheek. "I only wanted to be sure. I have never asked anyone to marry me, *ma petite,* and the sensation was such a strange one, I thought you might have put me under some kind of supernatural enchantment." He laughed slightly, and she stared at him, for it was a sad, incredulous sound. "I have led a mad, impossible life, Simone, and it is fit, I suppose, that I have made a mad, impossible marriage. It makes me almost believe in fate, and think this was meant to be." He took her hand. "Come back to bed. I know you will not sleep, but I would be pleased if you keep me company, and . . ." He cocked his head at her. "You will not be offended if I ask whether you will take blood from me as I sleep, will you?"

She looked away and closed her eyes, wishing he knew nothing of her need for blood. "No, monsieur, I will not, I promise you. I do not take blood often, and need it only when I am in a weakened state. If I am not worked up into a rage, then I will not hunt for blood, nor will I take it when I—when we—" She glanced at him. "I will use the dagger's sheath again if we—" She groaned, feeling more embarrassed. "I did hurt you. You made me angry, and then—I promise you, I will not do it again, and perhaps it is wise if we do not—" She pulled away, shaking her head, shame stopping all her words.

She found herself suddenly lifted from the floor, Michael's arms holding her securely under her back and knees. "Don't be silly, *ma petite,*" he said. "I asked because I don't know what you are capable of. I have only old legends and fairy tales to rely on as far as my knowledge of—" he hesitated, "—of vampires goes." He shook his head. "You see, even now it's difficult for me to comprehend. If I wish to know more, I need to ask you. I can hardly ask around the inn, after all. It might look peculiar, you must admit." She could not help smiling at the image as he set her gently down on the bed again. "There, that's better," he said. "You were right, of course, when you said we did not know much of each other. In fact, you have the advantage of me; I know nothing of the abilities you might have, whereas you already know what I am capable of."

"One might know a man for a lifetime and never know what he is capable of," Simone said gravely. "*En fait*, he himself may not know . . . and I doubt you are a man who freely reveals himself."

He chuckled. "There, you know that much about me. It is true I am not used to revealing much of anything about myself."

Simone smiled. "Reveal only what you feel comfortable revealing, then."

He cocked his head at her. "Even though I seduced information out of you?"

She frowned. "You did, but I think I wished you to know it, and it was not much more than what I had already told you, or what you could deduce for yourself."

"I could have seduced more out of you," he said, and gave her a wickedly sensual look.

She barely suppressed a shiver with that look, but then the laughter in his eyes made her understand he meant to affect her so. She gazed at him, amused. "I think you were too distracted to continue," she said in a challenging voice.

Michael laughed and held up his hands in surrender. "Yes, I was." He patted the bed next to him. "Come, sit with me."

She thought about how he was indeed reluctant to tell her much about himself, and, yes, how he had managed to turn aside her request that he tell her more about Pierre the Red's story. No doubt her instinct was right; there was something in the story that related to him. She watched as he returned to the bed and pulled the covers over his lap.

"If you wish me to stay with you, then you must tell me more about Pierre the Red," she said.

He gazed at her, a speculative expression passing over his face. "You are that fond of a silly child's story?"

"Yes," she said firmly. "I believe you cleaned it up for little Pierre and his mother—as you should have, of course. But you need not, for me."

He smiled slightly. "What if I should offend your sensibilities, *ma petite*?"

"If I had any sensibilities, after all I have done in my life, monsieur, I doubt I have any more to offend after working with you," she replied dryly.

Michael made an exaggerated wince. "You pain me, wife. Very well. Where shall I start?"

Simone thought over the story he had told earlier. "Did Pierre the Red truly run off to sea?"

"In a manner of speaking. He did not become a sailor but a soldier. He was eventually shipped off to the Americas, where he did indeed learn to hunt as the natives hunted, and generally became as much of a nuisance as a youth could be."

"How old was he when he ran off?" Simone asked softly. She moved toward him, then sat beside him, also resting her back on the head of the bed.

Michael sat still, his hands folded before him, silent while he looked away into the hearth. She wondered if she should move closer to him, but felt somehow he would not want her to. She bit her lip and looked down at her hands on her lap. For all that he teased her and called her *"ma petite*," he still felt . . . distant. More impersonal than he had been before their marriage.

"Pierre the Red was very young," he said at last, his voice taking on a long-ago and faraway tone. "I think he was no more than ten, but he was tall for his age, and easily deceived those who signed him on."

"That is very young," Simone said. "But I suppose he was eager to leave home?"

"Yes." The word was harsh. Ah, thought Simone, then his home was not pleasant. She raised her hand, almost touching his arm to comfort him, but returned it to her lap again. No, he would not welcome comfort, not now, and she was half afraid that he would stop his story if he thought she guessed he spoke of his own life.

"Did he become a pirate, then, in truth?" she asked instead.

"Of a sort," he replied. "He became well trained in arms, and was given dangerous assignments that made him almost indispensable, for there were few who could do them. He commanded a troop of men for a while, during a colonial war, but he lived a double life that not even his men were aware of. By day, he led his troop to war. By night, he sought out . . . certain targets to hit, for which he was paid much money. It was for the glory of his country, he was assured." Michael chuckled wryly. "Those were the idealistic days, when Pierre the Red believed he could redeem himself from his less-than-satisfactory childhood by deeds of derring-do, by eliminating the enemies of his country."

"Until—?" Simone asked.

Michael glanced at her, his smile still wry. "You are wise. There is always an 'until' with such things." His gaze returned to the fireplace. "Until his superiors asked him to eliminate a particular opponent, a great general of a ragtag colonial army, a man whom Pierre admired even though the man was considered a traitor to his country. In the past, you see, Pierre had only been asked to eliminate true cowards, men who had few virtues. This general, it seemed, was to be assassinated—an ignoble death for a good man, who was a valiant warrior and should properly have met his death on the battlefield. At the same time, Pierre the Red knew his government was being helped by that general's aide, a man full of greed and vanity." He shivered, and drew the bedcovers up over his shoulders. "Pierre understood, then, that virtue had no place in governmental affairs, but expediency did. And for the first time, Pierre the Red missed his mark."

Michael smiled cynically. "It was remarkable how he aimed and missed, and missed again. Surely, that general had a charmed life . . . or perhaps Pierre the Red was such a marksman that only the general's hat was hit, or his horse shot from under him. Pierre's superiors could not be certain, so they made sure he was punished by taking away his troop, and relegating him to the lowest and least honorable of occupations in wartime: that of a spy."

Simone thought of the war in the American colonies, and of a certain general and now leader of those states, of whom it was said that he led a charmed life. Michael had stayed his hand then, and now he was again involved in the turning of nations. She shivered, this time with an odd sense of prescience. She wondered if sometimes God used people in spite of themselves, to accomplish larger aims. Even one such as Michael? Or herself? No, not herself, surely not herself, with all the things she had done wrong in her life. She shook her head, and returned her attention to Michael.

His smile had faded, and turned into a thoughtful frown. "It is a strange occupation, betwixt and between, neither civilian nor soldier. It is assumed that you have no honor, even if you are able to withstand tortures and never betray your mission. If you are caught, your country will not ransom you. You are given not a soldier's death, but a criminal's. And yet, you are supposed to work out of loyalty to your country."

He shrugged. "Pierre the Red understood all this, and also understood that the life of a spy was often a short one. Therefore, since it was assumed he had no honor, and since he found he had a talent for espionage, he would take what he could from the situation, and soon became the highest-paid spy his country could afford. Quite a distinction, wouldn't you say?" he said lightly.

"Certainly very practical," Simone said. "If he survived his occupation, he could set himself up well after a few years."

Michael stared at her for a moment, then laughed. "Practical indeed," he said, and Simone wondered if he meant herself.

"And did he?" she asked. "Did he do well for himself?"

"He acquired some property, but I did not hear whether he had retired or not," Michael said.

"And what of his mother?" Simone asked. "Is she living on his property?"

The smile disappeared from his face. "No. She is dead." His expression had grown cold, distant, still. Simone wondered what had happened to his mother . . . Should she ask? She wet her lips, suddenly unnerved. Would he tell her?

The bedcovers rustled, and Michael threw them off, walking to the fireplace to throw on another log. Kneeling there, he held out his hands to the rising flames, and the light flickered over his face, now impassive and showing no emotion. Perhaps she could ask, after all. Perhaps it was only a story, a story he made up, and her intuition was at fault for thinking otherwise.

"How . . . how did she die, Michael?" she blurted.

He did not turn to her but continued holding his hands up to the fire. She heard him take in a deep breath.

"She died from her son's neglect," he said softly.

"I do not believe it," Simone said. "If Pierre the Red was only ten years old when he left home, it was not a matter of neglect on his part."

Michael still did not turn to her, and for a moment only the crackling of the fire sounded in the room. "A man once lived with Pierre and his mother, and this man was the boy's father. He was ambitious, and soon wished that his wife was not so lowborn. He sought to divorce her, claiming that she was unfaithful to him, which she was not. They argued, and this frightened the boy, and over time, the arguments became more violent. Finally, the man left. But one day, Pierre's mother received a letter, and a knock on the door soon after made her turn pale with fright. She bade her son hide himself in a closet, and made him promise that he would not come out, no matter what happened, until she came for him. The boy did. Soon, a visitor arrived, and there were once again the arguments that had frightened the boy, so that he was glad he had hid in the closet.

"There were screams, and then silence. Pierre stayed quiet for a long time, waiting for his mother. But soon hunger forced him from his closet, and he went to the kitchen."

A long sigh came from Michael. "There, he found his mother, broken and bleeding, near unrecognizable from the cuts and bruises on her face. She was also dead."

Pity tore at Simone's heart. Was this why Michael had left home? If his story was at all close to what he had experienced, it was no wonder he had decided to lead a rootless life, full of risk. She thought of the young boy wanting desperately redemption through honor, and who was not even given that chance.

She rose from the bed and knelt beside Michael. She put her hand on his arm. "Michael, I do not see how Pierre could have prevented such a terrible thing. He was only a boy."

He turned to her then, staring at her as if he stared into a dark pit. "Perhaps. But Pierre knew he was indeed his father's son, for he found a pistol, loaded it as his father had instructed him long ago, found his father, and shot him."

Simone for once was glad that vampires could not weep. She suspected that Michael would not welcome it. Instead, she patted his arm. "His father deserved it," she said firmly. "Was that when Pierre the Red ran away to join the army?"

Michael stared at her, and suddenly he smiled. "Yes. His uncle, wanting to get rid of the scandal as quickly and as quietly as possible, bought the boy a commission and shipped him out as soon as he could, despite his age." He gazed into the fire again. "So you see, it is not a story that I would have told to little Pierre and his mother, for—" He stopped, taking in a startled breath, and his hands suddenly turned into fists.

"What is it?" Simone asked.

"I—nothing. A random thought." He relaxed, and went back to the bed. She gazed at him, wondering if she should probe further, but she thought of what he had told her so far, and decided against it. They had two more days until they would come to Paris, and surely that was enough time to question him further. It was late, and Michael would need his sleep.

"Thank you for telling me the tale of Pierre the Red," she said. She went to the bed and sat on the edge of it. This time he lay on it instead of sitting up, pulling the bedcovers over himself. "It is a sad tale, to be sure, but I think Pierre will find happiness at some time."

He turned, and looked at her. "Hope. You believe in it, don't you?"

She bent down, and kissed him on the cheek. "Yes. Sometimes, that is all there is to fight for."

He sighed. "Hope is for fools, Simone."

She smiled. "Yes, I know. But have you not said more than once that we were both fools?"

He laughed then, and his face lightened at last. "Yes, I did." He sighed again, and she could hear a world of weariness in it. "Yes, I did," he whispered.

She said nothing in return, and thought that, though he did not seem to want comfort, she would give it nevertheless, and risk rejection. She took off her clothes, leaving her shift, and crawled into bed next to him, molding her body against his back. She closed her eyes, feeling the heat of him, the muscles of his back against her breasts and belly, and laid her cheek against his shoulder. His breath slowed for a while, and then he turned, facing her. He said nothing, but looked into her eyes as if searching for something. She touched his face with her finger, tracing the line of his cheek and chin, and he seized her hand. He held it tightly, as if he could not bear her touch, and would keep her from touching him further. But then he moved his hand behind her head, threading his fingers through her hair, and drew her into a kiss.

It was a gentle kiss, tentative, then exploring. Simone sighed and relaxed into it, and his kiss grew more demanding. Desire flared in her breasts and between her thighs. She sighed again, and it turned into a groan as his hand drifted down and touched her breasts and then her belly. She grasped his hand. "You need not, if you don't want to," she said, her voice trembling. She had not intended for him to make love to her, but she would welcome it . . . if he wanted her.

He shook off her hand, cupped her cheek in the palm

of his hand, and stared intently into her eyes. He did not smile, but kissed her after a moment, and she thought the kiss had a "yes" in it somewhere as he moved his mouth over hers and pressed her down upon the bed.

He made love to her carefully, as if she were made of glass and easily broken. His hands slid over her skin, upward from her thighs to her shoulders, pulling off her shift so that she was naked beneath him. He parted a moment from her to remove the rest of his clothes, and then he was again on top of her, rocking himself over her gently, persistently.

The heat within her grew, and she opened her legs to him, pushing upward urgently. But he did not enter her, only slid his hardness back and forth over her sensitive woman's flesh until she panted and grasped at him.

And then he thrust deep inside of her, thrust home. Home, she thought wildly. It was as if in taking him into her, she had opened a door in her heart and brought him home. The thought, and a sizzling clenching of her womb, forced a gasping laugh from her, and she arched her neck and pressed herself into him.

She had no true home, but as Michael thrust inside of her, kissing her and holding her tightly, she felt as if his arms held her in shelter, even as he brought her to a higher pleasure that made her groan deep in her throat. She moved her hand over his skin, feeling the smoothness of it, and pushed her hand between them, wanting to increase his pleasure. His lips made a line of kisses from there to between her breasts, and it felt as though he had poured champagne over her as he licked the tips of her nipples and took one into his mouth.

He continued to thrust slowly as he suckled, and the tingling over her breasts grew sharp and joined the burning in her loins. A pressure built inside of her, and it burst, making her press hard against him. His lips took hers, drinking in the cry she let out. His movements quickened, bringing her hard against him. She cried out again as another burst of pleasure made her arch her body, and he drove harder into her, his breath coming quicker, until one last thrust pressed her hard into the mattress and he breathed out a soft groaning sigh.

He rested his forehead on her shoulder for a moment, and Simone let her legs relax from around him. She closed her eyes, luxuriating in the feel of him on top of her, and caressed his back, marveling in the smoothness of his skin over the hard muscles.

She sighed. He had not rejected her, and she was glad of that. It was not love, of course, but at least he was not repulsed. And they had made love as a man and a normal woman would have, without fear that she would hurt him. Surprise seized her and she held herself still, not quite understanding how it had happened. She had been so sure she might harm him in the course of lovemaking, as she had done before. "Thank you," she said, grateful that she had not hurt him, that he had been gentle with her, that their lovemaking had been so normal.

He raised his head and looked at her, and his hair shifted down, forming a curtain around them. A chuckle shook his body, making her hips jerk, for he was still within her and the movement stimulated her still-sensitive flesh. "I was going to say that."

"You're welcome," she said, at the same time he said it, and they laughed. Michael rolled them to their sides, kissing her. He pushed back her hair from her face and gazed at her, a puzzled look on his face.

"What is it?" she asked.

He shook his head. "I don't know. I had thought this might be my last mission, and that it would be because I would die. And yet, I think perhaps I will not."

Simone shivered at his words, and put her hand over

his lips. "Don't talk of dying. We will complete our missions, and then we will be free, at least for a time."

"For a time," he said. "It is only two days until we reach Paris." He closed his eyes, then opened them again, and she thought he looked infinitely weary.

"You need your sleep," she said, and moved reluctantly away from him.

He did not protest, but rolled over onto his back, and pulled up the bedcovers. She lay beside him, merely watching the rise and fall of his chest slow until it was clear he was asleep. She bent and kissed him once again, her heart aching. If they finished their mission, and if she ever regained her humanity, she would do what she could to ease his pain, and be a good wife to him.

If. There was much hope in that word, and much doubt as well. She wondered if she were indeed a fool.

She sighed, pulled on her shift and the rest of her clothes. She walked to the desk near the fireplace, and carefully lit a candle. Taking out a piece of paper, a quill, and ink, she proceeded to draw a map. If they were at all to succeed in their mission to find the man who had killed her family and threatened Michael's country, then it would be best if she laid out what she knew of the Paris streets, and where they could hide if need be. Hope was all very well, but it fared better when accompanied by practicality.

She wrote and drew far into the night, until she heard the first cock crow. She looked at all the papers she had written on, sanded the last one, put them in order, and folded them in a neat packet. She tucked it into a pocket of Michael's coat, sure that he would find it when he put on his clothes.

She looked at him once again, sleeping in the bed. She still did not know his heart, and perhaps never would. She hoped they would do well, and come out of their missions alive. She went around the bed to where Michael slept on his side. She watched how his eyelids fluttered—perhaps he dreamed. Carefully, she bent and kissed him on his cheek. Moving silently away, she began to wrap her arms with her rag strips, in preparation for the day. Weariness tugged at her, and when she finally drew down the veil over her face, she lay down on the bed, careful to pull her skirts down over her thickly stockinged legs. She breathed deeply, and closed her eyes. She would sleep fitfully until it became dark, and no doubt when they came to the next inn—the last inn before they entered Paris itself. She drew in a deep breath. She would have to prepare herself for the on-slaught of human blood, for the streets were filled with the scent of it. She would refuse Michael's touch then, for her blood-hunt would seize her, and her senses would come to a high, intense pitch. Then, she would be dangerous to him, truly, until she fed once again.

She turned on her side, and put her hand on Michael's waist. She would touch him now and take comfort in it, for she did not know when next she could do so without danger to him. A tendril of warmth curled up around her heart, and her body relaxed and sank deep into the mattress, until the morning light touched the windows of the bedchamber and she fell asleep at last.

Chapter 15

CORDAY LOOKED AT SIMONE SLEEPING on the bed, thoroughly wrapped against the sunlight. They had made love last night, as any man and woman might, and it had given him comfort. Comfort. He had not thought he needed it, and never in the world had he thought that he'd receive it from one such as she. A vampire. He shook his head. She had drawn more of his history from him than anyone had in all his life, making him tell the story of Pierre the Red, which was really his own sorry, stupid tale. He wondered if she knew it—no doubt she did, for she was perceptive, even wise. She had said she was almost as old as he. Perhaps she was even older, though she looked little more than seventeen.

The notion sat oddly on him for a moment, and then, suddenly, it did not matter. It was only in brief moments that she displayed a knowledge and experience older than her appearance. The rest of the time, she looked and acted no differently from any young woman.

He put on his clothes, and frowned at the bulge in his coat pocket. He reached inside, and pulled out a packet of papers. He opened them, and his brows lifted as he read the strong, feminine hand. Simone had drawn out a map of Paris, with the streets and different prisons clearly marked, a route she thought might be the safest for them to travel, and where Père Dumont might be contacted if anything were to happen to her. Corday whistled softly in admiration. It was efficient work, and done well. He ran his finger over the list of her abilities that she had written on a separate piece of paper. Interesting, and very useful.

Corday perused the list, memorizing it as well as the abbé's address, then tore off that information and threw it into the fire, leaving the map. No need to put the old man in danger, or have any more information on paper than necessary. He thought of du Maurier and Hervé, and remembered they had mentioned they'd be stationed at one of the prisons. He suspected that the man he sought would be an agent as well; therefore, the prisons would be their destination. For Simone, it would be to release what prisoners she could to freedom. For him, it would be to seek out the man he was to kill.

It would take less time than he thought, for Corday believed he knew who this man was now, impossible though it seemed to him. The clues were in the way he had used the bodies he had killed. Sir Robert's description of the bodies sent back to England had sounded familiar. The familiarity had disturbed Corday when he read the report, though he could not place it at the time. He had remembered the method of death when he had told the story of Pierre the Red to Simone. He had in fact dealt with this man once, long ago.

Corday half doubted he would recognize the man after all these years. It would depend on how much he had changed. He was grateful Simone had pressured him to tell her the story—he doubted he would have remembered if she had not. He had seen a brief glint of pity in her eyes as he told it, however. His mouth twisted in irritation. He did not want her pity.

What do you want from her?

He thrust the question aside. There was no time left for contemplation, for planning and executing his mission. He brought his mind back to the man he was to hunt, the way the man operated, how he used the people around him, and of Johnson and Bramley, whom he had brought to the French side.

Johnson and Bramley. That was another thing he needed to solve. He would assume, for now, that the two English spies were in league with the man he sought. It was safer that way. He could trust no one except Simone.

Perhaps he would use Simone's supposed pregnancy as a reason for her absence when he began his search, and as a cover for her activities. He would say she was ill, and confined to her rooms in an apartment he had had one of his contacts reserve before he left for France. Then he would offer his scribing to those in the area who needed it, quite innocently, and prove to the very suspicious agents that he was not up to any wrongdoing. He'd make sure they'd not know he was using his business to find the man Sir Robert had directed him to eliminate.

He folded the papers again, and hid them in an inner pocket of his coat, then turned to rouse Simone so that she could go downstairs and then to the coach after their breakfast.

He picked her up, and shook her gently until she murmured a soft protest. "I am awake, monsieur," she said, and straightened, standing unsteadily at first on her feet.

Monsieur. He had asked her to call him Michael, but she had reverted to formality after their marriage. His heart twisted a little at the thought, then he shook his head. There was no room for sentiment. Her hand trembled as she moved toward him and he put her hand on his arm, supporting her weight as she leaned on him. She weighed very little, he noted, and rarely ate, although she did eat more heartily in the evening. No one could think that she was La Flamme, a strong and clever outlaw. He was glad, very glad, that she had come with him. Even if she called him "monsieur."

He led her down to the common room, where du Maurier and Hervé were already breakfasting. Both of them rose and bowed, and Corday noticed du Maurier directed a warm smile toward Simone. A brief shock of jealousy surprised him. His grip on Simone's hand tightened. Du Maurier turned toward him, and his expression became grave, though he nodded to Corday civilly enough. Corday returned the bow, and he fixed a smile on his face that he hoped looked better than the irritation he felt.

Du Maurier waved his hand at the still-laden plates before he sat again. "You are welcome to join me, although," he nodded at Hervé, "my good man here will be attending the arrangements for our journey shortly." Hervé bowed again, this time with an apologetic smile as he left their table and went out the inn door.

Corday pretended to hesitate.

Du Maurier smiled. "After our partaking of your meals, Citoyen Thibaut, it is only fair."

Corday nodded then, and guided Simone to a chair before he sat. "I thank you, Citoyen du Maurier." He watched Simone slump against her chair, and he wondered if she overestimated her strength during the day. He leaned close to her. "Simone," he whispered. "Are you well?"

A sigh emitted from behind he veil. "Yes," she said. "I am only tired." She waved away the biscuit he offered her. "I am not hungry."

Corday frowned, easy to do considering his earlier concerns. He looked at du Maurier. "I worry, citoyen. She does not eat much during the day, and this cannot be good for her, or the babe." He shook his head. "If this continues for the rest of today, I fear I will need to find a doctor immediately."

Du Maurier gazed at him thoughtfully. "We are but a little way from Paris, Citoyen Thibaut. More than a few good doctors are there, I am sure."

Corday put on an anxious expression. "You will excuse a husband's worry for his wife," he replied. "But I feel she needs to see a doctor soon. I confess I regret taking her along with me, but how could I leave her behind? She has no family to take care of her, I found, her uncle having recently died."

"You did the right thing," du Maurier said. He smiled slightly. "But I know a little of women and their vagaries during pregnancy. My own wife—" He paused and swallowed, looking down at his hands pressed flat on the table. "My own wife could not eat her breakfast without feeling extremely ill during the first four months of her pregnancy." He folded his hands in front of him. "She recovered her appetite fully in the fifth month, but not without much worry on my part."

Corday wondered if he should probe further. He glanced at Simone. Clearly she had made a good impression on the agent; it could not hurt to play on that impression.

"Your wife did well, then?" he asked. "The child—" He stopped. "I am sorry, Citoyen du Maurier. I recall that your family—"

A grim look came over the agent's face, then he sighed. "It was not from childbirth that she died, nor the child. The aristos— Hervé found them, dead and nearly unrecognizable from their injuries, and brought them back to me."

Corday froze, then drew in a slow breath. The injuries— and Hervé had found them. It was Guillaume Hervé. Dread crawled into Corday's gut, something he had not thought he would feel when he had taken on this mission. He hadn't recognized the agent at all, for he had not thought he would meet this man after all these years, nor that he would be *this* close. But of course; Corday had deduced that the man would most likely be a Public Safety agent for the utmost mobility, and it was so. It also explained his faint sense of familiarity when he had first set eyes on Hervé. Corday's dread increased. Had Hervé recognized him, as well? He heard du Maurier sigh, and looked at him.

Du Maurier evidently took his gasp for one of surprise and horror, for the distant manner he had taken with Corday dissipated. "So you see, it is necessary I find those aristos who did the deed and bring them to justice—and anyone else who has hurt the innocent."

Corday managed to nod. "Indeed. A laudable mission, citoyen," he said, barely conscious of the words he spoke. Guillaume Hervé. The man had had a different name, of course, and no, it was doubtful he recognized Corday, for it had been many years ago, and he must have changed much since then. He relaxed. In that, he had a slight advantage. He had recognized Hervé for what he was, and at most, Hervé knew him to be a spy if Johnson and Bramley had said anything about Corday to him. Dangerous enough, as he and Simone had discussed. It was a shock, nevertheless, for he had thought the man was dead; Corday had shot him, after all.

But neither Hervé nor du Maurier had made a move to arrest him, as they could very well have done this past week. A slight movement beside him—Simone—brought his attention back to the present again.

"Enough of that, however," du Maurier said, clearly closing the subject. He nodded at Simone. "I will see if I can recommend a suitable doctor when we arrive in Paris. You can be easy in your mind about it."

"I thank you, Citoyen du Maurier," Corday said, hoping he put enough gratitude in his voice.

Hervé entered then, and announced that the coach was ready. Corday was careful not to gaze at him any more than he would normally have. Now he could see the resemblance to the man Hervé had been; his hair had not been gray as it was now, he had grown stouter, and his face was no longer smooth of wrinkles. Du Maurier rose from his chair as Hervé turned and led the way to the coach. Corday helped Simone to her feet and followed them. His eyes strayed to Hervé again. It would be difficult not to stare at him in the coach. It had been a long time since he had seen the man, and Corday had thought him dead. He blew out a deep breath. He had the discipline he had cultivated over many long, dangerous years. This mission was no different from any others, with a few exceptions.

He smiled a little, thinking of the "exception" of Simone, then his smile fell from him. He didn't want to tell her about Hervé, but he would have to. He didn't have to tell her everything, however. He would tell her that Hervé was the man who had killed her family, no more. He suddenly did not want to tell her of his prior connection with Hervé; he did not know what to think of it himself. He closed his eyes for a moment, fatigue overcoming him. *Discipline, man, discipline!* he told himself. He would take refuge in it, as he had all his career.

The day was only a little overcast with clouds. But it was light enough so that Corday could hear Simone take in a painful gasp as she stepped outside. He mentally went over the list she had given him regarding her abilities and weaknesses. She had not written how weakened she could become from just a small exposure to light. He glanced at du Maurier as they entered the coach. It was clear that the agent was not inclined to let Simone and Corday out of his sight.

Still, he could play the innocent. He could ask the agent for names of physicians once they arrived in Paris, and then give him the address of the rooms he had let—the real address, not a false one, for he was sure that both du Maurier and Hervé would check to see whether the address was false. It was a risk, but it would deflect additional suspicion.

His eyes strayed to Hervé. Corday put his arm around Simone to distract himself, and she snuggled closer to him, laying her head on his shoulder. A sense of comfort eased into him, and he was able to take his attention from the man who sat in front of him, and look out the coach window instead.

The landscape had changed from rolling hills to flatter land as they had traveled from Normandy, and now it began to fill with houses and streets. They were nearing Paris, and Corday noticed more extremes of lifestyle than in the outlying provinces. In Normandy, an overall poverty seemed to cast a pall over the countryside, but here, so near the city, well-to-do mechants walked the street next to guttersnipes.

The horses picked up their pace, as if the coachman was eager to enter the city, perhaps for a glass of wine or cider. The buildings began to loom tall as they entered Paris, the houses and the occasional church shadowing the streets with their hulking forms. Corday had been in Paris before, but only briefly. He was glad that Simone was with him; she would be a good guide.

Especially now that he knew all she was capable of, her powers as a vampire. Hervé was the man he looked for, the man who had ordered the death of Simone's family, and the man who was financing the export of terror into England. He was sure of it. The victims' manner of death had been the same when Corday had first encountered it as it was now. And Hervé was the one who had brought the broken bodies of du Maurier's wife and child back to him. It could not be a coincidence. The man he had known had not refrained from brutalizing women or children, and his signature mode of imparting death was injuring them to the point of unrecognizability. And then the man would disappear, his identity change.

It was almost as if the man wanted always to remain in the shadows, and made sure that the dark shadow in which he existed reached out to draw the identity of others into the obscurity of darkness as well.

As you have yourself.

The thought dropped like a stone into Corday's gut. Who knew who he truly was, after all? And was he not a killer himself? He had known it since his first encounter with the man—Hervé's—ways.

No, no, he was not like this man. He went on missions, missions whose cause was just, and even then he held his hand from dealing out death if he deemed the recipients unworthy. And when he did kill, it was swift, clean, merciful, often done without the—the victim even knowing it had happened or was going to happen. He took no pleasure in killing; it was simply his . . . occupation, what he was ordered to do, and even then he did not always do as he was ordered.

What kind of occupation was it, after all? He thought of the simple people he had encountered in his travels, people who had served others in their inns, or the Abbé Dumont, who no doubt did good works. His eyes focused on the people he saw through the coach window, who streamed into the city, bearing goods for sale. They produced an object or gave service for their money. He . . . did not.

He glanced at the two men who sat opposite him in the coach. Du Maurier had fallen asleep, and a slight snore was issuing from him. Hervé cleared his throat as he turned the page of his book, his attention focused tightly on whatever he was reading. *So ordinary,* Corday thought. He looked again at du Maurier. This man also worked for his government, and though that government was possibly the most rapacious and brutal in Europe, du Maurier clearly believed he worked for a good cause and for the ideals his government claimed to support. Corday was sure du Maurier, also, had sent people to their deaths. But he would not be surprised if du Maurier had considered the evidence against these people carefully, and had been as just as he could be in his judgment.

Corday felt a sense of relief at the thought. He, too, worked for his government, carrying out missions that were in the interest of his country. His gaze drifted over Hervé again. And yet . . . and yet, he was more like Hervé than he had thought. At least du Maurier's activities were in the open, his identity known. Corday's, like Hervé's, was not.

Corday looked out the window again, not seeing the increasing numbers of people who flowed into the city, or hearing the cries of street-sellers hawking their wares. Despair winnowed its way into his bones, dragging out the fatigue he had so far been able to suppress.

"Are you well, Citoyen Thibaut?"

Corday looked up to see du Maurier gazing at him, his brows raised in question. He put on a slight smile. "Just the headache, citoyen, from lack of sleep. My wife—" he patted Simone's shoulder, "—sleeps much during the day and so is, ah, restless at night." He grinned, and du Maurier chuckled.

"That will change, citoyen, but not for long." Du Maurier's expression was amused. "Once the babe is born, you will have even less sleep than before, and it will not be because your wife is restless."

Corday rolled his eyes comically and let out a groan,

which made the agent laugh. They grinned at each other, and for a moment, Corday felt a kinship with this man, and regretted that they were enemies.

He glanced out of the coach window. The sunlight that had managed to seep past the clouds had become even more fugitive among the buildings, casting a dim light at cross-streets and fading almost to twilight in between. A sour smell came to his nose, the smell of dirt and the spill from chamber pots thrown into the gutter. He took out his handkerchief and put it to his nose; the smell was a strong contrast to the earthy smells of rain-washed countryside, and he hoped he would become used to the difference quickly.

Simone moved restlessly beside him, and suddenly stiffened. She had awakened, but then she relaxed against him again. Yet there was a tension in her body, and he wondered what it was that had disturbed her. He looked out the window again. No, not now. They were nearing their destination. He would ask her as soon as they came to their room at the hotel.

"Is your hotel near, Citoyen Thibaut?" said Hervé suddenly. His voice sounded mildly interested, as if he was only curious for conversation's sake. Corday suppressed a grim smile. Here it was. The man was clearly interested, as he had expected he would be.

"Yes," he replied. "It is the Hôtel de la Colombe."

Du Maurier smiled. "Well, then, the coach will go there first, and you may see your wife to the comfort of your rooms."

Corday bent his head in a brief bow. "I thank you, citoyens. And if I may be so bold, could I ask your direction?"

"But of course," du Maurier said. "You may visit me at my new lodgings at the prison I am to administer. It is close to the Abbeye—here, let me write down the address."

He pulled a small book of papers from his coat and wrote in it, then tore off a page and handed it to Corday. "I would be pleased to see you and your wife again."

Corday looked into the agent's eyes and smiled. Well. Was this a warning, then? But the agent's eyes were guileless, unsuspecting. Corday bowed again, glancing at Hervé. That man's gaze was searching, but only for a moment, before he opened his book and began to read again.

Du Maurier knocked on the roof of the coach, then opened the window and shouted to the coachman the address of the Hôtel de la Colombe. Corday watched the buildings pass as they continued into the city, and saw the prison that du Maurier mentioned he would administer. He quickly scanned the exterior, noting the entrances, the windows, and the guards. He eyed the men who guarded the exterior; they seemed well-fed enough, although they looked more like street rabble than soldiers set to guard prisoners. He hoped they were as lacking in discipline as he thought they might be.

The coach stopped soon after that at a freshly painted building that sported a large sign in the shape of a white dove. It was not one that had catered to the aristocracy, for the colors of the Revolution had been painted across the breast of the dove—or perhaps the enterprising owner had quickly painted the colors to avert suspicion. Nevertheless, it looked respectable, and the hotel was not far from du Maurier's prison.

Corday sighed as he opened the door, then turned and held out his hand. "It has been a pleasure to travel with you citoyens," he said.

Du Maurier smiled and shook it. "For me, also, Citoyen Thibaut." He nodded to Simone. "And you, citoyenne." She held out her hand, touching du Maurier's briefly, giving her thanks. "I hope you will regain your health soon," he said, and his voice was solicitous.

"You are very kind," Simone murmured, and sighed as if in tremendous weariness.

Corday held out his hand to Hervé as well. "A pleasure, Citoyen Hervé," he said.

The man gazed at him for a moment, then took his hand in a strong grasp. "I hope to see you soon, citoyen," he said after a moment.

Corday made himself nod and grin. "You have been most hospitable, citoyens," he said. "You may find it difficult to be rid of me. Do remember me if you need scribing services, or perhaps an entertaining tale or two."

Du Maurier chuckled. "To be sure, we will."

With a last grin, Corday descended the coach and helped Simone down from it. The door closed, and he watched the coach trundle down the cobblestones. Du Maurier and Hervé were no doubt going back to their lodgings, which they had passed on the way to the hotel. They could very well have gone to their lodgings first, and ordered the coach on to this hotel. Instead, they had let him and Simone out first.

It could be the two agents were being as hospitable as they had been during the journey. But Corday very much doubted it.

Chapter 16

BLOOD. THE STRONG SCENT OF BLOOD cut into Simone's senses, drawing out a piercing need.

She must be in Paris. She relaxed her suddenly stiffened body, aware of Michael talking beside her, but not listening to his words. Her whole attention focused on forcing down the blood-hunt.

Few other places had the scent of blood so persistently threaded through the air. Here, the mob madness, the mass murders, the work of the guillotine had drowned the earth and cobblestones in blood, and not rain nor tears had washed it out.

The tingling across her skin told her that it was still day, but the scent of blood tuned her senses to a finer pitch nevertheless. The rumbling of the coach wheels, mixed with the calls of the street sellers, pounded a mad symphony into her ears, and she felt almost mad herself with the onslaught of sensation. She clutched the cross at her breast. It tingled through the glove over her hand, but she murmured the rosary in her mind, and her thoughts gained focus again.

She sighed with relief. Her senses were still sharp with the blood-hunt, but the sensations ceased being a confused mass of sounds, sights, and textures. She shivered. She had seen another vampire once who had turned insane, and was sure it was because of the intensity of the blood-hunt. She had heard he had been shut in a church and died there from the holiness of it, and she had avoided other vampires since. And yet, she had come into a church and had not died. She shook her head. She did not understand it.

She closed her eyes, then felt a jolt of the coach. It seemed they were at their destination. She managed to focus her attention enough to say her thanks to du Maurier before she and Michael descended the coach to the hotel he had reserved.

Michael said nothing to her when they went into the hotel, although she noticed with amusement that the doorman, who came forward and took the large pack Michael had secured to the top of the coach, lifted his lip at the very devalued assignats and sous that Michael gave him. She noted the doorman's grimace, and contemptuous dropping of the pack to the floor as they entered the hotel. She had heard the assignats had devalued swiftly with each day; rumor had it that a bag full of assignats would only buy a few beets in the city, and it seemed this was true. Luckily, she had money in the form of actual livres, and then there were her mother's pearls, if need be.

She glanced at Michael's frown; he was clearly displeased with the doorman. He shrugged; no doubt he was used to inconveniences, she thought. But his frown persisted, and she thought he might have expected some little luxury here in Paris.

Simone focused on her surroundings: the calls of the customers for service, the décor, the scent of a meal cooking in the kitchens—it all helped keep the blood-hunt at bay. Michael had done well in choosing the hotel; the interior was thankfully dim, but it seemed clean enough, and the room to which the chambermaid led them well apportioned, though it was also dim, being situated across from a large church whose spires and towers cast a shadow on the chamber's window.

Michael put down his pack, then looked in another room—the bedroom apparently, for he turned to her with a smile. "You may rest well until the evening, *ma petite*. The mattress is of good quality—not made of straw. If I am not mistaken, it is a feather bed." He took her hand and led her to the bedroom. "There, rest. We will talk of what we must do when you awake."

She sat on the bed, but gazed up at him. "And you? What will you do?"

"I will rest also," he said, but made no move to the bed.

"I don't think you will," she said. "I think you will go about the city and look for the man you mean to kill."

He smiled slightly, but his smile did not reach his eyes.

"You are going out to find him—without me," she said, disgusted. "How will you find your way? Who will you ask?"

He walked to a chair and sat down, crossing his knees and folding his hands on his lap, obviously deciding to humor her questioning. His smile grew wider, and this time his eyes twinkled. "You were very efficient and thorough, Simone, in your descriptions of the city, and your map is very detailed. I believe I can go by what you have provided me." He hesitated. "The man I am looking for is no doubt connected with the Committee of Public Safety, and no doubt an agent. He will not be difficult to find."

Simone looked at him carefully. Neither his expression nor his voice revealed much, but for one moment his eyes shifted from hers. A moment only, but it was enough. She had known him for only a short while, but she had watched every move, every expression on his face in that time, and she felt she knew him as she knew her own heart.

And do you know your own heart? said the voice of her emotions. She gazed at Michael, at the eyes she had looked in while they made love, the lips she had kissed, the lean cheek she had stroked as they lay in bed. She sighed. Yes, she knew her own heart, alas.

She also knew he was going to search for the man he was to eliminate for the sake of his country, and he might well die. Her heart protested, her whole body and mind protested at the thought. She wanted to cry out at the pain of it all, her sense of danger and her love. But all she could say was "It is dangerous, Michael. You should not go alone. The prisons—for that is where I suppose you intend to go—are well guarded. It is best for you to go under the cover of dark, when the guards are sleepy, when the man himself is perhaps asleep. If you know at all who it is, and I doubt—" She stopped and gazed at him keenly, her heightened senses picking up an increase in his breathing. "You *do* know who it is," she said flatly.

His brows rose, and his smile faded. "You are perceptive." He looked down at his hands in his lap. "It is Guillaume Hervé."

"Hervé?" She stared at him, aghast. Hervé. Dear heaven. All this time, that insignificant, nondescript man. This was the man who had ordered her family killed. But he was wholly subordinate to du Maurier . . . surely Michael was mistaken. "How do you know? How long have you known? Why did you not tell me? Why did you not complete your mission while we traveled with him?" She stared at him, uncomprehending. Did he not trust her, after all they had been through together? After she had vowed herself to him before God and Church? Surely he knew what such vows meant to her?

He held up his hand in apparent surrender, his smile

returning. "My dear, I did not know until recently, and it was only after a few things du Maurier said during our journey that all the evidence I had been given before I came here to France fell into place. Du Maurier himself does not know—cannot know."

Simone shook her head, her mind awash in confusion. "Cannot know? How can he not?"

Michael stared at her, his mouth pressed into a grim line. "Hervé was the man who brought the bodies of Mme. du Maurier and her child to du Maurier."

"What of it?" Simone said impatiently. "I know this already."

"He was also the one who killed them, then blamed it on the aristos, no doubt to manipulate du Maurier into working for the Revolution."

A sick lump formed in Simone's stomach. "How can you know?"

"Remember the men you saw at the inn? The Englishmen?"

Simone nodded slowly.

"Their 'bodies' were shipped back to our headquarters, broken, and faces mutilated beyond recognition. The only things that identified them were their clothes and their effects. Yet, we saw them alive, in the same inn at which Hervé and du Maurier made their stop. Hervé must have convinced them over to his side, and worked to send some poor souls' bodies in their stead, to convince our government that our agents were indeed dead, instead of conspiring to bring down our country."

A chill went through Simone's heart. "Du Maurier described the bodies of his wife and child in such terms," she said.

"Exactly," he said, and looked approvingly at her.

Simone swallowed. All this time. All this time, the one who called for the murder of her family had ridden with them, had sat and dined at their table. Her hands began to shake with rage and blood-hunt. Hervé, the murderer, he who was so innocuous, so quiet and unassuming. Fire heated her gut and seared the edges of her mind. A prick of teeth caught the skin of her lower lip, and her hands opened and closed at the thought of gaining vengeance.

"Simone!"

Michael's voice, sharp and loud to her heightened hearing, made her jerk, startled, and a growing sting at her breast caught her attention. Her hand clasped the cross on its chain. It stung strongly through the glove on her hand, and she blinked. *No.*

She drew in a deep breath. No, she could not give in to the blood-hunt. She was not in danger right now, and it would not be in defense of anyone. She looked at Michael, and his eyes bored into hers, as if he willed his own control into her. She took in a deep breath and let it out.

"That's better," he said. He rose and sat beside her on the bed. "You had the same look on your face as you had when you went after Broussard. I assume you were about to get into as dangerous a state now as you did then."

She looked at him, then away. "Yes," she whispered. "I . . . I should warn you, the streets of Paris are seeped in blood. It . . . the blood-hunger—it grows the more I stay here, and my powers grow stronger with it."

"Good," he said. "It will no doubt be useful."

She raised her head and stared at him. "Good?" she cried. "How can such a curse be good?"

Michael cocked his head at her, then shook it. "Don't be silly, *ma petite,*" he said, his voice holding a touch of impatience. He put his hand under her chin, drawing her to him. "Look at me. Have you ever thought how effective you would have been if you had not your powers? How many people would you have saved if you had not had them?"

"I—I—" Simone shook her head, trying to find words

to refute him. Of course her powers were a curse, for they came with the curse of the blood-hunt, with her vampirism. If she were a normal woman, she would not have killed those men who had killed her family. She would not have . . .

If she had been a normal woman, she would never have gone the course of smuggling refugees. She would not have saved many people at all. She gazed at Michael, searching for words, not able to find them.

"How many have you saved? Fifty, one hundred, two hundred, more?" His voice was stern, and he stared at her, his brows frowning.

"I . . . I don't know," she whispered. "More, perhaps. I have lost count—I have not counted how many I have released from the prisons."

"How are your powers, which have saved so many lives, such a curse, then? Can a curse do good or evil?"

Her mind was a flurry of confusion. She had thought of her condition as a curse for so long. . . . "A curse cannot do good," she said at last. "But I thought—"

He shook his head, his smile ironic. "You did not think at all, *ma petite*. No doubt your priest told you this nonsense, bending you to his will—"

Quick anger flared, and she pulled away, glaring at him. "Père Dumont does not compel me. Indeed, it was he who said I should use my powers to save—" She stopped, the words she was about to say stuck in her throat. "To save others," she said finally after a pause. "To do good."

A groan burst from beside her, and she looked at Michael as he slapped his palm against his forehead. "Do you mean to say that all this time, you thought your powers evil, even when your own priest had not said it?"

"I . . ." Simone cleared her throat, suddenly thick with

tears she could not shed. "The taking of blood is a sin, Michael. Being a vampire is a curse. The powers are part—"

He shook his head in disgust. "How do you know that? And even if they came with your condition, did your priest not say you were to use them for good?"

"I . . . yes, he did."

"Then does it not make sense, my sweet idiot, that your priest sees your powers as mere tools, to use for either good or evil, as you will?"

"I . . . suppose he does," she said. A sprout of hope grew in her heart, a trickle of warmth. "I have been used to thinking of my condition as a curse, an evil thing, born of evil."

He shook his head, and took her hand in his. "*Ma petite,* you were more sinned against than sinning. You were a proud girl who fell into bad company, and who has not done that from time to time?" He laughed sourly. "Indeed, there are worse souls than you, who leap into bad company with both eyes open, and continue to use their powers, small or large, for wrong causes." He caressed her cheek lightly. "Listen, Simone. I do not know why it is you were cursed with this vampirism." His mouth curled skeptically. "I am far from an expert in the spiritual or supernatural. I only know we play with the cards that we are dealt. You were given a set of cards that were good and bad. So far as I can see, you have reduced the bad as much as you could, and used what good ones you could to the utmost. I doubt Père Dumont or even your God could ask for more." He shook his head. "Sweet Simone. Anyone else would have seen your powers as a gift, not a curse."

A gift. Simone gazed out the window of the bedroom. The sun had fallen far below the line of the buildings across the street, darkening the sky enough so that she saw the faint twinkle of a bright star high in the evening sky. She could feel her strength return to her as the night grew deeper. A gift—the idea was foreign to her, that a power based in her dark nature could be a gift. She shook her head slowly, the habit of fear and loathing of her condition warring with the hope that she might freely exult in her strength and swiftness. An odd trembling shook her for a moment at the thought, and she took a deep breath, stilling herself. She looked at Michael.

"I . . . I don't know. I had always thought—I am not used to—"

He put his fingers on her lips. "Hush, *ma petite*. Say nothing. Think on it for a while." He smiled, then took her hand and kissed it. "You are a mystery, Simone." The smile fell from him, and he looked out the window into the night. He released his hand and rose from the bed. "I must go."

"And I will go with you," Simone said.

He looked at her, his expression becoming cool. "I think not."

It was her turn to feel impatience. "Do not be silly, monsieur," she said. "It is night, and so my strength grows. I know these streets even in the darkest of nights, and know of passageways through which even the agents dare not go. I can go where no man has gone, and lead you through. I can show you a way to escape should you need it, and you must admit that a plan is all the more efficient if there is a way of escape."

Michael grinned suddenly, and chuckled. "You are right, of course, although I feel insulted that you assumed I had not planned an escape. I am not so much of a fool, however, not to look at as many ways of escape as possible. I am not that enamored of dying, after all."

Simone felt suddenly light, and her lips turned up in response. "Good. I am glad I did not marry a total fool."

His grin widened and he looked her up and down. "Why, *ma petite*, what a compliment! If I married you, could I be that much of a fool?"

"Perhaps," she replied, wrinkling her nose, but her heart still felt light nevertheless. She nodded toward his pack. "What do you have there that we can use?"

He shook his head. "Simone, this is dangerous. You know how many guards there are outside the prison. You also know how dangerous Hervé can be."

She let out an impatient sigh. "Only a moment ago, you talked of my powers as a gift. To whom? Both our missions benefit when we join our skills. Admit it, monsieur, my powers could help you gain entrance."

He gazed at her silently, apparently weighing her words. "I would protect you, *ma petite*," he said at last.

She gazed at him steadily. "And I, you."

He was silent again, then shook his head. "I am a fool to let you come."

"So you have said before, but that has not stopped either you or me, has it?" Simone said cheerfully.

He smiled wryly, and pulled his pack toward them. "Very well." He took it to a large escritoire whose surface was bare of writing material, opened the bag, emptied it, then went to a wardrobe that sat in one corner of the bedroom. "Ah, yes. My associate has been quite thorough." He pulled out another large sturdy bag of woven hemp, a seaman's pack.

She looked at him curiously. "You have associates here? Helpers?"

"Yes," he said, and poured out the contents of that bag as well. He said nothing else as he sorted the items he had spilled out of the bags, and it was clear to Simone he was not going to reveal anything else about whatever associates he might have in France. She shrugged. It was not important, but if they came out of their missions alive, she would see if she could find out more—of everything about him.

She walked to the escritoire and gazed at what he had spread over its surface.

A hank of slim but strong rope—more than thirty feet in length—lay there, obviously taken from the sailor's pack. She watched him as he laid more than a few knives, both long and short, in a neat line across the back of the escritoire, and then some long picks beside them. He opened a box—a brace of pistols, she noted. They were, no doubt, in addition to the one he carried on him. Shot, two bags of powder, the accompanying ramrod, two long wires, string, what looked like gum Arabic, a bottle of the spirit of alcohol, and hair.

"Hair?" she asked. He grinned, took a bit of the gum Arabic, applied it to his chin, then took a pinch of hair and stuck it carefully to the gum, forming a thin goatee.

She stared at him. He looked, if anything, more seductively satanic than ever. She closed her eyes, shivering. "Take it off. You look like *le Diable* himself."

"Like it, do you?" he said. "When we are done with our respective jobs, I will put it on for you."

"Don't," she said. "I do not think I would like making lov—" She glanced at him; his grin had grown wider. *"Tiens!"* she growled. "The night will not last forever, and if I am to release as many prisoners as possible before the Public Safety Committee decides to torture them, we need to go soon."

He nodded, wincing as he pulled off the false goatee and wiping off the residue with the alcohol spirits. He continued putting his equipment in order, then took out the pistols to prime them.

She watched as he carefully took the pistols out of their case, put in the powder, and then pushed the shot down the barrel with the ramrod.

"How many pistols do you have?" she asked.

"Three," he said shortly. She took no offense at his tone, for he was clearly concentrating on preparing his weapons and other equipment. Simone nodded, then remembered her brother's pistols that she had brought with her from the de la Fer mansion. It would be a good idea if she prepared them, too.

She pulled one out of the pocket of her dress, the other from her bag, and laid out her shot, ramrod, and powder as well. She quickly checked the action of the pistols, loaded them, and then laid them to the side.

She looked up at Michael to find him staring at her, his expression both bemused and slightly offended. "What is it?" she asked.

"You can shoot a pistol?"

"Yes," she said. "That is why I brought these with me."

"I thought you didn't like them," he said, still staring at her.

"I never said that," she replied. "I merely did not like yours, for you pointed it too many times at me for my liking."

"And you can shoot accurately with them?"

"Of course. Otherwise I would not have brought them," she said patiently.

His offended expression grew. "I thought you did not like killing," he said.

She gazed at him, her brows raised. "I don't like killing at all," she said, enunciating her words clearly, as if she were dealing with a recalcitrant child. "But nothing prevents me from self-defense or defending the innocent, and it is not necessary to kill with a pistol, after all, only maim." She looked at him with understanding, and patted his arm. "You thought I used only my powers? I am not that vain of them, monsieur! They have their limits."

"I did not know you could shoot." His voice had lost its aggrieved tone, but he still frowned.

She looked at him, surprised. "Did I not list it as one of my skills?"

"No, you did not."

She shrugged. "Ah, well. No doubt I forgot."

"I hope you remember to tell me of any other skills you might have left off the list."

Simone nodded. "If I remember any more." She looked about her and saw that he had rolled his tools in a cloth. "Are we ready, monsieur?"

There was silence, and then a sigh. "No, not yet," he said, and then she was in his arms with his lips on hers. "Not yet. Please." His voice was soft, almost a whisper, but there was despair in it, and it drew up the sorrow that seemed ever-present, pressing beneath her breastbone. He moved apart from her a hairbreadth. "I am not 'monsieur,' Simone. My name is Michael. Say it."

Simone could not say anything, for his lips came down upon hers again, kissing deeply. He moved his hand to her breast, and she couldn't say no, even though she had tried to keep him at a distance, had called him "monsieur" to remind herself they might not meet again after he—she hoped—completed his mission. She reached her hand behind his head, letting loose the queue in which he had tied his hair. It came loose, a lion's mane around his face, and brushed her cheek. Her senses were at their height now, and the brush of his hair felt like feathers upon her skin, soft and sensual. Desperation seized her, and she began to pull off his clothes, as he pulled off hers.

Michael pushed her onto the bed, making her sit, and kissed her lips again. His lips moved downward, making a sizzling trail down her neck to her breasts. She arched back her head at the sensation, and her hands trembled as she reached for him, but he seized her hands and held them to either side of her hips as his lips moved downward. He kissed her breasts and her belly, and then knelt between her knees, bowing his head until he reached the hub of her passion and kissed her there.

She dug her fingers into the mattress, convulsing instantly and crying out, for the pulsing pleasure was almost painful in its intensity. He rose, and as he kissed her, he entered her, moving hard and desperately. Suddenly he lifted her, and when she wrapped her legs around him, he turned and lay back on the bed, carrying her with him. Simone was above him for only a moment, however, for he rolled and she was beneath. She gazed at him, but he did not look at her in return, for his eyes were closed and he began moving again, with exquisite slowness. She could feel him inside, how he trembled within and above her, and his trembling sent pleasure like a warm mist of rain onto her flesh. The trembling translated itself to her, into her flesh and muscle, so that she also trembled, wanting to weep with the pleasure and the despair of possible loss. He moved within her, he kissed her, and she breathed his breath in a sob.

"Ah, Simone, Simone, what you do to me," he whispered. He kissed her again, his mouth tasting hers, and he pressed deeply inside her so that she gasped and twisted beneath him. "I cannot resist you, even when you ask me to let you do something that would make me risk losing you." He withdrew and sank deep again. "I am a fool indeed." He kissed her again, and then he moved faster, harder, until she groaned and moved against him as well, urging the pleasure from him.

Heat flared hot from their joining, and she arched against him, clutching his buttocks so that he would sink even deeper into her. She could not stand it, she must reach something—him, anything. Her hands grasped him tightly as he kissed her, and she bit his lip. She drew back when she realized what she had done—the blood-hunt had begun to seep into her sensations—but he kissed her once again, and put his forefinger on her lips and touched her tongue with it. She opened her eyes, and saw him gazing at her, his expression closed with despair.

"Take what you will," he said, and let his finger graze on the tips of her teeth. "At least I can give you this." She could taste a drop of his blood on his fingertip, and he brushed her tongue with it again.

She wanted to weep. "At least," he had said. As if they would part after this, as if he had not given her anything, when he had given her more than anyone had in all her life. She closed her lips around his finger, sucking lightly. He groaned, then pressed himself tightly against her, then withdrew and thrust again and again as she drew his finger into her mouth and licked down the length of it with her tongue.

Power flared through her, and it seemed Michael pushed his manhood into the core of her, where she burned and burned until she heard his deep groan and felt the spill of his release, and still he thrust until she cried out, releasing his finger from her lips and clutching his hips with her legs.

His head fell forward, resting on her shoulder, and then, with a sighing groan, he let himself down upon her.

Michael lay, unmoving, for a few moments, then moved to his side, taking Simone with him. He lifted his hand and brushed the hair that had fallen over her face, then kissed her once more. "Something to remember me by," he said. "Something for me to remember."

"Will you leave me, then?" she asked,

He said nothing, only looking at her as if he were memorizing her every feature, running his fingers over her cheek and chin, then over her shoulder and breasts. Once more he kissed her, then withdrew from her with clear reluctance, and rolled from the bed. He went to his pack on the floor next to the escritoire and searched within until he pulled out a large cloth. He returned to the bed then, and began carefully wiping the moisture from her body, and his touch was gentle, as if he were caressing a jewel of great price.

He kissed her once again, then gathered up their

clothes. She took hers, saying nothing, only savoring their time together and staving off the sadness that threatened to overwhelm her. She must not give in to the sadness, nor have regrets. All her attention must be on freeing what prisoners she could. It was her mission and her penance; she must be dedicated to it, heart and soul. She pulled on her clothes, abandoning skirt for knee breeches and stockings, then binding her hands with rags.

"La Flamme again?" Michael asked.

She turned to him and smiled. "Yes. The disguise works better than skirts when it is night, and you must admit it is not ladylike work that I do."

"True," he replied. "I imagine I would be much hampered by skirts if I had to wear them on my mission—unless I had a good reason to wear them."

Simone stared at him. "Have you— No." She laughed. "I doubt you have ever worn skirts, even as a disguise. You would make a rather ugly woman, Michael."

He put on a despondent expression. "You wound me. I had had an elegant image of myself in full court dress, and you have dashed it horribly."

She chuckled, and he grinned and kissed her once again. He held out her cloak. "There you go, *ma petite*."

She did not put on her cloak right away, but picked up her doll first, looking at it. She smoothed the hair from its face, still unmarred through all her adventures. She sighed. "I think I will give this doll to the next child I see," she said suddenly. She swallowed down an odd, tight feeling in her throat. Her words declared an end; not, she hoped, the end of her mission to free innocents from the guillotine, but perhaps an end to her disguise. She did not really need the doll, and it served no purpose but to further disguise her identity. She had held on to it to remember her family, but in truth it had only reminded her of her act of vengeance in killing those who had killed her family.

Wearing the doll had become a habit, and she realized she wanted to lose the habit of thinking of vengeance, to think of saving those who suffered instead.

Simone grinned suddenly. It would also confuse her pursuers, she was sure, if she suddenly appeared some day without the hump on her back. She tied the doll to her back with strips of rag, then pulled on her cloak.

She caught sight of herself in the bedroom mirror, her pale face peeking out from the darkness of the cloak's hood. She looked just as ghostly as she had before, except she had left off the rags on her face. It had never taken long for her to find her way into the prisons, for she had carefully charted her various paths and hiding places. And if she were caught . . . well, it would be easy enough to tie the cloak about her waist as a skirt, dirty her face, and pretend she was a servant, or a slattern for one of the prison guards. She glanced at Michael, who was tucking a pistol into his belt. It might be different with two people, but he was intelligent, quick, and practical, and she did not anticipate he would delay her.

She took her primed pistols and put one in her cloak pocket; the other she tucked under a belt. Then she took her dagger and strapped it to the side of her leg.

She glanced at herself again in the mirror and took in a deep breath. There. She was ready. Her heart beat faster with anticipation. If she were honest, she had to admit she liked the excitement of the hunt, the tricking of the guards, and the triumph she felt when she released prisoners. She looked at Michael and found he was watching her.

"Are you ready?" she asked.

He walked to the window and gazed out of it for a moment, then went to her side. He raised her hand to his lips and kissed it. "Yes. It's clear. Let us go." He opened the door, and bowed with an ironic smile as she proceeded before him.

Chapter 17

CORDAY WATCHED SIMONE WALK BEfore him, a small black form against the darkness of night. Though she had taken a small lantern with her just before they left the hotel, she did not light it, merely secreting a tinderbox in one of her cloak pockets. If there was a moon, he could not see it, for clouds once more obscured the sky that had been clear just a while ago.

A few candle lamps lit the outside of some buildings, but unlike in London; no linkboys offered to walk before them with their lamps, and he was half sure that some of the candles in the street lamps would be stolen by the time the night was over. He doubted many would be out at night; it was a lawless place, and what men policed these streets were just as likely to fleece one of one's goods as the street thieves themselves. Even if it were not so, few would want to be out at night like this. The wretched poverty of many of the people would be enough to incline them toward robbery out of sheer need.

Corday smiled cynically. He was beginning to think like du Maurier . . . . or Simone. He frowned. They were alike in their own ways, even though they were enemies. They thought of others more than themselves.

So unlike yourself! He mocked himself, mocking the touch of regret that tugged at him. He shrugged. There was no time to think on such things. He watched Simone, who glided from shadow to shadow, quietly, and with a graceful strength. She was focusing on the moment; it was best if he did the same.

It was clear that she could see in the dark, as she had said. She had no trouble wending her way through the alleys and the streets, and he followed, careful to keep himself as hidden as she did.

She stopped, then turned sharply away from the direction of du Maurier's and Hervé's prison. Corday seized her arm. "Where are you going?"

"Not far," she whispered. "I will lead you to a place that few enter. When—when we return, especially if we are followed, it would be good to go this way, for none would think we would enter it. It will take us half a street away from the prison."

He hesitated, used to distrust, then nodded. "Very well. Let's go."

"You will find it unpleasant, Michael, I warn you." He could hear the smile in her voice, a hint of mischief. "I am used to it, but no one except the graveyard workers go there."

"I will bear it, I assure you," he said dryly. No doubt she meant to lead him through a graveyard and thought he would be spooked. Yet, for all that he now believed she was indeed a vampire—the evidence of his senses could not be denied after all—he still had no faith in the supernatural. He had never seen evidence of ghosts; those he'd seen die stayed quite dead.

The street down which they turned was silent, more silent than others they had walked through, and few if any lights showed in the windows of the buildings they passed. Simone paused, then looked around. He heard a clink and a spark in the darkness and slowly a flame appeared, lighting her face. Carefully, she transferred the flame from the tinderbox to the candle in the lantern she had carried with her. She glanced at him.

"Sometimes even I have a little trouble seeing where we will be going. It is very dark." She closed the shade of the lantern so that only a slit of light showed. "Come," she said, and held out her hand.

He put his hand in hers, and she tugged at him. He followed her, and his feet met ground that slanted downward. He put his other hand out to the side—a threshold. He frowned. Not a graveyard, then.

"Where is this place?" he asked.

"It is beneath the city," Simone replied. Her voice sounded close, muffled, and then it seemed the space around them opened up, for he could hear the residual echo of her voice and that of their footsteps. A musty smell came to his nose, moldy, with an edge of rot. The air was humid and chill, and he could hear the dripping of water in the distance.

"It is a place that few venture into," she continued. "Prepare yourself, Michael, for I need to open the lantern shade. What you see will be unpleasant, but you need to see where we are going, so that if we need to escape you will know how to get through it."

He rolled his eyes with impatience. "You need not be so tender of my sensibilities, *ma petite*. Open the lantern."

"As you say," she said, and light poured forth. He found himself staring into the empty eyes of a skull.

"Bloody hell!" He moved back involuntarily.

"I do not understand 'bloody hell'—I think it is something you English say when you are surprised?"

"Yes," he said shortly.

"I told you, Michael." Her voice still held a note of mischievousness.

"No doubt you think this highly amusing," he said, gaining his composure. He looked around at the neatly stacked bones and skulls, forming the walls of the tunnel they had entered. He had heard that the cemeteries in Paris had grown to literal bursting with the newly dead, so that the authorities had been forced to make room for them. As a result, ancient bones were dug up and brought into quarry caves and tunnels under Paris. "The catacombs," he said.

"Yes." Simone moved forward. "You see how it is unlikely anyone would follow us here." She paused, and her voice became uncertain. "If . . . anything were to happen to me, Michael, if you must hide me, go through here to Père Dumont's lodgings, for I doubt anyone would follow us to this place, and I would not want to bring more danger to him than he is in now. But . . . but if I am severely injured, I would be shriven." She gazed at him intently. "Promise me this, Michael."

Corday looked at her, at how the light she held casting shadows under her eyes, making her seem older and more tired than she usually appeared. Pity stirred within him, and a desperate wish to save her, to make her life better after her unrelenting work and tireless effort. He touched her cheek.

"I promise, *ma petite,*" he said, and her look of relief and momentary joy made him . . . happy. He shook his head as she turned from him to continue down the tunnel. He was definitely not himself; emotions he was not used to feeling had seized him, shaking and rattling him like a rag doll. He was not sure when it had begun—perhaps with his discovery of Hervé's identity. No. It was with his first meeting with Simone. He smiled slightly. She had totally shaken his expectations, brought a certain . . . life to him.

An odd thought, but he had felt near dead with fatigue and that death would be a blessed rest. Yet, she was something outside of his experience, and had shaken all his expectations down to the ground.

He glanced at the walls of the tunnel, at how the bones were grotesquely arranged in decorative patterns, and thought there might be an artist among the graveyard workers. He gazed at Simone again, deftly wending her way past the eyes of the dead. Most definitely outside his expectations.

He noted the way Simone went, memorizing it with his eyes and his feet. He would keep his promise to her and bring her to Père Dumont to be shriven, if need be. He hoped there would not be the need.

The path rose beneath his feet, and moving air touched his face at last. The sky had cleared again, and he could see the moon rising behind the tall buildings and a few stars flickering above them. Simone stopped and looked about her, then doused the lantern. She put it down near the exit of the catacombs. "We will not need the light now," she said. "Besides, it will be too awkward to carry with us where we go." She looked at the moon and then at Corday. "Come. We must hurry."

The prison was indeed not far from the catacombs. It was—as were many of the prisons—a priory or abbey taken over from the Catholic Church by the government, for the old prisons were apparently not sufficient for the sudden influx of "criminals against the state." It was difficult to see in the dark, but Corday could make out general Gothic features of the building. Simone moved behind a nearby pillar, and he followed suit. She touched his arm.

"The prisoners are held mostly on the ground floor, but we cannot go in on those levels, for the guards come by frequently. This particular prison has a loose window in one of the storage rooms of the upper floors, which I always go through."

Corday looked at the sheer wall of the prison. "Which one is it?"

She pointed. "That one."

It was a large window on the second floor, with a protruding ledge, well able to let in a man of his size. However, beneath it was sheer stone, with no handhold he could see. He looked at her skeptically. "You go through that window often?"

She grinned at him. "Yes, did I not say so?" She looked about her again. "If we are to go in, we must do so soon. The guard will change with the turning of the hour. That is when we must go." She turned to him. "You brought the rope, yes?"

He nodded.

"Give it to me, *s'il vous plaît*. I will climb the wall, then enter into the room, where I will tie the rope to a cabinet. I will let down the rope, and then you may climb in." She grinned. "The guards look to see who might escape by the first floor, but they never look up."

Corday took out the rope and looked up at the window again. He could easily climb the wall with a rope; he had climbed up walls many times that way in his career. But Simone? He mentally went over the list of her skills she had given him. "Is *this* what you meant by climbing?" he asked.

Her brows raised. "*Mais oui*," she said. "What else could I have meant?" She took the rope and ran quickly to the wall.

Corday bit back a foul curse. She had used her damnable swiftness and left before he could stop her. . . . His eyes widened as he watched.

She did not stop her running when she reached the wall, and leaped as if she would jump a large fence. Her hands and feet seemed to dig into the wall, finding footholds, and she climbed nimbly up the sheer face of it as if she were a squirrel climbing a tree. Only a minute passed before she sat on the window ledge, then her hand reached out to open the window.

He grinned. "You, *ma petite,* are a miracle," he whispered.

Her arm seemed to disappear into the darkness, and then she, too, disappeared from the window ledge. Corday heard footsteps then, and moved back behind the pillar. The footsteps passed close; he could even hear the yawn coming from the guard. An idea came to him, and he smiled, pulling out his dagger. He flipped the knife in his hand and leaped for the guard.

"Oof!" The guard fell unconscious with a satisfying thump.

Corday flipped his dagger again and sheathed it. "Sorry, friend, but I have need of your clothes." He stripped the guard of his uniform, tied the man's hands and feet with the stockings, and gagged him with his neckerchief. Quickly he put on the uniform, wincing with dismay that he would have to leave his own clothes behind. Ah, well. One had to seize what opportunities one could.

Corday moved cautiously around the stone pillar, then glanced up. A face showed at the window, looking up and down the street, then a long snakelike shadow flowed down the wall.

"My cue," Corday muttered, and ran to the rope.

He did not climb the wall as swiftly as Simone; that was impossible. However, the rope was strong, and she had tied it to something clearly heavy, for it did not budge and gave him good support as he pulled himself up. He grasped the ledge at last, and a small hand extended itself to him when he was chest-level with the ledge. "I'll pull you down," he protested.

She grasped his arm and pulled with much more than average strength. "Silly man."

"Of course," he replied dryly, as he hefted himself up on the ledge and swung his legs around into the building.

The light of the moon spun thin threads of light into the room, and he could see it was indeed a storage room, filled with various types of furniture and supplies. Simone pulled up the rope, winding it around her hand and elbow, then tucked it away under a cabinet near the window. "We will leave the rope here, in case we need to leave through this window—if we do not find another way out." She looked him up and down critically, then frowned. "Did you kill the guard?" she asked.

"No, of course not, *ma petite*. I strive to please you in all things, and I knew killing him would upset you."

"Ha!" she said, then chuckled. "It does not quite fit you."

"It didn't fit the guard, either," he replied.

She grinned, then carefully opened the door of the storage room and peered out. She glanced back at him. "Come," she said. "There is no one here."

The door opened into a long hall, lit by weakly flickering candles in their sconces. Simone put her finger to her lips, signaling silence, and beckoned him to follow her.

The walls were spare of decoration, as Corday would expect of an old priory, but what he could see in the dim light was unkempt and smelled of dirt and urine. The mob that had raided the building had seemed determined to foul what they could not tear down. He thought of du Maurier's new appointment to this prison; he doubted the man would stand for this kind of uncleanliness.

He halted in his steps, for Simone suddenly froze. "Footsteps," she whispered. He could hear none, but she gazed earnestly at him as she tugged him to another door. Quickly they entered the room and Simone pressed her ear against the door. It was unnecessary. Even Corday could hear the voices.

"If he—or they—are not here tonight, I am sure they will arrive soon."

Hervé. Corday's hand went to his pistol.

"No." Simone whispered, seizing his arm. "Not yet. Not until we have freed prisoners. It is only Hervé."

"Only." His voice sneered.

"Du Maurier is not with them."

"True." It occurred to him that if he killed Hervé now, he would accomplish his mission. He gazed at Simone, at her eyes filled with urgency and pleading. It had not seemed to matter when he had begun it that he come out of his mission alive. He had felt indifferent, fated to it. Now, he wanted to escape out of the dark hole of France's Revolution into the green hills of England. If he killed Hervé now, du Maurier would be left; he would gather all his guards and alert the forces of the Committee of Public Safety to go after them. Their chances of escape—and that of any prisoners they managed to free—would be reduced drastically. He tucked his pistol back into his belt.

Simone rested her cheek against the door, listening. "It is safe," she said after a moment. They went out into the hall again. "This way."

Another door opened to a stone staircase that spiraled downward; they were in one of the towers at the corner of the priory. The air drew dank, and the smell of crowded humanity rose in the air. Low groans floated upward to their ears; clearly the prison entry was near.

Corday seized Simone's arm. "Stop," he whispered. "I am sure there are at least a few guards below. How do you usually get the prisoners out?"

She grimaced. "I usually knock the guards out, then take their keys and open the cell doors. Then I lead the prisoners out of a side door; that, too, is guarded, but I come out first, and dispatch the guards there before letting the prisoners proceed."

He grinned. "I have a better plan. Put your hands behind you and turn around. The less the guards suspect, and the closer we come to them, the better it is for us." She looked at him, then glanced at his guard uniform. Smiling, she turned and crossed her hands behind her. They descended the stairs.

There were indeed two guards at the prison door; one yawned and stretched, but they came to attention when they saw Corday and Simone. He assessed them; both were husky fellows, but it would not be difficult to be rid of them. He saluted.

"Marmont reporting, citoyens, with a prisoner."

One of them frowned. "Marmont . . . I do not recall a Marmont."

Corday put an anxious expression on his face. "Did I do wrong, citoyens? I am new, you see."

The guard's face cleared. "Ah, a new recruit." He looked at Simone and a smirk grew on his face. "What is this? She's a pretty one." He elbowed the other guard in the ribs. "Maybe I'll have a taste of this dove a little later, eh?"

Corday returned the smirk. "She's a feisty one, citoyen. She'll give you a good time, I'm sure."

"*Cochons!* Pigs!" Simone spat at them. "You will die first before you touch me!" She pretended to struggle, and Corday turned, facing her, lifting his hand as if to strike her for her insolence. He winked, and she pressed her lips together as if suppressing a laugh, then pretended to cower.

He swung his hand toward her. A quick twist of his body made his fist connect with a satisfying crack on the first guard's chin instead. A cut-off word and a thump to the side of him made him turn. Simone had knocked out the other guard, a fierce grin on her face. "Ha!" she said triumphantly. "That is what you get when you try to molest an innocent woman, *cochon!*"

"I don't think he heard you, my sweet," Corday said, rummaging about the guard's pockets for the keys. "From the looks of him, he will be out for quite a while." He peered at the guard's face. "A nice flush hit—Ah! The keys." He held up a ring of keys and tossed them to Simone. "A present for you, *ma petite*."

She laughed, caught the keys, and made an elegant bow. "*Merci*, Michael." She turned to the prison door and her expression sobered. "And now . . . the prisoners."

She looked over the keys, then pounced on one of them. "This one first." She fit it into the lock and turned. The door opened, and she slipped through. Corday followed.

The rank smell was worse here; these were the poorer prisoners, the ones who could not afford more than a pile of straw on the floor and slops for a meal. Simone peered into each window, and unlocked them swiftly. She pushed them open, and beckoned to each one. "Come out, come out. You are being released. But be quiet, and be quick, and do not go out of the main door until I say so." She looked intently at Corday, and he nodded, understanding that he was to stay at the door and watch for any more guards. She disappeared up another flight of stairs at the end of the prison hall after she opened the last door, and a brief cold dread caught him as he watched her. But she went with confidence, and he forced down his misgivings. She had released prisoners here before—that was clear by the way she knew exactly which key would fit into the main prison door. She knew what she was doing; he needed to trust her.

He breathed out a sigh of relief when he saw her slight form returning down the stairs, a crowd of people following her. Her face was filled with grief; he took her hand and squeezed it when she came to him. "Some of them . . . some of them did not survive the imprisonment, Michael," she whispered. "Some of them were children." She closed her eyes for a moment, murmuring under her breath, and he knew she said a prayer.

His heart constricted, and he held her hand tightly, kissing it. He looked at the tired, hopeful faces behind her, obediently silent. They were men and women, young and old, some clearly servants, others wearing rags of their former wealth. "We need to go, *ma petite*."

She drew in a deep breath and opened her eyes. "You are right." She turned to the people behind her. "Stay quiet, and follow me—at a distance."

Corday went a little ahead of her; at least he could see if the guards they had overcome had revived. He opened the main prison door—no, they were still unconscious. Good. He nodded to Simone, and she caught up with him, then paused at the side door that led outside. She pressed her ear against the door, then looked at Corday and nodded. "I can hear two of them." She paused. "Now," she said.

They opened the door, quickly. Simone took the first one as the door opened, and Corday took the one to the other side; neither guard had the chance to do other than gasp. She turned back to the waiting people within. "Go," she said. "Quickly. Hide where you can—the catacombs, if you know them well enough, or to the Seine if you can procure a boat. Go, now!" The people streamed out, eagerly, haltingly, as best as they could.

Simone looked at him. "They must make their way—there are many, and I cannot escort them all to the coast." She glanced back at the prison. "I will help you find Hervé."

He did not want her help. He thought of the agent, how he would face him, what he would say. No. He did not want Simone to come with him, or see what he would do once he found Hervé.

"No." He glanced at the prison as well. "No. There are other prisoners who need your help. I have my mission to complete." He turned back to the prison door, then hesitated. "Wait for me," he said, then despair made him seize her around her waist. He kissed her, deeply, a farewell. "I will meet you in the catacombs." He released her, and stepped across the threshold.

A click sounded next to his ear, and cold metal met his temple. "I think not, Citoyen Thibaut."

Corday froze. Du Maurier, damn him.

"Michael!" Simone cried.

"Go, Simone! Now!" he called.

"Citoyenne Thibaut. You will not go. If you do, I will shoot this man. Instead, you will come here." Du Maurier's voice was furiously cold—a man betrayed. Corday was quite certain he would do as he said.

He watched as Simone stepped closer, moving sinuously, catlike. She looked as if she was about to attack, then her eyes widened. Her eyes went from the pistol at Corday's head, to his face, and then to du Maurier. Even she could not outrun a shot at such close range. She walked slowly back to them.

Four guards came out of the prison, and two seized her by her arms. She struggled, but du Maurier's voice stopped her.

"Citoyenne, you will not resist. If you do, I will kill him. You will go with these guards and stay where you are put until you are called for. Do you understand?"

She gazed at him, and slowly nodded.

"Good."

Corday watched, gut twisting with frustration, as she twisted her body trying to look at him as she was led away. His hands were taken in viselike grips and brought behind him. Rope dug into his wrists, burning against his skin. A last tug and his hands fell, resting against the small of his back. Rough hands patted his body, and stopped at the pistols he had tucked into his belt. They took them away, as well as the packet of tools he had brought with him.

Hell. Hell and damnation.

The cold metal of the pistol at his temple disappeared. A hand seized his arm and pulled him around to face du Maurier. The man's face was pale in the moonlight, his lips thin with fury. He held Corday's packet open in his hands. "You, Monsieur Thibaut—yes, 'monsieur,' for I know you are no citizen—are under arrest. We will deal with you immediately." He turned to the guards. "Take him to Citoyen Hervé for questioning. I need to send soldiers to find the prisoners who have been released, but will join him later." His expression grew disgusted. "My first evening here, and prisoners escape. Clearly I need to make my first inspection of the prisons—and the prison guards—soon." The guards saluted, and pushed Corday roughly forward.

He blew out a deep breath. Well, he was going to see Hervé right away after all . . . just not in the way he intended.

The guards pushed him up the spiral stone stairs until he picked up his pace. They said nothing—no jests, no jeers, as he expected. He glanced at their faces. They looked uncertain, and glanced at each other, worry clear in their eyes. No doubt they feared for their jobs, perhaps even their lives, because of the prisoners that had escaped. The Committee of Public Safety did not tolerate mistakes.

They came to the same hall that he and Simone had walked through earlier, but turned to another door, just across from the storage room. The guards knocked.

"*Entré!*" The door opened to a brightly lit room, lavishly decorated with paintings—stolen from various aristocratic houses, Corday thought. Hervé sat at a desk, profiled against the window opposite the door, a brace of candles lighting a small pile of papers in front of him. He turned, and his brows lifted. "Ah. The spy." He pointed to a chair opposite the desk. "Put him there."

The guards shoved Corday forward, and he stumbled but regained his feet. He straightened, walked to the chair, and sat. He looked at Hervé, at his plain, ordinary features, his graying hair, and wondered if the man would at all recognize him from their encounter many years before.

Hervé looked at the guards, and waved a hand at them. "You may go." The guards hesitated, but the agent stared at them, and with a shuffling bow, they left.

The man was silent for a long while, steepling his fingers together in front of him on the desk. He cocked his head to one side, as if he were examining a strange sort of animal. "Well, Monsieur Thibaut," he said at last. His voice was soft, coldly so. "Though I doubt that is your name. What do you have to say for yourself?"

Corday lifted his head and gazed at Citoyen Guillaume Hervé, letting the silence grow long between them. Hervé said nothing; he merely waited. Corday drew in a deep breath and let it out again.

"Hello, Father," he said in English. "It's been a long time since I saw you last."

Chapter 18

❧ THE GUARDS PUSHED SIMONE BEFORE them, and she thought of how she might escape to save Michael. They had taken her dagger and her pistols, but it might be possible to disable both these men if she had a chance to turn and face them. She had developed a trick of leaping and kicking a man in the throat, enough to disable him—kill him if he posed a danger alive.

She did not know, however, if du Maurier still had a pistol to Michael's head, nor where they had gone. She had seen the betrayed and furious look on du Maurier's face, and was certain he would indeed kill Michael if she disobeyed. Then, too, even if she disabled the two guards, more had been stationed at the doors of the prison. She could handle two in close quarters; four or more would be more difficult. By the time she dispatched them, word would have come to du Maurier's ears of her attempt at escape, and more would arrive to try to subdue her. For now, she would have to sit in the prison cell and think of a plan. She closed her eyes for a moment, praying that she would find a solution, find a way to save Michael.

The guards pushed her up a few stairs to another set of prison cells. She peered in a few as they passed—they contained better than the pile of straw in the lower cells, for they had instead a pallet of straw on a rough wooden bed. One of the guards pulled her roughly to the right.

"This one," he said. "There is a girl and her brother—if they did not escape, that is—who might need a woman to tend them." He shoved her into the room and the door shut, clanging in the silence.

Simone turned and put her hands on the door, pushing it. It did not give much, just a little, but she could possibly force it open if she put all her strength against it. There were bars across an opening at eye level, and then a flap at the bottom through which she supposed food would be served, and the chamber pot changed. It was large enough for a small child to squeeze through, but she was larger than that.

Straw rustled, and she turned quickly to the corner of the cell from which it came. A dark-haired head rose from behind a pile of straw, and a smaller curly-blond head rose beside it.

"Who are you?" said the dark-haired one, a boy. Simone stepped closer, but the pair shoved themselves away from her. She stopped, dismayed and saddened. These children had learned to fear adults.

"I am Simone de la Fer." She did not think it would make any difference if she gave her real name . . . and she did not have the heart to tell the boy anything but the truth.

The boy swallowed and dashed his fist across his eyes. "You can't be. They are all dead."

A shiver coursed up Simone's spine. How could he know? "What . . . what do you mean?" she whispered.

The boy lifted his chin defiantly, and she shivered again, reminded of Auguste, her brother, who had had the same way of looking his defiance before he died. "I am Adrian de la Fer. The last of my family."

Pain struck Simone's heart, and she briefly closed her eyes. The boy was indeed Auguste's son. Dear heaven. All this time . . . "Hush, hush!" The little blond child shook· the boy's arm. "You must not give your true name, Adrian! They will take you away if you do, and then I shall be all alone."

The boy put his arm around the girl. "Do not worry, Thérèse. There is just this woman, and she is imprisoned like we are. The guards have left."

Simone moved carefully toward the pair, not wanting to frighten them. "I am indeed Simone de la Fer. I thought all of my family had died as well. How is it that you are here?"

The boy was silent for a moment. "I ran away, because Papa said I should or else the men would get me. There were screams, but I did as I was told. Then I walked and walked, until I found Thérèse, who could not find her *maman* or her *papa,* and then we walked until a lady found us and took us in her carriage. But she was taken away by the soldiers, and they thought we were her children." He looked down at his hands. "I did not want to leave her, because I was afraid she would scream, too, and she was kind to us. So—so the soldiers took us, as well."

"The lady told her real name, and they took her out of here, and see, now we are the only ones left," Thérèse said, and her lip trembled.

"But when the doors opened earlier, why did you not leave with the rest of the people?"

Adrian gazed at her gravely. "There have been other times when many people have been released, and when they left, I could hear the screaming and the cries. I thought it would be safer for us to stay here."

Simone's heart sank; of course the boy would interpret

such an event this way. She put out her hand to the girl, wanting to pat her on her shoulder, but Thérèse drew back. "I won't hurt you," she said.

The girl cocked her head. "You are pretty, but you have a strange back."

"Thérèse!" Adrian exclaimed. "That is rude. Mlle. de la Fer is trying to be friendly." He stood and bowed. "Adrian de la Fer, at your service."

Simone smiled, and curtsied. "I thank you, monsieur." She turned to Thérèse. "Thank you for saying I am pretty, but as you see—" She reached under her cloak and untied the rag strips that held her doll to her back. "It is not my back, but my doll." She held the doll out to the girl. Thérèse stood and leaned over cautiously to look at it. "You may have it if you wish, for I am too old for a doll." She smiled. Much too old, she thought. The doll is better in the hands of a little girl.

Thérèse gazed, round-eyed, at the doll. "She is beautiful, mademoiselle."

Simone laid the doll on the straw in front of the girl. "See, it is yours."

Thérèse touched it with a finger, then stroked the dress. She looked at Simone, then after a moment picked up the doll, cradling it in her arms. She gave a wobbly curtsey and said, "Thank you, mademoiselle."

"You are welcome." Simone went to the straw pallet and sat on it. She patted the place beside her. "Come, would you like to sit by me? Do you want me to tell you the doll's name, or do you want to give her a name?"

Thérèse hesitated, but at Adrian's slight nudge, went to the pallet and sat on it. She wrinkled her brow, then said, "If the doll already has a name, she should keep it." She looked at Simone expectantly.

Simone thought back to the days when she had played with it. "I believe her name is Bernadette."

Thérèse nodded. "That is a pretty name." She looked at the doll and smoothed back its hair from its face. "Bernadette."

Simone patted the girl's hand. "Well, now that I have told you my real name, and the doll's real name, perhaps you can tell me yours?"

Thérèse pressed her lips together, looking frightened. Adrian sat on the bed beside her. "Don't be scared, Thérèse. See, Mademoiselle's name is de la Fer, just like mine. I think she may be my aunt, or a cousin. Since she is in my family, she will not hurt you." He looked up at Simone, a warning in his eyes, and her heart ached with pity, for it was clear this boy, no more than twelve years old, had taken Thérèse under his wing and had tried his best to protect her.

The fear began to clear in the girl's eyes, and then she seemed to come to a decision. "Can I tell you my other name?" she asked. "Then perhaps later, when I am not so frightened, I can tell you my true name."

Simone smiled. "Of course, if that is what you wish."

Thérèse gave a big sigh of relief, and smiled in return. "My papa used to call me *Thérèse des jardins,* because I love flowers so much."

Thérèse des jardins. Simone swallowed. She remembered that name. Jacques du Maurier had spoken of his wife and his daughter, his daughter who had loved gardens so much. Surely it was not . . . he had said that his wife and daughter were dead. And yet, it was Hervé who had found the bodies of his family, and did not Michael say that the agents who had "died" and whose "bodies" had been returned to England were not dead after all, and in fact had perhaps conspired with Hervé?

How ironic if du Maurier's own daughter had lived—heaven knew how long—in the very prison of which he was to become an administrator. She looked at the girl, not more than six years old, and thought she could see traces of du Maurier's features in the blue eyes and the strong chin.

"Where . . . where is your papa, Thérèse?" she asked tentatively.

Fear returned to the girl's eyes, and she closed her lips tightly. Adrian moved closer to her and put his arm around her thin little shoulders. "Mademoiselle, she is very little, and easily frightened. Do not question her any more, for I fear she will cry, and . . . it hurts here"—he pressed his hand against his chest—"when I see her cry."

Thérèse suddenly twisted from his grasp. "I am not little! I am a big girl! Besides, my papa will come for me some day, for the bad men did not take him away, only my *maman*."

Simone wet her suddenly dry lips. She rose from the bed and beckoned to Adrian. He looked at her curiously and walked to the corner of the cell where she stood. "Adrian, I believe I know where her father is; that is why I was questioning her. She does not know me well, but she trusts you." The boy's sudden smile had a hint of pride in it. "You have taken care of her well. Could you . . . could you ask her for me if her father's name is Jacques du Maurier?"

Adrian's eyes widened. "Mademoiselle, that is indeed her father's name. She told me herself."

Dieu Merci. Simone closed her eyes in relief, then looked at Adrian, taking him by his shoulders. "Adrian, you must do as I say. I will see if I can make the guard bring her father, but I may have to leave you here for a while afterward. Make sure that she understands that when I leave with her father again, he will come back. Do you understand?"

The boy nodded, lifting his chin in the manner of her brother. She breathed out a painful breath of remembered grief, then gazed at him, thinking of what inheritance he had left. The house and grounds of the de la Fer estate belonged to him by rights. She thought of how she might help him escape, but a glance at Thérèse told her that she doubted the girl would want to be parted from him, or he from her, even though she would regain her father. She put her hand inside her bodice, where she carried the key to her home, next to her crucifix. She pulled it out and looked at it, shining in the light of the torch that burned just outside the cell door. She took Adrian's hand and pressed the key into it, closing his fingers over it.

"Take this. This is the key to the home of the de la Fers—your home. When Thérèse's father comes back, tell him that you wish to be returned to your home. Don't be frightened of it, even though people will tell you it is haunted." She grinned. "I have lived there for a while, pretending to be a ghost so bad men would stay away."

The boy's eyes gleamed. "That was very clever, Mlle. Simone. Were they very scared?"

"Very. One of them was so scared, he fell down the steps on his bottom."

The boy's solemn face split with a grin and he laughed. "I should have liked to see it," he said.

"Well, when you return, you must go to one of the bedrooms, the one with heavy curtains on the windows and the red velvet curtains around the bed. There, you must look in the wardrobe thoroughly, for I have hidden a treasure in it." Her mother's jewels, among other things. She gazed at the boy, and thought he would need the treasure more than she. "Some of the treasure is mine—my mother's jewels. But it is mostly yours, now that I know you are alive." The boy's eyes grew round, and she chuckled, for it was clear that a haunted estate with a treasure was a highly attractive adventure for him. "Do you understand what you must do?"

Adrian nodded.

She sighed. "Very well. Now, I must see about bringing Thérèse's father back to her."

She turned to the cell door and pressed her hands against it, testing the weight and the strength of it. She was not so sure that she would be heard if she called for the guards, and she doubted that they would go on their rounds any time soon. It opened inward, making it harder for her to knock it down, but the hinges were not in the best repair. It might be possible to lever the edge of the hinge and pull it off from the wood if she had a sharp piece of wood or metal. She looked about her . . . all she had was the pallet of straw, and that was no help.

"What are you doing, mademoiselle?"

Simone looked down to see Thérèse gazing at her. "I am trying to get out of this room so that I can call the guards and tell them to . . . find a man I think will help us."

Thérèse nodded, then pointed to the small flap at the bottom of the door. "You could go through there."

Simone grinned. "I am too big."

The girl looked her up and down. "Yes. But I could go through there and get a guard."

"No, Thérèse, you should not," Adrian said sharply. "It is too dangerous."

A mischievous look crossed Thérèse's face. "No, it is not. I have gone through there many times when you were asleep, and I have talked to the guards, too, and they gave me treats to eat."

"Thérèse!" the boy cried indignantly. "You did not tell me—or share the treats with me!"

The girl sobered. "I am sorry, Adrian, but they did not want me to take the treat back to our room, for they said they did not want anyone to see me eating it, or else a bad man would be angry with them." She turned to Simone. "I will go—if I may take Bernadette with me."

"I . . . it is too dangerous, Thérèse." Simone swallowed. It would be the perfect solution, and she needed to find Michael right away. But she could not endanger the girl.

The girl put her hands on her hips. "No, it is not. The guards are good to me, and they give me treats. They will do as I say. If I tell them you wish to speak to them, they will come." Simone suppressed a smile. The girl was full of spirit; she took after her father, surely.

Adrian threw an exasperated look at Simone. "See how she is. She—Thérèse!"

Simone turned, and swiftly grabbed for the girl's foot that was quickly disappearing through the flap door, but she collided with Adrian, who was trying to do the same.

"Ow! I am sorry, mademoiselle," Adrian said, rubbing his head.

"Thérèse! Thérèse!" Simone called. All she heard was the patter of the girl's footsteps.

"She can be very stubborn, mademoiselle," Adrian said apologetically.

Simone grinned. "So I see. Will she do as she said?"

The boy nodded. "Yes. You may trust her." He gazed at her shyly. "Are you truly a de la Fer?"

"Yes. Your family did not acknowledge me, only Marthe, my nurse—do you know Marthe?"

His face brightened. "Yes, she was my nurse, too, but she is very old. She saved me."

I have saved the heir of the de la Fers! Marthe had said when she gave Simone the doll, a year ago. Simone closed her eyes and shook her head, wishing the nurse had not been so mad with horror that she had indicated the doll instead of mentioning Adrian. "She gave me news of the family," Simone said instead. "I was—not good long ago, and so they asked that I leave."

The boy was silent for a moment. "It was fortunate,

mademoiselle, that they made you leave. You would not be alive now if they hadn't."

She gazed at him, surprised. "You are a wise young man, Adrian." She smiled. "I am glad you are the heir of the de la Fers. You will do honor to the name and the estate."

The boy blushed. "I am glad you think so, mademoiselle."

A jangling of keys sounded in the distance, then heavy footsteps, followed by the patter of small ones. A rough face appeared at the grated window of the cell door.

"Well?" the guard asked, his voice low and menacing. "The little citoyenne says you have something important to say. Tell me what it is, or else it will go ill with you. And if I find that you have used her for your own devices, then you will wish for the guillotine after I am done with you."

"No, no, Citoyen Lemieux, she is a good lady. See, she gave me Bernadette—is she not a pretty doll?" piped up Thérèse.

Simone suppressed a laugh. Clearly the girl had twisted the big guard around her little finger. The clock struck the hour and Simone sobered. Time was passing quickly. "Citoyen Lemieux, I wish you to bring Citoyen du Maurier here." She hesitated, hoping that it would not upset Thérèse. "Tell him I have found his daughter. And if he will not believe that, tell him—" She drew in a deep breath. "Tell him that I have information about the outlaw La Flamme."

The guard stared at her for a moment, then nodded. "The new administrator will know if you are lying." He looked down, apparently at Thérèse. "Go back into the cell, little citoyenne. I would not want my superior to see I have let you wander about the prison halls." He turned, and Simone could hear his heavy footsteps disappear down the hall.

The doll appeared first from under the flap, and then Thérèse's curly head appeared as she pushed herself through the opening. She stood up, and looked at Simone triumphantly. "See, mademoiselle? I said I could make the guard come here."

Simone chuckled. "So you did, and I am sorry I doubted you."

She waited, praying that du Maurier would come quickly. The time stretched out into what seemed an eternity, and Simone whiled away much of it talking with the children. She told them the story of Pierre the Red, the story Michael had told to little Pierre and his mother earlier in their journey, until Adrian's eyes drooped and Thérèse yawned and rested her head on Simone's lap, falling asleep just as she finished her story. Simone covered the two with her cloak; she did not need it, for she rarely felt the cold.

Finally, a clank and the jangle of keys sounded down the hall, and quick footsteps came toward their cell.

The guard's face appeared at the small barred window again. "Citoyen du Maurier has arrived, citoyenne." His face disappeared, and du Maurier's replaced it.

"Well?" he demanded, his voice angry. "Be quick, citoyenne. Tell me what you know of La Flamme, and do not try to divert me with nonsense about my daughter." He paused, then continued. "She is dead. Your lies will not bring her back."

Simone sent up a silent prayer, her heart pulled between dread that she was about to betray the hearts of a lost little girl and a bereaved father, and hope that these two were family and that she was doing the right thing. "Citoyen du Maurier, lies help no one, but the truth and the evidence of your own eyes will. If she is not your daughter, then I will gladly suffer whatever punishment you wish to deal me. If you think that I am any danger to you, you have your guard." There was silence, then the guard's keys jangled and the lock turned.

Light from the torch flowed into the cell, but Simone did not rise. She looked at du Maurier, his face in shadow, and gestured to the girl sleeping in her lap. "Look yourself, Citoyen du Maurier. She calls herself *Thérèse des jardins,* as I remembered you told me you named her in your love and your joy in her. If she is not your daughter, then I only ask that these two children—" she gestured this time to Adrian as well, "are released and their relatives found to take care of them."

Du Maurier stared at her, then nodded curtly. He did not move forward; he seemed frozen. At last he took a halting step toward her, and Simone shifted Thérèse and held her up to him. "Is this your daughter, Jacques du Maurier?" she asked.

The agent took the girl in his arms, awkwardly, then brushed the hair from her face. For one moment his face was as stiff as stone, and then he fell to his knees, his face pressed to the girl's body.

"*Ah, Dieu!* Thérèse, Thérèse!" Du Maurier's shoulders shook, and his voice was harsh. "Forgive me." He clutched the child to his chest, hard enough so that the girl awoke.

"Papa?" She opened her eyes and gazed at him. "Papa!" she screamed. Her arms came around his neck, and she sobbed. "See, see, Adrian, I told you my papa would come for me. I *told* you!"

The boy awoke, rubbing his eyes, and he looked at the girl and her father, then questioningly at Simone. "It is her father, as I hoped," she whispered.

Adrian nodded, looking wistful, and Simone sighed, wishing she could restore his family to him as well.

Thérèse's sobs died away, and she cuddled into du Maurier's arms, her fingers playing with the ribbons of the revolutionary cockade sewn to his coat. She frowned. "Papa, why do you wear the bad men's flower on your coat?"

He tenderly kissed her cheek. "Bad men?"

"The bad men who took *Maman* away wore this same flower on their coats." She tugged at the cockade for emphasis.

Du Maurier lifted his head and stared at Simone. His face paled. "They wore this cockade? These colors?"

Simone shivered at the look in his eyes, lost and dreadful. "Think, monsieur. Think who told you about your wife and child. Who presented their bodies to you."

"Hervé." His voice was low, harsh. "Guillaume Hervé." He closed his eyes, then stroked Thérèse's cheek. "Tell me, Thérèse—" He hesitated, then opened his eyes. "Tell me, do you know what happened to your *maman?*"

Thérèse shook her head mournfully. "No, Papa. The bad men with the ribbon flowers took her away, and she screamed and I ran away because she told me to." She sighed. "I think she went with the other people who scream when they are taken away. The bad men who took them away also wore the flowers."

Du Maurier looked ill. "*Mon Dieu.* Forgive me, Thérèse."

The girl looked at him curiously. "Why, Papa? Because you did not come soon? It is all right. You are here now, and I was lost many times, so I am not surprised you could not find me right away. Besides, Adrian found me and took care of me, and gave me his food, too." She nestled into the crook of his arm and closed her eyes.

Du Maurier looked up and gazed at the boy. "Thank you—" His voice shook.

Adrian bowed politely. "Adrian de la Fer, at your service, monsieur." He smiled. "She is a brave girl, monsieur."

Du Maurier looked startled. "De la Fer."

The boy's face grew stony. "They are all dead, monsieur, except myself and my—cousin, here." He nodded to

Simone, then looked wistfully at the girl. "I am glad Thérèse has you back."

"As am I, boy." He swallowed. "And I am grateful for what you have done for her. If there is anything I can do for you—"

Adrian nodded. "If you would be so kind as to return me to my home—"

"Of course!"

"And . . . I would like to see Thérèse from time to time, to see how she does."

A smile warmed du Maurier's face. "Yes, you may visit all you wish. But first—" He gently laid Thérèse down on the straw pallet again. "I must ask that you take care of her one more time. There is a man I must see before I take the both of you home." He gazed at Simone. "I thank you, citoyenne. After I deal with Hervé, I will need to talk to you again about the information you have on La Flamme." He turned to leave.

Simone grasped his arm. "Monsieur, I must go with you. I must find my husband."

He looked her up and down. "So, he is your husband, even though you are probably not with child?" A humorous glint entered his eyes.

Her lips twisted in a wry smile. "I am indeed his wife, though I am not with child."

"He is a spy, citoyenne."

Simone took a deep breath. "Do you know that for sure, monsieur? Who accused him?" She knew what Michael was, but it was not a lie to ask these questions.

There was silence for a moment, then he said, "Hervé."

She said nothing, but waited.

"Your husband's actions and yours speak of spying, citoyenne, but I see what you mean." He bent and kissed Thérèse's sleeping face once more. "As you say, lies help no one, but the truth and the evidence of my own eyes will."

"Let me go with you," Simone said. "I need to find my husband." She put all her yearning for Michael into her voice, and if she could have wept, she would have, for her fear for him hit her hard at last, and she felt sick with it.

Du Maurier gazed at her, and then at his daughter. "I do not think I can refuse such a request," he said, watching as Adrian sat protectively next to Thérèse and put his arm around her. "Not now." He sighed and nodded. "Come."

He left the door of the cell open and beckoned to the guard, who had obviously eavesdropped, for he hastily wiped a tear from his eye before he saluted. "Citoyenne Lemieux, please take my daughter and the boy to my quarters, and give them food if they wish. Find them some clothes to wear for the night, and warm blankets for their bed. And thank you for your care of her."

Lemieux grinned, saluted, and entered the cell.

Du Maurier led the way through the prison hall, then paused as he passed another guard. He turned and nodded to the man. "Do you have the weapons you seized from this woman and her husband?"

The guard saluted. "Yes, Citoyen du Maurier."

"Give them to me."

The guard raised his brows, but handed over the weapons. Du Maurier tucked one pistol in his belt before he went on his way, looking at Simone. "I suppose since one of these weapons was found on you, you are well versed in its use."

"Yes," she said. "And the pistol you have is primed."

"So I thought. Yet you claim you are not a spy?"

Simone hesitated. "I am not precisely a spy, monsieur." His brows lifted in question. She wondered if she should tell him the truth. She had risked much this evening; she did not feel like risking more.

"Is your husband La Flamme?" He led her up the spiral stairs, back to the hall she and Michael had entered before.

"No," she said.

He paused, giving her a penetrating stare. "Are *you* La Flamme?"

"I gave you your daughter back; is that not enough for me to ask that we find my husband?"

"I also owe a duty to my country, citoyenne."

"A country that imprisons innocents," she retorted angrily.

The agent gasped as if in pain and closed his eyes. "It will not be that way, not if I can help it," he said at last. "I vow this to you, citoyenne. I vow it by my daughter's life."

Simone gazed at him, at his eyes brimming with unshed tears, and she could say nothing to refute him.

"Are you La Flamme?" he asked again.

She watched him carefully. If he indicated by word or deed that he would do her harm, she would disable him and tie him up with his own cravat and stockings; she would find Michael herself and leave du Maurier's guards to set him free in the morning. She drew in a deep breath.

"I am La Flamme, monsieur."

His shoulders relaxed. "Thank you." He shot her an amused glance. "I suppose the reports exaggerated your powers?"

There was no threat or hint of it in his expression or his stance. She smiled slightly. "Yes, they exaggerated."

He nodded, seemingly amused. "So I thought." He turned toward one of the doors across from the storage room through which she and Michael had come.

"This is the interrogation room," he said. His face turned grim and pale. "I hope, if Hervé had anything to do with the state of the bodies he presented to me, that he has not gone too far into his interrogation."

Simone closed her eyes, feeling the pit of her stomach turn sour. She prayed, also, that the interrogation had not gone far.

Chapter 19

HERVE PEERED AT CORDAY DURING A long silence. "Ah," he said at last, in English. "I wondered if it might be you—you looked familiar to me from the time you joined du Maurier and myself. You look very much like your mother." He tapped his fingers together, as if contemplating the situation. "How interesting that you turned out a spy. It seems you have inherited some traits from me, as well."

Corday's gut turned at his words, and a bitter taste came into his mouth. At this moment, he would give the world to have inherited *all* his traits from his mother. But he could not deny that he was a killer, the son of this murderer.

Hervé stood up and walked toward Corday, making a circuit around him and coolly looking him up and down. "I wondered, too," the agent said, "when your compatriots described you, for the description tweaked my memory a bit." His voice was dispassionate, distant, sounding as if he were examining an interesting species of insect. He returned to the desk and sat, leaning back in his chair.

Corday was torn between a mad impulse to laugh and groan at the same time. He had blocked the memory of his father from his mind for almost two decades, hating him for what he had done to his mother. As he had grown older, and as memories of his father began to fade, his hate had cooled to an intellectual interest in gaining ways of manipulating the world around him so that he had a great deal of control at his fingertips, so that he need not despair. Now despair visited him again, for he was bound and sitting in front of this man, near powerless in his realization that he had not controlled his world at all, but had merely become a mirror of his father.

Powerless, also, in the knowledge that he had so far failed to kill the man who was behind the attempt to export the terror of the Revolution to other countries. He knew the truth: He could have killed Hervé and du Maurier at any time during his journey to Paris, never mind that he had not known Hervé's true identity until only two days ago. He could have done it, and his trip to Paris would have been merely a confirmation of what he had discovered during it. But he had refrained, mostly because of Simone's persistence in traveling with him.

No, he lied to himself if he thought that. She traveled with him because he had allowed it, because he had wanted her to be with him from the beginning. She had made him laugh, had given him comfort, and made him feel alive again so that he had wanted to live past this mission. She had given him hope.

Corday gazed at his father, and hope drained from him. Would she care for him still, knowing it was his father who had killed her family and ordered the deaths of so many others? He doubted it. He grew conscious of the ropes digging into his wrists and pulled at them. They seemed to loosen a little. If he could get his hands loose from the ropes, perhaps he could . . . He was not sure what he would do. Complete his mission? It would mean that he must kill his father.

Not that the man had ever acted as a father. Guillaume Hervé. It was not his real name. William Cunningham was. The dissolute second son of a nobleman, who had been forced to marry a virtuous Frenchwoman of good family after he had taken her virtue. It had not fared well. She was neither ambitious nor well-connected enough for Cunningham to advance in politics, and his own reputation kept him from achieving advancement. Corday gazed at the man before him. Apparently his father had decided to gain political influence in other ways.

"What did you do with them—my 'compatriots'?" Corday said at last.

Cunningham waved a hand. "They supplied what I needed; I am done with them."

"No doubt reneging on whatever you promised them by disposing of them," Corday said coldly. He worked the rope a little—yes, it was looser now than before.

His father shrugged. "My funds are limited. I must do what I can." He nodded at him. "You are an efficient man, from what I can see. Surely you understand that."

"Of course," Corday said, feeling nauseated. He did, indeed, admire efficiency, and had attempted to be as efficient as possible himself on all his missions.

Cunningham gazed at him, and a frown appeared between his brows. "I am curious. How did you discover who I was? It has, as you said, been quite a long while since we saw each other."

"It was not difficult, once I put the evidence together," Corday said, keeping his voice dispassionate. "You have a signature killing style, and have ever since you killed my mother. You beat and maim the bodies quite thoroughly, and then disfigure the face to the point of unrecognizability. It was the way you killed when I was a boy. Then there were the bodies you sent back to England that were supposed to be those of our agents. Finally, there was du Maurier's description of his wife's and child's bodies, and he mentioned you were the one who brought them back to him. The only reason why I did not think of you right away was that I was sure you were dead." He moved his fingers around the knot of the rope around his wrists. He could just reach one knot with the index and middle fingers of his right hand. It was knotted with what seemed to be a square knot. He pushed his finger between one section of rope and another; it barely budged, but at least it moved that much.

"Ah." Cunningham nodded. "So you would think, since you shot me yourself, Michael." It was odd hearing his father use his name. No one had used it for a long time, except for Simone. "However, your uncle saw fit to have me nursed back to health, and by that time, you had left for the army and he had covered up the scandal. Then he shipped me off to France. Quite circumspect, my brother." He tapped his fingers on the desk. "Very astute of you to guess."

"Decided to come to wider pastures after that, did you?" Corday said conversationally. The longer he could keep his father talking, the better chance he had of untying the rope around his wrists—thank heaven for guards who were incompetent with tying rope. "You could have killed my uncle, and inherited the estate and the title."

Cunningham nodded. "Yes, especially after the scandal was hushed up. But when I came to France, I could see larger possibilities. The country was in unrest from the poverty of its people, the king weak, the aristocracy ineffectual and thoughtless, the clerics corrupt. Naturally, it was ripe for profit in due course if one planned carefully."

Corday nodded as he worked the knot with aching fingers; it was not difficult to see the opportunities to seize power in the midst of such chaos. He had seen even the lowest of men seize what power over others they could during this state-declared Terror. "You do have a way with you, Father," he said. "Even du Maurier was fooled."

Cunningham's lip curled disdainfully. "It is not difficult to use idealists; such men are ruled by their passions more than their intellect, however intelligent they may be. One only needs to give them motivation to do as one wants, and voilà! It's done."

"You killed his wife and child, I assume."

A discontented look crossed Cunningham's face. "His wife, yes. His child—she escaped." He waved his hand again in dismissal. "It did not matter. I found a suitable substitute."

Corday clenched his teeth against the nausea that rose in his throat. No. No, he was not like this man. He, at least, did not kill children, nor did he kill or harm women, despite what he might have said to Simone at the beginning of their association. God, he had to escape, mission or no mission. Cunningham may have helped conceive him, but if the man had any shred of humanity in him, it was long gone. Corday worked the knot in the rope a little looser, though his wrists felt raw and stung with sweat and blood.

Cunningham gazed at him contemplatively. "That you came thus far undetected speaks well for you. I take it you have made a career of this?"

"Yes."

The agent nodded. "So I thought." He reached under the desk and brought out a pistol. "I have a proposition for you—son."

Corday's stomach turned. *Son. Dear God.* He stared at the man, then looked down at his lap, knowing that his eyes no doubt showed his hatred, and if not that, hatred for himself. He was the son of this obscenity before him; he had kept himself from sinking to the depths that Cunningham had sunk, but how long would it take before he walked the same path to the same pit? He gazed at the man before him; he must be in his mid-sixties by now, so ordinary looking that no one would suspect he had a soul as black as hell. How easy it would be for him, Corday, to do just the same. Blood would show, after all.

The thought made him want to vomit.

"A proposition," Cunningham continued. "I have a pivotal place now; I move men and events as I choose here. I have financed three insurrections so far—quite an accomplishment, don't you think?" A satisfied smile spread over his face.

"Quite." Corday raised his eyebrows, trying to look interested. The knot gave at last, and he moved his wrists apart experimentally—yes, the rope was loose. He would keep his hands behind him, however. He eyed the pistol that Cunningham had laid on the table. It was one of his own, therefore primed and ready to shoot. It was of German make, rifled and accurate. However, there would be a moment's delay between the pull of the trigger, the flash, and the shot. It was possible, barely possible, if he saw the man's finger pull the trigger, for him to move aside enough to avoid a deadly wound.

"I have a desire to form a dynasty," Cunningham said, smiling slightly. "Should you join me, you will be part of it. You are, after all, my son, and it seems you have inherited much of my intelligence and insight." He put his hand on the pistol. "If you do not, however, I shall be forced to kill you. You are a spy, after all, and this revolutionary chaos makes it very easy to justify the elimination of such enemies of the state."

Corday watched the man's hand curl around the weapon. He very much doubted that he would reap the rewards his father promised. More likely, he would be "discarded" as Johnson and Bramley had been when they ceased being of any use.

He put a thoughtful expression on his face, and loosened the rope further from his hands. He grasped a length in his fists. If he managed to dodge the shot well enough, he could come up and use the rope to disable the man. He swallowed. His duty was to kill him, father or not. His duty was to be a patricide, as he had always thought himself since he tried to avenge his mother's death as a boy. *Madness. What madness.*

He looked at Cunningham—Hervé—his father, and slowly shook his head. "No."

The man sighed. "You have made a terrible mistake, my son," he said. He pointed the pistol at Corday and pulled the trigger.

Du Maurier put his hand on the door, but Simone seized his arm. "No," she said. "Not yet. Listen first." She jerked her head toward the door and the sounds of voices within the room.

"Are you suggesting that we eavesdrop, Citoyenne de la Fer?" du Maurier whispered, but his expression lightened briefly with amusement.

"Yes," she replied. "Otherwise, how will you know the truth? The moment you enter, Hervé will act as he always has acted, and say what he thinks you wish to hear. If there are any secrets—either on his part or ... or on my husband's—then you will find it out when you listen."

Du Maurier nodded. "Very well."

The door did not fit well on the hinges; a product of the mob's vandalism of this priory building, Simone thought. A slit between the doorjamb and the door was large enough to peek within, and hear the voices clearly through it. She frowned. They were speaking English. She did not know the language fluently, but she could make sense out of most it. She gazed at du Maurier, watching his face pale as he listened. He looked ill, and the emotions of despair, fury, and horror flitted across his face. It seemed he knew English better than she did.

She watched through the slit in the doorway. Michael and Hervé sat, their profiles to the door. She watched as her husband fumbled with the rope that tied his wrists, never revealing what he was doing, and she smiled. He was clever, as always. She listened . . . "Father," Michael said, and Hervé said the word "son." She looked from one to the other and swallowed a lump in her throat. Surely not—? She thought of the story that Michael had told her of his life, the way du Maurier's wife had been killed . . . and yet, here was Hervé, with Michael before him, tied up instead of free.

But then Hervé moved, and put a pistol on top of his desk. His hand moved over the weapon in a caressing way, as if it were his lover. He looked at Michael, and she thought no father could look at a son in that way, as if he would enjoy killing him. She gazed at Michael. His face was cool, emotionless, as he gathered the rope between his hands, and he lifted his head to look at Hervé.

"No," Michael said.

She watched Hervé pick up the pistol—fear seized her heart. She was fast, faster than Michael. She needed less than a moment to run and pull Michael down before the shot reached him. She pushed on the door. It stuck, but she pushed harder and ran.

"Michael!" she cried, and her hands touched him as a shot rang out, and then a second one. Fire and pain seized her chest. Her vision blurred, turning red.

"Simone!" It was Michael's voice, harsh and raw.

"Michael . . ." she whispered. The red that obscured her sight turned black, and she knew no more.

Hervé's finger touched the trigger. Corday leaped to the side.

"Michael!" A shadow—Simone—ran toward him, and two shots rang out.

Her body jerked and fell. *No!*

Flames from the overturned candles angrily licked the desk on which Hervé—Cunningham—slumped. The papers on the desk caught fire and fell to the floor as the man slid off the desk and off the chair. Corday watched as du Maurier strode to Hervé and took another pistol from his pocket. He pointed it at the man on the floor and pulled the trigger. Another shot rang out, and though the pistol was clearly no longer primed or loaded, du Maurier pulled back the hammer again, and pulled the trigger again. And again. *Click. Click. Click.*

Corday pulled his gaze to Simone, lying lifeless on the floor. Blood oozed from her chest, and speckles of blood flecked her lips. She coughed and more blood appeared.

His breath left him, and his hands shook as he stripped off his cravat and pressed it, hopelessly, to the wound on her chest. Heat blew at his face, and he looked up at the flames that had crawled from the floor to the walls. *Bloody hell.*

He searched for du Maurier, and found him standing, staring at Hervé on the floor, the pistol loose in his hand. "Du Maurier—man, are you mad? There's a fire in here. Help me, damn you!"

Du Maurier lifted his head and looked at him, his eyes lost, dark, as if his soul had looked into an abyss. He gazed at the fire, then at Corday and Simone on the floor. He started, as if in a dream, and dropped the pistol.

"What—what happened?"

"The bastard shot her," Corday snapped. He glanced at the quickly growing fire. "We need to get her out of here, and anyone else who might be caught in this place. Women, children."

Du Maurier's expression stirred, and his eyes grew

alarmed, alive at last. "Thérèse, my daughter." He looked at Simone. "Your wife gave me back my daughter, and she tried to save your life. Come, quickly."

Michael lifted Simone in his arms; her head lolled sickeningly loose on his shoulder. *Don't let her be dead, don't let her die. Please. Not for me.* When had anyone tried to save him? He could not remember.

He moved swiftly out the door, following du Maurier to the base of another flight of stairs, where a guard stood at attention. "You there!" called du Maurier. "There is a fire in the far room—get what men you can to put it out, and if you cannot, leave. A . . . a traitor to the Revolution has set it, trying to burn us out of this place." Du Maurier pulled Corday in front of him. "This man stopped the traitor before he killed me, but his wife was hurt in the process. Make sure they are escorted to safety to their rooms at the Hôtel de la Colombe. Go, now." The guard saluted and ran down the hall.

Corday's eyes met du Maurier's. The agent nodded, then bent toward him. "Tell her . . . give her my thanks. Tell her I will free whatever prisoners I can. Tell her I will take care of the boy, Adrian, for I owe him my daughter's life. She will know what I mean. I know you are a spy, but—" His expression became grim. "But there are worse men than spies." He gazed at Corday for a long moment. "He was your father, was he not?"

Corday looked down at Simone. She still breathed, slightly. He raised his eyes to du Maurier's. "He has not been my father for twenty years." He gazed at the agent steadily. "My mission was to kill him."

"*Sacré bl—*" Du Maurier shook his head. "I am glad, then, to have saved you the trouble, if what I overheard was true."

Corday closed his eyes briefly, thinking of the madness of the last few moments. "It was true."

The stench of smoke seared his nostrils, and calls from

the guards sounded down the hall and in the stairwell. Du Maurier looked in the direction of the sounds, then back at Corday. "Go. No one will hinder you. If anyone stops you, tell them you have my authority to go as you please. Send them to me for verification." He smiled slightly. "You are still a spy, so I suggest you leave this country and not return, for your own safety and that of your wife. I will send word ahead to smooth your way. I swear it on my life."

Relief and sudden fatigue flooded Corday's body. "Thank you," he said.

The agent nodded. "Go, now." He turned, and ran up the staircase.

Corday hugged Simone to him as he went down the stairs, back to the entrance of the prison. He met no resistance; what few guards stood at the door had clearly been instructed to let them go, and merely nodded. One moved toward them, the one to escort Corday to the hotel. "A carriage," Corday said. "Quickly. My wife has been hurt." The man nodded and left.

It seemed ages before a carriage rattled up the cobblestones, and Corday opened the door before it had a chance to stop, and lifted Simone into it. He set her to lie down on the seat opposite him, and pressed the pad he had made of his cravat over the wound on her chest as the carriage moved away from the prison.

The pad he had made was soaked with blood. Hell. She needed a doctor, but he knew of none in the area, only—

Père Dumont. Many priests knew something of the healing arts, and Simone had asked . . . no. She was not to that point. She was not, please. He pounded on the roof of the carriage and leaned out the window, calling out the directions to Père Dumont's lodgings.

He took her hand, holding it tightly. It was cold, cold as ice, but her skin had always been cool to the touch at first. Her hand did not warm as he held it in his, however, and despair twisted its way into his heart.

She was a vampire. Surely that made a difference. Surely they reacted differently to injuries than did humans.

Human. She was more human than that bastard who called himself his father. Corday squeezed his eyes shut against the vision of Simone running, her face fearful for him—for *him*, for God's sake. He, who killed again and again, who had even made a jest of it from time to time. He watched as the moonlight flickered over Simone's face, and a thin dark line formed from the corner of her lips down her cheek. Pain stabbed his heart, and he frantically searched for a handkerchief in his pockets, then carefully wiped the blood from her cheek with the one he found. Hurry, he thought, listening to the wheels of the coach rumble—too slowly, it seemed—on the street. *Hurry.*

The coach stopped at last, and Corday gathered Simone in his arms again. He thrust the door open and ran to the town house in front of him. He banged on the door without stopping until a face peered out, a middle-aged woman wearing a nightcap.

"Bring us to Père Dumont, quickly."

The woman's mouth opened to protest, but she caught sight of Simone, lax and drooping in Corday's arms. "My wife—she is hurt. Tell Dumont . . . tell him that Michael Corday and his wife Simone are here, and for God's sake—" His voice turned harsh, then stopped. He swallowed, barely able to speak. "For God's sake, let us in, for I fear she is dying."

The woman backed away quickly, opening the door to the fullest, and Corday strode in. He looked about him as the woman ran up the stairs, and found a door ajar, leading to a room with a sofa and a fading fire in the hearth. He laid Simone down on the sofa, and her head rolled to the side.

"Bloody hell." He took her hand, which had fallen

limply to the floor. *Live, Simone. Live.* He put all his will in the words he said in his heart, all his love and fear and hope.

Footsteps sounded behind him, and he turned. Père Dumont rushed in, then stopped, his eyes widening as he saw Corday and Simone. His hand flickered in a quick genuflection, and he moved to the sofa, kneeling next to Simone. He gestured to the woman, who carried a brace of candles, to bring the light near.

The abbé crossed himself again when he saw the soaked pad over Simone's chest and the line of blood that oozed from her lips. "*Jésus, Marie,* help her," he whispered. He lifted her hand and put his fingers on her wrist. He looked at Corday. "It's hard to tell if she's alive." He stood up and walked to the door. "Bring her upstairs. I do not know what I can do, but at least she will be comfortable."

Corday picked Simone up once again, and climbed the stairs behind the priest, up to an attic room. A large cross hung at one end, and a makeshift altar had been set before it. At the other end of the room were four beds, empty, but apparently set there for those who might be ill or needing aid. Bandages and various cleaning elements and medicines were set beside each.

Corday strode to one of the beds and gently laid Simone on it. Père Dumont knelt at her side, easing away the blood-soaked pad from her chest, and cutting her clothes from the wound with a pair of scissors. He gestured to the woman again, who brought forward a steaming bowl of water; he dipped a towel into it. Gently he squeezed out the warm water on the wound and cleaned away the blood.

"Ah, *Dieu!*" He sighed and crossed himself again. "I do not know—it is very serious, monsieur."

A stone seemed lodged in Corday's throat, hard and hot. He wet his lips. "She will live," he whispered. He looked at Dumont. "She is not like us—she is a vampire. They are different, they have powers. . . ."

The priest shook his head. "I do not know, monsieur. She has great recuperative powers—I have seen a knife wound on her arm heal in hours, and her broken hand knit and move in a day." He took out a set of tiny pliers and put the ends into the candle flame. He glanced at Corday. "To cauterize the wound as I try to find the shot." He placed clean gauze on Simone's chest and began to search the wound.

Corday nodded, hope rising side by side with desperation. He remembered the blisters that had risen when her arm was exposed to light, and how quickly she had healed, in a matter of minutes. He looked at Simone, lying on the bed like a broken doll, her hair a mass of dark strands across the pillow, one arm crooked against her head, the other limp and dangling over the edge of the bed. He could not tell if she were alive or dead.

He watched as the priest used his instruments to search for the shot. After a while, Dumont withdrew a small mass of blood and metal. He shook his head and removed the rest of the instruments. "It went very deep." He inclined his head toward the blood that trickled from Simone's lips. "No doubt it pierced her lung." He washed his hands and put ointment on Simone's wound, then bound a pad over the wound site. He leaned toward Corday and pressed his arm. "This is very serious. I have not seen her this injured. Were she anyone else, she would be already dead, and her pulse grows weaker even now." He hesitated. "It would be wise, just in case, to give her extreme unction."

No. No. Rage boiled up from Corday's gut. She would not die; she did not need last rites. She could not leave him, not now, not now when he had begun to feel alive again. He turned to the priest, teeth bared. "No. She will live. Tell me what I must do." He seized the cleric's robes and shook him. "Tell me, damn you."

The priest looked at him with calm sorrow. "It is not up to you, my son, or to me, though we can only do our human best. It is up to God."

"God!" Corday spat out the word as he released Dumont. "There is no God if he allows her to die." He felt wild with rage, and his hands turned into fists. All his control, all his calculation had fled him, and he did not care. All he wanted was Simone.

The priest's face turned stern. "You say that out of grief, I know."

Corday did not hear. "God." He sneered. He went to Simone's side and gently arranged her hair about her face, stroking her cheek. "She deserves better." He gathered her in his arms and picked her up, and took a knife from the table beside her into his hand. She felt feather light, almost insubstantial. Her face was pale, almost translucent, her eyes sunken, her lips almost blue. He had seen the dead before, too much like this. He wanted to weep. He strode to the altar and dashed the items on it to the floor with his hand.

"Monsieur Corday!" Dumont protested. "This is sacrilege!"

He did not listen. Tenderly he placed Simone on the altar and kissed her lips. Anger blazed a fire in his mind so that he burned with it, so that he could think nothing but that *it was not right, it was not fair that she die,* over and over again. He fixed his gaze on the cross before him.

"I don't believe in you," he whispered. "But she does. *She* does." He almost laughed at the absurd madness of what he was saying, but did not care. "If you don't do something, I shall, do you hear me?" His voice rose. "I *shall*." He lifted his knife and slashed at his wrist. Blood dripped and he placed his wrist at Simone's lips and watched his blood mingle with hers. Her lips did not move, and her throat did not swallow. He groaned, despairing, and knelt, pressing his forehead on the altar and holding her limp hand tightly.

"*Monsieur Corday!*"

The priest's voice registered at last, faintly—an annoying buzzing in his ear. Corday turned his head, still resting his temple on the altar. He was tired, tired to death. "What do you want?"

There was silence, then a gentle touch on his shoulder. "My son, bring her back to the bed. She cannot be comfortable there. Surely you must see that?"

Of course. She needed her rest, and this hard bench was no place for his Simone. He lifted her gently and turned, almost stumbling, and then he regained his feet. He carried her to the bed again, smoothing her clothes and her hair after he laid her on the blood-speckled sheets.

He felt Dumont's hand on his shoulder again and he looked up. The old man's face was creased in sorrow and concern. "It is very much past midnight, Monsieur Corday. You need your rest." He nodded at Corday's wrist, still bleeding. "And you need your wound cared for, before it becomes infected."

Corday gazed at the priest, then looked about him. He felt drained, as if life itself had been wrung from him. His mind seemed eerily clear; each thing in the room stood out in sharp relief. He saw the candles flickering near the bed, the small fire in the hearth, the wreck he had made of the altar. His wrist stung—he looked down to see that the priest was cleaning the wound on his wrist, putting ointment on it, and wrapping it with clean gauze.

He looked at the priest's face again. The man's expression was sad, but his attention was concentrated on caring for Corday's self-inflicted wound. He looked up and met Corday's eyes. "You have done this before, *oui*? Given her blood?"

"Yes." Corday closed his eyes, remembering how

Simone had taken his offered wrist, how she had nestled against him afterward, warming him body and heart. "Yes," he said. "And I would give more, if she could live." He thought of his father, and how he had clearly taken some of his traits from him. *She deserves to live, more than I,* he thought. *More than I.*

He opened his eyes again, and the ruined altar caught his attention. He drew in a breath and let it out, forcing control over himself. *You've been busy, haven't you? You wallowing, self-pitying bastard.* He cast an apologetic glance at Dumont. "Sorry," he said. "I'll put it in order." He rose to his feet.

Dumont held his arm. "No, monsieur. Rest. I will take care of it." His eyes twinkled suddenly. "Besides, I doubt you know how to set up an altar properly. You will do yourself no good—or Madame, either, for that matter—if you do not rest and regain your strength." He gently took Corday by the elbow and pulled him to one of the other beds, near Simone's. "See, you may sleep here, near her, so you will know immediately if she wakes. You may even push your bed close to hers, if you wish."

The thought comforted Corday, and he nodded, moving the bed toward Simone, close enough to touch her. Weariness rushed into him like a strong tide, and he sat abruptly on the bed to which Dumont had led him. He tugged off his coat and his shoes, then lay down, the pillow a soft cradle for his head. He gazed at Simone across from him. Père Dumont had pulled a large blanket to her chin; she seemed like a wax doll under it. Her hand fell beyond the edge of the blanket, and Corday touched her fingers, then took her hand in his. Her hand was cold, but it seemed to warm a little in his. Perhaps she would live. *Please.*

Please. The word moved through his mind, through his heart, and as his eyes closed and as he slept, through his dreams.

Chapter 20

SIMONE DRIFTED THROUGH LIGHT AND dark, mist and emptiness. Sometimes she felt as frozen as snow-covered earth; sometimes she felt warm, as if she walked in a summer garden. She thought she heard voices: her mother, her father, her brothers and sisters. She had thought they were dead . . . but perhaps they were not.

She heard Père Dumont's voice chanting the extreme unction. She wondered who it was that was so ill or near death. The sound of the words comforted her. Then there was Michael's voice, strong and pleading, telling her to live. *Live*.

Live. The warmth grew, and she felt her feet move through soft grasses and the sun shone on her, as it had not for years, shone in this garden of flowers and light. She watched her bare feet skim the green blades, her toes scattering the petals of small flowers. The sun shone hot and she lifted her face to it, taking in the heat.

Strength flowed into her, faster and harder than the strength she gained from taking blood. Her feet flew over the grass, and Simone laughed as the flower petals whirled through the air, touching her cheek and hair with perfumed snow. She had not known living could be so wonderful, so beautiful.

Living. *Live*, said Michael's voice. Live.

Wistfulness drifted through her. She wished Michael was here to share this beauty and strength with her. He had been so tired, she could see that now. Tired even to death. She wondered if that was why he pursued death so much, just so he could rest some day. He needed to live, too. Her heart grew heavy. He was so alone. She had never known anyone so alone. Who would help him live?

Live. His voice grew stronger, she could hear it very clearly now. She turned, and her feet flowed over the grass again, and the mist and the light moved around her. The mist touched her skin with cold, and as the light faded, she grew colder still. She had not remembered such cold, not since before her time as a vampire. But she needed to help Michael live. He needed to live.

The darkness grew, until it was night. She felt a heaviness over her body, and then the heaviness became warmer, just a little. It itched. She opened her eyes, and saw fire in a hearth, and candles. She moved, and itched some more. Someone had put a wool blanket over her. She was thirsty.

"Michael," she whispered. She seemed not to be able to talk very well. "Michael."

"Simone?" Michael's voice. A shadow came between her and the firelight, and she shivered.

"Michael." She tried to raise her hand to him, but the blanket was too heavy to move. The shadow knelt, and Michael's face came close to hers. She smiled.

"Simone. Say you are alive."

Her smile widened. "I am alive," she whispered. "And you must live, too, Michael. Promise me this."

A shaking sigh came from him. "Ah, Simone, *ma petite*." She felt his hand take hers under the blanket, warm and strong. "I promise you I will live," he said. "As long as you promise to live, also."

She chuckled weakly. "I promise . . . if you bring me water. I am terribly thirsty."

He gave a short laugh. "God. Water." He rose, and she heard a clink and the pouring of liquid. A cup was brought to her lips and she drank. The water flowed down her throat like sweet wine, and she gulped it.

Simone gazed at his face. His hair was rumpled. Dark shadows lay under his eyes, and hard creases had formed around his lips and between his brows, as if he had tried to hold himself together through sheer will alone. She was right to come back from the sunlit garden. His face seemed a weary gray, and when he took the cup from her at last, his movements were stiff with fatigue. He needed to rest.

"Rest," she said. He nodded, and rose to go. She managed to grasp his hand. "No. You."

He looked a question at her.

"You rest," she said. "You are tired to death, Michael. Rest. Promise me."

"Promises again," he said, attempting to sound exasperated, but laughed instead. "Very well."

She watched him walk to a bed near hers, and he took off his shoes and his shirt, then lay on the bed and pulled sheets and a blanket over him. He yawned. "There, are you satisfied?" he asked.

She smiled. "Yes," she said. She watched him as he yawned again, and settled his head on the pillow.

He sighed. "Perhaps you are right. It has been a long two weeks." Weeks. She did not understand it. She had only been in the garden for a few hours at most. It did not matter; sleep pulled at her, and made her close her eyes.

She drifted in and out of sleep, for how long she did not know. Sometimes she saw Michael's face, sometimes Père Dumont's. Once she saw the face of the agent du

Maurier, and that of a little girl who held out her doll to her. A boy, strangely familiar, smiled at her, and patted her hand. She smiled in return, and the faces faded. Occasionally, she tasted food and drink, and from time to time Père Dumont would force a foul medicine down her throat or make her sip a soothing tea. When he brought the medicine, she often wished he would go away. One day, she said so.

"She must be getting better," she heard Michael say. "She is becoming impertinent and ungrateful; therefore recovery is imminent."

Père Dumont chuckled. "If those are the signs of better health, then she may be impertinent all she wishes."

Simone gave a tired laugh, and then sank into sleep. She woke again later to hear du Maurier's voice talking to Michael.

"I do not know when this Terror will end," the agent said. "The strictures grow tighter each day. It is not safe even for me. You must go, and the priest as well. I fear I will not be able to hold off investigation for much longer. I, myself, am resigning my position, and will leave Paris for Normandy." She heard him give a short, wry laugh. "I am pleading the bad Parisian air that is surely affecting my long-lost children. Yes, I will milk that cow for as long as I can, and have learned to show self-righteous indignation very well. Did I not, after all, find my poor children unjustly imprisoned and ill-treated in the very prison the Public Safety Committee set me to administer?"

"You are wise," Corday said, and she heard amusement in his voice. "No doubt the Assembly wept because of your grief."

Du Maurier chuckled cynically. "Indeed they did—the hypocrites." He sighed. "Take the boat I have procured for you on the Seine. It will be faster than going by land. From there—" He paused. "You may know more than I about transport out of this country. I will not question you, so you need not tell me the lies I am sure you would give me about such travel." Simone smiled at the amusement in his voice.

Michael laughed. "Thank you for sparing me an occasion for perjuring my soul."

She slept again. The next time she awoke, her bed seemed to rock back and forth as if it were a cradle. Sea air reached her nose, and the scent of chicken soup. She rose on one elbow and looked around. Michael sat on one end of her bed, a steaming cup in one hand and a spoon in the other. He smiled as he looked at her, and it seemed the sun from the garden she had walked in shone in his eyes, warm and strengthening. He lifted the cup toward her. "Are you hungry?" he asked.

Her stomach growled in answer, and she laughed. "I think I am," she said.

"Good." He brought the cup and spoon to her and she reached for it. "No, I will do it." She watched him as he dipped the spoon in the cup and brought the steaming broth to her lips. "Drink, Simone." She opened her mouth obediently, and he slipped the soup into it. The liquid flowed over her tongue, warmly rich and salty.

"Mmm," she murmured. "It's good."

He fed her until the cup was empty, and the feeling of fullness in her stomach made her feel sleepy again. She lay down on her bed and curled up on her side, watching him put away the cup and spoon. He kissed her tenderly, as if she were a rare and fragile creature. "Sleep now, *ma petite*. We have a way to go yet until we are home."

Home. She wondered what home he talked of. Her eyes drooped, and the *hush-hush* of water against wood soothed her, until she slept again.

She stayed awake longer the next time; it was difficult not to, for she found herself in a carriage, and the bumps and the jolts made her ribs ache. Michael sat across from her, squinting at a book he held to a crack of light that shone past the shuttered window.

"You will ruin your eyes if you squint," she said.

He looked up, surprised, then a grin split his face. "You're awake."

His expression was boyish, eager, and made her heart ache for him. But fatigue took most of her words. "It is not surprising I am awake, with the jolting of this coach," she said, and realized it was not what she had wanted to say at all. *I love you*, was what she had meant to say, fewer words, but they took more effort than a flippant reply.

He laughed, however. "A good morning to you, too, *ma petite*."

"Morning?" She had never fully wakened in the morning. She had always been drowsy, barely able to make conversation except through the sheerest of will, and if left alone slept an oblivious sleep without dreams.

A crease formed between Michael's brows. "Now that is a curious thing, *ma petite*. You have wakened briefly during the night, but as you have healed, you have done so more often during the day."

"Healed?" She became conscious of her aching ribs again, and a jolt made her gasp with pain.

He raised his hand and touched her cheek. A fleeting shadow crossed his face. "Healed. We—Dumont and I—feared you had died at one point, my love. Hervé shot you. Dumont believed the shot entered your lung, for you breathed your own blood, and then seemed to cease breathing altogether."

She frowned. She remembered the sunlight garden, but before that . . . she remembered the words of the extreme unction, and beyond that, remembered going into a prison, trying to save people. The mist across her memory cleared.

She had found two children in the prison she had entered with Michael; one of them was du Maurier's daughter, the other was Adrian de la Fer, her family's heir. Du Maurier had come to claim Thérèse, and then they had gone up to find Michael being interrogated by Hervé. Hervé had picked up a pistol, intending to shoot Michael, and she had pushed open the door and run— Ah!

She ran her fingers gingerly over her chest until they came to a painful dip in her flesh. She looked at Michael. "How long was I ill?"

He stared at her, his expression bleak. "Three, almost four weeks."

Four weeks. *Mon Dieu.* She shook her head. "I seem to remember du Maurier and Père Dumont. . . ."

"Yes. Du Maurier wished me to tell you that he has and will let as many prisoners go as he dared, but he cannot continue doing so without putting himself, his daughter, and Adrian in danger."

Alarm filled her. "Adrian—what has happened to him?"

Michael put his hand on hers, squeezing it comfortingly. "Du Maurier vowed to take care of him as he would his own son, for your sake and because the boy had protected and kept his daughter alive at the expense of his own comfort." He smiled wryly. "Jacques du Maurier is a man of the Republic, and though he detests the government that rules his country, he is still an idealist and hopes for a better future for France."

She relaxed. Du Maurier was a man of honor and of his word; he would do his best to carry out his promises. She thought of the house and the treasure she had left behind for the boy. He would be provided for, then, and perhaps be able to claim his inheritance in due time.

The coach jolted again, and she gazed at the line of sunlight streaming past the small crack through the shuttered window on Michael's side. She put her hand out to it, then drew it back. No. She was afraid, and if she was not well yet, putting her hand in the light would delay healing. She gazed at Michael, who was watching her. "Where are we?" she asked.

"England." He sighed, as if it held a world of relief in the sound.

She tensed. "No, I must go back—there are people who—"

He caught her hand. "No, Simone. You are too ill. Du Maurier said he would do what he could to release prisoners, so let him do it." He smiled slightly. "Besides, I am afraid your identity has been discovered. Du Maurier knows you are La Flamme, after all, and he would feel duty bound to report you if you returned, however grateful he is to you. I am sure he would not turn you in, but he would be sorely tried, I assure you."

She relaxed, but still felt unsettled, for she did not know what she was to do about her penance if she could not continue her bound duty. And . . . England. What was she to do here?

"Then, too," he continued. "Du Maurier knows me for a spy, and so I am useless in that capacity, at least in France. I will have to find a different way in the world." His eyes gleamed, however, and a mischievous look crossed his face.

Simone's lips twisted in a wry smile. "A different way? I am afraid to ask."

"I have a home now. It's the dower house I bought from my uncle."

"You have an uncle?" She lifted an eyebrow in mock disbelief.

"*Ma petite,* I do have family, for I hardly arose from the sea foam on a half-shell à la Venus."

She laughed even though her chest ached. The image

of Michael floating goddesslike from the sea—dear heaven!

He grinned. "I have a scandalous past, *ma petite*. I promised my uncle I would continue to call myself Michael Corday instead of . . . Cunningham. There, now you know my real name. In return, I could buy the dower house from him, and live there in relative comfort as Michael Corday until I inherit the title from him."

"Will your superiors allow it?" she asked.

A cynical smile formed on his lips. "He has. He had no choice . . . and the government owes me—and delivered—a favor." His expression grew cool. "Ask me nothing else."

He could still be dangerous, she thought, if he needed to. But he seemed changed, somehow, lighter and less careworn. She nodded. "I look forward to seeing your home, Michael."

He gazed at her, and seemed about to say something, but he merely nodded in return and opened his book once again.

Simone drowsed, and when the coach stopped once more, it was twilight.

It was Michael who carried her into the house; it seemed he would let no servant near her. She rested her head on his shoulder, taking comfort from his nearness and his warmth. She was nearly asleep again when she felt herself placed upon a bed. Gentle hands drew off her clothes until she wore only her shift. A soft pillow cushioned her head, and a warm sheet and comforter were drawn up to her chin.

"Sleep well, *ma petite*," Michael said, the last sound she heard before she fell deeply asleep.

The clink of china woke her up. Simone watched a maid put a tray of tea and biscuits on a table nearby.

"Thank you," she said, trying out her English.

The maid jumped. "Oh! Oh, you are awake." She gave a quick curtsey. "I am Betty, my lady. The master said you might awaken and that you might want some breakfast."

"The master?" Simone asked.

The maid gave her a quizzical look. "Sir Michael Corday, my lady." She gave another curtsey and hurried out of the room.

So, Michael was some sort of English chevalier. She remembered him mentioning inheriting a title, but that was all. She shook her head. He was not one to reveal much, not even to her.

A knock sounded on the door. *"Entré!"* she called.

Michael entered. "I am glad to see you awake." He glanced at the heavily curtained windows. "Even when it is morning. Interesting."

"It is the illness, perhaps," Simone said. "Perhaps it has changed my sleeping habits."

"How are you feeling?"

She sat silent, mentally going over her various aches, then nodded. "I feel as if I have spent too long a time in bed," she said. She moved from under the covers and to the side of the bed. Quickly she let her legs down to the floor.

"Simone—!" Michael rushed to her side.

Her legs trembled a little but stayed steady, and she waved away his helping hand.

"I can do it, Michael." She shuffled to the window, looking at the thin trickle of sunlight that tried to reach past the curtains. She put her hand out to it.

"No!" Michael grasped her hand in a hard grip. "You fool, what are you trying to do?"

She shook off his hand, easily, with her usual vampire strength and swiftness, and it depressed her. She was not cured of her vampirism, it seemed. She stayed where she was, however, and stared at the faint light. She cast a slight smile at Michael, hoping to reassure him. "I thought . . . I thought perhaps because I am awake during the day that I could tolerate the sun, just like I did in my dream." It must have been a dream, though it had been so very vivid. She put her hand out to the faint glow at the edge of the curtain, then frowned. She remembered other times when she had been this close to sunlight; her skin had tingled painfully then. She felt no pain now.

Her heart thumped hard, aching in hope. She put her hand to the curtain.

"Don't, Simone. Don't." Corday seized her hand again. "You've been ill. You cannot afford to hurt yourself."

She gazed at him. She was in his home, and she probably would not return to France to complete her penance. She did not know what else to do—what her future would be. Did Michael really wish to be chained to a vampire all his life? He might think he did now, but in years to come?

Simone drew in a deep breath. "I must, my love," she said. She shook off his hand once again, and opened the curtains with a sharp jerk. Sunlight flowed into the room and over her face and body.

Nothing. She felt nothing but the warmth over her skin, the warmth and strength in the sunlit garden of her dream. She spread her arms to it, taking in sudden power. Deep relief and abject gratitude burst in her, and her knees weakened. She sank to the floor, sobs bursting from her.

Strong arms gathered her to a solid chest. "Simone, Simone, you idiot, what have you done?" Frantic hands seized her arms, examining them, and he turned her to face him.

She raised her arms to him. "Look," she sobbed. "Look. There is nothing. I can see the sun again, and all the colors of the day." Tears streamed down her face, and she touched them, amazed. "And I am crying. Oh, Michael, I am crying."

She found herself suddenly crushed in his embrace, and a shuddering sigh came from him as he stroked her hair. "Don't cry, my love, don't cry."

She gave a watery chuckle. "But, Michael, I have not cried for years. It is such a novelty, I am sure I will do it often from now on."

Michael moved from her and gazed deeply into her eyes. A grin grew on his face, and he began to laugh. "Ah, God, Simone, you are a miracle. How I have lived my life without you, I do not know."

"With great difficulty, I am sure," she replied, and he laughed again.

"To be sure," he said, and kissed her hand. He sobered, and looked at her intently. "I suppose this means you are no longer a vampire?"

She rose and sat on the bed, and he sat beside her, holding her close. "I . . . I do not know." She put her index finger to her lips, then moved it to her teeth. "It's hard to tell. They grow sharp only when there is blood."

Michael leaned over and she saw his hand go to his boot. He pulled out a dagger. "There is one way to find out," he said.

"No—!"

But it was too late. He pricked his finger with the end of the dagger. A drop of blood formed on the tip and he held it out to her, gazing into her eyes. "Well?"

She shifted her eyes to his finger and wrinkled her nose. "Don't be stupid," she said, and quickly tore a piece of cloth from the edge of her shift and wrapped it around his finger.

Her hand paused in the tying of it, testing her sensations. She felt nothing. All she had wanted to do was wrap the wound before it became infected. She gazed at Michael. "I . . . I suppose I am not," she said. Tears overflowed again.

He took out a handkerchief from his pocket. "I will need to carry quite a few of these if you are going to turn into a watering pot," he said.

She took the handkerchief, wiped her eyes, and blew her nose. She looked at the sodden piece of cloth and grinned. "It is a long time since I blew my nose, too," she said happily.

"Oh, wonderful," he said. "No doubt I shall experience you honking like a goose three times a day at least from now on."

She laughed and hugged him. "No, for it hurts my nose. I am glad I do not have the blood-hunger any more." She shook her head, puzzled. "But . . . I do not understand. I am still swift and strong, as much so as I was when I was a vampire."

His stillness made her look up at him. "What is it?" she asked.

He gave her a crooked smile. "Perhaps this will help you," he said. "Père Dumont told me to give this to you, once you are well." He moved away from her and pulled out a folded, sealed paper from a pocket of his coat.

She looked at the seal. It was from Rome, from the cardinal to whom Père Dumont had written. She jerked her hand back from the letter he extended to her. No. She had to know the truth. Slowly, she reached out and took it.

The seal opened easily, and she gave Michael a suspicious look. "You opened it, didn't you?"

He shrugged and grinned. "Put it down to occupational habit," he said. "Have pity on me, sweet one; I have been much tried and troubled these past weeks."

Simone suppressed a smile, and turned her attention to the letter, scanning the contents quickly, fearfully. Her heart thumped painfully as she read it, then she put down the letter with a sigh and closed her eyes. The cardinal believed a cure would be dangerous, even deadly for her, and he feared that the conditions would be impossible to accomplish.

The condition for her cure required that she receive the holy sacrament of marriage in a church, or she needed to sacrifice her life for another out of love. The cardinal had doubted either would be satisfactory; both solutions could result in her death, and even if she were to survive a wedding ceremony, what man would willingly marry her for love, knowing what she was? Perhaps if she had done enough penance, she could survive it even if she were offered marriage, but the curse was strong, and faith often failed even the saintly.

But she had done it! Joy rose hard and swift in Simone's heart, and she opened her eyes and smiled at Michael. "I suppose . . . I suppose I should not worry about my strength and swiftness."

Michael smiled and touched her cheek. "*Ma petite,* did I not tell you that these things may be gifts? Admit it," he said, then continued, slowly and carefully. "Say it after me: 'Michael, I was wrong and you were right.' "

"It will puff up your vanity if I do."

He seized her hands and pushed her down on the bed. He put his lips on hers, and his kiss was hot and lingering. "Say it, *ma petite.*"

She smiled, gazing into his eyes. "Two more kisses, and then I might."

His eyes grew warmer and he pressed his lips to hers again, deeper, then again, and once more down her cheek and her neck. "Three more for good measure," he said against her throat.

She felt his hand caressing her breast, and she drew in a deep shivering breath. "Michael, I was—"

"Hush," he said, kissing her again. "I could not care less." He moved over her.

Pain crossed her chest and she gasped.

He rolled off her quickly. "Damn, I'm sorry, *ma petite*. You're not well yet." He drew in a deep breath and let it out again, clearly bringing control over himself. But the look he gave her burned, and his gaze traveled over her lips and her breasts. He leaned over and gave her one more lingering kiss. "I'll save it for later."

Simone gave a frustrated groan, and he grinned again. "Put on your clothes, *ma petite*. We have guests, and I think you might want to meet them." His eyes twinkled. "I thought perhaps we'd keep them until the evening, but they are impatient to see you."

"Who—?"

He put his fingers on her lips. "Don't ask; I won't tell you. It's a surprise." He rose from the bed and stepped toward the door. He hesitated, then turned again, looking at her.

He appeared a little pale, and a troubled expression entered his eyes, before he turned to look out the window, his face becoming cool and distant. He placed his hands behind his back, as if he were carefully pondering. Simone waited, saying nothing, for it seemed to her he struggled, wanting to tell her something she felt might hurt him.

"Simone, I—" He took half a step away from her. "Hervé—that was not his real name."

"Yes, so I suspected," she said.

"It . . . it was Cunningham."

She remembered the half-translated conversation between him and Hervé in the interrogation room. "Your father," she said.

He looked at her, and fear flickered across his face before it became still and cool again. "Yes," he said. "He had your family killed."

"I know."

"Of—of course you would know," he said quickly, his words stumbling. He looked away.

"And—?"

He glanced at her. "I am his son."

"Yes," she said carefully, as if talking to an infant. "I have concluded that if he is your father, you must naturally be his son."

He laughed, and the sound halted in his throat. "He did kill your family."

She let out an exasperated breath. "Yes, I know that. You have said it more than a few times. So?"

"And I am his *son*."

She stared at him, comprehension dawning. She pressed her lips together to keep from laughing. "Are you saying that you had something to do with their deaths?"

"No!" He almost yelled the word.

"So?"

He turned and strode to her, taking her by her shoulders. "Do you not understand? I am not worthy of you. I am born of a murderer, a monster, and like him, I have killed. And yet, I do not even have the discipline to keep my hands from you, from kissing you." His expression turned dark and hard.

She shook her head and smiled, then put her hands to his cheeks and kissed him. "Idiot man. Do you think I care? You love me, I know. You loved me even when I was cursed, and took your blood, yes, and you offered it to me freely. No one has done that, given me what I needed, knowing what I was. You told me my swiftness and strength were a gift, not a curse, and for the first time I came to enjoy them and felt free of guilt and evil. As for killing . . ." Her smile turned wry. "I am as guilty of that as you. Who am I to throw stones?" She reached up and kissed him again. "I love you, Michael. I would have no other . . . if you would have me."

He closed his eyes and took her into his arms, sighing deeply. "Ah, Simone. 'If I would have you.' " He kissed her tenderly, gently, careful of her wound. "I thought I did not know love, but if this heartache and this joy are part of it, I would not let it go for the world."

He parted from her at last, sighing. "We have guests, and I would be a poor host if I did not attend them. Call the maid, Betty, and she will help you dress." He gave her one more kiss and rose from the bed. He smiled. "Take as long as you wish, of course." He turned, and quietly left the room.

Simone gazed after him and sighed. She pulled the bell rope, and the maid quickly arrived.

"I will dress," she told the maid. "Although I am afraid all I have are my old clothes."

The maid shook her head. "Oh, no, my lady. Sir Michael has provided you with clothes, to be sure, for you are his lady-wife, after all." She opened a wardrobe that sat near the window, and pulled out a dress of cream and lavender.

Simone drew in a deep breath. The dress was lovely, and reminded her of the days when she had been brought to court and when she had danced at balls. She touched the brocaded cloth and looked at the maid. "I will wear this one," she said. The maid beamed at her and began to prepare her for the day.

She had forgotten how long such dressing took; she spent perhaps two hours between bathing and putting on the gown and having Betty dress her hair. She looked at herself in the mirror, and saw a different woman than she had remembered. She was not La Flamme any more, but Simone de la Fer, Simone Corday, married to Michael. She shook her head, smiling. She did not feel like herself at all.

She descended the unfamiliar stairs, Betty at her side in case she felt at all unsteady. But as she gazed at the well-lit and decorated hallway, and as she approached the drawing room, what weakness she had seemed to fade. She could hear murmurs of voices beyond the doors of the room, and she looked uncertainly at the maid.

"This is the room?" she asked.

Betty smiled at her reassuringly. "Yes, madame," she said. She put her hand on the doors and opened them.

Bright light streamed through them, contrasting with the darker hall, and for a moment Simone's eyes were dazzled. She put her hand above her eyes for a moment, screening out the light. She heard a footstep, and looked up—Michael. He looked devilishly magnificent, no longer in the drab scribe's clothes he wore during their journey, but all in black velvet, his coat edged in silver embroidery. His black hair was drawn back severely. It made his lean face look more ascetic, his lips more sensually sinful. She looked away, feeling her face blush . . . for the first time in decades. She heard him chuckle.

"How delightful that you can blush," he said, drawing her into the room. "I can now experiment to my heart's content and tease you so that I can see what makes you blush most."

She looked away, her face blushing hotter, then caught sight of the people in the room.

They were young and old, men, women, and children, all familiar. Père Dumont was there, too, smiling gentle reassurance. She looked, startled, at Michael.

"They are your friends, Simone," he said softly. "I brought them here—Dumont told me some of their names—so that you would see you need not fear living here in England."

She looked at them in silence. A sob suddenly broke from an older woman and she stumbled toward Simone.

She caught the woman and kneeled, holding her hands. The woman lifted a tearstained face—her name was Marie de Callander, Simone remembered.

"Ah, madame, madame! Merci!" The woman seized her hands and kissed them. "My family—I would have lost my son and my granddaughter if you had not saved them."

More people came to her, thanking her, taking her hands, kissing them. She shook her head, speechless, and tears rose to her eyes again. She looked at Michael, managing only a crooked smile. "Michael, you are making me cry again."

"I only wish to please, *ma petite*," he said, and his smile was tender. "You did say you wanted to experience the novelty of weeping again." He took her hand, and kissed it, then turned to the crowd in the drawing room. "Come, everyone, to the conservatory. The servants have set out luncheon for us—a veritable feast. I am sure, after all this waiting, that you are quite hungry." He put Simone's hand on his arm, near the crook of his elbow. "Come, my dear love, my sweet Simone. Luncheon awaits."

She smiled joyfully, and kissed him, blushing to hear a cheer behind them. She pressed her face to his chest for a moment, then turned to leave the room for the conservatory.

The sun shone strongly through the windows, and the flowers in the conservatory were bright with color, such as she had not seen in years. She looked at Michael as they sat among their celebrating guests. She would never tire of looking at the clear bright day, and never tire of looking at him, her husband and her lover. He turned to look at her and lifted his wineglass in a toast, the warmth of the sun in his loving gaze.

"To my wife, Simone de la Fer, Madame Corday, a woman of rare courage and intelligence. *Salut!*"

"*Salut!*" cried the guests, and Simone's heart was full at last.

About the Author

KAREN HARBAUGH lives in the Pacific Northwest with a wonderful husband and an alarmingly intelligent son. She has found that being a romance writer, wife, and mother, to be a lot more challenging than being a freelance technical writer or a Quality Assurance Analyst for a major HMO. On the other hand, she does enjoy challenges, and spinning tales for profit allows her to wear multicolored socks and Birkenstocks while she works, which is a definite plus.

Follow the
sinful and seductive adventures
of swordswoman Catherine de la Fer in
Karen Harbaugh's next mesmerizing novel . . .

Dark
Enchantment

by Karen Harbaugh

On sale now

Read on for a preview . . .

Vengeance. Desire. Bloodlust. A dark, erotic
journey is about to begin....

DARK ENCHANTMENT

From the author of *Night Fires*

KAREN HARBAUGH

Dark Enchantment

On sale now

Paris, Winter 1659

🌿 SHE BECAME A CREATURE OF MUD AND dirt, and though from time to time light glinted in her corner of the alley, she did not see it directly. Sometimes, the light would catch the edge of her blade and it would startle her, stirring a faint memory. It would stir something around her heart. But it hurt, this remembering, and she would push it away into a dark part of her mind.

Instead, she scrabbled for what food she could take from the rats when she could not find a dropped coin, and tried to avoid notice. Occasionally, she received kicks from passersby if she strayed too far from her corner, but the pain from this was only slight; nothing compared to the pain she felt when she saw pain in others. So she closed her eyes and tried to sleep when she was not searching for food.

She did not know what day it was, only that light and darkness passed one after another, and that it was very cold. When it became too cold, she was forced from her corner in her alley to the church, where she could sit in a far corner of the sanctuary and look at the light of the candles when she was sure no one was looking. This was more comfortable than in her alley, to be sure, and sometimes she would find a piece of bread that someone must have dropped on their way to confession. It eased the pain in her heart to be there, and she did not bleed from her hands, and her back did not ache when she slept underneath one of the pews. But a church was not for one such as herself.

It was on one such cold morning that she awoke to the sound of the priest yawning and opening the sanctuary. She stayed still underneath the pew until she was sure the priest had passed by, and she crept—she thought noiselessly—out the door.

"You, boy, stop!"

She looked wildly about her and stared for a moment at the plump black-frocked priest who had called to her. He looked surprised, then shook his head.

"Are you the one who has been sleeping here at night?"

Fear clutched her heart, stopping her voice, but she nodded slightly. "I am sorry, *mon père*," she managed to whisper after a while. "I will not do so again." She looked away, fear seizing her again, but this time the fear gave her legs motion and she ran.

"Wait!"

She would not wait. She knew what waiting would do. Waiting led to a place where she had no way to escape except through more pain. She ran to the alley that was her home, her sheathed blade tapping against her hip, hoping that no one had claimed her corner.

But just as the street she followed turned into her alley, she stopped abruptly. Tears began to build beneath her eyelids, and she drew in a deep harsh breath as she looked at the scene before her: A young girl sobbed while a man hit her across her face and another man pushed up her skirts.

Pain sliced across her back, making her gasp, and her hands prickled with the first flow of blood from them. She pulled out two strips of cloth from her pockets and tied them around her shaking hands. She slowly, carefully pulled out her sword while rage built underneath her ribs, rapidly pulling the air into her lungs.

It was the only way. The only way to stop the blood, the pain, and the rage.

She ran to the girl and to the men, snarling in her anger and at the almost blinding pain that surged across her back. It was the sound of fury, the sound of a cornered animal. The men turned, and she lashed at them with her sword.

"Get away from her." Her voice was a growl. "Get away, or I will kill you." She could feel the cloth at the palms of her hands dampen with blood, and pain grew there as well.

"Stupid boy. Go away—unless you want some too." One man sneered and the other turned back to the girl and thrust his hand underneath her skirt. The girl screamed.

The scream lashed at her, and she jerked as if whipped. She gripped her sword tighter, then her hand lifted and the blade's tip scored the back of the first man's neck. *His* scream lessened the pain in her hands and he released the girl, putting his hand to his neck and then looking with disbelief at the blood on his fingers. The girl ran, screaming and weeping. The other man's sneer grew into a frown, and he rushed with a knife at her, who had spoiled his sport.

Her blade sliced at his hand and knocked the knife from it. He cried out, and the pain in her back began to fade. She almost let down her guard in relief, but the other man came for her as well, more cautiously. He, too, had a knife. "*Jésu, Marie,*" she whispered. She had not ever taken on two men before. She had the advantage of a rapier that was longer than their crude knives, but her pain slowed her, and she knew if she were not swift enough, the strength of these large men would overcome her. She hoped her skill would be enough, as little as it was.

The second man circled her, and she could see he was trying to maneuver her so that her back was to his friend. If she could keep both of them in sight—

She turned the other way, but it did no good; both men had their knives in their hands now, and she was not sure she could deal with both of them. At least her back was to the street, not the alley. It would be possible to run if she needed to, cowardly though it was.

The thought of the two men raping another girl made her stomach turn, and the pain across her back increased. No. No, she could not let these men go free.

The men lunged as one at her, and she had no choice. She ducked under the arm of one and thrust her rapier clumsily at the other. A roar from the man on whom she'd used her sword told her that she had cut him. She glanced quickly at him to see that he was clutching his stomach, his clothes showing a spreading blotch of blood. Good.

She turned to the other. This man still had his dagger, and now had a large stick in his other hand. She bit back a groan—the rapier was heavy, and she had not the rage-brought strength she had long ago before she—before she . . . in the beginning of this fight.

She raised her rapier again, flexing her knees as she remembered she should, put her other hand behind her back to reduce fatigue, and wished she had learned to fight two-handed.

"Come, *cochon*, pig," she called out. "You can fight me now or later, but either way you will die. Make it quick, so you will not bleed slowly to death like your friend." She jerked her chin toward the other man, who groaned and vomited blood on the cobblestones.

The ruffian looked uncertain, but only for a moment before he, too, rushed at her. She was not so quick this time, and his dagger sliced her arm before she had a chance to move to defend herself. Fatigue washed over her, and she was glad her hands had stopped their bleeding and that the pain in her back had faded with the dispatching of the first man. This remaining man was wily, and stronger than the other . . . and what was worse, looked more well-fed than she. Hunger gripped her stomach at the thought, and her knees trembled.

Relief showed in the man's eyes—he had seen her trembling. He struck.

Again she put up her rapier in defense, and she whipped her blade at him—too slowly, for she barely escaped another cut of his knife. Blood dripped from her arm and sweat stung her eyes. At least it was not her hands that bled, or her back that stung now.

Her arm and legs ached, and the breath wheezed from her lungs. She could not stand much longer, she must fight with all the strength she had left. She swallowed down a sob and made a desperate lunge.

She missed and fell to her knees, her sword rattling on the street from her fatigued hand.

She would die now. It would be a blessed relief. She closed her eyes and waited.

And waited.

The killing thrust did not come, only the thud of a body hitting the ground. She opened her eyes to see a different man, cleaner, better dressed than the two she had fought, and frighteningly handsome. She looked blearily around her—the man she had fought was on the ground, a knife sticking out of his chest.

"Damned shoddy fighting," he said. "Bravely done of you, boy, but shoddy." He spoke French well, but she could hear an accent—English, she thought. "Not that my method was particularly elegant—a thrown dagger, you see." He grinned suddenly. "Fine aim, though, if I do say so myself."

He peered at her, then offered his hand. She could not seem to stand—her legs would not move. But she would not touch him. She sat, then willed herself to push up to her feet and take a step away from him.

The Englishman's eyebrows rose, but he gave an elegant bow. "Sir John Marstone at your service." He smiled at her, and his eyes were kind.

She closed her own eyes briefly. It was a long time since she had seen kindness. She remembered her mother had been so before she died, and had been gentle in her words and her touch. Remembering the kindness made her remember something else as well.

"I . . . *merci*, monsieur," she said, and sank into as much of a precise curtsy as she could, though she knew it would never do for a formal curtsy at the King's court. But this was not the court, or even her home. The Englishman's brows rose higher. "My name . . . my name—" A sob escaped her. "My name is Catherine de la Fer." Pain, old shame, fatigue, and hunger sliced through her, and her sight grew black. "*Dieu me sauve*, my name is Catherine de la Fer," she whispered, and fell into darkness.

* * *

Jack Marstone gazed at the still form before him and frowned. It'd be best if he left this alley; he'd hardly want to be caught with two dead bodies should anyone in authority decide to come down this alley. However, if he left the girl here, and said authority found her alive with the two ruffians—and a bloodied sword, no less—then she'd be as good as sentenced and dead. It'd be a waste of his efforts, and he disliked wasted effort.

Then, too, she was a mystery. He was curious about her, and he rarely resisted his curiosity.

He nudged the girl with his boot. "Up, girl, 'tis morning and no time to sleep. Indeed, we need to be awake on the moment if we're to get away with our skins."

The girl did not move, and Jack grunted in annoyance. God's blood, it looked like he'd have to carry the child—the girl looked not much more than a child, with her thin, delicate face. He bent over the still form and felt sticky wetness when he touched her arm. Blood. Worse, the girl was wounded.

Jack sat back on his haunches and shook his head. Good intentions were a damned nuisance. Well, there was nothing to do but to take the girl to his lodgings. He'd patch her up, get some food into her, and send her on her way to her mother—with a warning against playing with knives.

It was easy to pick her up and carry her over his shoulder—the child was as light as a feather, her bones easily felt through her clothes. He wrinkled his nose. She also stank. She'd be better for a washing. If he brought her back to her family in this state, they might just think he was less than a good Samaritan . . . and he intended to be a well-paid Samaritan.

Unless she was an actress and trollop and stole the clothes from some patron, she could very possibly have come from a good family. There was nothing coarse about her voice, her refined curtsy, or her manner, and that she displayed them even in the midst of extreme circumstances showed that she must be from a noble family. If so, then there had to be money in her return, and he was never behindhand in acquiring funds where he could.

The thought of money cheered him, and he whistled a tune between his teeth as he made his way down the narrow alleys to his lodgings. He garnered a few startled looks from passersby, but his rueful grin and response of "He's as drunk as a louse in a whore's bed" gave him a few chuckles as well.

His landlady only rolled her eyes at him when he entered the hotel, and he winked at her. "Yes, yes, Felice, yet another one of my charity cases, but this one will bring me into funds, you'll see." He jerked his chin toward his room upstairs. "I'll need some water for a bath—this one's filthy and possibly full of vermin."

"And you say this boy will bring you into funds, monsieur?" The plump landlady wrinkled her nose. "No doubt he will bring fleas into my house, and I will not stand for that!"

Jack grinned. "Aye, the faster the bathwater's brought up, the better. And it's a girl, not a boy, possibly run away from her family."

Felice frowned and put her hands on her hips. "*A vrai dire,* she will bring you trouble, not money. Her family will not want her if she looks like this."

"True." Jack hefted the girl more comfortably on his shoulder. "Therefore, I must have the bath." Felice shook her head, threw her hands up in exasperation, and bustled off as he went up the stairs to his room.

Once there, he laid the girl on the floor—Felice was

right, there was no need to risk a good night's sleep to fleas—and removed the belt that held the girl's scabbard and sword. He examined the sheath and the sword—both old and of excellent make. His hopes rose. She could not have come from anything but a well-to-do family. Surely they would pay a goodly sum for her return. The thought occurred that she might have been cast off from her family—but no. She must have run away, for a family would hardly have given her men's clothes or a sword.

Hope rose. He'd ask for a hundred livres, maybe more. It'd be enough to buy his way back to England—Cromwell and King Charles be damned. That much added to his savings would be sufficient to offer pay to enough of an army to take his lands back from the Roundheads, with the promise of more once he controlled his estate again.

Jack closed his eyes wearily. He almost wished he had not the obligation to regain his estate, but he was a Marstone—"seize and hold" was his family's motto, and he had failed to do just that, and worse, had abandoned his family—perhaps even let them die—in the process.

He opened his eyes, gazing down at the girl at his feet. No time to think of the past—it'd not gain him the funds he needed, and this girl would. Carefully he peeled her jacket from her unresisting body and threw it in the fire. It was beyond repair and beyond cleaning, as were the rest of her clothes. He frowned at her lack of movement and took her frail wrist in his hand, then breathed a sigh of relief. She was still alive. Good. It'd be too bad if he lost this chance to reclaim his inheritance.

A knock at the door sounded. "Come!" he called out, and the landlady peered around the door, her expression suspicious. "I'll need some help getting the rest of her clothes off, Madame Felice, if you'll be so kind. She's been hurt."

Concern and pity replaced the suspicion, and the woman bustled in, two footmen and chambermaid following with a small tin bath and hot water. Once the water was poured, Felice shooed the maid and footmen out with an order to bring back ointments and bandages, then turned to Jack.

"She is not a woman of the streets, eh?" she said, suspicious again.

He put on a pained expression. "My dear landlady. You know me better than that. The ladies I bring to my room are far better dressed and better smelling than this poor rat."

Felice frowned, then suddenly chuckled, slapping his arm. "You are a bad man, monsieur. I have indeed seen you with your ladies, and this *pauvre petite* cannot compare. Ah!" She gave a little cry as they peeled off the girl's shirt from her back, then crossed herself. "The poor little one! She has been badly treated."

· A crisscross of healing weals covered the girl's back. Jack's lips twisted. *There* was the reason she had run away . . . if indeed she received this from her family. Perhaps she was married—no, there was no ring on her finger, although she could have taken off the ring and sold it.

He shrugged. No matter. A woman belonged to her husband, and either way he'd be paid for returning her.

He caught Felice's worried look as they turned over the girl's body. He shook his head. "You need not worry that I have any lustful thoughts about this chit—I prefer plump beauties, as you know." He gave her a wink, and Madame Felice slapped his arm again and blushed.

"Eh, you think to charm me with your manner, but you know I am as one with my dear Robert, silly man."

He grinned and returned to the girl, gazing at her thin form. It was true; he could not be attracted to such a skeletal thing—her ribs were prominent above and below her thin breasts, and the bones at her shoulders and hips stuck out like the bones on a newly hatched baby bird, featherless and vulnerable. He shook his head. How she even managed to lift her rapier and kill a man he did not know; it seemed a miracle she was alive at all.

Felice sighed and clucked her tongue as she removed the simple cross the girl wore around her neck and then gestured to Jack to lift the girl into the warm bath. "Ah, the poor one! She has a sweet face; whoever beat her so must have been *le diable* himself—who but a monster would have beaten such a child?"

A soft pity moved in him . . . well, who would not feel such a thing? But it was a useless emotion. There were larger things at stake in his life than the fate of a girl from the gutter. He needed to remember that. He settled the girl in the bath slowly, half afraid she would break.

He moved away to bring the sponge that Felice had put on the bed, but a sharp gasp brought his attention to the girl again. She had awakened, and her hands gripped the sides of the tub with whitened fingers. She looked frantically about, then caught sight of him.

He could not help staring at her. Firelight flickered in her eyes, dark-fringed and green as grass. He had never seen the like—irises so green that they had no other color in them to mar their purity. The girl gazed at him, and her hands loosened from the sides of the tub, chastely covering her breasts, then slowly, finally, she looked away.

Jack closed his eyes and turned from her, fumbling

with the towels, then remembered that he was going to give Madame Felice the sponge. He did so, averting his gaze from the girl.

"Shhh, shhh, mademoiselle." Madame Felice's voice was soft and soothing. "You need not be afraid. Monsieur Sir Jack, he is an honorable man, and will not harm you, nor will I." The girl said nothing, but he felt as if she were looking at him again, her eyes boring into his back.

I hope she is not married, and that it was not her husband who beat her, he thought suddenly. He sat stiffly on a nearby chair, not quite looking at her except from the corner of his eye. Yes, she had been staring at him as if he were a wild animal sure to attack. Attack? he thought, disgruntled. Why, had he not saved her from certain death? He would hardly attack her, especially since she was means to bring him funds for the reclamation of his estates.

A thread of guilt wove its way through his thoughts, but he thrust it away. He was getting soft, and he could not afford that. There was no room for softness in the life of a mercenary. He turned and coolly gazed at her as if her eyes had not affected him at all, and examined what the tin tub did not cover.

She met his eyes and her gaze did not waver, but he forced his mind into an analytical vein and stared back. She was indeed too thin, as he had noted before, but she had a wide, intelligent brow, a stubborn chin, and a sensitive mouth. His gaze lingered at her lips, and he briefly wondered what it would be like to kiss them, for they were plump lips, unlike the rest of her. She gasped again as Madame Felice brushed the sponge against her back, but she bit her lip and closed her eyes, as if exerting discipline over herself. It worked; she had no emotion on her face when she opened her eyes again and looked at him, and he felt at once sorry and admiring of her fortitude. Surely she must have come from a noble family; few else were trained to such discipline except those groomed for King Louis's court.

"Ah! I am sorry, mademoiselle," Felice apologized. "I will be more gentle with your hurts."

Jack thought he saw a flicker of shame before the girl's face became smooth again. "It is nothing," she said, and he noted her voice was low and husky, smooth and sweet as sherry. "I thank you, madame, for your care of me."

Madame Felice chuckled and shook her head. "Ah, it is not I you should thank. It is Monsieur Sir Jack who brought you here and commanded that I bathe you."

"Why?"

Madame Felice raised her brows at the stark question and looked at Jack, clearly expecting that he answer. He stared at the girl coolly. . . .